LADY OF LIGHT AND LADY OF DARKNESS

COMPLETE IN ONE VOLUME FOR THE FIRST TIME!

In the sixth century after the cataclysm in the fair coastal kingdom of Westria, the dashing young king set out to find a bride, a lady who could be not only mistress of his heart but also Mistress of the Jewels.

The Jewels of Westria: whoever could master their mysteries controlled the awesome powers of the elements—and ensured the survival of the land.

And in a windswept northern province, a slip of a girl named Faris, beautiful but shy, humbly hid the powers she had long felt struggling within her.

She never dreamed that she would be the king's choice, and that love and magic would descend upon her, and transform the world.

THE
MISTRESS
OF THE
JEWELS

DIANA L. PAXSON

A TOM DOHERTY ASSOCIATES BOOK
NEW YORK

The characters and situations in this book are entirely imaginary and bear no relation to any real person or actual happenings.

THE MISTRESS OF THE JEWELS

Copyright © 1982 by Diana L. Paxson

A Tor Book
Published by Tom Doherty Associates, Inc.
49 West 24th Street
New York, N.Y. 10010

Cover art by Tom Canty

ISBN: 0-812-54866-3

First Tor edition: August 1991

Printed in the United States of America

0 9 8 7 6 5 4 3 2 1

Table of Contents

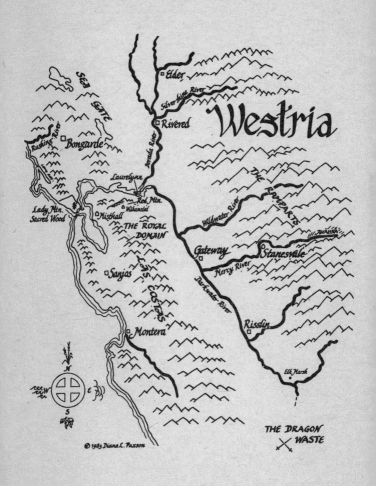

Elder

Silver-liver River

Rivered

Westria

Snyada River

Laurelynn

Rd. Mtn.
△ Wihanslai

Misthall

Sea Gate

Rushing River

Bongarde

Lady Mtn.
Sacred Wood

THE ROYAL
DOMAIN

THE RAMPARTS

Wildwater River

Gateway

Stanesvale

Mercy River

Darkwater River

Sanjas

LOS COSTOS

Montera

Risstin

Elk Marsh

N
W E
S

© 1983 Diana L. Paxson

THE DRAGON
WASTE

LADY OF LIGHT

To my husband . . .
Jon DeCles

Prologue

From the interaction of light and darkness, of spirit and matter, the world was made.

In the beginning, a spark whirled in the void. It slowed, cooled, became a sphere where the sovereign elements of earth, water, air, and fire combined and recombined in an endless dance. Continents grew, rivers carved paths to the sea, soil was formed, and living things appeared.

Each thing that came into existence followed the pattern of its kind, yet each was unique. Everything possessed awareness—a continuum of consciousness from the smallest particle to the Mind that had created all. Then the lesser minds, which were both cause and effect of the aggregate individuals, became aware of themselves and of each other and walked upon the infant world. They were the Guardians of their kinds. And above them all there was in every region a Guardian of the land itself, whose spirit determined its character, just as the Guardians were the patterns for the kindreds they ruled.

Species were born and disappeared. A new creature walked the earth who imprisoned consciousness in words, and whose name, in whatever language it made, was Man. For millennia men remembered their beginnings, revering the Guardians and living upon the earth without marring it. But at length the people began to change and desired to bend the earth to their own wills. Sooner or later in every place the new races pushed those who held to the old ways to the very edges of the habitable lands, and the Guardians withdrew from the knowledge of men.

Yet a time came when the land itself rose against men: earth trembled, and fires were fanned by the winds until the waters stilled them, and every plant and animal was at war with

Man. Then the remnant of humanity cried out to the Creator for fear that men would perish utterly.

And the Maker of All Things commanded those Guardians who were the souls of each land to appear. For each region a new Law was made, appropriate to its nature, but however the countries of men were henceforth to differ, in all of them it was decreed that humans should no longer be masters, but only the tenants of the land.

On a fair coast washed by a sunset sea, the survivors made a Covenant with the Guardian, and wishing to forget the past, they called Her, and their country, Westria. Those who remembered the old skills and the old rituals that would help them to live at peace with the land were made their teachers, and they began to build a world that was at once very old and very new.

Two centuries after the Cataclysm human wars threatened the Covenant of Westria. In those days a priestess made four Jewels of Power, one for each sovereign element, and her son wielded them to heal the land. In the years that followed there was always an heir of that line to bear the Jewels and to rule Westria.

In the sixth century of the Covenant the Estates of Westria petitioned the King to marry, for he had no child. And so the King and his companions set out to find a Lady for Westria—a woman who might be equally the mistress of the King's heart, and the Mistress of the Jewels.

I
Stormfire

Light slashed across the darkness, illuminating in bas-relief the snow-powdered mountains and the outworks of the Hold, the glimmer of Faris' face in the window she had just pushed open, and the livid scar that twisted up the inner side of her left arm. She took a deep breath of damp wind, blinking as the radiance faded and night swept back over the world. Thunder crashed and rolled around the fortress and Faris jumped, though she had been waiting for it to come.

"May the Lords of the Elements have mercy on the King, for surely they are at war tonight." Faris heard her friend Rosemary speak behind her, the customary calmness of her voice belying her words.

"Perhaps he has taken shelter somewhere," said Faris' brother, Farin. A few fragile harp notes echoed his words as he picked up the melody he had been playing when the thunder came. Reflected in the windowpanes she glimpsed a stretch of frescoed wall, Rosemary's owl on his perch, the gleam of the fire.

A gust of wind lifted Faris' dark hair away from her face. She heard the trees sighing in the walled orchard below as they stretched their arms to the storm, and a few petals, whirled up by the wind, clung to her hand. She wondered if any blossoms would be left for the Festival of the Lady of Flowers.

"Jehan promised my father he would be here in time for the ceremony tomorrow," said Rosemary.

"It would be a pity if he missed it—every girl in the Corona is hoping that the Lady will help her to attract the King," Farin replied.

"Not me—Faris is more beautiful, let her be Queen!"

"Hush, Rosemary! Don't encourage her to think such things. She will only be hurt." Farin's voice came too clearly as the wind eased. "Our family gained honor enough when our sister Berisa married your brother, who will be Lord Commander of the Corona one day."

Rosemary sighed. "You all protect Faris too much. No man worth marrying would care about her arm."

Automatically Faris tugged her sleeve down. Her eyes blurred and her disfigured arm throbbed as if the lightning had seared her flesh and not the sky. *My father cares . . . Berisa was right, I should have stayed at home!*

The wind was rising once more. Faris blinked as lightning flashed again and again above the white peak of the Father of Mountains, glowing through the boiling clouds. As if to escape Farin's words, she thrust the window fully open and leaned out into the rain, gasping as energy pulled her fine hair into a cloud about her head and tingled over her skin. The charged air dizzied her. *I must not do this,* she thought, but already her spirit was surging to meet the storm.

Thunder billowed around her, but it was a deep, unhuman laughter that Faris heard. She saw the sky people, bombarding each other with handfuls of cloud, spinning themselves out in lines of light that shattered as the lightning struck, then taking shape again. The elementals were playing, an abstract sport of force and pattern that she almost understood. Her spirit danced in the vortex of the storm, and she stretched out her hands to its power.

The heavens gathered themselves around her, then were torn asunder as if the fabric of the world had been rent to reveal the glory it veiled. Faris cried out and fell back as earth and heaven quaked to the thunderbolt.

"Faris! What are you doing? Do you want to get a fever again?" The ancient glass of the window rattled as Farin slammed it shut.

"Your hair is soaked—let me get you to the fire." Hardly aware of her own body, Faris felt Rosemary's strong arms half carry her toward the hearth. Her eyes followed the swing of the other girl's golden braids as Rosemary bent to poke up the fire and then pulled a shawl out from under the sleeping sheepdog and drew it around Faris' thin shoulders.

Now she could feel water trickling down her neck and the ache in her fingers as the circulation began to return. *A moment ago my hands had the strength of the storm,* she thought, ignoring her brother's scolding. *What a weak thing this body is. My father was right to forbid* . . . She closed her eyes against the memory of his words. Her mother had had the power to call the winds and talk to the trees, and her mother had died.

"That's better," said Rosemary, giving a last rub to Faris' damp hair.

"Please, Rosemary, I'm not one of the wild creatures you nurse so well." Faris found herself laughing as the owl's head swiveled and one golden eye blinked down at her. She could hear faint snufflings as the rabbits stirred in their wicker cage on the other side of the room.

"You might as well be," said Farin, but he had taken his seat again, and already his dark head was bent over his harp as he tested and tuned its horsehair strings.

"Father said that if the King did not get here before mid-evening, he would go out after him," said Rosemary.

"Then I'm going too," said Farin. "I wouldn't miss the sight of all the fine lords from Laurelynn half drowned in the rain."

"Don't laugh too loud. Eric of Seagate is coming with him, and some of the others who fought with Jehan against Elaya. And of course he'll have the Seneschal, Caolin. I doubt that *he* would be flustered by a second Cataclysm."

"But the Master of the Junipers is already here," put in Faris, thinking of the little gray-robed man she had seen at supper, sitting like a still rock in the midst of a busy stream.

"Yes, he had to prepare for the Festival."

Faris remembered the wind whipping the starry branches of the almond trees. This was the second week of February, but the winter had been a stormy one, and it was hard to realize that it was already time for the Festival, hard to believe in the coming of spring.

In the distance thunder muttered like a bear balked of its prey. Faris shivered, wondering how the King and his men fared now.

Thunder crashed as if someone had clashed two shields together above Jehan's head, and his horse plunged sideways, almost unseating him. The King swore softly as the clamor faded.

"Stormwing, you white donkey—I thought this kind of weather was your element! What are you afraid of, my swan? See now, it's going away . . ." Still talking, he gentled the horse with firm pressure of knee and rein. He saw his squire, Rafael, watching him anxiously and smiled.

Somewhere behind him he heard a squeal, followed by confused shouting. *Another horse down,* he thought. *I should have stopped at Badensbridge. What fool's pride made me believe I could get everyone to the Hold ahead of the storm?* But the place had been too small for all the lords and clerks and officers, the men-at-arms and supply train that the King of Westria must drag about with him in his quest for a Queen. *And I was a fool to agree to that too!* he thought, but he was past thirty now, and the Council had demanded that he choose a Lady for Westria.

Lightning flared, and for a moment he saw the confused mass of men and animals spread along the muddy curves of the road. Beyond them the land rose gently toward the mountains that gave the Province the name of the crown of Westria, dotted with scattered stands of liveoak and stunted pine. At least they were still going in the right direction!

Stormwing shook his head anxiously and the King loosened his rein, letting the stallion take a few steps up the road while he peered through the freezing rain. They must find shelter soon, but where? *When I was taking my training at the College of the Wise, I knew every twist of the road between here and Laurelynn . . . But that was a long time ago.* The border with Normontaine was quiet, and Theodor was an able lord. Without need to call him there, Jehan had not found time to visit the Hold more than twice in the fifteen years he had been King.

The next flash showed him jagged outlines on the horizon and he pulled the stallion to a halt. The ancients had built a great city here, destroyed when the earth moved and the dam below the Father of Mountains gave way, but he remembered some ruins that might give shelter. Had he seen them just now? Caolin, who knew everything about Westria, would surely know. He reined Stormwing around to find the Seneschal.

Caolin pulled his hood forward and hunched a little more in the saddle, his long legs gripping the brown mare's sides, his strong fingers steady on the reins. His body was settled to a patient endurance; his mind, having determined that there was nothing he could do to make sure that dispatch cases were dry, was focused on the next move in a chess game he had been playing with himself since they had left Badensbridge.

Then he heard his name called by the one voice that could always reach him. As he lifted his head to look for the King lightning struck again so close that he could smell it. In the flare of bluish light he saw a horse rearing and Jehan urging Stormwing forward so that he could grasp the bridle and bring the other animal down, his eyes shining and his face intent as he forced the beast to stillness and spoke to the trembling rider.

"You're not hurt, are you?" The lightning bolt had struck a pine tree beside the road, and now it blazed like a torch despite the rain. Caolin saw the boy whose horse the King had caught shake his head as he tried to smile. "Well then, see to your mount," Jehan went on. "He's frightened out of his skin!" The boy laughed then, for even in that dim light he could see the twitching of the horse's lathered sides.

"My Lord!" came a call. "Are we going to Hell or to the Hold?"

"*I* am going to the Hold." Jehan grinned. "But you are welcome to stay here! I'm just as uncomfortable as you are, but we'll get to shelter soon, so don't despair!"

Caolin saw the King's eyes gleam in the flickering light and thought that although he was cold, wet, and concerned for his men, the opportunity for action exhilarated him. The Seneschal sat still on his horse, watching as the King moved among his men.

"*Don't despair,* he says," came an anonymous voice behind him. "Why doesn't he use the Jewels then? He's their master; surely he could handle a little thing like a thunderstorm!"

"The Jewels of Westria?" came a shocked whisper in reply. "He would be breaking the Covenant if he used them to control a natural storm!"

"What's the use of having them then? In the old days men were masters of this world."

"Well, in the end this world mastered them. Leave well enough alone," his companion answered him.

Caolin peered through the darkness, but he could not see who had spoken. He had trained himself to ignore discomfort, but still he could sympathize with the first man's complaint. There had been many times, when villages were flooded or crops destroyed by fire, that he had wished for the power to protect them. The College of the Wise preached a slavish obedience to the Covenant, but Caolin owed no service to the College now. In other lands men lived by different laws—how different? he wondered. How much could men do without endangering Westria?

The wind shifted, flinging rain against his unprotected face, and lightning stalked across the horizon. Caolin huddled back down in the saddle. *Earth and water, wind and fire—there are the real powers. Might a man truly wield the lightnings if he bore the Jewels of Westria? But Jehan never uses them, so I may never know . . .*

"Caolin." The Seneschal started, turned, and saw the King. "We must find a place to stop. The men are tiring, and I'm afraid we'll wander off the road. Aren't there some ruins near that would protect us?"

Caolin closed his eyes, memory lying out before him the map of Westria with its four Provinces and the red lines of the roads. He could see the Free Cities spaced along the Dorada River like beads on a string, and fortresses like the Hold, where Lord Theodor ruled the Corona. His map showed also mines and grain fields and the ruins of dead cities, where they found metal and glass and sometimes books and strange mechanisms whose use no one in these times cared to know.

"Yes," he said finally. "The Red City lies this way, but there's hardly one wall left standing there now." He looked back at the King. Jehan was standing up in his stirrups, straining to see down the road. The Seneschal pushed back his hood, oblivious to the rain, and thought he heard a distant trumpet call.

A smile was growing on Jehan's face. "It doesn't matter now—don't you hear them? When we fought Elaya together three years ago, I got to know the note of Sandremun's horn—he and Theodor have come out to look for us!"

The King slumped in the saddle, allowing himself to feel the weariness of the long ride now that Lord Theodor and his son had taken over the responsibility for seeing them all to shelter. The excitement of battling the storm had worn off, and his shoulders ached as if he had been carrying half Westria. Now even Stormwing's steps had grown slow. More storm clouds were moving in from the southwest, but for the moment they were assailed by nothing worse than a cold, steady rain.

The lanterns of Theodor's men bobbed to either side of the line of horses, casting a fitful light on the road and briefly illuminating their Commander's beaked profile as he talked to Caolin about the economics of the wool trade with their northern neighbor, Normontaine. Seen in silhouette, without the jutting silver beard to betray his age, Theodor's erect figure could have been the shadow of his son's. Certainly the elder and younger lords of the Corona shared the same relentless good cheer. Jehan grimaced. His breeches were chafing him, water had somehow penetrated his boots even though they were laced halfway up his thighs, and Sandremun had not stopped talking in the two hours since the escort had found the King.

> I took the road to see the world
> When spring was fair and green,
> But now the winter winds do blow
> And I'm for home again . . .

Jehan turned to look for the singer and glimpsed the slight shape of a dark-haired young man who had come with Theodor. Sandremun broke off in the middle of a description of the perils of hunting deer on horseback in the mountains to join in the chorus.

> But I'll not care for wind and rain
> Nor will I fear the storm,
> If food and fire are waiting, and
> My love to keep me warm . . .

Jehan sighed, remembering the soft curves of the woman he had left in Elder and wondering whether he should have brought her along. But it had seemed discourteous to bring a mistress when he was supposed to be searching for a bride, and he doubted her temper would have withstood this journey in the rain.

The creaking of saddles and the splashing as the horses

plodded through the puddles made a rhythmic accompaniment to the singing. Forcing his attention back to the present, Jehan glanced back along the line, marking his men. Eric of Seagate's broad shoulders were unmistakable even in this gloom, but he did not recognize the smaller man riding beside him. He heard a familiar name and moved his horse closer.

"It is a pity we do not see people from the other Provinces more often," said the strange voice, the accent of Laurelynn overlaying the more relaxed speech of the north. "These visits provide such a useful opportunity to share our problems."

"I wouldn't know," said Eric. "This is my first trip around Westria."

"But you were down in Las Costas with the King, were you not? The Lord Commander Brian is such a fine man—such a valiant fighter, and with so many valuable ideas too. Did you spend much time with him when you were there?"

"We met."

Jehan grinned in the darkness. It was Brian's name that had attracted his attention, and remembering the instant hostility between the Lord Commander of Las Costas and the Lord of Seagate's son, he wondered how long Eric's restraint would last.

The stranger continued, "Yes, Brian is a truly admirable leader. I trade in furs from the Corona and even Normontaine, and I've visited all four Provinces. It is a pity that the King has not had time to know them as well. Some of the rulings imposed by that precious Council of his really display no knowledge of local conditions. In the circumstances it hardly seems right to insist on central control . . . That's why I mentioned Lord Brian. He's a strong man, and with a little support from the younger lords like yourself, he might win more independence for all of the Provinces. Don't you agree?"

"No, I *don't* agree!" Eric exploded. "I would remind you that Brian is a member of that 'precious Council' himself, as is my father. Let Brian take his valuable ideas to the King. He may find he is not as strong as he thinks!"

The other man opened his mouth to reply, looked beyond Eric, and saw the King. Without answering, he bowed and reined his horse away.

Eric looked around in confusion. "My Lord!" He glanced back at the empty space beside him. "Did you hear what he said?"

"Sandy," said Jehan, "who is the little man in the green cloak who just rode down the line?"

Sandremun turned, not needing to rise in his stirrups to see over the heads of most of the men. "Oh, that's only Ronald of Greenfell—Ronald Sandreson—he's a cousin of ours. Was he talking like a fool again?"

"With all respect to your family, he was talking like a traitor, my Lord," said Eric grimly.

"Treason, Eric?" asked the King.

"Well, sedition, at any rate. All about more freedom for the Provinces, and the like!"

"But, Eric, everybody knows how untrustworthy the Lord Commanders can be," Jehan said seriously, then grinned as Eric's face relaxed into a rueful smile. Sandremun was roaring with laughter.

"Only some of them, only some of them, Jehan!" said Theodor's son. "And only the loyal ones come to the Hold." He gestured up the hill, where an irregular outline bulked against the storm. A second cloud front was moving down on them quickly now, and Jehan thought they would be lucky to reach the fortress before the lightnings were playing about them once more.

The clear baritone of the singer soared above the roar of the storm as they began the last pull up the hill.

> And wanderers upon the road,
> And caravans and Kings,
> Are but the vagrant children of
> The Maker of All Things . . .

Sandremun put his horn to lips, and Jehan winced as the sound echoed back and forth between the walls that curved down from the protected side gate that was opening for them now. The Hold loomed over them in a confusion of walls and towers, built from every material and in every style known to the past three hundred years, according to no plan the King had ever been able to discern.

He kicked his weary horse after Sandremun's. People

were pouring out of the gate now, waving torches, and Stormwing snorted and reared. The air was full of thunder and the rush of rain. As Jehan fought down the prancing horse, the movement of a window opening drew his eyes upward to the chamber above the gate.

Then the lightning came. Walls and towers sprang into being around him, and in the midst of them a girl's white face framed in a cloud of dark hair.

For a long moment her eyes met his, as if time had been halted by that light, then the vision was gone. Dazzled, Jehan let Stormwing carry him under the arch of the gate, hearing the echo of hooves on stone and the cheers of the people of the Corona. When his sight cleared, he saw only torchlight and the welcoming smile of the Master of the Junipers.

The Master of the Junipers paused in the doorway of the paneled chamber they had given the King. Jehan's squire was helping him pull off his wet tunic. Boots, cloak, and sheepskin jacket already steamed before the fire, and the air was pungent with the smell of wet leather and wool. A partly demolished chicken carcass and a loaf of brown bread lay on a platter on the table beside a stoneware pitcher of mulled wine.

"Jehan?" He came into the room and let the door close behind him.

The King emerged from the tunic, still gnawing on a chicken leg, and reached for his blue robe. "My friend! Thank you for coming to me. I suppose you ought to be resting up for the Festival"—he grimaced—"and I should be in bed. But we'll have no time to talk tomorrow, and we—I thought we had better talk before you went up to the College of the Wise."

The Master had already seen Caolin, leaning against the battered blue leather of the King's traveling chest, blazoned with the radiant silver star of House Starbairn. Somehow the Seneschal had already managed to change into a dry tunic and to sleek back his short pale hair. He lifted his mug to the Master in ironic salute, his gray eyes veiled.

Jehan wrapped the robe around him, poured steaming wine into a mug, and eased down into a chair covered with fox pelts gathered over several seasons' rationed hunting. His squire hung the tunic on a hook to dry and took up a position by the door.

"Rafael," said the King without opening his eyes. "You need to get dry too. And when you've got your wet things off, go to bed."

"Yes, my Lord." The young man flushed beneath his brown skin, then bowed and went out.

The Master sighed and sat down in a straight chair across from the King. "I will visit the Mistress of the College as we agreed," he said, "to inform her about the problems in Laurelynn and Rislin and to have her report—"

"To have her reply!" corrected Caolin. In the firelight the straight folds of his robe glowed as crimson as the red stone on his right hand.

"The Mistress has ruled the College for over ten years, Caolin. I do not think she needs to be told her job." The Master kept his voice low, avoiding dangerous ground.

"She is a member of the King's Council, and accountable. This must be settled—my Lord, don't you agree?"

"Forgive me." Jehan looked up, but Caolin's glance fell too quickly for his expression to be read as he realized that the King had not been listening.

Jehan is tired, thought the Master, *and I think he did not choose to have this meeting now.*

"Do you agree that we must make a clear distinction between the areas of authority of the College of the Wise and of the Crown?" repeated Caolin.

"I thought we were discussing jurisdiction," the Master of the Junipers said quietly. "The only *authority* involved is that which both Crown and College exist to serve."

Caolin shrugged. "Call it what you will. But when you go to the Mountain tomorrow, tell the Mistress of the College that we will tolerate no more meddling. Take the case of the priestess in Elder who murdered her child—surely you will agree that no matter who commits it, murder is a civil crime?"

The Master shook his head. "You choose your examples poorly. You know my doubts that something so symptomatic of spiritual illness as deliberate murder can ever be merely a 'civil' crime."

The King eased off his golden circlet and ran his fingers through his dark hair, lines of patience hardening his face. The Master paused, knowing that Jehan had heard this argument too many times before, but there was a principle here he could not betray.

"Then what of the case where the Commander of the garrison in Rislin was arrested for having ordered his men to cut wood?" Caolin leaned forward, and the firelight burnished his hair to the same ruddy gold as the King's circlet. "The wood was on Crown land, the man was an officer of the Crown, and his removal jeopardized the defense of a major city of Westria."

"*Crown* Land? A *Crown* officer?" asked the Master wryly.

The King frowned abstractedly and poured another mug of wine.

"The officer was appointed by Jehan," continued the Master, "but the man himself is responsible for his exercise of that trust. Jehan holds the land on behalf of those who live here. *All* of them. You speak of wood, Caolin, but those were living *trees* until that man cut them down!" The Master remembered the fallen branches he had seen in the orchard. Surely the land was hard enough on itself without the intervention of man. His awareness, tuned to the tides of the earth, felt the movement of the clouds overhead, the hidden rising of the moon.

"So much that is wrong in Westria today comes because we forget that," he went on more quietly. "The King's authority, the duty of the College, the very survival of humankind—all depend on our keeping the Covenant our ancestors made with the Guardians of the other kindreds after the Cataclysm that destroyed the civilization the ancients made.

"We may not take a life—of any animal, of any creature of air or sea, of anything that grows from the earth herself—without apology or need. Not without need!" His voice grated and he tried to soften it for the sake of the King. Jehan was sitting with his head in his hands, and the Master remembered the many times he had counseled and comforted him since the boy of seventeen had become King. But he could not help him now.

"You need not repeat the Oath of the Covenant, *Master*!" snapped Caolin. "I too have studied at the College of the Wise!"

The Master's attention jerked back to the Seneschal, and his lips closed firmly on the words he would not say, knowing that Jehan heard him anyway. But Caolin could not communicate in that way. Caolin had not left the College voluntarily—he had wished to become an adept as the Master had done, but though his work had been brilliant, he had been denied. The Master had been in Laurelynn at the time, serving the old King. He had had no part in the decision, but he represented the College, and it seemed to him that Caolin had always resented him for that.

The King leaned forward as if he could protect Caolin physically from the memory. "We all live by the Covenant." His voice had deepened. "Assure the Mistress of the College that I have not forgotten what I swore when I first put on the Jewels."

The Master and the Seneschal both looked at him, seeking reassurance in his face, seeing the flicker of pain in the King's blue eyes at their disharmony. Jehan cleared his throat and went on.

"Tell her also that confusion results when communications fail. May the Lord of All forbid that I should usurp the responsibilities of the College, but I and my officers must know what the College intends so that we can know how to respond. If we do not, both Crown and College will forfeit the people's trust." Slowly, holding their eyes, he replaced the circlet upon his brow.

"My Lord King . . ." Caolin bent his head.

"I will carry that message gladly, Jehan," said the Master gently. He thought, *He is still Caolin's master—I should not have feared.*

"It grows late," said the King. "You must lead the Festival tomorrow, and Theodor has lined up every horse in his stables and every landholder in his Province to meet me. We both need sleep!"

"Yes." The circled cross of Westria on the Master's breast glittered gold in the firelight as he sketched a blessing. "Rest well, in the name of the Maker of All Things."

Jehan remained stretched out in his chair before the hearth after the Master of the Junipers had gone, staring into the flames. Images swam before his eyes as the glowing oak logs became coals, and coals fell into ash, fulfilling the natural life cycle of fire. Light and darkness patterned his vision. He saw again the bright face and dark hair of the woman who had appeared in the window when the lightning came. With such hair she was no kin of Theodor's. If she was real . . .

"He was right. You look half asleep, my Lord, go to

"He was right. You look half asleep, my Lord, go to bed," said Caolin.

"No." Jehan sat up and poured himself more wine. He could feel its warmth burning in his belly, but it did not ease him. His fingers twitched with undirected energy. He wanted to escape from the circlet that bound his brow, from the round of ceremony that would close upon him tomorrow, but he did not want to rest.

The sanded boards of the floor creaked as Caolin came toward him. He felt the other man's strong hands close on his shoulders and knead the taut muscles there. After a moment he let his head drop, trying to relax.

"I thought so," said Caolin. "Well, I can help you get rid of the effects of tension at least, even if at the moment I can do no more about its causes." He gave the King's shoulder a light slap. "Well?"

"I suppose so." Jehan got to his feet, pulled off the rest of his clothes, and stretched out face-down on the bed. The laced thongs of the bedstead gave to his weight as he eased down. Appreciatively he breathed in the spicy scent of the fine grass that stuffed the mattress, and the perfume of the rose petals that had been folded with the well-washed cotton sheets.

Caolin rummaged in the traveling chest and took out the flask of oil, tested it on his hand, and set it beside the fire to warm. Then he came back to the bed, lifted the King's dark hair gently to one side, and began to work on his shoulders again.

"I gather that Lord Theodor has planned quite a celebration."

"Yes, it's been a long time since I was here," answered the King. "It shouldn't take an order from the Council to get me to the far corners of the Kingdom." He remembered what Ronald Sandreson had said to Eric on the ride to the Hold. He ought to tell Caolin that Brian was playing politics, but he knew how the Seneschal would reply. Tomorrow would be soon enough to hear it again.

"Sandy wanted me to sit up and drink with him," he said instead, "but I have too clear a memory of the effects of Berisa's mead, or rather too unclear a memory."

Caolin laughed. "Sandremun *is* the sort of man one calls by his milk name for the rest of his life, isn't he?" He went to the fireplace for the oil, returned, and poured it across the King's back. Jehan felt hard fingers dig into the sensitive spot beneath his shoulder blade and winced.

"You're resisting it—remember to breathe."

Jehan grunted, releasing his breath and trying to draw it in again with the steady rhythm he had been taught at the College, letting go of all the worries that nagged him, letting tense muscles ease.

"Theodor will likely try to match you with his daughter. At least she has the family's golden hair," murmured Caolin.

Jehan shook his head a little. He had met Rosemary several times when her family came to Laurelynn for Council meetings and thought her a nice girl, but she was too tall for him.

"Or he'll find someone else for you," the Seneschal's cool voice continued evenly, inconsequentially, blending with the steady rattle of rain against the windowpanes.

Jehan let the steady murmur lull him as Caolin's fingers traced out the long muscles of his arms, worked down each finger until his hands lay nerveless at his sides. *Did I really see a girl at the window?* he wondered drowsily. *Or was it only a trick of the light?*

"Did you take care of that woman in Elder?" he asked suddenly. Thinking of her, he saw the shining waves of her black hair, but her face was already becoming vague in his memory.

"Yes," answered Caolin impersonally. "She had the bracelet and was escorted safely home."

Jehan smiled to himself. He was aware that Caolin often took the King's women to his own bed for a night before he sent them away. Jehan saw no reason to object to that, since none of the ladies had ever complained. They had, he thought cynically, probably been glad to cling a little longer to the source of power, however vicariously. Did Caolin know that he knew? Sometimes Jehan thought that his friend hardly seemed to remember it himself, as if the satisfaction of his body's need was unrelated to the life of his mind and soul.

Caolin's hands moved down the King's legs, loosing the knotted muscles of the calves, compressing the nerve endings in his feet. Jehan felt a sweet singing in his veins as his blood flowed freely once more. His body remembered the many times Caolin had done this before, and yielded gratefully. *Only one of the many things he has done for me,* thought the

King, knowing that Caolin's steady support had been perhaps the best thing in his life during the past fifteen years.

"You can turn over now."

Jehan roused himself enough to ease on to his back and smiled up at Caolin. "You should get some rest too," he said.

A little unaccustomed color rose in the other man's face as he returned the smile. "This is one of the few useful things I learned at the College of the Wise," he replied. "It rests me too."

Jehan let his eyes close as Caolin's fingers probed gently at the tightness in his forehead and the clenched jaw muscles beneath his short beard, then moved down his neck and began to work carefully around the old sword scars on the King's shoulders and chest.

The darkness behind his eyelids was shot with flashing lights that formed the face of the girl in the window, her hair full of stars. Darkness was her setting, but she was made of light. *My lady of light . . .* Words faltered in his consciousness and fell away.

He scarcely knew when Caolin finished and pulled the heavy quilts over him, carefully tucking them in. The darkness deepened as the other man blew out the lamp. He heard the click of the door latching and Caolin's soft good night.

Good night, Jehan. Caolin's own words reverberated in his awareness as if he had spoken them aloud. The palms of his hands tingled with the memory of Jehan's flesh; he brought them up to cover his eyes and breathed in the sharp savor of Jehan's skin. Dizzied, he leaned against the plastered stone of the wall next to the King's door.

The image of that hard, compact body filled his vision; the shape of every bone and muscle was imprinted in the nerves of his hands—he could have modeled the King's body from memory.

"Jehan, Jehan . . . my Lord and my King," he whispered, then pressed his clenched fists hard against his eyelids as if to suppress both touch and sight. *He is dreaming now and does not even know that I have gone,* thought Caolin. A shudder thrust him against the hard stone.

Once, Jehan would not have gone to sleep after Caolin had worked on his body. That contact might have turned to another kind of touching that would have eased them both.

But it had been a long time since Jehan had needed that from him.

"It does not matter!" Caolin said aloud. "What he needs now, only I can give to him. It is enough . . . it is enough for me!"

Slowly he lowered his hands to his sides and made his fingers uncurl, mastered his breathing, and waited for the pounding of his heart to still. He looked around to see if there was anyone in the corridor. Somewhere above him someone was playing a harp. Caolin could hear the notes faint but clear in the stillness of the sleeping fortress, like a memory of love.

Music had been one of those first bonds between him and Jehan. As he walked along the passageway to his own door, the Seneschal smiled.

Farin sat in the window above the side gate with his harp cradled in his arms, looking out at the steady rain. Rosemary and Faris had gone to their chamber long before, but though the long cold ride to bring the King to the Hold had tired him, he could not sleep.

"I sang to the King!" he told the harp triumphantly, "though he may never know it was me!" His fingers brushed the horsehair strings, drawing out the melody of the marching song, embellishing it with the little touches of harmony that his voice could not supply.

Then he stopped, plucked one string again, and reached for his tuning key. The harp was an old one that he had found in a storage room at home, and though he had oiled it, filled its cracks with resin, and carved new pegs for the strings, the sound was still a little dull sometimes and the strings went easily out of tune.

"But I would not dare to sing to him in public. You are not good enough, old friend, and neither am I." Here at the Hold they praised his playing, but Farin was too painfully aware of the times when his fingers stumbled, or his voice was a little less than true. The others heard the music that came from his fingertips but not the resplendent harmonies that soared in his heart. His hands dropped to the strings once more, plucking out the first lively chords of a war song.

"How splendid the King looked, shining like a star with the lightning around him. He would be wonderful in battle—I wish I could go with him to war! That would be something to sing about!" Realizing what he had said, Farin laughed. *What a fool I am,* he thought. *I can never make up my mind whether my hands are for the harp or for the sword.*

The lamp was flickering fitfully as the oil burned low, and the fire had sunk to red coals. Farin yawned, pushing his black hair back from his eyes, and gently set the old harp down.

Caolin sat at the table in his chamber and picked up the book of the stars he had brought from Laurelynn. It was very late, but he had less need for rest than most men, and only the use of his mind could ease him when tension kept him wakeful as it did now.

He turned the pages carefully, for the volume had been printed before the days of the Cataclysm and was held together only by its covering. The language had changed since the ancients described the workings of the stars—he was still puzzled by the distinction they made between astrology and astronomy—but he had become adept at translating it and at preserving pages that threatened to fall to dust in his hands.

He drew out his notebook, consulted it, then looked at the book again. It had taken him years of study to correlate the Westrian calendar with that of the old civilization. He was only beginning to trust his interpretations. Names, customs, even the contours of the land might have been changed by the Cataclysm, but the stars remained.

Caolin sighed, relaxing as he contemplated the mathematical beauty of the heavenly movements. Here was an order far removed from the confusions of men, yet governing them in a pattern that was plain if one had the wit to see.

There—the planet Venus was riding high in Cancer, the King's sign. But other forces were present: across the horoscope stretched the baleful influence of Mars. Caolin frowned, suspecting danger for Jehan. But from what source? In the years since the Cataclysm, Westria had become a Kingdom of four Provinces that honored the Guardians and kept to its Covenant. Normontaine, to the north, was ruled by a Queen and shared many customs with the people of Westria; they had always been allies. To the south lay the Confederation of Elaya, where instead of mixing, the people of different blood had formed five nations uneasily united under an elected Prince, who were always ready to fight Westria when they were not bickering with each other.

But that border, like the wasteland of mountains between Westria and the Brown Lands to the east, had been quiet for some years now.

From where then could danger come? Was Lord Brian of Las Costas planning some treachery? For a moment, intent upon the chart before him, the Seneschal smiled like a cat who waits for a mouse to pass his hiding place. Let Brian only try. He and Caolin had an old rivalry, but Caolin's ally was the King.

Then he sighed, checking the chart against the book again. The power of Mars would be brief and then Venus would reign. Was Jehan destined to find a bride here in the Corona after all?

Carefully he closed the book, eased it into its silken case, and pushed back his chair. He brought his thumb and fore-finger together around the candle flame. For a moment he held them so, savoring his own awareness of pain and watching the point of fire thin and lengthen as it sought to escape his touch. Then he smiled faintly and pinched the candle out.

Surefooted in the darkness, Caolin moved to the window, pulled aside the wooden shutters, and unlatched the multi-paned window to see into the night. The wind was hurrying the storm northward, and between the dim masses of cloud great patches of night sky showed now, strewn thickly with stars. Venus had set long ago, but for a moment he glimpsed the red wink of Mars. He stood still, dizzied by the glory that was alternately veiled and unveiled before him.

"When the Masters of the College of the Wise taught us to read the heavens, they never told us how to see the future there. Do they know? Is that a part of their secret lore?" Caolin spoke softly to the night.

"I may always lack the power to link mind to mind, and so they had an excuse to send me away, but I have this knowledge now, and I am not afraid to use it to guard the Kingdom and the King." Unvoiced came the memory of the one time that the doors of his spirit had been unlocked by another—by Jehan.

"Knowledge is power," he cried, "and with that power I can lead this land to a glory it has never known." Caolin spread his arms as if he would embrace the sky.

The Master of the Junipers spread his arms to the east, then slowly traced a star before him that his trained awareness perceived as a flowing pentagram of light. "O Thou Guard-

ian of the Powers of Air . . ." he murmured a Name, "guard
Thou the words of my lips and of my heart."

He turned then to the south, making the sign of warding
again. "O Thou Ruler of the fires of Earth and Heaven, keep
life's fire burning within me until I return to this body."

Moving again, the Master faced the west and, signing 'it,
commanded the Lord of the Waters to maintain him in harmony with all cycles and tides. Then he shifted to the north,
lifted his arms once more, and drew the line of light down
and up to the right, left and down and up to the point again,
finishing the star.

"O Thou Protector of Earth, my foundation, maintain the
bond between my spirit and my body until I take it up once
more."

He bowed, then seated himself in the center of the circle
he had made, legs crossed and hands open upon his knees.
His thoughts were still busy with tasks of the day, and for
the moment he let them run freely while he controlled his
breathing and relaxed his muscles one by one.

He had spent the afternoon rehearsing tomorrow's ceremony with the priestess from the town below the fortress.
He had learned all of the major ceremonies when he was at
the College, of course, but it had been long since he had
been a celebrant. They seemed to think that it would be an
honor for one of the Masters from the Father of Mountains
to officiate. It surprised him, for in the old days even the
head of the College had made a point of performing one of
the rituals somewhere at least once a year.

He turned his thoughts to the Lady of Flowers whose festival tomorrow would be, trying once more to bring Her into
focus as he had not been able to that afternoon. She was
not a physical being, even in the sense that the First People
who guarded the plant and animal kindreds could be. He
had been presented to the Lord of the Trees during his training, and once, on a journey to the sacred valley of Awahna,
had glimpsed the Great Bear, and he knew that they could
appear in many forms. But the Masters at the College still
argued over the origins of the gods.

Some said the great Powers, like the Lady of Flowers or
the Lord of the Winds or even the spirit of Westria Herself,
had returned to Westria after the Cataclysm. Others believed that they had always been there, and only those of
the ancients who knew how to worship them had been able

to survive to found the new nation. And there were some who felt that in truth, the gods were images that men used to focus and contact the universal forces by which they lived. The College itself did not require that men believe—only that they keep the Covenant.

But the Master knew that, whatever their nature, the powers he called upon were real. But in order to call upon the Lady of Flowers he must see Her clearly, and so he sought guidance where he had always found help before.

He straightened a leg that had been cramped by stillness, then crossed it over the other again. Smoothing his features into passivity, he deepened his breathing and willed it to resume the careful rhythm to which he had trained body and spirit to respond.

"In Thy Name, O Thou Source of All, and to Thy glory . . ."

Imperceptibly his open hands relaxed upon his knees. Images swirled across his consciousness and were banished. Releasing its grasp on the world of forms, his awareness retreated until all knowledge of his body was gone.

Within the darkness in which he floated now, he perceived a single point of brilliance. As he rushed forward it expanded until it dazzled his inner sight. Then he waited while the other world took shape around him, until at last he saw his Guide approaching, robed in light.

Light danced with darkness, and Faris' dreaming spirit soared on the wings of the storm. All her troubled dreams had resolved to this—the world spread out beneath her, the sleeping valleys of Westria where scattered points of light marked the dwellings of men, the mountains whose silver peaks thrust against the sky, oblivious to the tumults below.

I am free! she shouted. *Nothing can hold me now.* Not the anger of her father, her sister's solicitude, nor her own fragile body could stop her flight. Higher she rose, and yet higher, lifting her arms to the stars.

Then a bolt of lightning arched across the heavens toward her. She swooped and darted like a frightened dove but she could not escape.

But it was not lightning, it was a falling star, and when it struck, her flesh was ignited and she and the star burned with an equal flame.

Faris cried out as the force of its fall bore her downward, and she and the star upon her breast plummeted earthward in a single bolt of fire.

II

The Lady of Flowers

Faris shivered, feeling a draft though all of the windows in Rosemary's chamber were shut tight. She reached for the mug of green-gold yarrow tea that Rosemary had just poured for her, hoping that no one had noticed her chill. Steam rose from the mug in white curls that twined lazily in the thin morning light.

She swallowed gratefully as the warmth of the tea filtered through her, and pushed her breakfast about upon her plate so that it would look as if she had eaten. But she knew better than to try. She was paying now for her exaltation of the night before and for the dreams that had followed. Darkness and splendor warred in her memory, dimming the morning light.

Something gray and furry slipped by her. She stifled an exclamation as Rosemary's raccoon hooked a honeycake from the platter and, unimpeded by the splint on his hind leg, hopped back to the floor.

"*Scatter!*" Rosemary glared at the animal. "What shall I do with you? You need a good smack, but I don't want to spoil my doctoring!"

"If he tries to wash that cake it's going to come apart," said Farin, watching the raccoon warily. "And if he goes after my breakfast *I* will smack him!" He picked another sausage from the platter as deftly as the animal had taken the cake.

The Master of the Junipers laughed. He looked very much at home here, with the sunlight glowing in his face—a face not so much worn as lived-in, as if its owner had come to terms with his own strengths and failings long ago.

I wish that I could. Faris pushed her plate aside and picked up her embroidery again, frowning as she set neat stitches around the neck of the tunic she was making for

Farin. *Life would be easier if I could just accept my flaws.*
She shook her head to hold back tears.

"Faris, are you all right?" asked Rosemary. "Berisa will
send you home if you fall ill."

"Then don't tell her!" Faris answered rebelliously. She
admired her older sister's dark beauty and the efficiency
with which she had managed their home after their mother
died. Now Berisa bore the keys of the fortress, which Sandremun's mother had been only too happy to give up to her,
but when she was near, Faris felt what little confidence she
had slip away.

"I didn't sleep well," she added shortly.

"Well, that's no wonder, in such a storm—but at least the
Lady has given us some sunshine for Her Festival." Rosemary had finished eating and was feeding her animals. The
gopher snake coiled in its basket needed no attention, but
the cageful of mice were glad of the cake crumbs. Rosemary's maid, Branwen, was feeding two orphaned lambs in
a pen near the fire. The old sheepdog, who had been asleep
with his head across the feet of the Master of the Junipers,
thumped his tail on the floor as she went by.

"And we brought the King here safely, after all!" said
Farin proudly. When he had come in last night with the others, he had been shaking with cold, but he seemed to have
recovered his spirits now. "What a rider Jehan is! The
horses were half crazed with fear of the thunder, but whenever anyone needed help, he was there. Rosemary! Are you
listening to that owl or to me?"

Rosemary looked at him over her shoulder while the owl
swiveled its head forward to pick at the bits of sausage she
was offering it.

"Huw talks very good sense sometimes, and he has excel-
lent manners!"

The King. Faris could avoid thinking about him no longer,
and the vision of the rider on the rearing white horse whose
eyes had held her own replaced her awareness of the room,
as it had blazoned itself across her dreams. Had he seen her
as well?

"They say Jehan is a fine fighter. I wonder if he would
take me into his service," Farin went on.

"Shall I arrange for you to sing for him?" asked
Rosemary.

Farin looked horrified. "No! He heard me last night, of

course—but that was only a marching song, and he could not have known it was me. If I could be trained at the College of Bards, I might learn enough to perform for him . . . but Father would never let me go."

Branwen set down the bottle that had been emptied by one of the lambs and reached for another. Faris saw that she could not grasp it without losing her grip on the second lamb and got up to hand it to her.

"Thank you, my Lady," whispered the girl.

"Let me help." Faris sat down on the bench beside Branwen and coaxed the lamb to suck. She ran her hand across the soft wool of its back and felt her tension ease.

"Faris, you don't have to do that!" exclaimed Rosemary. The Master of the Junipers glanced over at her with one of his sweet smiles.

Faris tried to laugh. "Really, I am all right—it's just lack of sleep."

Her brother looked at her sharply. "Are you getting sick again, or did you have a dream?" She could not evade his eyes—he knew her too well. "What was it, Faris?" he said.

Faris stared at him, images and warnings conflicting in her memory. There had been a confused succession of visions of fighting—Farin had been in them, and the King. But she must not tell that. Once, she had dreamed that her mother was leaving her, and told her dream, and seen her mother die.

"Faris." His voice was soft, his eyes a mirror for her own. She heard his thought—*I will make her dream into a song*—and envied him, for in Farin all the intimations of power that tormented her had been channeled into the one gift of music.

"So that you can have something new to sing about?" she asked bitterly. Now she remembered her final dream, like an extension of the storm. "Very well. I dreamed that I was struck by a falling star—use that if you can!"

"You must not be afraid," the Master of the Junipers said gently, though his eyes had grown intent at her words. "Such abilities can be very valuable if they are trained. Didn't they tell you so at your Initiation? The College of the Wise would be glad to teach you."

Faris shook her head. She had gone through the classes that prepared all Westrian children to assume their adult names, terrified that the teacher would find out. But there was such peace in the Master's face. She gazed mutely at him, wondering how it would feel to enter the world of the spirit as a citizen.

"You don't know our father, or Berisa," put in Farin. "They would never let her go." A horse whinnied outside and hoofbeats echoed on the stones of the passage beneath the chamber. Farin sprang to his feet and went to the window to see.

"The King is riding into the town this morning so that everybody can see him, since there's not room for them all to come to the Festival," explained Rosemary.

The Master nodded. "That reminds me, it is time I went down to the Hall. Mistress Elisa wants to go over the litany again."

"And *we* should be going down to the orchard to see what blossoms the wind has left for us to use in the ceremony," said Rosemary. "If we hurry, perhaps we can see the King ride out." She began a hunt for the pruning knife while Branwen shut the lambs back into their pen and took down cloaks from the hooks on the wall.

Faris got to her feet slowly, finding herself curiously reluctant to go with them. She was still dazzled by the vision of the King's face in stormlight, and she did not want to see him grown ordinary in the plain light of day.

"Eric, will you go over to the stables and see if they have gotten Stormwing saddled yet?" asked the King, squinting into the sunlight. The rear guard of last night's storm clouds still trailed across the sky—towering silver-edged masses like floating fortresses, driven northward by a chill wind. But the sun shone with blinding clarity through air washed clean by the rain. Jehan breathed deeply, watching Eric stride through the puddles.

He turned to Caolin, who stood beside him on the porch that overlooked the courtyard. "Now that Eric's gone, I need to talk to you."

"I wondered when you would tire of his company," replied the Seneschal. He stood straight and still, the early light polishing the smooth planes of his face. "He is good-natured, but limited in his interests. I suppose it is a function of his rather appalling youth."

"I was appallingly young when I met you—don't you remember?" Jehan grinned. He had been thirteen when he had gone to be trained at the College of the Wise, where Caolin was a senior student. He had been only sixteen, back in Laurelynn with his ailing father, when Caolin, having astonishingly failed to complete his pilgrimage to Awahna and become a Master of the College, had appeared in the capital to take a post with the old Seneschal. Accepting no rebuffs, the prince had tried to penetrate the young clerk's loneliness. But it was in the following year, when King Alexander died and left Jehan to bear the crown, that Caolin had realized that Jehan needed *him*, and the bond between them had begun to grow.

"As a matter of fact, I find Eric's innocence refreshing," the King went on resolutely. "I wanted to talk to you alone just because I don't desire to disturb it. The Great Rebellion has finally approached him." Two of Theodor's men bowed as they passed and Jehan saluted them. Caolin waited until they had gone down the steps to reply.

"Oh? And what did he think of it?"

"Highly indignant, of course. You know how he feels about Lord Brian."

"I also know how Brian feels about him. They are too alike in strength and temper, and Brian is older. Was Roland of Greenfell the one who spoke to him?"

"Yes—how did you know?" Jehan rubbed at his beard, realizing that this was not such news to Caolin as he had expected.

"I've talked to him enough to find out he is Brian's man. Anyone who travels around the Kingdom as much as he does naturally interests the Seneschal's office, so I cultivated him. Hopefully he will keep me informed of his progress. He may be Theodor's cousin, but I doubt that the Lord Commander knows what he's up to."

The King nodded, remembering the light in the old man's eyes when he had greeted him. "I don't doubt Theodor's loyalty. Normontaine is too near, and the outlaws in the no-man's-land between the Kingdoms nearer still. He would not be able to stand alone." *How cynical that sounds*, he thought then. *Am I becoming like Caolin, to suspect lies whenever men offer loyalty?*

"Jehan, come down." Sandremun's call brought him back to the present. "The horses are waiting outside."

The King gave Caolin a quick smile, grateful that for once the Seneschal had forborne to accuse Brian of treachery.

Then he ran down the broad stairs, clutching at his green cloak as the wind filled it to keep from being blown away.

Faris hurried across the courtyard after Rosemary, head bent into the wind. She stumbled, then threw herself backward as hooves clattered like thunder and a dark bulk reared over her.

"You fool! If you don't know any better than to run under a horse's hooves, you should go back to your burrow in the hills!"

Gasping, Faris looked up, saw a large young man reining an equally massive black horse in tight circles, cursing her and the animal equally as it bucked and snorted, fighting his restraint. She knew that her cheeks were flaming, but she could not get breath enough to reply.

"There now, that's a boy—hold still. Maybe she's never seen a real horse like you." The stallion came to a halt at last and the young man's words died away as he focused on Faris standing there.

"My Lady," he said finally, after a moment of stunned silence during which his face became as red as her own. For all his size, Faris realized that he was scarcely older than she.

"I'm Sir Eric of Seagate, at your service. Did Thunderfoot hurt you?"

She shook her head. Why was he staring at her?

Someone called from the gate. Eric looked around distractedly, then back at her. "Are you sure? Will you be at the Festival?"

Faris nodded, smiling, wondering how long he would keep her standing here. Then his name was called again, and she took advantage of his preoccupation to gather her skirts and cross the courtyard before he could call out to her.

She slipped through the orchard gate and latched it firmly behind her, then stood still for a moment, catching her breath. It was very quiet here, out of the wind. Faintly she could hear shouts as the King's party set off toward the town, and more clearly, the voices of Rosemary and Branwen discussing which branches should be cut for the Festival.

She sighed, grateful to be alone. The plum tree before her was just coming into flower. She rested one hand lightly on its trunk, gazing into the lacy branches. She could feel a light throbbing through her fingertips—was it the response of the trunk to the wind, or the life of the tree flowing beneath her hand? Her breathing deepened, and the flush faded from her cheeks.

Looking from one tree to another, she let the memory of her encounter with Sir Eric slip easily from her mind, and with a greater effort banished the vision of the King. Here among the trees she could escape from the complexities of men.

Her ears buzzed with cold. Her eyes began to water, and the blossoms before her blurred. She blinked, looked up, and was suddenly still. For a moment in which she did not breathe she saw before her not a grove of trees, but a circle of maidens veiled and crowned in white, stretching out their arms to her.

Fear and longing warred within her. Her breath rushed back and, dizzied, she fell to her knees with her palms sunk into the soft earth and her forehead against the trunk of the tree. The air warmed around her and she recognized a subtle perfume. There was a moment then when she might have gained her feet and run away. But she did not move.

The Presence she had sensed approaching grew greater and the heat increased. A sweet fire melted all her stiffness. Faris kept her eyes shut tight, afraid of what she might see.

But words welled unbidden from the depths of her spirit. *Lady! Make me whole . . . let me be free!*

There was reassurance in the warmth that enfolded her, like a mother's arms. Faris bowed her head upon her crossed hands in wordless wonder, beyond self-awareness and beyond time. She heard distant laughter like a chime of silver bells, and the strange heat faded gradually away.

"Faris . . . Faris . . ." How far away the voices seemed. She did not want to move, but she made herself sit up and look upon a world whose splendor was once more veiled. And for that moment she *knew* that what she saw was only the appearance, and what she had sensed, the reality.

"Faris, what are you doing? We must get these flowers to the Hall, and then it will be time to dress for the Festival."

Faris slowly focused on Rosemary, standing before her with her arms full of starry flowers.

"Faris, you look so strange. What happened to you?"

But Faris could only shake her head and hold her face to the clean wind.

•   •   •

Wind swept the great Hall of the Hold, fluttering women's veils and ribbons, plucking white petals from the branches of almond and plum that garlanded the long room as the big double doors at its end were opened and shut again. People turned to see who had come in, asking each other if the families from the holdings on the northern border had arrived.

Jehan and Rosemary stood at the edge of a swirl of dancers, sipping white wine. "My Lord, I must apologize," said Rosemary, smoothing her azure gown a little nervously. "Things may begin on time in Laurelynn, but we are less precise in the Corona." The Festival had been scheduled for midday, but it was now halfway into the afternoon, and Theodor had told the musicians to start playing while they waited for the latecomers.

The King turned to her, lowering his voice. "Believe me, a more leisurely pace is very welcome. I am glad of the chance to learn more of the Province from you. For instance, you could tell me the names of some of the dancers. Only the heads of households were presented to me, yet I may have to lead their sons in battle, or . . ."

"Or their daughters in the dance?" Rosemary laughed.

For a moment Jehan's answering grin was as open as her own. "Your pardon, Lady Rosemary. I had not meant to be devious. It is a habit one gets into in Laurelynn." He met her steady gaze.

A boy came by with a wicker tray of sweet white cakes molded in the shapes of moons and flowers, blushing as the King took one and nodded his thanks.

"To be frank, the ways of the capital hold little interest for me. We live more simply here in the north. The companionship of the Master of the Junipers is the only thing I envy you."

"Yes, your father told me you study with him when he stops here on his way to the College of the Wise. I wish I could spare him more often, but my chaplain is like a peaceful clearing in the midst of a very tangled wood, to which I have sometimes great need to repair."

The music changed to the dance called the peacock, and the King offered his hand to Rosemary. Together they paced the length of the hall, the swirl of his dark blue mantle echoing the sway of her skirts. Across the room he saw the crimson splash of Caolin's robe and noted that the Seneschal was talking with Ronald of Greenfell. His gaze passed on, seeking among the dancers one white face framed in a cloud of dark hair.

"The couple ahead of us are Andreas Blackbeard, who is squire to Charles of Woodhall, and Woodhall's daughter Holly. Sir Charles is one of the latecomers we are waiting for. I think you know Allen of Badensbridge, and of course my brother and his wife, Berisa. Sir Eric is dancing with my companion, Branwen." Rosemary paused, scanning the crowd. Colors flowed and blended as the dancers moved, parting for a moment to reveal a white figure like a lily in a field of wildflowers.

Jehan's breath caught for a moment, but the rhythm of the dance carried him on. "And the dark-haired girl in ivory, dancing with the young man who so resembles her?" he asked softly.

"Oh, did I leave them out?" Rosemary looked at him speculatively. "They are relatives of Berisa, from Hawkrest Hold. She is Faris, and her brother is called Farin."

"Fair she is indeed, and her brother looks a likely lad," Jehan replied neutrally. "He is not knighted yet? How old is he?"

"He's nineteen, but he says he will not accept knighthood until he has earned it. I'm afraid he's had little chance to be a hero. Here, he's known for his skill as a singer and upon the harp."

"A singer? Of course, now I remember. His singing was the only thing bearable about last night's ride." Did Rosemary suspect that Jehan's real object of interest was Farin's sister? He was almost certain Faris was the girl he had seen.

The music ended with a flourish of flutes, and Rosemary gathered her azure silk skirts in a courtesy. Jehan escorted her back to her father, and for a moment they exchanged civilities. Her mother, Lady Amata, found events of this kind too great a strain, so Rosemary was acting as her father's hostess. As they talked someone came to her asking whether they should put out more cakes and wine now, or wait until after the ceremony, and Jehan took advantage of the distraction to move away.

He looked around him. The Seneschal had disappeared, and perhaps that was as well, for the King found himself unwilling to seek Caolin's help in meeting the girl in the moon-colored gown. A formal introduction would attract unwelcome attention, and he did not wish to embarrass her. But what about a chance meeting in the dance? Jehan cut through the crowd to find the Master of Musicians.

Soon the hands of the dancers were filled with flowers. Men and women danced together until the melody changed, then each must wander alone for a few measures until the music altered once more, and each gentleman offered his spray of flowers to the lady of his choice and took her as a partner . . . until the music changed again and it was time for the ladies to choose anew.

Like wanderers in some enchanted wood, each one sought the face he or she desired.

Sunlight slanted through the long upper windows, shafting through the dust motes in a haze of light. Dazzled, Faris peered at her partner, recognized him as Allen of Badensbridge, then laughed without replying as he asked her whom she had expected to see. Her pale gown swirled about her like a cloud as they moved forward. She moved as lightly as a cloud, as if she were dancing with the wind.

Ever since that moment in the orchard she had been acutely conscious of the insubstantiality of the veil between the worlds. And now the trees had come into the Hall to dance with her. Faris laughed again, forgetting her aching feet, answering the music. Nothing could touch her now. When the music lifted her, there were no more choices to be made, only the instinctive movement toward harmony.

The melody changed. Her partner left her and Faris waited, poised in the music, dizzied by the flowers' faint perfume. Sunlight blinded her. Then someone drew her into the shadow, and when she could see again she met the blue gaze of the King.

She took from him the spray of flowers, trembling suddenly so that only the steady pressure of his hand kept her from faltering in the dance. She fought for self-control, fear shattering her exaltation as she understood who her partner was.

They turned, and her unfastened sleeve fell back, revealing her scar.

The King turned to face her, almost breaking step. "You have been hurt!" His voice beat heavily across the music.

Faris nearly fell, waiting for him to show everyone her shame.

"How did it happen?" he asked softly. Still terrified, she looked up at him and could not look away. She found herself telling him the story that she had tried to forget, as she tried to forget her scar.

"It was long ago . . . our housekeeper had a baby whose gown caught fire. When I beat out the flames, I was burned too."

"Were you afraid?" asked the King, guiding her around the circle. "How old were you?"

"I was six," she said simply, held by his still gaze. Suddenly all that had happened to her seemed very small and far away. "I was afraid afterward, but when it happened everything was very clear, and I knew what I had to do."

The King gave a little sigh and nodded, his gaze releasing her to fix inward on some memory. "It is like that in battle sometimes."

He knows! Faris' heart shook in her breast. *He has seen my scar and still he is dancing with me.* She glanced at him beneath her lashes, and her breath caught as she realized that he was not only the King, but beautiful.

The music swept them forward, but breathless, she could not speak now. She let him lead her, attending neither to the figure nor to her own steps, for it seemed natural for his movements to be reflected by her own. The measure was endless, like music in a dream.

And then, like a dream, it stopped and left them standing together while all around them couples drew apart.

The King's hand tightened, as if he would have drawn Faris through the door behind them. But the breaking of the music had frightened her. Startled, she hung back. Immediately the pressure ceased and he raised her hand to his lips instead. Her left hand. Then he released her and was gone into the crowd.

Horns called, their clear summons dissipating into a buzz of comment as word spread that Theodor had tired of waiting and ordered the ceremony to begin.

Rosemary took Faris' arm and pulled her into place in the line of young women, but Faris scarcely noticed what she did, for even as the first notes of the processional began, the print of the King's lips still burned upon her hand.

• • •

"In the Name of the Lady of Fire, be this place purified and made sacred to our purpose here . . ."

While Faris stood dazed, the two priests and the other priestess had already sanctified the room with incense and water and salt, and now they formed three points of a square surrounding the altar where they had placed the most perfect of the flowers. The fire priestess finished her circuit, moved to the altar, where she used her taper to touch the tall candles to flame, and then took her place at the southern corner of the square.

"Thou earth, thou sky, thou sun, thou sea—I am the center of thy circled cross, be thou represented equally in me!" the people cried.

Mistress Elisa and the Master of the Junipers faced each other before the altar, mantled alike over their black and white robes in capes of pale green worked with embroideries of butterflies and flowers.

"Who is this that appears with the dawning?" the Master of the Junipers began the chant. "She is clothed in mist, Her hair is pearled with dew."

"She emerges from the sea, She rides upon the wind," the priestess answered him.

"Her strength is the strength of the seedling surging toward the sun; Her beauty blinds the eye." Back and forth ran the litany.

"Her beauty is as clear as water, Her fragrance stirs the heart like a distant song."

Yes . . . Faris breathed in the scent of the flowers. *I have heard Her . . . I have felt Her touch upon my soul.* The words of the celebrants blended with her memory of the orchard. Overlapping visions dazzled her. Was she surrounded by tree trunks or the carved and painted pillars of the Hall?

"When wind whispers in budding branches and the new moon swings through the sky, She is here."

"When blossoms open to the sunlight and earth receives the gentle rain, She is here."

The Master of the Junipers turned to the people, opening his arms. "O my brothers and my sisters, we are gathered here to celebrate the coming of spring and to invoke the blessing of the Lady of Flowers. But winter's sleep was peaceful, demanding nothing. Are you willing to wake, to grow, and with the world to face both the joy and the pain life brings? Is it your will to call the Lady here?"

"Yes! We will it, let the Lady come!" came the answer from a hundred throats, shaking the air and setting chills through Faris' flesh.

Do they understand that She will come? thought the girl, *that She is already here?* Abruptly she was afraid.

The Master stood before the altar, lifting his arms as a supplicant, and began to call upon the Lady by names that Faris knew and by others that she had never heard before. Tension charged the air like a gathering of lightnings as he focused the energies of all those in the room into one cone of power. The hair lifted on the back of her neck. The Master's voice rang like a bell in the stillness, names became images, and images a single shining form that stood before the altar, arms outstretched, veils floating upon an invisible wind.

Her cloak was a shimmering fabric of leaves like pale wings, like flames, like the petals of flowers, through which Her body shone like the new moon in a dawn sky. Her eyes were fixed on Faris with a terrible clarity, and Faris could not look away. This was the vision she had feared in the orchard, but she could not refuse it now.

Lady . . . The words trembled on her lips, but no sound came. *What do You want of me?*

Did no one else see Her? The Master of the Junipers stood rigid before the altar, arms lifted in adoration. His face was filled with light. Transfixed by his own vision, he had no help for Faris.

The priestess stepped past him to give the blessing, but Faris saw her slight figure cloaked in the Lady's glory. Her words sounded in the stillness of Faris' soul, answering her.

"I am the kernel in the husk and the seed in the ground. I am the shoot piercing the stone and opening its leaves to the sun. Come to Me, and grow . . .

"I am the rain in the cloud and the tides of the sea. I am the wind of heaven that bears seed to the earth and inspiration to men. Come to Me and bring forth beauty . . .

"I am the lightning in the storm and the star in the dark. I am the fire of earth in the coal and the fire of love in the heart. Come to Me and I will light the eternal flame within your soul . . ."

The words thundered and reverberated through the spaces

of Faris' spirit, opening before her vistas that she had never dared to look upon.

The herders were coming up to the altar now, bringing the firstborn lambs for the Lady's blessing, white and bleating with wide, curious eyes. The landholders came, bearing the sacks of seed they would soon put into the ground. Men and women came, smiling, with their children in their arms.

"The Lady blesses you. What will you give to Her?" asked the priestess.

In the midst of the people the unmarried men stood with crowns of flowers in their hands. As they came forward Rosemary led the young women before the altar to face them. "As we are all dresses of the Lady, so we accept your offerings in Her name," she said.

With her back to the altar, Faris was able to focus on her surroundings, though still she felt the Lady behind her as though she stood before an open fire. The men were grouped unevenly before them. Andreas Blackbeard came forward and, after a moment's hesitation, set the wreath he carried on Holly of Woodhall's head. Another young man stepped out and, blushing, presented his crown to the girl next to Faris, then another came. She saw Eric of Seagate towering over the others and smiling at her.

Faris found herself trembling. She had not realized before that it would be so public, that each girl would be singled out from the rest. *Lady, help me!* her spirit cried, and the answer came, *I am here.*

The next man in the line was the King.

Sunlight blazed from the gold that banded his forehead. A light was on his face, and his glowing eyes seemed to see through her to the One who waited beyond. With the stately deliberation of a dream figure he came to her, and in that moment she was not surprised when he stopped before her and set the crown of flowers he bore upon her hair.

He took his place again, and she saw beyond him her brother's astonished face, and in the features of Eric of Seagate a mixture of fury and despair. Other men came forward then, and Eric, mastering himself, strode up to give his wreath to Rosemary.

Then it was finished, and the musicians sounded the first measures of the danced hymn that the girls had been practicing.

"O Shining One," the sweet voices soared, "who from

afar bears beauty like the morning star; lend us Thy light who linger here, imprisoned by our pain and fear." Then they began the first verse and moved into the dance.

> O ye who wander in a barren land—
> Behold, the Lady stretches out her hand
> All that was comfortless is passed away;
> She leads the world rejoicing into day.

Faris' feet fulfilled the pattern without her will; her lips moved without her knowing if her throat made any sound as they repeated the chorus and began the next verse.

> Behind Her trail the lengthening daylight hours,
> And in Her footsteps spring the rainbowed flowers.
> Wise as the owl and tender as the dove,
> Her handmaidens are light and life and love.

Faris felt the presence of the Lady withdrawing now, like receding music or flower scent borne away by the wind, but the wreath of flowers the King had given her glowed upon her brow like a crown of fire. She wondered then, *Did the King see* me *when he gave me the flowers, or* Her?

> Hers is the rain that nourishes the soul;
> Her mirror shows us to ourselves, made whole.
> Out of death's sleep . . .

The great doors crashed open, sending tremors through the floor. A cold wind swept the Hall, blowing the candles into streamers of flame and swirling a cloud of flower petals over the people like falling snow.

> . . . She rises with the morn,
> And, waking to Her kiss, we are reborn.

The singers grasped at the melody and finished the verse, their voices rising resolutely over the confused shouting that was spreading from the direction of the door, but to Faris their voices sounded dull as a cracked bell. The Lady had left Her temple now.

The crowd parted like water breasted by a fleeing deer as someone pushed toward Lord Theodor.

"Commander, you must come." The man burst into the space before the altar. Through the mire that covered him blood showed, caked around a ragged tear in the shoulder of his coat, splashed across his legs and thighs. He fought for breath and clung to Lord Theodor's bony hands.

"Stefan, Stefan, be easy, lad, I'm here. What has happened?" the Commander's voice was low and steady. A little color returned to the messenger's face.

"It's raiders, my Lord, woodsrats from the mountains. They've taken Woodhall and set all the holdings along the Highwater in flames. My two brothers fought their way free beside me, but they brought them down with arrows on the road . . ." Sobbing, the young man sank to his knees, his head pressed against Lord Theodor's hands.

Holly of Woodhall whimpered once and then stood mute and shaking while the other girls tried to comfort her. But Andreas had cried out in a great voice and his hand struck at the air as if grasping for a sword. He looked around distractedly, saw Holly, and came to her.

"Holly—my lady—Sir Charles is a great fighter; he might be holding out still. I swear to you, we'll rescue him . . . or revenge him." He stopped short, swallowing.

After a moment her gaze focused on him and her hand came up to touch his cheek. Then her face crumpled and, giving way to her grief, she let the other women lead her away.

Two of Lord Theodor's guardsmen were helping the messenger to his feet. Rosemary left her place among the singers to take care of him. Some of the girls tried to finish the chorus, but the Lord Commander was shouting orders and they could not be heard. The Master of the Junipers and Mistress Elisa bent before the altar, hurrying through the closing ritual.

And only Faris, standing still amid the storm of activity, seemed to hear as if from afar an echo of silver bells.

• • •

The great bell of the Hold tolled from the tower. Caolin could feel its reverberations in the walls of the passageway two stories below. The ceremonies had been very pretty, but Jehan had looked like a sleepwalker at the end of them. Where had he gone?

Distantly he heard the neighing of horses and the shout of orders as supplies were readied for the war party. There was no need for Jehan to ride with them—Theodor and his men should be perfectly capable of handling this without the reinforcement of the King. But Jehan would think it his duty to go, and Caolin supposed that it was politically useful for him to show himself a warrior.

But he remembered the danger he had foreseen in the King's horoscope. *What is the use of all my knowledge if I cannot guard him?* he thought and quickened his pace.

He heard the King's voice ahead of him, the sound of the words oddly distorted as they echoed against the stones of the passage, and then someone else answering him. Caolin stopped, wondering who Jehan was talking to.

"You gave your flowers to the Lady Faris because you thought it might commit you too much if you honored Lady Rosemary, didn't you?"

Caolin recognized the voice of Eric of Seagate now, and as he rounded the corner he saw the young knight facing Jehan, half crouched as if he would spring at his throat. The Seneschal's hand moved to the penknife that was all the weapon he ever bore, but Eric had dropped to one knee before the King, and Caolin realized that he was pleading.

Jehan's reply was inarticulate. He looked dazed, like a man wakened too suddenly from a fair dream.

"I know that you must marry to serve the Kingdom." Eric spoke as if his throat were closing on the words. "But Faris is not like the other women you—" He broke off, blushing furiously. "She is so young! She would not understand!"

"Eric . . . do you truly believe that of me?" For a moment Jehan's voice shook. "I have known many women, but do you think I would play with a young girl's feelings for my amusement?"

Caolin stepped forward, watching Eric warily, but neither man appeared to notice him.

"Oh no, my Lord! Oh, I had not meant to speak at all, only I saw you here, and—why did you give her the flowers?" Eric sat back on his heels, looking up at the King, his eyes like those of a hurt dog.

Jehan sighed. The glory was gone from his face now, and he looked drawn and pale. "I don't know why. Or perhaps"—his grim look softened a little—"I did it because she stood like a white lily in the sunlight, and then for a moment I saw beyond her the Lady Herself, smiling at me . . . I gave her the flowers because she was beautiful."

"And you are the King," Eric replied bleakly. "She will see no one else now. I should have told you that I—well, it does not matter now." He got to his feet, pulling himself erect. "My Lord, will we be going with Theodor's men?"

"Yes, of course," said the King absently, "but Eric, please—"

"Then with your permission, I will prepare the men to ride!" Eric's face had gone rigid, like a statue of heroic despair. Without waiting for an answer, he saluted, strode past Caolin without acknowledging him, and went down the passageway.

It was no more than his usual response to me, thought Caolin wryly, but in this case he doubted that the young knight had seen him at all. He shook his head and went to Jehan, who stood with his hands clenched in the folds of his tunic, staring at the wall.

"My dear Lord," said Caolin softly, "what are you doing, playing at fighting cocks with Eric, of all people? Does he fancy himself in love with that girl?" He put his hand on the King's shoulder.

"A fancy? Oh no, Eric is perfectly sincere. Oh, Eric!" he burst out. "If only I had known!" Then he sighed and rubbed his eyes. Behind them came the clatter of hurrying feet and the jingle of mail. "They'll be needing me." Jehan straightened, then shivered suddenly.

Caolin's grip tightened on his shoulder. "Jehan . . . Jehan . . . it's all right! It's only a girl."

The King looked up at him, and for a moment his face held something Caolin had never seen there before, evanescent as the light reflected on leaves by moving water. Then his features settled into their familiar lines and his eyes focused on Caolin.

"Only a girl . . ." he echoed. Then he smiled. "And now I must go arm or they will leave me behind, and I would never be able to live that down."

The squire Rafael clattered down the passageway and slid to a stop, panting. "My Lord, there you are—I've been looking—" He caught his breath. "I've laid your arms ready and packed your gear. Please come now!"

"Thank you, Rafael. Yes, I will come." For a moment Jehan's hand clasped Caolin's. Then he moved from the Seneschal's side and was gone.

"Take care, my Lord," Caolin called after him, wanting to call him back, feeling the chill draft in the passage as the first breath of a wind that would sweep them all away, but he did not know if Jehan heard.

For a moment he stood irresolutely, wondering if there was something he should do. But war was Jehan's business, not his, and even his usual duties of support and supply were being handled by Theodor's people this time. He shrugged and went back toward the gate to watch them go.

A red sun was glowing beneath lowering clouds as the war band of the Corona prepared to set out. It glittered on helms and mail like a dying flame and painted the bright banners and formal battle gear the color of blood. The forces that Theodor had sent to reinforce the eastern strongholds were dwindling in the distance, and the men assigned to garrison the Hold muttered in disappointment from the walls. The hundred men whom Theodor had picked to accompany him held their mounts before the gates, waiting for the signal to depart. They included Theodor's own guard, men from the Highwater valley whose homes had been attacked, and the knights who had come with the King.

Faris drew her gray cloak more closely around her, but the bitter wind searched out every irregularity in its weave. She could not stop shivering, and her stomach cramped anxiously. Even the Father of Mountains, rising white-cloaked to the north of the fortress, seemed aloof and implacable now. She looked down at Theodor's little army, pitying the horses who stamped eagerly, not knowing the journey that awaited them.

She found it hard to think clearly. Too much had happened today. That morning Sir Eric had spoken to her like an eager boy, yet now he sat his black horse like a statue in armor. Once, he looked up at the wall, but it seemed to Faris that his eyes flinched from meeting hers.

Rosemary moved closer and took her arm. "Are you as

cold as I am? What are they waiting for?" she asked angrily. She was watching Sir Eric too.

There was a stir immediately beneath them, and the Lord Commander came through the main gate, his son by his side. With hair and beards hidden by their helms and coifs of mail, they looked uncannily alike—Sandremun was a trifle taller, with more padding on his long bones. Faris glanced at her sister, Berisa, who was standing with her mother-in-law nearby. They leaned over the parapet, waving as if their husbands went off to war every day.

But she must be worried about Sandy, thought Faris wryly, *or she would have seen me shivering and sent me inside!* Berisa had tried to be a mother to her after their own had died, but her well-intentioned tyranny had left Faris feeling more orphaned than before. For a moment the encompassing love she had felt in the orchard stirred in her memory like the scent of blossoms borne by a changing wind, but she stiffened, afraid to accept it, and it was gone.

The babble of conversation below them lessened momentarily and Faris heard the voice of the King. She had been watching Berisa and had not seen him come out, but now he stood just below them, talking to the Seneschal. Would he look up at her? What should she do?

Jehan and the Seneschal moved forward. Caolin bent his fair head over his master's hand. Jehan slapped his shoulder bracingly and he straightened again, shaking his head. The King let him go and swung up on to his waiting mount. He settled into the saddle and, seeing Lord Theodor's lady on the wall above him, waved a hand in salute. His eyes moved past her to the others, but if he hesitated when he saw Faris among them, she could not tell.

And as surely as she had known he cared for her that afternoon, Faris was now certain that he regretted his choice, that he remembered her scar. She schooled her face not to show her shame, staring out over the warriors without seeing them.

A man desires perfection in the woman he loves. Faris could not shut away the echo of her father's voice, the distaste in his eyes as he turned her marred arm and forced her to look at it. *If men say you are fair, knowing of this, they will be lying to you, and if you let them think you fair, unknowing, you will be living a lie.* Nausea rose in her throat at the memory, and she started to turn away.

Berisa hissed gently, and after a moment's disorientation Faris realized that she was pointing not at her arm but at the courtyard below. "Did you know about this?"

Shaking her head to clear her confusion, Faris joined Rosemary as she bent over the edge of the wall and saw Farin, fully armed, grinning up at them. He shifted his round shield to his other arm and waved. Rosemary laughed and waved back.

"He's too young!" exclaimed Berisa. "He has no experience in war, and who in that crowd will take care of him?"

"Really, Berisa," retorted Rosemary, "if it were not for his own foolish notions Farin would be knighted by now! Surely he is old enough to chase outlaws! They are unlikely to catch up with them, and if they do, not only your husband, but men like Sir Eric of Seagate will be at his back. Farin will be safer with them than he would be at home!"

"He wanted to impress the King," murmured Faris. Another vision superimposed itself upon the scene below . . . an image from one of last night's dreams. She saw Farin's face, not laughing now, but pale and intent as he swung at faceless men who came at him through the snow. Swords gleamed in the fading light. Farin was struggling to remain on his feet. She saw the King's squire, Rafael, beside him, and another man at his back. A blade flashed toward Farin's head, the third man turned to parry it, and Faris recognized Jehan.

I dreamed this battle, and now the King is going to war. Faris whimpered and hid her face in her hands.

The air quivered to the sweet summons of a horn. There was a confused murmur as those who were still afoot swung into their saddles. The hoofbeats became a rhythm as horses joined the line. When Faris was able to look again, she saw only their riders' rejecting backs. Involuntarily she stretched out her hand.

They had not all turned away. As she caught her breath Faris saw one figure still standing in the road and met the considering gaze of the Seneschal.

She stared at him, swaying a little in the strengthening wind, while her cheeks grew wet with icy tears.

III
Trust and Treachery

"By the Lord of Battles!" Eric exclaimed. "There is no honor in this kind of war!" He glared at the ruins of the homestead, whose still-smoldering beams were partly powdered with snow.

Jehan shifted in his saddle, trying unsuccessfully to ease muscles wearied by hours of riding, and smiled bleakly. *Oh, Eric,* he thought. *This is not how I taught you to make war when we fought against Elaya in the south.*

They had ridden northward from the Hold until past midnight and stopped for an uneasy rest beside the road until it was light enough to see their way again. Now the Father of Mountains rose to the east of them, and the beginnings of the Highwater's southern fork trickled through the pasture. A pall of smoke stretched southward, dimming the morning light as its acrid reek clogged the air. The red-stained snow of the yard was littered with household goods the reivers had not bothered to carry away. Nearby stood a single piebald cow, her bag heavy with milk, whose plaintive mooing made counterpoint to the cawing of the carrion birds.

"It is the usual practice of these woodsrats," commented Theodor grimly. "They attack at night, slaughter the people, loot the steading, and then burn it to the ground. They come down from the north in bands of fifty or more and work their way down one valley and up another and thence back into the hills. But we did not expect them at this time of year. I fear that too many of our fighting men came down to the Festival and the borders were left without adequate defense."

Jehan shook his head, anger burning impotently in his belly. He knew that these outlaws raided the Corona every year . . . and yet if he had not come to the north, this steading might have been better defended and the blood of his people would not have stained the snow.

"Where is Woodhall from here?" he asked.

"Perhaps two hours' hard ride up the road, my Lord. It guards the mouth of the valley, but I fear there is little left of it now," answered the Lord Commander.

"Please, my Lord, let me go and see!" exclaimed a stocky man with a bristling black beard who had been in the forefront of the riders. *Andreas Blackbeard.* Jehan's memory supplied the name from the presentations yesterday afternoon.

"My lord Charles is a valiant man, and he might have held them off! Oh, why did I go without him? He told me to bring Holly to the Festival . . . he said he was too old for dancing . . . but my place was by his side!"

"Peace, Andreas, peace!" said Theodor. "You have no reason to reproach yourself. Your duty was to do as your lord bade you. We will take the main force up the road to Spirit Falls—the tracks of the raiders seem to lead that way—but you take all the men from this valley and fifteen from my guard and go on to Woodhall. Guard the road out of the valley for me!"

Andreas bowed low over his saddlebow and turned his horse up the road, followed by the men Theodor had assigned to him. The others watched him go, pity in their eyes.

"To have one's lord die and be able to do nothing in his defense must be the hardest of all fates for a warrior to bear!" said Eric somberly.

Except to see one's people endangered and be unable to go to their aid, thought the King. A horse stamped behind him and he heard whispering.

"Doesn't this destruction bother them at all?"

Jehan half turned and saw young Farin leaning toward the King's squire, Rafael. They did not see him watching them.

"I would expect the King and the Lord Commander to be made of iron, but don't any of the rest worry about what is going to happen when we catch up with these devils? Do you suppose one acquires this calmness along with knighthood?"

Farin's thin face looked weary, but his eyes were bright. *That girl's eyes, in her brother's face . . .* The King faced forward again, shutting the thought away, while the whispering of the two young men went on. He wished he could tell them that the sickness and the fear never went away, or if they did, it was because a man's soul was already dead, though his body might fight on.

"I don't know," Rafael was saying. "Somehow I doubt it. All I know is that I'm afraid too. Ssh! Theodor's speaking."

The cow mooed mournfully again. A crow was cawing in the trees by the remains of the house. *The music of the battlefield,* thought the King.

"Will someone at least do something about that damned cow?" said Theodor.

Caolin the Seneschal rested easily in a low chair before the fire, his fingers plucking a sonata from the strings of a guitar. It was a beautiful instrument, its wood worn honey-smooth, inlaid around the sound-hole with a geometric design in jet and mother-of-pearl.

Faris, lifting her eyes from her embroidery, wondered at his ability to play with such evenness and accuracy when his attention was not on his music but on his audience. It reminded her of the way a deer fed in a meadow, ears constantly swiveling to catch any hint of danger—except that Caolin's alertness held no hint of fear.

When her brother, Farin, played his harp, he was oblivious to all but the music, and his fingers stumbled sometimes, unable to keep up with the passion he was trying to express. He had no harp to comfort him where he was now. Faris bit her lip and turned resolutely back to the faces around the fire, suppressing her momentary vision of mailed forms struggling painfully through the snow.

The late afternoon light was falling through the window behind her, gray and dim, but the firelight coppered Caolin's pale hair and chiseled profile and warmed the faces of his listeners. Lady Amata sat nearest, her gentle face, too plump to show the wrinkles of sixty years, flushed from the fire. Berisa was beside her, black hair drawn back from her face like raven's wings. Her hands were busy with a darning needle and a pile of stockings.

Beyond them, Rosemary was mixing a painkiller for Stefan of the Long Ridge, whose bed had been placed at right angles to the hearth. Two other men who had been left to guard the Hold were nearby. One of them held up his hands

for Holly of Woodhall to wind a skein of wool. In the corner
Rosemary's maid, Branwen, sat with her spindle forgotten
on her knee. Even Rosemary's old dog had managed to
evade Berisa's restrictions and now lay sleeping beside his
mistress' chair.

Berisa looked up as the music slowed. "You play well,
my lord Seneschal. We are grateful for the entertainment—a
welcome diversion from wondering how our lords fare tonight."

"Yes, we *were* distracted, until she reminded us again,"
muttered Rosemary.

Faris jabbed her finger with the embroidery needle and
sucked it hastily, looking around to see if anyone had noticed her agitation. This was ridiculous! Farin was only her
brother, and the link between them was such that she would
surely know if he were hurt. She had known it when he was
thrown from his horse and broke his arm, and the time he
was caught in a rock slide while out hunting.

*And yet I'm as nervous as if it were my lover, not my
brother, who rode away. But I'm no one's lady*, she
thought bitterly as she remembered how Eric's eyes had
avoided her, how the King had not seemed to see her at
all, *nor am I likely to be!* She picked up her needle
defiantly, but her hand was trembling so that she could
not set it in the right place.

"It seems unfair that I should dominate the entertainment," said Caolin, holding their attention with his eyes.
His clipped hair brushed the upstanding collar of his robe as
he turned his head to survey the company. "Will none of
you ladies give us a song?"

Faris thrust her needle slantwise through the shirt, folded
it swiftly, and dropped it into her basket. She stood up.

"I will sing if you will provide an accompaniment," she
said quickly, forcing her voice to calm.

"Indeed, my Lady, I will partner you with great pleasure.
What is the song?"

Her eyes met his, flicked away around the room. Rosemary seemed pleased, the others interested, except for Berisa, who frowned as if she were deciding whether or not to
approve. For a moment Faris wavered, afraid that her voice
would fail her before all these people, and knowing that her
sister would act on the merest hint of an appeal.

And tell me forever afterward what a fool I had been to

stand up at all!" "I will sing 'The Butterfly,'" she said clearly.
It was a ballad she had practiced with Farin a hundred times.
"Do you know it?"

"No." Caolin smiled. "But if you will sing the first verse
I will join in."

"Wait a moment." Rosemary looked up from her patient.
"Let us have some more wood on the fire. As the afternoon
fades it will be colder, and I don't wish Stefan to take a
chill."

Berisa's two daughters jumped up a trifle guiltily and
brought wood from the box to build up the fire. Soon its
light reached into every corner of the room, flickering on
the painted walls and making fantastic shadows on the
carven beams.

Faris' voice wavered as she began, then gained strength
and filled the room as the firelight had filled it.

Light is my flight as I float on the wind,
Like a flower given wings I will fly.
I sup on sweet nectar, my drink is the dew—
No creature goes freer than I.

And yet I have trailed all the weight of my fate
Over earth, over trunk, over tree,
Until, wracked by winter, I spun out my soul
For a shroud, and I dreamed myself free.

In beauty I rise as a child of the skies,
I feel the wind's chill without fear.
And when these wings, outworn, flutter earthward,
    reborn
And more gloriously robed I'll appear.

Faris finished the song and sat down abruptly, feeling her
heart pound with the realization that she had gotten through
it without losing her voice or forgetting the words. She
looked around her, focusing now on the faces that had been
a blur to her as she sang.

"Your brother is not the only one with talent in your family," said Caolin, studying her. "My Lady, your singing is as
fair as your face."

In her relief at having finished the song, replying to the

Seneschal seemed easy. "My Lord, I am not used to performing before such a company. Your playing made it easy for me to sing."

The others murmured appreciation. There was a scattering of applause. Stefan tried to lift his head to look, and Rosemary pushed him firmly down again.

"By the Mountain, Rosemary, I only have a sliced shoulder. You don't have to act as if I were dying," said Stefan fretfully.

Rosemary snorted disgustedly. "It's not dying, but living crippled that you're in danger of if you keep bouncing around like that. I've stitched the wound as well as I could, though I wish the Master of the Junipers were here to check it, but no binding will help you if you don't keep still!"

"I am sure that the touch of your fingers is the best medicine of all," remarked Caolin.

"I appreciate your gallantry, sir, but I have a more realistic opinion of my skill."

"Are you depending on the skill of the Master of the Junipers?" Caolin raised an eyebrow. "He did not specialize as a healer, you know. He has only the general training that all of us who studied at the College received."

"I have benefited from his advice in the past," Rosemary said stiffly.

"Oh, as an adviser, I am sure he does very well."

Faris saw that Rosemary was beginning to smolder. Her exhilaration still buoyed her, made it easy to intervene.

"Were you at the College of the Wise?" she asked Caolin swiftly. "Though we live so close, we know little of it—only that very few are accepted for training there." She smiled at him, suppressing her momentary discomfort at the thought of the powers those so trained were said to acquire.

"I was there five years," Caolin replied smoothly, "studying the things you were all told of when you prepared for Initiation—the doctrines of the Tree of Life, the ways of birds and beasts and the stars."

"I have heard you are a wolfmaster," said Holly of Woodhall.

"That came later," said the Seneschal, "when I was alone. You may meet my friend Gerol when he comes up from the south. It should be soon."

Lady Amata made a small, startled sound, and Caolin looked around him as if enjoying the sensation his announcement had made. Traders from Laurelynn had said that the Seneschal had made a great wolf his companion, but Faris had thought it only a tale.

Stefan grasped Rosemary's arm. "He's right—you've made me well. Let me get up and tomorrow I'll ride after the war band."

Rosemary detached his fingers and stood up. "Lie still and be grateful that your fighting is done for a while!" She turned away from him and went to the window, staring out at the falling rain while Stefan turned his head restlessly and sighed.

"Does the King mean to stay long here in the north, and will you remain with him?" Berisa asked the Seneschal.

"I will stay or go as the King's need requires."

Stefan muttered something and tried to push himself up with his good arm. Faris got up quickly and sat down in the chair Rosemary had left. "Lady Rosemary does not mean to be unkind," she said. "She is worried about her father and brother. But by the time you could reach them, they will have finished with the reivers and be on their way home," she said soothingly, readjusting the quilt around him.

His eyes fixed on her face. Faris smiled, and the lines of pain in his face eased. She continued to talk to him, surprised at how easy it was.

Stefan sighed. "I know that my lord and the others will do all that men can, but it is hard to lie here, wondering. You have been very kind to sit by me for so long."

Faris smiled and took his hand.

Caolin's voice rose above the general conversation once more. "The length of our stay will depend on what news the returning warriors bring."

"What do you think of the Seneschal?" asked Stefan as Faris turned her head to look at him. "He seems such a cold man to be the companion of the King."

"It's that look of his, as if he could see through to a man's bones!" said one of the other men, overhearing them. "And yet he has a name for efficiency, and no one has yet discovered any bribe that tempts him at all."

Faris considered Caolin—the stillness of his lean body within the claret-colored robe, his head poised as if his senses were instruments to be focused at will, the fair skin of his face fitted across high cheekbones and arched nose too neatly for any sign of strain to show. This was the man whom the King had chosen for his chief servant, or as some said, for his shadow, his soul.

As if he had felt her gaze, Caolin's eyes met hers, and Faris looked quickly away. "If they do not catch up with the raiders this time, the King will want to try again. He does not like unfinished business," said Caolin.

Faris listened to the rattle of rain against the leaded windowpanes. Higher in the mountains it would be snow. Where was the King now?

"Are you cold?" asked Stefan. "You are so slender, I would be afraid to let you face a winter wind."

Faris shook her head and smiled down at him, realizing with some surprise that she was still warmed by the success of her song. "No . . . I am very well. You should rest now, and don't worry about Rosemary."

"No . . ." His answering smile grew vague. Faris smoothed back his hair, and his eyelids closed as Rosemary's medicine took effect at last.

"Night is almost upon us, and I have work to do before we dine," said Caolin, rising and bowing to Berisa and Lady Amata.

"Oh, you must forgive us, my Lord—we have kept you too long!" Lady Amata fluttered. "Rosemary, darling, bring me my shawl—before dinner I must go to my own chamber and rest."

"Yes, Mother." Rosemary said a last word to her patient, then went to get her mother's fleecy shawl.

"Lady Faris, your singing gave great pleasure. I hope that you will join me again?"

Startled, Faris saw Caolin standing before her. She put out her hand; he bent over it, then drew her to her feet. For a moment he stared at her, and she fought the impulse to pull her hand from his grasp.

"He spoke truly," said Caolin softly. "You are indeed the lily of the north."

Faris drew herself up proudly, feeling as if his eyes had clothed her in silks and jewels. *Who* had told him that? Was it Eric, or Jehan? Then he bowed to her again, and she thought, *It means nothing . . . he does not know about my scar.* He let her go and she curtsied as he moved away.

She was still looking after him when Berisa's hand closed on her shoulder.

"In the name of the Lady, what did that performance mean?"

"My singing? I thought it went quite well." Faris faced her sister, holding her head proudly though her stomach was automatically clenching with the guilt her sister always inspired in her.

"Faris, you know very well what I mean. You were not brought up to lead men on." Berisa's heavy brows bent in a frown.

"Was I? Would they follow me?" She stared at her sister, waiting for Berisa to remember why Faris must not dare to love.

"Naturally they would. A pretty young girl . . ."

"Am I a 'pretty young girl'? You never told me that before." Could her father have been wrong?

"Well . . . you take after Mother," Berisa admitted reluctantly. She sighed and folded her arms. "It's for your own sake I'm saying this! If you court men's attention, they will want to make love to you, and then what will you do?"

Let them? wondered Faris bitterly. Might it be worth it to have the illusion of being loved, if only for a little while? And before they found out the truth, she could send them away, and if they suffered, then at least she would not be the only one.

"Oh, Berisa." She shook her head. "They only look at me because the King showed me his favor for a little while. They'll soon tire of the game. What does it matter what I do?"

"Will they?" Berisa looked at her, frowning as if she had never seen her before. She shook her head. "And if they do, won't it hurt you?"

Faris considered her, trying to decide whether she saw real concern or condescension, or perhaps a mixture of the two, in her sister's face. Her right hand had moved to cover the scar hidden beneath her left sleeve, and she made herself grasp a fold of her skirt instead.

"Compared to the risks that Farin is taking right now, what have I to fear?"

Berisa nodded as if Faris had conceded some point. "I told Farin not to go, just as I tell you to take care, because I'm responsible to Father for you both! If you run into trouble, don't blame me!"

Faris suppressed a shiver, remembering her dream. *But*

Farin is doing the thing he wants most—defending the King. And even if my Lord never looks at me again, he has given me courage too! And suddenly, though her Father's words were as true as they had ever been, they did not matter anymore.

"Father stays mewed in Hawkrest Hold like a bird afraid to fly." She laughed a little shakily. "Even if it freezes me, I'll trust to the wind."

A sharp wind drove the snow into the faces of the horsemen who were attempting to climb the curving road. Farin, riding with Rafael close behind Sir Eric and the King, squinted and wiped his face with the end of his scarf. Eric was standing in his stirrups, peering through the snow.

"We will have to stumble right over those bastards if we are to find them in this murk!" Eric exclaimed.

"Relax, Eric," said the King, hunched in the saddle beside him. "You will be worn out by the time we do." Stormwing snorted and shook snow from his eyes. Farin urged his horse closer, eager to hear how these legendary warriors were coping with the situation—eager, in fact, for anything that might distract him from the cold.

"I want something to do! My sword and my arm are both twitching, and there's nothing to use them on—nothing but this damned snow!"

"I'm not surprised," said the King dryly. "You must learn to save your strength, Eric," he went on. "One would think you were going into your first battle, and you a veteran of the Elayan wars!"

"If he doesn't watch out I'll try my sword on that viper Ronald." Eric pointed to two dim figures ahead of them. "There he goes again. 'Oh, my Lord, my Lord, please make haste, they may be burning my home even now! Come yourself, my Lord, and let us hurry to reach Greenfell in time!'" he mimicked.

Jehan laughed. "Don't be so hard on the poor man. You saw the raiders' work. Can you blame him for being upset? Besides, as he informed us himself, he is an archer, not a man of the sword. It wouldn't be fair."

"If he can keep his bowstring dry in this, I will begin to respect him," muttered Eric. His horse stumbled and he swore as he pulled the animal up. "Will this hill never stop?

The horses are sliding all over the road. At this rate we will never reach Greenfell before dark!"

"My Lord—" Farin's voice was a croak, and he tried again. "My Lord, I've taken this road before . . . I think there's a pass by the little waterfall ahead a bit, and beyond it the valley widens and levels out."

They all peered upward, barely able to make out the steep, tree-clad slopes that loomed over the road and then fell away sharply to the torrent that they could hear rushing over rocks far below.

But by the time another two hours had passed, it became apparent that it would be night before they reached Greenfell after all. Not only was the narrow road slippery with snow and mud from the banks above, but fallen fir trees blocked their passage, their branches interlaced as they lay. They had to lead the horses, picking their way one by one, step by step, through the tangled mass. The snow had stopped, but the light was fading fast by the time they were all assembled on the road that led into the upper valley.

"I wonder where Ronald is," said Sandremun as he and his father prepared to mount again. "He should lead the way from here." He swung himself up and then, suddenly, collapsed backward with a cry as the air hummed and a flight of arrows materialized out of the dusk.

Farin flinched and yanked at his horse's reins.

"Now we know why our scouts didn't come back!" gasped the King as an arrow snicked by his head. A horse screamed, and the King reined Stormwing sharply around after Farin, then slipped from his saddle. "Down!" he cried. "Get off your horses—the light's going too fast for them to shoot for long!"

Apparently the enemy thought so too, for as he spoke dark figures sprouted from the earth before them and the raiders charged. Swords gleamed dimly, and war cries mingled with the moans of those struck by arrows as the enemy closed in.

Theodor, surrounded by those of his guards who had been able to reach him, battled above the body of his son. His great sword scythed through his foes like grain. Eric stood back to back with the King, both of them cutting as the attackers came on and blocking their blows with neat movements of their shields.

Farin kicked his feet from the stirrups and slid off his hysterical horse, struggled to free his sword, and swung it up to block the blade that was slicing down at him. Another came at him; he slid his own blade over it and then onward, its momentum carrying it through flesh and bone. The raider screamed and toppled headlong at his feet.

Shaking, Farin looked down at the body, but before he had time to realize what he had done, the next man was upon him and he was thrusting up his shield, slamming his sword in the direction where he hoped an opening in his opponent's guard might be. He was gasping, but as he struck and parried he began to find the fighting rhythm that countless hours of practice had drilled into him. He glimpsed Rafael a few feet away. The squire had lost his shield and was defending himself with sword alone. Farin began to inch his way to the other boy's side.

Up and down the road, at the edges of the woods, and on the sheer brink of the riverbank, the fighting went on, and always the most furiously around Lord Theodor and the King. For every one they killed, two more came on, and against the shouts of "Death!" clashed the cries "Lord Theodor!" "Westria and the King!" and once, from Eric, "For the lily of the north!"

The leader of the raiders, a huge man with a fur cloak tied around him that made him seem bigger still, reached the space that Eric had cleared and paused.

"Ho! Plainsmaggot! Do you think you can stand against me in a single fight? We know that all this talk of honor is just a blind—there you are, clinging together like cubs whose mother is gone, afraid to come out and face a real man!"

Eric snarled but held his place, shield up and sword poised.

"I knew it!" the raider went on. "Cowards all of you, both you and that sniveling rat you call a King!"

Eric roared and sprang forward. There was a momentary lull as men drew back to watch the two champions, seemingly equal in size and strength. For a few minutes they dueled, trading blow for blow as if they had been alone on the field. Then the raider gave a cry and sprang backward. His men, disengaging themselves from their own battles, swarmed in to separate Eric from the King.

Rafael cried out in horror and began hacking his way towards his Lord, who was whirling like a snow devil, seeming to face in all directions at once. Attempting to follow his friend, Farin glimpsed Eric, roaring, light flaring around him as his sword swung. The enemy drew back before him as Eric charged like a grizzly enraged, and a swathe of bodies lay wherever his sword fell.

Like a hero in an old tale, thought Farin even as he parried, *I will know how to describe it now, when I write a battle song!* His thigh stung as someone sliced past his guard. *If I get out of this alive!*

Around the King the fighting boiled like an ant heap overturned. Rafael had reached his Lord at last, and the raiders were attempting to eliminate this slender reinforcement. The squire, helmet gone now as well, and black hair tossing, was fighting with an ecstatic fury that was in its own way as formidable as Eric's rage.

But Rafael had neither Eric's strength nor his skill. Many of the blows aimed at him got through, though his assailants often paid dearly for their success. But there were many of them, and he was only one. Farin, struggling to reach him, saw his parries slowing, his sword faltering as it fell.

Farin set his teeth and brought his blade down with all his strength on a raider's leather helm. It hit with a shock he felt all the way up his arm, but with only a fractional pause the downward force of his blow drew his sword on through the man's head like a knife slicing cheese. Farin stepped back and wrenched his sword from the body as the man began to fall, and leaping over him, he gained Rafael's side at last.

"Farin! Thank the Battlelord! See, they are retreating now that there are two of us to guard the King."

"If I can fight as well as you have, they will!" Farin gasped, but now that he was close, he could see that Rafael was bleeding freely.

"Have I killed many? It is hard to tell . . . I am so tired. But it is dark now," he added, "and the battle must end soon."

Farin glanced westward, where the clouds had broken and the sun, setting behind the mountains, glowed angrily. There was a pressure against his shoulder, and he turned as Rafael collapsed against him and slid gently to the ground. Farin bent over him, calling his name, and the raiders charged in once more.

Caught off balance, Farin began to fall as the foremost

struck his lifted shield and hurtled past it into the King. Jehan toppled, but Farin, recovering with a convulsive leap, was on his feet again and took the man in the neck as he raised his sword to strike at the King.

He swayed beneath a storm of blows, struggling frantically to guard.

"To the King!" he shouted desperately. "Westria, Westria, to the King!" He saw the blunt menace of a mace swinging at him, felt the shock as it struck his helm. As the world dissolved around him he thought he heard faintly the note of a horn, and he saw Eric striding toward them, breaking through the ring of his enemies like a swimmer breasting a wave.

Farin rushed upward through a well of darkness to become aware that somebody was hitting him on the head with dull, regular blows, and someone else was flashing lights in his eyes and calling his name. Why wouldn't they leave him alone and let him return to the peaceful dark? Farin moaned and stirred protestingly.

"I think he's coming back to us, sir," said a deep voice.

"Yes. He at least will live to fight another day."

Surely he should recognize that second voice. Painfully Farin opened his eyes and looked up into the face of the King.

"It is over then," he whispered, remembering. "And . . . you are safe . . ."

The King nodded. "The fighting is done, and I have taken less harm than you, so be easy. Your courage was not wasted. I have much to thank you for." He had said he was unwounded, but he looked weary, his eyes sunken and his face white above his short dark beard.

Farin smiled weakly. The King smiled a little. "You are very like your sister, did you know?" he said absently.

Farin stared at him. Why speak of Faris now? Had the fighting turned his wits? Then he remembered how the King had crowned Faris at the Festival. *Does the King want Faris? What will we do?* Jehan's love affairs were famous all over the Kingdom, but Faris would not know how to play such a game. It was too much to think about now. He closed his eyes.

"You must rest now, and I must see how the others fare," the King said quickly. "Sir Randal will watch over you."

After a few moments Farin opened his eyes and saw that the King had gone. Sitting by the little fire he recognized the owner of the deep voice he had heard—Randal of Registhorpe, who had come with the King from the south.

"We must have won," Farin concluded. "What happened after I went down?"

Randal put another piece of wood on the little fire, the light glinting like copper on his auburn hair and beard as he bent. Behind him other fires winked as men moved back and forth before them. Farin shivered, even though he lay on a bed of saddlecloths stretched over fir boughs, and several cloaks had been laid over him. He wondered whose they were.

"I'm not sure who would have won," said Randal, "if Andreas Blackbeard had not brought his men straight over the mountain between here and Woodhall. The woodsrats made off as soon as they heard his horn. Some of our people caught their horses in time to pursue, but I doubt they will find much in the dark."

"How are the Lord Commander and Sandremun?"

"Sandremun was struck in the chest, but the arrow missed his heart. They think he will live, with good care. The Commander has wounds, of course, but he can ride. He is a mighty warrior for a man of his years."

Farin lay silent for a little, then asked the question that had weighted his heart.

"And what about Rafael? He was beside me, and he fell . . ."

Silently Randal indicated a long shape covered by a cloak just outside the circle of firelight.

"There was nothing to be done. He had lost too much blood and he was dead when we took him up after the fight."

"If there were only something I could do!" Jehan told Eric as they made their way through the camp. "Rafael died for me like a knight before he had lived long enough to become one. And there's that boy—" He motioned back towards the fire where Farin lay. "He's alive now, but can he live through a night in this cold?"

"He's not the only one," said Eric grimly. "I think that for many, shock and exposure will finish what the woodsrats began. Five of the men I brought from Seagate are dead, and there's no shelter for the others in this wilderness. We came prepared for a celebration, not a campaign!"

"We should not have been caught this way!" the King swore again. "I should have taken command, but I did not wish to hurt Theodor's pride." He shook his head. "I should not blame him—his son's life may well pay for any mistakes he made. And I wonder if even I could have avoided this disaster. I would have relied on the Coronans' estimates of the enemy's strength and plans."

"Their tactics and their viciousness were certainly beyond anything I've ever heard of among such folk!" Eric agreed, pulling his cloak closer around him.

When they reached the Lord Commander, Theodor was saying much the same thing. "I tell you, the whole situation has the stink of a billygoat three days dead!" He turned to the King. "My Lord, I have fought these scum since I was old enough to carry a sword, and always they have hot-footed it down the trail at the first hint of resistance. Why stay and fight? They are after loot, not glory!"

"And why are all those who did not escape dead now? *All* of them are dead, Lord Theodor—I found no wounded at all!" said Serge of Greenforest. "Surely our warriors are not so deadly that none can abide their blows and live."

"I should like to examine those bodies by daylight," said Eric slowly, "and see just how they died."

"Have all our men been accounted for?" asked Jehan.

"Almost everyone, sir. Even those who tried to pursue the escaping raiders have returned. Of course, we could not look in the river."

"Was my cousin among those you found?" inquired Theodor, pulling at his short beard. "I have not seen him since before the fight."

"Oh, I am here, Theodor!" They all turned to look as Ronald staggered into the firelight and knelt before his cousin. His cloak was stained with blood.

"Ronald!" exclaimed Theodor. "Are you hurt? We were afraid you were slain. Where have you been?"

"Oh, it's nothing really. Indeed, I have a confession to make. I slipped away while the rest of you were still climbing the hill. I wanted to see if Greenfell was burning yet. Instead I saw the reivers attacking you. I scrambled down as quickly as I could, but by the time I got here the fight was almost done. I've been searching for fugitives on some of the paths I know. I'm sorry you worried about me."

Theodor snorted, but the others looked at Ronald with no expression at all. So he had missed the fighting, had he? And it was Ronald's holding that the rest of them were bleeding to save.

Something clinked faintly. They looked around and saw Andreas Blackbeard picking his way toward them. He was holding out, at arm's length, a leather bag.

"My Lord—" Andreas paused, but he already had their attention. "I was searching for the wounded, and I found the big man who challenged Sir Eric. He is quite dead, but this was on his body." He handed the bag to his lord.

Theodor hefted it, opened it, and with impassive features let a stream of gold flow onto the muddy ground.

"Well, now we know why, don't we?" said Jehan bleakly. "All that remains is to discover who."

In the silence that followed, they could all hear clearly the crackling of the fire, the muffled moans of the wounded, and the mournful whistling of the wind.

The north wind blew down from the mountains, gathered strength as it reached the head of the Great Valley, swirled impotently around the outthrust bulk of the Hold. Behind the thick curtains in the Seneschal's chamber, the shutters rattled as the wind tried to pluck them free.

Caolin shivered and looked up from the papers on the table before him—the reports on every aspect of the Kingdom's functioning that followed him wherever he and the King might be. He smiled as his gaze fell on the great wolf dozing fitfully before the fire.

"You and Ordrey arrived just in time, Gerol," he said softly. "This is no night to be on the road."

The wolf's grizzled ears twitched as Caolin spoke, but he did not open his eyes.

"Jehan was less wise than you. Unless they have found some roof unburned to shelter under, tonight the King of Westria lies on the cold ground." Caolin sighed impatiently. *There was no need for him to go himself, but he would not be ruled by me. Ah, Jehan, I cannot keep you from hazarding yourself, but if I ward the Kingdom well, perhaps one day no one will threaten you.*

He returned to the papers in his hand and began to read.

. . . at present the temper of the College is divided, the majority holding with the Mistress. This faction bases their philosophy on the teaching of the Master of the Deer Park, who held that the wise man concentrates on the truth beneath the appearances of things and lets the illusions of the world come and go as they will. Thus it is pointless for one who seeks wisdom to meddle in the affairs of men.

The opposing view is held mostly by priests and priestesses attached to the communities in the Free Cities or serving holders in the Marches. They wish to use the teachings of the College to influence the lives of those with whom they work, but they get little comfort from the College, since they have never made the journey to Awahna to become adepts themselves, and their vows are made only from year to year. Nor are they themselves united, since many lay priests are content simply to do their employers' will . . .

Caolin peered at the cipher with which the report was signed and began to laugh. "The man thinks I do not know him, but never mind, I will see that he is rewarded well. This is the kind of information I need. If I am to govern this land, I *must* know what is going on!" He laughed again. "The Master of the Junipers may be surprised at his reception in the College if he tries to find support for his ideas there!"

The Seneschal slipped the pages back into their oilskin envelope and reached for the next packet in the box that Ordrey had brought that evening. It bore the seal of Manuel of Orvale, Controller of Highways in Laurelynn.

"Why was this sent to the King?" wondered Caolin, opening it. The Controller's message sprawled across the page—obviously not a clerk's writing, but his own.

My gracious King—it is with pain that I write ill news of one whom you recommended to me.

Caolin frowned, then read on.

Three years ago I took one Waldan of Terra Linda, called Mole, into the service of the roads. He was assigned to maintain the way between this city and Riv-

ered in the Ramparts. I have now in my hands, and I
have seen with my eyes, evidence that instead of levy-
ing labor from the landholders along the way to repair
and improve the road, he has accepted gold from them
and spent it to maintain himself in splendor rather
than the road in safety. I have taken Waldan into my
custody, not wanting to give him to the judges since I
employed him at your request. I will await your instructions on how to deal with him.

Caolin laid the letter carefully on the table, whistling soundlessly. Thinking back, he remembered the man—a little nervous fellow with sleek dark hair and a livid scar down one
side of his face. He had gotten the scar in the southern wars
when he threw himself between an Elayan lance and the
King.

"The man faced death without flinching, but he could not
face temptation," Caolin muttered. "Jehan will take this
badly, I fear."

It had happened before, when the King's trust was betrayed. For several days he would have to be coaxed to eat
or sleep. He would spend long hours shut up alone. And
each time a little more of the youth went out of his eyes.

Oh, Jehan, thought Caolin, *fifteen years ago I swore to
serve you, and realized that to do so I had to serve Westria.
Sometimes I think that in taking on that burden, I have lost
you. But if I can spare you this pain, then I will do what is
necessary, even if it means deceiving you.* He tore a page
from his tablet and quickly began to write.

Deliver the person of Waldan of Terra Linda to the
bearer of this order.

Caolin scrawled Jehan's initials across the bottom, folded
the page, and held the candle to the lump of wax until
enough had dribbled onto the paper to hold the King's seal.
When it cooled, he fitted the order into an oiled envelope
and wrote the Controller's name neatly across the front.

"Gerol," Caolin whined softly, and the wolf sprang to his
feet. "Come." Gerol's nails clicked on the polished floor as
he came to the man, and laid his grizzled muzzle on the
Seneschal's knee. For a moment Caolin stroked his head,
his long fingers rubbing unerringly the sensitive spots behind
the wolf's ears.

"Yes . . . I know where it itches . . . indeed I do." Caolin made a sound low in his throat and Gerol's yellow eyes half closed. "You know all my secrets and care about none of them, do you?" said the Seneschal. "Well, I have an errand for you now."

He took his hand away and spoke in the wolf's own tongue again. "Ordrey—get Ordrey and bring him to me here. Go!"

Gerol sighed, lifted his head, and began to pad towards the door. Caolin growled, and with an impatient snort the wolf increased his pace, nosed open the door, and slipped through.

Caolin got up and began to feed the fire.

It was perhaps fifteen minutes before he heard sounds outside in the passageway and Gerol returned, followed by a short, spare man whose ginger hair was already beginning to recede, though his eyes were still as merry as a child's. The Seneschal stood up to greet him.

"Ordrey, I am sorry to call you at this hour. Were you asleep?"

"Well . . . I was in bed." He grinned reminiscently. "People here are not used to seeing our friend Gerol wandering about. I will have some explaining to do when I return."

"It may be just as well. You are going to need your rest. I fear I must send you off again tomorrow as soon as you can ride."

"Well, I'm sorry for it—they were giving me a warm welcome here. The kitchens are buzzing with gossip about Jehan's newest morsel. Is she just another diversion, or is he serious at last?"

There was a chilly silence. Ordrey looked at Caolin and lost a little of the fresh color from his face.

"Neither the King's name nor the lady's reputation belongs on your lips! I cannot stop the mouth of every kitchen trull in the Marches, but my servants should learn discretion if they wish to prosper. The King has made no decision, and I do not think he will seek your advice when he does." Caolin spoke shortly, his hands busy placing the packets he had dealt with already in the dispatch pouch. Ordrey stood uneasily, watching him.

"These messages must go south as soon as possible." Caolin's tone softened. "That candle is guttering so that it is hard to see. Could you trim it for me?"

Ordrey bent over the candle. Caolin brought his hand up beside it so that his ring of office captured the flame with a flare of ruby light. It caught Ordrey's gaze and held it. As he had done so many times before, he stilled. This was something else the College had taught him, thought Caolin, though they might have questioned the way he used it now. "You see only the light, Ordrey; you hear only my voice." Caolin's tone was very even. "What do you hear?"

"I hear your voice."

"You will listen and do what I tell you to do, won't you?"

"I will do what you tell me," said Ordrey tonelessly.

Caolin held up the letter to the Controller of Highways. "Do you see this packet? You are to disguise yourself and deliver it to Manuel of Orvale in Laurelynn. Wait there until he has read it. When he has done so, he will give into your custody a man called Waldan of Terra Linda. Evade his questions if Manuel should ask who you are and who has sent you—on no account tell him that you come from me. The order you bear is your authority. Do you understand?"

Ordrey nodded, looking at him with unfocused eyes.

"When you have this Waldan, take him to the Merchants' Caravansary in Rivered. You will find Gorgo Snaggletooth there—you remember him, we have dealt with him before. Tell him to hold Waldan with his other merchandise, guarding him carefully, and take him over the mountains on his next journey to the Brown Lands. When he has disposed of Waldan in the slave mart at Arena and has proof of the sale, tell him he shall have another forty laurels from you. Wait in Rivered until he returns. Remember, Gorgo must have the proof—on no account must Waldan ever return to Westria! Do you understand? Repeat what I have said."

Ordrey nodded and in an even voice recounted the orders Caolin had given him.

"Very good. In a moment I will show you the red light once more. When you see it, you will forget that it is I who have given you these orders. When you look at this packet, you will know what to do, but you will tell no one what you have done until I show you the light again."

Caolin stretched out his ring to the candle once more. Ordrey's dull gaze slowly focused on its red glow.

"You see the light, don't you?"

"Yes . . ."

"When I take it away again, you will forget that you have

seen it, or that we have just spoken, and you will regain your full senses once more."

Caolin covered the ring with his other hand. "Thank you for fixing the candle," he said. "You see it burns very well now."

Ordrey shook his head a little and looked at the Seneschal. "I'm sorry, what did you say? I have a slight headache, I'm afraid."

Caolin smiled. "I was only thanking you for trimming my candle. I should have warned you about Lady Berisa's mead." He slipped the letter for the Controller into the pouch and began to strap it up. He handed it to Ordrey and sat down again.

"Do you mind if I keep Gerol with me here? You will not need him on this trip, and I missed his companionship."

"Oh, of course. The reivers may haunt the mountains, but I doubt I will need protection on the road between here and Laurelynn." Ordrey laughed.

"Very well, then. Go now, and get what sleep you can." Caolin held out his hand and Ordrey bent over it respectfully, then straightened and went out. Gerol began to get to his feet, but at a sound from Caolin stretched out on the floor again.

Caolin eased back into his chair and rested his head in his hands. In the partnership that had evolved between King and Seneschal, Jehan was the war leader and focus of ceremony, the embodiment of the people's vision of Westria. But the King was free to pursue his pleasure when there was no festival or danger. To the Seneschal fell the daily drudgery of monitoring the life of the Kingdom, from the flow of commerce to the rotation of border garrisons. Instructing, evaluating, admonishing, he was responsible for the work of the entire government. He had set himself the task of forestalling or dealing with every problem, lest it trouble the King. And for the nine years he had been in office, he had exulted in his ability to do so.

But suddenly he was tired. *It is late . . . I should go to bed too. Yesterday Jehan joked about my vigilance, but he should have remembered that even I must sleep sometimes.*

He had done all that was necessary for now. In the morning Ordrey would be on his way. Strange that the man's reference to Faris had made him so angry. Caolin's thoughts went back to the girl's singing that afternoon. She had a subtle kind of beauty, like an exotic flower. Suitably dressed, she could be exquisite.

Caolin laughed softly. *If Jehan doesn't want her, perhaps I will take her myself. She would be a worthy ornament.* He looked at the windows and realized from the faint light that edged the shutters that it was almost dawn.

By the time the sun began to warm the northern sky at last, the men of the Corona were beginning the slow journey home. Jehan and Eric and the unwounded men rode in the lead while Lord Theodor held the rear, close to the litter where his son Sandremun lay.

"Andreas says that the arrow that hit Sandremun, and several others found, were black ones, military issue from Normontaine," said Jehan.

"By the Guardians! They wouldn't attack us—it would mean war!" Eric exclaimed.

Jehan nodded. "Yes, and I believe that Queen Mara has more sense than to do that—nor has she any need. Besides, if it means anything, we found no Montaner badges on the dead."

"Do you think someone else used those arrows to mislead us? Why?"

"I only have suspicions"—Jehan smiled—"and even a King should have some real evidence before he spreads accusations around. Whoever is guilty will probably try again though, and this time we will be on our guard."

They rode on in silence. Stormwing tossed his head and protested the slow pace, less wearied than his rider by the events of the previous two days.

"There is another thing about that skirmish that bothers me," said Eric painfully. Jehan waited for him to go on. "You remember when I fought with their leader . . ." He paused, and for a moment the King thought he would not go on.

"It was the kind of struggle the Bards live by writing about, from all accounts. I'm afraid I was too busy to give it the attention it deserved," Jehan said encouragingly.

"Don't make it harder for me!" Eric cried. "It should never have happened! I left you unguarded, and you could have been killed!"

"Has that been troubling you? Really, Eric, I do have some skill with a sword." Now was not the time to mention

Rafael, left behind in a lonely grave in the hills, or Farin in his litter at the end of the column.

"I swear to you I didn't realize what I was doing. I mean it wasn't because—" Eric stopped short, fighting for words.

The King shifted in the saddle to face him. "It wasn't because of jealousy over the lady Faris? We may as well face it, Eric. After all, she is bound to love someone eventually—it may not be you, and it may not be me either, you know."

Jehan frowned, remembering how many others had loved him, and how heedlessly he had received their gifts. Perhaps he should marry someone whose experience equaled his, who would not care.

"My Lord, I am unworthy of her! I have not spoken to her, and I never will!"

"But don't you think that would be unfair to *her*?" Jehan asked gently. "You can offer many things I cannot—youth, honor untinged by any compromise, a peaceful life. As knights, we are bound to fight our best no matter what the battlefield. You would insult me if you were to withdraw from the contest now."

Topping the shoulder of the Father of Mountains, they glimpsed in the distance the tower of the Hold, pink-tinged in the morning light. For the column, it was a full day's ride away, but a single rider on a fast horse might reach it by noon.

Eric reined in Thunderfoot and looked at the King with no wavering in his eyes. "Sir, I accept your challenge!" he exclaimed, bowing low over his horse's neck. Then he straightened, lifting the reins and driving home his heels, and sent the black horse galloping madly down the road.

"Eric, you are a true and honorable knight," Jehan said softly as he watched him go. "And by the Guardian of Men, Eric, if you are not I hope that you never let me know!"

IV
A Pledge of Faith

Faris shut the oaken door carefully and leaned against the rough stone of the wall, trying to catch her breath. From somewhere above she could hear the ripple of harp music, distant as a dream. She frowned and peered through the narrow window into the courtyard. Sir Lewis was still there, shifting from foot to foot and gazing hopefully at the door. Faris sighed as he shook his head at last and wandered off.

She supposed she was lucky. Some of the others, like Stefan or Sir Eric of Seagate, would not have given up so easily. She shifted the heavy folds of burgundy velvet to her other arm, shrugging the thought away. She had finished Farin's new cloak just in time for his knighting—surely that was enough to worry about today.

Faris started up the winding stair, passing alternately through the shadows and bars of sunlight from the slits in the stone. The warm breeze was scented with April flowers. The music came more clearly now, and her step grew lighter.

Farin had not practiced much during his long recovery from the head wound he had received in February. It was only in the last few weeks that his full strength had returned. He should have been sleeping now.

When she reached the landing, Faris was able to distinguish the melody, but the sound of the harp was purer and deeper than she had ever heard it before. She opened the door.

Farin was sitting by the window. The morning light glowed on his head and shoulders, glistening on the new streak of white in his hair that marked where the raider's blow had struck him . . . and on the harp, which in that moment seemed carved from living gold.

The door clicked shut behind her. A last trill escaped like a flight of butterflies and Farin looked up. On his cheeks she could see the glitter of tears. Silently he held out the harp. It was not the worn instrument he had brought from home.

This harp was a little larger, the soundbox deeper than broad, but it was the interlaced and inlaid golden wire that ornamented it, and the exquisitely gilded swan that crowned it, that sent back the blaze of the sun.

"*Swangold,*" Farin said simply, cradling it against his shoulder again.

"Where did it come from?"

"From the King . . . he sent it to me as a knighting gift!"

"It's magnificent—" Faris began.

"You don't understand!" her brother cried. "Since I went to war I have hardly thought about music. The King said he would make me knight, and I thought my way was chosen at last. I don't know if I have the genius to be a great harper, and what kind of life is that anyway—always eating at someone else's table and sleeping by a stranger's hearth? I want to be a warrior! To be knighted by the King himself is almost more honor than I can bear, and yet . . ." He rested his forehead against the smooth curve of the harp.

"And yet . . ." she echoed, sitting down on the window seat beside him.

"Yet if anyone tried to take Swangold from me now, I would die! What did the King mean by this gift? Is he trying to tell me I should not be a warrior after all?"

Faris looked at him helplessly. "Surely he wouldn't do that now?"

"He has been coming and going so constantly—chasing outlaws in the north, meeting with the Council in Laurelynn—perhaps he has had no time to think about it until now!"

"Farin . . ." She put her arms around his shoulders, pressing her cheek against his hair. It was the only way she could think of to comfort him. After a few moments he sighed and wiped his eyes with the back of his hand.

"At least you don't tell me I am being foolish, or upset from lack of sleep, as Berisa would do."

Faris smiled and kissed his cheek. For a moment the mirror across the room reflected their two faces, his paled by illness until it was almost as white as her own. Two pairs of dark eyes set above high cheekbones looked back at them, shaded by masses of dark hair, their inheritance from their Karok grandfather. But Farin's mouth was tight, his eyes haunted, while her own mouth was full and soft. Faris could not read the expression in her own eyes.

"In any case, it is the King I want to understand!" said Farin at last.

Faris laughed without amusement. "I don't pretend to interpret *him*—ask the Master of the Junipers what Jehan of Westria means."

"Yes," he said slowly. "Perhaps that is what I should do."

"Not now."

"I cannot sleep," Farin continued, "and there are two hours yet before I must dress for the ceremony. I will fret myself like a mewed hawk if I have to stay here." Abruptly he rose from her embrace and slung the harp across his back by a strap of soft leather stamped in gold. Before she could speak again, he had reached the door and was gone.

Faris sat for a moment, laughing helplessly. Then she got up and closed the door. She began to wander about the room, automatically straightening books and papers, picking up strewn garments and hanging them in the alcove. "Farin thinks that I understand him," she murmured. "I am glad, though I'm not sure that I do. He doesn't understand Jehan. Oh, Sweet Lady! I wish *I* understood the King. I wish I understood myself!" Her hand moved automatically to rub at the hidden scar on her arm.

As she bent to pull smooth the rumpled quilts on Farin's bed she saw a piece of paper on the floor. She picked it up, saw her own name, and began to read. She and Farin had shared everything for so long, it did not occur to her that he would mind her reading this now.

> My lord and father [he began], I write this letter during my night of vigil, not knowing whether you will arrive in time for my knighting ceremony . . .

Faris shook her head. Poor Farin. Did he delude himself that the old man would leave his eyrie even to see his only son knighted by the King? The lines were crossed and corrected—this must be a draft of a letter Farin had sent out some days before. She wondered why he had not told her he was writing so that she could add some dutiful postscript.

> I would be proud if you could be here. The King says

that I saved his life, and he would like to honor
you . . .

For a moment the letters blurred before her. "I love you,
Farin, even if he does not!" she whispered. She looked at
the paper again.

. . . and also because someone must speak to Faris before she comes to harm. Berisa has tried, but Faris
seems not to hear.

Faris stiffened, but she could not stop reading now.

Faris is flirting with fire. Men praise her, and now she
flutters from one to another like a butterfly. People
are gossiping about her behavior all over the
Province . . .

Faris flung the paper to the floor. "Love him! I *hate* him!"
she hissed. "How dare he judge me. He seeks no woman's
favor, though some seek his—what does he know of the
game of love?" Her skirts swished angrily as she stalked
across the floor.

"The King honored me—once—and so I am the fashion
now. But it is all a sport for the men. Not one has seen
beneath this surface mask I wear . . . not one has even tried
to see! What harm can it do for me to enjoy their company?
Of course Farin does not like it—he never had to share my
attention before. But it will not last. I am not *that* beautiful!"

She swept to the mirror and stared at her face in the glass.
She was already dressed for the ceremonies. Her sleeveless
over-robe, high collared and loose in the northern style, was
made of soft green Elayan brocade edged with goldwork.
But it was open down the front and cut wide at the armholes
to reveal the tight-fitting long-sleeved under-gown, made of
a silk that was so pale a gold it was almost cream, ornamented at the neck with a design in tiny golden beads.

It was the finest outfit she had ever owned. But her coils
of dark hair were already escaping from their pearl-headed
pins. Angrily she tucked the strands back in place. And her
face—her nose was too long, and she was even thinner now
than she had been when the year began. In truth, she did

not understand how her popularity had endured even this long.

"No . . . I am not beautiful enough." She closed her eyes so that she would not have to look upon the image in the mirror anymore.

Berisa's oldest daughter had brought the King a vase of lilies, creamy and golden-veined in their upright sheaths of green. Jehan looked at them, then forced his gaze back to the leather boxes on his desk. The last of them had just been locked and sealed for its journey back to Laurelynn.

"You said you had something else to show me," he said wearily.

"Yes," answered Caolin. The Seneschal reached into the case where he kept documents he was working on and drew out a little leather bag, curiously stitched around the top.

"Isn't that the bag that was found on the body of the outlaw leader who ambushed us? Why are you showing it to me again?"

"As it happens, it is not the same bag, which is why I thought you would like to see it."

"Then where did it come from?"

"It came," Caolin paused for effect, "with the taxes from Las Costas. I kept thinking that the other bag looked familiar, but I couldn't remember why. It's from the counting house at Sanjos. They have them specially made."

"That proves nothing, you know. Anyone in the Kingdom could have gotten one," said the King after a moment.

Caolin sighed. "I really find it hard to understand your refusal to suspect Lord Brian of treachery."

Jehan stood up and began to pace restlessly about the room. Suddenly he found the Seneschal's perpetual suspicion of Brian irritating. He had sometimes suspected that it was a reaction to Brian's loudly expressed scorn when he had made Caolin Seneschal. At the time Jehan had shared Caolin's feelings, aware of his need for Caolin's cool brilliance and loyalty, and himself fearing Brian's popularity. But surely they were all older and wiser now.

"Brian does not agree with me on how to run the Kingdom, but that is not treason. Our disagreements have always been open. Of course he tries to persuade people to support him, but he has never been secretive."

"*Somebody* paid the outlaws to ambush your war party.

You could have been killed, Jehan! Either you were their target, or it was Theodor, and I don't know of anyone who wants *him* out of his way."

"No. Brian may not love me, but he would no more do murder than you would! And certainly not at secondhand." The King went to the window and stood looking out at the Father of Mountains. As always, it was snow-capped, but the hills at its feet were carpeted gold and purple with flowers.

"Very well. I will drop the question of who sent the gold, and why. Let us pursue another line of thought," said Caolin patiently. "How did the gold get from Las Costas to the mountains? There's one likely suspect—one person who travels all over Westria, and who specifically told Eric that he had been in the south."

"Ronald Sandreson—" supplied the King. "He disappeared at a suspicious moment. We thought it was cowardice."

"Exactly. I hope that you will permit me to suspect *him*?"

"But you won't learn anything if he remains quietly at his holding. We should ask Lord Theodor to invite him for a visit here," Jehan said thoughtfully.

Caolin smiled. "I would like to question him."

"No, not yet. I'm sure Theodor will be willing to invite him on suspicion, but we cannot arrest him without some proof."

"Because he is the Lord Commander's cousin?" asked Caolin.

Jehan turned to face him. "No! Because he is Theodor's sworn man. I was thinking that if Ronald is guilty, he is more likely to betray himself here."

"By trying again to assassinate you? That's why I wanted to arrest him!" Caolin's fist struck the table. "Very well then . . . take the chance. But will you let me at least *investigate* Brian?"

"That would be unworthy. I will find the right moment and question Brian myself."

"And believe him if he denies it all, I suppose? In that case, why let him even know he has been suspected?" Caolin's chair rocked as he rose and crossed the room to the King. He grasped his arm. "Jehan! Why do you do this to me?"

Jehan laid his hand over Caolin's. For a long moment he

looked into the other man's gray eyes. "Mine is the responsibility . . . the risk must be mine," he said softly at last.
"We'll worry about Brian when we return to the south. In
the meantime, you have my leave to suspect Ronald all you
please!" He grinned suddenly.

Caolin pulled away his hand, controlling his breathing.
"You have a ceremony to conduct today and you are still in
your chamber robe," he said after a moment. "You cannot
mourn Rafael for ever—why haven't you taken a new
squire? Never mind. What are you going to wear? I'll help
you dress. Why not—I am your servant, my Lord!"

"I want to serve the King, and I don't know what I should
do!" Farin looked at the Master of the Junipers in appeal.

The Master ran his fingers through already rumpled hair
and looked at the young man quizzically. "Are you asking
me to tell you what to do with your life?"

Farin reddened. "I know—no one can choose for another.
But if the King doesn't think that I should be a knight . . .
I suppose what I really want to know is the King's mind."

"Why not ask him?" said a new voice from the door.

They looked up and saw the King. He was dressed in an
arming tunic of finely woven forest-green wool with no ornament, not even the circlet he usually wore. His voice had
been soft, but to the Master it seemed as if there was some
hidden tension in his stance.

Farin tried to speak, choked, and for the next few moments both King and Master were busy calming him.

"How . . . how much did you hear?" stammered Farin.

"Only that you want to know what I think . . . about
something," Jehan said soothingly, drawing up a bench.
"Are you still worried about whether you deserve knighthood? Believe me, you do."

"Not exactly. It was the harp . . ." Farin gestured at the
golden harp leaning against his knee. The King's eyes brightened with amusement, though his mouth remained grave.

"Do you like it?" he asked.

Farin's face grew radiant. "I don't know the right words.
My old harp and the Hall harp at home both gave me great
joy. But Swangold—you know, sir, how it is when you find
the one sword that feels like an extension of your hand?
This harp is like that for me. She *fits* me."

"Or like the woman who is your mate in body and soul," Jehan murmured. "Yes, I know."

"I meant to give up harping when I took up the sword. But if this instrument can stir me so . . . I do not know what to do!"

"Cannot you do both?" Jehan rested his elbows on his knees, his chin in his hands, watching the boy. His hair was backlighted by the tower window, through which the Master could see the Father of Mountains rising serenely above anxieties of men.

"I don't know," said Farin. "Being a Bard is not so high a vocation as that of a Master—" He glanced apologetically at the Master of the Junipers. "But the call can be as strong. I don't know what will happen if I let it take hold of me, and if it does, how can I fulfill my duty to you?"

Jehan took Farin's hands in his own and placed them on the curve of the harp. "Play for me!" he said.

Startled, Farin met his eyes, and his own widened.

"Much as I value your skill at guarding my back," Jehan said earnestly, "there are others who can do that. Swangold was a gift to me when I was a boy, but I could never make her sing. And yet I need music—being King is not all a Festival! Play for me, Farin, at feasts if you desire, but most of all when I am weary and alone."

Farin studied the floor. His hands were trembling beneath the King's. "I am not good enough."

Jehan shook his head. "I have heard you play! Will you do this for me?"

Farin lifted his head to face the King with shining eyes. "My Lord, to wield the harp or the sword, my hands are at your service to my life's end!"

"Or mine!" laughed Jehan. "So be it!"

For a moment they faced each other. Then Farin glanced at the window and straightened in alarm. "It's almost noon! They will be looking for me for the ritual bathing, and I must check my arms."

"Go then, and we will see you soon!" said the Master of the Junipers. They listened to his steps retreating down the passageway. "You handled him well," said the Master at last.

Jehan shook his head. "Maker of Winds! I wish there were anything I cared about as much as that boy does his art!"

"There is nothing? Not even Westria?"

The King buried his face in his hands. "Farin at least is free to choose his way."

"You could have refused election. Your older sister could have borne the crown."

"Jessica was newly married to the Commander of the Ramparts, and pregnant at the time. They told me that if she became Queen, the Ramparts would be too powerful. They said they wanted a war leader against Elaya. You were there! You know the arguments as well as I. Besides, I was a boy with dreams of glory. What did I know about responsibility and power?"

"You were only two years younger than the boy you just advised so wisely, and you had been bred up to rule." The Master smoothed the worn gray wool of his robe. "But whether the choice is forced or free, what does anyone know about the end of the road? Even the road to Awahna may branch many times. We can only do our best, whatever the path . . . and you did not answer my question." Gently he touched the King's bent head.

"Can there be two answers? I have sworn the oath . . . and I have worn the Jewels," the King said simply. "I care for Westria as I care for my own life, but that does not mean I find either of them easy to bear." His voice came muffled through his hands.

"If it were only Westria—only the land itself—that I had to rule! Sometimes I wish the Guardians would bring down a second Cataclysm, and this time destroy mankind. The animal kindreds act according to their natures and obey their own laws. I can deal with *them*. It is men whose deeds weigh on my soul."

Jehan sighed and looked up. "Sometimes it seems to me as if everyone in the Kingdom were engaged in some plot, that the strong are all out for their own advancement, and the weak are honorable only because they lack the power to do otherwise. I find myself plotting stratagems to make them reveal their plans, deceptions to unmask deceit—all the things I swore never to do or to be when I put on the Jewels. Open force would be more honest, and yet violence ignores the distinction between treachery and weakness, between those who are truly guilty and those who are merely misled."

The Master shifted on the hard bed to face the King.

"You must act with honor and forbearance to inspire it in others. If you use their methods, you will be no better than they. But, Jehan, do not close your eyes against evil. It does exist . . . and sometimes blind trust can be as dangerous as suspicion. Trust in the Maker of All—there only will your faith be secure!" He focused his voice to reach the King, but Jehan's face was closed.

"There have been too many treacheries," the King said in a dead voice. "I cannot afford to believe that there may be more. If I cannot trust the men I am supposed to lead, I may as well die!" His body was taut, and he stared through the Master into some vista of despair. "Can you understand what a burden the Crown and the staff can come to be?"

"Jehan . . . Jehan . . ." The Master took him by the shoulders and shook him until the King's blue eyes cleared again and met his own. "Surely it is so in every land. In Elaya the Prince fights for election from among the sons of the Royal House. In Aztlan they say that a man never knows if he is a chief until he begins to move and finds that others are following him. In Westria the throne passes usually from parent to child, as do the lordships of the Provinces, and of every holding down to the smallest steading in the hills. Ours is not the only way, but it is a way we chose from among the patterns of the ancients because we thought it would help us to keep our Covenant. If so many others have borne this, surely you can do as well!"

Jehan tried to smile. "Old friend," he said very softly. "I am afraid—not of pain or death—in battle at least I can see my enemy and I know how to defend myself. But when Caolin brings me an order to be signed, I am afraid. What if I have judged wrong? And when men come to me to be made knight, as Andreas and Farin will do this afternoon, I am afraid lest they betray the faith they swear to me, and I fail in my duty to them. Yet if I fail, the whole pyramid that is Westria may fall. I cannot go on like this!"

For several minutes they sat without speaking while the King slowly mastered himself. The Master was still as an image, his lids half closed. He had opened himself to the King's need, and now he felt his pain. What could he do to ease this agony? If only he could talk to the other Masters and Mistresses of the College of the Wise. But he remembered how indifferent they had seemed to his concerns when he visited there three months before. *There is no help in men,* he mocked himself, remembering his advice to the King. *Trust in the Maker of All.* He regulated his breathing, sending his awareness inward. The air was full of the scent of flowers.

He opened his eyes again. "No, I haven't fallen asleep." His gaze held the King's. "You came here to look for a Queen. Why have you left the lady Faris so strictly alone?"

Jehan brought up his left arm as if to ward off a blow. "You should have been a warrior!" he said, shaken by sudden laughter. "I did not expect that from you!"

"You are in love with her, and I think she is ready to love you," the Master continued calmly.

Jehan's hand clenched in the folds of his tunic. "Am I? Is she?" he whispered. "I thought I loved her when I gave Eric a clear field to court her. I owed that to him, and perhaps to her as well. I thought she would take him or reject him. I did not expect her to play him like a hooked fish for three months—him and every other male in the province!"

The Master sat back and let him run on.

"At the Festival of the First Flowers I saw her, not just with my eyes. I was *aware* of her, as if my soul had touched hers. I thought I knew her then. But when we came back from that first war party she seemed changed, encased in an invisible shell. Was it only my need that made me see her as the goal of my search? Or is the person I thought I saw still there, locked inside her?" He had seized the Master's hand. After a moment he released it and straightened, smiling. "You have forsworn wife and child—I should not ask these questions of you."

"I have not given up women entirely—only permanent companionship! That is what I sacrifice for my calling. Yours does not demand the same!" The Master laughed ruefully. "Perhaps a detached viewpoint can be of some value in this case." He grew serious again.

"What if Faris has begun to love you already? She cannot show it, since you have made no sign. All she can do is distract herself with others, try to make you jealous—which I think she has done. You should at least find out how she feels!"

"Maybe I am afraid even to do that, lest I find my worst fears true."

"Tomorrow is May Eve. Perhaps the fires of Beltane will kindle some courage in your heart. The festival is older than

Westria, and our ancestors knew their need for it when they chose to celebrate it after the Cataclysm. If you will not trust yourself, trust them!"

Jehan grinned. "I feel easier already. Do you know I have spoken to no one of this—not even to Caolin? I scarcely knew what I was feeling myself."

Not even Caolin? The close relationship between King and Seneschal had served the Kingdom well, but the Master wondered suddenly if Jehan was now finding that there were things he needed that Caolin could not give.

"I am here to listen," the Master said thoughtfully. "But there is one who can advise you better than I. The Beltane fires reflect the fires of heaven as love between men reflects the love of the Most High. Use the Jewel—ask the Lady of Fire."

"Use the Jewel of Fire for my own need?" The King stared at the Master.

"It is not for your need only, Jehan. The King exists for the Kingdom, but you need a mate to share the burden of the Jewels, to balance your energies, to make with you a child to bear the Jewels after you. You are the King—you stand for the people of Westria. But you have had no Lady to stand for the land. When the High Prince is mated to the Maiden, then will the Great Marriage be consummated at last, and both King and Kingdom will be renewed. Westria needs a Lady as much as you do, Jehan."

The King rubbed at his forehead as if he could already feel the Jewel in its coronet burning there. "I have been taught for so long not to touch the Jewels without the greatest need."

"Think about it. You have the time."

"I hope so," said the King. "But I know that it is time to leave you now. My duty today is to Andreas and Farin! Will you bless me, Master, before I go?" He slipped to his knees before the Master of the Junipers, his dark hair hiding his face as he bent his head.

The older man stood and traced in the air an equal-armed cross. "In the names of earth, of air, of water, and of fire"—he drew a circle sunwise around the cross—"and of the Maker of All Things! May your path be blessed: may you find faith, may you find love, may you find peace!" His rough voice deepened, reverberated against the bare stone walls of the little room like a bell.

He brought his hands down and rested them on the King's head, holding them there as if he could transmit through his fingertips all his love.

Faris unclenched tense fingers from the skirts of her gown, armoring herself with all the praises of her beauty she had heard in the last few weeks, then swept into the Hall like the Lady of Love appearing to Her worshippers. Comment echoed her passing as members of the household bent to tell her name to visitors who had come for the knighting. Her self-image wavered as their interest beat against her awareness. She fought the impulse to panic—she had never before found herself the focus of so large a crowd.

But if she ran away, or tried to blend into the background as she had always done before, she would be admitting that Berisa and her brother were right.

Rosemary was already in her place near the dais with the other girls, but the rest of the guests still swirled at random, waiting for the ceremony to begin. As Faris began to move towards her friend she glimpsed a stooped figure with lank, graying hair in her path, a worn cloak the color of dried blood. She stopped short.

It was her father, Gerard of Hawkrest Hold.

Faris did not need to see his face. He carried his own atmosphere about with him, a molting, broody falcon of a man in a roomful of songbirds. He sensed her presence, turned to stare at her, and her cloak of beauty dissolved. Gerard frowned, and her memory mirrored back the day he had beaten her for dressing up in her mother's abandoned clothes.

She flinched, feeling the familiar cramping of her stomach, the ache of her scarred arm. But his lifted hand and his mental summons compelled her. She felt people looking at them and forced herself to straighten as she obeyed.

"So it's true." Gerard's voice creaked harshly, as if he had not used it all the time she and Farin had been away. "I should not have let you come."

Faris shook her head, denying him.

"You are tricked out like a heifer at a fair, for any man to buy. Your mother played that game well—do you think to equal her? But she chose me after all." . . . *and left me,* came the unvoiced refrain.

Faris felt his shadows engulfing her and stifled her pity. "I am not my mother," she said clearly.

"No. *She* could charm the very trees!" Gerard bit off the words, an ancient anguish distorting his carven features. But Faris had overheard all that he refused to say once when her nurse and the housekeeper thought her too young to understand. Her childhood dreams and nightmares were formed from the story of how her mother had gone out one night to dance with the spirits of the apple trees, and thus took the pneumonia of which she died.

Faris tried to distract him with a laugh. "Now that Farin is being knighted, he will surely marry. His bride will not want to share her home with me. I must find a husband now."

Her father shook his head. "I do not think that Farin will marry. You must stay, daughter. *You* must keep faith with me!"

Faris shut her eyes. *I would come gladly if only you had said you loved me,* she thought. *But now I have learned how it feels to have people care about me—I cannot go back to Hawkrest Hold now!*

"Let my mother's ghost keep faith with you," she said aloud.

Drumsticks buzzed and spattered bursts of sound across the Hall. Faris looked quickly to the great doorway, saw the knights of Theodor's household filing in with a musical jingle of mail. The crowd was folding back before them.

"I must join Rosemary," she said distractedly, but already she was leaving Gerard behind. She reached her place, breathless, as the drumbeat deepened and the skirl of bagpipes overwhelmed all other sound.

The people stilled and turned. *The King is coming! The King . . .*

And then he was in the Hall, walking as if he were alone in the room, walking steadily, as if he could have gone on for ever despite the weight of the emerald mantle that dragged from his shoulders and the Crown of Westria binding his helm.

Lord Theodor marched just behind him, his eyes flickering constantly from the people to his guard, to his wife and family, and back to the crowd again, giving each one a genial smile. But Jehan's face was sculptured into stern lines, his eyes fixed on the circled cross that glittered on the royal banner behind the dais.

Awareness of her father's anger and her own fears slipped away from Faris as she saw the weariness in Jehan's face, the dark smudges beneath his eyes. She watched as he and Theodor took their places on the dais and turned, flicking their mantles behind them with a practiced swirl. Sir Eric and Sandremun, following, continued on to stand at guard behind their lords.

The pipes wailed to silence. Now there was only an expectant rustle of drums. Faris felt Eric watching her. He did not move from his post, but somehow he seemed to bow. Faris felt Rosemary stiffen, but when she looked at her friend, the other girl's face was closed and still. Then the crowd stirred with a sound like a distant wind in the trees, and Farin and Andreas Blackbeard came through the door.

Faris forgave her brother the letter, forgave him everything, seeing his face. His mail had been scoured to silver perfection, the helm he carried in the crook of his arm polished like a mirror, but his face was brighter now. He had called *her* beautiful, but now his face was as radiant as a bride's.

He passed without seeing her, and he and Andreas knelt before the dais. Their cloaks settled around them, Andreas' oak tree and the silver hawk alighting on a harp, which she had worked on Farin's red velvet, glittered in the afternoon light.

"Ye folk of the Corona, hear me!" The Herald stepped forward. "It is said that long ago men bore arms by chance and not by choice and were sworn to serve not their own lords but printed laws. But in the time of the Cataclysm all of men's laws were swept away. And in that time there were some who turned to a more ancient way of fighting that did not offend the earth. They were linked to their lords by loyalty and love, and the old way of war became the new. And so united, these warriors preserved a remnant of the people to establish Westria.

"Since then, those who prove themselves worthy of the service of the sword have been named knights in Westria. You see two candidates for knighthood before you. Will any speak for them and attest their right to the honor they seek here?"

There was a roar of acclamation from Lord Theodor's

guard. When the cheering had faded, the Lord Commander took a step forward.

"I will speak for them," he said gruffly.

"And I . . ." added Sir Eric.

"And I . . ." said Sandremun. He still moved stiffly, but otherwise he had recovered from his arrow wound well. Berisa, next to the dais, watched him narrowly as if afraid he would relapse before her eyes. Faris wondered if her sister knew that their father had come.

"My Lord."

Faris' attention snapped back as the King turned to Theodor.

"I would have your leave to speak for the youth Farin, and to make him knight with my own hand."

The King's voice was strong and beautiful. Faris looked at her brother with a terrible envy. He was the King's man now . . . he would go with Jehan whatever might befall. *I have lost my father and my brother—what will I do?*

Theodor bowed assent.

"Farin," said the King, "in recognition of the valor and skill at arms you displayed in the fight against the raiders in the Highwater Valley, which contributed not only to the defense of our party but also saved my own life . . ." His voice rose above the murmur of the audience. ". . . and because of your courtesy and the skill in all accomplishments befitting a gentleman which I have observed in you, I am minded to make you knight. Will you accept this from my hand?"

"Aye, my Lord," Farin replied in a low voice.

The King took from Eric his own great sword of war and poised it over Farin's bent head.

"You are honorable, courteous, and brave," said the King, striking him once on each shoulder with the flat of the blade so that he shuddered beneath the blows. "Rise, Sir Farin of the Harp!"

The Hall erupted in cheering as the new knight got to his feet, and Jehan, handing his sword back to Eric, gave Farin an equal's embrace. He took from his own neck a gold chain, which he passed over Farin's head. Berisa stepped forward to tie the white belt of knighthood about his waist, followed by Lord Theodor, who bent to fasten the golden spurs to his feet.

"My Lord Commander," the King said, smiling, "I am

minded to take this new knight into my service, for the sake
of his skill with the sword and with the harp. Will you release him to me?"

Theodor laughed. "The gift is already given, is it not so?"

Farin had been blushing, but his face stilled as the King
told him to kneel once more. *He loves the King,* thought
Faris, watching him. Her eyes moved to the faces of Eric
and the rest. *They all love him, and I think he loves them
all.* Tears made a blurred shimmer of their cloaks and silvered mail. Her mind shied from the thought of this pledging that was so much more real than any vow that had ever
been offered to her.

"I, Farin Harper, do swear to you, Jehan Lord of Westria,
to be your man in all things: to speak or to be still, to strike
or to stay my hand, to be faithful in wealth or in woe. To
your service I bind myself until you yourself release me or
my own life ends. In the Name of the Guardian of Men!"

He was trembling, but his voice came true and clear. The
King bent over him.

"And I, Jehan of Westria, do now accept you as my sworn
man, and take oath to you to be a true and loving Lord. I
offer you my hearth for your sustenance, my sword for your
defense, and for your trust in me, my heart. As you have
given your faith to me, I give mine to you—so witness the
four Jewels of Westria and the Maker of All Things!"

The King raised Farin to his feet and kissed him on the
cheek, then let him go. Faris could see tears on Farin's
cheeks, but the King's face was shining, as if in that exchange of faith he had gained not only a new servant, but a
new joy.

Farin stepped to one side, moving as if he were afraid he
might break. The applause died away.

Lord Theodor cleared his throat. "Andreas," he called
the other candidate. "You served my vassal Charles of
Woodhall long and well. In the battle on the Highwater your
reinforcement enabled us to drive off the enemy. You have
all the attributes of a gentleman, therefore I am minded to
make you knight. Will you accept this from my hand?"

"Aye, my Lord."

Lord Theodor took his sword from Sandremun and struck
Andreas' shoulders. "You are honorable, courteous, and
brave! Rise, Sir Andreas of Woodhall!"

Andreas looked up in surprise at the name. The Lord

Commander embraced him, but after chain, belt, and spurs had been bestowed, he held him there.

"Sir Andreas, you know, better than any, that the steading of Woodhall overlooks one of the main roads into Westria. It must be held by a strong man. For many years you helped Sir Charles to defend it. Will you bear the responsibility for it now?"

"My Lord, my Lord—" Andreas stammered. "It should belong to the lady Holly, not to me!"

Faris felt Holly trembling beside her and saw her expression as she looked at Andreas. *Holly loves him! I wonder if he knows.*

"I have spoken with the lady," said Theodor, "and she is willing for it to go to you. The Hold will shelter her, and I will act as her guardian as long as she has need."

"My Lord." Andreas' voice could hardly be heard. "I did not defend Woodhall before—I am not worthy to be trusted with it now." He bowed his head.

The King laid a restraining hand on Theodor's arm. "Sir Andreas, look at me!"

Face working, the young man raised his eyes.

"What shall the penance be for a man who has failed to defend his lord? You could not save Sir Charles, but to send you forth to wander would be too light a punishment, and, by the Lord of Battles, of no use to Sir Charles, to you, or to me!" Jehan took a breath, and his voice rang across the Hall.

"If it is by any fault of yours that Woodhall is without a defender, then the task of holding it shall be your punishment. If no fault was yours, then the honor of holding it shall be your reward! Sir Charles is dead, and no grief will bring him back. Take up his work, Andreas, and guard the land he left!"

Sir Eric had gone dead white, staring at the King, but Andreas gazed at him with shining eyes.

And that is why they love him, thought Faris, *because he reaches out to touch the best in them, and gives them hope again.*

The Lord Commander, his own eyes very bright, spoke then. "Sir Andreas, will you hold the steading of Woodhall for me, as I hold the Corona for my Lord the King, and as the King holds Westria for the Lord of All?"

"Aye, Lord Theodor, that I will!"

"Kneel!"

Andreas slipped to his knees and placed his clasped hands between those of his lord.

When the oaths had been completed, Theodor raised Andreas to his feet and presented him for the acclamation of those gathered in the Hall. All ceremony evaporated as the cheering crowd pressed around them.

The exaltation Faris had felt during the ceremony was suddenly gone. She knew she must go to the feast now—Farin had reserved a place for her. But their father would be there, watching her, shattering the illusion of beauty that had allowed her to respond to Sir Eric and Stefan and the rest. And when she gave them nothing, no word or smile or kiss, they would call her cruel.

But it is only a game . . . surely they will understand if I cannot play it now! Yet she could not still the inner doubt that added, *what if it is not a game for them?*

Faris slipped through the garden gate and latched it behind her, heart pounding as if she were being pursued. But no one was there. Even the babble in the Hall was only a whisper from here. Dim tree-shapes rose around her, mysterious in the darkness, and the air was heady with scent as the earth gave back its stored warmth to the cooling sky. She plucked a spray of lilac and, turning it back and forth between her fingers, began to walk.

The breeze cooled her burning cheeks, and the silence eased her soul. During the dinner her father had been seated by Berisa, who had kept his contempt focused on the people around him and left him no time to think of her. He had made his escape immediately afterward, and as soon as she could extricate herself, Faris had done the same.

Her neck and shoulders ached with the strain of resisting him, of the tension she had picked up from Farin, the myriad emotions of the crowd. A mockingbird began his song of courtship somewhere nearby, and more faintly she heard the beginnings of music from the Hall.

But she continued to walk. She could not face all those people again, and dancing would leave her vulnerable . . . memory shied away from the dance she had shared with the King.

The gate squeaked and gravel crunched as someone came towards her along the path. Faris froze, poised for flight, while she tried to tell her body there was no reason to flee. And as she hesitated she saw a tall figure silhouetted against the stars and recognized Eric.

"You startled me!"

"My lady Faris! I did not mean—" Eric broke off, peering at her. "May I walk with you?" he asked formally.

Faris fought the impulse to refuse, but something in his stance made her respond with a murmur he could interpret as assent. For some minutes they continued along the path in silence.

"Well, your brother is a knight now—it was a fine ceremony," he said at last.

"Yes. This meant a great deal to him." Faris began to relax, wondering why she had been so afraid. Already this conversation was moving toward ground they had covered many times before.

"The King needs good men around him, men who believe in honor—not more cynics like the Seneschal!"

"Yet Caolin seems very devoted to his master . . . in his way . . ."

"In his way—no doubt!" Eric spoke scornfully. "That's what is wrong with these clerks. They don't understand loyalty to an ideal if it means sacrificing one's comfort, much less one's life!" He strode forward as if expecting the forces of compromise to confront him on the path.

"I am sure you are right, but you can hardly expect that to be a popular attitude," said Faris breathlessly, hurrying to catch up with him.

"Oh, forgive me! I didn't mean to run on like that!" Two strides brought him back to her side. "In fact . . . well, now that Farin is going to serve the King, what will you do?" he added suddenly.

She stopped, staring at him, and unable to find a light answer, said at last, "I do not know."

"Faris, why don't you marry me?"

He stretched out his arms dramatically, and Faris, remembering her conversation with her father, found herself on the brink of hysterical laughter.

"Eric! I am not one of the causes for which you must be sacrificed!" They had moved closer to the Hall. Candlelight glowing through the windows laid golden bars across the path.

He seized her hand. "I can never say anything right. Now I've offended you."

"I am not offended, Eric. Don't apologize to me." She tried to smile.

"But you would say that—you are always kind, always gentle, and always beautiful—so beautiful, my Lady!"

His grip on her hand was painful. Faris tried to speak, but Eric charged onward.

"'My Lady' I always have called you in my mind, when I imagined myself finally telling you how beautiful you are, and how much I . . . love you, Faris . . ." He dropped to his knees beside her in the path, seized the trailing hem of her gown, and kissed it.

"Eric! Eric—you must not kneel to me!" His weight on her skirts reminded her of Rosemary's sheepdog. Stifling laughter, she went on. "Please get up!"

He gazed up at her, his face shining in the light from the Hall. As swiftly as he had knelt, he was on his feet again, seizing her in his arms. She looked at him in astonishment, and before she could catch her breath he kissed her.

Faris felt as if she were in the grip of some great force of nature—a whirlwind, a tidal wave, the Great Bear. She was too stunned to even try and break free. She felt the power of Eric's battle-trained muscles and was afraid. After a moment he let go of her and stood away, breathing hard. The spray of lilac she had been holding at her breast fell in fragments to the path.

Eric looked at her, and Faris realized in horror that perhaps it had not been just his height that had kept him from meeting her eyes before. She had no right to see the nakedness of his soul.

"Eric . . . no!" she whispered, raising one hand.

He stepped back as if she had pushed him. His great fists were clenching and unclenching at his sides.

"No. Oh, my Lady, I did not mean . . . I thought . . . Faris, I love you in all honor! Indeed, I love you as my own honor, and to have you for my lady and my wife would be an honor nearly too great for me to bear!"

His eyes were glowing and his curls had blown back from his brow. Faris looked at his broad shoulders and remembered the strength in his arms. Surely with him she could find honor, comfort, a strong rock on which to build her life anew. But he was looking at her as if he saw the Lady of

Fire, and she thought, *Does he really know me at all?*

She raised her eyes to seek his face again and saw in the window above him the silhouetted head and shoulders of the King. Her flesh ran suddenly hot, then cold again. *Jehan . . . Jehan . . .* his name rang in her heart like a knell.

She shook her head. "Oh no . . . what have I done?" and watched the anguished understanding of her answer dawn slowly in Eric's eyes.

"I cannot deceive you . . . I cannot deceive myself. If honor made a marriage, I would be yours—" she stumbled, "but I cannot be what you deserve!" She hid her face. "Oh, they were right—I have done evil—but I swear to you, Eric, I never meant you harm!" She dashed tears from her eyes and held out her hands.

He took her hand and kissed it as if it had been some rare flower. She felt him trembling like the trunk of a great tree in a strong wind.

"You have done nothing, my Lady," he said very patiently. "You, surely, have no reason to reproach yourself! It was all my own blind desire. Please do not weep for me!" His voice cracked and he dropped her hand. His face was shadowed now. "I have only one thing to ask. Will you let me serve you still? I ask no reward," he said with a terrible control.

"Oh, Eric," Faris said brokenly, "if you wish, of course you may, until you find another more worthy lady who will return your love."

He laughed grimly. "My Lady, have I your leave to depart?" At her nod he bowed very low and turned away into the darkness. It was only when she heard the far gate close that she realized he had gone to the stables instead of the Hall.

"Eric? Eric! Where are you going?" But no answer came from the night. "Sweet Lady, pity him, and pity me!"

She stood trembling where he had left her. She could no longer see Jehan in the window, but the strangely familiar music was clear. "Jehan . . . oh, Jehan . . . I love you," she murmured, shaking her head while the tears ran unheeded down her cheeks. Now she remembered the words to the song—*As I have pledged my life, so now I pledge my love, nor fate nor death shall ever break this binding.*

And she recognized the tune as the one that Farin had been playing that morning on the King's harp.

V

The Beltane Fire

The Master of the Junipers touched his taper to the green candle. *For the Lady of Fire.* He looked back at the King.

"Are you ready? We could do this later, you know—you will have a hard day."

Although the small windows set around the upper wall of the chapel glowed pale rose in the early dawn, the room was still visible only as dim masses of light and shadow. Scenes from the wall paintings glowed and faded as the candles flickered—men bringing blocks from the ruins of the Red City to build the Hold, Queen Auriane using the Jewel of Fire to turn a forest fire away from the Hold, the symbolic marriage of Julian the Great with the transcendent figure of the Guardian of Westria.

For a moment the King's face mirrored the exaltation pictured on that of the King in the painting. "I must know now," he said in a low voice. "Faris was not at the dancing last night. Her face comes between me and sleep." He placed upon the altar the redwood coffer he had been carrying.

"Since it was my suggestion that we seek the Lady's help, I can hardly deny you my help if you still wish me to be your guide," said the Master. He shook his head to clear it. The King had wakened him from a sleep filled by troubled dreams before the sun was up.

But Jehan did not look as if he had slept at all. His eyes were shadowed and his skin pulled tight above the dark beard. Had Jehan been suffering this torment since he and Faris met? Surely the Master would have known. But if this was new, it must have been the advice he had given the King the day before that, by sanctioning this passion, had unleashed its full force.

The Master's muscles tensed as he remembered a saying they had at the College—*Be careful what you ask of the gods . . . they may give it to you.* What would come of this morning's work? He breathed deeply, forcing himself to relax. Only good—surely only good could come if both of them held to the will of the Maker of gods and men.

The King turned full into the candlelight, and the Master flinched from the trust in his eyes.

He stepped back from the altar and spoke quickly. "In the Name of the Maker of All! The temple is sealed and the altar prepared!" He spread his hands wide. "Behold the Tree of Life, and obey its laws."

The tall candles set on the nearest corners of the altar flared as he moved, illuminating the male and female pillars, white and black, on either side. Behind them flickered the tapestry of the Tree of Life, which showed all elements and archetypes from earth to heaven.

Jehan stepped forward and laid one hand on the coffer. "Hail, Maker of All. May what we do here today find favor in Your sight!" He opened the coffer.

Inside were four compartments, each containing something wrapped in colored silk. The King's hand moved to the green, hovered a moment, and lifted it out. As he loosened his grip the silk fell away and a copper coronet uncoiled in his hands. The King held it up, eyes averted from the stone set at its center. It seemed dark and opaque, but as the King moved it caught the candlelight, and within its depths the Master saw an answering spark of flame.

"What must I do? I have not touched the Jewels more than twice since I became King, and never for something like this. At the College they said that there have been Kings who could use the powers of the Jewels without even touching them, but I am not one of them."

"Wait until we are in rapport," replied the Master. "I will tell you when to put on the Jewel of Fire." He motioned towards the chairs that had been set before the altar. Jehan took his place with the coronet in his lap, and the Master sat down across from him. For several minutes they were still, relaxing taut muscles one by one, easing their breathing into a synchronous rhythm.

The Master kept his eyes on the King, but he did not focus on his face, for it was not the body of the man that he wished to see. The charged stillness deepened around them. Their regular breathing was the only sound in the room. As the Master's awareness of his own body diminished, he began to perceive a glow around the King that changed gradually from dirty red to deep blue, lightening at last to a pale silver light. The Master closed his eyes and projected his consciousness towards Jehan.

Dim walls . . . a flicker of candlelight . . . the head of a warrior from the wall painting behind him . . . the Master moved deeper, saw Caolin and a blurred memory of Brian of Las Costas, then a glimpse of Faris.

Be still, be still! he sent his thought towards Jehan. *Focus on the Light.* The images in his mind fragmented into flickers of color. He visualized Jehan lifting the coronet and settling it on his brow. *Put on the Jewel!*

When the Master opened his eyes, he was dazzled by the blaze of the Jewel of Fire. The fires in its heart were awakened now, its dusky surface scarcely veiling the coruscations of emerald and flame. Even as he saw it with his eyes, he perceived the reflection of his vision in Jehan's mind and felt the echo of its burning on Jehan's brow.

The blaze flared around them until they were poised within the heart of fire, and for a moment the heat seemed too great to bear. *See flowers,* projected the Master, feeling the wavering of Jehan's will, and the flames shimmered and formed themselves into flower petals fluttering in a warm breeze. There was music around them, and the wind bore heady scents of cypress and sandalwood.

The Master saw the King beside him, robed in a garment the vivid gold of a poppy flower. His own garment in this place was paler, like sunlight shining through a cloud.

"Lead on, my Lord," said the Master then. "This quest is yours."

The flowers opened into a glade hedged like a garden, where the grass glowed as earthly grass glows in the light of the setting sun. All their fear was gone. They felt that they were walking only because it was the most familiar way to move—if they had desired, they could have flown. They hurried forward, their spirits swelling within them, and the music surged.

A scatter of white blooms on the ground before them quivered and rose cooing into the air. They watched the doves settle again, finding it suddenly hard to breathe. Someone laughed in a tinkle of silver bells.

They turned. Behind them stood a cluster of women, some barely budding into womanhood, some with the ripe beauty of an autumn tree, who smiled and sang.

> Mistress of Mistresses, bearer of beauty,
> And world's desire . . .
> The eye She blinds, the soul She binds—
> She is Love's Fire.

Laughter rang again and the women drew apart. Then they saw only one woman, veiled in robes that shimmered emerald and flame. Her face was too bright for them to look upon.

"Seeker, why have you come to Me?"

Jehan bowed. "Lady of Fire, I seek You as the Guardian of human love."

"That I know," she said tartly. "If you were concerned with any other of My aspects, you would see Me in another form. What is your need?"

The heat increased and the perfume deepened until the Master felt faint, but Jehan straightened and stepped forward.

"I must have a Lady to balance me as Lord of this land, and to ease the burden on my heart. But my eyes are too weak to pierce the illusions that surround me, and see truly my own need."

"You do not wish to know what you need," she contradicted him. "You desire to know whom you love. What you ask, mortal, is what you shall receive—do you choose the hearthfire that comforts or the heart-fire that consumes the soul?"

The Lady's voice sang like a viol, and the color of her robes deepened to crimson as she leaned towards them.

Jehan's voice rang in answer. "Show me the one whose soul will be mated with my own!"

The Lady seemed to grow. Her robes rippled away from Her body, and Jehan and the Master were dazzled by the brightness of Her limbs. But Jehan looked up. "Faris," he breathed, and seeing with Jehan's eyes, the Master saw—

Faris robed in green and glowing like the goddess of Spring . . .

Faris bearing the Four Jewels on loins and waist and breast and brow . . .

Farisheavywithchild . . .

Faris with eyes huge and burning in a ravaged face . . .

Jehan cried out and sprang towards her, and the Master leaped after him. But the Lady was gone. Her attendants swirled around them, drawing them into their dance. He saw their faces, the transfigured faces of every woman he had ever known . . . they were flowers . . . they were flames . . . and then even the flames were gone.

The Master opened his eyes.

For a few moments he could see nothing. When his sight cleared, the chapel was dim but clearly visible in the early morning light. Jehan lay slumped in his chair, and the coronet with the Jewel of Fire gleamed faintly from the floor.

"Jehan!" The Master grasped the King's shoulders and straightened him. As his head fell back the Master saw a red mark like a burn across his brow. "Jehan—come back!" He took the King's head between his hands.

Jehan's blue eyes opened, catching the new daylight as if they still held the Lady's fire. "Faris . . ." he murmured.

"Yes. I saw her too."

Jehan sighed and smiled, his eyes refocusing on his inner vision. The Master let him go and stood up. Faintly, like the beating of his heart, he could hear the pulsing of the Beltane drum.

On the other side of the field they were playing a dance tune—flute and tambour and the swift rat-tat of a hand drum. Faris pushed through crowds of people, come from the town that clustered below the Hold, or from the surrounding countryside, for the Beltane Festival. From time to time she stood on tiptoe and shaded her eyes to see. Bright awnings and pavilions were scattered about the field, making a loose circle around the Maypole and the two piles of wood stacked for the bonfires. But where was Rosemary?

Faris neared the trestle tables where they were distributing bread, cheese, and roasted mutton and saw her friend at last, her sleeves rolled up and a bread knife in her hand. Faris sighed with relief. She had slept badly, haunted by specters of her father accusing her, of Eric striding desperately into the night. But Rosemary would know what she should do.

"I have been looking all over for you," said Faris as Rosemary looked up.

"Where else would I be? Did you expect my mother to expose her delicate nerves to such a crowd? And Berisa is entertaining our noble guests." She glanced up the hill where the Lord Commander's black and white pavilion dominated the scene. "So I end up making sure that there are enough provisions and helping the people who are actually doing the work!" Her knife sliced through the bread in precise, vicious strokes.

Faris stared at her friend, then stepped quickly out of the way as a stout man with one child clinging to his tunic and another on his shoulder paused before Rosemary, who cut a long loaf into three pieces and sliced each lengthwise so that it could be used as a trencher.

"Here you are, Jack." Rosemary smiled brightly. "May the Lady give you joy. Have you brought animals to be blessed tonight?"

The man grinned. "Two heifers that we want to breed this year! But my wife won't go between the fires again—she is heavy with our fourth child."

"You finally found out what was causing it, then?" They both laughed at the old joke.

"Oh, we knew that well enough already!" Jack's grin grew broader. "And what of you, my Lady? We had hoped to see you dancing between the fires with the mothers this year instead of around the Maypole with the maidens."

"Everything has its proper season. Mine has not yet come," Rosemary said shortly. Jack coughed in embarrassment, handed the bread to his children, and turned away.

"Can I help?" asked Faris hesitantly. She handed Rosemary a loaf of bread.

The other girl glanced up at her. "Why aren't you on the hill with the rest of them? Are you hiding from your admirers? Or did you think that my company would drive them away?"

Faris stood with the loaf held uselessly in her hand, not knowing what to do. Now she observed the angry flush on Rosemary's face, the suspicious brightness of her eyes. *Have*

I hurt you too? I never meant to do anything wrong! her heart cried. She started to turn away.

"It's nothing," she said. "I only wanted to talk to you."

"I didn't think you needed any *female* friendship." Rosemary shook her head. "But now you don't know which of your suitors to choose, and you've come to ask Auntie Rosemary to tell you what to do? Well, I can't help you. My father's after me to pick any one of those men who are running after you, and I'm tired of competing like a heifer at a fair!"

Faris found her fingers digging into the bread in her hand and very carefully set it down. All the voices that had debated within her since that moment when she had seen the King's silhouette the night before had merged into one voice now. With a fearful clarity she realized that though there might be no future for her afterward, she knew what her next step must be.

"This heifer has just dropped out of the competition."

"What?" asked Rosemary blankly.

"You accused me of playing with men's feelings," said Faris. "I didn't mean to, and I didn't see how anyone could misinterpret me—" She faltered, reached for a mug of wine someone had left on the table. The stuff was too warm, but it eased her tight throat going down.

"But Eric did take it seriously, and I refused his proposal, and he ran away—" she blurted. "I came to ask you if you had heard whether he was all right."

Rosemary's knuckles whitened as she gripped the carving knife. "You came to ask that of me?" she repeated. Carefully she set down the knife and turned to stare at Faris. Her face was red from the heat, and though her golden hair had been braided firmly around her head, escaping strands clung damply to her forehead. But her gray eyes held the same dumb pain Faris had seen in her own mirror that morning.

And Faris heard the words that Rosemary could not say. "Sweet Lady!" Faris put her hand to her mouth. "You are in love with *Eric*! And you wouldn't tell him." She laughed a little hysterically. "Well, that makes two of us! Thank goodness I said no!"

Four boys crowded in front of them, clamoring for bread. Faris handed Rosemary two loaves, and for a moment she was kept busy carving. When the boys had gone Rosemary looked up, frowning.

"Two of us? Who are *you* in love with, the King?"

Faris knew that her own face must have betrayed her as Rosemary's frown changed to a kind of desperate mirth.

"And here I've been wishing you would take Eric and get it over with, while all the time—" Rosemary buried her face against Faris' shoulder, giggling.

"It's not funny," said Faris morosely. She indicated the scar hidden by her full sleeve. "I know better than to think that the King might want me. But at least now Eric will be free to look for someone else."

Rosemary straightened and sighed. "Do you think so? He is in love with an image he calls Faris. I'm not sure you can do anything about that. He might even prefer to serve a lost cause."

Faris nodded, remembering what Eric had said the evening before. Was it a mark of love to understand the beloved so well? Would she ever understand Jehan?

"You might try hitting him over the head," said Rosemary.

The wine Faris had drunk bubbled gently through her veins and buzzed in her ears. The sun seemed very bright, and there was something inexpressibly comic about Rosemary's smile.

"But Rose, I can't even *reach* his head," she began very seriously. Then her control slipped and she began to giggle. Rosemary whooped, and the two girls collapsed into each other's arms.

"I can't marry anybody, and I've quarreled with my father," Faris said at last. "Let's get a cottage together. You can keep your animals there, and I'll work in the garden."

"And we can sell advice to young girls suffering from unrequited love!" added Rosemary.

Trying to catch her breath, Faris brushed the loose hair from her eyes. Someone tugged at her sleeve. She looked down and saw Linnet, Berisa's oldest daughter, beside her.

"They want all the girls to come for the Maypole dancing," said Linnet, "and I promised I would find you. Please come, Aunt Faris—please, Aunt Rosemary?"

She looked up at them with Berisa's dark eyes, but the golden curls beneath her wreaths of flowers were her father's. Three wreaths. As Faris noticed that, Linnet took off the topmost, twined of the little golden lilies that star the grass, and offered it to her. The second, made of twisted rosemary strands, she gave to Rosemary.

They looked at each other, the wreaths held carefully in their hands.

"It is midafternoon. I suppose everyone has gotten something to eat by now," Rosemary said uncertainly.

"Did you make the wreaths?" asked Faris.

"Yes, me and my sister. We want to see you dance," said Linnet.

"Oh . . . well then, I see that we must go!" replied Rosemary.

They bent low while Linnet settled the wreaths on their heads and fussed with them until she was satisfied. Then they let her take their hands and lead them across the field.

The air was heady with the smells of crushed grass, roasting meat, and spring flowers. Faris tipped back her head and gazed beyond the crowds to the hills around them, vivid now with the mingled golds of mustard and poppy, slashed by drifts of purple or white lupine bloom. Behind them the mountains hung upon the horizon like silhouettes cut from blue silk. Except for a few clouds clustering around the Father of Mountains, the sky was clear.

The drum was beating already—the deep-throbbing ritual drum, not the little one used for dancing. The beat moved her feet faster, and the laughter she had shared with Rosemary still bubbled in her breast. *I will not ask for more than this hour, this day, this awareness of love,* she thought, and for the moment her fear was gone.

"Faris, I am so glad that you came to me," said Rosemary softly. "I was growing twisted as a crab apple, keeping all that unspoken. But we are two fools, you know. You should have accepted Eric, and I should let my father try to match me with the King!"

"No . . . Eric doesn't really know me. How could I ever trust him? He is too young. But you would make a good Queen, Rosemary—you manage things so well."

"Except my own life!" she laughed, then abruptly sobered. "You are thinking about your scar, but that's a surface thing. Can we ever really know each other's souls?" They walked for a few moments in silence. Then Rosemary added, "Well, we are all in the Lady's hand."

A little breeze coaxed the hair from its loose braid down

Faris' back and carried clearly the lowing of the livestock waiting for their part in the ceremonies. But the drum made it hard to think of other things now.

They reached the other dancers and took their places in the procession of young women and wives who had not yet borne a child. Someone gave them a horn of mead and they passed it from hand to hand. The pipers joined them, puffing and punching at the bags of their instruments until they swelled and the sweet skirling lifted above the beat of the drum.

The girls twirled in a flaring of flower-colored skirts, bent and leaped in place, stretching muscles to be ready for the dance. The piper settled into a frolicking march, and the crowd opened into an aisle before them with the flower-crowned Maypole at its end against the backdrop of the Father of Mountains.

At the retreat that preceded Faris' Nametaking and Initiation, the Master who taught them the history of the festivals of Westria had spent a long time on Beltane. Like many of the customs they used now, the Maypole dancing had been a practice of the old ones—the Edge People—in a land far away. Even the name of Beltane came from a land and language that were only legends now. But those who had brought the festivals to Westria before the Cataclysm were leaders among those who survived it. The Guardians protected those who knew enough to celebrate their powers. Faris knew that in five centuries the rituals had changed—they were not even precisely the same in all parts of Westria. But the purpose and the principle remained, and she realized that if she had refused to join the dancing, it would hardly have seemed like May.

Smiling, she moved forward with the rest. The people were throwing garlands to the girls and draping them with chains of flowers, for it was said to bring luck if one's token was borne in the ceremonies. The crowd cheered and made frank comments on the maidens' beauty. Faris tried to hide her embarrassment as she tied a string of dandelions about the waist of her white gown.

"Well, Ida," said one old woman as they passed, her cheeks burned red as ripe apples by the sun, "they look like a strong lot! They'll last till sundown surely, when it's time to light the fires! I remember one year when all the girls collapsed with an hour yet to go, and we had to wait until someone recovered enough to hold the torch. The rains were bad that year too, and my red cow miscarried of twin calves."

"Who's the warrior they've chosen to stand at the pole?" asked her friend, pulling her plaid shawl around her.

"Oh, it will be the King for certain this year. It's always a high man, and he's the highest of all!"

Ida cackled. "He'll have a fine time then, with all the lasses shaking their titties in his face and him bound too tight by the ribbons to move anything at all!"

"It's a small price to pay, don't you think? In the old days they would not have unbound him before they gave the pole to the fire!"

The King! Faris stopped short, fighting to retain her clarity. The girl behind her bumped into her and jolted her forward again. The drumbeat was deeper now. She could feel it shaking the earth, pulsing through her body from the ground to her heart. Another procession was starting down from the Commander's pavilion to meet them . . . all of the young men of the Corona, crowned with flowers. In the midst of them walked the King.

With much laughter and broad joking they thrust him against the Maypole. He stood still, his arms by his sides, while Sandremun loosed the ribbons that had been looped to the pole. They had dressed him in a new tunic of poppy gold, and there were poppies and lupines wreathed on his dark hair.

As the ribbons fluttered down around him he turned his head, and Faris met his eyes.

She wanted to run, to hide, but the music was moving her on. She looked away, followed the girl ahead of her until the circle was complete. For a moment the music stilled. Every second maiden turned until they were all facing each other in pairs. The ribbons were put into their hands.

The drum boomed twice, and twice again. Shivers ran up and down Faris' spine, and she clutched at her ribbon to still her trembling. The tension built, built, until the bagpipes let loose with a single exulting skirl. The girls facing sunward lifted their ribbons while the others bent. The drum began to beat out a swift insistent rhythm, and alternately lifting and bending so that their ribbons wove over and under each other around the pole, the dancers began to move.

They made the first circle, and Faris looked up and saw

Jehan smile. She stumbled, caught herself, tried to focus on
the music. She glimpsed her brother in the crowd, standing
with Caolin and the Master of the Junipers, and was obscurely grateful that her father was not there. Her wreath
slipped; she reached to adjust it and felt the tie slide from
her braid and her hair begin to fall free.

And still the music drove her forward, and the shortening
ribbons drew her inward to the pole. Faris was warming
from the dancing. Her limbs moved more freely now, and
she no longer tried to keep from looking at Jehan.

He stood still while the weaving of the ribbons crept down
the pole, but his eyes followed her. Faris felt them on her
even when she was turned away, burning hotter than the
westering sun. His forehead was beaded with sweat, his
throat like a marble column beneath his beard. Faris could
see a muscle in it twitch as she went by.

The ribbons were touching him now, lacing across his face
so that she saw only his eyes and the shape of his shoulders
and chest. The sun slipped towards the western mountains.
Its deepening glow lit pole and dancers, and the form of the
man bound to the pole, with the same fire.

They had to move closer and bend lower to weave around
him now. The lacing moved downward over shoulders,
chest, waist, molding the shapes of his loins and thighs,
tightening around knees and ankles. Faris brushed Jehan's
bare foot with her hand as she made the final circuit and
jerked away as if burnt.

The music stopped. The dancers straightened, backed
away from the pole, and let the long ends of the ribbons fall
so that they radiated outward from their center like the
spokes of a wheel. Now Jehan was only a swelling at the
base of the pole. Why could she still feel his eyes?

The rhythm of the drum changed again, becoming un-
even, enticing the body to respond to the lilt of the melody
the pipes took up now. The people joined in, clapping, shaking deerhoof rattles, jingling tambours.

Now the real dancing began as each girl tried to outdo the
rest. Young men called to them, hoping to claim partners
for the evening's revelry. Faris began slowly, meaning to
keep on for as short a time as custom allowed and then to
drop out. Some other girl could carry the torch and bear the
May Queen's crown.

The fading of the day should have brought a cool wind,

but the air that fanned Faris' cheeks was hot. Again she lifted the hair away from her neck, fanning it out so that it flared around her when she twirled, and loosened the lacings at the neck of her gown. Her eyes were blinded by the blaze of the setting sun. She should stop dancing now . . . she should . . .

High above the other music came the tinkle of silver bells.

Faris did not need to hear the drumming anymore. It was the pulse of her heart. She opened her arms, and flames ran along each nerve and sparked from her fingertips. She arched her back, feeling the delicious tension of breast and stomach muscles at full stretch. Her knees bent; her feet began to tap out the rhythm of the drums. Music rippled along her body, drew her arms, around her and out again as if they fluttered veils, lifted her into the air.

She no longer saw the sun, or the other dancers beginning to fall around her, or even the King. She was the sun; she was the flame of the torches eager for the pyre.

Faris danced.

The crimson sun sank rapidly towards the western mountains, its shape distorting as it neared the horizon, as if it were melting in its own fire. The clouds through which it fell stretched eastward in ragged banners of flame.

The ruddy light glowed on the faces of the people watching the dancing. The Master of the Junipers felt their emotion building as the pulse of the music increased, flowed back into the dancers, was focused by them and projected back again.

Rosemary stumbled towards him, wiping her forehead and fanning her cheeks. "That's enough for me!" she panted. "It's not fair—the pipers are playing in relays, but we have to dance straight through to the end!"

"I understood that one of the purposes of this exercise was to test endurance," said Caolin without taking his eyes from the dancers.

Rosemary looked at him coldly. "Who's left?" she asked the Master, getting her breath under control. "Oh . . ."

Only three dancers remained, and one of them was Faris, stretching and swaying like a living flame. As they watched, one of the other girls sank to the grass and was helped away by her friends.

"I didn't know that your sister could dance like that!" said

Sandremun to Farin, who was watching as raptly as any of them. His fingers twitched as if he were accompanying the dancing on an invisible harp.

The Master braced himself against the force of their emotion—not lust, for although Faris' movements displayed all the grace of her slender body, they were sensual rather than erotic; the desire they expressed was for something not quite attainable by mortal flesh.

"How she dances!" murmured Rosemary. "I did not know she had the strength. I told her that we never really know each other . . . now I wonder if she knows herself."

The Master shook his head. "I do not think that it is *her* strength."

The sun had become a flare of brilliance behind the hills, but the clouds were bright, glowing with opalescent flecks of crimson and gold and flame, purple, and a pale translucent emerald. *Like the Jewel of Fire.*

People looked eagerly towards the Father of Mountains, but the only light on its slopes was the rosy reflection from the snowfields at its peak. Up there the Masters and Mistresses of the College of the Wise would be waiting, but they would not light the Beltane beacon until they could no longer see the sun.

The second girl crumpled to the ground. Now Faris danced alone, and the Master felt the prickling at the back of his neck that told him something more than mortal was here. He glanced around him. Did none of the others feel it too?

At the College they taught that since the Cataclysm, the gifts of the spirit had become more common in Westria, perhaps as a compensation for the skill at making tools and engines that men had renounced. Those with great talent usually ended up in the College, but most people could sense emotion, or even link minds in moments of great joy or fear. But just as some people were deaf to music, some people had no psychic sensitivity at all.

"I have heard of this, but I have not seen it before," said Caolin thoughtfully. "The Goddess rides her hard— there are few who can serve so directly as a channel of Power."

The words focused the Master's attention on Caolin. He glanced sidelong at the Seneschal's clear profile, outlined now in flame. Only long practice in balancing amid the torrent of others' emotions enabled him to withstand those around him, but he opened his awareness momentarily to Caolin, trying to sense what the other man was feeling now.

As always, he met only a hard shell. *It is observation, not perception then that tells him what is happening here,* thought the Master. *What amazing barriers Caolin must have, and how well he compensates.*

A sound rose from the people around him, as wordless as the wind in the grass. Faris was dancing towards the pole and back again. The sky was darkening to crimson, but her pale dress still glowed. She began to circle the pole, and each circuit increased the tension in the watching crowd.

The Master forced an even rhythm on his breathing and fixed his eyes on the Mountain. He had faced the Lady once already today, and that was enough. Was this dancing the first fruits of the King's petition, or had they themselves been the Lady's tools?

The peak of the Father of Mountains blossomed with flame.

The people gasped. Then their tension exploded in a roar of triumph that engulfed the music and broke the rhythm of the drums.

"The fire!" they cried. "The Beltane fire!"

The Master saw Faris sway. He moved quickly towards her and found Caolin at his side. They caught her as she sagged and held her upright, feeling her body quiver to the racing of her heart. Her eyes were fixed, inseeing still.

Sandremun was cutting through the ribbons that bound the King. The Master shook his head. He had found it hard to withstand even the backlash of the power that Faris was channeling—what must it have been like for Jehan, who had been the focus of it all?

Caolin quivered as the ribbons fell away and Sandremun helped Jehan to step free. The King moved stiffly, his muscles cramped from his long stillness, but the exaltation on his face mirrored the look in Faris' eyes.

"Jehan," whispered Caolin, and the Master realized that this was one of the few times he had heard the Seneschal speak the King's name.

Rosemary and the other girls hurried to take Faris from their arms, to crown her with a wreath of early honeysuckle. Farin was bringing one like it for the King.

The Maypole quivered and groaned as the men worked it

free and, shouting, bore it to one of the Beltane pyres. They pushed Jehan after it and put a torch into his hands. The women half carried Faris to the other pile of wood. A second torch was given to her, and her hand closed automatically around its stock.

For a moment she and Jehan faced each other crowned like two woods spirits with flowers. The flickering torches revealed the same unearthly beauty on their pale faces and the same glow in their wondering eyes.

Caolin stood like an image, hands clenched at his sides.

"All hail to the Lady!" came the men's deep cry.

"All hail to the Lord!" the women replied.

As if that had been a command, Faris and Jehan swung high their torches and cast them on to the waiting pyres. The flames caught the sweet oils that had been poured over the logs and licked hungrily down to the tinder within the piles. With a roar the flicker exploded into a blaze of light.

A chorus of lowing and bleating, laughter and ribald commentary, mingled with the crackling of the fires. Two by two the couples who desired children passed between them. Women led their milk-cows, children their lambs, boys tugged at the noserings of the young bulls they had kept to raise. Some had brought chickens or goats to receive the blessing. Some of the young people rode their horses between the fires. One of the King's men led the stallion Stormwing through, snorting and rolling his eyes at the flames.

Over the sea of heaving backs and fire-flushed faces the Master could see Faris, leaning now against Rosemary. She blinked and moved her head, and he perceived warring in her face the bewilderment of the human girl and the terrible beauty of the Lady of Fire.

VI
Royal Hunt and Storm

Intent on his prey, Jehan slipped an arrow one-handed from his quiver and nocked it, guiding Stormwing with his knees as the white horse plunged through the trees. The pale early morning light shafted between the trunks of the firs; the King's eyes narrowed against the shift of bright, dark, bright, as he focused on the fleeting red-dappled form of the deer.

Light and darkness—the radiance of Faris' face, the shadows of her hair. Jehan's vision focused on the world around him again. Cold air rasped his throat, but the blood was singing along his veins. He was strung taut as his own bent bow, but soon he would flash free to his goal—the deer that flickered before him, the woman he had faced last night across the Beltane fire.

Farin and Randal crashed through the brush behind him. To his right he could hear Sandremun shouting and the calling of Caolin's horn. To his left . . . he did not need sound to tell him that Faris was there. He felt her presence, as if the dancing had forged between them an invisible chain.

The deer leaped ahead, slipping through the thickets as a salmon slips upstream. The hunters followed with more difficulty, forcing their way among the rock falls and the jagged stumps of branches as they strained to keep the dogs in sight. It was perilous riding, for the deer was avoiding the bald hilltops and meadows where they might have seen their way.

They emerged from the fir-wood and followed the chase down the mountain, through patches of manzanita and madrone. The hunters had laced their boots to the top and turned them up over their thighs, but still their legs were gouged and their faces welted as they crashed through.

Jehan let a madrone branch slide along his bent back, straightened, glimpsed the deer, and lifted his bow. Sensing his danger, the deer swerved, soared over a clump of manzanita, and disappeared. The King eased back in his saddle and Stormwing slowed, blowing noisily. He had outrun the dogs and must wait for them to give him a direction again.

Caolin pounded up and drew rein beside him. He spoke, but Jehan scarcely heard. The bushes across the clearing trembled; the pounding of his heart deafened him; Faris was there. She bent forward, quieting her black mare. Her hair had escaped its braid and blew around her face like a dark cloud, but in the sunlight her riding tunic and breeches glowed a vivid green.

The sun lifted above the trees and suddenly the clearing was adazzle with light. The hounds called like a chime of untuned bells and swept past them. Instantly Stormwing was plunging after them. Jehan gave him his head, letting the excitement carry him onward, knowing that Faris felt it too.

Sharp branches whipped at his legs as they plunged through the manzanita, up a hill, and down another rocky slope. The ground grew rapidly steeper, and Jehan thought the deer must be seeking some nearby stream in order to lose the hounds. He urged Stormwing forward. The music of the pack changed. Jehan swept after them and saw the deer hesitating, red flanks heaving, where the ground fell suddenly away.

The deer's muscles rippled as he gathered himself. Jehan raised the bow, bent it till its tension rippled along his outstretched arm. The deer lifted; the arrow slipped from Jehan's fingers, whispered across the top of the hand that clenched the bow, arced through the air to intersect the leap of the deer.

He heard the dull thunk as the arrow hit, saw the clean line of the deer's flight distorted. Then it disappeared below the cliff. The dogs milled at the cliff edge, their frustrated yapping drowning the tinkling of the little stream below. Jehan sighed, slipped the bow back over his head, and started looking for a way down.

He found the deer broken on the rocks beside the stream. He bent over it, hearing the others scrambling down to join him, Sandy calling his dogs away. The deer was not quite dead. The arrow had entered a finger's breadth from the joining of shoulder and neck, and its shaft quivered each time the deer took a breath. A little blood was trickling over the gray stones.

Jehan drew his knife. "Brother, forgive my clumsiness. I would have spared you this pain." The deer's dark eyes fixed on him in mute bewilderment. Kneeling, Jehan laid his left hand across them and held the deer's head down, murmuring, "Father, into Your hands I give the spirit of this my brother. His life will not be wasted, as I pray that my ending my own may not have been."

Then he drew his knife across the animal's throat. The body jerked for a few moments. When at last it stilled, the King lifted his hand and saw the deer's eyes already dull. He rose and stepped back, and Sandremun's men came up to begin the work of butchering, setting aside the offal for the dogs and any scavenger who might have need of a meal, and binding the carcass to a pole to be transported back to the Hold.

Jehan shivered. Clouds had come up from the west and were crossing the sun. He wiped his knife carefully and sheathed it.

"We have been lucky so far," said Sandy. "I think it will rain before noon. I'm going back—this morning's ride has tested my strength. I dare not return to my lady soaked to the skin!"

The King scarcely heard. Faris was watering her horse at the stream. The curve of her bent back, the flexed grace of her arm as she scooped water for herself, made a harmony of balanced tensions that drew him into its patterning.

"We have permission to take another deer," said Farin. "I would hate to turn back when we have come so far."

"I will take the King's deer back to the Hold," said Sandremun.

"We'll come with you," echoed Aramond. "Lady Holly is weary."

Jehan was still watching Faris. "I will stay," he said without looking around. But his thoughts were not on deer. Now he had other prey.

The hounds whimpered eagerly as they sought a new scent. Guided by Sandremun's huntsman, Caolin led the King, Randal, the girl Faris, and her brother through the oakwood. The sky had gone gray above them. Caolin felt moisture, looked up impatiently, then back to the hounds.

"What ails them?" he exclaimed. "We have been wandering for a half hour and they've not started a rabbit, let alone a deer! I should have brought Gerol—he would have found us some sport!" Caolin glanced at the King, who smiled faintly without replying. The King's eyes held the same inward focus that had been there since the night before. What ailed the man?

"You would make a free wolf help in your hunting?" asked Farin, astonished.

"Oh, Gerol is the lord Seneschal's willing shadow," said Randal, "but it might not be fair to the deer."

Caolin let the conversation flow by him, his attention on the King. "My Lord!" he began, but the King did not appear to have heard. "Jehan." He reached out to him.

The hounds gave tongue at last and Caolin's horse plunged forward. For a moment he and Jehan rode knee to knee. How could he breach the King's reserve?

"Ride hard, my Lord!" Caolin challenged at last. "Ride, or I'll beat you to this prize!" He drove his heels into the brown mare's sides.

The trail led straight through the oakwood, then up slopes steeper than any they had encountered, slanted and fissured from some ancient torment of the earth. The line of hunters spread and straggled as they tried to follow.

The air rang with the thunder of hoofbeats and the crying of the hounds. Caolin did not know how long they had ridden when he realized there was thunder in the heavens as well. He reined in and looked about him. He could hear the hounds ahead of him, but he had outpaced the hunters. He eased back in the saddle, waiting for them.

For a moment it was very quiet. Then he heard pattering in the leaves and felt the first raindrops strike his head. The clouds were dark with rain, and he knew this would be no mere uncomfortable drizzle, but a torrent that would wash every trace of scent away.

"Halloo!" he called.

In a few minutes Sandremun's huntsman appeared from among the trees ahead, the hounds frothing about his mount's feet.

"They've lost the deer," he said. "There's no good continuing in this, my lord Seneschal. We'll have to go back."

Caolin nodded. "Blow the rally then." Belatedly he pulled

his hood over his hair and fastened it. The rain was now falling so furiously that he could hardly hear the huntsman's summoning. Could the others hear?

A half hour's wait brought them Farin, Randal, and the huntsman's boy. There was no sign of Faris or the King.

Caolin urged his horse a little away from the rest, peering through the rain.

"My lord Seneschal, let us go back to the Hold! If the King and the lady are not there already, they must have taken shelter somewhere," said the huntsman.

"I cannot go back and tell them that I have lost the King!" said Caolin without looking around.

"This rain is too fierce to last long. When it lets up, we can return and look for them," said Farin.

"Who knows—maybe they don't want to be found!" Randal laughed.

Caolin turned on him furiously, and Randal's laughter ceased. The Seneschal forced himself to be calm. The huntsman was right. Surely Jehan could take care of himself. And yet, as he turned his horse downhill at last, Caolin's own words echoed mockingly in his mind. *I have lost the King.*

Faris reined in her mare at the top of the slope and knew that she was lost. The trees around her were half hidden by shining veils of rain. She dashed water from her eyes and peered at them. Faintly she heard the notes of a hunting horn, but the water roared so loudly that she could not tell from which direction it came.

Then the world turned to thunder about her, and lightning split the sky as if the sky-bowl were cracking and all the brilliance of deep heaven showing through.

The black mare, Sombra, threw up her head with a whinny of terror and slid backward down the farther side of the hill. Faris fought to control her and still keep her seat. By the time she had the mastery, they had come to rest in the midst of a small clearing. Far away, thunder continued to roll, but whether the hill provided some protection, or the clouds had simply moved on, in the clearing the rain was only a gentle pattering. She was alone.

Faris drew her cloak around her and relaxed, savoring the quiet that was somehow enhanced by the falling rain. She raised her face to the sky and breathed deeply of the rich scent of wet earth and leaves. She supposed that she ought to be trying to find the others or make her own way back to the Hold, but the forest seemed to welcome her into its peace.

It had been so long since she had sat quietly. The preceding days had been filled with frenzied preparations for Farin's knighting. She remembered her quarrel with her father as something that had happened long ago. At least he was gone home now, though he had left orders for her to follow him after the end of the Festival. But that did not seem important now. She remembered only the dancing and Jehan's eyes burning behind the ribbons. Her memories of what had followed were chaotic—fire, and more fire, and animals rushing past.

She supposed they must have carried her off to bed after that. The exaltation of the ceremony had merged into troubled dreams, into an urgency that had driven her unthinking to the hunting, as if she could outrun the memory of what had happened the day before. But now she had escaped the world and need run no more.

Her hood had slipped back and water was running down her neck, but she made no move to replace it. She became, instead, even more still. Her awareness expanded, touching spirits of tree and bush, of small animals burrowed snugly out of the rain. She felt another consciousness beating against her own and turned and saw the King.

He seemed to have materialized against the dark trees, sitting on his white horse as motionless as she.

"Come," he said softly. "I have found a cave."

The restless flicker of the little fire modeled the slabbed stone of the cave into a shifting frieze of light and shadow. It crackled merrily as flames singed wet bark and bit on the dry wood underneath. The cave was small—perhaps ten feet from its narrow opening to the closing of the fissure. A thin breath of cold air from that crack carried the smoke of the fire towards the outside. The floor slanted downward in a series of broken steps. They had built the fire in a crevice of one of them. Faris perched on another, her arms clasped around her knees.

Through the gap by which they had entered, Faris could see treetops bending under the rain. She felt a momentary pity for the horses, tethered to a manzanita bush below the cave. Their saddles were inside, upended on the other side of the fire with cloaks and outer garments stretched across them to dry. The air reeked comfortingly of horse and wet wool.

But Faris noted these things only subconsciously. Stripped to his breeches, Jehan was coaxing more branches into the fire, the smooth muscles of his back and shoulders defined by the light.

"What do you suppose has happened to the others?" asked Faris, stretching her hands towards the fire. She still wore a short sleeveless shift over her breeches, but her feet were bare. She had spread her hair across her shoulders to dry.

"If they are lucky, they have found shelter too—these mountains are riddled with caves. If not, they are probably swimming back to the Hold." He looked up at her, and her breath stuck in her throat. It was not fair for a man to have such thick black lashes and eyes like blue jewels.

"I hope they are not looking for me," he added, "or for you." His eyes went back to his work and she breathed again.

Faris considered him curiously. She was familiar with her brother's lean body, but the King was more compact, his muscular development more apparent. He stretched out his right arm to lay a larger branch across the fire, and she saw a long purple weal across the muscle of the fore-arm.

"You were hurt!" she protested, not quite touching it.

He placed the stick and turned his arm to the light. "That's a souvenir of the fight where your brother got his streak of white hair. It's healing well. Everything considered, I got off easily that time."

His eyes met hers. "Now I have a scar to match yours," he added suddenly. Instinctively Faris pressed the inner side of her bare arm against her body, but he took her hand and drew it towards him, turning it so that their two arms were twinned. "Faris, you must not be afraid. Do you think I would shrink from the mark of a deed that took more courage than any of my own? Don't you understand yet that there is nothing you need to hide from me?"

She stared at him, finding it strangely hard to focus on his face. For a moment awareness of his essence replaced all other sensation, though he had dropped her hand and moved away. She sensed mixed pain and laughter, an identity as vivid as any scent or color, though it was like none of these. For a moment she lost self-awareness, then, frightened, she looked away.

When she regained control, she realized that he was telling her the history of all of his scars, his voice light with the old note of self-mockery. He stretched out his arms and turned before her, *displaying himself,* she thought with sudden amusement, *like the peacocks at the Hold.*

His body had the lopsided development of the warrior—sword arm knotted with muscle leading to a bulging pectoral, while the shield arm, though more even in form, was supported by a wedge of muscle between shoulder and back. In comparison his hips and thighs seemed strangely slim. Looking at him, Faris found her breathing faltering and once more had to look away.

"Now this lump on my ribs"—Jehan pointed to an unevenness in his side where the ribs showed between the modeled muscles of belly and breast—"I got from an Elayan spear butt two years ago that sent me sprawling. If Eric had not straddled me until I got my breath back, I would not be here today." He sat down again, resting his arms on his knees.

"Eric told me," said Faris slowly, "that it was you who saved his life that day. He said he was surrounded, but you and Stormwing made so much noise that the enemy thought it was an army and ran away." She felt him watching her but continued to stare into the fire. "He was trying to explain to me why you are his model for courage."

"Caolin would say I was a model of foolishness—in fact, that is what he said to me at the time!" Jehan grinned. "And he's probably right. Eric may be a one-man army, but I have to use my head if I'm to stay alive on a battlefield!"

Faris shifted uncomfortably on the hard stone. Looking at him sidelong, she could see the faint white lines of other scars marring his bronzed skin and permanent discolorations from old bruises through his mail. She remembered suddenly his strong hands on the deer's throat that morning and the bright blood gushing beneath his knife.

"Eric—" she blurted. "He went away after Farin's knighting, and no one can tell me where he has gone!"

"Does it matter to you so much to know?"

Faris looked up quickly. Did he think that she loved Eric of Seagate? Was that why he had avoided her so long? Jehan's eyes were steady on hers beneath level brows. She felt her heart beating slow and heavy as a drum.

"He was . . . upset . . . when he left me. He had asked me to marry him and I refused. If it is my fault that he has come to harm—yes, it matters to me to know!" She stared defiantly at Jehan and saw the color leave, then rise again in his face, darkening a line like an old scar across his brow.

It had grown darker outside, though it was just noon. The rain roared against the mountainside so that there was no other sound. This was all that remained of the world—herself, and Jehan, and the fire.

"Theodor's Master of Horse says that Eric was asking the state of the roads between here and Seagate. He should have reached Bongarde by now. As for coming to harm . . . if you have rejected him, I pity anyone who gets in his way!" Jehan replied at last.

How heavy the air had become.

"Why are we talking about Eric?" Faris challenged. She was trembling. She folded her arms across her breast but could not still the shudders that shook her body. Where was the friendly flame that had made it so easy for her to approach him the day before?

"We aren't," said Jehan harshly, getting to his feet. He prodded the drying cloaks, glared towards the back of the cave where the cold draft stirred the air. "You're freezing! I have nothing to stop that crack, and our clothing is still wet." With a single fluid motion he stepped across the fire and eased down at her side.

She looked at him beneath her lashes, trying to speak. But the air was too charged . . . she could not breathe. She started as his arm went around her shoulders, then forced herself to lean against it, marveling at the hardness of the muscles.

It took a moment for her to realize that his arm was too taut and that Jehan was also finding it hard to breathe.

She smiled slowly then and turned in his embrace. The air's tension exploded in a flash of lightning that illuminated the cave and Jehan's face, now very near her own. In the darkness that followed he pulled her closer and guided her to meet his kiss.

The lightning had struck her and was tingling through every nerve. Jehan's arms held her in the center of a star and the world reeled away. After a moment that seemed an eternity he released her lips and she relaxed into his arms, her cheek against his chest. She could feel his heart racing. There was a long roll of thunder outside.

"Sweet Lady!" he said softly, his voice shaken between passion and laughter. "Did *we* do that?" He paused thoughtfully. "There's only one way to find out." He tipped up her head and kissed her once more. This time she wound her arms around him and tried inexpertly to return his kiss. After a little he released her and eased himself and her around so that they lay more comfortably against the rock.

Faris felt laughter sparkling within her, dancing more brightly than the fire. "My Lord," she whispered, "I'm not cold anymore."

His hold on her tightened. "Cold? No . . . not either of us . . . not ever again!" His mouth came to hers once more, gently, coaxing it to open, teaching her how to respond. The silence was longer this time.

When he let her go at last, his sigh was like that of someone who has put a heavy burden down. He lay back, and she wriggled closer so that her head rested on his shoulder. His left arm encircled her, holding her there.

"Blessed Lady," he whispered, his beard tickling Faris' forehead, "you have given me so much more than I asked!"

"You asked the Lady of Fire for *me*?" she said in wonder. "*I* only asked her to ease my heart."

He pulled himself up on one elbow and looked down at her anxiously. "You do love me, don't you? You don't feel bound just because we were linked in the ceremony yesterday, or because of what people may say when they know we have been together here . . . ?"

She smiled and ran one finger along the line of a little silver scar just above the line of his beard. "My Lord, without knowing it, I have been bound to you since you first claimed me in the dance. But I did not admit it until I sent Eric away. Now that I know you want me, do you think I could say no?"

He turned his head to kiss her fingers. "Faris, I *love* you! I asked the Lady of Fire to give me a Queen—someone to be Lady of this land as I am Lord, so that the Kingdom will rest firmly on both pillars once more."

She pulled at him, and he eased down so that she could snuggle close again, shutting out that reminder of a world outside the cave.

"I have been so lonely," he went on. "I have needed you so much."

She snorted. "Lonely! In the midst of such a crowd? They all love you—Eric and Caolin and the rest. My brother is your newest slave! I felt like a child peering into a Great Hall where the grownups were enjoying a feast that I could never share." Her hand moved across his chest, learning its contours.

Jehan turned to face her and began to kiss her forehead, her eyelids, the tip of her nose, and at last her lips. "This is the appetizer," he whispered. "The main course will be served . . . soon."

She clung to him, a sweet warmth loosening all vestiges of tautness from her limbs. Muscles that had been tensed all her life began to ease. For the moment she was content merely to feel him next to her. The wind still whispered in the trees outside, but the rain had ceased. It was perhaps two hours after noon.

"I know that they love me," said Jehan soberly after a while. "The weight of their love exhausts me. Caolin wants me to be his idea of a King, Eric wants me to be a hero, and now your brother thinks I'm a figure from some old tale!"

Faris pushed herself away so that she could look at him, feeling suddenly cold, as if a flower were turning to dust within her grasp. "Will my love be so good for you? I love you, but how can I be what you need?" So close, she could see the fine lines at the corners of his eyes crease as he began to laugh.

"You don't have to do anything, my love—only be Faris, and be here! When I hold you, I feel that at last I am linked with reality. With you as my Queen I will finally be married to this land!"

Faris shook her head, then nestled it against his shoulder again. She had seen images of the Lady of Westria, and She was tall, deep-breasted, and strong, with hair as golden as the ripening fields and eyes like the sea. If Jehan saw her as the Goddess, thought Faris, he must be in love with her indeed! She sighed. "I will try to be whatever you want me to be."

"Don't be afraid, my butterfly," Jehan said softly. "I will be with you, and together we will learn how to use the Jewels to make this land once more worthy of its Covenant. I have wasted so much time, trying to reclaim the youth the Crown robbed from me, and the land has suffered for my sins."

"Jehan! The sun still rises and sets and winter is followed by spring. The sins of men are their own to answer for!"

"Perhaps so—I *hope* so!" he said somberly. "But I have been raised to believe that the health of Westria rests on her King. What any single creature does affects the whole, but my actions more than those of others, for I have been taught the meaning of what I do. For a long time I tried to forget that—I've no right to be surprised if others in the Kingdom follow that example. But I will change—*we* will change things, my love!" He bent to kiss her again.

She shook her head helplessly. She laid a hand on his shoulder, let it slip across the hair on his chest and the smooth skin of his back and sides. His breeches stopped her; her palm came up and paused over the left side of his breast. She could feel his heart beating heavily beneath her hand, and his nipple harden against her palm. The sweet warmth she had felt before was becoming a fire. Her own breasts throbbed in response, and she moved restlessly against him.

"Jehan," she whispered urgently.

"Yes—" His hand traced the outline of her cheek, slipped down her neck, and paused above her breast. "But not quite like this, with stones digging into our backs! The Lady has been gracious to give us this time alone, but this is not my idea of a bower."

Ignoring Faris' protests, Jehan eased her aside, got up, and brought his cloak from the other side of the fire. He folded it and laid it along the stone step. It was nearly dry.

Faris fumbled with the ribbon of her chemise, then dragged it over her head. She felt a brightness in the air as the sun broke through the clouds outside, but she saw only Jehan's eyes.

He reached out and laid his hand upon her breast. "Yes . . ." Sunlight gilded the ragged edges of their door.

She moved towards him, exulting as his arms closed around her. The friction of their bare skins touching was incandescent, but still he was not close enough. She clutched at him as a circle of light began to form around them that would shut her darkness for ever away.

• • •

"Caolin, the King is not *lost,* only mislaid for a little while!" said the Master of the Junipers. "It is barely past noon."

Caolin shrugged impatiently and began to towel his wet hair. "'A little while' is too long." His voice came muffled through the cloth. "I will set out again as soon as this damned downpour stops."

"Don't damn the rain—there has been little enough of it this spring. Both farm and forest must be blessing those clouds." The Master smiled gently from an armchair by the fire in Sandremun's little study.

"Damn the farmers then, and the forests too!" Caolin retorted savagely. He threw down the towel and stretched his hands to the fire, shivering. A gust of rain clattered against the windows.

"Put some clothes on, Caolin! I expect that Jehan and Faris are warmer than you are right now." The Master ran his fingers through his cropped hair.

Caolin paused in the act of drawing on a gray wool chamber-robe of Sandy's. "You are so sure that they will be together! You have had a vision, perhaps? One of the Guardians has personally informed you? You pilgrims from Awahna have all kinds of powers, I understand!" He stopped short, slipped his other arm into the robe, and tied it around him.

The old sheepdog lifted his head from the Master's feet and pricked his ears, but the wolf, Gerol, continued to lie unmoving before the fire. Caolin sat down on the raised hearth next to him.

The Master's smile was troubled. "A vision . . . yes . . . though it was not mine. The Lady of Fire will finish what She began." He gazed into the flames as if indeed he saw a vision there.

Caolin glanced at the windows, where rivulets of rain magnified the distortion of the glass. Surely it was lighter than it had been a little while ago. His hand went out to caress the wolf's great head, rubbing the soft fur back and forth absently as he spoke.

"I agree that the ceremony yesterday was impressive. But surely you build too much on the chance pairing of Faris with the King. She is very sensitive, that is all. She should be trained."

The Master's deep eyes suddenly held his. "It was no

chance. The Lady of Fire *showed* us—" He broke off abruptly, frowning.

Gerol growled softly as Caolin's fingers gripped. The Seneschal removed his hand, his mind still on what the Master had almost said.

"The Lady showed *us*," he repeated softly. "Showed what? And who else did She show it to?" The Master's face revealed nothing. After a moment Caolin went on. "Yesterday the King had a mark on his forehead like the scar of a burn. *What did you do to him?*" Caolin's fingers twitched.

The other man's clasped hands were growing white. Caolin's will beat against his silence.

"You must have seen how Jehan has been worrying himself over Faris," the Master said at last.

No, thought Caolin, *I saw nothing of the kind! Jehan has hardly spoken to her for weeks.* But he did not dare to interrupt the Master now.

"He came to me . . . I told him that he had the means to an answer already in his hands." The Master's lips tightened, and Caolin knew that he would say no more. But he did not need to, now.

"The Jewel of Fire!" Caolin could not keep the wonder from his voice. "He used the Jewel? But he never touches them—not in all the years I have served him!" He sat back against the hearth, thinking.

In pictures the Jewel of Fire was set in a coronet—yes, that would explain the scar on the King's brow. And Jehan had used it to turn the element of Fire to his will. A log popped, and Caolin's eyes fixed on the flames. They warmed him now, but if he were to thrust his hand among them they would burn.

The Master sighed. "I know well that you love him, Caolin, so you should know that you have guessed right."

The Seneschal looked at him, wondering how much the Master did know of what had been between him and Jehan, then relaxed as the other man went on.

"I love him too . . . it was *his* will to use the Jewel, but I wonder now if I did well to encourage him. At the College these days they teach that it is better not to ask the gods to interfere in the fates of men. I wonder . . . Faris is so vulnerable, Caolin, can she give Jehan what he needs—what Westria needs?"

What Jehan needs is something to warm his bed, thought

Caolin. *After two and a half months without a lover, no wonder he was desperate!* But in sudden pity for the new lines he saw in the Master's face, he did not say so.

Lightning blinked in the window, and after a few moments thunder rolled faintly to the east. The storm was moving on.

"You may be worrying over nothing, after all," he began and saw the Master's body tense and his hands clench on the arms of his chair.

"Nothing!" he gasped. "Did you feel nothing, just now?"

"Lightning flashed," Caolin said blankly. "It does, in a storm."

"He has her! I have been wondering why I felt such tension growing, but *that* was unmistakable! He has touched her at last."

"No," Caolin whispered, but his vision was filled by the memory of Jehan and Faris mirroring each other's exaltation across the Beltane fires. He shook his head. "You are feeling nothing but your own displaced desire!" he accused. "I have lived with him for fifteen years—eaten and slept by his side and seen him take a score of women to his bed—and never felt . . ."

"This time it is different."

"How dare you feed your own deprivation by imagining Jehan in the act of—" Caolin could not finish that sentence either, remembering too vividly the light that filled Jehan's eyes when he made love. He leaped up, and Gerol sprang to his feet beside him, bristling.

"I will not stay to listen to your ravings! The storm is almost done—we must go!" He dragged off the robe, strode about the room snatching up half-dry garments, and flung open the door. "Sandy! Sandremun! I am leaving now, rain or no. Will you give me a guide or will it be said that the Corona could spare no one to search for her King?"

At Sandremun's mumble of agreement Caolin turned back to the room. His fingers were trembling so that he could not get the laces through his hunting leathers, and he forced himself to be still. The Master had not moved. Caolin reached for his cloak.

"I will forget what I have heard you say," he said coldly, "and I advise you to do the same!" But he could not forget the grave pity he glimpsed in the Master's eyes as he slammed the door.

• • •

Caolin wiped his forehead and strained to pierce the mists. The rain had stopped, but veils of cloud still trailed through the upper hills on the heels of the storm. Ahead, dark tree-shapes appeared and vanished again.

"I suppose that Gerol knows where he's going?" Sandremun said uncertainly, tucking his scarf around his throat.

Caolin made a sound deep in his throat and, almost on the edge of hearing, received the wolf's reply. "You are confused by the mists. Gerol is taking us by the straightest way to where the deer was killed. He says—"

"My Lord!" came the huntsman's cry. "There's a stream ahead!"

Caolin smiled. They had made good time through the forest, and now they had reached the place where they had been when the storm scattered them. It would not be long now. They clattered down the slope and splashed across the stream.

"I have a scarf of my sister's, if the wolf needs a scent," offered Farin, bringing his horse alongside.

"Do you think that Gerol is some foolish dog?" replied Caolin without looking at him. "He knows our scents as we know each other's faces, and those of our mounts as well!"

"The King and the maiden lost in the forest—it is like a legend," murmured Farin.

Caolin's heels dug into the brown mare's sides and, startled, she surged ahead.

"Ho! Look there!" cried Sandremun. Caolin reined aside and saw beyond the young lord's pointing finger a long white horsehair caught in a bramble bush.

"Stormwing, at least, has passed this way," said Farin.

The mare neighed suddenly, and from ahead of them came a deep whicker of greeting. Caolin set her at the slope. When he reached its top, Gerol was waiting for him, sitting on his haunches and grinning with lolling tongue. In the hollow before them he saw Stormwing and Sombra, Faris' black mare, tied to the same manzanita bush.

"They are near," breathed Farin. "I feel Faris' presence . . . but where?" He looked around in bewilderment. Trees grew thickly in the hollow except where a fall of rock had made a stony slope to the cliff. But though the rock face was knobbed and jagged, they could see no opening.

A damp breeze tore at the mist and ruffled their hair. Except for the sound of their own breathing and the creak and clink of harness as their horses moved, it was still.

"Could they have continued on foot?" began Sandremun, but Caolin motioned him to silence.

The air was brightening, and as they watched, a golden blaze of afternoon sunlight slanted through the parting clouds. Very clearly, they saw the slashed shadow of a gap in the face of the cliff.

Sandy whistled. "Well, Farin, I wonder how your sister will like being Queen?"

Caolin set his horn to his lips and split the stillness with a blast of despair.

Jehan let go of Faris, thrust her behind him, and whirled to face the entrance, his hand closing impotently as he groped at his side for a sword. The horn's bitter blare echoed through the cave, shattering their circle of peace. The shocked pounding of his heart began to slow as the sound was repeated, more mournfully, and he realized what it was.

Faris made a small choked sound behind him, and he turned to her. Her thin skin was pebbled with gooseflesh and her dark eyes dilated beneath the straight brows. Quickly he drew her to him again, wondering at the delicacy of her bones beneath his hands.

"Damn!" he said softly, then repeated it with more force. "Lady of Love, why are You mocking me!" he cried. His body ached with pent longing—he had waited so long! In another moment Faris would have been his beyond all questioning!

"Jehan?" she asked softly, clinging to him. He could feel the tension of anxiety tightening her body and that of passion draining from his own.

"That was Caolin's horn. We have been rescued," he said flatly.

"Oh . . ." Her laugh trembled. "Do we have to go? Can't we pretend we're not here?"

He shook his head. "I should have hidden the horses. They know where we are now!" He laughed suddenly and kissed her cheek. "Get some clothes on, woman, unless you want them to see you half naked. I told you that the Lady had a strange sense of humor, but next time I'll make sure we're not interrupted. We'll have time for our loving—and a far more comfortable bed!"

He pulled on his shirt and threw his cloak around him. Faris took longer to put on her chemise and settle her knee-length tunic over it, then delayed a moment, fussing with her hair.

"You look beautiful," he said, grinning. "Come on, I want to show them their Queen." He pulled her towards the entrance to the cave, then dropped her hand as she stepped into the flood of sunlight. Standing there with her hair loose on her shoulders and her green tunic glowing like peridot, she was as he had seen her in his vision, the goddess of spring.

One of Theodor's ancestors had planted a park to the east of the fortress. Its white oak trees had flourished, growing until their branches interlaced many feet above the forest floor and their leaves formed a roof through which the sun filled the air with green-gold light. As Sandremun led the triumphant searchers homeward with the King and Faris in their midst, they saw Theodor coming to meet them with Rosemary, the Master of the Junipers, and everyone else in the Hold who could sit a horse.

"You have found them, I see," called the Lord Commander.

"Indeed yes, Father," Sandremun replied. "Do you think our storehouses can provide a wedding feast?"

"A wedding?" Theodor reined in sharply, then his eyes lit and he urged his gelding forward. Farin pulled out of the way as the Commander reached Jehan, then trotted ahead to join the other young men.

"My dear." Theodor reached across Jehan's saddle to take Faris' hand and gave it a not quite fatherly squeeze. After a moment she freed it and took Jehan's arm. The King grinned. He wanted to whistle as Farin was doing now, but Theodor had seized his hand and was bending over it respectfully.

"She is the fairest thing in your Province, Lord—can you bear to let her go?" The King laughed. Theodor straightened and began to reply.

The air hummed. A black-feathered arrow appeared suddenly in Theodor's shoulder and his words became a cry. Jehan caught him as he slumped sideways.

Sandy twisted around to see what had happened, and a second arrow went under his arm and took the huntsman beside him in the throat. He looked back as the man fell, in his indecision turning his plunging horse in a tight circle and bringing the others to a halt behind him.

"Spread out and take cover!" cried Jehan, keeping his knees steady against Stormwing's sides and trying to hold the fainting Lord Commander on his own mount. "Faris, lie down on your mare's neck and get over to the trees! Caolin—help her!"

He glimpsed Caolin's tossing hair, turned at the sound of hooves, and saw Farin and the others galloping back to them. Farin drew up beside him, pointing towards the woods on their left.

"They're shooting from over there, Sir!" he cried, his cloak flapping around him as he waved his arm.

Jehan heard the wasp-whine of another arrow, but before he could look, it had pierced Farin's cloak, struck through the top of his own thigh with scarcely diminished force, through the saddle, and buried its tip in Stormwing's back.

Jehan gasped at the shock of the blow and instinctively reined in, soothing the horse who had begun to buck and squeal as he felt the arrow prick.

Sandremun and the others charged towards the woods. Farin slipped from his saddle and caught Theodor as he slid from the King's arms. A wave of agony pulsed dizzyingly from Jehan's thigh and he gasped, groping for the pommel of his saddle.

— "Jehan! Jehan! Lord of All, he's been hit too!" That was Caolin's voice. Jehan managed to focus on the Seneschal, who had grabbed Stormwing's rein now that Theodor's horse was out of the way. Beyond him Jehan saw Faris' white face.

"Get . . . her . . . out of the way!" he whispered through set teeth. There was a shout from the woods.

"They've found the bow—there's no danger now! Jehan, what can I do?" cried Faris.

"It's all right. Stormwing, be still—there's a fine horse—yes, it won't prick if you don't plunge about so," murmured the King, regulating his breathing to keep his voice calm. The stallion quieted, though every irritated stamp of his hooves stabbed Jehan anew.

"Rosemary, take the stallion's head. My Lord, where did it strike—oh, I see."

Relief washed through Jehan like a healing flood as he

recognized the voice of the Master of the Junipers. He felt Stormwing relax beneath him as Rosemary spoke to him, and shut his eyes.

"I will do well enough as soon as we get this arrow out!" He straightened, trying to smile, and grasped the arrow shaft. But he could not move it.

Sandremun trotted up, brandishing a quiverful of arrows and a broad warrior's bow. "My Lord, these are brothers to the one you cut out of me two months ago! Normontaine arrows, but did a Montaner draw the bow? I have a score to settle with him if it's the same man—he made me miss a good fight!" He saw the arrow protruding from the King's thigh and his next comment trailed off.

"The arrow's lodged too firmly—we'll have to kill the horse!" said Caolin.

"Oh no." Jehan shook his head. He looked over at Faris, who was growing steadily more pale. "Caolin," he begged, "please take her away from here!"

"Faris, tear some strips from your tunic for bandages—we'll be needing them," said Rosemary without looking around. Faris swallowed and began to obey.

"The arrow head is stuck under the saddle," Jehan told the Master. "If you can get it free I'll do until we reach the Hold."

The Master took his hand, looking up at him, then nodded. "You will have to hold your thigh away from the saddle. Sandremun, undo the girth and be ready to lift the saddle flap. Jehan, give me your knife."

Rosemary's murmur to the stallion made a soft background as the Master slid his hands beneath the saddle and began to saw at the arrow shaft. Jehan bit his lip as his thigh muscles screamed at his effort to avoid putting pressure on the horse's back. In a moment the Master brought out the arrow head.

"Now hold to the other end of the shaft so that it pulls no farther." The Master worked the broken end of the arrow shaft back through the saddle leather. "Caolin, Sandremun, help me to get him down!"

In a few moments they had settled Jehan on somebody's folded cloak with his back against a tree. Nearby, Andreas was trying to keep Theodor from sitting up. Jehan saw Faris, with her hands full of torn cloth, and Caolin kneeling beside him.

"Perhaps I should have asked Faris to help *you*, Caolin. I don't know which of you looks worse . . ." he said faintly. "It's all right. I'll be all right now."

Sandremun paused beside them and whistled. "You were lucky, my Lord—a few inches higher and you would have been little use to your lady!" He laughed uncomfortably, then turned to his father.

"Sir, the men who are tracking our attacker sent Barni back to report. He's still ahead of them, but several are sure they recognize him as our dear cousin Ronald." His voice was colorless.

"Invite him back to the castle," muttered Caolin, gripping Jehan's hand. "'If he is guilty he will reveal himself!' Sweet heavens!" he added in disgust.

Jehan's mouth twitched as he recognized his own words of two days before. "If I judged wrongly, I have paid," he whispered back, "and I promise you, if Lord Theodor does not arrest Ronald, you may do it with my good will!" But Theodor, his voice strengthened by outrage, was instructing his son to do just that.

Jehan could feel Faris trembling beside him. "My darling, don't be afraid—I have taken much worse in war," he said softly.

She shook her head. "It's my fault. It happened because you were with me."

There was a sound of voices as men from the fortress arrived with stretchers. Quickly he reached out to take Faris' cold hand. "My only regret is that those things are not wide enough for two!"

She tried to smile, and the color began to return to her face. Nearby Farin had just discovered the arrow hole in his cloak and was examining it in wonder.

"Well, Sir Farin, you tried," said the King, "but I fear you will not always be able to take the blows meant for me!"

He shut his eyes against the pain as hands that tried to be gentle lifted him on to the stretcher, remembering how they had bound up the deer he had killed that morning for transportation back to the Hold. Today all his hunting had proved successful, but now, grimacing, he wondered wryly whether he was the hunter or the prey.

VII

Ascending the Mountain

"To our future Queen—may your reign be memorable!" Caolin's voice was cool and dry, like Segunda wine.
As he lifted his silver cup men cheered his words up and
down the long table; goblets repeated its flash in the candlelight.

Faris detached her fingers from the crumpled moonlight
silk of her gown and clasped them carefully on the table.
Jehan laid his hands over hers and, stiff-lipped, she tried to
return his smile.

"I feel like a moth plucked into the full light of the sun,"
she murmured. The attention of those who had come from
all over Westria to see her pledged to the King beat against
her awareness. Now her oath was given, and she would
never be free of that scrutiny again.

"Are you already regretting your pledge?" teased Jehan.
His fingers tightened on hers, then he pried open her hand
and brought it palm-first to his lips. The contact shocked
through her body as though she held a coal. Did he think
this would answer her fear? She pulled her hand away.

He released her fingers instantly, but his darkened eyes
held hers. She saw in his face all the lines of pain that the
slow healing of his arrow wound had begun to smooth away.
And yet he had gone through the banquet without complain-
ing, and when he swore to make her his wife, his voice had
rung against the vaulting of the Hall.

Swiftly she raised his hand to her cheek and was rewarded
by an easing in his face as though a window had been
opened to the sun. She closed her eyes, turning her lips
against his hand, knowing that she could bear a lifetime of
judgment in strangers' faces more easily than one glimpse of
pain in his.

"I pressed you to this hurried wedding—have I been selfish?" he whispered. "I have kept the Kingdom waiting so long for a Lady, and I wanted them to honor you! See, even the Ambassador from Normontaine is here. I cannot even complete our marriage until my wound heals. But tomorrow we will go to the Mountain, and the College of the Wise—I promise it will be peaceful there."

She reached out to him. "If you are with me . . ." she began, but the rest of her reply was cut off by the introductory rattle of the musical consort's drums.

The sweet calling of recorders fluttered across the heartbeat of the drum. Caolin watched Farin Harper lead his sister into the dance and thought how haggard she looked. He wondered briefly if the stress of her new position would force her to something like Lady Amata's fragility. Jehan was watching serenely. If he minded having his lady taken from his side at their wedding feast he would never show it, but one might hope that Jehan was finding Faris less fascinating now that she was his. It was a pity that they would be going away together so soon.

"The King does not dance tonight?"

Startled, Caolin met the innocent gaze of the Ambassador from Normontaine. "My lord Rudiard." He bowed. "Had you not heard that King Jehan was wounded less than three weeks past? He is healing well, but his physicians advise against dancing." Caolin watched the other man, noting the shrewdness in his hazel eyes, wishing his mouth was not hidden by his fox-colored beard.

Sir Rudiard grinned. "We did hear something. I hoped you could tell me more. Naturally my mistress is concerned. This border has been peaceful for some years and Normontaine would like it to stay that way."

"Then you know it was a Montaner arrow that we pulled from the King's thigh," said Caolin. The music signaled a round dance. A circle formed among the crowd like a ring spreading from a stone thrown into a pond. Caolin eyed the approaching dancers and motioned to Sir Rudiard to follow him.

They moved casually through the crowd and slipped into the gallery that ran alongside the Great Hall. A small group of listeners surrounded a singer at the opposite end.

"The arrow . . ." said Sir Rudiard helpfully, stroking his beard.

"Did your Lady think we would accuse her?" Caolin raised one eyebrow. "My King knows that you need to maintain our alliance, and he respects Queen Mara's intelligence too highly to suppose that if she stooped to such a deed she would advertise her complicity." The Seneschal sighed. "Despite appearances, we suspect that the arrow's source was closer to home." The Ambassador's face showed polite inquiry, and Caolin went on. "In fact, we intended to ask Queen Mara's help in bringing the true criminal to justice."

The singing had been replaced by the ripple of a harp. At the other end of the gallery Caolin glimpsed a glitter of gold and Farin Harper's dark head. *Jehan's harp,* he thought. Its clear tones rang against the pillars of the gallery.

"Normontaine will be happy to assist you!" said Sir Rudiard as Farin began to sing.

> The mists are gathering in the hills and blotting out the
>   day.
> The embers of my father's Hall are smoldering far
>   away.
> Alas for me that I was born to set men's hearts afire—
> Death like a conflagration grows because of their desire!

"That's your new Queen's brother, isn't it? He sings well," commented Sir Rudiard.

Caolin coughed impatiently. "Are you familiar with Ronald of Greenfell, a dealer in furs? He has traveled much in this Kingdom and in Normontaine."

Sir Rudiard's hazel eyes came suddenly to his. "I've heard of him."

Farin's voice rang beneath their words.

> My father pledged me to his lord, nor would he change
>   again,
> Although the one King of my heart was also King of
>   men,
> Who ruler, was yet ruled by me, to carry me away,
> And slowly died beside the road as slowly died the day.

The Rock where I am brought to bay stands like a castle
  tower;
Below, that lord and all his men surround me in their
  power.
Alas, my love, thou hast paid dear to claim my heart
  and hand—
What wergild shall I pay to thee and to this lordless
  land?

"I cannot be specific, but you should know that we are
very interested in Ronald just now, and if you have word of
him in the near future, or . . ."

"Or if we find a reason to detain him . . . ?" asked Sir
Rudiard softly.

"You understand me well, sir. Of course, we would like
him turned over to us for judgment."

"The request seems reasonable."

"I hope that we shall have occasion to make it soon. Ronald's outlaw friends may be unhappy with him at present."
Caolin smiled slightly. "You might pay special attention to
disturbances along the border and be prepared to welcome
any 'refugees.'"

My last defender, true to thee, still stands here by my
  side,
Lest she who would have been his Queen should be
  another's bride.
My foe has scaled the Rock and now his great sword
  raises high—
Shall I not weep that two such men should war for such
  as I?

"I am only a plain messenger," said Sir Rudiard ingenu-
ously. "I'll tell my mistress what you have said." His eyes
fixed on the other end of the room. Caolin saw Faris and
Jehan in the far doorway, their arms around each other's
waists. As he watched, the King turned a little, his other
hand lifted to touch her hair.

"I dare say your King would be glad to have this Ronald
as a wedding present," said the Ambassador.

Caolin frowned. If Jehan were too involved with his
woman to pay attention to the Kingdom, then his Seneschal

must step in. "I am sure you will understand that my Lord is a little . . . preoccupied . . . just now," he said dryly. "I would prefer that you send news of Ronald directly to me. Be sure that I will inform my King when the time is right."

Sir Rudiard glanced again at the King and Faris, who had rested her head on his shoulder. As they watched, Jehan's fingers tangled in the dark masses of her hair and he drew her face to his.

"I understand," said the Ambassador blandly.

Farin's voice was louder now, with a bitter clarity.

The swords flash in the faltering light—I know that
    there will be,
If my knight's arm should fail at last, a last swordstroke
    for me!
The mists are covering the hills, spread like a leaden
    pall,
And I will reign in hell tonight, with thee, and him, and
    all.

"A strange song for a wedding feast, but Bards do not reason like other men," commented Sir Rudiard.

Caolin shrugged. "It's an old tale from Seagate. The incident described happened before the Crown was settled on my Master's House." He suppressed a shiver, felt the Ambassador watching him, and forced his features to an equally bland smile. But his eyes remained on the King.

Sir Rudiard made a strange, choked sound. Caolin turned then, followed the Ambassador's fascinated gaze, and saw Gerol sitting beside them with an air of having waited patiently for some time.

"Ah, Gerol," said the Seneschal genially, bending to stroke the wolf's grizzled head. "Do you have a message for me?" he concluded with an inquiring whine.

Gerol gave a short bark and growl. Sir Rudiard was edging delicately backward. For the first time during the conversation, Caolin grinned.

"Did my friend startle you?" he asked. "Remember, this is Westria—men and beasts deal as equals here!"

The Ambassador managed an answering smile, bowed, and walked quickly away. Gerol's ears flicked, but he did not deign to look after the Montaner lord.

Jehan had left the room.

"So Ordrey is come with messages," Caolin said softly, his pulse quickening. "They must be urgent for him to send you into the Hall."

He followed the wolf's swift trot down the gallery and through the passages to his own chamber. Ordrey was waiting for him, his freckled face thinned by hard traveling and his clothing stiff with dust.

Caolin let the door click shut behind him and held out his hand. Ordrey set down his wine cup and reached in the breast of his jerkin for a packet wrapped in oiled silk.

"It's from Ercul Ashe, my Lord—he told me to lose no time on the road."

Automatically Caolin ascertained that the seal was indeed his Deputy's, and untouched, then reached for his letter knife to slit the flap. Ashe's precise writing minced across the page:

My Lord—our agent Jonas Whitebeard is newly come with a load of goods from the south, and a tale that men from the fortress of Balleor in Santibar have raided over the border into Elaya. They say the Confederation is buzzing like an overturned hive. You must bring the King back to Laurelynn.

Gently Caolin laid the paper down. "Santibar is in Lord Brian's Province," he breathed. "Ronald is an arrow that may find its mark, but Santibar will be a sword to bring Brian down!"

He looked back at the letter. ". . . *bring the King back to Laurelynn.*" Ercul Ashe had a touching faith in his ability to influence Jehan's movements! And yet, in all the years of conflict between Westria and Elaya, the city of Santibar by the sea—the farthest (and some said the fairest) possession of Westria—had been the most frequent prize. It was a major gateway for trade between Westria and the south, and the taxes were valuable. But it had always seemed to Caolin that Santibar's allegiance to Westria was primarily an irritation to Elaya's pride.

In the time of Jehan's father, King Alexander, Westria and Elaya had gone to war and forced upon the Confederation what was supposed to be a binding treaty. Yet only three years before, the Conde de las Palisadas had laid siege to Balleor, and Jehan had gone south to fight for it. And even if Jehan had not shed blood for the place already, Brian would never let it go.

No words of mine could shake the King's infatuation, thought Caolin, *but if war is brewing in the south?* He smiled. "Faris may go to the Mountain," he added aloud, "but I think that the King will go to Laurelynn."

"Jehan lied to me! He promised to come with me to the College of the Wise. I have kept my word to come here, but you cannot make me learn!"

The Master of the Junipers heard Faris' voice from within the low stone cottage, and the murmur of Rosemary's reply. He took a deep breath of the crisp air, drawing strength from the clean line of the slope above the College and the clarity of the morning sky. Then he stepped inside.

His soft sandals made no sound on the stone floor, but Faris curled tighter, turning her face to the whitewashed wall. Rosemary shrugged in exasperation and brushed past him to the door.

Faris' dark hair flowed over the huddle of white wool blankets like an extension of the shadows. One thin hand clutched the sheet around her. She had suffered the two-day ride up the mountain to the College in sullen silence—he had hoped that their arrival would reconcile her to necessity.

"Will you spend the next month in this bed?" His voice grated.

"If Jehan wants me to learn about the Jewels, *he* can teach me." Faris' voice was muffled. The Master settled on the edge of the bed.

"Jehan serves Westria, and so must you and I. Would you give an infant his father's sword for a teething bar? You cannot wield the Jewels untrained, and the best of teachers will be hard put to prepare you to become their Mistress before Midsummer." He sighed, feeling her anger and fear, and doubting whether any words of his could reach her now.

She did not realize her vulnerability, and he knew only one way to persuade her. He frowned, but the thought returned. *Must I bend my own oath to serve Westria?* he wondered. *Lord forgive me, what shall I do?*

He closed his eyes and relaxed, breathing carefully. His sharpened hearing picked up Faris' sobs, the nervous shifting of Rosemary's feet, and the wind, sighing around the

buildings of the College like the breathing of the Father of
Mountains.

The Master let himself sink a little deeper, still aware of
his surroundings, but listening for the inner voice that never
failed him. His mind was like a still pool.

Jehan! Across the Master's stillness rippled the image of
the King. He saw the jut of his dark beard, the quirked eye-
brows that gave Jehan's face the illusion of laughter even
when it was quiet—but the Master had never seen such a
light in those eyes. This was how Faris saw him . . . and it
was the Master's answer. He had invoked the Lady of
Fire—he must use whatever means were required to make
sure no evil came of it.

Carefully he extended his awareness towards Faris. From
among the tumbled images emerged that of Jehan's chamber
in the Hold. Gold glittered as the King drew from his own
neck a circled cross, kissed it, and slipped the chain over
Faris' head. The vision dislimned and cleared. Then the
Master glimpsed Jehan's carriage beginning the journey to
Laurelynn and recoiled from Faris' despair.

He withdrew until her thoughts grew faint as the murmur
of conversation from another room, testing the texture of
her mind, sweet and shimmering as a butterfly's wing. Then
he focused his will.

Faris, listen to me . . .

No. But her refusal to speak made no difference now.

You have no choice—you cannot shut your mind. He
formed the picture of the Hall of Vision in the College,
where the Tree of Life glowed in colored glass. *You have
never seen this—whence comes the image then?*

Her wordless shriek rocked him. His own shields flashed
up and he rubbed uselessly at his ears. Rosemary started
towards them, unblocking the door. In the flood of light the
Master saw Faris' eyes roll like those of a frightened horse.
There were beads of perspiration on her brow.

"What's wrong?" asked Rosemary.

Faris sank back into her welter of blankets. "I thought it
was against your oath to do that!" she said bitterly.

The Master's hands clenched. *"Nor shall I ever use these
skills to dominate another's will . . ."* The words were graven
on his soul.

"It was like walking through an open door." He gazed at

her helplessly. "At the least you must learn to barrier your mind. How else could I convince you?"

Rosemary looked from one to the other and swallowed as she realized what had happened.

Faris shook her head. "I must not learn your sorcery!"

The Master rested his head in his hands. Justified or not, he was beginning to feel sick from reaction to what he had done, but he must make her understand! "You are wearing a Cross of the Elements."

Faris' hand went to her breast. "You saw it!"

"No. I saw Jehan give it to you, through your eyes. If you have no care for your own peace, still consider his. Will he be able to share with you only what he is willing for the world to know? If I could read you so easily, what might some enemy of his do?"

"I could resist! Read me now!"

Brutally, desperately, he breached the flame of her anger and saw beyond it almond trees that turned to maidens. Silver bells echoed in his soul. He recoiled, dropped his hands from his face, and looked up at Faris, whose eyes were glittering with tears.

"My poor child," he said softly. "So the Lady already had you in Her hand. No wonder She laughed at me." He felt the feather-touch of fear.

Faris whimpered and collapsed into Rosemary's arms.

Unwilling, he sensed her trying to soothe the wounded edges of her integrity. He knew that shrinking. Indelible in his mind was the face of the Mistress of the Madrones, before her beauty had crystallized to power and, becoming Mistress of the College, even that name had been lost. Only he still called her Madrona when they were alone. He had sought her willingly, prepared by training, and still he remembered the shock of that forced intimacy. But for them it had been a prelude to the union of the flesh as well. Would Faris ever trust him again? If only Jehan had been there—she would have surrendered to him with joy.

"Forgive me, Faris, for Jehan's sake," the Master whispered, pushing himself to his feet. "Once, long ago, this happened to me too . . ."

For a moment he sensed her outrage, and behind it the shadow of some deeper fear. Then she shook her head a little.

"I will try to learn to guard myself, but nothing more . . . for Jehan . . ."

• • •

The King braced against the jolting of the carriage, biting his lip at the twinge in his thigh and dipping his pen carefully into the inkhorn. Unappreciated, the meadows of the great valley rolled by, their green deepening to gold now, as May moved towards June.

> Faris, there are so many things I had no time to tell you. I wanted so much to share the peace of the Mountain with you. But if I can deal with this crisis while it is small, I may prevent a war that would keep me from you longer than the few weeks until you become my Queen.

Jehan frowned and looked up, taking comfort from Caolin's steady presence on the other seat. He picked up his pen once more.

> The wheels of the carriage lag as I long to be done with this journey, and yet they are carrying me too quickly away from you! This separation pains me worse that my wound, but I know we must be patient. We will have time . . .

The writing board jumped as the carriage wheels dropped into a pothole and jerked free. The quill bent, splattering ink across the page. Jehan swore and flung the pen through the window.

Caolin coughed. "I'm afraid that my attempts to write while riding in a carriage have always had a similar fate." His gray eyes warmed a little, and Jehan felt an answering smile tug at his own scowl and a rush of gratitude for Caolin's patience and support. They had been together for so long that he could hardly remember how it had begun, but surely whatever impulse had led him to befriend the aloof young clerk that Caolin had been fifteen years ago had been well rewarded.

Jehan sighed and slipped the ruined paper into his leather writing case. "I doubt that your correspondents were so fair as mine!" He grinned.

Caolin rummaged in his traveling case and pulled out a portable chessboard with holes in which one could peg the men. "Will you play?"

Jehan shook his head and laughed. "Distracted as I am, I could not even give you a battle, Caolin!" When he was playing well, he could sometimes force the other man to a draw, and once or twice he had even beaten him, though he always wondered if Caolin had allowed him to win. Caolin had a chessmaster's mind, adept to feints and deep-planned strategies.

"Never mind," the King added. "I'll finish my letter tonight in Elder. Tomorrow we'll be done with this carriage—perhaps we can play on the boat that bears us downriver to Laurelynn." He turned back to the window, where the shadows were already beginning to lengthen across the fields, and let his thoughts return to Faris.

Only a few students remained in the great hall of the College, their pale robes ghostly in the twilight. The remains of a simple dinner had been cleared away. Two young men were playing chess by candlelight while a woman made notes from an illustrated herbal. The Master of the Junipers and Faris stayed by the hearth.

Faris drew up her knees and clasped her arms around them, gazing into the fire.

"Are you tired?" The Master's voice was soft. Faris looked at him quickly to make sure that he had indeed spoken aloud, and saw him wince. She knew that her suspicion hurt him and supposed that awareness indicated that after two weeks her own hurt was beginning to heal. But she still shuddered with a sense of violation when she remembered that joining of minds. She would not give him the comfort of her forgiveness, not yet.

She shrugged and smoothed the folds of her undyed linen gown. "I don't know why my body complains when it's my mind that is getting the exercise. The Mistress of the Golden Leaves fills my head with every deed of every king since the Cataclysm, and then the Master of the Tidepool tells me to empty my mind of everything!"

There were new lines in the Master's face. "I am sorry—I told you that the time was too short. If you like, I will ask that you be spared the history. You can learn that in Laurelynn."

"I'd rather forgo the mental exercises."

He shook his head. "The mind rules all. Some hold that

if it were not for our belief, this world of forms would not exist at all."

She looked around her, reassuring herself with the sight of firelight gleaming on the grain of the oak beams, with the hardness of the stone upon which she sat. "I find that hard to believe."

"Believe? You must know it if you are to wield the Jewels!"

"I won't . . . I must not wield them," she whispered, staring into the fire. "Such things should not be meddled with. You cannot understand—I am so afraid—there are dark things in me that would be too powerful."

For a few moments she could hear only the occasional popping of the logs, mostly reduced to charcoal now, and the Master's regular breathing. Then something brushed her arm. Faris gasped as the Master of the Junipers reached past her and picked a coal from the fire.

Faris flinched from the fire in the Master's hand, looked at his face, and flinched again from the brightness of his eyes. He looked through her . . . he was too beautiful to look upon.

"Put it back!" she whispered, hiding her eyes. "Oh, put it back!"

"In the Name of the Lord of All!" he said suddenly, strongly, and dropped the coal back into the fire.

"It is not darkness, but light," he said when she dared to look at him once more. Light gleamed on the silver in his brown hair, warmed the weathered lines of his face. His eyes were quiet, focused on the outsides of things once more. "You can do that, you know."

She shook her head. "No—you have only convinced me that a Master from Awahna can do that."

"Don't you understand? If your road did not lead to Laurelynn, it might lead to Awahna instead! The power that you fear can be turned not only to darkness but to light! If you had the will, you could learn to do anything that is taught here." He laid his hand on her arm, the hand that had held the coal, and she was aware of him suddenly as a human being like herself. His brown hair was beginning to thin.

"Could you force me to it?" she asked quietly. "As you forced me to open my mind?"

His hand tightened. "No! I could not, not for Jehan's sake, or even for yours. And I swear to you by Those who dwell in Awahna that I will never touch your mind against your will again."

Faris looked at him in surprise, feeling his pain. Had their contact hurt him as well? She laid her hand over his, letting his face replace her father's accusing scowl. "Then I will open my mind to you, and you will show me how to pick up coals."

The Master drew a shaky breath and something eased in his face. He settled himself on the footstool. "Give me your cross." He held it before her eyes so that it caught the light. "Look at this, and listen to me . . ."

Faris stilled her mind, for that moment rejecting all fear. She rested in the Master's honey voice. She was still aware of her own identity, of the room around her. She knew that if she willed it at any time, she could rise and go. But she had no desire to will anything but what the Master told her to do. He hid the golden cross within his sleeve. She waited on his will.

"Do you see the fire?"

Faris nodded.

"There is a jewel among those coals—there, at the edge. It is yours. Take it up—it is the Jewel of Fire."

She saw it, glowing with crimson and purple and gold. *Fire burns,* said the distant voice in her mind, but she had seen the Master handle the Jewel and she believed in him. Her fingers closed on the coal. Without prompting she brought it to her forehead and saw herself reflected in his eyes, a Queen crowned in fire.

"Now put it down on the hearth again," the Master said gently.

Faris laid the jewel on the stone, and the swing of the golden cross drew her eye away. A moment later she was staring at the piece of charcoal that glowed beside her on the hearth. She reached for it and recoiled as the heat stung her fingertips.

"I will never force you," the Master said, "but there are others who might try. That is why you must learn."

She looked at the coal and then back at him, seeing now the strained set of his mouth and the shadows around his eyes.

"You have almost reconciled me to becoming Mistress of the Jewels." She smiled hesitantly.

"You must not be afraid of them," he replied. "Remember, there was a Mistress of the Jewels before there was a Master—it was a woman who *made* the Jewels!"

"They said so little of that when I went for my Nametaking." Faris looked at the Master in appeal.

"Very well . . . you, of all people, ought to know the tale." His gaze grew a little abstracted, and his voice fell into the cadence of the storyteller.

"You will remember that it happened in the days of the Troubles, when every great house fought to make its leader King, and in their fury men used whatever weapons came to hand, forgetting the Covenant. The College of the Wise tried to make peace, but the lords disregarded their words and slew their messengers and employed sorcerers to counter all they could do. So they determined to seek help from Those whose power sustains Westria—from Awahna."

A draft set the flames to leaping suddenly, and the Master paused and looked around. Faris followed his gaze to see the door to the Hall open, and a dark figure standing in the shadows there.

The Master frowned and turned back to Faris, his voice growing a little louder as he went on. "And so they sent a priestess, one wise enough to find the way to Awahna and young enough to make the journey quickly, to be their messenger. I think that she must have been beautiful as well," he added, smiling.

"For as she slept upon the road the sky blazed above her, and a being who shone like a star came to her and courted her and lay with her at last."

"But what *was* he?" asked Faris. "I have heard that he was one of the First People, but he gave her a child, didn't he? How could that be if he were not a man?"

"He could have been a mortal possessed by the spirit of star or wind, I suppose," the Master answered her. "But we have so many tales of such matings—I think that in the moment of union the energy of the Spirit transforms the woman's seed, so that the child, though fatherless in the usual sense, is yet not totally of humankind. In any case, the Lady bore a child whom she called Star until he named himself Julian. And her lover also left her a crystal, like the quartz crystals they mine in the Ramparts, but more perfect than any stone men have ever found."

"And that was the Wind Crystal?" Faris shivered a little, fancying that a playful breeze was stirring her hair. What must it be like to be possessed by such power? For a moment she was aware of profound gratitude that she was married to a mortal man.

"It became so," confirmed the Master, "when the Lady learned to use it to focus her mind on the powers of Air—to understand the structure of the universe, and by Naming them, to cause new things to be. In Awahna the Rulers of the Tree of Life showed her how to find stones worthy of the other elements, and to charge them with Power . . ."

"And ever since then, men have sought their answers in magic talismans and avoided the discipline that leads to true power!" The footsteps of the Mistress of the College rang on the flagstones of the Hall as she emerged from the doorway, but to Faris her dark gray robes seemed to surround her with shadow still. The Master bent his head respectfully as she came towards them.

"I cannot help feeling that Westria might be better off if the Jewels had never been made," continued the Mistress tartly. She pushed back her hood, and Faris saw the planes of her face gleam like polished walnut in the firelight beneath her silver crown of hair. "How can we tell people not to trust in charms and amulets when the King himself never stirs without his trinket box?"

The Master's head came up defiantly. "He doesn't use the Jewels . . ."

"His reluctance comes not from wisdom, but from fear! Jehan left this place without completing his training, and this child will have even less time than he did to prepare for her task."

Faris shrank back, sensing some undercurrent of passion in this argument. Could there be dissension even in the College of the Wise? Since coming here she had scarcely spoken to the Mistress, who reminded her uncomfortably of Berisa.

"She will be Initiated and receive the Powers," responded the Master. "A lifetime is scarcely sufficient to truly understand the Jewels."

"Or anything else of real value!" snapped the Mistress. "Initiation should confirm knowledge, not try to substitute. You may bend a young tree easily, but if it has not been trained it will snap back again when you let go!"

"My Lady," the Master said formally, "you agreed to the King's request. Surely this is not the time or place to question it . . ."

Faris folded her arms around herself, wishing she could become invisible.

"Well, I suppose it does not matter in the end," answered the Mistress of the College finally. "The purpose of the Maker of All Things will not be denied. It is our own fault if we suffer because we struggle against the flow."

Faris stared into the glowing heart of the fire. *Jehan . . . if you were here I would not be so afraid,* her heart cried out to him. But only the flickering among the coals answered her.

Caolin plunged a sliver into the coals that glowed on the hearth of his chamber, waited until it lit, then touched, one by one, the branch of candles on the polished table. Shadows leaped frantically in the corners until all the candles burned with a steady glow. He straightened and stretched, trying to ease muscles still cramped from the long journey, then turned to the other two men in the room.

Ordrey lay back in a padded chair with his feet towards the fire, his face a little flushed from the heat and the Seneschal's wine. Ercul Ashe sat like an image beside him, lank hair smoothed back, his maroon robe falling in carven folds, long eyes fixed on his master.

"You see that I have brought the King," said Caolin gently. "What have you to report to me?"

"I have made contact with two men in Brian's service—his butler and a clerk in the chancery at Sanjos. And the case of the misappropriation of revenues from the Ardello mill is almost complete. As you suggested, it was the clerk who was responsible." Ashe's tone was detached. "But we have found no evidence that Brian had any knowledge of what was going on."

"Hold the man then, but take no more steps against Brian's people—I have another key with which to unlock that door." Caolin sat down at last and picked up his goblet, turning it as he continued to speak so that the polished surface ran with rivers of light.

"Soon—very soon, I hope—we will receive from Normontaine a prisoner, a very special prisoner, Ercul, whom I want you to take in charge." Ashe nodded.

"He is one Ronald Sandreson, a cousin of Lord Theodor, though that will do him no good now. He gave the King the wound that has tied him to his bed this past month, and he has taken Brian's gold!"

Ashe's eyes narrowed, and Ordrey sat up in his chair, whistling. "Does the King know?"

"He knows who shot him, and he has been told about Brian, but he does not believe it—not yet. I want Ronald, and I want proof of Brian's guilt."

"Oh well," said Ordrey comfortably. "When you have the man, the proof will take care of itself."

"The King has given you full powers in this?" asked Ercul Ashe.

"He told me to arrest Ronald." Caolin shrugged. "It will give me the time to make a case."

"If we can spare the time ourselves to talk to him—Jonas Whitebeard has kept silence, but others have tongues, and the city is full of rumors about the fighting in Santibar," Ashe commented.

"Don't tell me," said Ordrey. "I am barely returned from a dash north and you would send me haring south again?"

Caolin looked at him, and Ordrey flushed and slumped back in his chair. "When I hold Brian in my hand, then you may have leave to lay yours on your lady friends!" snapped the Seneschal. "You know we must have more information than Whitebeard's report gives us." He ran his hand through his hair, dulled now with the dust of the road. What would he need to convince Jehan?

"You will go to Santibar," he told Ordrey. "Talk to the townsfolk, to the garrison, to the woman who washes the Commander's breeches. Hear it if anyone so much as whispers Brian's name. And when you have gleaned all you can—" His tone sharpened, and Ordrey looked up suspiciously. Caolin wondered whether he should bind Ordrey's will as he had in the past, but for this mission the man would need all his wits.

"You will slip over the border—you can pass yourself off as a clansman again," he said quietly.

"Oh, aye." Ordrey grinned. "I'm to survey the raided village?"

"In passing. I want you to go to Palisada, to the Red Crescent Inn. The keeper's called Arquino—tell him you're the Wolfmaster's hound. He'll give you a message for me. You'll need gold," Caolin went on, ignoring Ordrey's astonishment. "See to it, Ercul—fifty laurels for Arquino and another fifty for Ordrey's needs."

"The Wolfmaster's hound!" repeated Ordrey while Ercul Ashe smiled primly.

"Ordrey—look at me!" Caolin held his gaze. *You are mine, Ordrey, your will is my own.* Slowly the resentment faded from the other man's eyes.

"Just by the way," Ordrey said with a last attempt at bravado, "are we working for war or for peace?"

"The answer to that may lie in the information you bring!" Caolin said tartly. "Peace is good for trade, but a short war now might settle the border for a generation, besides bringing glory to our King." *And in the chances of war, who knows what mistakes Brian may make, and what chances I may find to bring him down,* his thought moved on.

When his servants had gone, Caolin went to the window. He could hear the muted noises of the palace, and the incessant gurgle of the river that surrounded the city, noticeable now because he had not heard it for so long. Laurelynn-of-the-Waters, city of the Kings, to which all roads, all news, came at last. It was good to be back.

He looked around the chamber. Volumes from the Royal library crowded the shelves on three walls; a chart of the heavens was tacked above a map of the four Provinces of Westria between the windows; cabinets full of correspondence and reports flanked the great desk. Caolin peered at the chart and then out the window again. A mist from the river veiled the stars.

The Seneschal frowned. There was not enough room here, nor the peace and privacy needed for mental work. He must find another place—out of the city, but not too far—where he could pursue the study of the stars and perhaps return to the study of ceremonial magic that had been denied him when he left the College of the Wise.

He considered the map of Westria with its cities and strongholds, its mountains and rivers. There were the four sacred mountains—the Lady Mountain for Seagate, the Mother of Fire in the Ramparts, the Red Mountain in the center, shadowing Laurelynn, and for the Corona, the Father of Mountains, greatest of them all.

We are going up the Mountain,
We are going up the Mountain,

We are going up the Mountain,
Seekers of the Way . . .

Faris' feet moved to the rhythm of the song, feeling out
footholds in the steep path. Ahead of her, Rosemary
stubbed her toe and swore softly, then hauled herself upward once more. One of the Masters started a new verse to
the song. First the women of the company echoed it, then
the men, then everyone joined in the chorus. If a woman
had begun the verse, the men would have echoed her. Off
and on, and singing had continued since they started the
climb at dawn, the verses growing more sacred in character
as they neared the summit of the Father of Mountains.

Faris readjusted her food bag and the piece of wood slung
across her back. They all bore logs—this was only one of
many trips that would be made to prepare the Midsummer
fire. The trail was too steep for any beast of burden, even
if they had considered it proper to use an animal for this
task, and the trail itself had been worn by the passage of
countless feet out of the living stone.

They were well above the snowline now, the scattered
stone buildings of the College three hours behind them.
Faris wondered at her own endurance. As children, she and
Farin had spent most of the daylight roaming the hills
around Hawkrest Hold, preferring the open air and each
other's company to the dark silences of their father's Hall.
Her feet had not forgotten their skill, and three weeks of
simple food, regular hours, and the training exercises of the
College had restored her wind. She laughed as she climbed,
breathing deeply of the pure air, feeling the cool breeze on
her face and the warm sun on her back as her body moved
to the rhythm of the song.

Jehan was right to make me come here! she thought suddenly, though her arms ached with the longing to hold him.
She wondered if his leg would have borne him on such a
climb—was it healed by now? Had he obeyed instructions
to rest it until it was well? If only she knew.

She had begun at last to accept something of the mind's
abilities, learned to shield herself from all but a determined
assault, or to try and reach another's soul. *Jehan!* She sent
the silent cry winging outward now. For a moment her

awareness embraced the bright world around her, flinging
it outward as a gift to him. Then she laughed at her own
presumption. The Masters, with their years of training,
could sometimes send messages that way. But three weeks
could hardly be expected to teach her to do so, unless the
message was indeed borne on the wings of love.

"We are children of one Mother . . ." The Mistress of the
College began the verse, pausing for a moment at the bend
of the path. Her robe was as gray as the bones of the mountain, but in the sunlight her hair shone silver as the snow
on its slopes above her dark face. Masters and students and
mountain alike were painted in monochrome, from the
sharp blacks and whites of priestesses and priests on leave
from their posts for further study, to the dull gray-brown
robes of the adepts who had returned from Awahna, and
the unbleached gowns of the students, dull as the discolored
snow at the edge of the path. The wind brought a whiff of
sulfur from the hot springs near the peak, then wafted it
away again.

Was that why they had chosen those colors? Faris wondered, for the Mountain was the crown of the Corona, which
was the crown of Westria. Her heart stilled and leaped again
as the path curved into the sky before her and she knew
they were nearing the top.

The Crown. She thought suddenly of the Hall of Vision
at the College, where the morning sun shone through the
great stained glass window, casting colored spheres of light
upon the polished floor. One could walk among them, ascending the Tree of Life through the spheres of Earth, the
Moon, then left to Mercury and right to Venus, and so onward, back and forth through every aspect of the Divine, or
else straight upward through the sphere of the sun and on
to the crown of all—the Light beyond all created things.

"Bless the Light and bless the Darkness," they sang.

Faris stumbled as the slope eased. There was a boulder
beside the path. She sank down upon it, dizzied by that last
effort in the thin air. After a moment she lifted her head
and looked around her.

Here, at the very top of the mountain, the sun had burned
away the snow. The peak held a slight depression, as if the
mountain's center had sunk from its own weight. Steam rose
gently from hot springs, melting the snow, and green grass
grew.

The Mistress of the College stood on the western lip of the hollow, arms uplifted, facing the Master of the Junipers on the other side.

> Now the Crown is our foundation,
> Now the Crown is our foundation,
> Now the Crown is our foundation,
> Seekers of the Way.

Those who had recovered from the climb began to clear away the ashes of the Beltane fire from the stone platform on the southern edge of the peak. After a few minutes Faris started across the hollow towards them. Weaving among the hot springs, she reached the center and paused, quivering as if some deep vibration shook her bones. The air tingled. Her eyes were dazzled by the noon sun. She held her breath, feeling the light grow around her. The air trembled with meaning . . . in a moment she would see . . . in a moment all would be clear.

She cried out and hid her face from the terrible clarity of that light.

When she opened her eyes again, she was lying on the ground at the edge of the hollow with her head in Rosemary's lap. Students crowded around her, but she sought the Master of the Junipers' clear gaze.

"The Light," she whispered desolately. "I have lost the Light . . ."

"I know." The Master nodded, taking her hand. "I should have warned you to stay away from the Mountain's center."

"Is it forbidden?"

"Does it need to be? It is a pole of power." He smiled.

Faris closed her eyes. "If only I could have endured it a little longer—it was so beautiful. I did not want to come back again."

The Master's hand tightened on hers. "We follow the Way to learn to bear that Light. Few reach it, and of those who do, fewer still return to show others the path."

"Some go straight to the Crown," said Rosemary. "But the Mistress says that is the hardest path. The rest of us must go from aspect to aspect, like a squirrel bounding from branch to branch of a tree." She laughed.

Faris struggled to sit up. The noon sky arched over them like a bowl of sapphire glass. Rosemary looked worried, but Faris smiled.

"Yet we all reach the same place in the end," said the Master. "Come." He drew Faris to her feet. "From the platform you can see half Westria."

Rosemary led the way, the sparkling breeze fanning the wisps from her braid into a golden aureole. "Look—there's the Hold!" She pointed to the fortress, set at the Mountain's feet like an amulet of rosy stone.

Faris shaded her eyes, gazing over the western ranges within whose misty tangle lay the Hall where her father brooded over her marriage, which he would not bless though even he could not break it now. The last ridge ran straight as a sword blade for sixty miles. Beyond it she saw for the first time the shimmer of sunlight on the sea.

"There, to the southeast, you can see the Black Glass Mountain, the Mother of Fire," called one of the students. Faris turned to see.

The other Mountain rose above her companions. Like the Father of Mountains, she was still tipped in white. A thin wisp of smoke curling from her summit reminded Faris that the volcano was still very much alive. Range upon range of mountains shaded into the blue vistas beyond it. The Master of the Junipers gazed into that distance with a curious sadness in his face.

"And there lies the Sacred Valley of Awahna," he said softly, "and the Pilgrim's Road that is never twice the same."

Faris averted her eyes from his face, but her shielding was not strong enough to barrier his longing. She forced herself to follow the glitter of the Dorada down from the Ramparts towards the golden haze to the south. There lay Las Costas and Seagate, and in the center of the Kingdom, the Royal Domain. There, her future lay.

The whole of the land before her dropped into focus, as one sees suddenly the picture inherent in jigsaw pieces spread out on a board. But it was a living picture, and the sunlight seemed to glow through it rather than upon it as if the visible Westria were yet only a veil over some fairer reality.

She stretched out her arms to Westria as she had opened them to Jehan. His words re-echoed in her heart—*I love you as my life, but my life is this land.*

"Behold your Kingdom, my Queen! May your reign be fruitful!" the Master of the Junipers said.

VIII
The River Passage

The river flowed with light. Through leaded windows Jehan glimpsed the dappled glitter of the sun, which reflected a glimmering net on the whitewashed ceiling of the room. It was the beginning of June. The river would bear his bride to him in three weeks' time.

The King's lips quirked as he realized that if Faris were already here, he would have had even less taste for the meeting he was waiting for than he did now, and he turned from the window.

"You told them to be here at ten?" he asked Caolin.

The Seneschal looked up from the papers he was sorting. "Yes. Lord Brian—"

"Lord Brian is here." The door swung open, and a shape like a valley oak tree loomed in the hall.

Jehan stiffened. As usual, he had forgotten just how big a man the Lord Commander of Las Costas was. Swiftly the King took his place in the tall chair at the head of the table so that the other man's advantage of height would be less apparent.

Brian moved into the room and stood, head thrust a little forward, poised on the edge of a bow. There was another step in the hall; the door reversed its backward swing and Eric thrust through.

He stopped short to avoid bumping into Brian, who had not moved. Jehan's lips twitched. A pair of oak trees . . .

Twice as many winters had thickened Brian's hide, and his luxuriant brown hair and beard were threaded with silver now, while Eric stood straighter and the beard he had started in the north was still a fringe. But they were of a height, and Eric's shoulders promised to equal Brian's breadth soon. This was the first time the King had seen Eric since he left the Hold. He was relieved to see him so well.

Brian looked the younger man up and down, nodded shortly to him and scarcely more deeply to the King. Then he took his place, his amber eyes glittering with amusement. Eric reddened, bowed deeply to Jehan, and sat down on the opposite side of the table.

Two other people, unnoticed until then, passed through the door. Jehan held out his hand to the sturdy woman whose silvered braids caught the sunlight.

"Lady Elinor—Lord Theodor sends you his greetings and his thanks for your reports."

The lady, who was Theodor's half-sister and representative in Laurelynn, smiled and bent over the King's hand. Her companion, Lord Diegues dos Altos, moved majestically forward.

"I suppose Eric can represent Seagate for his father, and this matter is unlikely to trouble the north, but what's Robert's excuse?" growled Brian. "I'd at least looked to see him here. With all respect to Lord Diegues, today's business is a heavy one to lay upon a delegate."

Lord Diegues stiffened. "The Lord Commander of the Ramparts instructed me—I have a letter from him here . . ." He fumbled in his pouch.

"Nay, my Lord. We believe you—be seated now." Jehan indicated the chair to his left. He glimpsed a flicker of irony in Caolin's schooled face. Lord Diegues' irate mumbling died away as the King's gaze rested on him, then passed to fix each of the others in turn.

"Indeed the matter is a heavy one, so we had best begin," he said quietly. "Lord Robert had duties to take him from Laurelynn just now, but we have spoken of this matter, and I know his mind." The King paused. *My brother-in-law will be escorting my affianced wife from Elder to the Sacred Grove, and if you waste my time I may leave you to your own devices and go to meet her myself!* Jehan's closed lips imprisoned the thought, but something in his expression compelled their attention.

"My Lord of the South," he went on, formally. "I believe you have brought us a letter?"

Brian looked at him levelly and proffered a roll of paper that had been lost in his hand. Caolin reached for it. The Lord Commander looked at the Seneschal for the first time since entering the chamber, and his eyes narrowed, but he did not speak.

Caolin inclined his head and smiled gently as he took the scroll, unrolled it, and in a clear, expressionless voice began to read.

My Lord Brian:

It is with sorrow that I report that on the second of May five men from the second patrol of this garrison left a tavern in Santibar and rode South to Elaya, looting and burning a holding a few miles the other side of the border.

I am told that the Elayan had a pretty daughter whom these men had seen when her family came to market in Santibar (as you know, many of the folk trade back and forth across the border, not caring whether Westria or Elaya holds the town).

They say that the girl was visiting kinfolk at the time, and the men burned the place from resentment at not finding her. I have placed them in custody and offered the smallholder compensation. I hope that you will approve this course. Please let me know your will as soon as may be.

I remain, your servant and true man—

Sir Miguel de Santera
Commander of Balleor

There was a silence when Caolin had done. Jehan heard the wind rushing through the poplars beside the river and the laughter of children, and wondered, *How long until a child of mine will play there?*

The paper rustled as Caolin set it down. "That is all he says." His voice inflected upward.

"That is all there was to say," said Brian, twitching the roll from the Seneschal's fingers as Caolin started to slide it into his case. "You have no need of this, Master Seneschal—I'm sure your creatures will provide you with the same information soon." Brian's teeth showed as he grinned.

"My *employees* can only tell me what happened," Caolin corrected, still gently, though his eyes grew hard.

Brian's head lowered and his beard jutted forward. "My men do not lie to me!"

Caolin shrugged. "I'm sure you know. But if that is indeed Sir Miguel's letter, and he is telling all the truth, why is Elaya so angry?"

"That's so," said Lady Elinor. "One does not like to think it of Westrians, but I have heard that soldiers often lose all sense of decency when they are stationed far from home, as if the natives seem less than human to them, somehow."

Brian's glare became a frown as he considered her words. "Perhaps I should recruit locally," he said thoughtfully. "Local control is what I believe in, after all—" His glance flickered towards the King and then away.

"*If* that was what happened," interjected Lord Diegues.

Brian's amber stare fixed Lord Robert's delegate. "I'll tolerate your presence, sir, but not your insults. I choose my men for loyalty, however your lord chooses his! One cannot spy on every breath they take. If Sir Miguel has betrayed me, he will suffer for it, but I'll not judge the man unheard." The Commander's right hand closed over the massive gold ring he wore on the forefinger of his left, and again his eyes sought the King. It was the ring Jehan had given him when Brian had sworn fealty to *him*, fifteen years ago.

"An effective leader controls his subordinates so well that they *cannot* do wrong!" said Caolin dryly.

Eric looked from the Seneschal to Brian, clasping and unclasping his broad hands on the table before him. "If a lord's example inspires his men, he won't have to *control* them."

"Well said, cockerel," growled Brian. "But a Province is not a tourney field. Men will not follow you for glory alone! They must have a stake in their work. You win their loyalty by protecting their homes and families, or even, sometimes, their good opinion of themselves."

Eric grew red again, struggling for an answer. The dappled reflections off the river underlighted his face.

Jehan cleared his throat. "Westria stands by the bonds between man and man, between man and the land, each one bearing responsibility for his own part. But there are some matters that affect the Kingdom as a whole."

"We differ only in deciding which matters they are," said Brian with the glint of a smile.

"If Elaya comes against us in war because of this, they are more likely to strike the Ramparts, as they did two years ago, than to attack Las Costas," put in Lord Diegues.

"*If* Elaya uses this as a pretext for war," said Lady Elinor.

"Will they? It seems to me that this is what we must consider, and try to avert."

The voices of the children outside grew louder, then faded. Jehan heard the smack of a ball.

"I would just as soon avoid a major war right now—mail makes an uncomfortable wedding garment," he said, smiling.

"Pay them off then—more gold for the landholder and a hundred laurels to sweeten the Governor at Palisada. Flog the men involved," said Caolin.

"I suppose that would satisfy *you*?" Brian bristled.

"If we do that, they will think we are weak. They'll conclude we are paying because we cannot fight." Eric's fist jarred the table and he looked at it in surprise.

Brian ignored him, his eyes on the King. "I will transfer Sir Miguel if you insist, Jehan, but let *me* handle this. The responsibility for Las Costas is mine."

They were all looking to the King now. Jehan focused on the play of light on the wall, marshaling his thoughts. He drew breath to reply.

"Jehan!" Faris' voice blazed in his mind and her love rushed over him like a bright wind. Impressions of white-glistening slopes and an endless arch of pure sky were netted by the light on the wall. Light and space overwhelmed him; Faris was more real to him than she had ever been when he held her in his arms. Then, as swiftly as it had come to him, the sense of her presence was gone.

He released his breath. His lips began to move in words prepared in some other part of his mind. "No, I will not insist on Sir Miguel's transfer. After this he should be as watchful a Commander as anyone could wish." Jehan's eyes were still dazzled. The room was filled with light that glistened on Brian's curling hair, glowed steadily in his eyes, modeled the enduring strength of his frame.

"Send no more money to Elaya—send the men. When they have rebuilt what they destroyed, we will transfer them. They will find ample outlet for their energies in the Ramparts, guarding the Trader's Road," Jehan went on.

The light was everywhere. The line of Eric's brow was almost too pure to look upon, and his eyes were like clear pools. Jehan forced himself to finish.

". . . and I will write to the lord of Palisada and to his prince, as one lord to another, equals in honor and strength." Loyalty shone in the faces of Lord Diegues and Lady Elinor.

My people, thought Jehan. *How beautiful they are.*

"Do you wish my office to draft the message, my Lord?" asked Caolin. The planes of the Seneschal's face were polished; his long fingers flickered as he shut papers into their case; the light struck brilliance from his gray eyes.

Jehan stretched joyfully, resting his palms on the tabletop. "No. I will want your opinion, but I will write the letter myself. I bear responsibility for Westria." He smiled at Brian, wishing he could share his joy, and the other man's eyes dropped to his scarred hands and golden ring.

"Are you well, my Lord? You look . . . strange," said Caolin when the others had gone.

"Did it show then? It was so brief, between a breath and a breath." Jehan thrust back his chair and stepped lightly to the window. "I have my Lady's love and I am very well!" he half sang.

"Jehan . . ." Caolin said carefully. "You are not being very clear."

"Faris is learning things, there on the Mountain, and she has forgiven me for leaving her. She called me just now, and I saw the snowfields of the Father of Mountains through her eyes. We were together." Jehan shook his head, unable to explain, though even the memory of what he had felt sang and shimmered along his veins. "Oh, Caolin—you should fall in love!"

Light rippled across the surface of the Seneschal's face. "No . . . that is not my Way. Besides, someone must keep his eyes on the earth while yours are filled with stars."

The sunlight on the river was too bright. Jehan's eyes had been like sapphire stars. Caolin shut his eyes and leaned back against the balustrade, focusing once more on Ercul Ashe.

"And so, my Lord, Hakim MacMorann has invited me to supper Wednesday eve at the Three Laurels Inn, and I am to give him his answer then. I thought I should appear open to his offers, in case you wanted to know more."

I would like to know if those drunken troopers were inspired by any encouragement of Brian's, or even by any negligence. Balleor is Brian's responsibility—there must be some way to hold him culpable for what has happened there! thought Caolin.

"Yes—you've done well, Ercul," he said at last, looking

at the other man through lids slitted against the sun. "And so Hakim MacMorann thinks we do not know that the simple Elayan trader he pretends to be has been sending regular reports to Prince Palomon in Alcastello along with the goods he buys here!"

"It appears that he does not, sir. Naturally he would not be very explicit talking in the street, but I suspect that in the current crisis he feels a need for more detailed information than he can find in the marketplace." The cool wind rushing up the river from the distant Bay tugged at the stiff folds of the man's robe but did not sway him.

Caolin nodded. "The King intends to write to the Prince of Elaya, but if they want war, I doubt—" He broke off—that had come perilously close to criticizing the King.

Caolin had never seen Jehan look so beautiful, not even when he had first seen him as a boy more than fifteen years ago, shining with love for the world. Now the King added to that radiance a man's settled power.

"Go to the meeting, Ercul," said Caolin quickly. "Tell Hakim that your worth is unappreciated by me, and if I do not reward you then you will find a master who will. I will be happy to give you information for them . . . and some of it may even be true!"

"Very well, my Lord." Ashe permitted himself a small smile. "There is one other thing. The Master of Signals reports that the Beacon-Keeper on the Red Mountain has died and wishes your recommendation for a replacement."

"The Red Mountain," murmured the Seneschal, gazing beyond the city walls, across the tangle of hill and meadow to the west of Laurelynn. The Mountain rose behind them, its red earth slopes darkened by distance, a looming presence so familiar that it was sensed rather than seen. Caolin had been to its top years ago. He remembered the stillness, the sense of being poised above the turning world.

"Yes, I know someone—a poor creature who hears badly and whose tongue has been twisted since birth. But she will not need to hear or speak to watch the beacon, only to see. Margit can hold the post for the time. I will supervise her while we seek a more permanent keeper. Send workmen to make sure the living quarters in the old fort are in repair."

Caolin's gaze came back from the mountain to the river beside him. Several boats were docked below the balustrade, being repainted to celebrate the arrival of the new Queen.

"Very well, my Lord." Ashe turned to go, paused when Caolin did not follow.

The Seneschal shook his head. "I'll join you soon in the Offices. Just now I have some thinking to do."

The Queen . . . Caolin forced his mind from the way Jehan had looked, to what he had said. To touch the King's mind from so far away, Faris must have in one month gained powers it took most adepts years to master. Could she read the thoughts of others as well? When Jehan held her in his arms, did she touch his soul?

"King's choice or no, Faris is not ready to become Mistress of the Jewels!" The Mistress of the College of the Wise spoke crisply. As she turned, the Master of the Junipers saw her clear profile drawn like a sword against the silver pre-dawn sky.

"Madrona, we cannot stop it now," he replied in a low voice. "The people await her at every holding between here and Laurelynn. From all over Westria they are already traveling towards the Sacred Grove. And any further delay would break Jehan's heart."

"Is it his heart that's so impatient, or another part of him?" she asked dryly. A horse whinnied outside, and another answered it.

"You had Jehan under your eye here for three years and yet you think that of him?" the Master asked bitterly.

After a moment she sighed and laid her hand on his shoulder. "Very well, that was unworthy . . . but you know that I am right about Faris. She should stay here the full year at least. A regular priestess would stay here for four and receive her initiation then!"

Through the window behind her, the Master saw riders in Theodor's black and white forming up in the courtyard, and after a moment Sandremun, reining in his restless mount. Two of the men led riderless horses, and the Master recognized Faris' black mare.

"Faris has learned the basics, and she knows how to shield her mind now. Initiation will give her the spirit of the Jewels. Their history she can learn in Laurelynn," he said evenly.

"Spirit! History! And what of the discipline and detachment she will need to master them? Do you think she will learn those at Court?"

"Why not?" he flashed. "She is not called to renounce the world but to serve it. Her goal *is* Laurelynn!"

"Do not preach the Way of Affirmation at me! Do you regret your own choice now?" The Mistress turned her head without moving her body, and his memory mirrored the movement back across the years, to the days when he had been only a student, and she already a Mistress of Power, and later when he returned from Awahna with a new name and the mystery of the Valley still in his eyes, and she had met him as an equal and given him her love. But that had been long ago, before she had become Mistress of the College of the Wise and he had gone to serve the King in Laurelynn. The light behind her made a nimbus of her hair but left the polished mahogany of her face in shadow. Almost he could see there the flicker of lost laughter, and his throat ached with the weight of words unsaid.

He shook his head, whispering, "All roads lead to Awahna in the end."

A bell rang from the tower. Through the window he saw Faris come out of the dormitory, swathed in a green riding cloak, with Rosemary behind her. The morning light glowed on her face.

The Mistress of the College followed his gaze, and the bolder light picked out all the weariness in her face, all the scars of her struggle to acquire that serenity. For a moment the old face of renunciation, the young one of affirmation, the aspiration that had once shone in the Mistress' eyes, and the tragic vision of Faris that the Master had seen through the Lady of Fire flashed alternately before his eyes. Then they mingled fractionally in one face and were gone. He thrust out a hand, whether in protest or petition he did not know, and when his eyes focused once more, he found that the Mistress had taken it in her own.

"You must go now," she said gently.

"You will not come with us?"

"Between the escort and the baggage, you will be two weeks on the road. I will continue my work here a few days more, then ride across-country to the Grove."

There was a soft knock at the door, but he did not let go of her hand. "It is a punishing journey."

"Has lying in palaces softened you?" She laughed. "I am

not so frail—I will be at the Grove before you, never fear!"
Lightly she touched his cheek, and he turned to go.

Faris came down the stairs to the commonroom of the
Stonecross Inn carefully, clutching at the skirts of her new
green gown. It was one of several Berisa had made for her
while she was on the Mountain, cut close at the waist in the
fashion of Laurelynn, with sleeves tight to the wrist as she
had asked, its trailing skirts supported by petticoats. After
the simple tunics she had worn at the College of the Wise,
its constriction was almost unbearable.

But at least she was clean; the lingering soreness of muscles bruised by six days' riding had been eased by the hot
bath that had awaited her here at Tamiston. The worn stairs
creaked beneath her feet—Sandremun had said the inn was
one of the oldest in Westria—and every few steps a slitted
window opened onto the innyard and the circle of the common beyond, now bathed in a rosy sunset glow. Shadows
from the houses on the western side of the common pointed
across the grass to an upright half-arch of that composite
stuff the ancients had used instead of stone. Local tradition
held that it had once supported a road that arched through
the sky, though no one could say why.

"Faris, wait for me."

She heard Holly clattering down the stairs behind her and
paused, gathering the folds of her skirt. The muted roar of
conversation from the commonroom rolled and ebbed in the
stairwell, but the minds of the people down there were
louder than their voices. Faris felt their curiosity, excitement, or boredom, and above all their anticipation, and
knew that they were waiting for her.

She closed her eyes, visualizing a golden curtain that
would veil her from them without cutting off perception entirely. Carefully she drew it around her and for a moment
stood still, fixing the physical image so that it would continue
to function mentally without her attention.

"Lady of Earth—something smells good down there,"
said Holly, stopping behind her.

Faris smiled, glad, even with her barriers up, not to have
to face the crowd alone. Together they made their way to
the foot of the stairs.

At the table nearest the door a big gaunt man with a
wolf's grizzled hair paused with a beef bone in his hand. His

stillness spread to the four younger variations of himself who
flanked him. Beyond them several men in the leathern jerkins of drovers saw Faris and pulled off their knitted caps.

Faris looked around the room as the silence spread, finding at last the long table where they had seated Sandremun
and Rosemary, Farin and Andreas, and the others who had
come with them from the north, with some of the notables
of Tamiston. Empty places waited there for Holly and
herself.

Jehan would have had a smile and a greeting for them all,
she thought. But Jehan was not here. Faris lifted her chin,
gripped her skirts, and started across the room.

"There is rich land along Bear Cub Creek—I could get a
good crop of corn from it without stinting the forge, my
Lord, if you would let me try." The man's fringe of black
beard wagged as he talked. Faris recalled him from the introductions—Jonas Ferrero, the smith.

She turned back to the task of eating enough of her meal
to satisfy her host, though her stomach was uncertain. Dietrick of Wolfhill, the holding within which Tamiston lay, was
replying.

"I might allow it, but Mistress Esther at Elder would not.
She has already warned us about exceeding our bounds."

"Let her! She may be priestess at Elder, but I don't notice
the College of the Wise backing her. What's the objection
anyhow? The earth was meant to be tilled, and I could trade
the corn for more iron. Men from all over Westria have
praised my swords—I could make Tamiston famous if I had
the metal to work." The smith drained his beer mug and
sighed. Faris remembered arguments she had heard at the
College and echoed the sigh, grateful that the Master of the
Junipers had gone ahead to Elder and could not hear this
one.

"Master Smith, that is not quite so!" Rosemary frowned,
her spoon stopped halfway to her lips. "The earth sustains
all things in her own way. We should be thankful that sometimes she suffers men to impose their ways as well."

Dietrick's eyes glowed as he looked over at her. Down
the table his movement was echoed by his sons. "I was bred
by this land, and I think I understand it."

"Your pardon, my Lady," Jonas Ferrero broke in, "but
we have been frightened by legends too long. The world is

wide and men are few—we could accomplish so much more!"

"Have you forgotten the Cataclysm?" Rosemary's voice was very low.

"If indeed the powers of earth ever came near to destroying man, it was a long time ago. I have never seen one of the Guardians, nor has anyone I know."

The murmur of conversation in the rest of the room had stilled. Faris saw an old man watching them, his dark eyes cold in his brown face. Beside him a woman with hair like the fall of night fed her small daughter. Edge People, thought Faris—Old Ones like her own mother's kin. She wondered of what tribe and village they came.

The smith went on. "Even the King has no need to use those magic Jewels of his—" He stopped suddenly, remembering who Faris was.

Her hands clenched in her lap and she turned to the innkeeper. "I saw a pillar of concrete in the middle of your marketplace. What is it for?"

"Well, my Lady," said the woman eagerly, "that's what gave this place its name—Tam's Stone, not Tam's Town as most people think. As to what it's for—it survived the Cataclysm, and who can say for sure how the ancients used the things they made? The booths are set in rings around it when we have our August market fair. Caravaners are always coming through, but there are hundreds of them here then." She waved a hand at the group sitting at the long table nearest the fire. "I wish you could be with us for the Fair." Her gray eyes creased to slits above her red cheeks.

Faris sipped a little wine and smiled. "I would like that." She recognized the men and women she had seen unloading packmules when she arrived. They were carrying cloth of cotton and silk from the Free Cities, salt-fish from Seagate, worked tools and jewelry from Laurelynn, and iron ingots all the way from Elaya. Their destination was the Hold, where their goods would be exchanged for furs, raw wool and leather, and cured meat and cheese.

Two boys in sacking aprons began to clear away the meal.

"We keep no minstrels, my Lady, but we enjoy what cheer our guests can share. Would it please you if I asked whether someone would like to entertain the company?" the innkeeper asked.

Rosemary cocked her head at them. "You could start with

Sir Farin over there. His harp was given to him by the
King." She grinned.

After Farin had played, the caravaners sang for them,
their voices linking in close harmony they had beat out to a
mule's pace over scores of weary miles. Imperceptibly Faris
began to relax. Some of the candles had burned out, and
the dimmer light from the rest flickered on the faces of the
company, touching them with mystery. At the College, Faris
had learned something of the other kindreds that dwelt in
Westria. Now she thought suddenly how little she knew of
its men.

The caravaners finished. There was a little silence as people looked for the next volunteer, then the black-haired
woman Faris had noticed before rose from her seat, giving
her little daughter to the old man to hold. There was a pattering of applause from the local people as she came
forward.

"That's Tania Ravenhair, our healer. She's a rare herb-
mistress, though she was never at the College of the Wise,"
whispered the innkeeper.

"Then where did she learn?"

"From her own people, from her uncle—the old man
there. He is Longfoot, leader of the Miwok village at the
head of Bear Cub Creek."

Tania stood in the center of the room, shaking back her
long hair. She wore an ankle-length shift dyed saffron and
held to her narrow waist by a woven sash, but her arms and
feet were bare. One of the serving lads produced a little
wooden flute from his belt while the other lifted a drum
from the wall.

Tentative at first, the drumbeats settled to a rhythm. For
a while the dancer scarcely seemed to move. She swayed,
her feet brushing a pattern on the floor. Then the flute eased
into the rhythm of the drum, lilting around its steady beat
like a butterfly fluttering across a meadow, and Tania
opened her arms as if to draw the company into her embrace.

Faris did not know how long the Miwok woman danced
or when it was that Farin's harp entered the music, supporting and enriching it with a delicate courtesy like a lord at a
village feast.

Faris felt her feet twitch. Her heart went out to the
dancer, and the golden shell she had locked around her

misted away. She felt the stretch of Tania's muscles, the
spring of the worn oak floor. She glowed with the dancer's
joy as she gave herself to the music, making sound visible,
shaping the space around her and drawing her audience into
the pattern she made.

Faris was aware of their presence, but it did not frighten
her now. Each man or woman brought to the pattern something of his or her own. The dancer, the pattern, the world,
were refracted through a score of visions, framed by a score
of memories. And Faris knew them all, and through them,
Westria. *Jehan's people,* she thought, and then with surprise,
my people too.

When the dancing was over, Faris stumbled up the stairs
and fell into a dreamless slumber. But later she wakened,
needing to relieve herself, and paused at the window, looking out at the waxing moon. In its little light the heap of
unburied refuse behind the inn seemed inoffensive as a
nameless burial mound. Beyond it the common stretched
dimly, deserted except for the ambiguous shadow that was
Tam's Stone.

Two days later they crossed from the Corona into the Ramparts and transferred to the boats waiting on the Snowflood
at Elder. They were met by Robert, Lord Commander of
the Ramparts, a sturdy, square man with the weathered
strength of his own mountains in his face and their stillness
in his eyes. With many good wishes for Faris in the future,
Sandremun's escort of Coronans left them, to be replaced by
the axemen of Lord Robert's guard. However, Sandremun
continued with them, along with Farin, Rosemary, and the
Master of the Junipers. They were now two days from Laurelynn and a day farther from the Lady Mountain that
watched over the great Bay.

The barge bore them with dreamlike smoothness between
banks where ripening grain fields rippled towards the horizon as if the river had overflowed its bounds in waves of
gold. People lined the landings as they passed, but the royal
barges floated onward without pausing, letting the gentle
current bear them down the Snowflood to the Dorada, then
on to the Dorada's confluence with the Darkwater.

The misty shapes of the Ramparts disappeared as the river
curved. Lower hills darkened to the west and south, and one
peak slowly reared itself above the rest—the Red Mountain,

Lord Robert told her. Soon they would be there.

They came to Laurelynn-of-the-Waters when dawn was painting the city's brick walls an even deeper rose and were immediately surrounded by a flock of boats as bright as butterflies. Bunting and banners whipped in the river breeze, and flowers were blown from garlands to turn the river to a meadow through which the barges cut their stately way.

Faris gazed wistfully at the city as it brightened in the growing light. Was Jehan still there, where the banner of Westria marked the residence of the King, or had he gone to the Sacred Grove to wait for her? She wished they could stop here. The serenity in which she had left the College of the Wise was ebbing now. She had scorned her father's disapproval of this marriage, but what if he were right? How would she live among strangers? Instead of the Father of Mountains' familiar clarity, there was only the dark mountain that rose above the river's southern bank, its slopes glowing garnet in this dawn.

"I am sorry that my lady Jessica could not be with you now," said a quiet voice. Faris turned and saw Lord Robert, cloaked as she was against the early chill, the wind ruffling his silver-veined brown hair.

"You need not worry, my Lord," said Faris. "She will meet me soon enough, and there is no reason why she should suffer now."

Robert frowned. "It is not so for all women, I know, but Jessica is always so ill the first three months she carries a child. She wished to come with you—she grew up in Laurelynn and could no doubt tell you many things you wish to know."

Could she tell me what Jehan wants me to be? Could she tell me how to be a Queen? Everyone had been very kind, but she found it hard to believe they really approved of the King's choice. She turned away, not knowing how to respond to Lord Robert's scrupulous courtesy.

The deck vibrated to the pull of the river as the polemen thrust them away from Laurelynn and into the main channel, where the force of the Darkwater's contribution to the river could now be felt. To either side water eased through myriad arms and channels around the ephemeral islands of the delta. Only brick-armored Laurelynn resisted the river's power, and that only by dint of ceaseless vigilance.

The channel was too deep for poling now. The barge

jerked as four tugs eased ahead of them and the lines drew taut. Oars flashed in the sun. From the corner of her eye Faris saw something—perhaps a river otter—slip silently into the stream. Red-winged blackbirds dipped around the barge as it passed; the graceful neck of a white heron glimmered among the reeds. This was their land—whatever floods passed over them, they would remain. Faris shivered, thinking with what ease even a minor cataclysm might sweep the works of men away. Robert looked concerned and added the weight of his gray wool cloak to her own.

A little past noon they slid by the narrow strip of Spear Island and drew in to change rowers at Julian's Isle, which was high enough to bear a small village on its back. Faris and the others left the barge for a last chance to stretch their legs before they entered the Bay.

"Was the island named after Julian Starbairn?" asked Farin, slinging his harp across his back and hurrying after them.

"In Seagate they say that King Julian created it," said Lord Robert, pausing to wait for them. "According to the legend, he was caught by his enemies on the riverbank and the Dorada was too swift for him to swim. So he used the Earthstone and the Sea Star to raise up an island from the riverbed."

They began to stroll forward along the path at the edge of the island, turning their faces to the stiff wind and holding on to their cloaks. Wind rustled in the reeds, sighed across the rushing waters, whispered of the not-so-distant sea.

"Is all that Seagate land?" asked Rosemary.

"Everything to the north of us, from the west bank of the Dorada to the sea."

Faris followed Lord Robert's gesture from the bare hills they had just passed, smooth as eggs in a basket with their spring green crisping to summer's gold, to the more rugged hills in the west whose brushy slopes hinted at damp breezes from the Bay. Between them a rolling valley opened to the river's edge.

"Rich land," said Sandremun, peering under his palm at a distant cluster of buildings and a herd of fat cows.

"The field would be a good place to hold Games." Farin eased his harp forward and began to pick out a martial tune.

"It would be a good place for a battle," said Robert. "This is the last crossing calm enough for barges before you reach the Bay, and there's no fortress here to guard it."

Faris turned her gaze back towards the western hills. *Seagate* . . . She wondered how Eric was, and Rosemary's closed face told her that her friend wondered too. The Sacred Grove was in Seagate, and all of the Marches were bound to send representatives to see their new Queen invested with the Jewels. Rosemary would surely see Eric there.

And I will see Jehan.

Tonight she was to keep vigil on the Lady Mountain. Tomorrow she would be initiated and invested with the Jewels, and become Westria's legal Queen. Suddenly the day she had awaited with such longing seemed too soon.

She took a quick step towards the river's southern bank and stopped short, facing the mountain that from this vantage point alone reared free of its surrounding welter of hills. As a dark cone on the horizon it had haunted her journey southward. Here its presence overwhelmed her. She cowered back as if even across the waters its shadow could reach for her.

"You are right—the Red Mountain is a place of power." The Master of the Junipers spoke softly at her side.

Faris swallowed. "Is it evil?"

"Few things are evil in themselves—but many can be used for ill. The power of the Red Mountain is only alien to the needs of men. But we have built a beacon there, for it is the center of Westria." He smiled a little. "Do not be afraid. You will find the Lady Mountain very different."

Faris gazed hopefully downriver, where the hills framed the shimmer of sunlight dancing on the Bay. Yet even when they moved out onto the river once more, she felt the shadow of the Red Mountain following her.

Caolin leaned on the parapet of the beacon tower, watching toy boats creep along the river far below. He recognized the green and gold paint of the barge, but even without that he would have known whom it bore—Faris of Hawkrest Hold, on her way to be made Queen. Soon now Jehan would ride down the road from Misthall, the hunting lodge his father had built on the hills overlooking the Bay, and set sail across it to join her. Caolin envisioned them converging, imagined their meeting tomorrow morning at the Sacred Grove.

No horn call of his could stop their union now.

He felt a pang in his fingers. Curious, he looked down

and found them pressed white against the guard rail. He detached them one by one and saw etched into his hands the pattern of the stone.

Caolin stepped back, his gaze passing over the swept platform piled with logs for the Midsummer fire, over the lower slopes of the Red Mountain, moving to the folds of the coastal hills and across the stretch of the Great Valley and the veiled ranges of the Ramparts to the east.

Returning, his eyes found the city of Laurelynn glowing in the afternoon sun. Each toy house was picked out clearly by that golden light. Upriver lay toy villages, to the south a fortress the size of the castle in his chess set. How easy it would be to move them on the board of Westria if only he had the reach.

One could see so clearly from this place! The whole world lay at Caolin's feet. The mazes of politics, the morass of human hopes and fears in which men floundered, unable to see the Kingdom's good and their own, all seemed so insignificant from here. Why did he allow himself to be troubled by a toy woman and a toy man?

Caolin's fingers throbbed and he turned abruptly to the stairs that led down from the beacon to the buildings atop the lower peak. The pale wood of new shingles patterned the weathered roofs, but the red stone walls had needed no repair. He hoped that the workmen had followed his directions about the interior.

He passed the door to the main building and turned a corner to a smaller house where a woman was hanging wet sheets on a clothesline. He pursed his lips and whistled a high, shrill note, then waited as she turned and came towards him, wiping her hands on her apron. The sun was warm here, and her full breasts were half revealed by the loosened lacings at the neck of her gown.

"Hello, Margit," he said pleasantly. "Are you comfortable here? Do you have everything you need?"

Her eyes fixed on his face, brightening as she read his expression. Her mouth twitched and she nodded jerkily, trying to force out the sounds that struggled like trapped birds in her throat. On the right side of her face the pure line of cheek and jaw seemed to have slipped, pulling down her right eyelid as if her features were melting.

Caolin sighed impatiently and with a flicker of his fingers caught her gaze. She was still trying to speak, but he bored into her consciousness with images—of himself entering the Beacon-Keeper's dwelling, of faceless others being turned away, of Margit going into the first room to clean and turning away from its inner door.

"Except for you, no one shall enter that place, and except for me, no one shall enter the inner room at all!" he whispered. "See, here is the key." He drew from his pouch a key of wrought brass, waved it before her, and drew it softly down the marred side of her face, watching shame flare in her eyes. Then, as casually as he had reached into his pouch for the key, he slipped it into the cleft between her breasts.

"Guard it well, Margit, for if ever you fail me, fair one, it will become a serpent to pierce your heart!" Caolin's mind sent image with word, and as she tried to jerk away his other arm held her against him. The warmth of her breast soothed his bruised fingers, and her heart beat heavily under his hand.

"But you won't do that, Margit—because who would take care of you if it were not for me?" He released her and stood smiling while the fear left her eyes.

He went back to the main dwelling and used his own key to enter the outer room. The walls were lined with bookshelves as he had ordered; a long table stood to one side of the stove and a narrow bed at the other. The mattress was a thin pallet stuffed with straw, and there was no rug on the floor.

He hung his cloak on a hook on the door and, scarcely glancing at the room, pulled out a second, smaller key on a chain at his neck and opened the door to the inner room. Then he stopped, smiled, and turned back to light a candle before going in.

The room was windowless, from floor to ceiling painted a featureless black. At present its only furnishing was a square, blood-colored block of native stone. But Caolin, looking around him, envisioned the altars of the elements that he would fit up in each corner and the glowing lines of the pentangle he would inscribe on the floor.

Now it was only an empty room, echoing his footsteps and smelling faintly of paint. When he had consecrated it, tomorrow, it would become a fortress within which he could build his power. Midsummer was a good time for beginnings.

That was why Jehan had chosen it to make his lady Mistress of the Jewels.

Caolin picked up the candle abruptly and went out again, locking the room carefully behind him.

The porch at the back of the house was braced out over the cliff. Although it was lower than the beacon platform, one could see almost as far. Caolin leaned against the wall, breathing deeply in the still air. The afternoon was softening to a golden dusk. There was a bright haze on the valley, and the river glittered like a stream of gold. His eyes followed it through the straits and were drawn onward where the Lady Mountain watched over the bay with her back to the sea.

The west blazed as if the sun had expanded to fill the sky. Caolin shut his eyes tightly against the glare, but the after-image of the Mountain remained imprinted there.

Jehan stood in the bow of the *Sea Brother,* his eyes fixed on the Lady Mountain. His arm was around the dolphin figurehead and he balanced easily as the ship leaned into the wind, her zigzag course bringing him ever nearer to his goal.

Faris should have reached Seahold, he thought—they should be half way up the Mountain by now.

The sky-glow had deepened to a lucent orange like one of those great opals that were sometimes traded up from Aztlan, and the slopes of the Mountain were draped in a purple veil. Radiance flooded across them in a tidal wave of light, spilling down to edge the forested curves of the islands at the Mountain's feet with ruddy gold.

Jehan heard the sailors laughing together, Sir Randal telling his friend Austin, Lord of Seahold, about the girl he had met in Las Costas. But his heart beat in his chest like a ceremonial drum and he could not move.

Often as a child Jehan had had moments like this, when the world held still and the Source of All Beauty was only a breath away. Only now did he realize how long it had been since he had felt this surge of Joy.

"Lady of Fire," he breathed, "You are beyond all praise—only be as gracious to Faris as You have been to me!"

The ship heeled on to a new tack and Jehan blinked at the light, hearing the sounds of the world around him once more. He straightened a little and shaded his eyes with his hand.

They were sailing through a sea of fire.

IX

Mistress of the Jewels

Faris trembled as chill water trickled over her bare breasts, across her belly, and between her thighs. She saw her reflection drawn in pale strokes on the dark surface of the pool and erased again as the water moved, like a vision of something not quite in this world. And in this moment that seemed as likely as the idea that she was really here, being readied for her union with the King.

Smiling, the young priestess from Bongarde rubbed rose soap on a sponge and began to scrub Faris' back. The long day was fading at last, and sunset jeweled her pale skin with drops of crystal fire. Another priestess dipped water in a shell and tipped it over Faris' shoulders, while a third combed out the long, shining strands of her hair. The dark robes of the older women made deeper shadows among the laurel trees that edged the pool; their chanting focused the hush of the mountainside.

Faris stood rigid, though each soft touch seared her skin. She ought to welcome this cleansing after her long journey. Why did she feel as if they were stripping away layers of her soul? She had undergone such ritual baths before—at her puberty ceremony, and before that first Initiation that all Westrians shared, when she had chosen her name. Was it because these strangers could see all her imperfections, her scar? But here were none of those shocked glances too quickly turned aside that she had learned to dread. She was being judged by other standards now.

Goosebumps pebbled her skin as the water touched her again.

"Are you cold, my Lady? Tomorrow you will be warm."

The sponge caressed Faris' side. She felt the other

woman's memories of hard flesh pressing her own—a man's flesh, like that alien body that would soon possess hers.

Am I afraid of that? she wondered. *I wanted Jehan to take me when we were in the cave, but then it was something between him and me, not this ceremonial offering to the service of Westria!*

"Surely the Lady has favored you," said one of the priestesses, her eyes dwelling on Faris' delicately modeled breasts.

Faris' memory shied from the chime of silver bells. The barrier she had tried to draw around herself shimmered and misted away. Her flesh felt scarcely more substantial, as though her essence were diffusing through it into the soft summer air.

Across the water she met the cold gaze of the Mistress of the College of the Wise, the dark planes of her face as unyielding as the slopes of the Father of Mountains. Faris straightened, wondering if the old woman sensed her fear.

I am Faris! She clung to her identity. *I am thin and scarred and pale. There are things inside me that must not get free, and I know nothing of men and the world. What am I doing here?* Her father's accusations haunted her.

I am going to be Mistress of the Jewels, came the answer, and she did not know if the words were hers or those of another will.

Faris stepped forward in involuntary protest, but the priestesses surrounded her and drew her down to the cold embrace of the mountain pool. For a moment she lay still, her rosy nipples peeping above the surface of the water and her black hair swirling about her like waterweed, then she struggled to her feet. The laughter of the other women echoed against the trees.

I am Faris and I will not let you steal my soul! Warm tears slid down her cheeks to mingle with the cold waters below.

Still laughing, the girls helped her out of the pool, rubbed her dry, and clad her in an undyed linen gown. The sky had deepened to a translucent blue edged by a black fretwork of trees. Through their branches Faris glimpsed the mocking twinkle of the Lady's star.

By the time they had brought Faris to the meadow where she would keep vigil that night, day was only a memory in the west and scattered stars were blooming in the sky like the first daisies in a field that will soon be white with flowers. The faces of the priestesses glimmered pale within their hoods as they embraced her. Then they turned away and their black robes merged with the shadows, but Faris heard their singing long after they had disappeared.

> Queen among mountains with head star-crowned
> Above the sea,
> Blue-cloaked, your vigil guards the land—
> Watch over me!
> As a mother lays her child to sleep
> Upon her breast,
> Oh, let me seek your shelter now
> And give me rest. . . .

Faris cast herself down among the blankets they had left for her, buried her face in the rough wool, and cried.

A cricket sang nearby, then another. Tree frogs chirred in deeper harmony from the woods on the other side of the meadow. Faris sat up, sniffling, but the concert went on, oblivious to her pain. A last shudder shook her, then she set herself to fold her blankets into a bed.

When she lay down again, she found that the earth still held the warmth of the day, though the hay-scented breeze that played with her drying hair was cool. The steady pressure of the ground was obscurely comforting. This at least was dependable and real. Through the trees she glimpsed the rising moon. Her eyes closed.

When Faris became aware once more, the world was filled with light.

Halfway across the heavens the white moon rode like a queen, paled the stars, and awed the earth to still humility. Her cold light glittered on the tops of leaves. It iced the edges of the bending grass, yet lit the world to deeper mystery.

Something dappled shadows through the trees. Faris thought of maidens crowned with bloom she had seen dancing at the Hold. She heard a singing like the top note of a viol, played at the edge of sound. She shivered then—shapes wavered at the limits of her sight, more luminous than moonlight. Sweet they sang, and drifted towards her through the crystal grass, and beckoned to her with hands that brimmed with light.

Faris' memory strained for the sound of human song, the

taste of fresh-baked bread, Jehan's hard strength to hold her. But the moon's strange music drew her to her feet. She freed the gown that weighed so heavily and loosed the shadowed masses of her hair and danced.

Faris woke to a world of shadows, struggled free of her blankets, and looked around her, yawning and rubbing her eyes. She had dreamed—what had she dreamed? Through a gap in the trees she glimpsed mist-shrouded slopes falling sheer to the Bay. The water had the soft sheen of the inside of a shell, an iridescent lavender that shimmered into rose as the light increased. Then the sun lifted above the eastern hills and the transparent world grew solid once again.

Still bemused by the memory of music, Faris began the salutation to the dawn. Then she stopped. Before her she saw the dewy glitter of the meadow scrolled by the printing of a single pair of feet. She *had* danced then—it had not been only a dream. She shivered, wondering, if such things could come to her in her dreams, what the focused evocations of this Initiation would do.

The sudden pounding of her heart was echoed by the inexorable beat of a ceremonial drum. Faris stood still, waiting for them to come for her.

Caolin saluted the dawn from the top of the Red Mountain. Then, ignoring the golden-misted valley stretched below, he went back into the house. To finish the task for which he had stayed on the Mountain, he must not waste a single moment of the day.

He had bathed the night before. Now he carefully combed his fair hair and put on a new robe of undyed linen that he had sewn himself. His tools were laid out neatly on the table. It was time to begin furnishing and consecrating the temple in which he could become a Master—of his own powers.

Taking a deep breath, Caolin picked up his sword. He smiled a little as light quavered its length and picked out his own name etched into the blade. He had filed it from a blank of Elayan steel himself and bound it on a hilt of bone. He doubted that it would stand up to use in battle, but it was not intended to defend him from tangible foes.

The floor creaked beneath his bare feet as he moved to the open door of the inner room. His heart was beating a little faster than usual, but his movements remained graceful and deliberate. He was depending on careful study for his results today, not on intuition or the chance assistance of friendly powers.

Carefully he set the point of his blade to the jamb of the door.

"In the names of the four elements and of that Power that rules them all, I enclose this temple for my own uses by means of this barrier."

Drawing the blade deosil along the base of the wall from right to left as he faced it—the way of the sun—he visualized a mist rising from the scratch it left along the floor, which shone faintly and hardened as it grew. When he reached the corner, he poked the blade through the open window, went out to the porch where he picked it up again, and continued around the outside, reentering the same way and finishing at the other side of the door.

Caolin's mind firmed and strengthened the barrier, bringing it over the building until the inner room was enclosed by a gleaming shell. He could not see it with his physical eyes—it was a mental construct, the foundation of a series of images that would establish his temple at once on the physical and psychic planes. According to his studies, the temple was now sealed everywhere but at the door to entry by any elemental, thought-form, human suggestion, or spell.

He leaned the blade against the wall and rested for a moment, shrugging his shoulders to release their tension. Then his mouth firmed and he cleared his mind of all but his task. He prepared to go in.

"You are to go in." The priestess of the Grove slipped her hands into the green sleeves of her robe and nodded to Faris.

Sunlight, filtered and refracted by countless leaves, bathed their faces in greenish light. The clearing before her was bare except for a veiling of emerald moss. She looked up at a single redwood, huge-girthed and scarred by many winters, yet green as a sapling that has just unfurled its leaves to the sun.

Faris took a few uncertain steps forward, then stopped short.

Like a reflection broken by a falling leaf, the great redwood dislimned. Like an image forming as the water stills, it took shape once more. But now it was a man—crowned with green locks, clothed and skinned roughly in reddish-brown, but human in form. His eyes were as deep as the well of time.

Faris clasped her hands to still their trembling, knowing that she stood before the Lord of the Trees.

"Fair as the lily flower, daughter of the north, I welcome you." His voice whispered through her understanding like the rushing of wind through many leaves.

"My Lord, I thank you."

He sighed. "I was first among the First People to sign the Covenant your mothers made, and it is my right to question all who come here to be sealed to the Jewels of Power. Here they begin their task, and here they are laid to rest when their work is done."

The rich smell of damp earth dizzied her. What did he want her to say?

"You will have honor when you rule this land—will you honor us? You will keep men from sinning against each other—will you punish them when they sin against the other kindreds? Will you be willing to lose all that all may be saved?"

Yes . . . no! What do you mean? Faris struggled with questions, but a great wind roared about her, and when she could see again, both the Lord of the Trees and the clearing were gone.

A pit gaped before her feet. Beside it sat an armed man whose sword gleamed upon his knees. He rose and extended the sword till its point hovered above her heart.

"What is your name?"

"My name is Faris," she whispered, peering at him to see if it was Jehan.

"Not here," he said in a voice like iron, a stranger's voice. "Here your name is Seeker After Truth, until you shall earn a greater one." He lowered the sword and grasped her hand.

"Wait—" She was not yet sure what she had promised to the Lord of the Trees. She needed time.

"Enter in the name of the Maker of All Things!" The warrior stepped into the pit. She tried to hang back, but he drew her after him down the steps and into the darkness.

Caolin paced sunwise around the dark room, scattering pinches of salt from the earthenware bowl in his hand.

"Be this temple cleansed of all spirits of whatever kind! By all the powers of earth I bid ye begone!"

When he had finished his circuit, he replaced the bowl in the other room, returned with the aspergillum filled with consecrated water, and repeated the procedure. The cleansing was performed a third time with a censer smoking with myrrh, and lastly with a candle that searched every corner of the room. Then swiftly he drew the sword across the entryway.

Caolin stood still in the midst of the room, hearing no sounds but his own breathing and the sigh of wind on the mountaintop. It had been long since he had allowed himself to regret the lack of extra sensitivity that would have given him firsthand knowledge that the room was cleansed. But he had based his life on the ability to do without it. He was depending now on both his learning and his will, using the knowledge of the College of the Wise while rejecting both their support and their authority.

"It will succeed," he murmured. "It must!" He turned to each corner of the room and lifted his arms in invocation.

"I, Caolin, do dedicate this temple to the search for knowledge and mastery—of the powers that lie in the world around me, and of those that lie hidden within me! In the names of the four elements I dedicate it, and through that Power by which the elements were made, and on the foundation of this Mountain upon which I stand. If I betray my own truth, may it betray me!"

The floor quivered. Caolin stepped to keep his balance, wondering if the excitement had dizzied him. The blood was singing along his veins.

The temple was ready now, and it was time to furnish it.

Four steps down, then Faris stumbled across an open space heavy with the smell of damp earth. She bumped into a wall of dirt that crumbled at her touch and struck out in panic as her hood was pulled over her eyes.

Metal knocked hollowly against wood nearby. From some unimaginable distance came a reply—"Who comes to the sacred circle?"

"The Guardian of the Gate brings a candidate to the Mysteries." The sentinel's voice was very close. Faris groped, touched cold armor, and clung to the arm it covered.

"Has she been purified according to the Law?"

"All things have been done as the Law prescribes."

"Then enter."

Wood scraped on stone. Gasping, Faris stumbled upward and realized that she had come within the sanctuary.

"Seeker, what are you looking for?" The voice vibrated around her. How must she reply? Jehan would be ashamed if she could not remember, and whatever must happen could not be as terrible as her imaginings.

"I walk in darkness and I seek a door . . . the elements within me are at war." She took a breath and added uncertainly, "The Jewels of Westria have summoned me, and now I seek the wisdom to obey."

There was a short silence. "Who speaks for her?"

"I speak for the College." Faris recognized the harsh sweetness of the voice of the Master of the Junipers.

"I speak for the Jewels!" The second voice was young, and she vibrated to it like a harpstring whose mate is plucked.

A gentle hand put back her hood and she blinked in the sudden light.

All was well. This was still grass beneath her feet, and a circle of redwoods around it, the same sun and sky. She was still in the world she knew. Gradually her eyes adjusted and she saw the Mistress of the College watching her across an altar of granite. She glimpsed other figures positioned around the circle but could not look at them. To either side of the altar two pillars, black and white, pointed to the sky. Beyond them—was that Jehan? Her eyes dazzled again.

"Come."

The Master of the Junipers gave her a welcoming smile and led her to kneel at the central altar with her fingertips touching the stone. Atop it sunfire danced in a golden bowl. The Mistress of the College began to administer the oath, and the clarity of her voice calmed Faris; the words echoed in her soul to affirm an orderly reality.

"I, kneeling in the presence of these mysteries . . . knowing nothing and having now no will, promise thus—not to speak foolishly of what I may learn or to cease my striving towards the eternal goal, and never to debase what powers I gain, however tempted, to any creature's harm or to the weakening of the Covenant.

"And if I break this oath, then strike me down ye, who journeying upon the winds, can strike where no man can and slay where no man may!"

There was a pause, and Faris saw the shadow of the sentinel's sword poised across the stone. Her throat dried with the knowledge that her own lips were sentencing her, but she went on.

"And as I bow me now beneath this sword, I bind me to their justice with my word. This by my name and by my soul I swear and by that which is All and Everywhere."

Faris clung to the stone altar for her life. Gently the Master of the Junipers helped her to rise. Through her weakened barriers she felt the gentle glow of his concern for her.

"Having been so spoken for, and having so answered, and having so sworn, you may now see the hidden things," said the Mistress in a voice like sunlight. "Let the Mystery of Earth begin!"

Caolin knelt before the northern corner of his temple and lit the yellow candles in front of the tiered altar there. At its top lay a chunk of rock from the Red Mountain's peak. Lower steps bore an earthenware dish of salt and a wicker platter holding a clod of earth with a rooted stalk of grain.

All of these represented aspects of the strength he wanted to claim—the vigor of the soil, the ordered structure of salt crystals, and above all the enduring and eternal resistance of stone.

Slowly he spoke the words of consecration.

"I am Earth, the foundation, the sphere in which all the elements are conjoined."

The words came from the figure before Faris, but the sound vibrated from the ground on which She stood. Her gown folded green-flecked russet highlights and umber shadows around the curves and hollows of a body as rich as the land in flower, below a face like weather-sculptured hills, stripped of all but beauty.

"Hail, Lady of Earth, in whom all things take form!" The litany echoed from the lips of the Mistress of the College, of the Master, of all those within the circle, and as it seemed to Faris, even from the leaves and blades of grass.

"I am Earth. My body is the living soil, the rocks are my bones, the metals flow in my veins. The waves may beat against me, the winds buffet me, the fire sweep over me, but I abide."

Faris slumped beneath the weight of earth. Into the darkness of the Lady's shadowed eyes she fell; rock formed around her bones. By countless colored strata she was pressed; she felt the interplay of stress and shift and cherished the integrity of jewels that would never see the light. She sensed the elementals' inner forms, which told stone how to grow. She slept a million years.

"I am Earth. I am the Bride and the Mother. Sun and rain quicken me; life springs from my womb to ascend into the heavens once more. From me come all green and growing things."

Faris felt life tingle through her veins, thrust with fierce persistence towards the light, knew warmth, and swayed to a pine-scented breeze. Once more she bowed before the Lord of Trees and danced with spirits sprung from leaf or flower. In joy she rose to life, in joy returned herself to pregnant darkness once again.

"Child of Earth, from Me all your substance comes. Until the end of time when I am united with the Lord of Heaven once more, Earth I am and will remain."

Faris' eyes dazzled. She looked away and remembered who she was and where.

"As you have seen and understood, so shall you be consecrated." The Priestess of Earth sprinkled her with salt, and the Master of the Junipers draped a robe of brown linen over her and turned her towards the altar again.

Someone was coming to her through the light. Faris bit back a cry of greeting as she saw Jehan, holding a girdle whose clasp bore a jewel that shone like sunset shining through leaves. His lips shaped her name, shaped a smile for her. Then she felt the cool touch of the Earthstone on her forehead, her breast, her loins.

Light and shadow swirled around her. For a moment she felt all the growing things in Westria rejoicing in the sunlight, reached with their roots into the earth, knew the structure of the rock beneath that soil as she had never known her own bones. Understanding Earth, she knew suddenly how one might work with it—not forcing it to her will but willing in harmony with its nature and her own.

"Initiate of the Mystery of Earth, I invest you with its power."

Carefully Caolin poured the consecrated water from its crystal vial into the chalice of silver set with moonstones. He raised it reverently and set it on the altar he had placed in the western corner of the room. Water, he thought, so soft, so necessary, which could yet strip branches from great trees in its fury, and in its patience wear away stone. He needed water's strength.

He lit the silver candles and set them down. From the depths of the chalice glimmered a star of light. Like the Sea Star . . .

Caolin thrust the thought from his mind. Let Jehan and Faris play with their toys—he would make his own magic!

The cool touch of water on her face brought Faris back to the clearing once more. She shook her head impatiently, looking for Jehan.

I am Faris, and this is the Sacred Grove of Westria. This is solid earth that I am standing on.

But she felt the strength of that earth flowing up from her bare feet through her bones and knew with a tremor of panic that she was not entirely Faris . . . not anymore.

Water touched her again and she focused on the figure before her.

His pale face filled her vision as the moon had filled the sky. His gray robe shimmered with half-seen rainbow tones—purple, blue, and green—and he bore a silver chalice in his hand.

"I am Water—water of the sky, water of the sea, water of life in man's blood, of death in his tears."

"Hail, Lord of the Waters, nourisher of all things!"

"I am the mist on the mountains, the rain that soaks the earth, and the storm that washes all away. Drop by drop I conquer the hardest rocks; my floods overwhelm the nations; I sink forests and fill plains; from the shores I carve new dominions for the sea."

The grass before her swayed in waves of gray. She sank; bright-armored fish escorted her beyond great forms that stirred dimly in the deeps. She floated, wondering. Then dolphins came and whistled challenge till she joined their game. From sapphire depths in dazzling bursts of spray, she fountained skyward, shimmered as a cloud, rejoined the earth as rainfall, trickled through its hidden places, and became the steady flow of a dark stream that sought the sea.

The cycle was repeated until Faris realized that it was water from the chalice that was drenching her, and that her brown robe had been replaced by one of silky sea green. Light blazed from a stone all the colors of the sea. She tried to see Jehan beyond it, but its touch plunged her into the depths once more.

She felt at once the waters flowing through her own body and through the sea and answered with the waters to the call of the moon. She knew how to flow with them now, to share their power.

"Initiate of the Mystery of Water, I invest you."

Caolin coughed as the sweet smoke caught at his lungs, swirled away from the incense in the brass bowl, and billowed around the room. He went on with the ritual, intoning both dedications and responses as he set in place the wand, the feather, and the bell. The Lord of the Winds was also Lord of Magic, ruler of airborne words that shaped being out of will.

His hand trembled a little as he lit the blue candles, and he forced himself not to hurry, not to give way to the strain of so long a focusing of his will. At the Sacred Grove the joined power of half the College of the Wise was bent on the Initiation of one weak girl. Caolin felt a bitter pride that he must do all alone.

For a moment he wished he had brought someone to assist him. But whom could he have asked? It was no crime for a man to make a temple for the perfecting of his own soul, but building it on the Red Mountain might be considered a presumption by some. Whom could he have trusted not to tell a busybody such as the Master of the Junipers what he had done?

Caolin's mouth quirked as he thought of Ordrey stumbling in this darkness, pictured the responses coming from Ercul Ashe's prim mouth. No—better to be alone than to work with such faulty tools, even though his back ached with weariness and the smoke stung his eyes.

Faris turned her face to the wind and breathed deeply, slowly, trying to reorient herself. The spicy scent of the redwoods drifted through the air; the warm breeze was drying the water from her face and hair. The Master of the Junipers had brought her to the eastern side of the circle, she did not remember how.

But she no longer wondered whether Jehan was there— she felt at once the yielding femininity of earth in her own body and its unyielding strength in his; the gentle tides of the sea and the fury of the storm. She looked back over her shoulder at the two pillars—feminine and masculine, dark and light—and understood why they were there.

The breeze chilled, nipped her cheeks as if it had swept down from snowfields or through the starry reaches of the sky. The air she breathed in tingled through her body, sharpening hearing and sight.

"I am Air—the wind of heaven and the breath of life."

The priest before her had the smooth features of a boy and ageless, merry eyes. The wind whipped his orange robes around him and ruffled his pale hair.

"I draw both heat and cold across the world, carrying the clouds from the sea to give their blessing to the land, to bear seed to the earth and pollen to the flower. Terrible as thunder I can be, or softer than a feather on a breeze." His words were lost in a roaring of wind.

Faris felt the world whirl away, tossed upward with a speed that took her breath, then sank in lazy spirals; felt the wind ruffle feathers, stretched, and spread her wings. She eyed the scrambled patterns of the land with an eagle's vision. Disdaining gravity, she sported with the wind, found in the sky a kingdom freer than mere men could ever know.

"And yet I also bear the sounds that stir your soul—the words by which you understand the world."

A bell's sweet chime divided sight from sound, and sudden harmony of harp and horn laid note by note a pattern on the air that drew her trembling earthward once again.

"What is your name?"

"Seeker After Truth."

"Who were you?"

"Faris."

"What are you?"

"A woman."

Question and answer followed without cease. Word by word he drew from her the names from which she had built her identity—asking, comparing, and denying them till she no longer knew which ones were true.

Nameless, she stared at him while the soft clouds of incense swirled around her and they laid the orange robe across her shoulders. Jehan held out to her a crystal filled with light, and as it touched her she knew her name, and his, and the names of every thing and creature in the land.

"Initiate of the Mystery of Air . . ."

The light of three pairs of candles danced among the shadows. It gleamed fitfully on silver and brass, glowed on cloth and earthenware, alternately revealing and disguising the trappings of the altars of earth and water and air. Caolin breathed carefully, steadying himself for the final consecration.

Gently he set the large candle on the highest tier of the altar above the sword. The candles were red; the candlesticks of polished copper, the Lady's own metal.

The Lady—whose blessing was being invoked on the union of Jehan and Faris even now. Caolin's head ached with the effort to keep from crying out, to retain control. He brought the taper to the candles on the altar of Fire and touched them to life.

"What can warm can also burn," he breathed. "The spirit of fire is no one's possession, and it too will serve me."

He stared into the candlelight, but all he could see in its steady flame was the light of Jehan's eyes when Faris' message came to him. Caolin remembered a time, long ago, when Jehan's eyes had held such a glow when they looked on him.

Had that also been the work of the Lady of Fire?

Jehan . . .

"Now begins the Mystery of Fire!"

Her heart still ringing with his name, Faris looked from Jehan to the Mistress of the College, and beyond her to the figure towards whom the Master was now leading her. She felt his tension as they approached, glanced at his face and wondered what he feared to see. Then she met the eyes of the Priestess of Fire and sensed Jehan's joy as he sensed hers.

"I am the fire of light and life, and love."

The priestess' robes were made of some shiny stuff shot interchangeably with emerald and flame. They fluttered around her in a blast of heat that seemed to come from the copper lamp she held. Its flame caught Faris' eye and drew her into the heart of fire.

"I am the fire at earth's core, the fire of life in man or animal, the fire of passion and redeeming love."

Shadows circled Faris. Breaching them, she flared against the heavens in a burst of flame. She soared among the stars, became the sun, became the light that fell to earth once more. Burning in each leaf, from light new substance formed; consumed by living things, their bodies made; burned in their blood, gave them the heat to move and join in union with their kind.

And still the fire burned before her eyes, the heat surrounded her, consuming her until she felt herself only a shell through which the light could glow. The brilliance focused to a point, it neared till she could scarcely see. Then she felt fire sear her brow and saw herself reflected in Jehan's eyes.

"Initiate of the Mystery . . ."

Faris scarcely heard. Nor did it matter when Jehan removed the Jewel of Fire from her brow. She walked with his feet, felt him walk within her as she was led around the circle once more. She radiated the steady warmth of every hearthfire in the land; she burned in the veins of every moving creature, transforming matter into energy; she felt the gentle glow of affection between long-wedded pairs, the trust of comrades, the ecstasy of lovers who were each others' fuel. For a moment she sensed the passion of Caolin's mind, bent on his task.

She stood and burned with unconsuming Light.

Caolin had put on a white robe. He stood before the naked stone in the center of his temple and bowed before it. The golden vessel upon it was empty still, as the altar beneath it was still merely stone. He had consecrated the four corners to the four elements upon whose interaction all earthly life depended, but the parts were still less than the whole.

His business was with the center now—the balance, the integration, the focusing of power.

Caolin turned to his left, continued the circle to the altar of Earth, and laid his hands on the heap of coal piled there.

"Creature of Earth, into you I summon all Earth's power." He visualized all the strengths with which he had hallowed the altar flowing through the hard, powdery surfaces of the lumps of coal. Then he turned again and bore them to the golden basin on the altar.

He moved to the altar of Water then, felt for the brittle heap of dried seaweed he had placed there, and willed into it all the slow strength of the sea. Then he added this fuel to the coals. From the altar of Air he brought incense, placing special intensity in his invocation of the element whose presence was as vital to the life of the fire as it was to his own.

Then he turned to the altar of Fire, whose flame, like all fire, had come originally from the incandescence of the sun. He took a white taper and touched it to the candle, holding his breath as the spark ran down the wax-coated fibers, strengthened, and became a flame.

"Creature of Fire, you are the seed of Light, the catalyst in which all elements will join."

He stood and, holding the taper carefully, began to pace around the room. Softly at first, he intoned names of the elements, the attributes with which he had invested them. As he moved his voice strengthened until it rang against the confines of his skull as it echoed from the walls of the room.

Dizzy, his pulse still pounding with the rhythm of his march, Caolin turned to the central altar at last and thrust the taper into the fuel laid in the golden bowl. It flared in blue sparks and fizzled, flared once more. Caolin's breath caught as he willed it to live. His nostrils prickled with mixed scents of sandalwood and sea wrack as light flickered across the surface of the bowl and the fuel crackled, hissed, and then settled to a steadier glow.

Caolin let the taper rest on the edge of the bowl, forced everything from his mind except the powers on which he was drawing now, and set his hands flat upon the naked stone to either side of the bowl.

"In the name of Earth!

"In the name of Water!

"In the name of Air!

"In the name of Fire!"

His shout became a scream as he willed the forces of all the elements into the altar stone.

Breathless, his sight darkened, his balance gave way. Then he realized that it was not his own weakness but the stone itself that trembled beneath his hands. The floor quivered; there was a deep rumbling, like some great animal stirring in its sleep. Caolin's body convulsed as he received back through his hands all the focused power he had sent through the altar stone into the Mountain's heart.

Caolin cried out again, unable to take his hands from the stone. For a moment he knew the interplay of the elements not with his conscious mind alone, but with every cell of his body, and the passive power of the Mountain balanced the positive energy of his will.

For an instant the sealed rooms in his soul were thrown open, and for the second time in his life he was not alone.

Mistress of the Jewels!

Faris stood before the central altar in the Sacred Grove, eyes dazzled by its pure flame. Her pulse jumped to the steady beating of her heart; her ears throbbed; the ground trembled beneath her feet.

"Mistress of the Jewels!"

Her sight cleared and Faris knew that it was the beating of a drum she heard and that the ground was being shaken by dancing feet. They had clad her anew in a priestess' black robe.

She stood still, trying to master her body—her sight, her breathing, her balance on the earth. But too much had been added to her awareness. She felt within her the interplay of the elements; her consciousness slipped back and forth between Faris the human woman and the Lady of Westria, whose body was the land, whose blood was its rivers and streams, whose breath was the wind, whose life was the light in which it grew.

The priests and priestesses of the four elements had disappeared. Faris saw instead two circles—men robed in white, women robed in black—moving around the pillars and the altar stone. She and the pillars formed two sides of a square at right angles to the square that the elements had made. The opposite angle—Faris glimpsed something white beyond the dazzle of the altar fire . . . was it Jehan?

Blinking, she tried to find among the dancers' faces some she knew, but all were strangers, closed upon a knowledge she did not share. The black circle drew inward; she saw the Mistress of the College reaching for her, pulling her into the dance. She followed unresisting, her bare feet carrying her sideways to the steady beat of the drum. The circle bore her to the other side of the altar, but now there was no one there.

And yet she felt the presence of an Opposite that orbited the center just as she did, balancing her. And in response her awareness of the elements within her changed. She felt the sweetness of the Lady of Flowers and the riches of the Harvest Queen, and across from Her, the hard strength of the Lord of Stone. The chaste simplicity of the Moon drew through her body the tides of the sea, and then she bowed to the driving power of the Lord of Wave and Storm. She was the breath of Spring upon the air, and she fled before the force of the Wind; she was the gentle hearthfire, reflecting the wildfire's flame.

Though her skin burned, she was shivering. She felt a Presence in the air around her, and in some still untouched corner of her mind remembered the Beltane ceremony and how she had been possessed, and was afraid. What waited to use her body now, and for what ends? Where was Jehan?

The other dancers were leaving, black and white robes pairing and disappearing through the trees. But Faris could not follow them. The drum held her in the circle and the Presences around her became greater—the Lady of Wisdom, the Lady of Stars, and She who is the Darkness from which all is born and to which it must return.

Then Faris was alone, and the drum stilled at last. She swayed, trembling. The energy that had sustained her ebbed. She slipped to her knees.

Have mercy upon me, have mercy upon me, O Thou Who Art . . . But she knew not to whom nor for what she prayed. All the goddesses who overshadowed her were merging into one Goddess in response to that other Presence that approached her now. Westria waited for the coming of the King.

Be not afraid.

Faris turned slowly to face it, saw a figure edged in light. It moved into the shadow of the pillar and she recognized Jehan. Light and shadow transformed him as he came towards her. He had shed his robe, and his broad shoulders and narrow hips, his triumphant masculinity, belonged equally to man and to god.

The air burned.

He came to her. His hands loosed the clasps of her gown and it pooled about her knees. His lips saluted her brow, her breast; he bent to her thighs. She reached out to him and tried to shape his name.

But as He rose again to press her down upon the earth, His features were lost in a blaze of light.

Jehan . . .

Her flesh glowed with an answering radiance into which her consciousness pursued his name and was consumed.

The Goddess opened Her thighs to receive the God.

X

The Evening Star

They say a star has come to rest
In peace at last upon your breast—
Oh, sister, will you be the same . . .

Farin muttered the lines, broke off, and shook his head.
Faris' dream of the star, dimly remembered from what
seemed a lifetime ago, had haunted him since dawn. He recalled promising to make a song about her dream if she
would tell it to them, and suddenly the need to write it was
troubling him, not for her sake, but for his own. He stood
alone in the midst of the throng that milled before the garlanded platform where the King would shortly show the new
lady of Westria to her people, struggling for the words that
would tell him what he wanted to say.

Like an accompaniment beneath the melody of his
thoughts, he felt the patient benevolence of the Sacred
Wood, charged now with something more—a tension as if
the world were about to explode in terror or in joy. A chill
brushed Farin's skin.

Oh, sister, are you now the same
In any aspect but your name,
As she . . .

"Surely the ceremony should be finished by now. Do you
think something has gone wrong?" Rosemary paused beside
him.

Farin lost his thought and peered impatiently at the slant of the sunlight through the redwoods. The trees shone in that golden light as if they had acquired an extra measure of reality.

"Is it so late?" he muttered. "How long should it take? Why don't you ask Eric—he came here with his father to see Jehan invested with the Jewels fifteen years ago."

As she . . . As she who was my other self . . . He tried to concentrate, but the tension around him was making it hard to breathe.

Rosemary looked uncertainly at Eric, who stood before the platform like a sentinel. The vulnerability in her face struck Farin with sudden misgiving. It was too like the way Eric and Stefan and the others had gazed at Faris not so long ago. Did Rosemary love Eric? If so, he pitied her and felt an obscure gratitude that he had escaped being kindled by the passion that spread like wildfire around him.

Beyond Eric, Sandremun was talking with Lord Brian of Las Costas. As Farin watched, Brian turned to Eric, grinned, and started to take his arm. Eric stiffened and jerked away with an oath. Brian's face reddened and his hand drifted towards his sword, but Sandremun moved between them saying something that made Brian laugh, and led him away.

"Never mind," Farin said quickly. "I'm sure things are going well. Faris and I have always been so close—remember, she knew I was going to be wounded. I would feel it if she came to any harm!"

The sun backlighted Rosemary's hair to a halo of gold but her eyes were shadowed. "I know that you and she *were* close . . ." She gestured helplessly.

Farin stared at her. *As she who springing from one birth, was twin in soul as twin on earth . . .* No, that was not quite what he wanted to say.

The tension broke.

Farin gasped and staggered like someone turning a corner out of a strong wind. He felt Rosemary's grip bruise his arm, but his eyes were dazzled, his spirit a fountain of joy. The crowd stilled, then broke into excited chatter once more.

"Did you feel that?" he whispered when he could speak again.

"Yes. They must have felt that all the way to the College of the Wise. The Goddess has merged with the God and made a channel for the One. Such a joining renews the world!"

The crowd around them shouted in a babel of accents from every Province in Westria. Farin relaxed and found himself able to focus on the world around him once more.

"Praise to the Maker of all Things that the King has given us a Lady!" came a woman's voice with the lilt of Las Costas. "They say she's from the Corona—one of the Lord Commander's daughters."

"No, Dorian, it was her sister that married the Lord Commander's son—you can see him over there talking to Lord Brian."

Farin sighed and looked after the two women as they passed. *As twin on earth . . .* That was not quite it. He tried to find another line, but his mind homed on what he had just felt. Had Faris caused that? What then had she become?

"Rodrigo said that Lady Faris is as beautiful as the Lady of Light. She must be, considering the women who have been in and out of Jehan's bed!"

Two men laughed, and Farin stifled an impulse to wipe the names of his sister and the King off their lips with his fists. How could they understand?

He sighed instead. Already the legends were beginning—soon reports would name Faris as beautiful as Auriane the Golden Queen or Fiona Firehair. He knew that she could be pretty, but he remembered too vividly other times—Faris smudged and sweaty from working in the garden, or with her face blotched from fever. He remembered how she had looked last night when they took her up the Lady Mountain, pale as paper and bowed beneath the weight of her own hair.

And yet Jehan had chosen her for his mate from among the beauties of a kingdom. That was the mystery. What had the King seen in Faris that her brother, after twenty years of living as close to her as one breath to another, could not see?

> As she who was a twin to me
> In birth, in face, in memory?

Rosemary made a stifled sound beside him. Farin groped

for the next verse, swore, and then stopped, hearing what she had heard. Silence was spreading through the crowd as spilled oil calms a troubled pool. And deeply, as if all the people of Westria shared a single heart, came the steady pulse of the ceremonial drum.

Step by step the people moved towards the platform from the groups in which they had been talking. Farin grasped Rosemary's hand and drew her towards Eric, around whose tall figure people eddied like water around a rock. The three of them stood together as the crowd packed itself around them and the last whispers died away.

The drumbeat grew louder. Farin felt a collective sigh as the lines of priests and priestesses in their white and black robes appeared through the trees.

"The Mistress of the College." Rosemary nodded towards the woman who led them, her hair like a silver crown above her black robe. Her dark face held a remote gentleness now.

Farin glanced towards the priest who walked beside her and his eyes narrowed. Surely that was the Master of the Junipers, but how strange he looked. Was it the white robe that made him seem so tall, that gave him the air of a prince as he came towards them?

> Praise the Lord and Lady, praise the One
> Who Self-divided, is at once Self-known,
> And from that knowledge manifests the world!

Farin's song disappeared like a raindrop into the sea. "Praise the Lord and Lady, Praise the One!" The earth trembled as the people responded to the litany.

"They're coming." The whisper stirred the crowd. Faris swallowed, straining to recognize the black-and-white-robed figures as they mounted the platform and spread out to either side of the thrones.

They're coming.

Farin saw the King first, looking tired but triumphant, with the four Jewels of Westria glittering from his loins and waist and breast and brow. His face held the joy of a man who has achieved his desire. He disappeared momentarily behind the platform, then Farin saw him climbing the stairs.

"Sweet flowers of spring, will marriage do that to me?"

Rosemary's shaken whisper drew Farin's attention from Jehan to his Queen.

It was not Faris.

Certainly this woman wore his sister's slim body and shadowy hair and eyes, but the expression in those eyes was none that he had ever seen Faris wear—none that any human woman could wear, at once sensual and innocent, infinitely compassionate and proud. Farin remembered the Beltane Festival and understood that it was the Goddess looking out of Faris' eyes.

Oh, sister . . . are you now the same?

"All hail Jehan, Lord of Westria and Master of the Jewels!" the people cried until he smiled and held up his hand to still them.

"As I am King of Westria, I have chosen my Queen; as I am Lord, I have given you a Lady for this land—does any here deny my choice?"

"All hail the Queen!"

The sunlight glistened on Faris' hair as she stepped forward and smiled at the people whose cheering shook the trees.

"As Master of the Jewels, I declare to you that she has been initiated into the Mysteries and may now bear the Jewels of Power," Jehan added when at last they were quiet again.

There was no response to this but a hastily stifled whisper as someone hoped that the Initiation had been a thorough one, since it was said that the Jewels would blast any who bore them otherwise. Tension grew.

Jehan unclasped his girdle of embroidered linen and bound it above the swell of Faris' thighs. The Earthstone flickered suddenly like a forest in the sunlight as she turned to face the people again.

In Her footsteps spring the rainbowed flowers . . . Words trembled on Farin's lips, but whether they were his own or some hymn he did not know.

The silver mail of the belt that bore the Sea Star flashed in the sunlight as the King fastened it around Faris' waist, and the great stone flared with sapphire light. He drew the Wind Crystal in its eagle-winged setting from around his neck and passed the chain over her head.

Farin's breath caught, seeing it flame like a star upon her breast. He had heard once that the Wind Crystal was the first of the four to be made and that its power gave the others their potency. But he cared only for the fact that the Lord of the Winds ruled not only magic, but song.

The Jewels glowed against the dark stuff of the Queen's gown. Jehan, gazing upon her face, hesitated a moment as he lifted the coronet with the Jewel of Fire from his head. Then, very carefully, he settled the circlet upon her brow, stepped back, and sank to his knees.

She stood still for a few moments while the breeze sported with the skirts of her gown and blew out her hair. Then she paced forward, gently blessed Jehan's bent head, and lifted her white arms to the crowd.

"People of Westria!" she cried in a voice like a golden clarion. "I stand here before you—will you receive me as your Queen?"

Eric groaned and hid his face in his hands. Rosemary's head was moving in denial even as her lips opened in the cry of assent that seemed to surge from the earth on which they stood.

But Farin could neither cry out nor look away. As he gazed at the Lady of Westria he felt her image replacing that of the sister he had loved, and his eyes stung with tears.

Jehan rubbed at the fatigue that filmed his eyes and took another swallow of mead. Before him the Midsummer Fire roared like a furnace, as if the sun had indeed come to spend the night on earth's breast. The last light of that longest of days had faded from the sky, and the stars danced along their sunways road as the people of Westria danced below. The air throbbed with the beating of drums and quivered to the high note of the flute as they circled sunways around the fire. The dancing had been going on since sunset, and it would continue until dawn.

He felt sweat trickling down his neck and turned to look up at his Queen, enthroned beneath a canopy of green boughs. Although the heat of the fire was scarcely less where she sat, she showed no signs of feeling it.

Jehan gazed at her and sighed. Her skin glowed and her eyes gave back the light of the fire as if she burned within. She smiled on all, she spoke, she sipped a little water, but she did not eat, and men left space around her as if by coming too close they would be consumed.

"Her beauty is beyond the beauty of women, and she is

now in all ways both Mistress and Queen, but you miss the maiden you found in the north," said a harsh voice.

Jehan looked around to meet the unexpected warmth of understanding in the Master of the Junipers' eyes. Seeing himself and the Master robed alike in white, he felt a sudden kinship with the older man, as if the different mystiques of King and Master could for a time be set aside. Both men looked up at Faris.

"I have made her Lady of Westria as I promised," said Jehan thoughtfully, "but though I know that I possessed her in the ritual only a few hours ago, I am as awed in her presence as any man in Westria. We are all her subjects tonight."

"You don't remember lying with her this afternoon?"

Jehan shook his head and the Master smiled. "I have no certain memory of what I did either," the Master said, "though I can guess. It is always so in the rite, when we become the channels for something greater than ourselves. But afterward we are merely human again."

"Not Faris—not yet," sighed Jehan, considering the terrible radiance of her face. "I am married to a Goddess, and all I want is the girl I held in my arms in that cave!" He tried to laugh. For a few moments the two men kept silence in the midst of the revelry.

Then the Master spoke again. "I remember a boy who sat where Faris sits now, with the Jewels of Westria on his body and the god-light in his eyes."

Jehan flinched a little from the Master's keen glance. "I remember a boy who woke the next day," he replied, "weary as if he had borne the whole weight of Westria, not only the Jewels, and knowing only that the glory with which he had been united was gone. And there was nothing between me and despair in that hour, no one who understood where I had been, but one little gray-robed man." He groped for the arm of the Master, who covered the King's hand with his own.

"But at *her* waking she will have you," the Master said.

Jehan felt his heart ease. "Yes. She will always have me." A girl offered them a platter with steaming chunks of roast venison, and Jehan smiled at her and took a piece. He and the Master leaned back against the platform to watch the Festival.

"I had expected Caolin to be here," said the Master after a little while.

"No—he has allowed me a holiday, but he says that the business of the Kingdom must go on, although I think myself that the most important business of Westria is being accomplished here." The King laughed.

"Jehan . . ." The Master shook his head. "You need not always laugh with me. Is Caolin upset by your marriage?"

"Caolin?" For a moment the flames of the bonfires seemed to form the face of the King's friend, bidding him farewell from behind the smiling mask he wore for the world. Strangely, at this moment Jehan could not help remembering times when that face had been opened to him—in the cold loneliness of a mountain cabin, in Laurelynn after the old King had died, and other times. But not recently, not since he had lain with Ronald's arrow sticking out of his thigh.

"I don't think so," he answered reluctantly. "He has given no sign. It's true we are not so close as we once were, but that is natural enough—both of us are older now. He knows that when I have loved someone, I don't change."

"Did you ask him to come?"

"I asked—but I did not want to make him see Faris wear the Jewels." Jehan's voice sank. "That was the first thing I could not share with him, you see, when I became King . . . the thing that he could never understand."

"Be gentle with him now, Jehan. I would be his friend, but I represent the College that rejected him." The Master passed his hand through his thinning hair.

Jehan smiled. "I will. For too long I have left him to hold the helm while I played. Now that I have my foundation, I can begin to pull my weight in the government. Caolin will have the time to play or study, or maybe even find himself a bride."

"That is not entirely what I meant . . ." the Master began, but one of the younger priests came up to them, bowing respectfully.

"Is it midnight already?" asked Jehan. "Well, I know you will be needed to lead the singing, my friend. You must go now." He clasped hands with the Master and watched him follow the other priest through the crowd before mounting the platform and taking his place beside his Queen.

The people drew into a great circle as the white-robed

priests came forward, marching together sunwise around the
fire. Gradually the great meadow grew still, and when all
was quiet but for the crackling of the fire, they began to
sing. The music was majestic, and the singers matched its
beat as they sang.

> We hail thee, brother sun, whose conquering light
> Hath captured for the day so many hours,
> And dance our triumph over dwindling night,
> Surrounded and constrained by daylight's powers.

The melody rose triumphant towards the velvet sky as the
marchers completed one circle of the fire and the first verse
of their song. But as they started around again, a line of
black-clad priestesses approached them, moving in the other
direction around the fire and singing in their turn.

> Think not, oh, man, because the sun is now
> Triumphant, that his power must still increase;
> For it is not in nature to allow
> Growth unchecked, or motion without cease.

The voices of the men confidently replied:

> And yet it is the sun whose burning kiss,
> Touching earth, makes fruitful wood and field;
> Lord of life, by whose bright power it is
> That this world in its beauty is revealed.

The melody with which the women replied was like that
of the men, but moderated with a certain bitter harmony.

> But that same sun whose splendor fills the sky
> At noon, must sink upon the evening's breast
> When the force that lifted him so high
> Has drawn him once more downward to his rest.

From male and female, from white robes to black, the
chorus passed back and forth.

Though he may rest, his warmth enfolds the land
In witness to his power. The barren cold,
Night's offspring, is o'ercome. On every hand
The orchards redden, and the corn turns gold.

The women replied—

Maturity is followed by decline,
And in the eternal cycle of the years,
Earth will sleep in darkness yet again
As the sun's power grows less and winter nears.

The music ceased for a little then, although both groups
continued to circle the fire. Then the women paused in place
as the men sang once more.

If this must truly be, then on this fire—
Sun's image—herbs of fortune let us lay,
And as we make it greater, may this pyre
Retain some power to guard each lessening day.

One by one each man took off his wreath of twined rosemary and vervain, mint and thyme, and threw it into the
flames. As they did so, the women turned to follow them.

Oh, worshippers, fear not, for one thing dies
In order that another may be born.
The sun from his defeat at last will rise
And make the darkest night give way to morn.

The women sang, tossing their own wreaths into the fire.
A little wind fanned the newly fed bonfire and the flames
surged towards the stars. Jehan led Faris down from the
platform, and as soon as the priestesses had finished singing,
the King and Queen came forward, followed by the rest of
the people, to add their own leafy crowns to the blaze. Faris,
laughing joyfully, threw her wreath in a high arc above the
bonfire, where it was caught by an escaping spark so that it
plummeted back into the flames like a crown of fire.
Jehan grinned and sent his wreath to follow hers, then

turned away to lead her into the dance. Caught in the up-draft, his wreath was blown sideways and fell on the edge of the flames, where its greenery slowly shriveled until it flaked into nothingness without having been consumed.

Caolin yawned, winced, and forced himself to sit up. The damp dawn wind brushed goosebumps across his skin and swirled ashes from the remains of the Midsummer beacon by which he had watched since sunset the night before. He took a deep breath and winced again at the complaints of muscles cramped by sleeping on the stone platform and strained by yesterday's ceremony.

Automatically he began the salutation to the sun, then stopped and stretched out his hands to the Mountain.

"Mountain of Power, I salute you, and I claim your strength this day!"

Caolin smiled then, fancying he felt an answering quiver beneath him, and got to his feet. The mist-wrapped lands of Westria stretched north and south, east and west below him, sleeping at the feet of this mountain whose strength was now linked to his. Jehan's mating with Faris was intended to sym-bolically marry him to the land. *But I have touched the land directly,* he thought in wonder. *What will that mean to me?*

The roofs and towers of Laurelynn glittered in the early light. If he started now, he could be there before last night's revelers had started their day.

He had what he had come here for and more. He knew his power; it was time to use it. He had been too long away.

"By the time you reach the other shore it will be day," said the Master of the Junipers, looking across the Bay. Jehan followed his gaze to the blue folds of the eastern hills and the dawn-colored cone of the Red Mountain just visible be-hind them.

"It will be good to be home," he sighed, feeling the accu-mulated weariness of the past two days weighting his limbs. Faris stirred against him and smiled without opening her eyes as his arm tightened around her. The *Sea Brother* butted hollowly against the jetty as the sailors moved about, readying her to sail.

The Master grunted, rose from his place in the bow beside Jehan, and grasped the rail to step back to the dock again.

"You are sure that Faris will be all right?" said Jehan.

The unnatural vitality had left her with the coming of day, and she had ridden from the Grove to the shore like one in a trance, doing as she was bid but making no reply.

"Let her sleep—that's what I will be doing." The Master's worn face creased as he smiled down at the King. He looked familiar and friendly in his old gray robe, and Jehan reached out to him.

"You would be welcome at Misthall."

"I know, and perhaps in a few days I will come to you. But for now"—the Master turned to gaze at the Mountain from which they had come—"I need to spend a few days at Juniper Cottage." He gestured towards the brightening slopes where lay the only bit of land that Jehan had ever heard his friend call home.

"I have never been there," said the King. He wondered suddenly what the Master of the Junipers did when he was not helping other people deal with their lives. Were there those who gave him comfort? Were there things he desired? Jehan glimpsed the dark figure of the Mistress of the College waiting among the trees and thought that perhaps she knew the answers to those questions.

"Perhaps the next time you cross these waters, it will be to visit me," said the Master. Jehan smiled, then shivered in the freshening wind.

"My Lord, we are ready now." Austin of Seahold bowed before them.

The Master jumped back to the dock and waved as a ribbon of water widened silently between them. Jehan waved back, then his arms tightened once more around Faris and he turned to face the sun.

Sunlight barred the worn tiles of the floor in Caolin's office and gilded the edges of the papers stacked on his desk. He had washed away the dust of his journey and changed to fresh robes, but some lingering tension kept him from sitting down to the work that awaited him there. He paced nervously to the window, glanced at the courtyard below, and stiffened as something that looked like a large dark dog trotted through the gate.

Gerol! Caolin peered through the wavy glass, then smiled just a little as he saw Ordrey riding in with someone whose head was hooded and whose hands were bound. He moved slowly back to his desk and sat down, feeling the tension leave him to be replaced by a great certainty that he had indeed tapped into the force that powered the universe. For he knew who that prisoner had to be.

He was sitting at his desk, seemingly absorbed in the work before him, when a timid knock disturbed the door and a clerk answered his summons.

"Tell Ordrey that I will meet him in the lower chamber of the Keep in fifteen minutes' time," he said as the woman was still opening her mouth. The mouth slowly closed; the faded eyes above it rounded with wonder. The clerk hesitated, then nodded and slipped from the room.

Now she will tell her friends that I am a sorcerer, thought Caolin wryly, then sobered, realizing that it was true.

"Well, my Lord, it took a long time, but I have had good hunting at last."

Caolin folded his arms and frowned at the man who slumped in the chair before him. His hair was matted and his clothing torn and splattered with mud. The bound hands seemed thin beneath their grime. All in all, this Ronald was a very different creature from the man who had accosted Eric on the road to Lord Theodor's Hall.

"A sorry prey to have given you such a chase," he said to Ordrey. "Where did you find him?"

"In a midden—no, truly!" Ordrey added as Caolin laughed. Ordrey was thinner too, but his pale eyes sparkled. "He had been hiding in a borderer's barn, and when he heard us breaking down the door, he leaped through the nearest window, which happened to be above a dung heap. It had been raining, and the pile was deep, and besides, Gerol was waiting beyond it. We had to sluice the poor man thoroughly before we could stand his company—it did not improve his beauty, I fear."

"It seems an appropriate way for him to end," said Caolin. "You say you found him on the border of the Ramparts? Then he did not go to Normontaine."

"If he did, he didn't stay there long." Ordrey shrugged. "He hasn't told me much, though I suggested that it might be easier to talk to me than to you."

"He should have believed you," said Caolin softly. He placed a finger beneath Ronald's chin and lifted it until the man must meet his eyes. The prisoner's face was pale and as thin as the rest of him now. He was sweating already and began to tremble as Caolin held him, but he could not move his head or withdraw from the Seneschal's gaze.

"I have done nothing," he whispered at last. "What are you going to do to me?"

"If you have done nothing, you have nothing to fear," said Caolin pleasantly. "I would like to help you."

"I'm the Lord Commander's cousin, and I have my rights!"

Caolin straightened and turned away. Rights! This wretch prated of his rights as loudly as Brian himself . . . as if the world owed him something for having been born. He heard Ronald's breathing grow a little ragged and came back to him.

"I know who you are," he said soothingly, "and it's my duty to see that you get what you deserve. But you must be frank with me. There are several points about the past few months that I find hard to understand." He smiled.

Ronald swallowed and attempted to smile in return.

"We know already that you shot the arrows that wounded Lord Theodor and the King," Caolin went on without a tremor, though he was seeing again Jehan's blood bright upon the grass. A pulse began to pound in his throat. "That's a terrible crime, you know—to harm the King. If you want mercy, you will have to be very cooperative from now on."

Ronald stared back at him like a trapped bird.

"Did you bribe the outlaws to attack Lord Theodor's war party on the way to Greenfell? Why?" Caolin asked suddenly.

Ronald muttered unintelligibly. Caolin gestured to Gerol, who padded forward with his muzzle wrinkling in a silent snarl.

"Yes—yes, I did!"

"But why? What could you hope to gain?" repeated Caolin.

"Theodor is a hard man, and Sandy a young fool. I was their own cousin and next heir, but they never gave me my rights. I lived like Theodor's poorest liegeman. Theodor does not deserve the Province—if he and his son were gone it would be mine! But I swear I never meant to hurt the King!" moaned Ronald.

"It is a pity you cannot prove that, friend." Caolin paced towards the door, then turned suddenly. "And what about the gold? You say yourself that you are not a rich man—where did you get the money to bribe those vermin?"

Ronald started violently and stared at the Seneschal.

"You just admitted that you bribed them. Where did you get the gold? From someone in the south, perhaps? From someone who would just naturally put his money in a Sanjos bag?" Caolin drew a suede pouch from the breast of his robe and dangled it before Ronald.

Brian . . . the name pounded in his head until he thought that Ronald must hear it. He must speak! As long as Jehan refused to blame Brian for the incident at Santibar, Ronald was Caolin's only weapon against him. The man's life was forfeit in any case—why could he not make himself useful and give Caolin the proof he needed to break Brian's pride?

But Ronald was shaking his head. "It was my own money," he repeated. "I did not mean to hurt the King!" His lips closed like a miser's strongbox and he hunched back in his chair.

The Seneschal regarded him silently, but Ordrey, who had been lounging against the wall, stood up and began to grin as Gerol did when the table scraps were being cleared. Ronald looked from one to the other and grew pale.

"I've told him already, my Lord, that if he didn't talk to me on the journey, and he wouldn't talk to you when we arrived, you might let me try to persuade him."

Ronald's eyes closed and his color became something nearer gray.

"You see, he remembers," Ordrey added happily. "Is it time?"

Caolin looked at him with distaste. Not for the first time, he wished he had the ability to force rapport—but it was not information but a confession that he wanted now. He could rule minds like Ordrey's or Margit's, but they were willing tools. Breaking Ronald's resistance mentally might break his mind.

Unless his life had been made such a burden to him that he would consider Caolin a deliverer.

Images chased one another through Caolin's memory—Jehan's face as the Master dragged the arrow from his thigh . . . the face of another prisoner after Ordrey had "persuaded" him . . . Brian's scornful smile.

His fingers twitched and he clasped his hands, remembering how power had flowed through them on the Mountain. But power was useless if not used.

"You must not be rough with him, Ordrey. I have business elsewhere now. Perhaps you could help him consider the matter until I return." Impassive, he met Ronald's relieved smile and Ordrey's understanding grin.

The door behind him closed on Ronald's first astonished gasp of pain, and Caolin found the Red Mountain, seen through the long windows of the staircase, obscurely comforting as he returned to his Offices to wait.

Jehan raised himself on one elbow to contemplate Faris once more. In the dim light of his bedchamber her face glimmered with an elusive beauty, the clear modeling of her brow and chin belied by the vulnerability of her lips, and her eyes, which might have resolved the contradiction, veiled by the thick lashes that shadowed her cheeks. When they opened at last, what would those eyes say?

Crossing the Bay, Jehan had managed to doze while Faris slept in his arms. But now that she lay in his bed at last, he found himself unable to sleep and unwilling to leave her lest she should wake and find him gone. And yet he felt no impatience. He was content to wait, if need be for ever, till she should come to him.

He heard Farin playing Swangold, the notes as faint and clear as if the wind were singing to itself, and wondered if the boy had found the bench at the end of the balcony, which was his own favorite place here at Misthall. Like the shuttered windows in his chamber, it looked out on fields sloping down to the Bay and across the sweep of the water to the gracious silhouette of the Lady Mountain.

The harping stopped for a moment. Jehan heard voices, then light footsteps passing his own door and going on. He smiled. A small staff kept Misthall for him, and beside Farin and the girl that Rosemary had brought to be Faris' maid, only Rosemary and Sandy were staying here now, waiting for the upcoming Council in Laurelynn. But after the threats with which he had closed his door, he doubted that any of them would dare to disturb him. This time was for him and Faris alone—the time he had been longing for since their aborted tryst in the cave.

Comparing that setting to this one, Jehan's eyes followed the complexities of the embroidered flowers that twined across the green linen curtains of the great bed, then returned to Faris. This was a sanctuary, and she the goddess worshipped here. It only needed candles to reveal her beauty.

Then for a moment he saw her lying still upon a bed of flowers with candles at her head and feet. He held his breath in contemplation, then grew cold as he realized that silver threaded her midnight hair, saw her face pared to an unearthly beauty by pain, and paler than the lilies upon which she lay. He shut his eyes against the vision and groped frantically for the living reality.

His fingers closed on Faris' warm shoulder and he collapsed upon the bed beside her, burying his face in the dark masses of her flower-scented hair. Faris muttered sleepily, turning and folding in upon herself like a flower closing its petals against the dark. Jehan released her then, but it was several minutes before he could lift his face from her hair.

"Oh, my love," he whispered shakily. "With such fancies I will end by waking you myself."

He rolled to the edge of the bed and slipped his feet into the welcome of the sheepskin rug beside it, then padded across the room. His clothes lay tumbled across the chair, but he felt in the darkness of the wardrobe for the familiar folds of a long loose robe that, after having been discarded by his father, had been worn by him till its weave was bare, its blue uncertain, and its shape a mold for his own. He drew it around him, thrust the clothes from the chair, and sat down.

He could just see Faris from here, her long hair spread on the pillow beneath the dim shapes of battling warriors that he had painted on the wall long ago. The picture showed the battle in which Julian the Great had slain the last of the warlords and checked the fires they had loosed upon the world. The figure of Julian, with the Jewel of Fire upon his brow, was fully colored, and the blood of his enemy spilled crimson on the ground, but the rest of the figures were incomplete, some of them mere outlines on the wall.

Jehan remembered that he had been working on the mural just before his father took him on his first campaign, against the barbarians from the Brown Lands to the east. After he returned he had not cared to paint pictures of battles anymore.

He looked across the room, smiling at all the clutter he had never allowed anyone to disturb—musical instruments he couldn't play, sketches of animals tacked to the walls below dusty trophies of weapons. He had been very proud of the graduated set of throwing knives from the Ramparts, and the Elayan group, complete with tasseled assegai. He even owned, in a special case above the fireplace, the barrel and mechanism of a weapon from before the Cataclysm, which was supposed to have projected pellets of metal as one would shoot a bow.

The shelves to either side of the bed held more collections—shells, feathers, rocks from different parts of Westria, and complete or half-made models of boats and buildings and weapons for besieging them—his own work and gifts from people all over the Kingdom. Looking at them, he tried to remember the boy who had retreated to this room to enjoy the luxury of loneliness, dreaming of a distant future in which he would be the greatest of Westria's Kings.

But the Kingship had been closer than he dreamed, and as for the greatness . . . He looked back at Faris, remembering all his wasted hours. *You are my greatness,* he thought. *For you I will be a true Lord of Westria.* His throat ached with words unsaid, knowing that he must not disturb her with them now.

He rose suddenly and went to the work table below the western window, next to the doors opening onto the balcony, and began to search through the books and papers piled there.

Below a sheaf of reports on trade between Seagate and the Corona, which should have been filed in Laurelynn, he found a treatise on the art of the longsword and the blade of a dagger with a broken tang. He came to a book of love poems by Hilary Goldenthroat, smiled, and placed it on top of the pile. But that was not what he was looking for.

On the other side of the desk he found a notebook into which he had carefully bound all the letters Caolin had sent him the first time he went on progress alone, leaving his newly appointed Seneschal in charge in Laurelynn. He ruffled the pages, seeing in the exquisitely formed letters the man who had written them. Even when Caolin was writing about his struggle to get Lord Brian to acknowledge his authority, the handwriting remained as legible as a printed book from ancient times. Jehan thought how fortunate it was that Caolin's detachment had been able to foil his own impulsiveness, especially in the first years after he had become King.

Jehan's hands, sifting through the pile, encountered something hard and drew it out. He adjusted the shutters to give him a little more light. The smoothness of the rosewood case he was holding tugged at his memory. Almost reluctantly he opened it.

The lilac scent that clung to the silk scarf and the letters inside had even now the power to bring back memories. Jehan closed the case without needing to reread the letters, testing, as one feels the gap where a tooth has been drawn, the edges of his old pain.

He remembered Mariana of Claralac as vividly as the lilac scent she had always worn and the words in which she had suggested that if her old husband were given a post on the borders, she would be the sooner freed to become Jehan's Queen.

Is that why I delayed marrying for so long? wondered Jehan, considering how desperately he had loved Mariana and how desperately he had suffered when he understood that she loved nothing of him but his crown.

He put down the case and rested his fingers on a leather-covered notebook beside it, smoothing the nap of the suede back and forth. The only clear memory he retained of the period just after Mariana's betrayal was of the time he caught Caolin trying to smuggle two giggling girls into his bedchamber. As he recalled, he had not taken either of the girls, but he had laughed at Caolin's attempts to conceal them, and the two of them had gone out together and gotten drunk.

And Mariana had black hair too—Sweet Lady, help me!
Jehan shook his head as if he could shake the memory away, picked up the book, and opened it. Except for a few notes on the countryside of Las Costas, it held only blank pages. Swiftly Jehan tore them out, then picked up his writing case and went back to his chair. For a moment he sat, staring at the empty page, then he dipped the pen into the inkwell and began to write.

My beloved, I dare not wake you, and yet there is so much I need to say. Will I ever show you these scribblings? Will I find them useful notes, when, beholding your beauty, I can find no words? Or will I find that after all, none of this even needed to be said?

If I had your brother's gift I would make my longing into music and sing it away. But I can only fumble for ways to explain how you are the light that shows me that there is a future—and that the fear that I may fail you is the shadow that darkens it. Your beauty of body and soul stands surety for the world.

I have shared my body with many—too many, perhaps, if I cannot even remember them all—but how few are those with whom I have dared to share my soul.

There had been Caolin, he thought, and the Master of the Junipers, but since his mother died there had been no woman to whom he could reveal himself as they surrendered to him. Until Faris. But she was so fragile, so vulnerable—he must go carefully.

The fading light made it hard to see the page. Jehan went to the shutters and half opened them. Bars of rosy sunset light added new color to the worn Elayan rug on the floor, slipped between the bed curtains, and glowed on Faris' outstretched hand.

Jehan stared at it, knowing that all reality lay focused there. Blindly he replaced the book and writing case on the table. Then he moved to the bed and with pounding heart bent to kiss Faris' open palm.

The harpstrings flashed and flickered as Farin's fingers moved over them, as though he were drawing from the air not only music but fire. For a long time he had played without words, evoking the silken stillness of the Bay and the perfect line of the Mountain, whose blue slopes shaded imperceptibly to mauve and purple as the sky burst into flame.

Images moved in his mind like great sea creatures beneath the surface of the Bay, sometimes almost breaking into consciousness, then sinking unrecognized into the depths once more.

Farin played without trying to think while the harp sang of a beauty beyond tears.

"My Lord."

Farin's fingers trailed a descending shimmer of strings and

stopped. With an effort he turned from the sunset to the girl beside him.

"My Lord, we have laid out a supper in the hall if you wish to come." She looked at him shyly, her straight brown hair coppered by the sunset, her features in shadow.

Farin remembered vaguely seeing her with Rosemary. She was called Branwen and had been brought south to be Faris' maid.

Supper . . . he focused on her words and realized that his stomach had already responded to them.

"Thank you. Just . . . give me a little longer. I will come."

She looked at him uncertainly, then curtsied and made her way back along the porch to the stairs.

Farin sighed. He had been so close to . . . something. His fingers settled on the strings, kissed from them a minor chord, then a matching harmony. Above the hills he saw suddenly the steady glitter of the evening star.

Melody distilled from his random music, words from his tumbled thoughts, like some spell that only the starlight reveals.

          Oh, Beauty like the evening star—
          Oh, sister soul—however far
          You rise above your earthly twin
          (Bright star without, dark star within)
          Still will I follow you, until
          You blaze upon my breast as well.

XI
The State of Westria

A wind off the river dappled the poplars and rattled the opened shutters of the breakfast room. The Master of the Junipers took a deep breath, savoring the coolness retained from the night just past; the aromatic response of curing grass in the fields around Laurelynn to the first rays of the sun; the heady sweetness of roses climbing the palace walls. The wind drew his awareness outward till the distinction between self and surroundings blurred.

He felt the presences of the others in the room—the clarity of the Mistress of the College; Robert of the Ramparts' solid strength and the wry cheerfulness of his wife, Jessica; Farin Harper's single note in the midst of the others' harmony; Jehan, burning like a torch; and Faris herself, like all the roses in Westria in full bloom.

Her red robe folded like petals around the whiteness of her breast. She was talking to Farin, but she turned to Jehan as a flower to the sun, and the Master was dizzied by the pliant sweetness of her passing glance.

He savored the moment as he had savored the wind, able for now to forget that it was the nature of both to pass.

"Will you have some honey muffins, or some tea?" Jessica's words and the scent of the food brought the Master gently to the present again. Her blue eyes—less brilliant than Jehan's but with the same sweetness—met his with a friendly smile. He wondered if she had noticed his abstraction—it was always hard to tell how much Jessica knew. He reached out for the muffins, took one, and passed the basket to Farin.

"I was just remembering the first time I met Faris—at breakfast in Rosemary's chambers at the Hold," he said.

"Yes," added Farin, "and Rosemary's raccoon made off with the cakes. Did you know she brought that damned owl of hers south?"

"Huw?" asked the Master.

"Who?" said Jessica.

"Exactly!" answered Farin, laughing. "She's collected another menagerie here in Laurelynn. Don't expect her to show up for breakfast until she's fed them all!"

"What's the joke?" asked Jehan from the head of the table. As Farin began to explain, the Master looked past him to Faris again and was stopped by the considering brilliance in the eyes of the Mistress of the College, as if she had laid a sword between them.

"I don't mean to interfere," Lord Robert continued to speak to her, oblivious to the pause, "but naturally Mistress Esther and I work together, and I share her concerns. Perhaps other Commanders would resent the involvement of the College in the affairs of their Marches, but I welcome you."

"If I were to answer you now, we would be talking until the Council begins. I prefer to reserve my explanation until then," said the Mistress.

The Master of the Junipers looked at her with sudden misgiving. In the weeks they had spent on the Lady Mountain, she had said nothing of politics. He remembered with abrupt clarity waking in the still mornings, content to know she was there; the sweet blending of their two voices making a litany of the daily rituals. And he remembered with a deeper wonder the times when they had shared the gifts of the body as well as of the soul—equals bringing to the act of love the stored richness of their lives.

They had talked as he had never been able to talk to her in the days when she was the teacher and he the pupil seeking his way, a dream of youth flowering in maturity. But the conversation had been all of the hidden ways of the soul. She had not spoken of the affairs of the College, and he had been relieved to forget them for a while.

I did not want to ask her, he reflected bitterly. *I was afraid of the answers.* Her dark face was closed to him, her mind impenetrable now.

"Robert, the Council will be on everyone's mind at the feast tonight, and tomorrow will be given over to it entirely—let us at least leave it out of the conversation now!

Faris," Jessica went on, "you aren't eating. Believe me. You will need your strength today."

Faris shook her head. "No, I couldn't now. But don't worry about me—I've gained weight since coming here."

Jessica smiled commiseratingly, but the Master sensed her interest focusing on Faris. "Where have you put it? Shall I help you alter your clothes?" She laughed, setting her hands on her own belly, rounding now as her child grew.

Faris shrugged, embarrassed. "Across the bust, mostly, but Jehan says he likes it that way."

Jessica's glance crossed that of the Mistress, then returned to Faris with a speculative gleam that reminded the Master of a herdsman surveying his ewes. Suddenly he realized what she suspected. It was possible, he thought. The King and Faris had first come together just a month ago, but the Midsummer ritual was known to enhance fertility or hasten it if a woman was near the time.

"I also have finished my meal," said the Mistress of the College. "Let us go to your chambers and you may show me your gown for the feast."

Faris stared at her. Her small acquaintance with the Mistress must still be enough for her to know how uncharacteristic this suggestion was. She looked at the older woman uncertainly.

Awkwardly Jessica pushed back her chair. "I'll come with you." She smiled at Faris and led her out of the room.

Robert had begun talking to Jehan about the Elayan situation. Farin was gazing into space, his fingers tapping out some music only he could hear. The Master sat frowning for a moment, then softly rose and followed the women.

Jessica stopped her questioning and Faris looked up accusingly, face flushed, as the Master came into the room. The Mistress of the College was sitting at the window, disapproval marring the remoteness of her face.

"Is it not enough that I was made wife before the whole College?" asked Faris bitterly. "Cannot Jehan and I wait together to learn what came of it?"

"My poor sister!" Jessica shook her head. "Don't you understand what it will mean to Jehan tomorrow if he can announce the coming of an heir to Westria?"

Faris still looked mutinous. The Master moved forward and took her hand. "If you do not wish anyone to know, I am sure Jehan will abide by your decision—but this would give him such joy."

"But it's too soon. I was sure it was only my stupid stomach again." Faris sighed. "Very well—what must you do to me to find out for sure?"

The Mistress rose. "Lie down and be still. There is nothing to fear." She gestured to the Master. "You may as well assist—you have little practice in this, but you will most likely attend her." Her unspoken thought reached him— *She resists me, but she already knows the touch of your mind.*

Faris looked up at them, lips tightening as fear grew in her dark eyes.

"Lie still," the Master repeated gently, projecting wordless reassurance until Faris closed her eyes. He stood and let his eyes unfocus, breathing deeply until he saw Faris' body veiled in a glow whose muddy red deepened into purple, then cleared to blue as she relaxed.

The hands of the Mistress poised a few inches above Faris' head in a blur of golden light. The Master extended his awareness until he felt her presence. *Madrona,* he named her, *Faris. . . .* Mentally he drew the two together until they touched through him.

The Mistress passed her hands from Faris' crown to her neck, her breast, her stomach, loins, knees, and feet, and the Master's perception deepened until he saw the golden glow of each power point and the energy flowing between them in rivers of light. He had done this himself, to diagnose illness, but not since his student days had he traced the energy flows in someone so healthy.

See, came the thought of the Mistress, *power pulses already around her womb.*

He focused his awareness on the flare of light and stretched out his hands. Radiance pulsed around them, spiraling the womb, brightening as his perception sharpened. He probed deeper, until he came at last to the tiny core of brightness beyond all color, like the light that crowns the Tree of Life, and knew that the seed of life was indeed planted there.

The spark glowed, as yet unaware of anything save that it lived and grew. The Master gazed, aware of nothing but the miracle.

• • •

Sunlight flamed in the glass flagon as Caolin lifted it to pour the second goblet of chilled wine. He had seen Jehan crossing the courtyard. Now he recognized the King's step in the hall and heard the door open, but he continued to pour steadily until, the twin goblets filled to precisely the same level, he turned with them in his hands.

Jehan stood by the window, light blazing from the gold tracery at the neck of his tunic and the brooch that closed it, gleaming on the smooth planes of profiled nose and brow, aureoling hair and beard. For a moment Caolin was dazzled. Then the King moved out of the sunlight to the table and sat down. Shards of light danced in the goblets, and after a confused moment the Seneschal realized that the movement came from the barely perceptible trembling of his hands. Quickly he set the goblets on the table, where the surfaces stilled to pools of shadow once more.

"You are early," Caolin told the King, taking his own seat and reaching for his wine.

"Am I?" Jehan's eyes glowed, though he was no longer in the sun. He indicated the goblets. "I thought you were waiting for me."

"I wait for you always, my Lord," Caolin said quietly.

Jehan shook his head a little, drank deeply, and set the goblet down. "We must plan well for this Council—there have been few so important since I was crowned. At least it will be well attended. They tell me Lord Hakon has dragged himself from his sickbed to come; Lord Theodor will be here by tonight; the other Commanders and the lords of the cities have already arrived." He continued to list those he knew would attend while Caolin reached for the agenda his office had already compiled and laid it before him. Jehan glanced down the list.

"Presentation of the Queen . . . yes, that must certainly be first." The King smiled.

"They will approve her," said Caolin.

Jehan had risen and was moving about the room, still reading the agenda. "Yes, there can be no doubt about that now." He smiled again.

"After that, the reports from the Estates of Westria," said Caolin from memory. "I'll have copies ready for you." He waited for Jehan's customary sigh of resignation, but the

King had wandered to the stacked coffers at the far end of the room.

"You keep the cities' records here, don't you? They must fill whole libraries! How many years' worth of accounts can you store in this room?"

"Five years," Caolin began, but Jehan had come back to the table.

"Can you tell whether my traveling this past year has had any effects? Are there any changes in the reports, increases in trade?"

"The places you visited certainly reported it, if that's what you mean," said Caolin slowly, watching the King move about. "Trade figures . . ." Automatically his memory transferred the information to his lips while his mind searched the past days for some clue to the King's unusual diligence. Jehan had crossed the room and pulled a map from its pigeonhole, unrolling and rolling it again as Caolin continued. It was a forest map of the Corona. Had the King found out about Ronald?

"You'll have summaries of all this for the Council," repeated Caolin. "Next comes new business, petitions, and the like," he went on before Jehan could ask any more questions.

The King looked at him intently, then began to laugh. "My poor friend. You must think I've gone mad. The fact is, I think I'm just becoming sane. I ought to know these things as well as you do, but I've had all the pleasure of being Lord of Westria, while the labor has been yours. That isn't right, and I mean to make it up to you, Caolin." He laid his hand for a moment on the Seneschal's shoulder, then turned away again.

Jehan is going to be his own Seneschal? For a moment all other thoughts were blanked out by sheer astonishment. Then Caolin recalled other fits of Kingly efficiency and relaxed. This energy was unlikely to last long, but in the meantime . . . Caolin frowned, wishing that the one man whose questions he had to answer had not chosen just this moment to remember his responsibilities.

"I am told that Lord Brian intends to present a petition tomorrow," Caolin said neutrally.

Jehan put down the folder he had been leafing through. "You are 'told'? Is your evidence sure?"

"I am sure he has completed it, at least," Caolin replied.

"The assistant to his Seneschal copied it out for me." He pulled a paper from the pile before him.

"You have a *spy* in Lord Brian's house?"

"I have a subordinate," said Caolin stiffly. "As all the lords of this Kingdom are your men, all the Seneschals and their deputies are mine. It was his duty to inform me of this, as it is mine to inform you." He held out the paper again. "What action will you take?"

"I will hear the petition." Jehan took the paper and set it face down, unread.

"My Lord! Why will you not be warned? Is it dishonorable to feather your arrows until the enemy comes down the road, or to wait for snowfall before you get the harvest in?"

"No . . ." Jehan answered slowly. "But Caolin, it is foolishness to waste those arrows on what may be only the wind in the trees, or to gather the harvest unripe for fear of early storms. Let Brian speak before all the people, and we will know how many follow him. If we strike in secret, secret whispers will call us tyrants—and judged and judges alike will be unheard."

Caolin's eyes fell before the appeal in Jehan's and silently he replaced the copy of the petition in its file. *No,* he thought, *now is not the time to tell the King about Ronald, but it is time to draw from that man a confession that will force Jehan to believe.*

For a moment he longed for the stillness of his temple on the Red Mountain. Since Midsummer he had not found the time to return to it. Coordinating, negotiating, manipulating, he stayed in Laurelynn like a spider caught in its own web and longed for the pure stroke of power that would set him free. Had he imagined that pulse of power? Could he draw it forth once more? Perhaps when next he questioned Ronald, they would see.

Jehan was still waiting for him to reply. "What about the Elayans?" the Seneschal asked softly. "Will they underestimate our strength, seeing us so mild?"

Jehan straightened, head lifting so that he seemed suddenly taller, and his features sharpened. "They will not underestimate *me!*"

The King was not standing in sunlight now, but to Caolin he seemed to glow. *I have been too concerned with my own secrets,* he thought. *What is he hiding from me?* He waited, staring up at Jehan until the grim look was transmuted into a joy so transcendent that the Seneschal must look away.

"I would have waited to surprise you with the others," Jehan said quietly, "but we have shared so many sorrows, more-than-brother, let us rejoice together now. Westria will have an heir, Caolin—I have just learned that already Faris carries my child!"

He knows about the child, thought Faris, seeing Caolin's eyes turn from Jehan to linger on her breasts, so clearly outlined by the clinging green gown. She tightened her grip on Jehan's arm and returned the Seneschal's smile.

Jehan turned immediately. "Are you tired? Do you want to sit down?" Colored lanterns reflected rosy light off the awning that had been set up on the palace lawn on to Jehan's face; brightened the robes of councillors and their families and followers who were the King's guests tonight.

"No." Faris shook her head, torn between apprehension of his solicitude and a need for the reassurance of his touch. The crowds had given them a respectful space, but Faris felt their curiosity like the touch of moth wings upon her skin. Tomorrow they would be curious about the coming child as well. Why had this had to happen so soon, when she was just becoming used to the idea that she was Jehan's Queen? She shut her eyes, reaffirming the golden barrier that kept her safe from the pressure of so many minds.

Jehan looked at her doubtfully. "Perhaps Caolin will get us some wine." They turned, but the Seneschal had gone.

Caolin slipped through the crowd, looking back only once at the two green-clad figures who stood so close together, like an island around which the people of Westria flowed. Still dazzled by the King's radiance, he had seen Faris abruptly as Jehan saw her, as if he *were* Jehan.

But he told himself that to stay talking to them would waste time. He was not at this feast for his own pleasure, but to see and hear—to flatter this one, to draw information from that, to plant a suggestion in the mind of a third, and to test the temper of the crowd before tomorrow's council began.

Expectation strings them like a bow. Even I can feel it, tonight. He breathed deeply, automatically easing his own unrecognized tension as he had learned at the College of the Wise, and veered towards a shimmer of brocade at the edge of the crowd.

The Elayan envoys stood a little apart, Emir Akhbar's dark, deeply lined face impassive, Rodrigo Maclain's fair skin flushed above his red beard, but garbed alike in jeweled caps and flowing robes and guarded by four dark warriors whose plumes towered even above the Seneschal.

"Westria is honored by your presence at the proclamation of our new Queen." Caolin paused before them, searching their faces for the flicker of speculation or contempt that would tell him that Ercul Ashe's careful confidences had reached their target, and they now underestimated the strength of Westria and her King.

"Indeed, there comes a time when every warrior must turn his mind to more pleasant things," the Emir rumbled in reply, but Caolin was watching Lord Rodrigo's eyes.

"My Lord looks forward to receiving the message of your Prince," the Seneschal replied, continuing to smile even when Lord Rodrigo's face told him for certain that the message would be a challenge Westria could not ignore.

Quickly Caolin disengaged from the Elayans and moved onward. It would not do to be seen too much in conversation with the enemy, nor did he want Maclain to realize how he had revealed himself. Caolin caught sight of Sir Eric's brown curls and turned towards them, schooling his features to concern.

"My Lord." Eric looked around and Caolin went on, "I am told that your father is not well. I hope that the effort he has made to come to this Council has done him no harm."

Eric's surprise faded and he shrugged helplessly. "He is very tired, but he would come. He tells us he will be in his seat tomorrow if we have to carry him there."

Caolin shook his head. "I had hoped that the session would be uneventful, if only for your father's sake. But I am told that Lord Brian intends to present a petition. Of course I don't know what it says," he went on as Eric's face grew red.

"I can guess." The young man shook his head. "It will enrage my father, but he will never listen to me if I ask him to stay away."

A clarion announced that supper was to be served, but

Eric was still in the same place, scowling darkly, as Caolin slipped away.

"Will you come to my father?" Eric asked anxiously. "He wants to attend the Council tomorrow, and he is very ill!"

The Master of the Junipers looked up from his dinner, feeling the young man's concern but finding it difficult to reassure him. He had seen the old lord of Seagate when he arrived in Laurelynn and had recognized mortal illness in his face.

"Indeed I will visit him. It's been long since we talked, and I can easily forgo the rest of this feast. I promise nothing, Eric, but I will do what I can." Beyond Eric, he saw Farin with Sir Andreas and Holly of Woodhall. Randal of Registhorpe and his new lady were close behind. "Go with your friends now, Eric. Your father would not wish you to miss the feast."

Eric tried to smile. "Indeed, in these past weeks he has often told me I am like a dog with one sheep to guard and has sent me from his room."

The Master saw Eric join the others and then started towards the wing of the palace where the Seagate party had been lodged. He skirted the crowd, climbed the grassy slope beyond the long table, stopped as a shadow stepped from among the fir trees that edged the lawn.

For a moment the Master's neck hairs prickled—knowing more than most men about what things might come in shadow form, he had both more and less to fear. Then he recognised low laughter and the glint of silvered hair as the Mistress of the College put back her gray hood.

"Madrona, must you hover like a spirit of the night? I would have thought to find you at the High Table."

"Night is my Kingdom. Some things are clearer in darkness than by day."

His skin chilled. Not so long ago she had joined with him in service to the Lady of Fire, but she was totally a priestess to the Wisewoman now. He repressed a shiver. A man might court the Maiden and mate with the Mother, but the Crone knew all the secrets of death and darkness, and only the Sage could deal with Her on equal terms.

The Master looked away. With an effort he forced calm into his reply. "Sir Eric of Seagate asked me to visit his father. I think that he is right to fear for the old lord if tomorrow's Council goes ill."

"Lord Hakon will live yet awhile. It is the woman you diagnosed this morning who should be your concern."

"Faris?" He looked at the Mistress in astonishment, then down to the table behind which Faris and Jehan were enthroned like a tapestried King and Queen. "You yourself said that she was in perfect health."

"While you were contemplating the mystery of life, I was examining the vessel that bears it," she said tartly. "Faris may be with child, but her responses are those of a half-awakened maid."

"But that will come. Many young wives—"

"Look at her," the Mistress interrupted, "leaning on her husband's shoulder, hanging on his every word. Today they hail her as Queen of Love, they will hail her as Mother tomorrow, but when will they hail her as Lady of Westria?"

The Master shook his head. "What do you want of her? What do you want of me? Faris is harnessed already to Westria; do not make her draw that load before it is necessary. She will have little enough time to play."

"Go back and learn your catechism." She leaned forward and whispered the name he had borne when he first entered the College, the name that perhaps only she remembered now. "If Faris were 'any young wife' her maturity would be no concern of yours or mine. I said that she was not ready, but not one of you would listen to me." The Master saw the gleam of her eyes as she stared at him.

"The King of Westria stands for all the people of this land, but his Queen must be able to act for the land itself! She receives his service, but she must be his steady reservoir of power, otherwise the Great Marriage is a sham, no matter how impressive the ritual has been. You are her teacher— you must make her understand!"

"No!" He shook his head in revulsion, remembering how he had stripped Faris' soul in order to teach her the need to guard it. His own oath barred him from attempting such a violation again. "I awakened her soul," he said hoarsely. "Her body is Jehan's."

"Do you wish it was yours?" The voice came softly as if the darkness whispered those words. The Mistress of the College withdrew into the shadows once more.

The Master stood, fighting outrage, fear, and then a hysterical impulse to laugh. "Madrona?" he whispered finally in a strangled voice. "Old woman! Are you envious of what you threw away?" he cried out suddenly. But there was no reply.

"My Lord . . . Jehan . . ." Faris pressed her face against his shoulder and felt his lips brush the top of her head.

"Are you sleepy, my love? Soon they will let us go." He tipped up her face, kissed her forehead, her cheek, and then, very slowly, her lips. Around them other couples sat close, listening to singers from the Ramparts twine a love song in close harmony.

"I will be ready," she whispered, "whenever it is right to go." She felt the familiar sweet lassitude relaxing her as his arm went around her again. Her mind shied from memory of the ceremony in which Jehan had made her Lady of Westria. She knew that he was disappointed because, afterward, her passion did not match his. But she did not want that ecstasy that stole the soul away, only the safety of his arms around her and the awareness of his joy.

"Tonight," she whispered, kissing the palm of his hand. "Tonight."

A hunting owl called once, then slipped by the tower on silent wings. In the basement chamber, covered lamps glowed dimly in niches in the walls, casting shadows that seemed darker than if there had been no light.

"I have been patient with you, Ronald," Caolin said softly. The prisoner's hand moved wonderingly across the velvet of the cushioned chair. Caolin peered into his eyes, saw them beginning to dilate, and held the goblet to his lips again. Ronald drank greedily. The Seneschal had chosen a wine heavy and sweet enough to cover the taste of the drug he had mixed into it and to dull the prisoner's pain.

"My Lord," croaked Ronald. "I have told you what I could. Don't let him hurt me again."

"He will not touch you." Caolin had sent Ordrey away and Gerol as well when he saw how the captive's eyes followed every move the wolf made. He set the goblet back on the table.

Ronald grinned foolishly, triumphantly, but the oblivion he expected did not come. Caolin hoped he had mixed the right dose. When the man was so weak, it was hard to tell what would be enough to loose tongue from will without loosing spirit from body as well.

"We will talk instead," he said pleasantly. "I need clever people to help me, people who have been passed over while foolish men sleep in silk. I know how that feels, Ronald. When I came here, I was only a clerk, and people who could scarcely write their names jeered at me because I would not swing a sword."

"Clever . . . I'm clever," mumbled Ronald. He looked up at Caolin. "I should be Lord Commander of the Corona, you know."

The Seneschal nodded. "Of course. All you needed was some money, and when Lord Brian gave you that gold . . ."

Ronald shook his head, and Caolin let out his breath again as the man went on. "The gold was to get the Coronans to talk about independence from the Crown. The outlaws were my idea, I thought—" Ronald choked and stopped.

Caolin had moved away and was pouring himself a cup of wine. "It's all right, Ronald," he said gently. "I already knew where the money came from. If the outlaws killed Theodor, that would help you, and it would help Brian if they killed the King." With an effort he kept his voice steady, his body still. There was a long silence.

"No . . . it was not that way . . ." The words dragged from Ronald's lips. Caolin stole a glance and saw that the prisoner's eyes had closed. "I could not control the woodsrats once they had taken my gold, and I thought that perhaps it would be better that way. The King did not like me. He would never have made me Lord Commander. Brian would have supported my claim as I supported his cause. But Brian was too soft to do what had to be done. I did it for Brian, but Brian did not know!"

Caolin's fingers clenched on the silver goblet until the slender stem bent. He recognized the ring of the truth. He too knew someone who was too soft to do what had to be done.

Brian had begun by teasing a nameless clerk, had protested Caolin's low birth when the new King proposed to make him Seneschal, had sneered at him or ignored him at every turn. He would end by challenging Jehan's own right to the throne. Whether he had conspired to kill the King or not, Brian must be implicated now.

Caolin sighed and touched a taper to one of the wall lamps, then to the unlit candle that stood on the table. Then he slid off his Seneschal's ring.

"Ronald," he called softly, turned the man's face to the flame. The prisoner's eyelids quivered, and he moaned. "Ronald, here's something pretty—open your eyes to see." The ring focused the flame to a ruby glow. Ronald's dull eyes moved towards it, remained there as Caolin kept up a stream of commands. "You see nothing but the light, Ronald. You hear nothing but what I say. You will speak the words I tell you now . . .

"My name is Ronald Sandreson. Say it." Caolin waited tensely as the man whispered his own name.

"Lord Brian gave me gold to kill the King." Caolin visualized his will as a glowing rod extending to pierce the other man's soul. *Say the words!*

"Lord Brian . . . gave me . . . gold . . ." The voice faltered. Ronald's breathing rasped the still air. Caolin left his ring on the table and gripped the man's face between his hands.

"Say the words!" Will and voice thrust through the link between their minds. "—gold to kill the King!"

He felt Ronald's head twitch between his hands, and the eyes that had been fixed on the ruby lifted to his own. *Speak!* Caolin stared as if he could see through Ronald's eyes into his very soul.

"Lord Brian . . . Brian . . . my Lord!" The anguished whisper grew suddenly clear.

Caolin trembled with frustrated fury, holding Ronald as he had held to his altar on the Red Mountain. And as if that thought had released a force greater than his own, he felt rage flare from his feet to his fingertips. Ronald's body jerked, convulsed again and again, and Caolin felt in his own flesh the echo of his victim's pain and the final moment of release in which the pain became an ecstasy.

After long, silent moments Caolin realized that Ronald was dead and very gently laid him down. He looked at the slack face wonderingly. Had his ritual on the Mountain done all this? After so many years in which he had felt nothing, the spirit of the Red Mountain had touched him, and now the death struggle of this fool—this fool who yet had died without betraying his master.

Did you love him? he asked silently. *I could forge a confes-*

sion in your name, but I will let your fate remain a mystery. You were at least a loyal fool. And what am I? he wondered suddenly. What am I?

He sat down by the table and picked up his goblet, but he found that he could not drink. Instead he rested his head in his hands, and so Ordrey found him when he came, some hours later, to tell the Seneschal that it was dawn.

The early morning light had a unique purity, unfiltered by the dust of the day, and soft enough so that one could see things in their true colors without squinting against the sun. But it could be a pitiless purity, thought Jehan, peering into the glass to see if last night's celebration had indeed left a puffiness around his eyes. He picked up a towel and began to rub at his hair, still wet from his swim in the lake that was the heart of Laurelynn.

A ghost of a headache reminded him that he had done due homage to Lord Hakon's gift of Seagate wine. But a sense of ease in his body brought back even more pleasant memories of the night that had followed the feast. His body was content, if not his soul.

Jehan threw down the towel and looked for his robe, then laughed as he realized that even the memory of Faris' sweet yielding was enough to stir new desire, intensified by the yet unfulfilled need for her ecstasy to match his own. He told himself to be grateful for what he already had.

He had asked his sister Jessica whether Faris' pregnancy might account for her passivity and winced, remembering her comments on the way he had hastened Faris into marriage, loosing the wonder of her initiation into womanhood by submerging it in her initiation as Lady of Westria.

"Perhaps after the child has been born," Jessica had ended her lecture. "Give her time, and you will both have your desire."

Mik Whitestreak, who took care of the King's wardrobe in Laurelynn, came into the room with the garments Jehan would wear for the Council today. The King drew on the fine cotton loinguard, raised his arms so that Mik could slip over his head the sleeveless undertunic of white silk ornamented with drawnwork at neck and hem.

It was followed by a full-length tunic of gold silk woven with a pattern of green laurel sprigs, cut fuller than the style was now. Jehan glanced at the emerald velvet Cloak of State draped across a chair, his skin prickling already at the thought of its weight in the summer sun. Fortunately he would do no riding today, and so needed neither boots nor breeches. He slipped his feet gratefully into the sandals of gilded leather Mik held out to him.

"Thank you, old friend, the rest can wait until I've breakfasted. Will you find out if the Queen is ready? That is, if she wants to eat at all!"

Mik's grin answered his own and the old man went out.

Jehan picked up the great jade brooch incised with the circled cross of Westria, which matched the ring that for fifteen years had never left his hand, and pinned the neck of his tunic. The door opened again.

"What does she—" Jehan turned and fell silent as Caolin came into the light, that unpitying light that showed the color drained from his fair skin and marks like old bruises beneath his eyes.

"Well! I thought I had done some carousing, but you look as if you had been through all the taverns in Arena," said the King. The Seneschal's eyes evaded his too swiftly for Jehan to read them, but he realized that they were clear. He caught Caolin's shoulder, pulled him forward, and grasped his other arm. "What is wrong?"

"I . . . was up all night questioning a man who had been badly used . . . and he died."

"Here in Laurelynn? I'll have something to say to the City Guard. But you must not dwell on it," Jehan went on, "the memory will pass. The first battle I was in, I felt everything, but I learned."

Caolin raised his head, and something in Jehan grew very still at the look in his eyes. "You don't understand," said the Seneschal. "It was I—"

"Jehan, I'm ready for breakfast, I'm even *hungry*! And isn't this gown beautiful? Your sister helped me fix it—" Faris drew breath. "I'm sorry, Jehan, I didn't mean to interrupt. Let me wait for you in the breakfast room."

"No," said Caolin. "Interruption is the privilege of beauty."

Somehow he had slipped from Jehan's grasp. He turned and bowed to Faris, and for a moment both men stood still in acknowledgment of the truth of his words. The Queen's tight-sleeved crimson gown was woven with golden roses, cut low across her breasts to display a royal necklace of garnet and gold. But her dramatic coloring and the brilliance of her eyes enabled her to dominate the gown.

"Oh, damn," Jehan said softly. Had he for a moment seen vulnerability in the Seneschal's still face? "Caolin, we must talk about this—maybe after the Council?"

"If, after the Council, we have voices left to talk of anything at all." Caolin smiled. "You remind me—the Council begins in an hour and I still have things to do." His hand brushed the King's sleeve, then he was moving toward the door. "Be easy, my Lord. I am supposed to do the worrying for you!"

"Health and long life to Jehan, King of Westria!"

"Health and long life to Faris, our Queen!"

"Lord and Lady of Westria, all hail!"

Jehan groped for the armrest of the throne behind him, momentarily dizzied by the waves of energy flowing from the people to him. *This is for me,* he thought wonderingly, *not for a poor stand-in for a great King lost too soon, but for the man who has given them a Queen to adore and begotten a child to follow him.*

For once the weight of the Crown, hammered from Ramparts gold and ornamented with medallions enameled with the emblems of the Estates of Westria, did not oppress him, nor did the shepherd's staff he held seem heavier than a sword. He was the guardian of the fairest of all lands, King of a great people, and their belief in him renewed an old ambition to become for them a great King.

At length the cheering died away. Jehan assisted Faris to her throne and was reminded of her radiance when she had first put on the Jewels. He gave silent thanks to the Guardian of Men who had thus rewarded Faris for having consented to become his Queen.

"In the name of the Maker of All Things, and in the presence of the King and Queen of Westria, I command order in this court. Let the business of the day begin!" The Herald's staff rang on the marble pavement.

With a rustle of robes and a last murmur of comment, the seven councillors and the several hundred others—relatives, followers, great landholders from the four Provinces, and Guildmasters from the Free Cities—took their places. For each Estate there was a wedge-shaped section that rose in the fashion of an amphitheater from the circular floor, where smoke curled gently from a perpetual hearth, to the eight-sided walls of the Council Hall.

Behind him Jehan heard the whisperings of his household and holders from his own lands, the Royal Domain, cease as the Herald called the gathering to order once again. The King glanced across the hearth to where Caolin sat at his desk, crimson robe glowing in the brightness from the skylight, fair hair glistening. The Seneschal looked up, and Jehan was relieved to see that though he was pale, he seemed quite self-possessed. Caolin smiled faintly and handed a sheaf of papers to a page to carry over to the King.

Reports—Jehan remembered the agenda and settled back to hear the yearly tally of gains and losses among the population of humans, their animals, and the other kindreds with whom they shared the land.

Lord Hakon of Seagate, as senior Commander of the Provinces, usually reported first. But Jehan saw that Eric's concern was justified. The old warrior lay back in his chair with nothing moving about him but his eyes, while Eric read his report in a voice that gathered certainty as he went on. When the west had reported, came the turns of the south, the east, and the north. Caolin had marked points in the reports where Jehan or one of his officers might want to comment, but there was little that called for questioning.

The King having already given his principal news when he presented his Queen, the floor then passed to the Free Cities, whose place was on the building's southwestern side, for whom Frederic Sachs made a report that the Herald finally had to curtail. Next came Caolin, speaking for the government of Westria, reporting briefly on the status of roads, bridges, foreign trade, and relationships with foreign powers. Most of those present had already noticed the Elayan envoys sitting impassive in their roped-off section, but Caolin's mention of their visit nonetheless caused a little stir. Last came the turn of the College of the Wise, whose Mistress represented not only the College but all priests and priestesses, all shrines, and a link with the Powers who dwelt in Awahna itself.

She rose in her place, waiting a few moments while the silence deepened. Jehan's gaze sought the Master of the Junipers, sitting with other members of his Order in the ranks behind her.

"Fellow-children of this land of Westria . . ." The voice of the Mistress came softly, yet it filled the Hall. "I will not recite facts or figures that you already know. There is little of importance in the world of the spirit that can be described in that way. But I must speak to all of you—and to my own people as well—regarding the role that this College is called to play in our lives."

Jehan thought he saw apprehension on the Master's face and leaned forward, watching the speaker intently.

"My priests and priestesses in the holdings and cities complain to me that men are returning to superstition or fanaticisms from the past and abandoning the rituals of Westria that keep us in harmony with the other kindreds. Lords and holders complain that the College interferes with their legitimate struggle to win a living from the land.

"But I say to you, the only soul that a man can win or lose is his own. If those who are called to the priesthood illustrate their belief with their lives, the lesson will be clearer than any commandment or coercion. Once a ritual becomes a form to be followed, it loses power, but if even one believer walks the path convinced of its truth, its power will endure.

"Look into your own hearts, you leaders of Westria. I will not pass judgment upon you. You will be judged by your own actions, so consider them well!" She gathered her black and white robes around her and sat down.

I must speak to the Master of this. Jehan bit at his lip. *If each man and woman must save his or her own soul, what of their lords? What of the King who is responsible to the Maker for all?*

It was Caolin who signaled to the Herald to proclaim the Council open for new business at last. Jehan watched Brian rise to his feet, deliberately as if a mountain had decided to move. Still shaken by the words of the Mistress, the King did not know whether to be glad or sorry that he did not know what the Lord Commander of the south was going to say.

Lord Brian did not read very effectively, but he did not have to. Copies of the proposal had been passed to each councillor, with a carefully copied list of those who supported it.

"As I understand it," said Caolin, "this proposal of yours is intended to decentralize the Kingdom—to give the Provinces more independence in certain areas, such as relations with those on their borders, and to extend the jurisdiction of the Commanders' courts to cover all except disputes affecting other Provinces?" The others were still checking back over their copies to be sure they understood. Brian nodded shortly.

"But where do you draw the line as to what affects your neighbor and what does not?" asked Lord Robert.

"My Lord of the south and I do not share a border," said Theodor, "so I have not that concern." Laughter was muffled in several places in the Hall. Theodor went on, "But I do have to deal with a foreign power, and I would rather have the weight of a Kingdom behind me than stand alone."

Lord Brian looked down briefly, then turned, surprisingly, to Faris. "My Lady, since you are a strong man's choice, I will credit you with his strength. This Council has always been a place where we might speak freely, without courtly phrases or poisoned compliments"—his eyes flickered in Caolin's direction—"so you must believe that I mean no discourtesy when I suggest that your relationship to Lord Theodor encourages him to support the Crown."

Jehan stiffened, feeling Faris' confusion and fear. He half rose, and Brian sent him a startled glance, but Theodor was already on his feet, his face purple, crumpling his copy of the petition and flinging it down.

"Lady Faris may be too gracious to call that discourtesy, but I am not! Lord Brian, I had heard about your opinions before the King ever came north, and my reaction to them was the same. The strength of Westria lies in unity under a strong King!"

"It depends on how that strength is used. It is well enough when the King is young and honorable, as I believe our Lord to be—"

"You had better!" Eric's whisper was audible across the floor.

"But even when he is," Brian continued as if he had not heard, "the Kingdom is large, and no one man can know it all well enough to be certain of judging rightly all the time. You will say that the King has Deputies to be his eyes and ears, but how shall he know if their reports be true?"

By this time Jehan had gotten his temper under control. He reached for Faris' hand. "Don't be afraid, love—wait, and I will show you how I play the King." She looked at him and smiled, and he wished them back in the cave in the mountains or at Misthall, or even in their bedchamber in the palace.

"I speak for the Free Cities," rumbled Frederic Sachs, smoothing the fur on his robe. "If you ask more freedom for the Provinces, the cities must be protected."

Eric was on his feet now, looking anxiously at Jehan. "My father bids me speak for him." He continued before the King completed his nod, "You say that frankness is a virtue, Lord Brian. Well, I can be frank too. You talk about other people's motives, but what about your own? When your boats came into our fishing grounds, the dispute was settled by the King. If we had been under your new system, what would have judged between us, your sword?" His father was pulling at his arm, but Eric charged on, "Frankness indeed—I could give this kind of talk another name."

"Eric, be still!" Jehan found his voice at last. "Westrians do not challenge each other's loyalty in this Hall." Eric looked at him open-mouthed. Someone tittered and he reddened, but seeing the King's gaze soften, he recovered himself and sat down. Jehan looked over at Brian, holding the man's yellow eyes until some of the fierceness went out of them and he too took his seat.

Then the King rose from his throne and stood before them. "Ladies and Lords—such a question will not be settled by hot words. I hold power by the will of Awahna and of the people of this land and may not lightly renounce it—I am as bound by the law as you. If my people find me blind to their needs, I must strive for amendment. But I will not do so by giving up or delegating my responsibilities. So far I will agree with Lord Brian that power and knowledge should be one, and how shall I judge, or you follow, if I pass all my life in Laurelynn?"

Slowly he paced around the circle, drawing their attention to him, to his words. "Therefore look for me not in my own Hall but in yours. For my Lady and I will come to you, and our children after us, and so we shall rule."

He held them. He knew it by the shining eyes of the people in the ranks above him. He would not relinquish leadership of this Council again. He turned, saw in Caolin's face a mixture of admiration and apprehension, followed his gaze upward to the Elayan envoys.

Jehan's arms twitched as if he could protect his people with his bare hands. *Even from Elaya.* He paused below the strangers' box. Everyone was looking at them now, and he nodded to the Herald to announce them.

Emir Akhbar came slowly down the steps, followed by Maclain.

"I bring you the greetings of my Prince, Palomon Strongbow, head of the House of Ottavie and lord of the confederated states of Elaya. He felicitates you on your marriage and wishes you many children, for the husband of a beautiful wife will wish to enjoy her, and the father of a family to teach his children, unlike young bachelors, who think only of war." His dark eyes paused on Eric's fascinated face. Jehan shifted uneasily, waiting for the insult all this politeness hid.

"And yet young warriors must be kept under control, if fathers of families are to enjoy their homes in peace," Akhbar went on. "In times past the town of Santibar belonged to Elaya. Twenty years ago there, there was a war, and your father, my Lord, put his hand to the treaty of peace, and swore"—the Elayan's eyes grew distant—"*that the town of Santibar and the fortress of Balleor should belong to Westria so long as the border between our lands be well and peacefully kept,*" he quoted.

"My Lords of Westria—" The Emir's voice rang now against the painted timbers of the ceiling, and men's fingers twitched for the hilts of swords they had left at home. "That oath has been broken, and Santibar and Balleor are now by right Elaya's! These are the words of my Prince, and we bid you peacefully accept our claim . . . for if you do not," he added softly, "be assured that we will write you a new treaty in your own blood with the points of our spears."

"You call the treaty broken when five drunken soldiers burn a barn, when the walls of Santibar still bear the scars of your catapults not four years old?" Brian's fist crashed on his table, and Rodrigo Maclain, beard bristling, moved forward.

"The envoys were addressing me." Jehan focused his voice to the knife edge they had taught him at the College, which could be heard through battle or storm. He stared

Brian down, compelled even the envoys to wait on his words. He wished that Faris were not here. He would have to leave her Regent if he went to war.

"My Lords of Elaya," he said evenly, "remember that men fight most fiercely when they defend their homes. Tell your Prince that my marriage but makes me more dangerous as a foe, and reconsider what you say." He stood up, the step on which the thrones were set allowing him to look down on them, and grasped his shepherd's staff. "While the men and women of Santibar wish to remain Westrian, I will not betray them."

Jehan looked around him, seeing anger, apprehension, or excitement in the faces of his people, and knowing to what he committed them if the Elayan challenge were no bluff. "I have offered reparation to the man whose barn was burned, but I have had no answer," he added slowly. "Therefore to the south I will send an embassy, to see this man and have his story from his own lips, to question the accused soldiers and send them to me for judgment, and to hear from the people of Santibar their will." He avoided Caolin's eye, but he could see the forced stillness of the Seneschal's hands.

He turned to his right. "My lord Brian. You desire to take care of your own. You, therefore, shall head this embassy and face yourself whatever your deeds have wrought." Something broke like a snapped twig in the silence that followed. Jehan watched Brian pale and redden, then go pale again as he bowed his assent. "Lady Elinor of Fairhaven shall go with you." He named three others, all well known and respected in peace as well as war.

"Tell your Prince what has passed today, and if you will, send wise ones of your own to join my embassy. The people of Santibar shall decide, and their decision will be backed by all the swords in Westria!"

As the echoes of his words died the King grew still; a vigilant stillness, which held the Elayans silent as they bowed and withdrew, held even the Westrians, until the Herald had declared the Council closed.

Jehan drew a deep breath, trembling now that it was over, and reached out to Faris. She came into his arms and he held her as if he could draw strength from the thing that his strength was meant to guard.

Beyond Faris he saw Caolin stacking the papers on his

table and packing them into a portfolio with swift, precise motions as if he were imprisoning enemies. A pen lay broken beside the portfolio, and Jehan remembered the snapping sound he had heard.

"Caolin, I would rather have consulted with you about the choice of delegates for the embassy, but there are times when one must seize the moment for action."

The Seneschal looked up, his eyes rounding in surprise. "My Lord, it is your decision—you are the King." His voice was colorless.

"Jehan . . . can we leave?" Faris murmured against his shoulder.

The King looked around him. The council floor was clear, but crowds still milled at the upper doors. *My people,* he thought, *my people who would follow Brian or any loud fool who promises something new . . .* He sighed.

"Soon, my love—this herd would trample you now."

"Young cockerels must crow, but not in royal council halls! I have a mind to whip you like a half-grown boy!"

The Master of the Junipers paused in the corridor, recognizing Brian's angry tones. He had hoped for a word with the Mistress of the College, but she was past him now. He turned towards the voice, wondering who Brian was talking to. The long windows he passed were open to let in the cooling air, and the evening wind was beginning to rustle in the willows outside.

"I am old enough to teach you the meaning of loyalty!"

The Master rounded a corner, saw Eric facing Lord Brian. Both men stood with feet apart, hands open and ready to strike.

"You named me traitor before half Westria—do you think to go unpunished?"

"On the field or off it, you are not the one who will lesson me!"

Brian tipped back his head and gave a bark of laughter. "I may lessen you, however, for all they call you the new champion. Men are wagering on the outcome if we fight. You hope for glory, but you will find humiliation."

Eric quivered like a leashed hound and took a step forward. Brian laughed again.

"Brian! Is this how you repay the King's trust? Eric, do you think the King will thank you for brawling in his name?"

The Master stepped between the two men, stretching to meet their eyes.

"Prayersmith, keep your sermons for your own flock." Brian did not take his eyes from Eric's.

"I am the King's chaplain, and you are both the King's men. Victory for either would bring honor to neither of you, nor would you get any sympathy in defeat."

The silence seemed long before Brian snorted in disgust and stepped away. "Very well, grayrobe, but one day I will face this cockerel on the field with a good blade in my hand!" His head swung back and forth as he glared from the Master to Eric, then stalked away.

"I will be ready, Brian, only name the day!" Eric cried after him. He turned to the Master, the sparkle dying from his eyes. "And he will be the one left lying on the field."

"Save your strength for the Elayans," the Master said tiredly. "They are even more eager to fight than Brian is. Go away, Eric," he added, seeing interest return to the young man's eyes.

Eric flushed a little, bowed, and turned away. The Master listened to his receding steps, wondering if he should go to the rooms where the Mistress of the College had stayed. There were words between them that needed to be unsaid. He went to the window, looking across the gardens to the Guesthall, but the Mistress' window was dark.

He rubbed at his eyes and sat down on the window ledge, hearing now no voice but the lonely sighing of the wind.

XII
The Lord and the Lady

Faris lay against the low rail of the barge and trailed her fingers in the dark water, shattering the reflections of the lanterns into a swirl of multicolored flowers. Petals dropped to add to them from the garlands of red roses on her hair and at her breast. She raised herself, turned back to the boat, and Jehan's arm went around her. She grinned then and flicked her wet fingers so that droplets caught like crystal in his hair and beard.

"For that, a kiss," he murmured, drawing her to him. After a moment he let her go, and she settled into the crook of his arm with a contented sigh, smoothing the gold silk of her loose gown to admire its embroidery of fruit and flowers. For a moment she hardly dared to breathe, poised upon the balance-point of content. *Be still,* she thought, *lest the moment pass.*

"Is everyone comfortable? Do you all have your desire?" the Mayor of Laurelynn asked earnestly, by echoing her thought, destroying it. His dark hair, showing just enough silver for respectability, lay sleeked against his head.

"Indeed, Master Joaquin, Laurelynn has outdone itself. I cannot remember when I passed the Feast of the First People so pleasantly," replied Jehan dryly.

The Mayor's wife stifled laughter as her husband frowned, and pulled nervously at her stiff skirts. She looked older than her husband, perhaps because of her rouged cheeks and the henna with which she tried to cover the gray in her hair. But her gown had the tight sleeves that were now all the fashion in Laurelynn. Faris had not meant to encourage anything so hot and uncomfortable, but she wondered how many would still praise her beauty if they knew of the disfigurement her own sleeve hid.

But surely that did not matter now—she must not allow herself to think of it on such a night as this. She smiled encouragingly at the Mayor's wife, aware of Lady Gwenna's anxiety at playing hostess to the royal party, but it seemed strange to be offering comfort instead of needing it. She heard Frederic Sachs' bray of laughter from one of the other barges across the water—obviously the other guests were enjoying themselves too.

Caolin poured yellow wine into the King's cup and handed it to him as Jehan reached out. Faris looked at the Seneschal under her lashes, wondering how long it would take for her to know what Jehan needed so instinctively. She eased herself closer to Jehan and was rewarded as his arm tightened around her.

"Oh, look—it's a deer!" Rosemary's exclamation focused all attention on the lake, where rafts bearing large lanterns in the forms of plants or animals were being poled across the glittering waters. They floated among the barges and then along the shore, where the people of Laurelynn were gathered. Beyond the lawns that sloped down to the lake the windows of the city glowed.

"Indeed, my Lady, like everyone else in Westria, we open the gates of the city on this night, but it is so rare for any of the other kindreds to accept the invitation that we make these toys to show the children what the Festival means," Master Joaquin explained.

"You should let Rosemary invite them for you," said Farin. "She keeps the Festival all year round. You've collected a family of quail and a lame coyote cub since you came to Laurelynn, and of course you have that damned owl!"

"Should I refuse my help because I am no longer at home? All my doors are open tonight, and if the animals stay with me, it will be because they so choose!" Rosemary turned to Master Joaquin again as Farin picked up his harp and plucked a trill like the call of a bird.

"I expect that Laurelynn has too many people for the other kindreds to feel at home here," she told the Mayor. "The Hold is a way above the town, and so we never know who our visitors will be. One year a great boar came down to our pig barns and sired a new breed on our sows."

"Has Gerol gone to keep the Festival?" Jehan said to Caolin.

The Seneschal smiled. "When the moon rises, listen and

you will hear music from the hills. Gerol goes to sing with his pack each year, but he has never told me the meaning of the song."

Farin plucked a series of chords. "In the north we have legends about humans who have gone to the hills on Festival night. When someone is missing from his or her bed the next morning, we never ask where they have been, but the old women are careful to examine the children born at Beltane."

"But why?" asked the Mayor's wife, wide-eyed.

"To see if any of them have pointed ears, or a skin that glows green in the sun!"

Even as she laughed Faris found her arms moving to shield her belly.

"Don't worry," said Rosemary, "your baby will be born in March!"

Faris smiled and shook her head. If the child had been conceived at Midsummer, more than the kiss of a wood sprite had gone into its making. But she remembered only the dreadful sense of loss with which she had awakened, merely human once more, to realize that she remembered only fragments of the ceremony that had mated her to Jehan. Was the child indeed hers, or was she only a vessel to bring it into the world?

All you Powers of light and darkness, be far from me! she prayed. *Give me no dreams, no ecstasies that set adrift the soul. Let me only be human, and in love, and Faris.*

Jehan's face shone like one of the torches; his eyes gleamed like the stars sewn on to his blue robe. He set his hand gently over Faris' belly, then looked back at the others.

"I only wish I could have offered more today," he said softly. "I have been given so much. I have a wife and Lady for my heart." He turned then and grasped Caolin's hand. "And I have my mind's twin—so much more than friend, and the child who will be my first-fruits, born to the service of Westria."

Lady Gwenna's fingers flickered in the sign to avert ill luck, and Rosemary stretched out her arm and tipped wine from her goblet over the side.

"May the Powers accept our offerings," Rosemary said softly, "and not grudge us the achievement of our desires."

Her eyes moved involuntarily towards one of the other barges.

Faris knew she was thinking of Eric and wondered what could change the reproachful devotion with which he served his Queen to love for the girl who loved him. If only everyone could be happy tonight!

Her gaze moved on to Caolin, who sat looking into his wine cup, his face unreadable, his hand passive beneath that of the King. In the north he had seemed as finely tuned as the instrument he played for them. Now, though his dress was still meticulous, he had a faintly ragged quality, as if his flesh were no longer so neatly fitted to the spirit it housed. She let her awareness expand to include him, drew back in surprise as she felt the blank surface of his shield.

Did he accept what Jehan had said? What did he think of her? Once it had seemed that Caolin was going to court her like the rest, then he had seemed almost hostile. But tonight he had left off his brittle mask, and she began to understand why Jehan cared for him. *Let nothing change that. I would not have Jehan lose anything because of me.*

"Caolin—" Impulsively Faris drew the wreath from her head, plucked two white roses from Jehan's wreath, and worked them in among the rest and held it out to him. "We all have flowers tonight except you. Wear this wreath—see, I will take the flowers from around my neck and wear them so we shall be all alike."

Caolin looked up at her then, his gray eyes darkening, holding hers. Then he straightened. "My thanks, Lady. Few can boast of having received such a crown from such a Queen." He took her hand as she reached across Jehan, and she felt the cool touch of his lips on her palm before he settled the bright roses on the gold of his hair.

"You are fortunate indeed, my Lord," said Master Joaquin. "My lord Caolin will keep good watch while you and your Lady travel in the Provinces." He bowed towards the Seneschal, whose eyes gleamed sardonically for a moment as he nodded in return. Loud laughter and a splash told them that someone had missed his step in getting from one of the other barges to the dock. Now other barges were turning towards shore.

Jehan nodded. "The time for celebration has been well spent, but it is the season for work now. The harvest will be starting, and I must keep the promise I made in the Council Hall."

"Then let these last moments of pleasure be spent well," said Caolin softly. "I remember the first time I heard my Lady Faris sing . . . if she is willing, let her sing again."

Startled, Faris looked from Caolin to the others. Farin grinned. "I have done my part of the entertaining this evening, now it is your turn. Sing, Faris, and I will play for you."

"Please," said Jehan. His eyes burned like blue stars.

"Very well," she answered slowly, trying to recapture the words she remembered her mother singing long ago. She cleared her throat and began, so suddenly that she had finished the first verse before Farin caught the tune and began to accompany her.

Where shall the flower turn, if not to the sun?
Where shall the river run, if not into the sea?
Where shall the leaf fall when summer is done,
If not to earth's bosom? And so it is with me—

For if I sing sweetly, it is because you hear;
If I have beauty, your seeing makes me fair;
If I know laughter, then you have banished fear,
And if I am fruitful, it is your seed I bear.

As you have chosen, so will I decide;
The same path that you tread, my feet will follow still.
Where you are dwelling, there will I abide—
Oh, my beloved, I wait upon your will!

She finished and sat with bent head while Farin rounded out the ending with a series of descending harmonies and a final chord. She could feel approval from the others, and from Jehan, passion that built like a climbing wave.

The music ended. Faris looked up at Jehan and shut her eyes against what she saw in his face. His hands closed on her shoulders; he pulled her to him and her lips opened beneath his as he bore her back amid the cushions.

Her body yielded to his as if in illustration of her song, and yet some separate compartment of her mind was noting the changed motion of the barge as it followed the others towards the shore, the gentle bump as it reached the dock.

There was a short silence, then a rustle as the others rose and made their way to the side.

"We thank you, Master Mayor, for a most memorable evening. Since this is the King's barge, I think it will be no discourtesy if we leave before he does," Caolin said blandly. Feet echoed on the dock, and Faris heard a shocked giggle from the Mayor's wife.

Jehan's lips released Faris at last and he began to trace the line of her throat. She turned a little to accommodate him and saw Caolin, silhouetted against the stars.

"Good night, my Lord . . . my Lady," he said softly. Faris fought an impulse to laugh—had Jehan even heard? There was a faint sigh, then a light step on the dock, and Caolin, too, was gone.

Jehan had pulled down the loose neck of her gown, imprisoning her arms and baring her breasts to the warm night air. As his hands moved over her body Faris breathed deeply of the scent of crushed roses and felt the familiar sweet lassitude unstring her limbs.

Her heart pounded as the ceremonial drum had pounded in the Sacred Wood. She flinched from the heat of the sacred fire. She felt a pressure against her mind as Jehan's body possessed hers, and grew still in his arms, knowing the Power that waited to overwhelm her if she opened her last defense.

Oh, my beloved! Her body waited on his will, but her spirit remained barriered. She felt his longing as he held back, seeking to kindle her with his own flame, but in such a blaze they could both be consumed. In that mating of god and goddess Faris and Jehan would be whirled away like sparks upon the wind, and she refused to be used in that way again.

She moved in Jehan's arms, and he cried out, holding her fast within the tempest of his love. When he grew still at last, she worked her arms free of her gown and held him, murmuring his name.

"Jehan!" Caolin turned abruptly, brushing the Queen's wilted wreath from the table to the floor. "Is something wrong?"

The King shook his head as he came forward, running his finger along the backs of the leather-bound volumes in the bookcase, touching the velvet of the drapes Caolin had just opened, as if he expected them to have changed since the last time he had visited Caolin's chambers more than a year ago.

"I didn't know if I would find you still here," Jehan said at last.

"There's little point in going to my offices until my staff has had time to recover from the Festival," Caolin replied dryly. That was not really true—he rather preferred working alone, but he did not wish Jehan to know that he had slept badly, haunted by the scent of roses.

Jehan looked around him, noted Gerol stretched snoring on the hearthrug with a streak of mud along his side and burrs in his plumed tail.

"He appears to have celebrated rather thoroughly too," the King said ruefully, then met Caolin's eyes. "I'm sorry! I didn't mean for you to have to end the party for me last night. It was the wine, perhaps, or the Festival—" He shrugged helplessly. "I have no reason to hide my feelings, but my control is usually better than that!"

Caolin looked at him curiously. Jehan had never concealed his passions before—why was he worrying now? "It's all right. They all understood."

"I wish *I* understood!" Jehan tried to smile, the beautiful bone structure of his face highlighted by the clear morning light. "What Faris and I have now is all that any man should desire, but if we ever join completely, all Westria will shake!"

"My dear Lord, you should be saying this to your wife, not to me!" said Caolin uncomfortably, picking up his belt and drawing in the full folds of his mulberry-colored robe, but his heart kept saying, *Whenever I turn to you, she is there between us now. What is it you want from her that I could not give you, my Lord?*

The King laughed, and Caolin realized that the moment when he might have asked him such a question had gone.

"Actually," said Jehan, "I wanted to talk to you before I leave Laurelynn this afternoon. Brian has not returned from Sanjos, and people are preparing for our visits throughout the Ramparts. I cannot wait for him. I fear you will have to instruct the Embassy we are sending to Elaya."

"Appoint someone else to lead it and your problem will be solved."

"I was afraid you would not like my choice." Jehan

sighed. "But I would rather occupy Brian with a real problem than leave him to invent one while I am elsewhere. If I give him what he thinks he wants, he may change his mind."

Caolin made a sound that was not quite a laugh. "If the Red Mountain fell on his head he might notice. Otherwise . . ." He shook his head. "Well, I will do my best."

"You are the diplomat—I would depend on your advice in this in any case."

"Perhaps, but do you think Brian will be willing to do so?" Caolin asked.

"He will have to." Jehan grinned suddenly. "Caolin, you must be mellowing—we have been discussing Brian for five minutes without an accusation of treachery. Are you waiting to catch Ronald before you go after Brian again?"

Caolin's fingers tightened on the buckle of his belt. *Does Jehan know?*

"Nothing has been heard of Ronald for some time. I doubt we will get any evidence from him now," he said carefully. "I know that you will not suspect Brian until he implicates himself. Maybe he will do so on this trip to Santibar—I only hope the price of the evidence is not too high."

Another half-truth. Caolin moved to the bureau, picked up the Seneschal's chain of office with its golden key.

"Caolin . . ." Jehan spoke with difficulty. Caolin stilled, waiting for the words that would accuse him. "Caolin, the morning of the Council you came to me with some trouble—we had no time to talk. I did not want to go away without giving you a chance . . ." His voice died away.

Does he know? Caolin asked himself once more. *Does his heart feel what he will not let his mind understand?* Slowly he turned.

"So much was hanging on the Council—I was too easily upset. It does not matter now. You must not worry about me."

Jehan took his arm, a smile lighting his blue eyes. "You worry enough for two, my friend. Do not work too hard while I am gone, and if you have difficulties, follow me."

Caolin's arm still tingled with the pressure of the King's hand when Jehan had gone. He stood unmoving, staring at the door. *I did not lie . . . I said nothing untrue,* he told himself. *Oh, my Lord, I do not find it easy to conceal my soul from you.*

The bell in the palace tower tolled ten o'clock. Caolin

stirred at last and bent to pick the Queen's wreath from the floor. Something glistened, and he saw tangled among the red and white roses a strand of his own golden hair.

Brian of Las Costas returned to Laurelynn six days after the Royal party had left for Rivered, guarded and provisioned as if he were setting out on campaign. Caolin leaned from the window of his Offices to watch the escort clatter by, wondering which of the Lord Commander's people would have the thankless task of informing Brian that even when the King honored him with a commission, its terms were to be mediated by Caolin.

The next morning, when Brian met with Caolin and the other members of the embassy to Elaya in the small council chamber overlooking the river, the Commander appeared to have recovered from the shock. Despite the open windows and the early hour the day was already hot. Caolin found his fingers sticking to the paper he held and laid it down, considering the other man.

The Lord Commander's face seemed unusually red, and his hair bristled rebelliously from whatever order he had tried to impose on it. Brian looked up, and Caolin let his gaze shift away from the amber glow in the other man's eyes. The fire was only banked, then, not out.

"The King has laid out the purposes of this investigation and asked me to discuss its points with you before you go," he said.

Brian reached for the paper and the Seneschal twitched it back, holding it up. "Copies have been prepared for each of you, my Lords, my Ladies." He gestured to Ercul Ashe, who moved quietly along the table, passing them out.

Lady Elinor slipped a small glass on a chain from around her neck and peered through it at the paper. Ras of Santierra, one of the senior Masters of the College of Bards, leaned back in his chair, moving a dark finger from point to point on the page. Alessandro Cooper, a Guild-master of Laurelynn whose family had traded with Santibar for generations, pursed his lips as he read. Caolin waited as the others looked through their copies, suppressing a smile as he saw Brian's lips silently forming the words.

"As you see, our Lord wishes you to accomplish two things—to find out what really occurred in the so-called

'raid' on Elaya, and to learn whether the people of Santibar
wish to remain with Westria. In addition—"

"Whose addition? I'll grant the first two, for the King has
put his name to them, but I take no orders from you," said
Brian.

"I am sure that our Lord has discussed this matter with
Master Caolin, and I for one would be glad of further counsel now," Lady Elinor said quickly.

"Let us discuss it then, but I warn you I will not be bound
by what he may say."

"I would never expect that, my Lord," Caolin murmured,
slipping his ring of office from his finger and turning it back
and forth so that it captured the sunlight in ruby flares.

"I will only offer suggestions for you to listen to . . . only
listen to what I have to say," he soothed. Brian's glance
fixed on the ring. "There's no need to be upset . . . listen."

"Stop that!" Brian's roar jerked everyone alert. He glared
around him like a hunted bear when the arrows begin to
sting. Caolin kept his face expressionless. Apparently Brian
was sensitive enough to feel that something was being tried,
but too strong to be affected. Unobtrusively Caolin slipped
the ring back on to his hand.

"My Lord of the South," said Kimi of Longbay, lady of
a fishing village in Seagate, "we have no time for this—let
the Seneschal have his say. I want to know how we are to
be certain of what the people of Santibar desire." Her almond eyes flashed.

"Your people are fishers too; you should be able to win
their confidence," said Lady Elinor.

"After I finished at the College, I polished my craft upon
the roads," said Master Ras. "I could arrive separately from
the rest of you and listen to people's comments as I play for
them." They looked at Caolin.

"You speak as my Lord hoped you would," said the Seneschal. "And you, Master Cooper, could find time to talk to
the merchants with whom you trade."

"That's all very well, but all this skulking won't convince
the Elayans. Let the people of Santibar tell me to my face
whether I have been a good lord to them, and then let us
look to our arms!" Brian's tone was surly.

Caolin frowned. Could the man be driven, then, since he
could not be led? "Seek a fight and Elaya will be happy to

oblige—but if the King wished to declare war he could have done so himself three weeks ago!"

"Let them—" Brian began, but Master Ras cut in.

"Our instructions say that we are to report only, to take no action that will commit Westria to any course."

Be quiet, man. Let Brian go on like this and he will condemn himself! thought Caolin, then said, "You are to take your time—gather information, inspect the entire border, delay if you can until the autumn rains begin to fall."

"You would like that, wouldn't you, to keep me away from Jehan while you poison his ears against me. How many other lies have you told in the King's name?" Brian seemed to expand as he leaned across the table.

"In the King's name?" Caolin was startled into response. "I will deal with you in my own name some day!" He gripped the arms of his chair to keep from flinching as Brian rose.

"Don't try me! I could break you, clerk!"

"Lord help your embassy," said Caolin very softly, "if you think you can search out every truth with the point of a sword!"

Caolin heard the scrape of a chair as Master Ras tried to grasp Brian's arm and was shaken off as easily as a bear beats off hounds. He waited, almost eagerly, for his enemy to strike.

But Brian stilled. "No! No—I will not soil my blade." He took a deep breath and sat down again. "I will use your weapons, snake. One day I will find the King alone and tell him what you are."

Caolin looked around the table. The others were beginning to relax, sensing that the quarrel was over for now. He shook his head. *When I have gone to my temple a few more times, I will know how to master you. One day you will learn what I am, Brian, to your cost!*

The remainder of the discussion was subdued and quickly over. Caolin sat still in his place after the Commissioners had gone. *At least Brian no longer discounts me.* He stretched out his arms and flexed his fingers to relieve their tension. *I suppose that is an achievement.*

Ercul Ashe came into the room and set down his papers. "Well, they are on their way."

"I must be on my way as well," said Caolin with a little laugh. "Tell someone to prepare my mare for travel and pack some food. I think I had best ride myself to report on this meeting to the King!"

Rosemary shifted uncomfortably in her saddle. "Oof! I feel as if I'd been riding for a week."

Faris laughed. "No, dear, we spent the week at Rivered, being pampered by Jessica. We left there only three days ago, and we have been riding for only two hours today. If I can bear it, surely you can survive." Her morning sickness had ceased before they left Laurelynn, or Jehan would never have let her ride, and in some ways her health was better than it had ever been. And yet there was something oppressive in the morning despite its brightness, and she understood Rosemary's complaint.

She patted Sombra's dark neck and glanced behind her. Dust rose in a steady haze behind the baggage carts, drifted across the dun-colored fields that stretched to the eastern mountains, shimmering in the heat. To her right the shrunken trickle of the Darkwater coiled through the reeds. She closed her eyes against the glare and shook her head a little, trying to clear it.

Hooves clattered behind them. It was Philip, the oldest child of Robert and Jessica, who was Jehan's new squire. He handled his responsibilities remarkably well, Faris thought, although his behavior alternated disconcertingly between that of boy and man.

The black mare tossed her head as Philip reined up beside them. Faris gave her a warning tap and smiled at the boy.

"Do you see that bird?" He pointed. "That's a red-tailed hawk. I have one at home, and a peregrine. Did you see them when you visited us?"

Faris shook her head. Philip looked momentarily disappointed, then continued, "Perhaps next time you visit us we can go hawking—after you have the baby, that is. I'm glad you are going to have a child," he added in the same tone. "I got awfully tired of being told to be careful because I was Uncle Jehan's heir."

Faris stared at him. "You didn't want to be a King?"

"It's bad enough to be Lord Commander of a Province! I want to enjoy life! Being King—well, now that he's married Jehan's mood doesn't change so much, but still . . ." Philip shook his head.

Faris rubbed at the small of her back, which was beginning to ache despite Sombra's smooth pace. They had told her that easy riding would not harm the baby, and she refused to be cooped up in a cart, but she found it hard to be concerned. Yet lately the idea of the child was taking on more reality. She looked doubtfully at Philip and wondered what kind of life her child would have.

For a moment the boy was silent, and Faris realized that his chatter had distracted her from a growing sense of oppression, as if a headache were coming on. Almost, she recognized the feeling. *No!* She barriered the awareness away. *I escaped such visions when I married Jehan! I don't want to know!*

"Do you see that peak—the one that looks almost transparent in the haze?" asked Philip. Faris shaded her eyes to search among the shapes that wavered in the heavy air, then nodded.

"At Initiation they told us it guards the road to Awahna, but they could not tell us how one gets there. Do you know?" he went on.

"Ask the Master of the Junipers," said Rosemary, pointing towards the Master, who turned his mount towards them when he heard his name.

Faris felt her oppression lighten as she focused on that distant silhouette. "Is that the road to Awahna?"

The Master's gaze followed hers, and the lines in his face eased as if a younger man looked out through his eyes. "It lies close by there, but no one can say for sure where it is."

"But you have been there," said Rosemary.

"I have made my way to the Secret Valley, as all who enter the Second Order must do, but I know only the signposts on that path. The road itself is never the same to any two who travel it . . . and unless the Lords of that Valley please, the path will not appear at all."

"At the College they spoke of it as a valley of wonders—a place not entirely in this world," said Rosemary.

Faris watched the Master, remembering how he had looked when he held out the coal to her and seeing a reflection of that brightness in his eyes now. Involuntarily her awareness sought his, and for a moment she glimpsed granite ramparts laced by silver waterfalls, the reflection of trees and sky in a still pool, faces like those of the priests of the elements who had sealed her to the Jewels. She closed her eyes against the memory, but the echo of the Master's longing had shaken her.

His thought came to her through the link she had made. *Each of us is Called to a different road, nor do we know our true direction until we reach its end.*

The link shattered as a rush of alien impressions broke through. *Run! Death is coming—get away!* Faris clung to the mare, cowering back from the tide of fear, and cried out.

Jehan reined Stormwing back on his haunches, whirled, and set the big horse speeding back, followed by Farin and their escort. He reached for Faris, who was trying to still her horse and herself. She grasped at his hand, a steady point in a spinning world.

"What is it? Are you ill?" They milled around her, overwhelming her with irrelevant concern.

"It's not me!" she cried. "Jehan—Master—reach out! Can't you *feel* that something is wrong?"

They stilled then, staring around them. For a moment the creaking of the approaching baggage carts was the only sound.

"It's very hazy," said Rosemary at last.

"But we often have dust storms here in the Valley," offered Philip.

"Not at this time of year," replied the Commander of the escort, "and not above the hills."

Faris felt the Master's touch on her mind, picking up her memory of fear.

Farin lifted his head, sniffing the air. "Fire—" He voiced the knowledge that had been growing in them all. "It must be fire."

The Master sighed. "The land's self-cleansing is not always gentle, I fear."

They loosened their reins, let the horses move forward again.

"We are expected for the noonmeal at a holding called Ravenhill," said Jehan. "We'll be there soon, and you can rest."

Faris nodded but kept hold of his hand. Twice during her childhood lightning had sparked forest fires that swept the mountains of her home, consuming deadwood and underbrush and clearing the ground for new growth. Men and animals alike fled before the flames and afterward returned to rebuild their lives. Faris had been able to bear the pain of it then—was it because of the Jewels that she felt it so sorely now? Her scarred arm throbbed with the memory of fire.

As they turned up the road towards the holding they saw a rider.

"I hope that's someone from Ravenhill—I could use a welcome!" said Farin. The rider had seen them and was galloping now.

"A very eager welcome." Rosemary tipped back her broad sunhat so that she could see. "It is a priestess."

The woman pulled up before them, wiping sweat from her soot-streaked face. Her dark robe was brown with dust, and strands of her graying hair hung around her face. She nodded to the Master of the Junipers, but her attention was on the King.

"I am Mistress Ramona from the Community at Rivered, sent south by Mistress Esther to serve the people here," she said, catching her breath. "My lord King, I summon you in the name of the Covenant!"

Faris felt Jehan's hand tighten on hers while his face grew paler beneath its tan. "In the name of the Covenant I hear you," he said steadily. "Is it fire?"

Mistress Ramona nodded. "Lord William's younger son decided to carve out a new holding and set fires to clear the land. In high summer!" She controlled her anger and continued, "And with no knowledge of the winds or the lie of the land."

"And no authorization?" asked the Master of the Junipers.

The priestess shook her head wearily. "I have tried to call the clouds, but they are too far away." The woman looked up. "Two hours ago word came that you were traveling this road. I came as fast as I could—the fire is likely closer by now."

" 'The evil that men do men must repair,' " the Master quoted softly from the Covenant, looking at Jehan. "The Jewels are with us."

"I will gladly help fight the fire," said the King, "but the Jewels? I have never used them so—I do not know what must be done here." Faris trembled in the backwash of his uncertainty.

"Let us go and see," said the Master of the Junipers.

• • •

Sunlight refracting through the evil gray of the sky bathed their faces in a coppery glow. Before them plumes of black smoke signaled the advance of the fire, and the nearer ridges were edged with flickers of light like the vanguard of an army of flame.

Faris coughed and lowered her head, but she still heard the futile scrape of shovels as men and women tried to clear a firebreak that would stop the flames. Lord William had set up a movable camp on the hill, with food and water on wagons, and pallets where the firefighters could rest.

An old man with hair singed off one side of his head and his arm in a sling was ladling stew. He looked up, saw the King, and started a cheer. The Master of the Junipers smiled a little. He had spent the hour's ride to the fire-camp reviewing with Jehan the means by which the Jewels might be used to control the fire.

"Your presence will give them new strength, but it will not still the flames," he said.

Someone called. A man and a woman ran down the hill and returned in a few moments, helping to bear a rude stretcher. Rosemary stifled an exclamation and Faris swallowed, realizing that the blackened thing on the stretcher had been a man. The scar on her arm began to hurt once more.

"He's still alive!" called Rosemary. "Have you salves and bandages?"

"My work is here," the Master told Jehan. "Only you can decide how to do yours." He hurried towards the burned man, rolling up his sleeves.

"Jehan . . ." Faris followed the King to the madrona tree where he was standing with his hand lightly resting on its trunk.

"I know that I must use the Jewels, but I would rather lead a charge against half Elaya!" he said ruefully. "That's my kind of fighting!"

She relaxed her shielding a little to sense his mood and shuddered as she felt the terror of fleeing animals, the pain of dying trees. Jehan touched her arm.

"Go help Rosemary and the Master, and keep anyone from disturbing me here." He glanced down, and Faris saw on the ground beside him the redwood case that held the Jewels. For a moment she hesitated, torn between fear for him and a shamed relief that he had not asked her to stay.

As she moved away Jehan knelt and opened the chest, oblivious to her anxious gaze or the hushed murmurs of the others. Slowly he traced the sign of the pentangle upon his breast and began to bind on the Jewels—the dimly glowing Earthstone, the moonlight glimmer of the Sea Star, the white blaze of the Wind Crystal, and the ember that was the Jewel of Fire. Then he paced forward to face the line of flame. Tremors shook his body as he strove to focus the powers he bore.

After a few moments Faris could no longer bear to watch him and turned to the Master of the Junipers.

The man on the stretcher lay very still. The flames that had engulfed him had somehow missed his face, but his skin was gray, and the eyes he fixed on the Master were dilated with pain.

Faris stopped next to Rosemary, who gripped her hand. "He is dying—too much of his skin has been lost." But Faris had already known that, feeling the man's agony as she felt the martyrdom of the land, which buffeted her shielding until it was gone. She whimpered as if she were still the six-year-old feeling the fire bite her own flesh as she tried to beat the flames from the gown of the housekeeper's child.

"Be still . . . be at peace. I will come with you. There will be no pain," the Master said softly. Wood clattered as Lord William started to pack up the wagons, preparing to retreat from the fire.

Faris began to shiver as the eyes of the burned man dulled. The Master eased back on his heels, his hands resting open on his knees, and his eyes took on the fixed, in-seeing expression she had seen at the College when he had picked up the coal.

She felt in her own flesh the dying man's agony fade, to be replaced by an expectance, as if a sweet melody had just ceased to play and might at any moment return. She stilled; for a moment there was something, as if she heard brightness. Then she fell back to consciousness and saw from the slack features that the man had gone.

"Hurry!" cried someone. "The fire is getting too close!"

But the Master did not move. Several minutes passed before his eyes refocused on the outside world, and Faris read in them a last longing for the place to whose gates he had accompanied the spirit of the dying man.

She looked around her, painfully aware of the Master's weariness, the despair of the people around them, the energy of the fire and the torment of the land it devoured. But above all she felt the surges of unfocused power that racked Jehan, the desperation of his battle to control the Jewels. Silence throbbed around her. She knew that Rosemary spoke to her, but she heard no words. Hoofbeats vibrated in the earth, but she did not look to see who had come. Jehan was afraid. The Jewels were mastering him. Faris began to run.

As she reached him the King moaned and dashed the circlet from his head, tore the Wind Crystal's chain from his neck, and fumbled to loose the Sea Star and the Earthstone from his waist and loins. He sank to his knees, clutching the earth, while the Jewels blazed malevolently beside him. Taking care not to touch them, Faris knelt and held Jehan until his shudders ceased.

"I'm all right," he muttered. "Give me a moment and I'll attack again." He looked up, his eyes registering awareness of her presence and the realization that he was not on a battlefield. "Faris, you and the others must go!"

Faris shook her head, though her cheeks were already smarting with the heat of the nearing fire. "Not unless you come too!" She gripped his hands to keep him from reaching for the Earthstone.

"Faris!" Anguish darkened his eyes. "I do not know if I can win this battle, but I cannot run away! Let me go—how can I fight if I must fear for you?"

She felt his torment, and beneath it, as she had known the Master's longing for the Gates of Light, a yearning for the agony that would justify all pain and end all questioning.

Desire and denial flowed back and forth through their linked hands. To those who watched they did not seem to move, but Faris countered power with power as though she and Jehan were swinging each other in a dance, and imperceptibly their conflict became a balancing of forces. Her expanding awareness began to recall how the Lord and Lady of Westria had come together in the Sacred Grove.

For a moment she faltered, fearing to lose herself again if she accepted this power. Some inner voice whispered, *He cannot do it alone.*

Faris tightened her grasp. "Then I will help you."

With a little sigh she laid down the burden of her fears

and stepped into stillness, as she had done so long ago when she saved the child from the fire. Around her the hills blazed like a vision of doom. The sounds of that burning reached her as if from another world. But where she was now all was simple, and she reached for the Earthstone and in one smooth movement bound it on.

"Faris!" cried Jehan, but already she was rooted to the earth and could not be moved.

"You must take the Sea Star and the Wind Crystal and bring wind and water to our aid"—she held them out to him—"and I will bear the Jewel of Fire. Do not fear for the child." She answered his thought, "He was conceived in the presence of the Jewels. He will take no harm."

Still staring at her, Jehan began to put on the Jewels. Faris picked up the coronet and for a moment hesitated as the red glow of the Jewel stirred the embers of an old fear, then she settled it on her brow.

This time there was no warning, no gradual building of power. At once she *was* the earth, screaming within her garment of fire. She felt the agony of every small creature caught by the flames, the extinction of each blade of grass, the heat that seared even the life within the soil. Stones cracked; clods were fired to rock; earth powdered to mix with the ashes of those it had fed.

This was what had defeated Jehan. She heard him calling but could not get free, for the flames were calling to her too, promising freedom in a frenzy that would not fade until all was consumed. And still she struggled, her fear of the pain lost in her fear of the dark fires in her own soul.

Faris . . . Faris . . . turn and come to Me.

And with a last effort she turned and saw a form whose garments pulsed with green and scarlet fires, whose skin glowed like a lantern, whose eyes were flame. The Lady of Fire . . . Faris shrank from the welcome of her outstretched arms.

To save the man, to save the land, to save yourself . . . you must come through the fire. The soft voice seared her soul.

And for that moment Faris knew the answer to her fears. She moved into the Lady's terrible embrace, but her eyes were on Jehan. For a moment there was terror and a pain beyond words, then all the agony of her flesh was transmuted to music, and all the passion of the flames to love.

"My Lady!" said the King. His eyes widened as he recognized her transformation. Still looking at her, his hands closed on the Jewels he bore. He took a deep breath, seeming to grow taller as he drew in their power.

"I am Earth and I am burning—cool me with thy kiss," said Faris, holding out her hands.

"As the wind I will caress thee," he replied.

"I am Earth and I am burning—fill me with thy sweet waters."

"As the rain I will bless thee." His hands clasped hers. Opposing forces arced between them and vibrated to equilibrium.

"In the name of the Maker of All Things!" they cried as one.

Faris set her feet in the earth and held fast as Jehan's awareness whirled outward, coaxing heated air away, drawing cooler air down to replace it and create a wind that would drive the flames back upon themselves. Her head throbbed with the anger of the fire. Like a mother seeking wayward children, she reached out to the fire elementals, set them to herd the flames inward until they exploded in fantastic filigree against the sky.

Jehan's spirit sped westward to bring damp air from the sea, to draw moisture from the waters into the clouds, to raise a wind to bear them back across the land. Cool air soothed Faris' burning cheeks and replaced the acrid breath of the fire with a sweet sea breeze.

Now, my children, be still, for it is time to rest, she whispered to the flames, and over four thousand acres the fires sagged, flickered tiredly, and winked out. Faris staggered, feeling the agony of the earth anew, now that the fire was gone. She looked at Jehan in appeal.

Already the dark smoke that had billowed around them was being invaded by pale swirls of gray as low clouds rolled across the land. Faris turned her face to the sky as the clouds folded the tortured earth in their cool embrace. Very gently it began to rain. Faris drew deep, sobbing breaths, feeling the earth's pain ease as moisture soothed its surface, feeling its grateful expansion as rain penetrated soil seared by the fire.

As the elements mingled Jehan reached for her, and Faris came into his arms. The mists veiled them from the ravaged land and the camp where the others waited. Now all four Jewels were pressed between their bodies. Faris trembled with the powers of the Wind Crystal and the Sea Star as well as those of the Jewels she already bore. Her spirit yearned towards his, striving to pierce the flesh that separated them. Now they were linked not by their own strength but by the flow of power, and the mists around them sparkled with a light more radiant than that of the fire.

Then the clouds thinned and were gone. Voiced and unvoiced, the calling of those they had left behind in the camp reached them, and the Lord and Lady of Westria turned.

Oh, fairer than the evening star! As from a great distance, Faris perceived her brother, Farin, helping support a wounded man.

Lord and Lady, bless me and bring me to the one I love. Rosemary stood with a bowl of soup forgotten in her hand.

Oh, my King! Why did you never tell me what it meant to be Master of the Jewels? That was Caolin—she had not known he was here. His hair clung damply to his skull as if he had been caught in the rain. His eyes were dark hollows in a face that seemed pared to the bone. *Oh, my Queen! You are filled with light—love me also, and set me free! My Lord and my Lady . . .*

Lord and Lady, now I bow before You, the Master's voice echoed, affirming, and the others joined him in the hymn.

> Your radiance burns the darkness from my soul;
> I stand upright between You and am balanced,
> When I embrace You, then I am made whole.
> Lord and Lady . . .

But Faris did not hear the rest, for the Light was becoming a blaze in which she could no longer see the humans below. The air stirred with music. In a moment she and Jehan would be free.

"Faris! Jehan!" The shout of the Master of the Junipers shattered the radiance into shards that fell about her like rain. Faris staggered as the Jewel of Fire was lifted from her brow.

"You must take them off or you will be consumed!" The Master reached past her to slip the Wind Crystal over Jehan's head and unclasp the Sea Star, then he turned to

Faris to take the Earthstone. "I should have warned you, but the power held me too."

Sick and shaking, Faris clung to Jehan.

"No," Jehan whispered, stopped the Master, and unclasped the belt himself. "There is something left to do." He took Faris' hand and drew her a few steps towards the charred, rain-soaked land. Together they lifted the Jewel.

"Lady of Earth! Be gracious to this land!" said Faris.

"Lady of Earth, forgive us, and do not deny your blessing to men," Jehan echoed her. They held their breath, waiting, and for a moment the reek of smoke gave way to a hint of apple blossom, and they heard a shimmer of silver bells.

Answered, they let their hands drop then, let the Master take the Earthstone and replace it in the casket. In the stillness the only sounds were an occasional pop as moisture penetrated some smoldering log, and the patient patter of the rain.

Wonderingly Jehan lifted a hand to touch Faris' cheek. His lips soothed the burn on her forehead, then his head drooped to her shoulder.

Faris looked around her, but the glory was gone; even the memory of what had come to her was fading, as if she were waking from some bright dream. Every muscle in her body was aching, and she knew that she was only a human woman, who could be afraid.

But Jehan was beside her. Because of him, she had been safe in the storm of glory, and now his arms held her in a circle of peace. Beyond him she saw Caolin and the others, and like a glimmer from the future she sensed how the Lord and Lady of Westria might guard them, as the memory of how they had mastered the fire was now a glimmer from the past.

But not yet. For now, it was enough to sigh and bend to heal her scorched face in the raindrops that jeweled Jehan's hair.

LADY OF
DARKNESS

ACKNOWLEDGMENTS

I would like to thank David Hodghead for information regarding the habits and hunting of wild boars, Ken DeMaiffe for data on the capabilities of both horses and carrier pigeons, Clint Bigglestone for suggesting the strategy used in the Battle of the Dragon Waste, and Paul Edwin Zimmer for arguing with me about the right way to do a fighting scene.

Prologue

The Master of the Junipers tucked his grey robe under him and settled himself beneath a live oak on the sunny hill above Misthall. Carefully he shook out the silk cloth and laid his deck of tarot cards down. Beyond the silvered shake roof of the hall the land fell gently to the Great Bay. The Lady Mountain seemed almost to float above the water, its lower slopes veiled by autumn haze. With the marriage of King Jehan to the Lady Faris, the past year had been eventful, and it was good to rest.

He took an appreciative breath of air scented with the Harvest feast they were preparing for this afternoon and shuffled through the worn cards. He was seeking the *Queen of Wands*—dark, slender and ardent—to represent Faris. She had been so young and fearful when the King had married her that many had wondered if she would ever make a Queen. But the Master had seen her face when she put on the Elemental Jewels of Power to help Jehan master a forest fire a month ago, and he thought that she understood what it meant to be the King's counterpart at last. No urgency drove him to read the cards for her now, only the knowledge that they were sometimes useful, and lack of practice must not dull his skill.

But perhaps he had not lost it, for the first card the Master drew—the one showing the influence that ruled the subject now, was the Empress, surrounded by the fruits of the field. He thought of Faris, growing more luxuriantly beautiful as her pregnancy advanced, and knew that she *was* the Empress now.

As the pattern required, he picked another card from the deck to cross her. The *King of Cups?* This card indicated a fair man in a position of responsibility. Was crossing the same as reversal of the card? *That* could mean treachery.

More important, whom did the card signify? Westria had its share of politics, but the King and the Seneschal, Caolin, had always kept the worst plotters under control. Brian, the Lord Commander of Las Costas, was agitating for greater independence, but he was more an enemy of Caolin's than of the King and Queen. Did the card point to the Elayans, who were now claiming Westria's southernmost city, Santibar? But how could they threaten the Queen?

With a sigh he went on to the card which should show the best that could be achieved. It was the *Seven of Cups*, and usually indicated the insubstantiality of earthly wealth. Here was another puzzler, but perhaps later cards would make its meaning clear.

The card for past achievements was the *Two of Cups*, whose emblem was a youth and maiden pledging their troth. That was better—the pictured couple even had the look of Faris and Jehan, and the appearance of the *Lovers*, following it, seemed to confirm the reading. If this was the influence that was now passing away, perhaps it showed that their love would now mature.

The sixth card was for the future, and as he turned it over the Master found his stomach muscles tightening, for it was the *Queen of Swords*, and she means mourning. The seventh, for the subject's attitude, proved to be the *Two of Wands*, showing a great man sorrowful in the midst of his wealth.

Keep on, the Master told himself. *Only when it is complete will the pattern become clear*. Swiftly he set out the next two cards that should show the environment within which all should come to pass and the subject's desires, and shivered as he saw the *Tower* and *Death* on his dark horse. *Death* could be interpreted as a card of transfiguration, but there were no hopeful meanings for the *Falling Tower*.

And what of the end? The air seemed to have chilled, though the Master saw no cloud across the sun. He forced his clenched fingers to release and put the last card down.

The *High Priestess* gazed up at him from the silk cloth, her eyes mysterious below her crescent crown. She had Faris' face—why had he never seen that in the card before? But what road could lead from the opulence of the Empress to this? As he stared, the enigmatic features of the Priestess were momentarily dimmed by the flickering shadow of a late butterfly.

It has been too long since I tried this—I have lost my touch with the cards, The Master told himself. He heard his name called and looking down the hill saw Faris herself waving from the garden gate. Beyond her a rider was coming up the road, his fair hair glinting in the pallid sun. It was Caolin.

I will read the cards tomorrow. Surely they will tell a different story then. Briskly the Master began to gather them up and fit them into their case, ignoring the bitter wind that ruffled his thinning hair.

I

Harvest

Fire leaped from the taper in Faris' hand to a twig, exploded in the tinder and flared through the kindling with a soft roar. Startled, Faris snatched away the flowing wings of her orange robe, but the fire's beauty fascinated her, its sunset colors veined by dark branches like the wings of the monarch butterfly she had found that morning, killed by the cold.

I could draw those flames into a cloak to warm me, she thought. Her hands throbbed with the memory of power. She took a quick breath and stood up, careful because of her pregnancy, and turned to the others who were seated in a semicircle before Misthall's great hearth.

"On this day the powers of light and darkness are balanced and we celebrate the feast of hearth and harvest. We honor not only the hearthfire but the earth from which both reaper and harvest come. Therefore let us reaffirm the Covenant that binds us and Earth's other children, our kin . . ."

The words flowed freely, as if some other part of Faris' consciousness were conducting the ceremony. With doubled vision she saw the firelit faces of the household she and Jehan had gathered around them, and her own prismed reflection.

To Jehan's steward Patrick and his wife Carlota she was the stately priestess of the hearth. Her friend Rosemary was seeing herself, tall and fair, at the hearth of Eric of Seagate whom she loved. To her brother Farin, Faris blazed with more than mortal beauty, but the trained awareness of the Master of the Junipers perceived her as the Queen of the Harvest with her hair earth-dark and her body ripening with child.

Curiously her awareness moved onward to Caolin the Seneschal and halted, finding no reflection in his cold eyes. *But Jehan loves him,* she thought, *and therefore I must love him too*—she sought to draw him into their unity and glimpsed a confusion of the glory she had worn when she and Jehan mastered the forest fire and a coarse and animal opulence that was its opposite.

Frightened, she sought Jehan's familiar strength and stilled in his contemplation of a flame-robed Goddess, the Lady of Fire. Dazzled, her awareness expanded to encompass the fire on the hearth and the earth below, the golden hills of Westria and the life they bore. She was a redwood tree breathing in the sun, a salmon thrashing up the stream, a boar that coughed challenge as it scented a sow. She was the Lady of Westria . . .

Then the King's presence balanced her and she realized that the ceremony was almost done. The others were setting before the hearth the offerings of salt and water, milk and honey, bread and wine, and squash and corn.

"We have laid these gifts before our hearth," her words came clearly, "yet we cannot hallow that which is already more holy than we. Let us therefore take these separate elements into our own bodies, and as they become one in us, let us join with each other and with the earth from which we come . . ." She raised her arms in invocation, feeling the air throb around her. She knew herself at once servant and sovereign, and glimpsed a way of transcending the fear of self-surrender that had kept her from matching Jehan's desire.

"Let it be completed in the names of earth and water, air and fire, and in the Name of the Maker of All Things!" With a gasp she brought down her hands and bent to touch the floor, grounding the energy she had raised.

"Now is my Lady Mistress of her own hearth!" cried Jehan. Faris sighed and went gratefully into his arms, ignoring the others' indulgent smiles, while Carlota dashed for the kitchen and Caolin rose stiffly and turned away.

"Make way for the garden! Make way for the feast!"

Caolin stepped backward abruptly as Jehan's squire Philip strode past, hands to his lips as if he were blowing a trumpet, while Rosemary and Branwen staggered behind him with an enormous wooden bowl of salad to match the tureen of shellfish stew.

"Poor Caolin!" Jehan laughed, drawing the Seneschal toward the table. "We will have to put off our discussion of Lord Brian's mission to Santibar." It did not matter, Caolin told himself as he sat down. As long as the lord of Las Costas was in the south there was little he could do against him. He smoothed back his fair hair and sighed.

"You really do have a garden here." The Master of the Junipers hitched up his grey robe and took his place next to Faris at the foot of the table.

"Well, most of it—" she smiled, serving him a generous portion. The wreath of gold chrysanthemums was already askew on her dark hair. *She was like a Goddess when she wore the Jewel of Fire,* thought Caolin. *What is she now?*

He picked at a slice of duck that had been baked in clay and stuffed with wild rice and herbs and waved onward the dish of zucchini sauced with cheese and dill. He had already eaten at this meal as much as he usually did in a day. Jehan was at the sideboard, slicing the haunch of venison.

"This is my contribution to the feast."

"It was a wonderful shot!" exclaimed Philip. "We tracked the buck for five miles, and my Lord was just drawing when the wind changed, and—"

"Peace, Philip!" said the King, "It was the deer's fate, not my skill."

The boy's mouth closed abruptly, and Farin looked at him in sympathy. "There will be more hunting—it has been a fat year and we help maintain the balance like any other predator. I hear that sometimes wild pigs from the coast come into these hills."

"Wild boar!" Philip's eyes began to sparkle again. Caolin toyed with his meat and took another swallow of Wilhamsted wine as fruit and cheese were passed.

Jehan loosened his belt with a sigh. "Surely there has never been such a feast in all this land!" He smiled the length of the table at Faris.

"That's because it's your own, my Lord," said Carlota, setting before him a bowl of raspberry cream.

He clasped her hand. "Thank you, Carlota, for waiting all those years when it seemed I would never bring a Lady to this Hall." He looked around him. "I know when I am a happy man!"

There were food stains on the King's tunic. Caolin saw in Jehan's full stomach the beginning of a paunch, saw a softening of the clear lines of cheek and jaw, and something within him contracted in pain. He remembered too clearly the clean beauty that had been Jehan's long ago. But the memory of the young King's clear skin and slim grace were replaced by a vision of thickening body and greying hair, a face reddened by good living, and eyes that sought nothing beyond a plump wife and children around the hearth. Alarmed, Caolin looked down at his own belt, tighter now than it had been this morning, but still buckled firmly in the same notch that had held it for ten years.

"For me, happiness is being safe among the ones I love," said Faris tremulously. "I haven't felt this way since my mother died."

Farin pushed aside his pumpkin pie and reached across the table to clasp her hand. "I'm happy as long as I have my harp and my sword!"

Caolin listened with increasing irritation. Did they all believe that the purpose of existence was a full belly and a place by the fire?

"Happiness comes to me when I am part of the harmony of all things," said the Master of the Junipers in his voice that was at once both rough and sweet. "But my life has been laid in pleasant places—contentment is no virtue in me."

"Then you must seek a challenge that will make you earn your happiness!" the words burst from Caolin's lips. "It is the struggle to achieve more than one has that proves to us we are alive! Don't you understand that—" he stopped abruptly, seeing the surprise on the faces of those who were still listening, and tried to laugh. For a moment he met the grave gaze of the Master of the Junipers, then looked away, realizing uncomfortably that of them all, the man he disliked most was probably the only one who had understood.

Presently people began to leave the table. Philip and the Master started a game of chess. Farin brought out his harp. Caolin stood apart, watching the colors change while the room darkened around him. After some time, he turned back to the fire, meaning to ask Jehan when they could discuss the report from Santibar.

He found the King sleeping with his head on Faris' lap, her hands upon his dark hair. Jehan lay utterly still, vanquished by the feast and the softness of the woman's arms. Caolin fought an impulse to haul him to his feet and out the door, away from the murmur of women's voices and the warmth of the fire.

But it would do no good. As long as Jehan could seek oblivion in Faris' dark eyes he was lost to him as surely as if the traitor's arrow had found his heart last spring. Faris was as earthbound as the pumpkins that flanked the hearth, her arms like clinging vines that in time could crack stone.

With a stifled groan Caolin strode from the room. His brown mare tossed her head skittishly as he led her from the stall, but he cuffed her and cinched the saddle tight before she had time to swell her sides. The road was dim, but the mare knew the way. Caolin pressed her over the pass and spurred her into a canter as they reached the level ground beneath the walnut groves. They were galloping as they passed Wilhamsted, nearly knocking over a small boy herding sheep along the road.

Caolin's body jarred as the mare leaped forward, and the regular motion imposed at last a kind of order on his memories. *Jehan's slack body . . . Faris' complacent gaze . . . the silver in Jehan's hair . . .* As the road curved over the lower slopes of the Red Mountain he let the mare slow to a walk. The peak bulked dark against the early stars. He controlled an impulse to turn the mare toward the temple he had built there at Midsummer, where he had touched the Mountain's power, the one place where he need not pretend.

Pretend what? The horse paused as Caolin's fingers tightened on the reins. "Since Jehan married Faris I have been pretending that all is well, when every day he loses more of his youth, his beauty, his spirit. When they fought the forest fire they were like a god and goddess, but Faris has bound him to the earth again now." He urged the mare forward again. "Will Jehan be so happy ten years from now when Faris has become a fat sow like her sister, and he realizes that he has thrown his manhood away?"

And yet what could he do? Caolin let the mare amble, staring into the night until his thoughts acquired substance again. The King was required to have a Queen and an heir. It was Jehan's *obsession* with Faris that must be cured. His passion must be killed or turned to something that would kill Faris' smothering need for him. Yes, that would be better, since it would free Jehan from guilt.

But Jehan will suffer . . . Something twisted in Caolin's belly as he remembered Jehan's grief when love disappointed him before. Did he want more days like that, searching frantically for something to bring back Jehan's smile and fearing to leave him alone?

But Faris might betray Jehan in any case. Last spring her heartlessness had been the talk of the Corona. Considering it that way, Caolin realized that he must make Jehan invulnerable to such a loss and let his own love compensate as he had before.

In the library at Laurelynn there were books unknown even to the Masters at the College of the Wise. Surely Caolin would find a way there to turn Jehan's love to hate and save him from his folly.

He dug his heels into the mare's sides and whipped her neck with the reins until they were stumbling down the river road. Then Caolin let the reins slacken at last and eased back in the saddle, feeling the wind chill his damp brow and seeing in the distance the lights of Laurelynn.

"You should take care, my lord. I think that Brian is as much your enemy as you are his." Ordrey eased further down in the soft chair, brushing dust from the muted plaid of the Elayan kilt he still wore. He was a little, gingery man and Caolin's most trusted servant.

Caolin tapped the papers Ordrey had just brought him against his palm, wishing it had not taken the man until mid-October to get them here. Brian's writing sprawled across the page— ill-spelt, but legible enough to one who had an interest in deciphering it. It had been addressed to Brian's lady, Alessia of Moonbay, but its tone would have suited any comrade-in-arms.

We have done what we can here, and you may expect me back before November ends. I think now that my quarrel is not with the King but with his Seneschal. Caolin is no warrior. When Elaya attacks us, what if I tell Jehan that I will not ride to war—not I nor any man who swears to me—while Caolin bears the Kingdom's keys? Will Jehan choose his Seneschal above his throne?

Caolin stared through the window, his thoughts as fragmented as the courtyard seen through the leaded glass. If it came to a choice, what would Jehan do?

"Brian means to make my head the price of his sword . . ." he said softly.

Ordrey nodded. "It's true Elaya is arming. They are beating crude iron from the desert mines into blanks for swords and the impis are practicing maneuvers below Palomon's citadel. We will need Brian's sword, come spring."

"We will need my head as well!" snapped the Seneschal. "If only to make sure they don't lose at the peace table what they win in war!"

Ordrey shrugged. "I will not argue with you, but why not pretend to let Brian have his way? Agree with the King to 'resign' until this war is done. After bearing the load alone for a time he should be only too eager to reinstate you."

Caolin moved closer to the window. Clerks scurried across the courtyard and carts bore the produce of Westria into the Royal City and the products of Laurelynn out again. He touched the glass as if he could feel the pulse of the Kingdom through his fingertips and knew it was more than a metaphor.

The heart of Westria beat here in his building through which records of all the comings and goings in the Kingdom passed; in this mind that compared, evaluated and understood them all. But would Jehan see it that way?

And what would happen if he followed Ordrey's advice? Would Brian be content with that victory or would the taste of power only whet his thirst for more? King and Seneschal might share the responsibility for a Kingdom, but in an army there could be no divided command.

Caolin shook his head. "I do not think that Brian will let go once he has Westria in his grasp." He looked back at the letter.

Therefore, my lady, be vigilant, and set our friends to examine Caolin's doings as formerly they watched the King. I do not think he will be cast off easily . . .

Caolin suppressed the desire to crumple the thin sheets and laid them carefully on the desk once more. *You are right in one thing, Brian*, he thought, *I will never willingly give up Westria!*

He turned to Ordrey. "Brian and I have only been playing until now! But Jehan will never be able to rule him without me, and I do not want him free to breed trouble here while Jehan is at war! Brian's own weight will drag him down, but I cannot wait that long—" he went on more slowly, "if Brian will not incriminate himself then we must help him!"

Ordrey grinned. "Oh, indeed! And what happens when Jehan finds out?"

Caolin did not answer. He moved back to the window, staring unseeing at the glass as the day faded to dusk. He remembered Jehan as he had last seen him, supine in the arms of his Queen.

Jehan must never know . . .

In times past, each god made sacred certain birds and beasts to signify his powers . . . In the north, the god who ruled men's generative powers had as symbol the boar, by reason of his fierceness and fecundity.

Caolin replaced the marker and carefully closed the book, brushing age-powdered leather from his fingertips. Each book on his table had passages similarly tagged, the result of a month's work in the library at Laurelynn. He rubbed at eyes reddened by lack of sleep—he could only do this research after the day's work was done, in the moments when he was not searching for a way to trap Brian.

In his mind the two problems had become the same—to destroy Jehan's trust in Brian, that threatened Caolin's position; to destroy Jehan's obsession with Faris that had diverted his love. The tools for his second purpose lay here.

Beside the books lay the notes on rite and symbol upon which he would base his ritual. He would have liked more time, but Samain was only a week away, and Jehan would be returning to Laurelynn. He must act soon.

It was long since he had applied the principles of ceremonial magic he had learned at the College of the Wise. Still it was simply a matter of patterning the symbols to focus the power of the mind until the alternate reality envisioned achieved an existence of its own. The most effective rituals used many minds bent toward the same end, but a single sorcerer could achieve as much with sufficient strength of will.

Caolin rested his head in his hands, remembering the warnings against solitary sorcery. A man working alone was apt to forget that he was only human and that the power he exercised was a gift to be used for the good of all.

"And so it shall be!" he exclaimed, "though I doubt those fools at the College would say so! Are a flock of sheep wiser than the shepherd just because there are more of them?"

He pushed back his chair and began to pace about the room. He must wait until sundown to begin his work, and though anxiety was foolish, he could not sit still. He opened another box and leaned the stuffed boar's head he had found in the palace at Laurelynn against the wall.

"You shall help me, old tusker!" he turned the head so that its glass eyes glowed red in the sunset light. "This is not so different from the skills I use to rule Ordrey and others . . ." He stopped, remembering that he had not used his ability to control men's minds since he questioned Ronald Sandreson and the man died.

"I misjudged Ronald's weakness—" he addressed the boar's head as if it could absolve him. "That does not mean my technique is wrong! I cannot touch another's mind, but there are things I *can* do. Why should I stop my studies—it is all for the good of Westria!"

The door creaked and he whirled. Then he realized it was only the deaf and dumb woman, Margit, with his dinner. She turned the ruined side of her face away and smiled shyly.

"Well, Margit," he said genially. "You must feed me well tonight, for I've a great work to do—transforming a King's passion for his Queen from love to lust!" He gestured toward the boxes, laughed as she peered at him uncertainly and showed her a tunic of Jehan's, a gown of the Queen's. And seeing Margit next to the gown, he realized how much she looked like Faris, despite her handicaps.

"Oh no—don't go yet, my pretty one . . ." he pulled her toward him, ignoring her trembling. "You live to serve me, don't you—well you shall serve me well! My plan was sound enough, but I think I see a better way!"

"Would you like to be beautiful, Margit?" he went on. "You shall be—as beautiful as a Queen. Put on this gown!" Holding her eyes, he projected commands until she obeyed, modestly pulling the gown over her head as she dropped the last of her garments, as if her body had been as maimed as her face. Then she stood before him, nervously smoothing the green silk that clung to her breasts and sides.

He twitched the kerchief from her head, loosened her coiled hair. "Dark hair, like *hers* . . ." he murmured. "Now you shall *be* Faris."

He closed his eyes, summoning from all his memories the image of the Queen. She was small, her head just reaching his chin . . . her neck was long and her shoulders slim, the bones fragile as a bird's. Dispassionately he reviewed Faris' body, shaped her face with its smooth curves of cheek and brow, and the fold of her eye-lid that gave the almond shape to her brown eyes. She had a little mole just where one straight eyebrow ended, he remembered, and paused, a little surprised he could visualize her so well.

So—that was Faris—an ordinary woman in whom Jehan for some reason saw the Goddess revealed. That was what he wished to change.

Deliberately, Caolin lifted his ring to catch the last sunset light, and held Margit until her eyes focused on the spot of light. Then he began to project into her mind an image of Faris, subtly distorted from that of the woman he knew to the one he wished Jehan to see. And finally he pictured this green gowned Faris looking in the mirror, and drawing Margit to the small glass that hung beside his door, he took away his hand and let her see her own reflection there.

For a moment he wondered if it would work, then schooled his thoughts, knowing that his own disbelief could make it fail. His breath stilled for the long moment that Margit stared into the mirror, until, very slowly, she smiled.

Caolin's breath eased out in a long sigh. The woman's stance was altering now, her spine straightening with shoulders drawn back to display her breasts. The Queen's birdlike turn of the head became a provocative tilt, her smile more shallow and sensuous. Both more and less than Faris, Margit stretched luxuriously and began to preen before the mirror. Caolin found himself smiling as well, and thought that the role he had set himself might not be so distasteful after all.

But the light was fading. Quickly Caolin pulled on Jehan's tunic, picked up the boar's head and pulled Margit after him into the inner room. Soon candles were flickering on the Altar of Fire, lending a malevolent life to the boar's mask which he had set there.

"Lady of Fire—" his voice echoed dully in the little room. "Light in us a self-consuming flame! Lady of Fire—help me take this woman in violence, in pain, until she hates and fears the thing that she has loved."

His voice rolled on as he fired coals and laid upon them an incense that eddied chokingly around the room, rehearsing all the evils men could commit in the name of passion, evoking every image of lust he knew.

He lit candles until the room was blazing and he was sweating. Margit was perspiring too. Did he dare hope that another kind of fire was kindling now? The reek of the incense dizzied him. Margit's eyes were half-closed and a pulse beat heavily at the base of her throat. He had made her believe herself Faris. Now he must make her believe that he was Jehan.

The image of the King's face came to him immediately, every feature memorized. For a moment the memory of Jehan's beauty stilled his spirit, then Margit sighed, and Caolin remembered what he had to do.

Swiftly he searched his memory for every expression he had ever seen Jehan wear, from laughter to the sick anger that shook the King when he encountered treachery. He passed quickly over the memory of the tender amusement that focused the King's face when he was making love—that look would never be for Caolin again, but it did not matter, not if he could separate him from Faris.

In frustration he realized that it was Jehan's inability to look at a woman with greed that made this work necessary now. Margit must simply see the King's face then—its expression would be Caolin's. He sent the image of Jehan to Margit's mind.

I am Jehan . . . he shivered as he dared imagine what it would be like to inhabit that beautiful body, to lead men who loved him, to rule Westria and bear the Jewels.

He ripped Margit's gown sharply from shoulder to knee. Laughing at her attempts to cover herself, he passed his hands over her body, his fingers closing brutally on her shrinking flesh. Then he thrust her to her knees, and hitching up his tunic, pictured to her what he wanted her to do.

He had thought to prolong her humiliation, to enjoy the sight of that dark head pressed against his loins, but the passion he was evoking grew too quickly. With a gasp he threw himself upon her, battering her with his body until the spearhead of his attack found her vulnerable core. Her lips writhed in a soundless scream, but her struggles served only to impale her more securely now.

Caolin felt power build within him, possessing him as he possessed the body beneath him. Lights danced crazily and the boar's head leered with its red eyes. Then the woman's arms tightened, and he saw not Margit but Faris—no, not Faris, but the completion of her transformation.

He had sought to evoke Love's darker shadow, and its Goddess was here—Her eyes were black fire; Her red lips fastened hungrily on his and Her legs vised around him. Something in the depths of his soul that had only been touched by

Jehan screamed, but his flesh belonged to the Dark Lady now. A brazen clangor clamored in his ears, and he was sucked into the heart of a volcano. His body exploded in a convulsion that engulfed his world.

There was a sharp "pop" as the walnut shell cracked. Faris picked out the nutmeats and dropped them into the bowl, and the broken shell into the fire. Carlota was making walnut pastry for the Samaine feast, and they needed a week to prepare. Rosemary missed the fireplace and bent, her golden braid swinging, to cast the shells again. When she straightened her face was flushed.

"Faris . . ." she swallowed, "now that you are so well settled it is time for me to go home." The nutshells crackled, then the fire returned to its steady purring again.

Faris stared at her. "But Rosemary, I need you here!"

"You have Branwen and Carlota to help you and Jehan to love you, and soon there will be the child."

"If Jehan had to be my constant companion even his love might fray! Besides, he spends so much time on business of the Kingdom which I cannot share."

"Cannot, or will not, Faris? Have you tried?" asked Rosemary.

Faris sighed and clasped her hands over her belly. "No, not yet. I suppose you find that hard to understand—you have been managing a great house since you took your name. But I panic at the thought of even ruling the palace at Laurelynn."

Rosemary touched her hand. "Poor Faris—I did not mean to be unkind. Perhaps I too am afraid."

"Afraid of meeting Eric?" Faris saw Rosemary's stricken look replaced by laughter.

"Haven't we had this conversation before?" Suddenly they both were laughing.

"Well?" said Faris at last, "If my dream came true, why can't yours?"

"Oh very well, I promise to stay with you until the baby has its milkname!"

Faris smiled and picked up another walnut, her eyes returning to the glowing tapestry of the fire. Here with Rosemary it was warm, and tonight she and Jehan would kindle another kind of fire. But as she watched she seemed to see painted in lines of flame a boar's wicked muzzle and glowing eyes. The shadows swept around her like dark wings, and she knew a moment's desire to sink into them.

Jehan, her heart cried, *come soon—I am afraid of the fire . . .*

II

The Samaine Boar

Gouts of fire danced across the darkness. Images flickered in and out of focus—the weathered wood of a wagon . . . Jehan's face white above bloodied bandages . . . blood everywhere . . .

Faris shrieked denial, fought the restraints that would not let her go to him.

"Faris! Wake up—it's all right now . . ."

Faris saw shadow and firelight. She relaxed as she realized that Jehan was holding her and turned to him with a shuddering sigh.

"Faris, my darling, don't cry—it was only a dream."

"A dream!" For the past week she had slept badly, haunted by images for which she had no words. "You were hurt and there was so much blood," she said. "Must you hunt the boar on Samaine eve?"

He laughed softly and pulled her against him so that her head nestled in the hollow where his neck and shoulder joined.

"Is that what troubles your sleep? We will be a dozen men against one poor animal, however fierce he may be. You should pity the boar!"

"But he killed a little boy—" she began.

"Yes, the child of one of my people. That is why I must go," he replied as she whimpered and clung to him. "Darling, I am solid—touch me all you will."

She took his head between her hands, feeling the hard bones beneath his skin and the strong neck where the long tendons merged with the heavy muscling of chest and shoulder. Jehan's skin was fine-textured, satiny to her touch, with the faint taste of salt that had become so familiar to her.

She moved down his body, her hands confirming the contours that covert glances had taught her to reverence. She wondered anew at the corded strength of his forearms, and the roughened texture of those long fingers that could control a plunging stallion or stray like a butterfly's wing across her cheek.

Her hands tried to compass his waist, slipped along his thighs. He held himself still, only his breathing growing a little ragged as her hand closed on the velvet skin of his phallus. She felt it swell beneath her fingers and her terror for him turned to tenderness. She bent to kiss him and recognized in her own body the beginnings of a desire that reflected his.

Farin was sharpening the two-foot blade of the boar spear. His hand stopped as he heard a cry from the room shared by Faris and Jehan, and he tensed with the backlash of his sister's fear. Then the murmur of voices blended with the normal night noises of Misthall.

Farin returned to his task, punctuating the other sounds with the steady rasp of stone on steel. A breath of air touched his cheek. He looked up and saw Faris' maid, Branwen, at the door, clutching her robe around her against the chill.

"I heard something—I thought the Queen called . . ." Hesitantly she came into the room.

"Faris must have had a nightmare. It is too bad she woke the King."

"*You* are awake." Branwen knelt, holding out her hands to the fire.

Farin lifted the spear so that ruddy light ran along the polished surface of the blade, forged from a piece of steel that had been dug from beneath the ruins near the shore. "I'm too excited to sleep," he admitted. "I've never hunted boar." Firelight gleamed on the use-smoothed eight-foot oak shaft as he lifted it and tested the blade.

"Be careful!" Branwen twisted her long braid of brown hair. She looked curiously vulnerable, with the firelight lending her its own soft beauty.

"The boar has a thick hide . . ." Farin tentatively touched the tip of the spear.

Branwen shivered and glanced at the window as if she expected the beast to come ravening through. "I wish you did not have to go."

"The boar has broken his own Covenant, killing a man. The

King must destroy him. Well, we will have roast pork for our Samaine Feast!" He blew dust from the surface of the blade.

Low laughter drifted from the King's room and he heard the creaking of the bed. Branwen took wood from the basket and as she leaned forward to place it on the fire her robe fell open and Farin saw the curve of her breast.

Farin felt his face flaming, not wholly because of the refuelling of the fire. He bent again to his work, but he could not keep from hearing the rhythmical creaking of the King's bed, and looking at Branwen's breast beneath her gown.

Jehan's hand slipped across Faris' breasts and over the curve of her belly, leaving a record of its passing in the tingling of her flesh.

"You still want me, even though my waistline has almost disappeared?"

"Is a ripe pear beautiful?"

"But I am becoming too round for us to be comfortable," she protested.

Jehan turned his head and his breath tickled her ear. "There is a way . . ."

Faris raised herself and moved above him, gasping as her flesh encompassed his. For several moments she held her breath, gazing down at the mystery of his face.

"It is all right for you to move now . . ." Jehan breathed at last.

Faris felt him trembling with something more than laughter. She could see him more clearly now, as if his body were becoming luminous. Her flesh radiated heat and she stilled, remembering other times she had felt such a glow—when she danced at Beltane, and when she put on the Jewels of Power. But this time she could choose whether to feed or to snuff the flame, and surrender herself completely at last.

Deliberately Faris set her hands upon Jehan's shoulders and began to move her body against his, riding waves of sweet fire that swept her toward some unimaginable shore until she no longer knew whether it was she who moved or he. She bent over him, seeking his spirit as her awareness of his separate body disappeared. Glimpses of her own face refracted from his consciousness to hers, blazing with a splendor in which her beauty was not so much transformed as revealed.

A cry swelled in her throat and she felt, rather than heard,

Jehan call out her name. Then she was falling, and her shout of triumph vibrated through every level of her being like the reverberations of a great golden bell.

Hearing that cry, Farin dropped the weapon he held. Branwen clutched at his arm, he turned and found himself kissing her. She gave a little sigh and her arms crept around his neck, and Farin, panting from a heat grown suddenly unendurable, tore at his clothing and sank down upon her before the fire.

The Master of the Junipers, meditating in his room on the floor below them, found his thoughts turning to festivals at the College of the Wise and smiled.

Rosemary stirred restlessly in her sleep, and turning her head into her pillow, murmured Eric's name.

Caolin moaned and ground his body against his crumpled blanket. The sound of ripping fabric woke him and he lay still, waiting for his pounding heart to slow and wondering angrily to whom he had been making love in his dream.

After a few moments he stumbled to the window, shrugging into his robe. There was a fresh, dawn smell to the air. He shivered, for the October air was chill, and rested his head in his hands. His body was still bruised from the ritual he had performed the week before, and since then he had known no peaceful sleep. Strangely Margit had been affected less than he . . . what had happened to Faris and Jehan?

When he opened his door, he saw a square of white upon the floor. The graceful writing was Jehan's—someone must have brought it during the night and feared to wake him. But the King was supposed to return to Laurelynn today—could he have learned somehow of the trap the Seneschal was forging for Brian? Caolin tore off the wrapper, cursed as the lines of writing dimmed and swam in the half-light, and fumbled with flint and steel.

"My dear friend . . . a rogue boar at Wilhamsted . . . enough men gathered to hunt the beast on Samaine eve." Caolin's eyes moved quickly over the candlelit paper. "Please make my apologies to the Lord Mayor and the others."

Samaine eve . . . thought Caolin. That was today. Jehan's delay would give him more time to seal Brian's fate. And yet . . . He stopped, wondering why his heart was pounding so heavily, and looked at the letter again.

"I will be going after a rogue boar . . ." An image of the

boar's mask that Caolin had used in his ritual swam before Jehan's words. And Wilhamsted lay at the foot of the Red Mountain . . .

"No!" Caolin swung his head back and forth in denial. "It is only a natural beast, and Jehan is a skilled hunter!" But he whimpered at the vision of the boar's head he had left on the Altar of Fire charging down the mountain to rend and slay.

"It is not my fault!" he cried again. "There is nothing I can do!" But already he was searching his wardrobe for a hunting tunic and hauling out his riding boots. Outside, the mists of morning dispersed before the growing light of day.

Jehan took another bite of bread and cheese, marvelling at the quantities of food with which the folk of Wilhamsted had weighted the table. This time, there was a grimmer meaning to the festival of the dead which they celebrated every year. Two of the men who had promised to help them avenge their son had yet to arrive, and Jehan knew they would need time to get organized. He forced himself to eat, stifling his impatience to get back to Faris. The memory of their lovemaking still shimmered through every nerve—what need had he of food?

"If this were war I would be going into battle with the King."

Jehan glanced across the room and saw his squire Philip standing with a girl of sixteen whose fingers played ceaselessly with the dagger at her belt.

"This *is* a war," she said grimly. "Neither of us has the weight to face the boar, but my father has assigned me to lead the beaters who will drive him into the trap. We will have plenty to do." Sir Walter of Wilhamsted's daughter spoke with a gloomy pride, fully aware of her status as sister of the boy who had been slain.

"My father says I make enough noise to wake the dead— I guess I can scare the boar . . . I hope we can see the men finish him." Philip said eagerly.

Jehan suppressed a smile, remembering how excited he had been to serve as a beater when his father hunted peccary in the south.

"Would you like some ale, my Lord?" A woman with thick iron-grey braids bound about her head stood holding out a tankard and smiling like an old friend. Jehan thanked her, frowning as he tried to remember her name.

"Oh, it was a long time ago, in the old King's time. Your

horse went lame near my holding and you stayed the night."
She laughed.

"Mistress Martina!" He took her hand, grinning as he remembered that he had slept that night with her. "Forgive me—
you have changed less than I."

"Well, you're a married man now, and with a child coming,
I hear."

Jehan smiled. "But for that, I would have brought my Lady
with me today." He was aware once more of muffled weeping
from the other room. "I wish Faris were here—when I spoke
to the boy's mother I did not know what to say."

"You are our own lord here, not only the King. It is enough
that you came."

There was a clatter of hooves and sounds of greeting from
outside. Jehan turned as the door opened and was surprised to
see his Seneschal there.

"Caolin!" The King's steps slowed and he frowned as Caolin
put back his hood. "Is something wrong?" The Seneschal's
pale hair bristled about his ears and his tunic was half unlaced.
But it was his face that stirred the quick throb of alarm.

Faris! he thought, then realized that Caolin had come not
from Misthall but from Laurelynn. "Are we invaded?" he laughed
with relief. He held out his hand and Caolin pressed his fingers
as if to reassure himself of the King's solidity.

"No—why should anything be wrong? You wrote you would
have some sport today and I thought I might join you. I know
the countryside hereabouts fairly well." The Seneschal straightened and passed a restraining hand over the disorder of his
hair. The King peered at him, wondering at the marks like old
bruises beneath Caolin's eyes. Even the flesh of his face was
subtly altered, as if it were losing its hold on his bones.

"Have you been ill?" Jehan handed him a tankard.

The Seneschal shook his head quickly. "I've been having
trouble sleeping. Perhaps I need exercise."

"Are you sure that is all? You must have *some* other reason
for coming here." Jehan looked at his friend narrowly but could
not interpret the color that came and went in Caolin's face. "I
can't believe you don't intend to seize this opportunity to talk
politics!"

Caolin took a long drink and shrugged. "I have no papers
with me, but there is always news." Jehan raised an inquiring
eyebrow. "The Lord Commander of Seagate is ill again, and
this time he is not expected to live."

The King sighed. "I shall be sorry to lose Hakon, and the lordship will be a heavy burden to come to Eric so young—I should know."

"And the Commissioners from Santibar will be returning soon," Caolin went on.

"Yes, I expected that," said Jehan absently, his thoughts still on Eric. Perhaps he could send the Master of the Junipers to him for a while.

"I thank you all for coming to me in my need—" Sir Walter's voice boomed around the room and Jehan and Caolin turned. "The afternoon is passing, and I have sworn not to lay my boy in the earth until I can bury the boar's head at his feet!"

Jehan stared, somewhat appalled at this passion for vengeance. *But what if one of mine were killed?* he wondered. *How would I feel?*

"You have marked the boar's run?" he asked quickly.

Sir Walter nodded. "He lairs on the slopes of the Red Mountain, but there is a gully through which he comes to wallow in the stream. We have the nets to span it and entangle him—"

"And *we* have the spears to pin him once he is caught!" said Farin.

"And the hounds?" said the King.

"Fifteen of them—the pack that I keep for the valley," said Jaime of Palodoro, a neighbor. "They will track anything on legs."

"And we have something to give them the scent," said Sir Walter with grim pride. He was holding out a boy's knife to which a few reddish bristles clung. "My boy marked him, and I swear that I will kill his slayer without delay, without pity—"

"Without breaking the Covenant." Jehan's quiet voice stilled the others as they remembered who and what he was.

"Then make the petition, and let us go!" whispered Sir Walter hoarsely.

Jehan lifted his weapon from the rack of spears, clasping his hands around its shaft, and the others followed his example with their own. The King took a deep breath and closed his eyes, reaching out to the men who stood with him.

"In the name of the four elements whose balance signifies the proper balance of all things; in the name of the Lord of All; may that Being who rules the Pig-tribe hear us now," cried the King.

"Hear us now!" the others echoed him.

"Upon these blades we swear that we begin this hunting not in malice nor for idle sport, but to enforce the Covenant that sets for each creature his own bounds. With our weapons we will come to grips with this boar, body to body, tusk to steel. And if he should prevail, we forgive him our deaths, as we ask thy forgiveness for his." In the silence that followed, the speartips touched with a succession of metallic clicks. Outside the dogs yapped eagerly, but the Red Mountain waited, unmoved.

"How long must we sit here?" Caolin peered through the screen of laurel branches at the slope of the Red Mountain above them.

"Have patience, old friend—" said the King in a low voice. "This hunting is not unlike war—a great deal of marching and waiting and a few flurries of action that finish before you quite know they've begun." He had not moved.

"Sir Walter says that every evening for the past week the boar has come this way to feed." Farin was sitting on a pitted curve of concrete that had been part of some ancient wall. "They are holding the dogs upwind until he enters the gully."

Caolin looked at Jehan's bright eyes and calm face and wondered if this was how he appeared to the men he led to battle. Both duty and inclination had always assigned the Seneschal what he considered the thornier problems of supplying the King's forces or negotiating a conclusion to his wars. Here was an aspect of Jehan's nature he had never had a chance to know.

Jehan smiled. "The waiting galls me too. My Lady and I have achieved our full joy at last, and I would be home again."

Caolin winced at the triumphant wonder in Jehan's eyes.

"Why not come home with me, Caolin?" the King went on. "We can give you a good meal and a soft bed."

The scraps from your table and a pallet by your door . . . how long can I live on the leftovers of your happiness, my Lord? The words trembled against the barrier of Caolin's lips.

Before he could voice a reply, the stillness was broken by the hysterical yammering of the hounds.

The three men sprang to their feet, reaching for their spears, all senses subordinated to hearing as they tried to interpret the confusion of barking and shouting and the boar's occasional deep grunt of rage.

"What's happening? We've got to see!" cried Farin. He swung himself into the bay tree and Jehan's protest was lost in the thrashing of branches. "Lord of Battles! He's a monster! They're all around him now, trying to drive him this way—" They heard a yelp of agony. "He's got one of the dogs . . . another . . . oh! Philip barely got out of the way!"

"Farin, get down! We must be ready—"

Jehan's order was interrupted by Farin's moan, "He's broken away!"

"What?"

"The boar—he charged straight up the bank!" The tree shuddered as Farin danced on his branch.

"Which side?" snapped the King.

"Ours!" Farin's voice squeaked unexpectedly.

"Down!" cried Jehan, "He must not catch us here!"

Caolin followed the King to the comparatively open ground of the canyon floor while Farin flung himself from his tree and crashed after them. They listened again, tracing the boar's progress by the yapping of the hounds.

"Sir Walter—" cried the King, "the boar is past the net! We must cut him off further down the canyon!" He drew his short hunting sword and began to hack at the ropes that held the net. In moments Sir Walter and his three men had joined them. When it was free they dragged it after them, hoping they could still use it to entangle their foe.

There was a patter of footfalls and Jaime of Palodoro stumbled around the bend behind them with Philip and the other beaters.

"Walter, I'm sorry—he's too crafty—" Jaime broke off as a dog burst from the bank beyond them, bleeding from a gash along his side.

"My Lord, we'll run down the canyon. You follow if the dogs flush the beast and we'll surround him—" Sir Walter led his men at a trot around the bend.

Caolin leaned on his spear, glancing nervously at the tumbled rocks of the gully's sloping sides. They were glowing now with the fiery light of the dying day.

"Jaime says that sometimes a boar will turn and hunt his hunters. They can move silently, he says, and—"

"Farin, be still." Jehan's quiet voice cut off the harper's babbling and steadied Caolin so suddenly that he wondered if the King could control the boar too. Then he jumped at a sound like a covey of quail taking flight—the noise of a heavy body penetrating brush at high speed.

The red boar erupted over the edge of the slope in a flurry of dogs. But before the hunters could seize the advantage he was on his feet again. Crimson-tusked he faced them, swiveling as they circled him, ears flicking and head swinging to track his enemies. His shoulder bore the festering wounds of some mating fight. Had that pain maddened him to invade the lands of men?

Caolin met the animal's furious gaze and took a step backward. Sir Walter shouldered past him and only the King's restraining hand kept him from charging the boar alone. The dogs danced about their foe, deafening the men with shrill yapping, but those that remained were more cautious now. The boar moved only enough to keep them from hamstringing him, rumbling his defiance at the men.

Sir Walter's daughter and Farin ran forward with the net, but the boar's rush drove them back again, tripping on the loose stones. Caolin felt the spear haft grow slippery in his grasp; every taunt with which Brian and others had ever questioned his courage echoed in his memory. Surreptitiously he wiped his palms—no one should doubt him now—but the reality of the boar was worse than its image in his ritual. His desperate glance sought the King.

Jehan balanced on the treacherous ground, spear poised, lips curving in an interested smile, his eyes never leaving the boar. "Drop the net," he said softly. "We will have to attack *him*."

"Then he'll charge for certain!" gasped one of the men.

"Jaime! Can you call the dogs to one more attack?" asked the King.

"Well, my Lord, I'll try." Jaime whistled sharply. His pack leader, a brindled bitch whose flanks were already splashed red, whined unhappily, then leaped forward, snapping at the boar's tender ears.

"Now!" shouted the King as the boar's head jerked and the dog was flung over their heads. Sir Walter screamed his battle cry.

Caolin found himself running forward with the others, aware of a blur of rocks and the vivid bulk of the boar. His spear hit as if he had struck a stone wall, the boar heaved and he felt his foot slip. Frantically Caolin tried to hold on while the boar twisted himself further onto the spears.

Battered by the struggles of the beast as he had battered at

Margit in his ritual, Caolin clung to his spear. The remaining dogs leaped in to hamstring their hampered enemy. The boar jerked convulsively and Caolin's mouth shut with a snap. There was a sharp crack and Jehan flew backward with a broken spearshaft in his hand.

The King rolled to his feet and drew his hunting sword. The boar swung to face him, eyes glowing furiously. The hunters swore, knowing they had not the strength to hold him if anyone withdrew his spear to try a new stab and give the King a safer opening.

"Don't attack from the front, my Lord—" called Jaime. "They cannot stop him if he goes for you!"

"Use the net!" screeched Farin.

"Jaime cannot throw it without tangling you. If I wait he may break loose and savage you all." The King crouched, still smiling. "Hold fast!"

The blood drummed in Caolin's ears. "Jehan, don't!" he found his voice as the King lunged. His swinging steel flared in the light of the setting sun.

Time expanded with a terrible clarity as the bright blade fell. It struck the vulnerable crease where the boar's neck and shoulder met. Then the fury in the boar's eyes dazzled Caolin with flame and darkness and his fingers lost their hold on the spear.

The boar surged forward, his bright blood spattering the men who were no longer enough to hold him, and struck the King. The huge head lowered to gore his foe. Sir Walter tugged the axe from his belt and brought it down with all his strength upon the animal's spine. The boar seemed to rock upward, then dropped, jerking until the mortal message of his wounds finally reached his limbs.

Blood covered the boar, the ground, Caolin's eyes. He groped for a twitching foreleg and found other hands beside his, hauling the body of the boar from the King. *I did this . . . it came of my ritual . . .* Accusations reverberated in his brain. Then the red bulk was gone. Caolin collapsed to his knees.

"Caolin—" Jehan was breathless. "Now you can use what you learned of healing at the College of the Wise. Quickly, before I begin to feel the pain."

The tumult in Caolin's mind stilled. "Yes, Jehan," he heard his own clear reply. Dark blood was welling from beneath the King's leather tunic. Caolin lifted it and saw the red tear cutting raggedly from his groin up his side.

"First we must stop the bleeding. Give me your shirts—" He pressed the wadded cloth they gave him against Jehan's side.

"Is he dead?" Farin's voice wavered. Caolin's heart thumped as he saw that Jehan's eyes were closed.

"It is the Feast of the Dead!" said one man with a superstitious shiver. "He is the Sacrifice!"

"He's just fainted!" said Sir Walter bracingly, pulling his shirt over his head.

Mechanically Caolin cast away the soaked rag and applied another, putting all his weight upon it, willing the bleeding to ease. If the boar's tusk had torn the femoral artery there would be nothing he could do. His lips moved soundlessly in the first petition he had made since he left the College of the Wise.

"Do you need another bandage?"

Caolin looked up and felt an obscure pang of sympathy for the terror in Philip's face. Then he realized that the stain on the pad pressed against the King's side had ceased to grow. He took Philip's shirt and swiftly used it to replace the one that had stanched the wound.

"The bleeding is under control," he breathed. "Give me strips to bind the bandage on." Caolin felt down the King's body for other injuries.

As their shock eased the others began to talk. Caolin heard the dull, regular blows with which Sir Walter was hacking off the head of the boar.

"By all the Guardians, Jaime, why didn't you stop the King?" asked Farin.

"I couldn't reach him in time! Why didn't you all stand fast? The beast shook you like dogs and the Seneschal let go of his spear."

Caolin tensed, but Farin was already protesting, describing the boar's strength with a bard's flow of imagery that silenced dispute.

"I believe the King's leg is broken—" Caolin finished his examination. "Let me have the broken spearshaft to splint it before we move him. And we will need a litter to carry him home."

"Bind that damned net to some spears to make a hammock," suggested Sir Walter. "We might as well get some use out of it."

Caolin bent over Jehan, gently stroking his hair. The King's head turned restlessly and his lips moved.

". . . forgive him our deaths as we . . ." the blue eyes opened and focused upon the headless body of the boar, ". . . ask thee to forgive us his," he finished. "How badly am I hurt?"

"I have done what I could, Jehan," said Caolin. "Your leg is broken and there is a hole in your side, but I think there is nothing that cannot heal."

The King breathed in carefully. "You must get me home, to Faris. Take me to Misthall!" He was growing paler, and sweat beaded his brow.

"Yes, my Lord," said Sir Walter. "We are making a litter, but it will be a rough ride and I am afraid we will cause you pain."

"Never mind—" said Jehan with a ghost of his old grin. "If I am lucky I will faint again."

They stumbled homeward through the gathering dusk, Caolin walking beside the litter with his eyes on the pale face of the King while his feet found their own road. An east wind chilled the back of his neck as if the Mountain were sending its cold breath after them. Caolin looked back and shivered, for the slope above him reproduced the silhouette of the boar against the dimming sky.

A cold wind was blowing through the open door of the Hall. Faris drew her shawl more closely around her, wishing she could close it, but on this night every household in Westria left open one door, as they set candles flickering on their window-sills, to guide the returning spirits of the Dead and to welcome them home.

The scent of Carlota's walnut pastry wafted enticingly from the kitchen. She should be in there, gossiping with the others, not waiting here alone in the darkened hall. They would have a fine feast tomorrow, with a ham from their own cellars if Jehan did not bring home a haunch of the boar.

But where was he? Whether or not they had killed, he should have been home before dark. Was he so excited by the hunt that he had forgotten her? He had never had a wife to consider before. But how could Jehan forget her after last night—when even the warm flush of memory felt as if it would melt her bones?

"Faris—what are you doing here?" The Master of the Junipers was like a shadow himself in his grey robe. She turned to him, wordless, and he put his arm around her. "It will be all right, Faris—Jehan is too courteous to rush away from his hosts, no matter how eager he is to be home."

He brought her a cloak and built up the fire since she would not go to a warmer room. But it was long past sunset, and the rest of the household had joined them there, before they finally heard the sound of hooves on the road.

Faris went to the doorway. Torches were bobbing through the mists that blanketed the hillside without visible support, as if they were being borne by the spirits of the dead. The damp air caught in her throat and she coughed.

"They don't seem very jubilant—" said Rosemary brightly. "Do you suppose the boar got away?"

"Be quiet, Rosemary." Peering through the shrouding fog, Faris stepped slowly across the porch, down the first stair . . . the second . . . Then she waited, unable to move.

The Master of the Junipers hurried past her as the procession neared. Like images in some evil dream Faris saw Caolin's haunted eyes, saw the wagon beside him and the blood, blood everywhere. They halted. Carefully they lifted a litter from the wagon. She saw Jehan's white unconscious face and the moisture glittering on his hair and beard.

Faris tottered forward, screaming his name. But they would not let her go to him.

III

A Season of Pain

>   My greatest pleasure has become the simple release from pain . . .

Jehan's pen slipped and carefully he moved his good leg to brace the Journal in which he was writing. The wound in his groin still throbbed dully, though the boar hunt had been a month ago.

For convenience they had put him in the old King's bedroom on the first floor of Misthall, with its great carved bedstead and heavy curtains of faded blue brocade. Jehan turned a page, marvelling that he had filled two-thirds of the Journal since June.

> I dream that I am in my own bed with Faris beside me— just holding her, breathing the mountain-flower scent of her hair. And then I wake in darkness and remember that my parents both died in this bed . . . Farin's music would help me, but I don't want to wake him in the night.

Farin was playing for him now, his fingers wandering across the harpstrings in a seeming random pattern through which a melody threaded like the gold in the curtains' brocade. Through the window beyond him Jehan glimpsed morning sunlight glittering on the blue of the Bay, very welcome after a week of rain.

The King put down his pen. "What is the tune?"

Farin looked up, color rising in his cheeks. "Just a harpsong, my Lord."

"It sounded like a love song to me."

"I suppose, in a way, it is . . ." Farin's fingers caressed

the gold inlay of the harp's frame a moment before they settled once more on the strings and he sang—

> *"My little harp, for thy great gift of music,*
> *I offer now this faltering song to thee.*
> *More faithful hast thou been than any lover,*
> *And sweeter thy companionship to me.*
> *I seek thy touch when worn by fear or sorrow,*
> *And ever comes thy answer cheerfully—*
> *For thee I must forgo all tears and anger—*
> *Thy nature knows no bitter harmony."*

Farin played the harp as though it had become a part of him, modulating the end of his first verse, then continuing—

> *"To me thou art the very shape of beauty,*
> *Thy weight against my breast delights my heart.*
> *And when my roving fingers wake thy music,*
> *My ears rejoice. Obedient to my art,*
> *Thy sweet response is yet more sweet unbidden,*
> *And when, unwilled, I hear thy singing start,*
> *I know not which of us has made the music,*
> *Or if the god of love plays now a part."*

Jehan remembered times when he and Faris had made such harmony . . . He roused as the last notes died away and looked at Farin.

"Don't you ever want a human being who can return your love?"

Farin rested his forehead against the smooth wood of the harp. "I have been with women, and it was good, but when I am playing Swangold sometimes music comes that I never heard before. I don't know what we are reaching for, but I think that together Swangold and I may find it, someday . . ."

Faris and I found it, the night before I hunted the boar . . . thought Jehan, *But now she seems so far from me, and it is all to do again.* He sighed, remembering how he had feared he would never succeed in giving her joy, and now he feared she might tire of waiting for him to be able to make love to her again. Human beings were so vulnerable—perhaps Farin had made the better choice.

"I am selfish to keep you here, Farin," Jehan said abruptly. "You should be studying at the College of Bards."

"Oh my King, let me stay!" Farin exclaimed. "Perhaps one day I will follow the Bard's road, but not yet, not now!"

"Where is he going?" Faris gently closed the door behind her. She was wearing a loose gown of a blue as pale as the rain-washed sky and her arms were full of chrysanthemums whose spicy scent filled the air.

"I only suggested . . ." began the King, but Farin's "No-where!" interrupted him.

Faris shook her head in exasperation and began to remove the old flowers from the vase beside the bed.

"I've no need to ask what you've been doing this morning," Jehan smiled.

"Oh, it's a beautiful day! The poplars are all pale gold, and the firs look black against this sky. After a rain everything glows and you forget how dreary it was before." She kissed him and he breathed in scents of damp leaves and rain-fresh wind. There was a splash of mud on her sleeve.

"Yes, and I suppose you have forgotten to change your shoes, too."

"Oh Jehan! They will dry soon enough. You are the one who has been ill—why do you worry about me?" Her voice came muffled through the fall of her hair as she bent over the vase. "I could nurse you as well as Rosemary . . ."

"You were always sick when we were children—" said Farin.

Faris dashed her hair from her eyes and turned on him, "And *you* were always breaking bones—but now you go to war."

Jehan stared at her uncomfortably. He had told the Master of the Junipers to keep her away because he feared to let her see him weeping with pain.

"Faris," he faltered, "we wanted to spare you, because of the child."

"Spare me!" She slipped to her knees beside the bed and hid her face against his arm. "Perhaps you are right! I might have begged to be allowed to go away! But you never gave me the chance to try . . ."

Jehan turned on his side to stroke her hair, murmuring her name, and she twisted suddenly to meet his lips. He felt a familiar stirring in his loins, and though it was a faint reflection of remembered fires, his arms went around Faris exultantly. For a long moment they remained so, until the strained position tired his weakened muscles and he lay back on his pillows.

"Is everything ready for Eric's ceremony?" he asked a little breathlessly.

"As ready as we can make them," said Farin. "I wish he could wait."

"Eric could wait, but he should not," replied Jehan. "Every day we put off his investiture as Lord Commander will make it harder for him to step into his father's shoes."

"I think Eric will be happier with a small ceremony." Faris smiled.

"It won't be that small—" her brother replied. "Eric's family is coming, and people from Seagate, and the other Commanders. At least Robert of the Ramparts will come, and Lord Brian if the Commissioners get back from Santibar in time."

"Yes, and Caolin will be here too. I will be glad to see him again." said Jehan.

Caolin picked up the letter and compared it with the one on his desk. The sprawling writing was the same, and the signature that covered half the page. Even the seal showed a realistic variation in depth and angle. The man whom Ordrey had found to write the letter was indeed a master of his craft. Brian himself would have cause to wonder if he had penned these words. Caolin flattered himself that he had fairly caught Brian's blustering style. It was a pretty style for treason.

But would Jehan believe it?

The Seneschal rested his head in his hands, kneading the taut muscles in his forehead. After the first shock, Caolin had realized that Jehan's accident gave him time to prepare a weapon against Brian. And it must be used. With Jehan too ill to control him, Brian was even more dangerous.

But his plot was horribly uncertain. What if Brian's agents learned of the forgery? What if Brian evaded arrest and led the south into rebellion, or even joined forces with Elaya?

Tomorrow he must go to Misthall to see Eric of Seagate invested as Lord Commander of his Province. Caolin fingered the forged letter, wondering whether he would have the courage to give it to Jehan. Brian had left Santibar with the other Commissioners over a week ago.

He was running out of time.

It was time to begin.

Jehan nodded to the herald of Seagate, and the old man stepped out before the company whose bright robes glowed in the afternoon sunlight, the petition trembling in his hand.

"We, the people of Seagate, having lately lost our beloved lord . . . do now desire Jehan, King of Westria to give to us another, to be our gracious governor in time of peace and our leader in time of war . . ."

"Whom do the people of Seagate ask for their Lord?" The Seneschal's calm reply carried the ritual forward.

"They ask for Eric of the Horn, accepted by the landholders of Seagate as Lord Hakon's heir." The herald bowed to the King.

Jehan shifted uncomfortably in his cushioned chair, avoiding the eyes of the Master of the Junipers. Caolin turned to him.

"My Lord, is it your will to grant this request?"

"It is my will."

Caolin shifted smoothly to face the company. "Then let Eric of the Horn come into the presence of the King."

Jehan pulled himself upright—Eric must not see him slumped in his chair. The far doors of the Hall were flung open and the steward of Bongarde entered, followed by two men and three women who represented the landholders of the Province. After them came Eric's mother, the Lady of Seagate, and his sister Astrid.

There was a silence as Eric came through the door, robed in white. Jehan flinched before the exaltation in his eyes as the young man knelt before him and bowed his head. *Lord of All!* he thought, *Did I ever look like that?*

The Master came to stand beside the King's chair, his almost ugly features made beautiful by some inner light above the splendor of the green cope he wore.

"My Lords and Ladies—" he said gently. "To make a man responsible for the welfare of part of Westria is a heavy thing. It has been long since you needed a new lord, so it is meet that we consider the reasons for this ceremony."

Jehan relaxed a little, listening to the harsh sweetness of the Master's voice repeating the words they had prepared together.

"In the time of the Cataclysm, most of those men who had survived the onslaught of the elements wandered naked and desperate, for without their machines they did not know how to live. But even in the time of the Ancients' power, some had sought other ways. And in the land we now call Seagate they gathered, and in the Sacred Wood they signed the Covenant. Thus the oldest names, and laws, and faith became new, and this was the foundation of Westria."

Jehan remembered the beauty of the Lady Mountain, and of the Sacred Wood at its feet. If only he could go there now, surely peace would come to him.

"Westria is like a body," the Master went on, "all of whose parts must be healthy if the whole is to survive. But each part of the body has to have its own health too. If the Kingdom, the Provinces and the holdings are well-nurtured, then all will thrive. The animal kindreds are governed by the wills of their Guardians, but men have need of more formal bonds than they."

The King tensed, knowing what was coming now.

"Yet paper laws are easily forgotten," said the Master, "and so we live by words sworn, hands clasped, eyes meeting without fear. Holders swear by their land and bear responsibility for it to the Lord or Lady commanding them. The Commanders, having responsibility for the Provinces, are protected by the King or Queen, who stands for Westria before the Maker of All Things! By each to each the bond of faith is sworn, a chain of loyalty that is the strength of Westria . . ."

And the whole weight of it rests upon the King, Jehan thought bitterly.

"Knowing to what you commit yourself, are you, Eric of the Horn, ready to pledge your faith to the King of Westria this day?" asked the Master.

Jehan leaned forward to meet the young man's clear gaze.

"I am ready, my Lord . . ."

The King gripped the clasped hands that Eric offered him. "Eric, swear now to me these things—" his voice strengthened as Eric echoed his words. ". . . to provide such support in goods or men as I may need to preserve Westria . . . to obey my lawful commands in peace or in war . . . and to speak only truth to me, whatever may befall!" The King swallowed and took a firmer grip on Eric's hands. "By what will you swear these things?"

Eric looked up at him and smiled. "I will swear by the land of Seagate that bore me, and by the sword which I have never drawn in an evil cause, and by my love for you. May my own sword turn against me if ever I fail!"

Jehan's breath caught. "Listen to me well then, for the things I promise you must swear in turn to those who will call you lord . . ." His voice trembled.

"I, Jehan of Westria, do pledge to you, Eric, these things: to come at your call and support you with goods and men, saving only the greater need of all Westria; to rule you according to the Covenant and traditions of Westria, to judge you mercifully; and to answer your truth with my own."

His eyes were dazzled by golden light. He felt the strength of Eric's hands between his, and as he went on, it seemed only natural that he should for a moment feel the firm pressure of another pair of hands clasped over his own.

"This I swear to you, Eric, by the Four Jewels of Westria, and by the help of the Guardian of Men. And may all who have sworn to me deny me if I fail!"

Eric's hands slipped from his grasp and Jehan fell back in his chair, the words of his own binding ringing terribly in his ears. The sun had gone down and he could see nothing in the sudden dimness of the room.

"By what tokens shall the people of Seagate know that Eric of the Horn is truly their lord?" asked the steward of Bongarde.

"By the token of the sword—" Robert of the Ramparts stepped forward, solid as one of his own mountains, and held out the blade that Eric's father had worn. "Your forebears never used this weapon but with all their strength and never bore it in flight from a battlefield. Now it is your turn—use it well!" He bowed and gave the sword into Eric's large hands.

"By the token of the mantle—" Faris shook out the folds of a cloak dyed so dark a green it was almost black and draped it across Eric's broad shoulders. "As this mantle covers him," she said softly, "so shall he spread his protection over all beings committed to his care."

"By the token of the coronet—" said the Master of the Junipers, bringing out a roundel of twisted gold. "As it crowns the Lord Commander, so shall he be the head of his people, as the King is above him, and beyond the King the Lord of All." Gently the Master set the golden band upon Eric's brown curls.

"And by the token of the ring, which I give to him as symbol of the contract made this day between him and me," said Jehan, drawing from off his thumb a heavy golden ring. The last person for whom he had performed this ceremony had been Brian of Las Costas. How could he keep his oaths when those to whom he had sworn them were at odds? Even the Jewels had no magic to deal with this. Carefully he slid the ring onto the little finger of the younger man's left hand.

"Eric, Lord Commander of Seagate, rise!" he said then, and

Eric got to his feet, looking around him as if he wondered how all those people had come there. Gold shone on his head and on his hand, and the dark folds of his cloak set off the golden hilt of his sword, but none of the gold shone as brightly as his eyes.

"People of Seagate, behold your lord!" cried the herald. "Recognize the tokens of his leadership, and as you return to the west tell all what you have seen." There was a blast of trumpets from somewhere outside the Hall.

"Hail Eric of Seagate!" cried the steward, and others echoed him. Robert gave his new peer a hearty hug, then stepped back to let Eric's mother take him in her arms. Jehan saw Rosemary watching them wistfully and wondered if Eric could be persuaded to marry her. A babble of congratulation filled the air.

"My Lord, we should get you back to your bed," said Patrick in his ear.

"Very well, but give me those crutches. I'll not have them see me being carried out of here."

Jehan managed to leave the Hall with fair grace, but by the time he had hobbled down the corridor to his room he was sweating. He rolled himself onto the great bed and lay waiting for the pounding of his heart to slow.

"Jehan . . ." It was Caolin's voice. The King opened his eyes and made out the gleam of the Seneschal's fair hair in the shadows by the door.

"Please my Lord—can't you see he is exhausted?" protested Patrick.

"Yes. I know . . . but this cannot wait," blurted Caolin, coming toward the bed. Jehan had a fancy that the shadows were following him, and knew that he must be very tired. If he pretended to be asleep, Caolin might go away.

"Jehan, I need to talk to you."

The King sighed and opened his eyes. "Let him stay." When he heard the door close he rolled over. Caolin still stood in the middle of the room. "Well—pull up a chair so I can see you— quickly, or I *will* go to sleep!"

Slowly Caolin came to the bedside. "While our Commissioners were collecting evidence in Santibar, the Elayans seem to have been searching too. They hold to their accusations, and this paper was sent to me."

Shadows swam before Jehan's eyes. "Light a candle—do you expect me to read it in the dark?"

The flickering light made a mockery of the planes and hollows of Caolin's face, but the words on the paper were only too clear.

> . . . the time has come now for the move we agreed on when I visited you in Balleor. The King is grown weak and thinks only of this woman he has found in the north. Therefore raid into Elaya now. Help me, and you shall have the holding I promised you, and I . . .

Jehan's gaze jumped down to the signature, but he had already guessed what it must be. The note was addressed to Sir Miguel de Santera, Commander of the fortress at Balleor.

"I suppose that Brian did visit Balleor last spring?" he whispered hopelessly, and then, "I cannot believe it. I did not know he hated me so."

"Jehan, Brian must be punished." Caolin said gently.

"Why? No one can stop Elaya from attacking now . . ."

"Jehan—Brian is dangerous to *you!* He gave Ronald Sandreson that gold!"

"What?" Jehan seized on the distraction of Ronald. "You mean you found him?"

Caolin's face was in shadow. "It was just after your wedding, my Lord. Ronald was weak already, and . . . he died. I was the only one who heard what he said, and I had no proof. I did not think you would wish to be bothered then."

Jehan stared at him. The news that Ronald had died while a prisoner connected with something that had happened in Laurelynn last summer. He struggled to remember, but the significance slipped from his grasp.

"Caolin, are you sure that Ronald got that gold from Brian?"

"My Lord—" the Seneschal sounded faintly offended. "I will swear if you like."

Jehan sighed. "No. I have had too many oaths—only look at me . . ." He gripped Caolin's arm as his eyes fixed the other man's and saw what might be relief there, but no wavering. "Have I been so poor a judge of men?"

"You must execute or imprison Brian now."

"His peers will judge him, not I."

Caolin turned his ring of office around and around. "What of Las Costas? Shall a traitor's spawn hold the power?"

"A boy of six? He has done no wrong, and his mother is a strong woman who can rule until he is grown. I will not interfere with another man's inheritance."

Caolin drew another paper from his pouch and Jehan turned his head away.

"No, Caolin, no more. Have you not shown me treason enough for one day?"

"This is the order to summon Brian for questioning," the Seneschal spoke softly. "Jehan . . . I swear I did not *want* to do this to you . . ."

The King could not answer him. The candlelight seemed powerless against the darkness in the room. He grasped the pen Caolin thrust between his fingers and without really focusing on the words on the paper managed to scrawl his name.

The Seneschal picked up the mug that Patrick had left and slipped an arm beneath the King's head. "Drink this now, my Lord. Now you can rest."

"Sleep perhaps . . . but I will get no rest unless I wake to find that Brian's treachery was only a dream. Oh, Caolin—I trusted him!"

The Master of Junipers shut his book of medicine with a snap. "I trust my own skill less and less the longer this illness of Jehan's goes on!" he exclaimed, moving restlessly to the window of his chamber and staring out through the narrow panes of old glass. Low clouds rolled across the Bay and over the hills. He had gone over his notes and the books sent from the College of the Wise, and found no certainty. One passage echoed in his memory—

A hidden pocket of infection can sap a patient's strength.
If found and lanced it may be cured, if not, it may burst
and poison him, causing fever and death . . .

But how did one know if that were the cause of the trouble, and how could one find such a spot once the wound closed? Something had weighed on the King's mind ever since Eric's investiture. He was a more cooperative patient now, but he would not tell them what troubled him, and he did not heal.

The Master tried to think of someone who might know more. His own teacher was dead and the College presently had no one who specialized in healing. Though every landholder knew enough to deal with ordinary maladies, few studied the curing of more subtle ills.

"In Westria we are like the beasts with whom we share the land. Either we recover quickly or we die and let others take our places here," he told himself wryly. "But no one can take Jehan's place . . ."

He rested his forehead against the cool glass. Once he had been linked with the Mistress of the College, but remembering how they had parted in Laurelynn, he did not know if she would respond to his call.

"And I do not even know if pride makes me hesitate to call her, or fatigue makes me wish that I could . . ." Jehan had awakened him with a nightmare the night before, and he had found it hard to sleep afterward. He had even sought comfort in laying out the tarot, but the cards were all at odds with one another, and they ended with the *Moon*, whose reflected light showed only error and uncertainty.

But now it was time for him to return to the King. The day was still gloomy, but his heart lightened as he heard the cheerful murmur of women's voices from the Hall, and he was smiling as he opened the door to the King's room.

"I feel as if it has been cloudy forever, and as if I have been pregnant forever!" exclaimed Faris, hunting through her workbox for a skein of green silk.

Carlota laughed. "I know, but spring will come, and when it does the baby will come too!" Her foot continued its steady pressure on the spinning wheel and the cloud of wool in her capable fingers twirled into an even thread.

"And the cold season is half gone—next week will be the Midwinter holiday." said Branwen. "The King sat in his chair most of yesterday, do you think he will be well enough to preside over the feast?" she looked at Rosemary.

Rosemary finished threading her needle and smiled reassuringly, but Faris did not think the smile reached her eyes. *I will not ask her why, if everything goes well, the shadow stays in her face*, Faris told herself. *Jehan has made it perfectly clear he does not want me in his sickroom, so I will be good, and hold my tongue.*

"Yes of course Jehan will be well," she said aloud. "If Eric's ceremony had not exhausted him he might be up now! Why couldn't he wait?" She jerked her needle through the fine cotton of the baby gown she was embroidering.

"It wasn't Eric's fault!" exclaimed Rosemary. "The King insisted . . ." she stopped, realizing that Faris had not accused Eric.

"Oh, my lord was always willful—even as a lad," said Carlota comfortably. "But so well-mannered you'd done what he wanted before you thought. I daresay he doesn't realize himself how much he's had his way."

Oh my beloved, I wait upon your will . . . the needle trembled in Faris' fingers, scattering light from the little fire. *I wait for your child to be born and I wait for you to return to me.*

"Is that thunder?" asked Branwen. Carlota took her foot from the spinning wheel. "No, someone's coming up the road from the Bay, and fast, by the sound."

Rosemary dropped her mending and went to the window. "There is a horse-ferry down at our pier. The banner . . . is blue," she finished in disappointment.

"From Las Costas, then," said Carlota.

"Has Lord Brian come a week late for the investiture?" Branwen giggled.

Without conscious decision, Faris folded the baby gown and replaced it in her sewing bag. She stuck her needle in its case and latched her workbox shut. Did she hear hoofbeats, or only the thudding of her heart? What did the horseman want? Was it someone who would drain the strength Jehan had so hardly regained? Faris straightened her skirts and moved slowly to the entrance hall.

The great door crashed against the wall and Brian strode through, head down like a bull looking for something to charge. Faris braced herself.

After a moment he focused on her and sketched a bow. "My Lady—I must see the King."

"My Lord is ill—if your affair is urgent you should go to Laurelynn." Faris lifted her chin as she saw a yellow glow begin to smoulder in Brian's hazel eyes.

"To Caolin? Nay, Caolin's master must answer me now!"

"*Must* answer you?" Faris heard a rustle and knew Rosemary was behind her.

"He must answer me or be forsworn—it is a matter of my honor, and if you cannot understand what that means you are no fit mate for a King!"

"Your honor will have to wait! I am fit mate enough to protect my Lord, and that is all that matters to me!"

"Could you write your message, Lord Brian?" asked Rosemary.

Brian seemed to see her for the first time. "Nay—I cannot put such a thing into scribe's talk! It must be my voice to his ears—my eyes meeting his. Paper can carry too many lies!"

Farris barred the passageway, her hands clenched in the

skirts of her gown. "Go back, my Lord—you shall not enter here!"

"If you wished to spare the King you should have kept your voices down—" said a tired voice behind her. Faris whirled and saw the Master of the Junipers.

"King Jehan says that he will see the Lord Commander of Las Costas now . . ."

Brian hesitated as if suspecting some new obstacle, but Faris stepped aside, still trembling with rage. Lowering his head, the Lord Commander stalked past the Master toward the open door of the King's room.

Faris covered her face with her hands. "I tried to help him! Why is there nothing I can do?"

The Master put his arms around her and she leaned gratefully against him, feeling his concern as she felt the rough texture of his robe.

"I know . . . my dear, I know. He has shut me out too . . ."

"You *are* ill!" exclaimed Brian. "I thought it was a tale to keep me away!"

"I am well enough to deal with you!" said Jehan icily. "If the Queen has taken any harm I *will* have your head!" He struggled to push himself upright, Faris' furious voice still reverberating in his ears.

Brian shut the door of the chamber and took a few steps into the room. "You did ask me to come in . . ." he said a little more quietly. "But you have little cause to chide me, since you ordered me imprisoned without cause."

"I ordered you held for trial—" said Jehan bitterly. "If you are innocent that should be no heavy thing. And how did you know what the order was?"

"Not all in the Seneschal's Office are his creatures. I have friends who would not see injustice done." Brian dragged a chair to the King's bedside, but remained standing, gripping its back.

"Friends like Ronald Sandreson?" Jehan saw Brian's look of scorn tempered by surprise. "That touches you, does it?"

"If Ronald implicates me, bring him to trial—if he *does* accuse me . . ."

"You would rather be tried for what you and Ronald did than for what you wrote?"

"Wrote? Where?" Brian sat down.

Jehan stared at him. He would not have thought that Brian

could feign such honest indignation. "The letter you wrote to Sir Miguel de Santera at Balleor, ordering him to raid Elaya and provoke a war," he said very distinctly.

Brian's cheeks went pale and red again above his beard. "I see that you think me a traitor, Lord, but do you think me a fool? I dealt with Ronald Sandreson, but do you think I would have set my seal to treason?"

"You might think treason to the Kingdom worse than treason to the King . . ." said Jehan tiredly. "But do you think the lords of Westria will acquit you of paying Ronald to assassinate *me?*"

Brian surged to his feet. "That's a lie! That . . . I gave the man gold to gather support for my petition—if he tried murder it was on his own, and if Ronald said I ordered it he is trying to save his own skin." He paused for breath. "Or Caolin has made him implicate me! Let me face Ronald and we'll have the truth."

"That's a safe request . . . Did not your spy in Laurelynn tell you that Ronald died?" said Jehan softly. "And I have seen the letter myself."

"He died! How fortunate for you!" said Brian sarcastically. "And I wrote no letter . . ."

"Brian! I have *seen* it!" cried Jehan, no longer able to suppress his pain. "It was in your writing, with your signature and your seal!"

For a long moment Brian stared at him and the King saw the fire fade gradually from those yellow eyes. He sat down and remained still for several minutes, slowly shaking his head.

"All the way here I was storing up accusations . . . thinking you had broken your oath to me . . ." Brian whispered at last. Jehan felt suddenly dizzy, as if he stood on the edge of a precipice.

"Oh my dear Lord—I see that we are equally betrayed."

Jehan shivered. What had Brian said?

"My Lord, I swear to you by my knight's honor and by the head of my son, I paid Ronald only to persuade men to my cause." Brian leaned forward, forearms braced on his knees, eyes fixed on Jehan's. "Oh Jehan—my writing is an ill-formed scrawl that anyone could imitate, and impressions can be taken from seals!" Brian's rough head bowed and the rest of his words came muffled through his beard. "But if you cannot believe me, I will go into exile from Westria . . ."

Jehan felt his spirit swing like an unmoored boat. Caolin

had not said that Brian wrote the letter, he had only given it to the King. He had not said that Ronald accused Brian—only that Brian had given Ronald the gold. He had told only the truth, but that truth added up to such an overwhelming lie . . .

"I meant to spend the winter repairing the southern fortresses . . . somebody should . . ." his look was suddenly piteous. *"Do* you believe me?"

Jehan stared at him. It would contradict all he knew of Brian, all he knew of men, to think that this man could dissimulate. To serve the Kingdom's good, was Caolin capable of denying all that Westria was good for?

"Yes, I believe you . . ." Jehan whispered at last. "I did not wish to condemn you, Brian—you always opposed me honestly, and I trusted you. But you see, I trusted *him* too . . ." With a kind of dim wonder he saw the other man's fierce eyes brighten with unshed tears.

"My Lord!" said Brian, "We have had our differences, but I have always been your true man!" He dropped to his knees beside the bed. "Jehan, King of Westria—I, Brian of Las Costas do swear to you . . . to spend my goods, my men, my very life for Westria . . . and to speak only truth to you, my Lord, whatever may befall!"

"And may all who have sworn to me . . ." Jehan's voice broke on the words from the ritual of investiture and he reached out blindly to the other man, bruising his fingers on the ring he had given Brian so long ago.

"It will only be justice if I fall in this war . . ." said Brian at last. "I should have kept Ronald under control."

If it be a crime to trust one's servants, then I am guilty too, thought Jehan. A memory of a morning in Laurelynn when Caolin's face had looked like a badly erased manuscript surfaced suddenly. Caolin had said that a man had died under his questioning, and Jehan's heart cried, *How did Ronald die?*

The King shook his head. "No, Brian—is such a price required of lords whose men do ill? Live, Brian! I think you will be needed soon."

Brian met Jehan's gaze and his face twitched as if its strong lines were about to disintegrate. "Jehan, you are tired . . . I have stayed too long. But we will sort this thing out somehow." He stumbled toward the door.

"Brian—say nothing of this . . ." called Jehan.

The Lord Commander turned. "I understand, and I trust you, my Lord."

*But do I trust myself? I trusted Caolin—there must be some
explanation, something he can say* . . . Jehan's mind flinched
from the thought. Rain pattered against the windows. The King's
hands and feet twitched with reaction. He swung his feet over
the side of the bed and pulled himself upright as the Master of
the Junipers came into the room.

"Jehan, what is going on? What did Brian say to you?"

The King shook his head and made his way to the window.
Hoofbeats thudded dully on the muddy ground outside and he
heard Farin half-heartedly wishing Brian a good journey. How
could he tell the Master what had happened today? He was no
longer sure what was true.

Lanterns glimmered down the road—Brian's men must have
come to light him back to the pier. Jehan peered through the
rain. Someone shouted, the King fumbled for the catch and
threw open the window.

". . . name of the King!" he heard, and then, more clearly,
Brian's deep reply, "I have just come from the King! Stuff
your damned order of arrest . . ."

There was more yelling, then the clash of steel.

"Treachery!" cried Brian, "Las Costas, to me!"

"No!" muttered Jehan, "Not treachery, not mine . . ." he
stopped, remembering the order he had signed for Caolin without reading it. He flung open the door to the porch, anger
burning all awareness of weakness away, then hobbled across
it and swung himself down the half-flight of wooden steps to
the rock garden.

His picked his way through the darkness, cursing the clumsy
cast. When he fell he clambered back to his feet, ignoring the
shouting behind him. The Master would not know this path,
they could not stop him now. Lanterns bobbed before him.
Jehan heard the dull smack of a sword biting a wooden shield.
Brian was the Kingdom's champion, but he was alone. How
many were attacking him? Gravel pricked his bare feet and he
forced his legs to carry him forward.

"He resisted—cut him down quickly in the King's name!"
A small man reined a piebald horse around the edge of the
fight.

"In my own name I command you—put down your swords!"
Jehan cried in the voice he had trained for the battlefield.

"It is the King!" shouted Brian.

"The King . . . the King is here . . . but they said . . ."

voices faltered as the riders fell back to either side and they saw Jehan standing in the road.

The man on the piebald horse was Ordrey, still clutching a bit of paper in his hand. "But the order . . ." he began.

"The order is void! Lord Brian is under my protection." The lights dimmed and whirled around him. "Go back and bid your master come to me!"

Ordrey's horse squealed as the man reined it sharply around and slashed at its haunches with his riding whip. In a moment he was clattering down the road. One of his men swore, then followed, and the others went after him.

Footsteps splashed on the road as Farin ran toward him, then the bulk of a horse blocked the light. Brian threw himself from the saddle and caught the King in his arms.

"Oh my Lord, my Lord, what have you done?" murmured Brian, lifting the King as easily as if he had been a child.

That is a silly question, thought Jehan. "I have honored my oath to you . . ." The pain slashed through him, freeing him from consciousness at last.

When Jehan became aware again he was in his own bed, washed, rebandaged, clad in a clean robe. He knew that it must be very late, for the Master of the Junipers lay asleep in the chair and the candle was nearly burnt away. Pain nibbled at the edges of Jehan's awareness and there was a bitter taste in his mouth. If he moved the Master would wake and give him another dose of willowbark tea. But the candlelight illuminated all the weariness etched in his old friend's face.

No . . . thought Jehan. *Let the pain come. Relieving my body will only open my mind to a less endurable agony. Caolin has lied to me. Time will heal my body's wounds, but what is the cure when the soul is in pain?*

IV

The Sun Road

The north wind lashed the windows with whips of freezing rain, but inside Misthall everything was still. The Master of the Junipers closed the door to his chamber quietly and turned to Rosemary. "I think the King will sleep now."

"I wish you would not try to contact the College of the Wise now, when we are both tired," she replied.

The Master knelt by the hearth, building up the fire. "Rosemary, you are enough of a healer to understand what I tried to do just now . . ." His nerves were still twitching from the blacklash of energy he had tried to project into Jehan. "The King's mental shields are like the walls of Laurelynn! And when I tell him so he only apologizes and asks me to wait. What for? What does he fear I will see?" He drew the curtains more closely across the window, shivering again.

Rosemary sat down beside the bed. "I will remember to keep up the fire and keep you covered . . . and call you back if Faris needs you, or if you do not return by dawn," she repeated his instructions to her.

The Master removed his belt and sandals, drew off the golden chain with his circled cross, kissed it and laid it on the mantelpiece. He wore no other metals nor anything that would constrict his body. Then he pulled the blanket over himself and closed his eyes. *In the Name of the Source of All I set out . . . by the power of the Source of All I travel . . . may the mercy of the Source of All bring me safely home again . . .*

He mastered his breathing, systematically released each muscle, strove to drive from his awareness the messages of his senses and the crowding visions of the day. But it was hard to banish the image of Jehan's haunted eyes. What if he could not get free? Hastily, the Master thrust his awareness outward.

He flinched as he touched a current of energy, then reached again and jerked as successive rings of energy passed along his body and waves of fiery sparks exploded in the darkness of his mind. Then all was suddenly, blessedly still.

The Master opened his eyes. Below him he saw his own inert body and Rosemary, looking around her with an uncertain frown. He stretched, relearning the senses of this second body, then he dove outward, focusing his sight beyond the physical surfaces below him to the patterns of energy that defined them.

Between the Red Mountain and the Lady Mountain to the west of it ran a vein of light. Other lines rayed out from them, crossing and connecting to form a network within the body of Westria. Flowing beneath him the Master saw the energies which were the life of the land, as he had traced the energies within the King's body a little while ago. The lines of light gave him a map to follow, over the curve of the horizon to the white radiance of the Father of Mountains, and the pulse of power on its breast which was the College of the Wise. The Master focused his will on the College and sped toward it.

The Mistress of the College was asleep when he came to her. He drifted downward, hoping to arouse her energy body with his. A tremor shook his spirit as he remembered the times when their bodies had joined physically and he paused, knowing that such feelings could draw him back to his own body.

"Madrona . . ." he called her by the old name only they two knew now, sensing her weariness though he could not afford to pity her. *"I need your help! Answer me!"*

She stirred. He drew away and saw her other body emerge from her sleeping form. *"Calm yourself! Why have you disturbed my rest?"*

He was still for a moment, ashamed of his fears. *"The King has ceased to try to heal himself and he will not let me try. There is evil there whose source I cannot identify, and I am afraid."* he said at last.

The Mistress turned a little away. *"What would you have me do? I cannot force the King to love his life, and neither can you."*

"If his body has time to heal he will be able to rule his own soul."

She nodded, but she would not meet his eyes. *"Men should take responsibility for themselves . . . We can form a healing circle here and send you our power, but we have now no regular link with the priestly communities in the towns."*

The Master moved uncomfortably. When he had first come to the College of the Wise a network had linked all the adepts of Westria. But he had done nothing to keep it up—why was he surprised?

"At least you can call to Awahna!"

"I can call, but Those who dwell in the Secret Valley answer in Their own times and ways. Why do you always look for help to others? Pray to the Source of All!"

He wanted to protest, but his uneasiness distracted him, as if someone were tugging at his sleeve. He found himself drifting toward the wall and realized that Rosemary must be calling him back to Misthall.

"Madrona—I will do all I can. But come to me—I will need you so very badly if I fail!"

"You called me, my Lord . . . and I am here," said Caolin, entering the King's room. Although the curtains had been opened to let in the early morning light, the great bed was still shadowed. Jehan did not move. Had he heard?

Caolin struggled with a desire to turn and run, his mind replaying alternate visions of confrontation or flight as he had been doing ever since Ordrey had returned to him the previous morning, without Brian. He could not forget the vivid picture Ordrey had given him of Jehan, dominating them all as he stood mud-smeared and half-naked in the rain.

A board creaked in the corridor behind him. *That upstart Farin*—thought Caolin, *or the Master of the Junipers—spying on me!* He struck at the door, then turned again as the click of its latching was echoed from the bed.

"Caolin . . ." the King's voice was almost bodiless, but very clear. Caolin remembered countless other mornings when he had come into the King's chamber. For the first time in all these years he did not know what to say.

Before he reached him, the King spoke again.

"Caolin—did Ronald tell you *why* Brian gave him that gold?" Jehan moved his head on the pillow, and the Seneschal stopped short as he saw the King's face. "Did *you* believe that Brian had written that letter you showed to me?"

Caolin knew that little frown of bewildered pain. He had seen it before, when the King found men less noble than he believed them to be. Long ago Caolin had vowed to keep Jehan from ever having to look like that again. *And this time it is me* . . . His fingers closed blindly on the bedcurtains.

"Caolin, I *will* have truth from you!"

The ancient fabric parted in Caolin's hand. He brushed dust from his palm, staring unseeing at the King. What was the truth? *I loved you, my Lord* . . .

"Jehan, I was afraid!" he said aloud. "Brian meant to make my dismissal the price of his support in the war!"

"But you lied to me—"

"I did what you forced me to do!" Caolin flinched from the flash of Jehan's eyes, but he could not hold in all the resentments he had never realized he bore. "There has always been some reason for me to carry your load—"

"You tricked me into breaking my oath—" Jehan's words crossed Caolin's.

"Who would keep the Kingdom in order if I were not here?"

"—I would have had Brian's blood on my hands!" Both men paused. The King's face was flushed and he breathed rapidly as he glared back at Caolin.

"Did you hear me?" shouted Caolin suddenly. "Have you *ever* listened to me?" The high color began to fade from Jehan's cheeks. Caolin pressed the heels of his palms over his eyes. "No, that's not true. Once you heard what I did not even know how to say . . ." He dropped his hands, moved awkwardly to the chair by the bed.

"Are you saying this is all my doing?" whispered the King. "Whatever I laid upon you, you only smiled and asked for more . . ."

Caolin looked down at his tightly clasped fingers. The garnet in his ring of office caught the light as they trembled and he turned it to hide the stone. "Yes . . . power is a heady draft for one who had none. You set the cup to my lips, my Lord, and I cannot cease from drinking now . . ."

"Have I indeed done this to you?" Jehan asked again. "I thought our strength was that we both had our desire . . . And Faris—how have I failed with *her?*" His last words came almost too faint for Caolin to hear. "It would be better for me to die now and leave you all in peace!" the King cried then.

Caolin looked up quickly and saw Jehan's face contorted, his cheeks frosted with tears. His own turmoil resolved into a single fear. "Jehan, no! Don't you understand that you also gave me the only real joy I have ever known?

"When I came to you after the College of the Wise had rejected me, my life was no good to me," he continued with some difficulty. "But you cared about me, you courted me

even, and when you took my body—an easy thing for you—
you also touched my soul. No one had ever been able to do
that for me before . . ." This was not the time to tell Jehan
of his rituals on the Red Mountain and the other power that
had touched him there, scarring his soul. He went on, "You
gave me something to do with my life, and a reason for wanting
to do it!"

Jehan's face twitched painfully. With a pang Caolin saw
how the new silver in his hair glistened in the merciless morning
light. He brought the King's hand to his lips, stroking the thin
fingers that lay inert within his own.

"Jehan—if I have erred it is because you seemed so far
from me. I need your trust . . ." Jehan's gaze met his at last
and Caolin's tongue faltered. The King's eyes seemed more
black than blue—pools of darkness where he could drown.

"How can I give my trust to anyone? I have no faith in my
own judgment now."

"I need you, can't you understand?"

"Then you must give me truth . . . Oh, Caolin, your face
is like a locked room—" Jehan's voice shook. "I must know
what you have done."

Caolin stared at him. In nine years in office he had done
so many things. How would they look through Jehan's un-
practiced eyes? Truth, like beauty, lay so often in the beholder's
view.

"My Lord, where shall I begin?" he said wryly. "Shall I
raise all the little veils with which men cover the nakedness of
reality? This sin of mine—if it is a sin—is what has allowed
you to live with your conscience unstained!"

"Until now—" replied the King bitterly, "when I find that
I must bear the guilt for what you have done without ever
having chosen what you would do! Caolin—" he shook his
head despairingly, "can't *you* understand?"

Caolin rubbed at his eyes. "To understand what I have done
you must know why. You read my soul once, Jehan—do it
again now!"

Jehan's strained look eased. "Will you open to me?" he
asked wonderingly.

Caolin tensed, knowing that this time there would be no
ritual or sexual arousal to help them. "My Lord," he whispered,
"I will try." He closed his eyes, seeking to darken his mental
vision. He counted until his breath was regular again. In all

the world there must be no reality but the warm pressure of Jehan's hands.

He checked a surge of joy as something brushed his awareness like wind ruffling the surface of a pool. He marshalled his memories—all his strategies and decisions, all the skirmishes in his war with Brian, all his paths to knowledge . . . And the memory led inevitably to the Red Mountain and the boar's head that still gathered dust on the altar of the Lady of Fire.

He shuddered with vertigo, as if the floor had slipped, and clung to the King's hands. His ears buzzed. In a moment—if only he could open himself, it would be as it had been when Jehan came to him before . . .

The sense of self-awareness being overwhelmed shook him in sickening reiteration of the climax of his ritual—the infernal Lady's embrace that had poisoned all sexual or spiritual contact for him now. Past and present terror resonated through his mind and body and the fear that he had learned on the Mountain wrenched his hands and Jehan's apart.

Caolin's next thought was a dull awareness that someone was pounding on the door. He jerked upright, focusing on the King's still face, grasped his wrist and felt the pulse flicker like the heart of a wounded bird.

"Jehan!" he cried aloud. The door slammed open and the Master of the Junipers hurried past him and bent over the King.

"Who screamed? What have you done to him?"

Caolin shook his head. "The scream was mine. We tried—he wanted to touch my mind . . ."

The Master's hands were passing swiftly above the King's body. After a moment Jehan stirred a little and mumbled, as if in sleep. "Fools, both of you! He had not the strength for this now . . ." The Master laid a hand on the King's brow.

Caolin's head bowed. "Save him—" he whispered. "I need . . ." his voice failed.

The Master's expression softened. "We all need him, Caolin." His hand brushed the Seneschal's shoulder, then he turned to Jehan once more.

Faris bent to take the folded cloth from Jehan's forehead, wet and replaced it, then picked up the half-knitted sock she had dropped beside her chair. But for the sound of Jehan's harsh breathing the house was very still.

As she began to knit, Jehan muttered Caolin's name. She tensed, but in a moment he was still once more. Four days ago, when the infection of the King's reopened wound turned to fever, he had struck at anyone who tried to restrain him. Now he could no longer even stop her from nursing him. She focused her mind on the repetitive movements of her fingers and the irregular spatter of sleet against the windowpanes. On the mountaintops there would be snow. She could bear this waiting as long as she concentrated on the surface of things, knowing that beyond it howled a darkness deeper than the night outside. As long as Jehan was alive she could hold madness at bay.

"Faris . . ."

For a moment she thought that Jehan was speaking in his delirium. Then she heard her name again, faint as if the air had shaped itself to words.

"Why are you here? What is the hour?"

"It is nearly dawn. I am here because I could not sleep and the others needed rest! Oh Jehan—is that all you have to say to me?" Her shawl slipped from her shoulders as she rose awkwardly and bent over him. "Are you better?" She took the cloth from his head and smoothed back his lank hair.

His gaze seemed to turn inward. "No . . ." he whispered at last. "My left side doesn't seem to belong to me, and everything else—Faris, if I am dying, the Council must be called!" He swallowed painfully.

"The Master sent for them three days ago—" she started, then the sense of his words got through to her and a spasm of terror stopped her breath. She gripped his hand. "But you will live—they are praying for you all over Westria!"

"He sent for them . . ." For a long moment Jehan lay very still. Then he gave a faint sigh and what could have been a nod. "Who is here?"

"Lord Robert and Lord Brian, and Frederic Sachs of the Free Cities, and Eric . . ." she answered slowly. "But the Master did not say—"

Jehan shook his head. "If the Master has summoned them, he knows already that this body is too poisoned to heal," he said heavily. "How he must hate to admit that, after he has tried so hard. Everyone has tried, except me."

His eyes closed tiredly. Faris stared down at him, willing herself to see the browned skin she remembered instead of this face that had no color but the fever spots on his cheeks. She took his head between her hands and pressed her lips to his as if she could breathe life into him with a kiss. He lay unresisting, but as she let him go she saw he was weeping, soundless tears that channeled through the fever-sweat on his face until they were lost in his silvered beard.

"I have faced death in battle—" he groaned, "why is it so hard now . . . is it because I have left so much undone?" He paused, fighting for breath.

"You cannot leave me alone!" Faris exclaimed. "I would have been your mistress gladly, but I cannot be Mistress of Westria!" She slid to her knees beside the bed, hiding her face in his pillow. She felt the clumsy touch of his fingers on her hair.

"Faris . . . I accused Caolin of sheltering me too much, but I have done the same to you. My beloved—we cannot change it now! You *are* the Lady of Westria!" She felt him trembling. "Have I failed my trust also in choosing you?"

She wept into the pillowcase, still shaking her head. He could not mean to leave her to carry the burden that had brought him down! His breathing hoarsened and he coughed convulsively. Faris sat up and held the cup to his lips.

He swallowed painfully. "Faris, you must promise to guard Westria or I will be not only dead but damned! Others will help you rule, but only you can be Mistress of the Jewels!"

Faris shuddered as she saw his face twitch spasmodically. Surely nothing could be worse than to remain a powerless audience to his pain.

"Oh my love—if you say I must . . . I will do whatever I can . . ." She kissed his brow, thinking, *now I am doomed too* . . . Jehan's body grew limp, and Faris felt a moment's terror, but she could still feel the life in him, trickling unevenly like water in a polluted stream, but there, still there.

"I must do what I can to order the Kingdom . . ." he murmured after a little while. "Take my Journal from under the table and write out what I say . . ."

Mechanically Faris noted his words, but they made no sense. How could a body exist without its head? How could Westria exist without her King? How could she exist alone? When he seemed to have finished, she laid the book on the table.

"Jehan, do you want something to drink now?" She bent over him anxiously.

He smiled a little and laid his hand upon her breast. "The source of life . . ." he murmured, but his touch was as sexless as that of a child. His smile grew vague, but when she straightened his fingers closed on the front of her gown. Gently she eased down beside him, cradling his thin body against her own. After a little his fingers relaxed and she turned to him in alarm.

But he was only asleep.

Faris hesitated in the doorway to the Hall. Her brother lay fast asleep on a bench by the wall; Eric sprawled in a chair nearby. Before the fire at the near end of the room Lewis the herald was playing a listless game of chess with Speaker Sachs, while Lord Brian and Robert of the Ramparts maneuvered troop counters across a map of Westria. In the far corner Caolin gazed out at the falling rain. Then Eric saw her and sat up suddenly. The others, hearing the scrape of his chair, stared anxiously. Faris swallowed, for to speak would give her words reality.

She was doing Jehan's bidding, though every act thickened the film of ice around her heart. Did she still hope that if she did everything correctly Jehan would relent and get well?

"The King is awake now and his mind is clear."

"Is he better?" asked Brian hoarsely.

Faris barriered herself against the tide of grief she felt from him, from all of them, and spoke coldly, knowing it was the only way to survive the next hours. "He . . . summons the Council of Westria to hear his will." Abruptly she turned back across the hallway and down the corridor to the King's chamber, hearing by their heavy footfalls that they followed her.

The Master of the Junipers sat at the head of the bed, his grey robe falling in carven folds. Faris took her place on the stool next to it. Jehan breathed shallowly, gathering his strength; the curtains had been looped back, making it only too clear how small and still he lay. Benches scraped as the others sat down.

Caolin entered last, marched up to the bed and halted, his face going ashy as the winter sky. "Jehan . . ." he whispered, "how is it with you?"

The King's clear gaze held him. "I do not blame you, Caolin," he said softly, as if continuing a conversation interrupted a moment before, "only you must forgive me, too . . ."

Caolin began to tremble so violently he could not reply. He shook his head and made his way to the back of the room. The others looked at him in wonder, but to Faris it seemed natural that when so much else was disintegrating, the Seneschal's iron composure should shatter too. For a few minutes the only sound was the drumming of rain on the roof of the porch outside.

"Councilors of Westria—" said the King at last, "I will not sit in the high seat at Laurelynn again, and it is my duty to order this Kingdom as best I may." He waited for their silence. "My heir is the child that stirs in my Lady's womb. The Queen will be his regent and rule this kingdom until he is grown. If he does not become Master of the Jewels you must choose another Sovereign. But I think that the child will be a greater King than I! By this token I declare my will . . ."

The royal signet slipped easily from Jehan's finger and he held it out to Faris. After a moment's hesitation she clenched it tightly in her fist, still warm from his hand. "Under Faris, Caolin shall exercise the supreme civil power," added the King. Brian stirred angrily and Caolin jerked upright.

"My Lord—" the words seemed wrenched from his lips. "You must not—you must not give me such power . . ."

"Who else can teach Faris what she will need to know?" Jehan answered gently. "You will be each other's safety. It is for Westria, Caolin . . . If you have loved me, swear that you will serve the Queen and her child!"

There was a long pause. "I swear to serve . . . the Queen . . . and her child . . . as I have served you." Caolin's words seemed chipped from the stone mask of his face.

Jehan sank back and the Master gave him a spoonful of something from a vial of blue glass. Faris held up the book where she had written his notes.

"To lead the Kingdom's armies I give you Robert, Lord Commander of the Ramparts, for I believe there will soon be war . . ." Lord Robert sighed and nodded. "Elaya will think Westria weak now, and they will attack us in the spring . . . attack *you,*" he corrected, adding, "may the Lord of Battles protect you, since I have failed." Rain thundered suddenly outside like galloping hooves.

"Brian of Las Costas will be second-in-command," the King continued. Eric stifled an exclamation, but Brian's head came up proudly. "If any of you have heard rumors against Lord Brian you must forget them, for I say to you, while I am still your King, that I have examined him and find his loyalty unstained."

Brian's amber eyes fixed on Caolin. Faris could feel the Lord Commander's defiance even through the shield of her abstraction, but the Seneschal did not move until Jehan murmured his name. He roused then, and bowed to Brian, but there was no recognition in his eyes.

"Brian, you must remember your promise to me." said Jehan. The Lord Commander stiffened, then returned Caolin's bow. Jehan frowned a little, seeming about to speak again, then closed his eyes in exhaustion. After a few moments Lord Robert rose to go.

"No—" said Faris. "He only rests. There is more . . ."

"My Lady Queen—" Robert nodded acceptance. Faris slumped beneath the authority with which his deference had invested her. The room grew brighter as the rain thinned.

Jehan's eyes opened. "Eric—will you be my Lady's champion?"

"My Lord, you asked this of *me?*" Eric stammered. Rosemary winced and looked away.

"I would ask it of no one else," Jehan answered gently. Mechanically Faris held out her hand. Eric knelt before her awkwardly and kissed her fingers, but as he rose the King spoke once more. "Eric . . . there is no more time for rivalry. Offer Lord Brian the embrace of peace. You are both true men and I think that you will know it before the end."

Eric flushed again and stiffened, but as Brian stood he cast a swift look at the King and quailed before the pleading in his eyes. They gripped each others' arms like two mastiffs whose masters have ordered them to be friends.

Jehan coughed spasmodically and the Master gave him more medicine. For a moment he breathed harshly, then appeared to ease, trying to smile.

"Lord Robert—I thank you for the loan of your son. And Rosemary, give my farewell to your father. You already have my gratitude for nursing me—such an effort should have had a better reward. But I will leave Faris with less pain, knowing that you are near her . . ."

Rosemary stared at him, her face working, then turned blindly to Eric, who after a moment's surprise held her against him, patting her awkwardly.

"And you, Lewis, and Master Sachs . . . and all those others who have served me and Westria so well. Receive my thanks for it now." Jehan sighed. "My Lords and Ladies, I have done what I can to leave you in good order—to cover my retreat!" he added with a glimmer of humor. "I see now how often I failed you. Sometimes I shrank from the resolution to steer a safe course. Where I have been blind or unjust . . . I ask you all to forgive me now!" he looked around the room.

"Forgive you!" cried Brian, "Oh my dear Lord do not go without forgiving us!"

"What is there to forgive? I was your King . . ." Jehan's tone held faint curiosity. His voice faded and his eyes closed and for a moment Faris thought he slept again. Then he spoke once more. "Now you will have to be responsible for yourselves . . . Preserve Westria until my child bears the Jewels. Serve the Queen!"

"I swear now to be faithful to your Lady and your heir—I and my heirs after me!" cried Brian.

"And I!" said Lord Robert. The others echoed him.

Jehan sighed a little then and looked at Faris like a child wishing to be told that his work is all done and he may go out to play. Somehow she was able to smile at him, but her voice broke as she turned to the others.

"The Council is ended. You may go."

Crystal drops still flashed from the eaves of the porch and the window frames, but the clouds had gone. Golden light streamed through the western windows to light Jehan's sleeping face. The fine bones of his hands and skull seemed veiled rather than covered by flesh, as if he were illuminated by some light within.

Faris' own pregnant body seemed grossly physical in comparison. *Oh my beloved*, she thought, *how can I dare to try and touch your spirit now?*

"They say we have an immortal body hidden within this one . . ." whispered Rosemary. "I think that his is very close to the surface now."

The King's household had remained in his room to keep vigil while the other members of the Council waited in the Hall, speaking to the steady stream of people who had come to wait for the news that no one could, even now, quite believe. As they watched the peace of the King's face was broken by another ripple of pain, as a fish swimming in the depths disturbs the still surface of a lake.

"He suffers!" Eric accused the Master. "I thought you gave him something to stop the pain!"

"He said he would shut it away no more. It is the body laboring so that the spirit may be born," the Master said wearily.

Faris felt his gaze turn to her, but she would not meet it. *You could not save him and you are helping him to leave me now . . .*

As the sun descended they waited silently, hating each passing minute even as they hoped it would bring Jehan to consciousness again. The storm had washed all impurity from the sky and left it a glowing gold.

There was a sudden indrawn breath from Caolin, and Faris saw that Jehan's eyes were open and the lines of pain smoothed from his face at last.

"My Lord, how is it with you?" Farin asked shyly.

Slowly the King focused on him. "Very well . . ." he answered, as one answers the silly question of a child. They flinched beneath the clarity of his gaze.

"Faris . . ."

She reached out, but did not quite touch him. "I am here."

"You have done more than I deserved. Now I think that I can at least end my life well. Remember your promise to me, my darling. And if I can . . . I will be with you . . ." His hand moved, just a little, so that it touched hers. Faris bit her lip to keep from crying out a denial that would break his peace.

"Have you no word for me?" said Caolin with an odd desperation.

The King smiled a little. "Only remember that I have loved you, Caolin . . ."

The Seneschal turned away abruptly and seemed to collapse until Faris could see only a huddle of robes at the foot of the bed. She felt the Master of the Junipers trembling behind her.

Jehan shifted his head on the pillow to look at the older man. "Be still—you know better than anyone that this parting is not forever. Will you link with me to set me on the road?" The Master nodded silently, but his face showed his struggle for control.

"What day is this?" asked the King.

"It is the eve of the feast of Sunreturn," said Rosemary, surprised.

"The longest night . . ." Jehan sounded faintly alarmed. "Open the windows!"

Eric looked to the Master, and as he nodded, moved reluctantly to force outward one of the windows that faced the Bay. Cold rushed in and they shivered, but Jehan breathed deeply. The setting sun laid a path of gold across the Bay.

"The darkness shall not have me!" Jehan exclaimed. "See—

the sun road is prepared and I must follow the light . . ." His eyes fixed on the descending sun.

Faris shut her eyes against that brilliance. Shimmers of light and darkness pulsed across her vision in time to the heavy pounding of her heart. Though her ears buzzed with pressure, she heard the change in the Master's breathing as he slipped into trance. Desperately she cast her consciousness outward, seeking Jehan's spirit as once she had sought it from the Father of Mountains.

Jehan's fingers quivered in her own, and through her eyelids she felt a sudden brightness in the room. Faris opened her eyes.

Figures moved before her like ships on a sun-dazzled sea. The Master . . . and Others, whose radiance burned away her fear. She stood up. The air around her vibrated with her name. She turned. As if she had tasted the sound of his voice, or felt the blue of his eyes, she knew Jehan . . .

She took a step forward, but the other figures were swirling around him, drawing him away.

Faris cried out, and her vision was lost in a blaze of light.

"Now indeed is our long darkness come." Caolin repeated the words softly, finding an odd satisfaction. He had said them to himself many times in the two days since he had looked on the empty shell that had been Jehan. He rested his crossed arms on the sill of the window next to the hearth, watching three riders pick their way down the Misthall road to the King's road that edged the Bay. The King's funeral procession had passed that way, only a few hours before.

He heard the door to the Hall open and turned angrily, blinking as his eyes tried to adjust to the shadows. He glimpsed dark hair and a shapeless blue robe.

Jehan's robe . . .

He stood up too suddenly, groping for the solid stone of the hearth as the blood left his head. When he could see again he recognized Faris.

He struggled to school his face, but the Queen looked blindly past him as she stepped into the room. Except for her pregnancy she was as he had first seen her in the north, her face colorless, the skin stretched across her cheekbones. There was nothing here of the voluptuous quality that had offended him at Harvest—the thing he had simulated in his ceremony.

He must have made some sound, for her head came up like a startled doe's and her shadowed eyes slowly focused on his face. "I . . . I thought that everyone had gone . . ." She pulled the robe more closely around her and turned.

"No, stay—" Caolin found himself moving to stop her.

The Queen looked as if she expected that the carved timbers of the Hall, the pewter and brass dishes shelved along the walls, even the needlepoint cushions on the benches at the sides would be different now.

"I thought you had gone to the Sacred Wood with the others," she said.

Caolin shook his head. "Someone had to speak to those who come for news." In reality, someone else could have stayed, but Caolin could not have watched earth cover Jehan's body, knowing what must happen to it now.

Faris held out her hands to the fire. There was gooseflesh on her thin arms. "I did not want to see his body . . ." she said slowly. "I told the Master I was too tired to go to the burial, but I cannot sleep, and I cannot lie awake in that room, remembering . . ." She shivered violently.

Caolin nodded. "They will lay him in the earth of the Sacred Wood, and sing songs, and come away comforted. But Jehan will still be gone!" For the first time he met her gaze fully. There was nothing she could take from him, now.

"He went away and left me alone." Faris said in a still voice. Caolin felt suddenly dizzied, as if his own soul had spoken to him through her lips. She moved restlessly away from the fireplace, realigned the game table, then began to replace the tumbled chess pieces. One had fallen, and she bent awkwardly to pick it up.

But Caolin was there before her. He knelt to reach the piece and held it out to her. It was the queen. Still kneeling, Caolin set the bishop beside it on the board.

"Our King is taken," he said softly, "and Queen and Minister must fight on alone . . ." His fingers clenched on the chessman.

"You loved him too." Faris' words pierced Caolin's darkness.

He stared up at her, reading in her eyes a kind of grief he had thought no one else shared. Surely it was true that they had both loved Jehan, and perhaps received from him something which that much-loved man had not given all the others as well. He had built his life on that belief, but now Jehan was gone, his honors fallen to this thin woman who huddled in the King's old robe.

"My Lady, I am *your* servant now—what is your will?" he exclaimed. Eyes burning with unshed tears, he kissed her hand. *This is what I promised Jehan . . .*

The Queen tried to smile. "I have no will. I do not know what to do." She began to straighten the cushions on the benches against the wall. Caolin got to his feet. She must speak—she must tell him what to do!

Faris pulled something from behind one of the pillows and stilled, staring down at it. It was a doeskin glove, the fingers molded by use to the shape of a man's right hand.

"Everywhere . . . everywhere I turn I find his things, as if he had only gone away for a day's hunting!" she exclaimed. "I cannot bear it—I must get away!" She looked at him, pleading, her fingers digging into his arm.

Caolin braced himself and put a tentative arm around her shoulders. "Yes . . . In the morning we will go to Laurelynn."

"It seems very far from the high seat in Laurelynn to a scrape in the earth beneath a tree," said Lord Theodor harshly.

The Master of the Junipers, struck by the pain in the old man's voice, turned from watching for the wagon that bore the body of the King. The meadow was full of people who waited to see Jehan enter the Sacred Wood for the last time as once they had waited to see him put on the Jewels.

"The journey from Hall to Hallows will be the same for you or for me . . ." said Brian grimly.

"I know that, but Jehan could have been my son! If these old bones could keep me from reaching here in time to see him, I have lived too long!"

"You are not old! I saw you swing a sword in the north!" exclaimed Eric, but the Master noted the lines graven so deeply into Theodor's face and the new hint of fragility in his bearing, and knew that he *was* old, now.

If a simple hunting accident could destroy Jehan, what can be counted on to endure? The Master wondered. He shivered in the chill wind and moved toward the Mistress of the College, but she was deep in conversation with the Priest of the Wood. He had not spoken with her alone since she had arrived with Lord Theodor the day before. His stomach knotted, and he wondered what she could say to him that would be worse than his own self-blame.

There was a murmur like distant surf from the crowd as the wagon appeared, and the Master struggled to barrier himself against the intensity of their sorrow. Robert of the Ramparts climbed down from the driver's bench, his face set. Brian touched his arm in brief sympathy, then bent to remove his boots. When all were barefoot, the lords of the four provinces went to the wagon and lifted out the bier on which the King's body lay, scattering the flowers that covered it.

"How can he be so light . . ." whispered Eric as they settled the poles on their shoulders, but no one answered him.

The green-robed priest had taken his place between two redwood trees that stood like pillars at the entrance to the Wood. "Human kind, why have you come?"

"We bring Jehan, King of Westria, for burial," replied Robert gruffly.

"What is the King of men to the People of the Wood?"

The Mistress of the College stepped before them. "We come to return the body of the Master of the Jewels to the elements from which it came."

"Enter then. A place has been prepared for him." The priest stepped aside and the little procession moved into the darkness of the wood.

The Master of the Junipers took his place behind the bier, his bare feet feeling the way. The forest sighed around him as if it too were lamenting for the King. The Priest of the Wood chose the easiest way through the trees where since the Cataclysm no path had been made. As they moved more deeply into the forest the cries of the people faded and even the wind diminished to a distant rustling. The air stirred with the sharp perfume of new redwood needles and the richer scent of decaying leaves. Sunlight was slanting through the branches and kindling the trees with rich tints of carnelian and green when the procession entered a circle of young redwoods and halted at last.

This clearing was much like the one in which they had buried Jehan's father, but landmarks shifted strangely in a Wood where some of the trees could take the forms of men. Once they had gone, only the Lord of the Trees would know for certain where Jehan's body had been laid. In the midst of the circle was a trench just wide enough for the naked body in its linen shroud.

The pallbearers knelt to set their burden down. The Master reminded himself that there was nothing on the bier that he would wish to retain—not when he had seen the living soul depart—but still it took an effort of will for him to help the Mistress ease the body into the grave. She stood looking down at it for a moment, then began the prayer.

"Mother Earth! We bring to you this form of flesh whose substance is your own. As each bodied creature consumes the bodies of others, so each has the same debt to pay. Receive then what remains of him we loved, that from it new life may spring."

The others linked hands and chorused—"Give the flesh to the earth, the blood to the waters, breath to the winds and the fire of life to the Maker of All Things—we go as we have come!"

The Master scattered a handful of damp earth across the shroud. The others followed him, their fingers furrowing the soil as their faces were furrowed by tears. The shallow grave was soon filled. But as they knelt, redwood twigs began to shower down upon the scar in the earth, though there was no wind. The Master felt his skin prickle and saw looming over them a redwood tree that had not been there before, and with another kind of vision, a green-crowned, red-robed figure whose eyes comprehended all the sorrow the world had ever known.

"My Lord of the Trees . . ." he whispered, bowing his head until the last needle had settled to the ground and there was nothing to show where the grave had been.

When they emerged from the Wood it was dusk and most of the mourners had gone. Robert and Eric began to hitch the horses to the wagon again. The Mistress of the College waited, her dark face unreadable. The wind whipped back the cowl of her hood so that the Master saw her profile outlined against the dim sky.

"You must go back with them to Misthall," she said.

The Master shook his head. "I failed Jehan. He had some sickness of the soul that I did not understand. Since I saw him depart I have not been able to meditate. Perhaps if I go to Juniper Cottage alone I can restore my soul. As I am, I have nothing to give to anyone!"

Her fingers closed on his arm. "Do you think so? I have lived in that darkness for five years! But you can still walk even if you walk blind. If you failed the King, that is between you and the Maker of All—but you must not fail Faris as well! I no longer see clearly," she murmured, "but I think a great wind is coming that will sweep away much that we have known. That may be just as well, but if there is anything you want to preserve, you must not run away!"

Abruptly the Master remembered how he had read the cards

for Faris the morning of the Harvest Festival, and the cold
premonitory wind that had chilled him then. Thus far the reading was proving itself—Faris was the Queen of Swords now.
He stared at the Mistress of the College. "Is my task then to
stand against the wind?"

"To stand against it or to ride it . . ." the Mistress replied.

V

The White Queen

Firelight flared on the bronze harpstrings as Farin shifted Swangold in his lap. He dipped his rag in the oil jar and smoothed it along the sound box's polished sides. The interlace of golden wire edging the soundholes shone softly like the embroidery on a King's gown. His hand stilled. He remembered how Jehan had shone in his Council robes the summer before. But now January was half-gone—they had come back to Laurelynn without the King and everything was changed.

A footstep echoed on the stair—Faris, coming from the entry hall below, followed by Caolin.

"—and so when Lord Robert returns from speaking with the holders in the south, we must hold a council of war," said the Seneschal.

Farin returned to his work, his polishing cloth caressing the pillar's curve.

"Yes, I suppose so—" Faris said in a low voice. She slipped off her white cloak. Her gown was of undyed wool as well, the mourning color. "I did not know what it all meant when the Elayan envoys spoke at the Council last July, and afterward . . . I suppose Jehan did not want to tell me . . ." She leaned toward the fire, holding her arms and shivering.

Caolin looked down at her. "We *can* win," he said softly. "We *will* win, if hotheads like Brian listen to reason."

"Jehan trusted Brian . . ." said Faris, her eyes fixed by the leaping flames.

"He said he did." Caolin stared into the shadows of the entry hall below.

"But Brian broke into Jehan's sickroom," she continued, "and when Jehan went out to him, afterward—"

Two strings spoke softly as Farin's cloth brushed them. Caolin whipped around, his eyes flicking to the golden gleam of the harp on the table by the windows.

"You have chosen a strange place to practice in!" the Seneschal said sharply.

Farin's hand paused in its downward stroke. "These tall windows give the best light."

"Not at this hour," replied Caolin, looking out at the bare branches of the plum orchard that sloped toward the central lake of Laurelynn. The pink light of sunset was already fading into the dim winter dusk.

Farin's hands tightened on the harp. "Then if I play, it will be in darkness, now."

For a moment Caolin stared at him in silence, his hands hidden in the folds of his robe. "I must go back to my offices," he said suddenly to Faris. She nodded and held out her hand. Caolin bent over it, then pulled his cloak around him and went softly down the stairs.

Farin picked up a clean cloth and began to wipe down the harp. The wood glowed as if it had absorbed the light of the fire. He looked at his sister, wanting to speak to her, and noted with shock how the firelight glistened on a new veining of silver in her earth-dark hair. Her silence walled her from him now as it had since the death of the King. Once he would have been able to touch her without words.

The stairs creaked deeply beneath a rapid tread. Eric sprang up the last step and stopped short as he saw Faris by the fire. "My Lady!" She looked up, her eyes wells of shadow, as Eric knelt to kiss her hand. Farin plucked the bottom note of the harp, then the other three that made the octaves, but he did not turn. After a moment Faris smiled vaguely, rose and fumbled for her cloak. She allowed Eric to help her to put it on, then, still without speaking, went to the stairs that led to the plum orchard.

Eric stood looking after her, his big hands hanging open at his sides. "Should we let her go out there? It is getting cold."

Farin shrugged, plucked a string and made a minute adjustment with the tuning key. "She will not freeze. Are *you* going to order her to come in?"

Eric slumped. "She smiles past me as if I were not there . . ."

Farin considered him and thought wryly that it took uncommon abstraction to ignore something Eric's size. "I think she listens to Caolin . . ."

Eric snorted. "I suppose she has to! His conversation certainly wouldn't amuse me!" He paced back and forth along the gallery, then paused by a chest beneath the windows. "Jehan used to keep a chess set in here—I wonder . . . yes, here it is! Farin, will you play a game with me?"

Farin shook his head, remembering the many games of chess he had played with the King. "No—" he saw Rosemary and the Master of the Junipers coming up the stairs. "No, but you might ask Rosemary."

Eric looked surprised, but after a moment Rosemary agreed, and he began to arrange the chess board on a bench before the fire.

The Master of the Junipers came over to Farin and ran a gentle finger along the curved top of the harp. "Was Faris here?"

"She has gone to walk in the orchard again," Farin replied. He plucked a minor chord, adjusted two of the strings. The Master sighed, and Farin thought that for the first time since he had known him the chaplain seemed old. He went to the windows and stood staring down at the orchard, his robe blending with the shadows of the coming night.

Farin's left hand lifted to the strings, touched a note, then two more. No—not that tune. He had played that one the afternoon before Jehan died. He tried another combination, but the notes throbbed to silence as his fingers stilled. The fire glowed like the King's eyes, and there was no tune he knew that did not carry its own bitter harmony of memories.

The lord I loved is gone . . . and he has taken all my music away. He rested his head against the curve of the harp and his closed eye-lids stung with hot tears.

Faris eased back in her chair, feeling her aching feet throb against the softness of the sheepskin rug, letting the lassitude of exhaustion still her body. To achieve this numbness she had walked in the orchard until the damp cold bit to her bones—perhaps tonight she would sleep without dreams. Branwen hovered by the door as if looking for some further excuse not to leave the Queen alone.

"I need nothing else, Branwen—you may go—"

"My Lady—" the girl drew from the pocket of her apron a book covered in green leather. "I found this with the things we brought from Misthall." She set the book on the table and turned away.

If it was a book, it should go to the library or to Caolin, thought Faris. Then she opened it, and Jehan's graceful writing flashed up at her.

"My Beloved, I dare not wake you, and yet there is so much I need to say . . ." The date was Midsummer, when he had brought her home to Misthall as his Queen. Faris whimpered and let the Journal close, but Jehan's words resonated in her mind, shattering her illusory acceptance of his loss. She covered her face with her hands.

"You had so much to say to me, and yet you could not stay till everything was said . . ." She opened the book again.

Today we set out for the Ramparts. Has Westria always been so beautiful, or is it Faris who lends beauty to all I see in her company? Was it cowardice that made me leave Caolin to deliver my instructions regarding Santibar to Brian? The land dreams under the summer sun and I want only to lie beneath the oak trees with my wife in my arms. We must avert war with Elaya! The land needs peace, and so do I . . .

Faris remembered those days, when the sickness of her early pregnancy had passed and she flowered beneath the sun of Jehan's love. Now wind rattled the windows. Soon the clouds she had seen overwhelming the sunset would bring sleet or rain. She shivered and reached for her shawl. Golden summer was only a fantasy. Reality was cold, and a lonely bed, and the threat of war.

I try to find words to describe you, my beloved, but all my words have been tarnished by too much use. Your brother Farin has the words and the music, but no love . . . and so in the end I can only climb back into bed and praise you with my body like any other man!

No! She could not bear to remember the acts with which he had praised her, not now . . . Swiftly she turned the page and stopped, seeing not words but a picture—a few simple strokes which resolved themselves into the curve of a woman's bent head. Her own ivory comb was in the figure's hair. She wondered, *How could Jehan find in me such serenity?*

The mural on the wall above her swam in and out of focus as her eyes filled with tears—a woman and a harper, facing a wolf-shape with three fierce heads . . . She recognized the old tale, more ancient than the Ancients, of Orpheus, who had won his lady back from the Lord of the Underworld. If only she could do the same!

The woman in the painting stood with bent head and lifted hand. The style of the drawing was the same as that on the wall of Jehan's chamber at Misthall and in the book on her lap. This room had been the old Queen's, and Faris found herself smiling as she imagined Jehan painting the walls of his mother's room.

Still smiling, she set the Journal aside and snuffed her candle.

One by one, the Master of the Junipers put out the candles in his room. He had learned to fear the shadows this past month, and yet darkness was his only road back to the Light. It was still early in the evening, but the palace was already quiet. He remembered how it had been filled with light and laughter when Jehan was there and sighed as he sat down on the matting, crossed his legs and laid his hands open upon his knees.

"In the Name of the Source of All!"

That was the key, the phrase with which he had been taught to begin. Did it show him his error as well? Has he been seeking his own desire instead of that of the Maker of All Things? He breathed in and out, out and in, easing his body muscle by muscle until there was no distracting strain.

"Ruler of earth and heaven, of the world without and the world within—hear now my prayer!"

So the litany began, the first thing he had learned at the College of the Wise when he sought to chart a path to the Glory that had overwhelmed him spontaneously at times since childhood. And he had succeeded—the ecstacy that had flooded him, unexpected and unwilled, had become a fountain to nourish him whenever he had need. Until now . . .

"Thou art the Foundation of Being, in Whom all times and places are One—therefore hear now my prayer!"

The Master closed his eyes, reaching for stillness, letting

the senses go. He knew that the darkness which had come upon him was no uncommon thing. Indeed, it was an expected obstacle if one pursued the Way. If even the Mistress of the College suffered it, why should he complain? But why must it come to him now, when Faris wandered in her own darkness and needed him?

"From Thee have I come and to Thee will I return—therefore hear now my prayer!"

Surely that was true—he had been blinded by the brightness of Those who had taken Jehan away, and he remembered it as a man in a dungeon remembers his last glimpse of the day. But then the sun had gone down.

"I will seek the Darkness that is the gateway to Thy Light—so hear now my prayer!"

The Master voiced the words and let them go, let his thoughts dwindle and drift until only the fact of his existence remained, sinking through the darkness . . .

Into Nothing . . . There was no foundation, no boundary, no gateway. He fell through the gulfs he had once traversed so easily, and That which was Not began to dissolve his soul.

No! Awareness exploded in terrified rejection. *I exist . . . I am*—his Name reverberated through his returning consciousness. His body convulsed as all senses resumed functioning simultaneously, and he collapsed.

After a time, the Master painfully opened his eyes. It was still dark.

Faris stirred in the great bed, half opened her eyes on the darkness, then slipped back into sleep. The shadows in her chamber changed to shapes—columns soaring to a hidden sky. A forest deeper than the Sacred Wood surrounded her, and hushed all hint of sound.

Why am I here? she wondered suddenly and answered, *I am looking for Jehan.* And at the thought she turned her head and found him walking at her side . . . *He is not dead! I knew it was not true!* Her spirit sang.

"I only fainted when they thought I died—" he said, "and never lay within that shroud—"

She looked at him and said, "I've made no change . . ."

"How does the kingdom?"

"Well enough," she said. "But southern skies still rumble threats of war."

He held her arm. "I would not have them know that I am here—you must still hold my place. But I will tell you all that you must do!"

"But I cannot command your men, my Lord—"

She was being shaken, and brightness stung her eyes.

"My Lady! My Lady Queen!"

Faris stilled, reaching inward to Jehan. But he was gone, and daylight dissipated the shadows of the trees. She sighed and smiled. At least Jehan was not dead. It had all been a mistake after all.

Then she opened her eyes upon sunlight, streaming into the Queen's room in Laurelynn, and knew that not her dream but reality was the nightmare.

The clouded sky filtered a dull, even light into the small council chamber overlooking the river, revealing without illuminating the faces of the four people in the room. Caolin found it comforting.

Faris sat huddled in the King's chair at the head of the table. With her wan face and pale gown she looked like a ghost herself, but at least not like Jehan's ghost. Indeed they were all sombre today—Robert of the Ramparts in grey and Brian in scuffed leather. Caolin had instinctively chosen a robe whose red was so dark it was almost brown. Only the memory of Jehan held brilliance now.

Robert set down the report he had been reading aloud. ". . . and so I was at Elk Crossing when I learned that Prince Palomon is mustering his men," he said. "I had thought that they would want to negotiate when they learned of our loss . . . I wish I knew where and when their attack will come!" He looked to Faris.

Say something! thought Caolin. *This man is waiting for you to command him . . .*

"The road to Santibar has been open all winter," said Brian. "It is obvious they will strike there!"

"The winter has been cold, it's true, and though it is the beginning of February, the Dragon's Tail pass is still blocked with snow." Robert rubbed nervously at his greying beard.

Caolin cleared his throat, thinking of the coded message that lay locked in his desk. "Nonetheless, they will come that way as soon as they can."

Brian's yellow eyes began to glow. "Have you read Palomon's mind? Or perhaps you are such great friends that he tells you his plans?"

Caolin stiffened and looked to Faris for support, ignoring Robert's shocked exclamation. The Queen's clasped hands whitened, but she remained still.

"Lord Brian, I remember *my* promise to the King . . ." he said softly at last. "I suggest that you do the same." Brian's whole body quivered, but the fire in his eyes dimmed and he eased back into his chair.

Robert looked at them both conciliatingly. "It is true that knowing the source of the information would help us to evaluate it."

Caolin frowned, thinking of the patient effort that had developed those sources. Could Robert and Brian be trusted?

"There is someone in Palomon's court," he said carefully, "who talks very freely in a certain tavern where he is never asked to pay for his wine. The inn-keeper passes what he hears to someone who sends it to me." He shrugged. "I cannot swear to its truth—but the information has always been good before. I knew that Elaya had decided on war a week ago," he finished baldly, watching Brian.

The Lord Commander of Las Costas leaped to his feet, leaning across the table. "You should have told us!"

Caolin smiled slightly. "Why Brian, can I do nothing to please you? First you doubt my sources, then you criticize me for wishing to check them!" He turned deliberately to Robert. "I have made what preparations were in my power, my Lord, awaiting your return." His glance flicked back to Brian. "I informed the Queen Regent—I did not know I was accountable to *you*."

"*Someone* will hold you to account one day . . ." growled Brian, his hands clasping and unclasping as if they hungered for Caolin's throat.

"My Lords, be still!" cried Robert. He ran his fingers distractedly through his hair. "Save your hostility for Elaya, in the name of the Lord of All!"

"Robert . . . Brian . . . Caolin . . ." Startled, they turned to Faris, who went on, "This is no pleasure to any of us, and I . . . am becoming tired . . ."

Or ill—thought Caolin, considering her. The Queen had drawn her cloak about her as if she were cold, but perspiration beaded her brow.

"What decisions can we make now? We must make plans for either attack—where does the greatest danger lie?" Faris went on.

Caolin swallowed—for a moment she had sounded like Jehan. Robert nodded gratefully and straightened in his chair.

"If they come up the coast they can attack Santibar immediately and it will take us longer to move an army to meet them. But they will find it hard to pass beyond Santibar to the rest of the kingdom."

"Do they want Santibar?" asked the Queen.

"What else have we been fighting over for the past twenty years? Palomon and I are old enemies." muttered Brian.

You are good at making enemies, my Lord . . . thought Caolin.

"And if they come through the Pass?" Faris went on.

"A heavy storm could delay them, and our fortress below the pass can hold for a little while. But once through, in two weeks they could reach Laurelynn."

"Santibar has been regarrisoned and the fortifications at Balleor improved," said Caolin quickly. "They should be able to defend themselves. We cannot leave Laurelynn unprotected."

Robert nodded slowly. "That makes good sense . . ."

"But I promised the people of Santibar—" Brian began.

"You promised? In whose name?" snapped Caolin. "Will you break your oath to the King to defend your own lands?"

"Brian—we cannot divide our strength!" protested Robert.

The Lord of Las Costas seemed to wilt. "I know . . . I know . . . but it is hard when they are depending on me . . ."

Robert touched his hand in comfort, but his eyes went to Faris. "My Lady—you must decide . . ."

"How can I know what to do? I have never held a sword!" She was shivering.

Brian shrugged. "I obey my lord's will, and he gave you the power. But you will have to lead if we are to follow you!"

Caolin realized wryly that he and Brian agreed on that. But if Faris would not, or could not, exercise her power, someone else must guide her. He took a deep breath.

"We must gather our own armies . . ." whispered the Queen before he could speak. "We must be ready to relieve Santibar or to defend Laurelynn." She stared through Robert, who shifted uneasily in his seat and looked away.

"It will take at least a month for everyone to arrive . . ." he said.

"War . . ." Faris spoke again. "Slaughtered people and burned homes . . . Cannot we send to Prince Palomon and ask for peace?"

Brian gave a bark of laughter. "Peace, with Palomon?"

Robert shook his head sadly. "This is an old quarrel, and now they think themselves stronger than we. What price would we pay for safety? Would you give Prince Palomon the Four Jewels to adorn his wives?"

For a long moment the Queen was still, her eyes dilated and unseeing. "But there will be a price . . ." she said in a dead voice. Caolin watched her intently, feeling a stir of excitement as he recognized the fixed stare of trance.

Faris seemed to focus on Brian. "You desire battle, but I see only blood and death and the arrows of treachery . . . Blood—" She shuddered violently and recognition came back into her eyes. She clutched at the table's edge and looked fearfully around her. "What—what have I been saying? Brian . . . I'm sorry—"

"Why?" replied Brian with surprising gentleness. "I would not grudge the price if I paid it with sword in hand and it brought victory."

"I will send out the battle summons . . ." said Robert at last, shuffling his papers uncertainly. Faris nodded bleakly. Her eyes were bright with tears.

Caolin considered her with a wonder beyond envy. All the gifts of the spirit and all temporal power had been given her, and she seemed neither to value nor to have the will to use them.

Faris looked up, her gaze going from Robert to Brian and resting at last on Caolin. "Help me . . ."

The Seneschal rose, pity and triumph warring in his heart. "Yes, my Queen. Now you must rest. But be easy—I will make sure that everything is done."

For a moment she rested her face against his shoulder, then straightened and held out her hand to the other two men. "Thank you for your counsel, my Lords."

Robert and Brian stood up and bowed. Caolin took the Queen's arm, but he could not keep a gleam of triumph from his glance as, just before the door closed behind them, he looked back and read the smouldering anger in Brian's eyes.

* * *

"What is it?" asked the Queen. The Master of the Junipers followed her into the chamber, cradling a wooden box in the crook of his arm.

Faris sat down, relief from the chronic ache in her lower back momentarily distracting her. The child within her roused at the change of position, his movement ridging the round of her belly. It was almost mid-February, and her delivery was little more than a month away. The Mistress of the College had said it was a son. His birth would lift her physical burden, but what weight would he place on her heart?

She sighed and looked up at the Master. "Is something wrong?"

Only his eyes seemed to be alive in a face which was not so much aged as used-up, his hair and skin as nondescript as his grey robe. Carefully he set the box on the table between them. "I should have given you this before."

Something about the box nagged at Faris' memory. The front fell open and stepped trays slid back as she touched it. Gently she lifted a corner of the silk cloth. There was a glimmer from within. Faris flinched from the blaze of leaf green and mud brown and gold.

"The Earthstone! You have brought me the Jewels!"

The Master nodded. "You will need them for the Feast of the First Flowers."

She fell back, her memory invaded by the fragrance of plum blossoms and the vision of the King coming to her through the sunlight, a crown of flowers in his hands. "I won't wear them. I won't go to the Festival."

"The people have lost their King—will you deprive them of their Queen?"

Faris remembered her promise to Jehan. "Very well, but I will not need the Jewels for the ceremony." Her gaze moved unwillingly to the redwood box. She could *feel* the presence of the Jewels tickling the edge of her awareness like the roar of a waterfall so distant it was sensed rather than heard.

The Master was silent, his hands twisting in the folds of his robe.

"Well?" she asked bitterly. "Is that all you had to say?"

"What do you want me to say? You are now the only guardian of the Jewels, and you have barely begun to learn their powers. When you left the College of the Wise we agreed that you should continue to study. You know what you should do!" His voice held harshness, not honey, now.

She gripped the arms of her chair. "If I do not it is not for want of being told. Caolin wants my approval for supplies, and Robert my orders for those who will consume them. Petitioners come from all over to present requests they did not dare show the King, or just to gape at the kingdom's prize broodmare!

"I am not the King! Whenever I must act in his place I know that people are thinking what a poor substitute this pale misshapen creature is!" She bit off the rest of her complaint. She must not tell him that every night she dreamed that Jehan had come to her seeking an accounting, and every morning she faced the pain of losing him again.

"And if a time came when you must put on the Jewels?" the Master forced the words from his silence into hers. "Could you rule them?"

"Alone?" She shook her head. "Once more Jehan has left me alone with you, as he did when I went to the College of the Wise, and again you are trying to make me grasp power. But this time you cannot threaten me with his need; you cannot force me to do anything! As you reminded me, I am the Queen." Her laughter became a sob and she covered her face with her hands.

"Then let me go!" the Master cried. She thrust out her hands futilely as his barriers slipped and she felt the full force of his despair. Darkness . . . darkness . . . different but in its own way no less dreadful than her own.

From some yet unknown well within her came a swift rush of compassion, diverting the tide of his pain. Rising awkwardly, Faris put one arm across his thin shoulders.

He shuddered, and the pressure of his emotions abruptly eased. "I'm sorry—" he whispered. "I never meant that to happen . . ."

Faris pushed him back down into his chair, but remained leaning against the table, holding onto his hand. "Where would you go?"

Awahna . . . She scarcely noticed that he had not said it aloud. Then she caught her breath as images rushed from his mind into hers—massed trees greater than those in the Sacred Wood, through which clear streams ran sparkling to green meadows where the frisking deer grazed unafraid. Above the meadows sheer cliffs of stone dwarfed the trees, and everywhere one heard the distant whisper of waterfalls . . .

Faris trembled, recognizing those trees, and the meadows

in which she walked nightly with Jehan. "Awahna . . ." she said aloud.

The Master sighed. "As I am I think I would never reach it. The Guardians only welcome the worthy, and the way to the Valley is never twice the same."

"Stay with me—" Faris murmured. The baby kicked sharply and she set her hand to her side. "Stay at least until the child is born." That would be soon enough, now, and perhaps she would die of it and be free.

The Master looked up at her, a memory of his old smile warming his face like sunlight reflected off a stream. "When you need me, I will be here . . ."

When the Master of the Junipers had gone, Faris stood for a long time gazing down at the Jewels. Her shielding had been breached by her contact with him, and she felt their proximity as an almost painful attraction. Without willing it, she found herself putting them on. It was very still in the palace. In this moment, when no need, no other presence distracted her, Faris felt for the first time the undiluted power of the Jewels.

Earth . . . Water . . . Air . . . Fire . . . Her body throbbed with their untapped potency, poised in a moment uncompelled by either fear or desire.

Slowly she turned to face the mirror. The Jewels were awakening, colors shifting, radiating a deepening glow until her body was bathed in rainbow fires. She stared at the terrible beauty of her image in the glass.

This is not me . . . She felt something waken within her soul as the child in her body stirred, some Other that smiled mockingly with her lips and sparkled with a reckless excitement in her eyes.

I am Power . . . it said. *I have always waited within.*

Images pulsed through her awareness: darkness that heaved with emergent life, nameless forms that flowed outward on irresistible tides, tossed in the winds, flared in incandescent fire, and sank into darkness only to be born anew.

I am the Lady of Darkness . . . the voice within her said then.

Faris gasped as the child in her belly kicked sharply. For the first time she felt the touch of his mind, like a flare of clear light. Suddenly terrified, Faris fumbled to free the Jewels from her body and flung them into their box.

Then she sank shuddering into a chair. The right side of her head had begun to throb sickly, but she welcomed the pain. Now she understood why Jehan had feared the Jewels, but more than their power she feared that of the Shadow-self who had desired it.

Caolin grimaced at the paper in his hand and crumpled it, wishing he had the power to do the same to Brian. This was the third time in a week that one of his requisitions to Las Costas had come back with a note that the Queen must sign it before it could be obeyed. The Seneschal sighed and ran his fingers through his fair hair. Damn Brian! Whether this interference was meant to keep him from performing his duty to provision the army by the beginning of March or merely to remind him of his dependence on the Queen Regent, it was irritating him.

"It is your men who will go hungry, my Lord, if I fail!" Caolin muttered, getting to his feet. Faris was presiding over the Feast of the First Flowers this afternoon. He slipped the requisition into the folder of things to discuss with her and began to pace restlessly to the shelves of files and back to the desk. The wolf Gerol's ears pricked and he lifted his grizzled head, watching the man. There was more sound outside the Chancery today than within—even with a war approaching the Seneschal could not deny his staff their holiday, though he had managed to hold a few to their tasks. But none of them could help with the decisions he had to make now.

"Our army can best Palomon's . . ." Caolin said aloud, considering the forces that were already swelling the encampment outside the city. "And Brian will return a hero. Will that satisfy him? Or will he use his popularity to try to divide me from the Queen?" Gerol's head sank back upon his paws, but his amber eyes continued to follow his master back and forth across the room.

Caolin moved to the window and looked down at the revellers crowding the streets, crowned with early apple blossoms or wreaths of silk flowers. Three soldiers went by arm-in-arm, singing raucously.

"Palomon has rivals at home. If he does not conquer outright he will not dare to press a campaign. But Robert and Brian do not know that—Palomon will seem strong to them. Brian accused me of being Palomon's friend when it was not true, but I think that he and I might have some interests in common.

There might be subtle advantages I could grant him without endangering Westria, in return for concessions that would support my claim to power . . ."

His gaze unfocused, as if he were trying to see all the way to Elaya from Laurelynn. "Such a contact would be too delicate to entrust to Ordrey or to Ercul Ashe, yet I dare not compromise myself . . ." He saw his own face reflected dimly in the windowpane. *I must be myself and not myself, as I was to Margit in the ritual* . . . Time was dimming the memory of that ceremony, and he found himself longing for the Red Mountain again.

Across the roofs of Laurelynn he could see its peak and part of the southern slope, still dusted with snow from the last storm, though fruit trees were beginning to bloom in the sheltered orchards of the Valley. The westering sun stained the peak with rose. He had not been there since Samaine.

A shift in the wind brought him the sound of women's voices massed in song and he moved back to his desk and sat down. Could he change his semblance while retaining his will? He closed his eyes, thinking. First he must make his barriers an opaque surface upon which to paint the persona he wanted others to see. Then he would withdraw so that only the simulation could be seen. If he visualized the other identity sufficiently vividly, the strength of his will might be enough to impose that impression on others.

He pictured the face of a little clerk who logged in documents at the Chancery, a foxy-haired man with a missing front tooth. Caolin must slump in his chair—so—and wet his lips with his tongue as he hunched over his work . . .

Gerol whined perplexedly in the silence. The man at the desk reached for a pen and began to trim it with clumsy twitches of his knife.

The door swung open. "Waren, what are you doing here? I thought you were off today!" A stocky young woman with an armful of papers and a pen stuck behind one ear stepped into the room. "Don't let Lord Icicle catch you in that chair."

A flare of triumph breached Caolin's concentration. He lifted his head.

"Oh, my Lord!" Papers spilled from the clerk's arms in a crackling waterfall. "Forgive me—I didn't realize—this dim light!" stammering, the girl scrabbled for the papers, thrust them onto the Seneschal's desk and fled.

Gerol snorted disgustedly and began to scratch while Caolin threw back his head and for the first time in months, laughed aloud.

"I can do it! I *will* do it! Ah, Brian, how will you plot against me now? I may be anyone . . . beware, Brian, lest I creep into your bed and you tell me the secrets you intend for your own wife's ear!"

For a little while he sat smiling as the winter day dimmed around him. Then he rose, and lighting his lantern, prepared to go. His reflected image winked at him from the slubs and swellings of the window glass. He peered at it, moving the lantern slightly, projecting a score of images on the pane—

—Until he glimpsed for a moment a face with dark hair and eyes like blue stars. Caolin's hand moved of itself to shutter the lantern, and he turned and went quickly from the room.

Farin stared into the candle flame, but he saw only the image of the King. It had been two months since Jehan died—two months since Farin had been able to make Swangold sing. He had come to his own chamber tonight just after dinner and now it was past midnight, and silent, still silent, with no music at all.

The strings shimmered gold as his grip tightened on the harp. If he could not break this paralysis he might as well smash the instrument and destroy himself afterward. He would be going to war soon, death would be easy to find. But once a fisherman from Seagate had told him, *You must go through the breakers to reach the open sea* . . . If only he could fight this sorrow with song!

The lord I loved is gone . . . The phrase echoed in his mind. Farin turned abruptly from the candle as once more he realized Jehan was dead, but the brilliance of the flame still dazzled him. His fingers moved blindly on the strings.

"But he is *not* gone!" Farin exclaimed. "If he were gone, we would be able to forget him. My own heart harbors the ghost that haunts me!"

His vision was clearing now, but he was not focusing on the chamber around him. His silver-streaked hair fell across his face as he bent over the harp, testing phrase after phrase of music, shaping and setting the words that lay waiting within. They had always been there, but he had not had the courage to look for them before.

Words and music linked with the sweet simplicity that one felt sometimes when the arrow sang true from the bow, and Farin knew that it was not he, but that Other within whom he and the harp were joined, that made the song.

> *"The lord we loved is gone*
> *His brilliance dimmed by death,*
> *But in our hearts his image does not die;*
> *Just as a candle flame*
> *Is snuffed out by a breath,*
> *But still its after-image fills the*
> *eye . . ."*

VI

Maneuvers in a Mist

"Soon we will know who is to have the mastery of Westria!"

Caolin half-turned to glance at the doorway to the grain shed, thinking he recognized that deep voice. Hoofbeats clattered and faded on the packed ground outside—another company off to the muster on the plain outside Laurelynn.

"My Lord, this wagon's full," said the black-bearded man from Las Costas.

"Yes, yes, go on then." Caolin ticked off another space on his tally sheet as the next wagon rolled into place. The loaders were already heaving twenty-pound bags of corn onto their backs and staggering forward. He glanced down the line— only two wagons to go—they could be finished by the time the army moved out this afternoon. He wiped his brow on his sleeve. It was only the tenth of March, but the air inside the shed was very warm.

"Well! I hardly expected to find you here!"

Caolin whirled and saw Brian's dark bulk silhouetted in the doorway. The Lord Commander passed through a shaft of light that barred the dusty air and paused, surveying the Seneschal with a broadening smile.

Caolin returned his stare impassively and flicked chaff from the scarlet wool of his sleeve, uncomfortably aware of the dust in his hair and the perspiration running between his shoulderblades.

Brian was already dressed for the formal departure of the army of Westria. The rivets that held the steel plates beneath the russet suede of his hauberk had been gilded, and gold thread outlined the crimson arrows that flashed across the black shield embroidered on his breast. Light glanced from his golden spurs.

"I promised that your supplies would be loaded. One of my clerks fell ill so I came in her place . . ." The Seneschal checked off the last of the wagons and waved it on. The loaders picked up the weapons they had stacked in the corner and trooped after it. "Are your men as ready to fight as they are to eat?"

Brian grinned. "Prince Palomon will be sorry he challenged us . . ."

"Indeed?" Caolin closed his notebook and slipped it into his pouch. "They have two thousand foot soldiers, three hundred crossbowmen from the eastern desert and a brigade of axemen from the mines, besides their light cavalry."

"But we have more—" Brian stopped, his yellow eyes narrowing. "My last report gave them only fifteen hundred foot!"

"Well, perhaps they lost some when they took the fortress at the bottom of the pass . . . Good hunting, my Lord," said Caolin agreeably.

Brian thrust his head forward and grinned, his teeth surprisingly white in his brown beard. "Good hunting indeed! But you need not play-act now, Master Red-robe—we are alone. I know well that you hope I will not return!"

Caolin stilled, straining his ears for any sound beside their own breathing. Warpipes wailed in the distance, summoning some contingent from the Ramparts or the north, but inside the shed there was only the buzzing of a fly that faded as it flew out into the sunshine. The Seneschal's gaze paused uneasily on the heavy sword that hung at Brian's side.

"I should be sorry to see Westria deprived of such a strong arm . . ." he said unevenly, and truthfully.

"Would you?" Brian laughed shortly. His advance brought him from sunlight to shadow again. "Then no doubt you will rejoice when I present the Queen with Palomon's coronet. You seek to become her only councilor; I will not allow it . . ."

Caolin's eyes narrowed, suspecting this restraint, but he must not let Brian think him afraid. "I can defend myself—is your own place so secure?"

"Are you threatening me?" Brian's eyes began to glow and he straightened. "I have never yet drawn back from a fight!"

"I know that." Caolin smiled slightly, seeing his enemy revert to type. This automatic response to provocation could be Brian's greatest weakness. "Fortunately I am not so constrained. Fight or flight are equally valid if they serve my purpose."

"Or treachery and subterfuge?" Brian spat.

A pulse began to pound in Caolin's temple, but he held his features still, forcing himself to ignore all the provocations of the past three months. "Did you come here to quarrel with me? There has never been love between us, but we promised Jehan to cease our enmity. He left us both in positions of trust. Help me do my job, as I have helped you to do yours . . ." He gestured toward the empty storage bins, trying to read the smouldering in Brian's eyes.

The Lord Commander shook his head. "How very reasonable. I think you even believe it yourself, for now! I begin to see why Jehan believed in you for so long." He set one foot on a grain sack and leaned forward, resting his gauntleted forearm on his knee.

"But do you think I would trust anything you say?" he went on. "Did you think Jehan trusted you? I know that you forged evidence against me, and he knew it too!"

A warhorse trumpeted and the ground trembled as a troop of cavalry went by. Caolin felt the tremor pass through his body. A muscle twitched in his cheek and he could not make it cease . . . Jehan *had* trusted him—Jehan had loved him! He could not afford to doubt that, now.

"I might even forgive your attempt on my honor," Brian's deep voice battered at his ears, "but I saw Jehan's face when he understood what you had done . . . *you* killed him, Caolin, with your treachery!"

"No!" Caolin's shout sent dust motes swirling to kindle in the light. This was the one accusation that could break his control. He saw again the boar's mask on his altar, felt the spear give way between his hands, heard Jehan's voice pleading . . . pleading . . . His hands shot out and Brian recoiled.

"No one shall say such things of me!" hissed Caolin. Brian retreated before him, step by step, his hand hovering above his sword. "Your own words have released me from my oath to spare you!" The Seneschal's voice lowered, focused, till it vibrated the tines of the pitchforks in their racks.

"You have warned me—now I warn you! If you trip, do not laugh, for I will have dislodged the stone . . . If thunder rattles in the sky, beware my lightning bolt! And when you feel your death upon you, then curse me, for I will be its cause!" He stood trembling, glaring at his enemy.

Brian straightened, his eyes glinting with something halfway between astonishment and satisfaction. "Hah—" he barked, "so the worm can turn? Do you bear the Four Jewels of Westria, that you think to bend all Nature to your will?" He shook his head. "Perhaps I should kill you now, but I will let you live to see my victory!" He threw back his head like a bear scenting the breeze, turned abruptly, and strode away.

Caolin collapsed to his knees in the dust, feeling the sweat chill upon his skin. What was happening to him? He had never given way to such fury . . . never, since the day he found the gates of Awahna closed to him. He was changing—nothing was certain, now. He heard Brian speak to his horse as he mounted, then a shout of greeting.

"You should have killed me, Brian . . ." Caolin whispered through teeth that chattered with cold. Pipes keened in the distance, bittersweet as the promise of revenge.

In the shock of the silence after the warpipes had ceased to play, the banners of the Army of Westria snapped like whips against the turquoise sky. All morning the forces of Westria had been maneuvering across the plain near Laurelynn. The reviewing stand trembled as the wind caught at its canvas sides. Faris shaded her eyes and tried to hear what Robert of the Ramparts was saying to the soldiers ranked before him.

". . . and whatever the price, we will accept only Victory! Those who sought to take advantage of our loss must fear our sorrow!" Robert paused for breath as a murmur swept the massed troops he faced. The sun caught their mail in myriad twinkling points of light.

Faris' shielding tingled with the force of their emotion. *Do they think to punish Elaya for the death of Jehan?* she wondered. *But perhaps they are fortunate to have a physical enemy upon whom to expend their grief . . .*

Robert's horse tossed its head with a clashing of bits as the Commander went on—"Our King swore to defend the people of Santibar, but we cannot help them, for the enemy has taken the fortress at the foot of the Dragon's Tail Pass, and they march northward even now. We must redeem King Jehan's oath! We must defend our land!" He stretched a gauntleted hand to Faris as the cheering deafened them. "My Lady," he cried. "I present to you this Army of Westria!"

Faris felt the attention of the Army transfer from Robert to her, as if she had become the focus of a burning glass. The clamor stilled. The three wings of the Army rayed out to form a half circle with the pavilion as its hub. How could she reach them all?

Her thoughts raced in panic, but Caolin had already explained to her that the canvas sides of the platform would reflect her voice outward. Her white gown would stand out against the colors of the other ladies—Rosemary, Jessica of the Ramparts and Alessia of Las Costas. Eric's mother and sister were there too, and her own sister Berisa who had come down from the north with Sandremun. Caolin had even written out a speech for her to memorize.

As she hesitated, she felt Caolin's hand beneath her elbow, helping her to rise. There was a smudge of dirt on his brow. Faris coughed, and Rosemary handed her a cup of wine. It went down like red fire, easing her throat, but burning in her belly. She moved to the railing.

"Warriors of Westria—the Prince of the South has come against us, and now indeed we feel the loss of our King . . ." her voice wavered, then steadied. "But the strength of a King is in his people—" light flickered across the field as the crowd moved forward, and she felt their attention intensify.

"My lord foresaw this war, and it grieved him more than his wound . . ." Faris forced herself to continue. "But he made what provision he could against this day. Come forward Lord Robert, and Lord Brian, whom my lord appointed second in command."

The two leaders turned their mounts until the horses' noses touched the stand. Lady Jessica and Brian's wife Alessia came forward to stand by the Queen, purple gown and blue, one on each side. Faris took from Jessica a baton of polished wood whose ends were adorned with knobs of gold. She held it out to Robert.

"My Lord, receive from me now the insignia of your command. Come back to us victorious and unharmed." She glanced sidelong at Lady Jessica as she spoke, and drew strength from her sister-in-law's steady gaze.

Faris turned to Lady Alessia a little shyly—she had met her only the day before and found her competence unnerving—took from her the silver-ended baton, and held it out to Lord Brian.

"My Lord, take this baton as the King desired, and serve Robert and Westria well," she said quickly.

"My Queen, we will drive the enemy from this land even if we must spend our lives. We swear this by our homes and families, and by the memory of Jehan our lord, and by the Guardian of Men!" The voices of the two generals sounded as one, and as one they wheeled their horses to face the Army again.

Faris took a deep breath. Rosemary offered her the wine, but she waved it away. "Let Eric of the Horn come before me . . ."

Thunderfoot danced and sidled toward the stand, half-rearing as the streamer of white Faris had drawn from her sleeve blew out in the wind. Eric reined him down severely and brought him to a halt before the platform.

"I accepted you as my Champion at the King's word. Here is my token . . ." Faris said faintly, holding it out to him. Eric took it as if she had put a white butterfly into his hand, and held it against his heart.

"Wear it into battle as a true knight, as my lord would have done . . ." she whispered brokenly.

But Eric had heard her. Faris felt Rosemary stiffen beside her, and through her faltering barriers came a momentary picture that was Rosemary's sight of Eric's face. Faris blinked away tears and saw him herself, less beautiful than in Rosemary's vision, but wearing the same look of ecstasy. She shook her head, rejecting that adoration, but Eric had already reined Thunderfoot away.

Faris clung to the railing. Her back ached, and there was a pain behind her eyes. "You must go out to battle," she said, "and I must stand in the place my lord left me to hold until his child can take his throne. But as your time of testing comes, remember that my time is close as well. As you labor on the battlefield, remember that I will soon be fighting to deliver your new King . . ." She set her hands on her belly and added, "Pray for me then, as I will pray for you." Her hands dropped to her sides and she swayed a little where she stood.

A hush stilled the host, as if they had been the mirage of an army. Then Eric bowed low in his saddle, and the movement swept through the lines with a flicker of multi-colored surcoats and a flash of steel like sunlight on the wind-ruffled surface of the Great Bay.

Robert turned in his saddle and held up his baton. "My Lady, is it your will that we depart?"

Faris leaned forward. The tension was building, building, and only she could give it release.

"Go forth to victory!" she cried with breaking voice, "In the name of the Lord of All!"

Robert swung down his baton.

"Faris! Faris!" Trumpets blasted on her left. Robert reached his men and they began to move—forward, then a wheel to the right that resolved itself into a steady southward flow. The beat of their marching feet pulsed in her blood.

Robert, the commander, cantered in the van. Above him flared his banner, with its golden bear, ramping over horsemen who laughed and shook their spears. Behind them the holders from each mountain vale marched in loose formation, axes in their belts. Spears were in their hands and bows across their backs; they wore scale or leather, and bright steel caps. Cavalry came with them from the sloping plains that spread between the mountains and the river's edge. Hoofs dancing in the dust their mounts curvetted by and the pennons on their lances fluttered cheerfully.

Faris raised her hands to salute them, received back a flood of exultation that dizzied her. Lady Jessica abruptly returned to her place.

But Lady Alessia, still standing by the Queen, stirred suddenly and Faris saw Lord Brian's forces—the folk of Las Costas, come forward, wheeling to join the march. Caolin took the place Jessica had left, his robes crimson as blood in the March sunshine. Faris felt him and Alessia trade glances above her head, but the cheering of the warriors before her claimed all her attention.

Brian sat his mount at ease and laughed, motioned with broad arm sweep to his men, reined in to rear in homage to the Queen. The southern coasts bred bowmen, lightly armed, and mounted on scrub ponies good for miles. Each bore a shield and sword—both men and girls, with steel caps covering tightly braided hair, and they were no less fierce, for being fair.

They cheered as they passed, and Faris felt the hairs lifting on the back of her neck. Her heart pounded to the beat of Brian's drums, and she suppressed a desire to leap from the stand and follow them. She thought, *What have I begun? Is this what Jehan felt when he led his men?*

As the last of Brian's forces passed, Caolin gave a little sigh and moved away, his robes clashing violently with Berisa's

berry-colored gown as she brushed by to take his place at the
rail. Faris looked around and motioned to Rosemary and to
Eric's family to join them as Eric signalled the third wing into
motion, Sandremun of the Corona by his side.

Out of three smaller forces the last wing had been formed.
Their van was bright with banners, led by Seagate's green,
black and white for Theodor's men and blue for the Domain.
Eric led the horsemen, well-armored for a charge, mounts glittering with plates of steel and strong enough to bear their own
weight and the weight of men with sword and lance and mace.
He led also Jehan's own men as champion of the Queen—
picked men, grim-faced with grief, for they had known and
loved their King and lost him to an enemy they could not meet
with sword. Behind them came the northerners—above the
hoofbeats' drum, they heard the swift chords of a harp, and
suddenly a song—

> "With hearts aglow to strike the foe
> The warriors sally forth,
> And their delight shall be to smite
> For the Lily of the North—
> Oh, 'For the Lily of the North'
> Our battle cry shall be,
> And our refrain, when home again,
> We come with victory!"

They paused as they came by the stand, and Eric wheeled
and turned. They saw on his lance fluttering the favor of the
Queen. White it burned against the sky and Eric cried again—
"For the Lily of the North we fight, and for our lord, Jehan!"

The northerners echoed him, and the cry spread forward to
the contingents from Las Costas and the Ramparts. Waves of
sound rolled across the plain until it seemed to Faris that the
earth itself was shouting her name. Her name, and Jehan's . . .

Berisa sniffed. "I thought they were fighting for Westria! I
hope Farin comes home in better frame than he did last time,
and my dear lord too . . ."

Faris' exaltation vanished. She shuddered and groped for
the rail, the brightness before her warring with the darkness
surging within. She felt Rosemary's firm hands assisting her
to lie down.

"I told you it would be too much for her—" said Berisa

with gloomy satisfaction. "But at least she did not have to watch her lord ride off to face those savages . . ."

"Berisa!" came Rosemary's shocked whisper. "That was thoughtless, even for you!"

But Faris only shook her head and turned her face against the cushions. *Oh Thou who made life and death as well*, she prayed, *help them all through the next weeks. Oh Lady, help me!*

But though she covered her ears against the sound of their going, still Faris felt the vibration of marching feet through the wood of the platform and the bench, through the very earth of Westria.

"I think that tonight the Army will camp here—" Ercul Ashe's finger brushed the map of Westria to hover above a bend in the Darkwater. "Lord Robert's message was dated noon today, and it would have taken the pigeon something over an hour to bring it here. They are going so slowly!"

Caolin peered at the map. "For a newly formed army, fifty miles in three and a half days is not bad time. They could go a few miles further today—why do you think they will stop there?" Ashe seemed oddly concerned for so dispassionate a man.

"There is a ford and a meadow that would make it easy to water and graze the horses."

"You seem to know the country well," observed the Seneschal.

"I was brought up in Risslin, my Lord, and my parents live there still. Naturally I want to know whether our forces will arrive in time to defend it from the enemy." Ashe said stiffly.

Caolin nodded. "They are nine days' march from Risslin. If Palomon persists in stopping to capture everything in his path, they will meet somewhere in the Dragon Waste south of the city. Your family should be safe." He smiled. Was there some way he could use Ashe's interest in the campaign?

"Thank you, my Lord." Ercul Ashe did not quite hide his surprise at being answered so kindly—Caolin had never encouraged his staff to confide in him.

The Seneschal was rolling up the map with swift, precise twirls. He slipped it back into its niche. "When is your next meeting with Hakim MacMorann?"

"Tonight, at the Three Laurels Inn. He returned to Laurelynn two days ago. I suppose he has an answer to the letter I gave him when he left in January . . ."

Caolin looked at the other man sharply. He had enclosed the letter in a blank outer wrapper, to be opened only when the trader reached Elaya. Could Ercul Ashe have opened it and seen that it was addressed to Prince Palomon?

"Things have changed since then . . ." he said abruptly. "Do not meet with the Elayan tonight or again."

Ashe nodded. "Good. There seems little point in secret diplomacy now that we are at war!"

Caolin looked quickly away lest the other man should read suspicion in his eyes. Inwardly he blessed the instinct that had inspired him to remove Ashe from any part in the communications that, far from ending, had hardly begun.

In his letter, he had offered Palomon a kind of alliance— a chance to trade Elaya's recognition of the Seneschal as spokesman for Westria, for Caolin's help in arranging a generous settlement after the war. There were concessions that would impress the Elayans without weakening Westria, and his own position would be strengthened if he were the only Westrian leader who could handle Elaya. How would Palomon reply?

Afternoon was fading into evening before Ercul Ashe gathered up his papers and left Caolin alone. The Seneschal went to the cupboard and exchanged his crimson robes for a plain gown of brownish wool . . .

The clerk at the side door looked up as he came down the stairs. "Master Ercul, how can you be leaving again so soon? Have you found a way to do two days' work in one?" She laughed. "Surely even our master does not require such efficiency!"

Caolin stilled, concentrating on the image of Ercul Ashe, willing the young woman to hear the other man's dry voice as she obviously saw his thin shoulders and greying hair.

"I came back in by the other door." he said stiffly. "There was a paper I had not put away."

Her laughter followed him as he started down the street toward Ashe's rendezvous at the Three Laurels Inn.

"I am the broodmare of Westria, bound to her service more surely than any slave in the Barren Lands . . ." murmured Faris bitterly. Her distorted reflection stared back at her from the dark waters of the lake of Laurelynn.

The sliding surface of the water revealed nothing. If Faris should cast herself in she would vanish without a trace . . . She sighed, knowing that they would only pull her out again and add reproaches to the weight she bore. She knew that she was watched. Even now, if she should turn to look across the expanse of lawn to the Palace, a face would flicker at a window or a door would click shut. They watched her as avidly as a farmer watches his best cow.

But with the Army gone a week, what else was there for them to do? Faris knew that today there were only two questions being asked in all Westria—Has the Army met its foe? Has the Queen delivered her child?

A mallard swam quacking from among the reeds. Faris turned away abruptly and began to walk along the shore. The messages Robert sent to Caolin told them that the Army was two days north of Risslin and had seen no enemy. Sometime in the next week then their course would intersect with Palomon's.

Sometime in the next week . . . A cramp rippled across her belly and Faris froze, holding her breath. Was it to be now? The child within her kicked painfully and turned, but though she waited, her own body remained still.

Faris glared up at the eyes of the Palace and cried suddenly, "You will have to wait, damn you! Nothing is happening— stop looking at me!"

Caolin put down Palomon's letter, finding the same meaning there on the twentieth reading as he had seen when he received it from Hakim MacMorann three days before.

"If I should need to trust anyone, why should it be you?" wrote Palomon. *"How will you prove your good faith to me?"*

How indeed? Both commanders wanted a great victory, but the Westrians still outnumbered the forces of Elaya. What if something happened—some mischance to Brian's little army, for example—that would even those odds until the margin of victory would be narrow no matter who won. Both sides might be glad of a mediator then. Could he win over Palomon and destroy Brian with one blow?

If only he could go south—he would know his chance when it came . . . The Seneschal smiled ruefully, recognizing an impossibility, for though he might pass unknown in the Westrian camp, he must be known to be here in Laurelynn, and no one could impersonate *him!* He must take the riskier way of making another his instrument.

The opening of the door cut short yet another iteration of his figuring.

"My Lord—I have been in the library, and—"

"Ah, Ercul!" interrupted Caolin. "I am glad you are here. The dispatches for you to carry to Lord Robert are ready." He slipped Palomon's letter unobtrusively into his desk and pulled out the green dispatch case.

"I found some books on strategy, just as you thought—but no one has opened them for centuries!" Ercul Ashe came forward, a surprising amount of color in his worn face, and set two mouldering volumes on Caolin's desk. Dust rose in a visible cloud. Ordrey, entering after the deputy, coughed loudly and sat down on the other side of the room.

"In the dispatch case is the analysis of the Elayan—oh very well, Ercul—" Caolin gave in to his Deputy's eagerness to speak feeling that he had frustrated Ashe sufficiently for the man to be certain that the idea he wanted to discuss was his very own.

"Thank you, my Lord." The deputy opened the book and began to carefully turn the pages until the volume fell open as if its back had been broken at that spot.

"Here is an analysis of battle plans for different weather conditions," said Ashe. "I know the lower valley, my Lord, and I have found accounts of battles of the ancients which duplicate anything our forces are likely to face!"

"That's all very well . . ." said Caolin patiently, "but I doubt that Lord Robert will have time to come here and consult them."

Ashe shook his head. "You don't understand. I could take the books with me . . ."

The Seneschal began to laugh. "Very well, Ercul—take them. Perhaps they will add enough weight for the horse to know you are on its back. If Lord Robert finds he doesn't have time to read up on strategy, you can tell him all about it!"

"Yes, my Lord!" Ashe collected himself with an effort, resumed his customary imperturbability. "I will be ready to leave in the morning. It should take us a week to get there, and allowing a few days for me to visit in Risslin, another week to return. You may expect me back within three weeks, my Lord Seneschal." He picked up the two books and the dispatch case and turned to Ordrey. "I will meet you at the Chancery stable tomorrow then, at six o'clock in the morning promptly." He bowed and went out.

Ordrey bent in his chair, his shoulders shaking with silent laughter.

"Did you have to pour quite so much dust on those books?" asked Caolin, brushing off his robes.

For a moment Ordrey simply shook his head, unable to speak. "At six o'clock promptly!" he gasped finally. "Does he think I keep a clock in my chamber? Oh my Lord, what have you saddled me with!"

Caolin smiled a little, knowing that Ordrey was quite capable of waking up in the middle of the night if necessary, but that he would complain no matter what time he rose. "It's the horses that you will be saddling. I hope you have good ones— it will be hard to make the trip in that time."

"We should be able to make thirty miles a day on those roads," Ordrey replied. "Your plan seems rather complicated—" he went on, "why not just send a description of the strategy to Lord Robert?"

"Because Robert will discuss it with his other commanders, and as soon as Brian knows where it comes from he will reject it out of hand."

"But he will know that Ercul Ashe comes from you," objected Ordrey.

Caolin sighed. "Yes, but Ercul's honesty is so transparent that even Brian should believe him when he swears I had nothing to do with it . . . You *will* remember the strategies?" he added anxiously.

"I wore out my eyes on them last night," said Ordrey cheerfully. "I memorized everything that could possibly apply. A word from Ashe will let me know which one they choose."

"They may not choose any of them. You will have to wait and see how the troops are stationed before you slip away to Palomon. And remember, be careful what you say to Ercul Ashe!"

Ordrey looked hurt. "I understand." He smiled a little wistfully. "Ercul Ashe only serves Westria . . . I serve *you*, my Lord."

The ground was wet. Farin could feel its dampness even through the thick wool rugs covering the floor of Lord Robert's tent. He drew his knees up and clasped his arms around them, trying to stay awake. He wondered whether Faris had started to have her baby yet. The commanders were making their reports, a soporific account of men and supplies, and their lieutenants and couriers had been ordered to listen to them.

A draft of cold air struck his face and he looked up as someone pushed the tent flap aside. He glimpsed a cloaked figure outside, ghostly in the mist.

"My Lord Commander—" Robert's squire poked his head through the door. "Here's a messenger from Laurelynn." The cloaked man bent to come through and straightened as the flap fell behind him, pushing back his hood and blinking at the light. His hair was as grey as his cloak, his face like an old shoe.

"Is it the Queen?" asked Robert anxiously. Farin dropped his arms and leaned forward.

"She is well, but there was no news when I left six days ago."

"They will light the beacons when the child is born," Brian reminded them.

The messenger fumbled at his belt for a green leather case. "I come from the Lord Seneschal."

"Of course—" said Robert as Brian stiffened. "I believe I remember you. You are one of the deputies, and your name—"

"Ercul Ashe, my Lord." The deputy bowed and handed the case to the Lord Commander, who unlocked it, drew out the papers within, and began to read. Farin's heart sank as he saw Robert's normally dour expression become graver. At last the Commander looked up, sighed and passed the paper to Brian.

"I could wish that your master had given me this information sooner . . . but I suppose it makes no difference. We have already done all we can."

Farin shivered, remembering the cruel pace of yesterday's march, the confused maneuvering to take advantage of this ground, and the shock when the dark line of the enemy army appeared suddenly on the southern horizon in the afternoon. For a while they had thought they would have to fight them, but the Elayan advance had stopped a mile or two away, and they appeared to be settling in for the night. Now their camp-fires glowed like a line of fire in the shadowed fields.

"I am sorry, my Lord," said Ercul Ashe. "We had to wait until all reports were in before we could make this analysis."

"You know what it says? Then you may as well stay," said Robert as the Deputy Seneschal nodded. He sighed again and looked bleakly around.

"I hope that you have not all been feeling overconfident because we outnumbered the enemy two to one. The Seneschal informs me that a better estimate of Palomon's numbers would be 3,500 men, and as you already know, he has had all winter to train them."

"But surely invaders will not fight as well as men on their own ground, defending their homes!" exclaimed Eric.

"Our own men are courageous and willing, but they are more used to skirmishing with bandits than fighting pitched battles. We still outnumber them, but I beg you to give up any notion that this makes us the superior force!" Robert snapped.

Brian shook his head with a pitying smile. "Spirit is valuable, but if you think it a substitute for skill you are even more naive than I thought. Courage can turn to panic only too quickly when they are untried and the enemy is strong. Even a veteran would be foolish not to tremble when the *Impis* advance."

"I have fought these people before—" said Eric sullenly, "three years ago below Santibar!"

"That was no war! That was a formal exercise. Besides . . ." Brian added more soberly, "then we had the King."

Farin dropped his face against his knees, overwhelmed by memories of the King fighting in the snow, hawking in the hills above Misthall, falling beneath the tusks of the boar. *Oh my Lord . . . my dear Lord . . .* his spirit cried.

In the silence he heard Ercul Ashe cough dryly. "My Lords, forgive me—I have no right to speak here, but I have been searching the military library at Laurelynn . . ."

"Speak, man! This is no time to worry about etiquette!" said Robert.

"I brought a book with me, my Lord—" Ashe gestured toward the door.

"I'll look at it later if the idea is a good one!" Robert growled. "What does it say?"

Ashe took a deep breath, his dull eyes beginning to glow.

"In a distant land, there were two armies that waited to do battle on a night when there was a great fog—and you see, my Lords, the mists are already rising here." He twitched the door flap aside and they saw the moisture in the air glitter in the lantern light.

"They were encamped facing one another, as you face Palomon, ready to charge in the morning. But one of the commanders had an idea. He left his campfires burning, and that night he sent part of his force, perhaps a third, to one side, on a little rise where their numbers could not be clearly seen. He marched the rest very silently in a large circle, so that they emerged, still hidden by the fog, behind their foes." He paused.

"Well, what happened then?" asked Sandremun, pushing his fair hair from his eyes as he leaned forward.

Ashe smiled a little. "In the morning the enemy saw the lesser force before them and attacked, thinking them easy prey. They never knew about the rest of the army until it fell upon their rear. They were caught between hammer and anvil, my Lords—they were destroyed."

"We would have to find a guide who knew the country here very well . . . or we might get lost ourselves." said Robert after a few moments' thought.

"Elnora of Oakhill's holding is a mile back up the road . . ." said Esteban Swift, Brian's lieutenant. "And she is with us here."

"Well Brian, what do you think?"

"I think . . ." said the lord of Las Costas slowly, "that we should look very carefully at any plan that comes from the Seneschal . . ."

"Brian!" Robert's shocked reproof crossed Ercul Ashe's protest—"But it came from the book!"

"I dare say!" Brian turned on the Deputy. "But where did the book come from? Who sent you to tell us about it when we would have no time to think it through?"

"Brian—I know that you and Caolin are not friends, but do you really believe that he would betray the Army of Westria?" said Robert in frank wonder.

"Not friends!" Brian shook his head and laughed, and Farin felt hairs lift on the back of his neck at the sound. As it faded, everyone in the tent turned to stare at the Seneschal's Deputy, who still stood in their midst, twisting his hands.

"My . . . my Lords!" he stammered, then continued with a curious dignity. "I am no warrior, but my integrity is dear to me. I will swear by my honor, by anything you like, that I found the book in the library with the dust of centuries thick upon it. I tried to tell my Lord Seneschal what I had found, but he would not listen. It was my idea to tell you—you do not have to listen either . . ."

He straightened and looked at Brian. "I have served in the

office of the Seneschal since I took my name, and with the Lord Caolin for seven years. You who rule the Provinces know something of what government requires, but can you imagine what it is to keep watch over the entire Kingdom? I have seen Lord Caolin laboring while other men slept—if you think that such a man would betray what he has served so long I think that you are fools!"

"But he might try to betray *me* . . ." muttered Brian.

"It *is* a good plan . . ." Robert sounded as if he were pleading.

Eric's eyes were shining with excitement. "Lord Robert! Let me be the anvil, let me take my men and hold the hill!"

Robert frowned down Brian's bark of laughter. "You would do it well, Eric, but we must not waste our heavy cavalry so. We will need you to spearhead the charge. No—for the anvil we must have infantry, a wall of spears!"

"As Commander you should stay with the main force," said Brian abruptly. "But I have forty companies of spearmen from the lands along the river—it is their lands that these vermin have been wasting—give the honor to them!"

Farin's heart lurched as he realized that the decision had been made. The waiting would be over only too soon.

"I think you are right," nodded Robert. "And you have archers to make the welcome hotter. Give me your light cavalry and I will hold my foot soldiers in reserve. In exchange you may have my mountain men. They have spears too, and heavy axes, and they like close work best."

Through the murmur of comment that followed Farin could hear Robert giving orders to specific commanders—they must let the men sleep until midnight, move the main force out first, leave the campfires alight. He tried to listen.

"I thought you disapproved of the plan—" said Sandremun to Brian. "Why did you volunteer for the most dangerous post?"

Brian laughed, and Farin felt the force of his lust for the coming fight. "Do you think I will let that man go back and tell his master that I was afraid?" He pointed at Ercul Ashe, who still stood in the midst of the commanders, a reed among oak trees. He saw Brian's gesture and turned to go.

"Oh no!" growled Brian. "I have not lost all sense—you will go guarded to my tent," his great hand crushed Ashe's shoulder. "The one thing that would certainly bring disaster would be for this plan to be betrayed!"

Ashe began to protest feebly as the Lord Commander marched him out into the night.

It was night in the Queen's garden. The air was rich with the smell of wet earth and growing things. Faris breathed deeply as she walked. They had tried to make her stay inside, but her arms and legs twitched with an energy that had no outlet. She walked quickly, as the Army had marched on its way south, but the latest pigeon had brought the message that the Westrians were resting now, about to face the enemy. Only she could not rest, tonight.

Faris reached the wall and paused. Where was she going, after all? No haste of hers could bring her more quickly to her own battle. She reached out to touch the velvet surface of a leaf, but her legs wanted to move. She turned, breaking off the leaf and rubbing it. It was mint, and the sharp scent was heady in the darkness.

Jehan's child would be born soon . . . She felt it move within her and tried once more to imagine it as a real being made from her flesh and his, a new person whom she could learn to love. But she had only wanted the baby because Jehan wanted it . . . He had written—

> The child has begun to move. I can lay my hand against Faris' belly and feel a flicker of movement like the birth of a candle flame. I think it will be a greater thing to hold this child in my arms than to bear the crown of Westria . . .

But now she must bear the child and the crown of Westria too. Muscles cramped deep within her, but she did not pause. This was weaker than the warm-up contractions she had been having for weeks. She only stopped when a second, slightly stronger pang made her gasp.

Was it to be now? Was this rainy March night the culmination of that golden afternoon at Midsummer in the Sacred Wood? She shivered and began to move forward again, but more slowly now. Another contraction stopped her, then she went on.

She ought to go in and tell them that it had begun, but she could not. Perhaps it was only a false alarm—was she to upset the entire kingdom for no cause? And if it was not . . . She knew how they would close in on her, fussing, questioning. If she went in, the belief of the others would make this thing that was happening to her real, and there would be no escape.

Somewhere in the darkened city, midnight tolled.

Faris walked determinedly, shutting thought away, while the ache that periodically rolled through her belly became harder and harder to ignore. It came again and she gasped and fell heavily to her hands and knees in the mud of the path.

She let her head sink upon her crossed hands, bowing before the plum trees as she had bowed to them at the Hold the day she met Jehan. Wind sighed in the branches, or was it only the blood roaring in her ears? Wind touched her damp forehead like a caress.

Her body ached in protest at a new contraction and the seal that had held the waters within her womb broke. As they flowed to the earth on which she knelt there came a roaring in her ears like waves upon a distant shore.

"Oh Lady, help me! Help me . . ." Panting, she tried to get up. Faint as a whisper of wind in the trees she heard a chiming of sweet bells. Warm hands helped her to rise, and for a moment she thought it was the Lady. Then she heard Berisa's voice, as gentle, surprisingly, as her hands.

"You are a walker like me, love, and now your labor is well begun—come, sister, it is time to go in . . ."

The Army was moving out of its encampment, through fog that rose from the river like steam. It drifted from hoof prints sunk in the mud where the spring rains had fallen and the waterlogged earth had let it stand. From the foothills of the Ramparts to the first swellings of the coastal mountains, from the sodden earth fifty feet upward into the sky, fog covered the Great Valley, and from its misty depths the campfires of the two armies glowed like angry eyes.

Shivering, Farin pulled his cloak around him, watching the fog writhe about the hurrying forms of men. The air rustled with confused whispers, for only the commanders knew why they were moving at such an hour.

"Farin—find Lord Brian and tell him he can have two hundred of my archers, but I need to know where he wants them to go!" called Sandremun.

Farin nodded and set off to the knoll where Brian stood in the torchlight, compensating with dramatic gestures for the force he dared not put into his voice. Droplets of fog glittered in his bristling beard.

Farin waited while Brian thought, then answered, "Have them join Dorothea of Montera's troop, toward the end of the line." Farin sketched a bow, but the Lord Commander was already turning away.

"To be under guard is an insult, but to be bound and left here is an infamy!"

Farin saw Ercul Ashe spluttering at the man-at-arms who was looping rope about his ankles. As the soldier began on his wrists, another man paused beside the tent, shaking his head sympathetically.

"What's the trouble, Ercul? Didn't the lords like your plan?"

"Oh they liked the plan well enough—but Lord Brian doesn't trust me or the Lord Seneschal!" Ashe began to struggle in new indignation.

"Brian doesn't like the Seneschal? You astonish me!" said the other man. The soldier laughed, made fast a final knot, rose and walked away.

"Ordrey! Untie me—you cannot leave me here!"

"My dear man, if I let you go, Brian would never forgive *me!*" Ordrey also laughed, and still grinning, stepped back and disappeared into the mists.

Farin repressed a smile and remembering his duty hurried off toward Sandremun's tent. It did seem cruel to leave the poor man helpless while a battle was raging, but the chances were that the fighting would not come that way. Ercul Ashe was more likely to be safe than any of them, he thought, but he made a mental note to check up on him after the battle. *If I survive* . . . and suddenly his belly was cold.

With a murmur of creaking leather and jingling mail Brian's forces moved out toward the hill where they would huddle through the rest of the night, regretting their abandoned fires and longing for dawn. Soon they were gone.

Farin checked his saddle girth and his weapons and swung up onto the chestnut horse, swearing under his breath as the excited animal snorted and plunged. He urged him quickly into the line of Robert and Eric's men who were already moving, like an army of ghosts, southward through the mists.

They had been cautioned to keep silence, so when the dank air caught in their throats they stifled their coughs. Jingling mail was muffled by heavy cloaks, and even the bits of the horses had been wound in strips of wool. What sound they did make was swallowed by the fog as their own forms were engulfed by the darkness. Presently even their own campfires disappeared.

Fire leaped fitfully on the broad hearth of the Royal bedchamber. Caolin paused in the doorway, blinking away the darkness of the corridor. The room was full of women, moving purposefully about like soldiers preparing for battle. Caolin smiled a little at the simile—he was preoccupied with warfare tonight—then realized that it was true.

Rosemary saw him, bent over the bed for a moment, then stepped away. Faris was lying there, the sheet drawn over the distorted mound of her belly and up to her chin. As the Seneschal hesitated, she moaned and bit her lip, turning her head against the pillow, and her belly changed shape beneath the cloth. Her face was puffy and her hair lank with sweat.

Shocked, he turned to lady Jessica. "Is she dying?"

Jessica raised an eyebrow, then her lips quirked. "I suppose you never have seen a woman in childbed before. Doesn't a man at hard labor look the same?"

Caolin's eyes moved back to Faris. Her spasm seemed to ease, she sighed and relaxed while Rosemary sponged her brow. Then she opened eyes that were like smudges of shadow in her white face, and looked at Caolin.

He made himself go forward and sit down in the chair beside her bed. He took her hand. "How are you?"

Faris grimaced. "They tell me I am doing well . . . I am glad that you came." Her eyes fastened on his as if she could draw strength from his soul. He fought an impulse to pull away his hand.

The Queen caught her breath and her gaze turned inward. Her hand tightened painfully on Caolin's and he looked quickly away from the heaving of her body to the pure flickering of the fire.

Berisa bent from her seat by the hearth to pick a new ball of wool from her basket, and turned to lady Jessica. "I had trouble with my legs when I was carrying my first child and my third. But the second one was the hardest to deliver. I was in labor for two days . . ." she said proudly, then glanced at the writhing figure on the bed. "Something always seems to go wrong."

Caolin swallowed and shut his eyes, but he could not keep from smelling the sharp odor of sweat, the too-sweet scent of the women's perfumes, the musky female smell that permeated the room.

Faris' hand relaxed and he snatched his own away, rose and stood looking down at her. Jessica had said that all was well, but what if something *should* go wrong? Jehan on his deathbed had been more beautiful than Faris was now.

"You should go—" said Rosemary softly at his elbow. Caolin fancied he saw pity in her eyes, but at that moment did not resent it.

"Will the child come soon?"

Rosemary shrugged. "I am a maid among mothers, and so no expert, though I have midwifed animals often enough. From all accounts a first child takes a long time. It will be tomorrow before the baby comes, I think—we will call you."

"Be grateful—" said lady Jessica, grinning. "If you were the child's father we would make you stay!"

Caolin shuddered and turned away, nearly running into the Master of the Junipers at the door. The Seneschal stepped back and bowed. "This is one task I will gladly leave to you," he murmured as the Master went by him into the room.

The darkness of his own chamber was a refuge from the sights and sounds of the labor room, but not from his own thoughts. He could not forget the Queen's racked body. Women did die in childbed—What would become of him then? Desperately he lit a lamp and rummaged through the papers on his desk—records of stores sent with the Army which had not been tallied yet.

He forced himself to the work, figuring where he would find grain to replace what had been used . . . how many bushels from which holdings . . . how many harvests . . . But he could not keep from glancing at the window, from listening for footsteps in the hall. In the Palace the Queen was laboring to bring forth an heir to Westria. In the mists south of Rissiin, the Army was preparing to meet the challenge of Elaya. By this time tomorrow, the answers to so many questions would be clear—whether Brian would live to torment him, whether the Queen would live to uphold him as Seneschal and whether or not a living child would make her own position secure.

Surely tomorrow would decide who was to have the mastery of Westria. He had only to wait.

VII

The Queen's Battle

The rising sun blazed like a beacon on the high edge
of the eastern mountains. Farin wondered how long it would
take to burn away the fog that suffocated the Valley below. A
sea of mist still lapped the hill where Brian's command waited
for the day. People were beginning to stir, stretching legs grown
stiff with damp, wiping the dew from swords and bows. An
archer combed out her brown hair and braided it again; dawn-
light glistened on the silky strands.

Farin flexed his cold fingers and longed for his harp. But
by the time he got Swangold tuned, he thought wryly, the battle
could be lost or won!

He heard Brian's deep voice and turned. What he had seen
of the Lord Commander of Las Costas at Misthall had left him
with a hearty dislike for the man, but his army obviously adored
him.

Brian paused to speak to an axeman from the Ramparts,
and there was a gust of appreciative laughter from his mates.
At the noise Farin jumped, then remembered that there was no
need for silence any more. Even if the enemy heard them, it
was too late to change position now.

"So, Sir Farin—I see you are still with us." Brian came
toward Farin and glanced approvingly at the chestnut horse,
who was pulling eagerly at dewy hummocks of grass. "Well,
I daresay Robert and Eric slept no softer than we . . ."

"Slept?" said Farin in wonder. Even if his body had been
at ease, visions of the coming battle would have kept him
awake.

Brian shook his head. "I hope you got some rest—you will
need your strength today!" He peered down the hill.

The archers were unwrapping their bowstrings from around

their waists and fitting them to their bows again. One offered Farin some of his bread and cheese, but he shook his head and wondered if his belly were cramping from fear or if Faris had gone into labor and he was picking up some echo of her pangs.

The silver veil of mist drew steadily away, revealing hummocks and standing pools carved by the feet of cattle now eaten by the Elayans or driven away from the path of the war. The new grass glistened in the growing light.

"*They* are sleeping soundly enough, the bastards—" said an axeman near Farin, gesturing toward the enemy camp. "You would think they'd be stirring by now."

They listened. Farin's horse shook his head and began on another clump with a juicy sound of tearing grass. A bird flashed out of the mist, twittering cheerfully, and sailed over their heads into the sunny upper air.

Brian frowned. "What's that down there—the black spots on the grass?"

"Cow pats?" suggested somebody, sniggering.

"They're too big . . ." Brian ignored the laughter as he squinted into the thinning fog. Farin was reminded oddly of a herd bull alerted by a shift in the wind. Silence spread around Brian like ripples in a pool.

"Those are Palomon's watchfires . . ." came the whisper at last.

"Cold . . ."

"Palomon may have slept soft last night, but he did not do it here!" Brian's voice grated on Farin's ears as if someone had scraped a fingernail across his soul.

"My Lord! My Lord!" There was a clamor from the troops on the other side of the hill. Farin dashed in Brian's wake as the Commander plunged toward it through the buzzing ranks of men. Then he halted. Farin swerved to keep from caroming into him and slipped to his knees in the wet grass.

For a moment his eyes were dazzled by a glimmer of light that grew momentarily more brilliant as the mists drew away. Then he realized that the dim shapes on the grass below him were figures, warriors, whose spear points sparkled cruelly in the sun. The Elayans! Rank upon rank of them were formed up on the Westrians' left flank about a quarter of a mile away. The outlines of a great crescent were emerging from the fog— surely Palomon's entire force must be here!

"So . . ." said Brian very softly. "The worm *has* turned!" Sorrow flickered across Brian's face so swiftly Farin could scarcely believe it had been there. Then the Commander seemed to root himself into the earth and turned to Farin.

"I see that Palomon can also play at strategy. Lord Robert was going to march behind them—behind where they used to be—and he should be somewhere beyond the abandoned camp by now. Find him! In a moment they will charge us—we are outnumbered, and not properly formed up to meet them. Robert must bring the rest of the army quickly or there will be none left here to aid!" He gripped Farin's shoulder for a moment.

Farin swallowed, shivering as the murmur around him swelled to a roar. As he made his way back to the chestnut horse he heard Brian's voice lashing through the tumult—

"Everyone, face me! Everyone on the end of a line begin moving to your left—you others, follow—march, you fools!"

With surprising coordination, Brian's force shifted to face its enemy. As Farin mounted, a shiver of movement rippled through the ranks of the Elayans beyond them as they readied themselves. For a moment both forces were still.

Farin wrenched his gaze away and slashed at the horse's neck with the reins. The indignant animal squealed and plunged down the hill, bounding erratically among the hummocks toward the abandoned campfires. Farin did not dare to look back, but he heard the ominous *clack, clack* of spears beating on shields as the *Impis* advanced.

"How long will this go on?" asked Faris shakily. She gasped for breath as she felt another contraction begin, then fought to keep from breathing, to avoid any movement that would conflict with the wrenching that was reshaping her body.

Jessica sponged her brow as the pain eased and smiled. "The gate is only half-open, my dear. For nine months your body has been learning to carry this child—it takes time to reverse the process!"

"What is the hour?"

"Near dawn—" replied her sister-in-law.

"Morning!" corrected Rosemary, pulling open the curtains. Lady Alessia of Las Costas had taken Berisa's place by the fire. The midwife from the Community at Laurelynn was adding water to the pot that had been heating over the fire.

Pale light filtered into the room, silvergilt on Rosemary's head, lighting a stray strand of silver in Jessica's darker hair. In the cradle by the window Jessica's three-month-old son stirred, made faint sucking sounds, then slept again.

Faris shuddered. "I thought it would be over by now . . ."

"If your brother were here he could play us a tune to pass the time," said Jessica.

"I expect that Farin must wish he were here too, by now!" Rosemary came back from the window. "Unless he can find music in the clashing of swords."

Branwen looked up from her needlework. Jessica's face stilled and her glance crossed Lady Alessia's, then she smiled resolutely.

"Here we are concerned with the *giving* of life! Branwen, you have a sweet voice. Why don't you sing for us?"

"What shall I sing?" stammered the girl.

"Why not a lullaby?" suggested Alessia.

Their voices blurred as Faris' body reasserted its dominance. When the contraction eased, Branwen was finishing the first verse—

> *"Here there is peace, though the weather be wild—*
> *Sleep in my arms, oh my darling, my child."*

Jessica rose, lifted her own child from his cradle and sat down in the rocking chair to nurse him. The creaking of the chair kept time to Branwen's song.

> *"If your father were with me, then close to my breast*
> *I would hold him, and singing, watch over his rest.*
> *But now he has left me for war's bitter field,*
> *Where my love is no guard and my arms are no*
> *shield . . ."*

The last note was choked off as Branwen realized what she had sung. Embroidery silks cascaded to her feet as she stood and ran from the room. Jessica's baby whimpered as her arms tightened around him, and Lady Alessia's hand closed on her marriage-ring.

"The song was ill-chosen for this company—" said Lady Alessia at last. "But why did she run away?"

Rosemary had gone rather pale, but she replied steadily, "She loves Farin, and he went to war without saying good-bye."

Faris turned her face against her pillow. *Why should they be spared?* She thought, *My own lord will never return to me . . .*

"May the Lord of Battles hold them all within His hands . . ." said Alessia.

Brian's hand closed on the hilt of his great sword and he drew it in a single shining motion. His gaze focused on the bright array of the Elayan army below. Still watching them he turned a little so that his own men could hear his voice.

"Warriors of Las Costas and the Ramparts!" he cried. "We, who have suffered most from this enemy, were chosen to bait a trap for them. But it seems that they can be clever too. Soon we shall learn if they can fight as well. If we can hold them until Lord Robert comes they will be surprised indeed. Stand fast, therefore, for the honor of Westria!"

He was shouting at the end, his voice ringing across the rhythmic thunder from below as the Elayan infantry banged their spears against their shields.

"Archers, release your arrows when I drop my hand!" His great sword flickered in the morning sunlight like a living flame.

The *Impis* were moving now, the men almost hidden behind oval cowhide shields. Their leather corselets gleamed with oil and the bright plumes of their helmets tossed above the rims of the shields. There were cavalry on either side of the main body of foot soldiers, their brimmed helmets glinting in the growing light. There would be mounted archers among them as well as the lancers with their great round shields. Brian motioned to the man at his side.

"Douglas, find Sir Edgar Whitebeard and tell him to turn four companies of archers—whoever is in back—to guard our rear!"

The enemy were beginning to climb the hill now, their deep chanting seeming to vibrate from the earth. He glimpsed a glitter in the midst of them. "Palomon . . ." muttered Brian, "Palomon and his household in their silvered mail . . ."

From the corner of his eye he was aware of Palomon's horse archers drawing ahead of the rest, swinging wide to circle the Westrian rear as the infantry advanced. He had one moment in which to hope that Sir Edgar's archers were ready for them, then he saw that the infantry was within range and swung down his sword.

The archers, positioned behind the Westrian spearmen on the highest point of the hill, drew and released. Arrows buzzed

toward the foe like a flight of angry bees. In the moment the
cowhide shields bristled with their stings. Some of the plumed
helmets disappeared, but there was no faltering in either chanting or advance.

Arrows swarmed again and again while the enemy came
on. Brian could make out individual features clearly now. The
blood raced in his veins, his feet seemed to sense the pulse of
the earth below him. Now he remembered—only this imme-
diacy of destruction could make one feel so alive! Grinning
savagely, he swung round the shield from his back and slipped
his left arm through the straps.

They were very close now.

"First rank, ready—" Brian cried, "and—*charge!*"

He leaped forward, his sword swinging up as if lifted by
the shout that burst from his chest. He was carried forward on
a wave of sound as his men echoed him, their feet beating a
thunderous undertone as they used the slope of the hill to gain
momentum.

The enemy swirled around them. Black eyes glared into his,
but already Brian's sword was lashing forward. He barely felt
the shock as the Elayan's shield rim crumpled; the honed edge
sliced through leather armor and flesh to be stopped finally by
hard bone. White circled the dark eyes as they widened. A
scream tore at Brian's ears as he ripped his blade free and ran
on.

Faris cried out as the giant's fist squeezed her again.

"Relax your muscles! Take a deep breath! Ride with it, my
Lady—don't fight! Now pant—the contraction is coming, now
breathe deeply, and again . . ."

Faris tried to relax, for a moment moved with the contraction
as if she were poised on an enormous wave, then lost the
precarious balance and plunged into a sea of pain.

"No!" She threw out her arms as if she were indeed drowning. Hands pressed her back with gentle force and her body
tensed, muscles of back and abdomen tightening in a vain
attempt to block the mighty constrictions of the womb that was
working to bring its burden into the world.

The contractions strengthened, peaked, and a scream rasped
Faris' throat, faded to a moan, rose again and again. She gripped
Rosemary's and Branwen's hands and never felt them wince.

"Faris—the first part of your labor is almost over, but you

must get back in control. What do you think those exercises were for, girl? You know what to do! Relax, count, breathe!" Berisa's face swam before her.

"Jehan . . . I cannot do it." Faris murmured as the agony receded a little. "I cannot rule the pain . . . Jehan! I eased your dying, can't you help me now?" She whimpered, feeling her womb begin to tighten once more. Something cold touched her lips, but she had not strength even to sip the lemon-water Rosemary was offering her.

She jerked as the midwife applied hot cloths to the birth opening, hoping to relax the muscles. They had removed her nightgown to ease her and when Faris realized that she did not even care if the other women saw the scar on her arm, she knew how completely this agony now governed her. Then pain slashed through her again and she forgot even to be afraid.

"She is bleeding again . . ." the midwife's voice sounded very far away. Faris closed her eyes.

"Master! Can't you give her something to ease the pain?" cried Rosemary. "She has not the strength to endure so long!"

"It is too soon—" his voice was strained, "it would harm the child . . ."

"But there must be something you can do!"

"If she will let me . . ." Faris felt the cool touch of the Master of the Junipers' hands, and for a moment a memory of stillness eased her torment. *Awahna* . . . Her spirit groped for the Valley's silence, the cooling mist that veiled its waterfalls. Mist engulfed her. She heard the Master calling her name, but she was already beyond him, as if his touch had given her the excuse she needed to break free. The sound of frantic voices faded, and then, awareness of pain.

Farin reined in the chestnut horse, batting futilely at the mist that swirled around him. He peered over the horse's sweating shoulder at the trampled ground. Clearly a large force had been this way, but whose? The hoofprints of Westrian and Elayan horses looked the same. He tried to remember the details of Elnora's map. The chestnut shook his head and took a few steps forward, tugging at the reins as he reached for grass.

"You hog—" muttered Farin. "If I am killed will you push my body aside to get at the grass I'm lying on?"

A glint of silver in the mud caught his eye and he swung down from the saddle to see. It was a medallion of the Mother, bare-breasted with Her child upon Her knee. On the reverse was the circled cross of Westria.

Something cold and sharp pricked the back of his neck. Farin stilled, drew breath again as the pressure eased, then turned. For one moment he thought he saw an Elayan's plumes beyond the short shaft of the lance. Then he realized they were quail feathers and recognized Sir Randal of Registhorpe.

"Randal—where's Eric?" his voice cracked and he steadied it. He scrambled to his feet and hauled himself into the saddle, still talking. "The Elayans marched around us and everything fell apart—"

"This way!" Sir Randal was already jerking his mount's head around. Farin felt for his swordhilt and realized he still held the medallion in his hand. He thrust it into the breast of his tunic, thinking suddenly of Faris. "Mother of All! Protect us both today!"

Free at last, Faris floated forward through the dim swirls of mist that became the spray of waterfalls flowing over towering cliffs of grey stone. For a time it was enough to be there. Then Faris remembered why she had come and called out Jehan's name.

"My beloved . . . I am here."

This was not like her other dreams of him. Just as this Valley was vaster than the Awahna she had seen before, its very stones pulsing with light, so Jehan seemed taller and more beautiful than he had been.

"Has it been so many years?" he said wonderingly. "I waited here, though they wished me to go on. Are you dead too?"

"I . . . do not know," she answered slowly. "I had been laboring so long."

Jehan's features twitched, but the memory of her own pain was too vivid for Faris to pity him. "My darling, I never wanted you to have to bear that alone!" he paused. "And what of the child?"

"Let them tear it from my womb!"

"Can they?" he said doubtfully, not seeming to hear her bitterness. "Would they be in time?"

She stared at him, anger replacing her awe. "You would send me back to that torture? Not alone, my Lord! Not alone!" Her hand closed on his.

She felt herself moving then as if the mist had become a

current. But still she clung to Jehan's hand, making it the focus
of her consciousness even when she heard the Master of the
Junipers calling her name.

"For the Lily of the North!" cried Eric. Even through the
heavy saddle he could feel Thunderfoot's muscles surge as the
stallion leaped forward, glorying in freedom after the long hours
of waiting in the cold. At his heels thundered all the heavy
cavalry Westria possessed.

Words echoed in Eric's memory as hooves beat out the
rhythm of the charge—Farin's gasped message. He remembered the stricken look on Lord Robert's face and the orders
that Eric was turning to obey before they were past Robert's
lips. It hardly registered that this was Brian he was riding so
furiously to save. He only knew that he was free to fight at
last.

Thunderfoot charged over the last rise and Eric saw the hill
on which Brian had made his stand. The sun, almost overhead
by now, glinted wetly on blood-slick swords. The pitiful remnant of Brian's command were still struggling in the midst of
a sea of waving plumes around which horse archers circled like
wolves.

"Westria! Westria and Jehan!" The battle cry swelled from
five hundred throats. The enemy horsemen saw them now and
came swiftly toward them, their arrows glancing off the heavy
armor of the Westrian knights.

The two forces shocked together. One of the lighter southern
horses squealed and went down as the black horse crashed into
it. Another was before him now, throwing up his shield in a
hopeless attempt to ward off Eric's spear. As they sped past
the spear struck, stuck, and was jerked from Eric's fingers. A
horseman came in from the side. Thunderfoot swerved and his
iron-shod heels lashed out, the rest of the Elayans whirled
helplessly aside and they were through.

Eric felt Thunderfoot's stride lengthen as they shot toward
the beleaguered Westrians. Beyond them Palomon watched
with his reserves. Eric wrenched his sword from its sheath and
reined to the right, burning with desire to reach that silver
figure and run it down. The air hummed around him and something flickered by his head. Startled, Eric took his eyes from
Palomon and saw beside him a group of men on foot—sturdy
bearded men with leather jerkins, steel caps, and faces burnt

red by the sun. They carried crossbows.

The air sang again and the black horse shuddered. Eric cursed as Thunderfoot faltered. There were cries behind him as bolts pierced plate and mail. The horse rocked at the impact as another arrow struck him in the flank, just missing Eric's thigh. Thunderfoot threw up his head with a scream and Eric saw a fourth bolt transfix his neck.

Eric kicked his feet from the stirrups and cast himself from the saddle as the stallion fell.

For a moment there was no one near him. With stinging eyes Eric knelt by Thunderfoot's head. He remembered kneeling in the straw beside the newborn black foal and giving him his name.

"Brother, forgive me for bringing you here," he said swiftly. "May I fight as well as you have done . . ." He laid his sword on the grass, ran his hand one last time along the sweated neck, and drew his dagger for the mercy stroke.

A shadow dulled the blade. Eric's hand shot out to close on an arm and jerk the attacker down across the body of the fallen horse. In another moment his knife had sliced through the man's throat.

"Here's an escort for you, old friend!" he said harshly, but the stallion's eyes were already dull.

Eric picked up his blade and got heavily to his feet, swearing with grief for the horse and for himself, because he knew he would not get his chance at Palomon now. But above the clang of swords and the screams of dying men he could hear Brian's battle cry, and up the hill, he saw the blurred swing of a great sword.

Eric settled his shield more securely on his arm, and shouting, he began to run toward the fight.

"For the Lily of the North, Jehan, and Westria!"

"Jehan!" Still calling his name, Faris felt herself sucked downward. Colors whirled madly around her, but he was still there. She felt his presence even when she opened her eyes and found that she was clutching the Master of the Junipers' hand.

"Thanks be to the Lady!" murmured the Master. His brow was beaded with perspiration, but his face was very pale.

"I brought Jehan . . ." said Faris clearly, ignoring the shock on the faces of the women who hovered at the foot of the bed.

"I know . . ."

Faris felt her body begin to tense and tried to withdraw into the mist again.

"No—The waiting is over and you must work *with* your body now!" cried the Master. "Are you willing to link with me and let me help block the pain?"

Faris nodded, biting her lip as the contraction lifted her. *Jehan!* Her spirit still held his.

"*My Lord!*" the Master echoed her.

"*I am here . . .*"

Faris moaned, feeling the pain begin, but another presence slipped between it and her awareness of it. Was it Jehan, or the Master, or both of them? It did not matter now.

"The contractions are changing!" exclaimed the midwife, laying her hands on Faris' belly. "The door is opening at last. Breathe in now, my Lady, and hold . . ."

Let the ocean bear you to shore . . . the Master filled her mind with the image of a vast surging sea on which she rose and fell. Faris reached out for Jehan, and thought she felt his lips touch hers.

She was vaguely aware that someone was thrusting cushions behind her back until she was half sitting, and placing clean cloths beneath her on the bed. Jehan guided her while the Master helped her bear her pain and the waves grew higher and faster, seeking the shore.

Suddenly she understood their urgency. She was not riding the waves, she *was* the wave. Her moan became a grunt and she bore down.

For a moment she was free. She opened her eyes and looked around her, seeing with unusual clarity the strained faces of the women around her, sunlight pouring through the windows, the Master of the Junipers' bowed head.

"Well, it's about time!" exclaimed Berisa.

"*Now we can begin to fight!*" said the presence within her.

Faris hesitated, her whole being poised as the contraction began.

"*Now!*" The command rang from without and within. Faris cried out as fiercely as any man upon the battlefield and bore down. Light flared and shattered from the windows, on the sea, in Faris' eyes.

The air seemed to glitter as swords rose and fell. Eric squinted against the noon glare and hewed downward with his sword.

A spear thrust at him, he lifted his shield to knock it aside, staggered and set his feet again as Brian was thrown against him. Eric could feel the other man's muscles bunch against his back as Brian recovered and swung. Eric slashed at a contorted face, missed and realized that the man was retreating. They were all retreating.

Dazed, he stared around him. A breastwork of heaped bodies bore mute testimony to a stand that had lasted, how long? One hour? Ten? He glanced up and saw the sun directly overhead, and against the sky's pure blue tiny specks that circled waiting for their time to come.

Eric's arm ached from striking and he lowered the tip of his sword to the ground. He was covered with blood, and though he knew that some of it must be his own, he felt only a vast weariness. He heard a long sigh from behind him.

"Hmmn—would you agree this is a better place to compare our skill than the dueling field?" Brian asked with a tired grin.

Eric blinked, forcing his muddled brain to remember his challenge to Brian the summer before. After a moment he shook his head and smiled hesitantly. "I think you are the winner, my Lord."

"The pile is as high on your side as on mine."

"Yes, but I feel nearly done, and you were fighting for hours before I came." He looked at Brian's profile, the hazel eyes sunken, the brown beard matted with blood, and felt a sudden jolt as if he had seen his own reflection.

"I'm glad you came. *Bare is brotherless back.*" Brian repeated the old slogan of fighting men.

"Brian . . . I'm sorry we quarreled. I . . ." Eric stammered and fell silent.

Brian grinned. "You will make a man, cockerel—if you get the chance. Jehan predicted this, but I do not think we will enjoy our friendship long."

They looked around them. Beyond the piled bodies there was an area that was almost clear, and beyond that the men who had drawn off from the attack with Palomon and his reserves behind them. Eric nodded, trying to accept the fact that he would be dead soon, but the idea did not seem real. He could imagine himself fighting on and on, but his mind shied away from the darkness at its end.

"If by some chance I should fall and you survive," Brian said quietly, "take the ring, the King gave me, and give it to my son to wear until Westria has another lord." Eric realized that it had been hours since he had even thought of the Queen. Her child could be born by now . . .

"Yes . . ." he said hoarsely. "And you take mine."

They were silent for a little, gazing at the waiting enemy. They could not see southward beyond them to tell if Robert and the army were on the way.

Suddenly Brian laughed. "Well—at least we can make our last fight a thing for the poets to sing about. That lad—the Queen's brother—perhaps he will do it." He began to murmur an old battle chant.

> *"The foe gathers round us, red run their spears*
> *With blood of our brothers slain in this battle.*
> *Strike, men of Westria! Swords cease not swinging*
> *While valiant warriors' will does not falter . . ."*

They could see Palomon clearly now, his silver mail unstained, his black eyes gleaming. Brian fell silent, staring at him.

Eric nodded. "I tried to reach him too . . ."

"I don't suppose he will accept a challenge, but I must try . . ." Brian stepped forward, lifting his sword.

"Palomon of Elaya, I call you to combat," he shouted. "This quarrel is chiefly between you and me—why should these others suffer too?"

Palomon continued to look at them, no change in his face to show if he had heard. Then he raised his hand and called out a command. There was a movement in the waiting ranks and a file of men appeared and took up position facing the two Westrians. Eric growled deep in his throat.

"The crossbows . . . the crossbows! Faris saw it, poor lady—my doom!" Brian said softly. He turned to Eric. "I have no proof, but if you live, remember this—Caolin did this somehow! He swore he would kill me. I never thought he could succeed . . ." he shook his head like a wounded bear. "The cowards! I owed Jehan my life, but not like this—" He gripped Eric's arm.

"They shall not do it! Brother, come with me and let us charge *them!*"

Eric nodded and the sick feeling in his stomach was replaced by a fierce joy that ran along his veins like wine. The two men clasped hands briefly and then, as the crossbowmen raised their weapons, turned to face their foes.

Brian shook his head and started forward, and he chanted as he ran—

> "Strike now, my comrade, closer than kindred—
> Foemen who fell us will weep ere night falls!"

Close behind him, Eric cried, "For the Lily of the North," once more, and the arrows came.

Brian stumbled as a bolt struck him, but went on. Eric heard a bee snick past his ear and pounded after him, remembering the courage of his black horse. Then he felt the shock himself as an arrow nicked the top of his shield and grazed his shoulder. The missiles were coming fast now, but still Brian staggered forward and Eric followed him.

Some of the arrows bit into Eric's shield. He was hit in the arm once more, and the legs. He did not count the arrows now, but only thought of that line of men he must reach somehow.

His legs did not want to carry him. He swayed and slipped to his knees. Ahead of him he saw Brian stopped at last, saw the sword drop from his hand. More arrows pierced him, then he spread his arms as if to crush his foe and toppled face forward into the mud.

Eric crawled toward the fallen man. He shook his head, trying to get rid of the black patches that crawled before his eyes. It was only a few feet, but his head was swimming when he got there.

He crouched over the body and carefully touched the face. There was no response, no change in the other man's grim smile. Ignoring the roaring in his ears, Eric tugged the ring from Brian's finger and thrust it onto one of his own.

He tried to get up, but the darkness rose about him like a sea. His limbs gave way and he sank down on Brian's body instead. The black wave burst over him, but just before it drowned all awareness he heard, as from a great distance, the sweet music of Robert's horns.

"You are the sea . . ." Faris heard the Master as the bright wave lifted and receded again. They had tied a rope to the bedposts for her to pull on, and Jessica and Rosemary were bracing her feet. She felt the child being forced through her body—outward and then back again as the surge faded away.

"You are the earth, and the child a sapling striving for the sun . . ." said Jehan. Faris braced herself with the strength of earth, visualizing a shaft of light that streamed upward from her body until it took the shape of a broad-shouldered man with Jehan's features and her own dark eyes.

"I see the baby's head! It has dark hair!" cried Rosemary.

"Just a few more heaves now—" Berisa bent to check her progress. The midwife was already crouched by Faris' knee with hands outstretched. The contraction eased and Faris let out all the air she had left in a shuddering sigh.

"Take a deep breath now, my Lady—" said the midwife calmly.

"You are the wind!" cried the Master.

Faris filled her lungs, felt air rush through her, tingling in every vein. She braced herself, hauled on the rope and pushed, and her breath exploded in a shout that rattled the window panes.

"Now, my darling, now! We are fire!" Pain and ecstacy were one.

Faris' body convulsed and her spirit flared. And in that brilliance she saw a woman whose body glowed, whose hair rippled like flame. She felt Jehan and the Master cower before that Presence, but she opened her arms to embrace the fire. Then the Light grew, until Faris saw only a pair of eyes that were neither male nor female, but something more than either, incandescent with love.

She felt a tug and something slippery against her thighs. The flame that enfolded her eased to a steady glow and her body stilled at last. A warm weight was laid upon her belly. The midwife moved quickly around her.

Then she heard a smack and a thin outraged cry. Faris' eyes focused and she saw the midwife lift high an infant whose face was contorted in protest and whose genitals, seeming from that angle unnaturally large, were unmistakably male.

"A boy! An heir for Westria!" cried Jessica. "Faris, see!"

"Jehan, we have done it . . ." murmured Faris. "There is your son . . ."

"Yes . . . he is beautiful."

From Jehan's thought came a hint of sadness and Faris wanted to ask him why, but every nerve was relaxing in the golden glow. *Our son . . .* she thought drowsily. The women around her were laughing and crying out, a hubbub that spread to those waiting in the corridors and ran along the streets of Laurelynn like flame.

"The child is born! The waiting is over! At last! At last!"

"At last!" shouted Sir Randal. "Look at them—they are running at last!"

Farin squinted at the dark figures moving across the glare of the plain. Someone tossed a sword glittering into the air and caught it with a shout.

"Victory!" the cry was repeated up and down the ranks of bloodstained men who paused, panting, realizing that they held the field.

"You men from Las Costas and the plains—anyone whose horse is fit to run—get after them. I want Palomon!" Lord Robert gestured toward the fleeing foe.

Farin dug his heels into his horse's sides. The chestnut shook his head and took a step forward, stumbled and stopped, whickering unhappily.

"You'll never catch Palomon on that one, Farin—he's gone lame in the off foreleg," said Randal.

Farin swung down from the saddle and inspected the strained leg, then patted the horse's bronze neck. "I'm sorry, old hog . . ." he looked up at Sir Randal. "I didn't notice it before, and I don't think he did either."

A raven sailed overhead, cawing disconsolately, and settled on a dead horse. It looked at them watchfully with its yellow eyes as if wondering whether they would dispute its meal.

It is over . . . Farin rested his head against the shoulder of his horse, who was nosing distastefully at the bloody grass.

"Well, there's plenty of work for us here . . ." Sir Randal looked at the wreckage of the field. "They can't all be dead."

"Where's Eric?" asked Farin suddenly. He and Randal had been sent on to guide Lord Robert's men since neither was armoured heavily enough to join Eric's charge. "Could he have gone with the riders after Palomon?"

But Randal's gaze had fixed on the raven, which was beginning to tear at the black flank of its intended meal. Randal urged his tired horse toward it and Farin ran after him, flapping his arms to drive the bird away.

"Sweet Lady! It's Thunderfoot!"

With an identical motion they turned to look at the little hill upon which Brian had made his stand, then started toward it through bodies strewn haphazardly as if some insane reaper had been harvesting corn. For every Westrian whose face Farin bent to see there were two from Elaya, their bright trappings trampled into the mud. Crows flapped away resentfully as he passed, then hopped back to resume their meal. He saw a condor as well, and heard coyotes howling in the hills, waiting for the protection of night to claim their share of the feast.

He shook his head. How could there be so many dead here and yet have been so many left when Robert and the rest of the army had arrived? His arm ached from striking, but except for a few gashes he had come through without wounds. Had the bards who wrote so cheerfully of battles ever seen one?

Swallowing, Farin plodded determinedly on. In the west the sky was beginning to glow with rosy streamers, and the coastal hills were shadowed. Soon it would be dark, and how could he recognize anyone then? Across the field he saw men with wagons, gathering the dead for the pyre.

Farin paused as he came to a ring of piled bodies, Elayan infantry, and wondered what brave man had raised such a monument. Shuddering, he climbed over them to see who lay in the center and stopped, puzzled, because there was no one there, only the marks of two pairs of feet sunk deeply into the mire.

He stood still a moment, wondering. To the east he could see the place where Prince Palomon and his reserves had awaited Robert's charge. His gaze moved downward and across the curiously empty space between Palomon's knoll and where he was standing now. A flicker of movement caught his eye. Farin's breath stopped, he stared, then clambered over the corpses and began to run.

What he had seen was two bodies, lying quite alone. They both looked dead—with so many arrows in them they must be, and the movement he had seen only a garment fluttering in the wind. Then the one on top moved again.

Farin threw himself down beside it and with trembling hands heaved it over to see the face. Even in the rosy evening light it was pale, but not cold—not yet.

"Eric . . ." he breathed. "Eric!"

". . . the bastards! Go on!" Eric muttered without opening his eyes.

"The Lord of Battles be praised! Randal!" Farin lifted his head to shout. "He's over here!" He bent to the wounded man. "Eric—it's me, Farin! It's all over, Eric—we've won!" Eric's arm fell limply as Farin moved him so that it rested almost protectively across the body on which he had lain.

"No . . . no!" he murmured, "Don't touch him."

Farin lifted the head of the dead man and saw Brian's face. After a moment he laid it down, confusion and wonder struggling in his heart.

"Is he dead?" panted Randal, stopping next to them.

"No! Not yet . . ." Farin added, "but Brian is. Get the wagon over here—get a healer—get someone!"

Somewhere across the field men were cheering Robert, cheering their victory. Farin shook his head and stroked back the matted hair from Eric's brow, wondering whether they would still cheer when they learned its cost.

Even in the palace they could hear the cheering that swept the city, mixed with smatterings of song. The Prince was born and there were rumors of victory in the south.

"Well, they have waited for their festival," said Rosemary, turning away from the sunset glory of the window. "If I were not so tired I would be out there too!"

"Tired!" exclaimed Branwen, "But Lady Faris did all the work!"

Faris, lying warm and euphoric with her child nestled in the crook of her arm, closed her eyes again. They had washed her and dressed her in a clean gown. After the Master of the Junipers had blessed the baby they had swaddled him and laid him beside her. Now she wanted only to sleep. There was a rustle in the doorway and the Master of the Junipers came in, robed in a cope of green damask.

"Don't disturb her—" cautioned Jessica as the Master bent to take the baby in his arms. Faris stirred and half-opened her eyes.

"I will return him safely my dear, sleep now . . ." He smiled with almost his old serenity. The baby nuzzled hopefully against his breast and he laughed. "No, my cub, there is nothing here for you. Let me show you to your people and then you may go to your mother again." He turned to Jessica. "Has someone told Caolin? He will want to light the beacon fire."

Faris heard the door shut behind them. Sunset blazed beneath her closed eyelids like a memory of the Lady's fire. "Jehan, do you hear them rejoicing for our child?" she murmured drowsily, but she was asleep before she could wonder why he did not reply.

*   *   *

The last light of sunset was fading above the western hills when Farin came out of Lord Robert's tent where the physicians were still fighting for Eric's life. Across the way lights shone in Brian's blue and gold pavilion, whose lord now lay in state with torches at his head and feet. But Brian's horsemen were still away after Palomon, and of the archers who had stood beside their lord, pitifully few survived to mourn him. There would be weeping up and down the Great Valley when this was known.

At least Farin had been able to rescue Ercul Ashe. The man had been gibbering after that long day without food or drink, or news, and was pitifully grateful to his liberator. But Farin had hastened him out of the camp, afraid that Brian's men would blame the man who had brought them this disastrous strategy.

He gazed northward, wondering vaguely whether the rest of Westria had heard the news. On the brow of the hill beneath the pale glitter of the early stars he saw a point of orange light. Another star? But surely it had not been there before.

As he watched, light flared and he saw a second orange glow. It was larger—nearer, perhaps? A third blazed from the hill before him, and Farin realized stupidly that he was looking at bonfires—beacons signalling each other from hill to hill all the way from Laurelynn.

"Faris—" he muttered in confusion. "She's had the baby and I didn't even know!"

All around him men were pointing at the mountain tops, swearing delightedly and pounding each other's backs. "The child is born!"

Farin looked beyond them to the growing mound which would shortly become a pyre to rival the fires on the hills, and wondered whether the lives of so many men and women were a fair exchange for the one that had come into the world. It was the kind of question he would have asked the Master of the Junipers if he had been there. Or, he thought unhappily, the King.

He stood alone, staring at the cheerful twinkling of the beaconfires. "Fire burn bright and light us all to home again . . ." he murmured at last.

VIII

The Chessmaster

The shadows of the scattered chesspieces wavered across the board in the candlelight. Caolin wondered why he had thought that working through the deliberate strategies of a chess game would calm him. The wolf Gerol lifted his great head as his master turned restlessly to the window, then laid it on his forepaws again.

Outside the night sky glowed with light from the beacon fire. Caolin had come to the top of the Red Mountain to light it as soon as he knew that Faris' child was born. He fancied he could hear the rejoicing all the way from Laurelynn, but it was only the crackling of the great fire. Here there was only stillness. But there was no peace.

He turned back to the little bare room in which the chess set was the only thing of beauty. Why had he stayed here instead of returning to the revels in the city? He had not used his temple since Jehan died—since that terrifying ritual to the Lady of Fire. Had he come to the Mountain because he knew he needed the power that waited here? Perhaps, but he was not yet ready to re-enter that room.

Idly, the Seneschal picked up one of the white chess pieces— a rook, and turned it between his long fingers. Light warmed the polished ivory of the little tower as he set it down in its proper place at one end of the board.

"One rook—Lord Robert of the Ramparts, that worthy man . . ." he murmured. "He moves in a straight line to his goal, once he knows what it is. He is the hero of the day— will he know what to do with his popularity?"

Gerol's eyes followed Caolin's movements, but he could

tell when the man was speaking to him and when he was only making noises and he remained where he was.

Caolin searched out the other rook and set it on the opposite end of the board. "Two—Theodor, the bastion of the north. Here he is set and here he stays, mourning because he has outlived his powers."

Caolin's hand hovered above an intricately carved knight. "And here is our champion, Eric." He lifted the piece in the knight's move, three squares ahead and one to the side, "who never knows where he is headed until he gets there." His eyes sought the other knight, which had fallen on its side, and he thought of the message which Ordrey's pigeon had brought him that afternoon.

"And the other knight?" he picked up the piece. "Sir Brian . . . is off the board!" There was a faint snap as his fingers tightened on the chess piece and the helmed head rolled across the floor. Caolin smiled, just a little, and set the torso aside.

"Now we must have our bishops—the Mistress of the College . . ." he set one hooded figure next to the knight, "and the Master of the Junipers . . . who finds no comfort in his own counsel anymore." He set down the second bishop, remembering the lost look he had seen lately in the Master's eyes. He understood the other man's pain but could not pity it.

Nonetheless his face grew very still as he looked down at the two places left empty in the center of the line.

"The king . . . no King—" he shook his head, gently placing the white king on the table beside the board. "But we do have a queen—" he added swiftly, his fingers moving caressingly on the intricate detail of the gown.

Now there were only pawns scattered upon the board. Frowning, Caolin picked one of them. "And the child—" he said then, remembering the red-faced thing he had seen squirming in the Master of the Junipers' arms. "Will the child be a pawn, or a king?" Shrugging, he put the piece on the king's empty square and swiftly began to set the other pawns in place before the line of principals.

Then he repeated the process with the black figures, pausing only when he came to the ebony king. "Palomon . . . " he muttered, setting the figure down. Caolin smoothed back a strand of pale hair and considered the chessboard.

"And what about me? Well, Gerol—what is my place on this board?" Caolin leaned back in his chair as the wolf got up and padded across the stone floor to nose at his hand. Smiling, Caolin began to stroke the rough-furred head, his knowing fingers moving over the smooth dome of the skull, scratching behind the flattened ears, sinking into the thick fur that hid Gerol's throat.

The wolf made a deep sound of pleasure, then, as the caresses grew more abstracted, sighed gustily and lay down again with his head across Caolin's foot. The Seneschal was staring at the board. In the wavering light the black and white ranks seemed waiting for the signal to charge.

"They are waiting for someone to move them, Gerol, though they may never recognize the touch of his hand," said Caolin at last. He remembered another chessboard, at Misthall. Then as now, Faris had been the Queen, but Caolin had identified himself as a bishop, her chief counselor. And he had tried— surely he had tried to play the role of one piece among many on the board.

He picked up the white queen, fancying he saw a resemblance to Faris in the tilt of her carven head. "The queen is the most powerful piece on the board, but even she is vulnerable . . ." his glance went to the headless knight.

With Brian gone Caolin had no great enemy—strange, how now he almost missed that blustering bully of a man! At least Brian's hostility had been open. Now there remained only a host of pawns who could be turned against him. And he had no ally but this vulnerable Queen! If Faris had died in childbirth what would have become of him? Lady Jessica was next heir, and she would surely have leaned on her stupid husband rather than on her brother's Seneschal. Even now, Faris could choose some other counselor.

"No!" Something in Caolin's voice brought Gerol's head up, ears twitching for sound of an enemy.

"*I* must be the chessmaster!" Caolin picked up the black king and weighed the two pieces in his hands. "Faris and Palomon must both move at my will . . ."

Westria's victory in the battle of the Dragon Waste would force Palomon to negotiate. And once he had met the man Caolin would know how to manipulate him. But before Caolin could make the peace he must make absolute his power over the Queen. He set the black piece back on the chessboard, but kept the white queen, turning it over and over between his strong fingers, considering how it might be done . . .

How can I be father and mother to this child and rule Westria too? Sighing, Faris looked down at the baby's dark-fuzzed head. Oblivious to her doubts the child butted his head against her breast and seized her nipple again. This was all he wanted from her now—from being the broodmare of Westria she had become its most exalted cow. And the worst of it was, they all expected her to *like* it.

Her arm began to cramp. She shifted position against the cushions with which they had padded the big wooden chair so that she could lie on the terrace in the early April sun. The lawn that ran down from the terrace behind the Palace to the lake was starred with dandelions across which the Master of the Junipers was walking with Rosemary.

Over the roofs of the city Faris saw the slopes of the Red Mountain flaring with the varied golds of mustard and poppy fields. Everywhere she looked new life was bursting from the earth even as it had sprung from her. Why then could she not rejoice? *I would rejoice if Jehan were here* . . . She stopped herself from forming a mental call to him. He would not answer now. He had waited only to see his son safely into the world and then he had left her once more.

"Praise the Lady for this fine weather!" said Jessica from her chair. "Soon we can put the babies on a blanket and let them tumble like puppies in the sun . . . Now that my lord has defeated Elaya we will soon be going home. Faris, why don't you visit us in Rivered? You spent so little time there, and in the spring one can see at a glance the snowfields and the flowers . . ."

"Your lord had help with the Elayans," said Rosemary with some bitterness. Her eyes sought the room in the Palace where Eric lay. After a week of her careful nursing he was out of danger, but it would be long before he could ride again.

Faris shook her head. Weakness from her own battle weighted her limbs and she winced where her torn body was still healing from having given birth.

Jessica interpreted her gesture and smiled. "Of course you're still weak—you had a hard time—but you'll mend."

Faris closed her eyes. "What is there to recover for?" She felt the easy tears run down her cheeks. She waited for a scornful answer but felt instead Jessica's swift kiss on her brow.

"I know, you're depressed—well, that's natural just now." The chair creaked as Jessica sat back down. The other woman continued, "It will pass."

Rosemary laughed. "My mother told me there was one day when she was so discouraged she nearly dropped me out the window!"

Faris let their chatter wash over her without bothering to reply. Jessica's husband had returned to her, and Eric, however oblivious to Rosemary's love, was still *there*. But Faris had lost her own love when he died and again when his presence was withdrawn from her, and now she was condemned to live at the mercy of this mewling creature who champed in frustration on her breast.

"I think he's still hungry—try shifting him to the other side," said Jessica.

Wearily Faris complied, rearranging her gown to expose the smooth curve of her right breast, bursting with milk like the bosom of the Mother in a statue. Faris bit her lip as the baby's mouth clamped her nipple and braced herself against the pang in her breast as the milk began to flow.

"Master—can't you persuade her to treasure this time? He will grow up so soon!" said Jessica.

He laughed. "I am only an honorary member of your company, and though few men have shared the privilege of giving birth, among womenfolk I am no expert!"

Faris looked at him in wonder, gingerly recalling the confusion and agony which were all she remembered of her lying-in. Did he consider *that* a privilege? The baby had fallen asleep, his head tipped back in satiation, pink mouth pursed and lashes lying like smudges across his cheeks.

"Let me take him," said the Master. "Having helped you bear him should give me some instinct for the task!" He eased his strong hands around the child's head and bottom and laid him against his shoulder, patting industriously.

"He is probably wet . . ." warned Faris, lacing up the front of her gown.

The Master explored the wrappings. "A bit damp perhaps— let's wait until he has digested a little before disturbing him." He began to walk up and down.

"Have you decided on a milk-name yet?" asked Jessica. "His Naming ceremony is only a month away. *Star* is traditional in the family . . ." her sister-in-law went on, "after Julian Starbairn. Goodness knows who Julian's father really was, but it's a pretty title, and this child is certainly our morning star!"

Rosemary laughed. Faris leaned back against her cushions, watching a stray gull sweep down to the lake to rest before returning to the sea.

"Good morning, my Queen . . ."

Startled, Faris looked up and saw Caolin, his crimson robes glowing like a pillar of fire, his hair a golden cap in the morning sun. Seeing his elegance, she was suddenly glad she had done up her gown and wondered how badly the wind had tangled her hair.

"Here is your daily tribute, my Lady." He bowed and held out to her a bouquet of miniature irises, ivory mixed with an almost slate blue, as delicate and precise as his gesture presenting them. The day before it had been multi-colored poppies, and before that, violets.

"They are beautiful," she said smiling.

"No more so than the hand which receives them."

Her eyes went to his face. Did he really think so? Perhaps now that she was regaining her figure men might find her fair . . . The women had kept him from her when she was in labor, so he had no memory of her in her agony . . . he had not seen her scar . . . On his face she saw only the look a man wears when considering a finely crafted jewel.

Faris laughed suddenly, looking down at the irises. How beautiful their colors were, and how bright the air! She was vaguely aware of Jessica rising and moving away, but when she thought of saying farewell the other woman had gone.

"Have you nothing better to do than turn compliments, my Lord Seneschal?"

"I have been preparing to talk to Elaya, my Lady." He handed her a paper at which she glanced as he went on. "This letter invites Palomon to come here for negotiations two weeks from today."

"It seems well enough . . . what does Lord Robert say?" asked Faris.

"Robert?" He raised one eyebrow mockingly. "Robert is warleader—the council table is *my* battlefield. The decision is yours, my Queen, not Robert's. If they come here your beauty will finish the conquest that Robert's sword began."

She shook her head. "I doubt I will be well enough to appear."

He offered her the paper again with a pen and inkwell and she rather shakily signed in the space he showed her.

"But you must come, even if only for a little while. I will have the cleverest seamstresses in Laurelynn make you a new gown."

"I had no idea that the duties of a Seneschal extended so far!" she mocked him. "Perhaps I will attend, if only to see what kind of a dress you would design for me!"

"A dress that will make the Elayans know that indeed we have a Queen in Laurelynn!" Caolin replied, kissing her hand.

"The Elayans are very fine . . . you would think they had never been near a fight!" said Farin, looking down on the first rank of Prince Palomon's guard.

"They looked pretty on the field too . . ." muttered Eric.

Farin turned from the window to glance at his friend, bound and bandaged so that little of him was visible. But Eric's eyes were very bright, and there was a flush on his cheeks. Rosemary frowned and put her hand to his forehead.

The tramp of feet gave way to a clatter of hooves on cobblestones. Farin looked back to the street as the plumes of the guard disappeared around a corner and the Elayan envoys appeared. Mail glittered from beneath their silken robes and Farin blinked as their silvered helms cast back the sun.

"They do well to come armed," he said, listening. "Hear the crowd . . ."

From the people who lined the street came a murmur like the sound when the wind changes and one hears the thunder of a distant waterfall. The Westrian soldiers who had been stationed along the way looked around them uneasily.

"Can you see Palomon?" asked Eric.

Farin waited while the first four horsemen went by. Another came after them, sitting like a statue on his dappled mare. "I see someone . . . a dark man with a face like an eagle and silver brocading on his blue robe."

"Palomon . . ." Eric sighed. "I wish I could see him up close—I tried to get to him on the battlefield, but they shot Thunderfoot and then afterward . . ."

"Eric! It's over now—please don't try to move!" Rosemary gripped Eric's shoulders, holding him down. He quivered for a moment then stilled, tears of weakness glistening on his cheeks. Rosemary's hand moved gently over his brow and slipped behind his head to smooth the pillow.

"They ride in honor . . ." she said bitterly. "They should enter this city yoked and in chains!"

"Well, they did come in under truce—we never captured them." Farin pointed out, though he found his own hand twitching as if it wanted his sword.

"Whose truce?" Eric's whisper strengthened. "Did the Council meet while I was ill?"

The last of the Elayans had passed from view. Farin frowned and closed the window. "I don't think so." He picked up his harp again.

"Well who decided it then? Robert? Damn this weakness!" Eric added, "I should know what is going on—I should be there!"

"You're here—you're alive! Be grateful for that," exclaimed Rosemary. "The Master says that if you lie still now in a few months you will be riding again. Even fighting, if that's all you want to do!" She bit her lip and turned her face away, but Farin saw how she struggled to regain her usual placid smile.

Eric's eyes rested on her golden braids. "I know I have been lucky . . . But you see, I have never had to lie still before," he said simply.

Rosemary reached blindly for the half-full bowl of broth on the table and began resolutely to spoon it into Eric's obediently opened mouth. Farin, lowering his head to hide a smile, struck up a cheerful melody.

"I know you hate being fed—" said Rosemary, "but soon you will be strong again!" She leaned over him, clutching the empty bowl. "I saw the King slip away from us, but I shall not give up until you are well again!"

"Nay love—I'll not doubt you! If you had been with us in the south the enemy would have run for fear!" Eric grinned as the hot color rose in Rosemary's cheeks and watched appreciatively as she stalked to the other end of the room. She stepped backward suddenly as the door opened and Branwen came in.

"Why are you here?" she snapped, "Have Faris and the child no need of you?"

"Rosemary! Let the poor girl at least get through the door!" said Farin, rising to shut it behind Branwen and reddening in turn at the warmth of her grateful smile. Jehan's sickness had driven memory of the night he had lain with Branwen away, but lately it seemed as if she would like to recall it again . . .

"The Master of the Junipers is playing with the baby—" explained Branwen. "Sometimes I think he is more a mother

to him than the Queen! As for my Lady, she is with Caolin."
She sat down on the stool that Rosemary had vacated and gave
Eric a cheerful smile.

He stared past her. "Caolin . . ." his eyes focused on Farin.
"Did I ever tell you exactly how Brian died?"

"Eric . . ." began Rosemary, but he shook his head.

"No, I'm not raving—it will ease me to talk about it. Anyway I must tell *you*, Farin, because Brian hoped you might
make it into a song . . ."

Farin tried to laugh. "I thought he didn't like me—" but
Eric was already speaking. Farin leaned forward as passion
colored Eric's fumbling phrases with the hues of an epic from
the ancient days.

"And so I took his ring and promised to avenge him if I
lived." Eric lifted his hand and they saw Brian's ring glittering
on his middle finger, next to his own.

Farin rested his forehead on the smoothly curved top of the
harp. Indeed the tale was worth telling, but could it be told by
him? He had never ventured more than a ballad before.

"And you say that Brian accused Caolin of causing his
death?" asked Rosemary in the silence that followed. "I don't
understand—Caolin wasn't even there . . ."

"I don't know how he did it—neither did Brian—but he
did say that Caolin had sworn to kill him. Remember, Farin,
how he suspected treachery even when that Deputy of Caolin's
first suggested the battle plan?"

Farin nodded, hearing again Ercul Ashe's precise voice warm
to enthusiasm as he explained the fatal strategy.

"But I still cannot believe it!" repeated Rosemary. "I have
never *liked* Caolin, but . . ."

"Faris likes him," said Branwen suddenly, twisting the end
of her brown braid.

"What do you mean by that?" Farin set down the harp.

"Sir Farin! Don't be angry with *me*. It's just that he visits
her every day and brings her flowers . . . and she laughs at
his jokes . . ." her voice trailed off.

"But Branwen, what's wrong with that?" asked Rosemary.
"If he cheers her, why not be grateful? It is more than we have
been able to do!"

Branwen shrugged resentfully and fell silent. Farin sighed,
wondering why he had been so angry.

"If there was no Council meeting . . ." said Eric after a

little while, "then it must have been Caolin. With Faris' consent, of course, but the idea would have been his."

"Well, she *has* had other things to think about . . ." said Rosemary.

Farin shut his eyes, remembering how Jehan had galloped up the road toward the Hold, and the bright splash of the Seneschal's robe as he followed the King. Caolin had always been there a step behind his master, always serenely in charge.

"But . . . the King was always going off and leaving Caolin to run things . . ."

"The King is gone," said Eric bleakly. "Do you think Faris can rule such a man? I am her champion—I should protect her!"

"But—this is ridiculous—do you realize what we're saying?" Rosemary blinked and rubbed at her eyes. "If Caolin is such a villain, do you think you can protect Faris with the edge of your sword? Brian's sword didn't protect *him!*"

Farin watched Eric's eyes brighten as the idea took hold. He tried to picture his friend skulking in corners spying on Caolin, and began to laugh.

"You are laughing at me and you are right," said Eric. "I don't have the right kind of mind to be a good conspirator. I could never out-think Caolin by myself—but together we might . . ." he looked at them with eyes as bright as those of a dog hoping to be taken for a run.

"I'll help you," said Branwen. "I don't like the way Caolin makes the Lady Faris laugh."

Rosemary was still shaking her head. "Even supposing Caolin is guilty of—something—how do you propose to find him out?"

"Well, what about that Deputy we were talking about before. Did he betray the plan to Palomon?" asked Eric.

Farin frowned, pushing back the silver lock of hair from his eyes. "I think he offered that plan sincerely, Eric—he really believed it was brilliant. And he had no chance to betray it afterward. I should know—I untied him myself after the battle was all over. Poor man, he had spent all day trussed in Brian's tent, wondering whether he would be spitted or rewarded, and by which side."

"Then you know him, and he would be willing to talk to you again . . ." said Rosemary thoughtfully.

"Well yes, but . . . He is loyal to his master."

"At least you can talk to him, Farin. It's hard to believe

that the Elayans just *happened* to move that way!" said Eric.

"Talk to him, and we might find out," added Rosemary.

Farin gave her a sidelong glance. "It sounds as if you have joined the conspiracy."

Rosemary looked at him, her fair brows lifting in surprise. "Are we a conspiracy? Caolin would die laughing." She shook her head.

"I only want to learn the truth . . . for Faris . . ."

But her eyes went to Eric's eager face, and Farin thought that her decision had been made more for his sake than for the Queen's.

"I appreciate the trouble you have gone to, Caolin. The gown is beautiful," Faris lifted a fold of brocade, watching the afternoon light pick a new pattern from its gold threads, "but I am not going to wear it." She let the fabric fall and the gold rippled back into the swirl of opening butterflies whose wings fluttered across the brocade in shades of scarlet and deep purple and rose.

Faris looked up at Caolin. His grey eyes were a little hooded so that she could not tell what he was thinking. But then Caolin's thoughts were rarely apparent even when one met his gaze.

"But you will receive the Elayan envoys . . ." It was not quite a question. Was he disappointed because she had refused the gown?

"I suppose so . . . yes . . . they are all expecting me to go," she replied wearily.

He turned to the window, sunset flaring in his ring of office as he latched it against the cooling air. "What will you wear then? What do you want the Elayans to see?" he asked quietly.

Faris shrugged, looking down at the gown that hung loosely about her. "They will see me as I am." She was abruptly conscious of the scar hidden beneath her sleeve, her pallor, and the silver that was beginning to weave through her hair as gold threaded the brocade. "Why should I put on a show for them?"

Why indeed should she put on a show for the Elayans or for the Master of the Junipers and Rosemary and the rest? They could force her to do this job but not to enjoy it!

Caolin took her hand and turned her toward the window, kissing her curled fingers respectfully. The garnet in his ring glowed like the Jewel of Fire.

"Faris . . ." Caolin's voice was very even and low. "Let

them see a Queen . . . Listen to me Faris, and do as I say."
She waited, eyes held by the ring, while he lifted the brocade
overdress with the midnight purple of its undergown folded
inside and held them up to her.

"See a Queen, Faris!" he repeated. His eyes, grown suddenly luminous, held hers. For a moment she saw herself reflected in their surface.

"You are beautiful and proud—" he went on. "Make them
bow to your power!"

Faris straightened from the slump with which she had walked
since her delivery and raised her chin. *Yes . . . let them all
remember that I am the Queen!* The door to the chamber clicked
open and Faris started. Caolin swung away from her, still
holding up the gown.

"Branwen, you are come in good time! I have brought the
new robes for your mistress to wear tonight and you must help
her into them." He smiled brilliantly.

Faris twitched at the faded dress she was wearing with
sudden distaste, wondering how she could have considered
wearing it.

"Yes, Branwen, and quickly!" she said as the girl hesitated,
watching Caolin. She began to fumble at the lacings that closed
her gown.

Caolin bowed. "I will return within the hour to escort you
to the Hall."

In the Great Hall of the Palace at Laurelynn, candles had
been lit in the sconces along the walls. But not all of them, so
that the light was not quite sufficient to drive the shadows
away. On the musician's balcony a consort of stringed instruments were playing something soft and low without marked
rhythm or melody to catch the ear.

Farin listened to them with part of his attention, giving the
rest to Rosemary's commentary.

"I wonder how Caolin got people here—" she looked around,
nodding to Mistress Gwenna, the Mayor's wife, as she passed.
"Everyone was saying that to feast the enemy would betray the
dead . . ."

"Is this a feast? It does not seem very festive somehow."
The muted music and the shadows lent a sombre air to the
proceedings and no food had been set out, though servants
were circulating with goblets of a pale chill wine.

They stopped for a moment while Rosemary greeted Lady Elinor of Fairhaven. But when Farin would have gone Rosemary tugged at his sleeve.

"Look at them!" She pointed to the glitter of Elayan brocade below the great banner of Westria that hung on the wall. Farin stiffened as he recognized Prince Palomon and his men.

They were easy to see, for the other guests had left a space around them like the plowed strip that brakes a fire. Palomon chatted easily as he sipped his wine, his manner as unconcerned as if he had been in his own hall.

There was a pause in the music, then the consort began a pavane.

"Oh! Why must they play so mournfully!" Rosemary shook her head as if the music pained her.

Farin focused on it and recognized the tune of an old love song. "Surely the musicians know better than to play a pavane as if it were a funeral march, unless . . ." Rosemary looked at Farin curiously as he slowly smiled. "Unless they are doing it on purpose. I think that Caolin has planned it this way."

"Well he has succeeded, then. I feel almost too hopeless to be angry. If Eric were here he would not be so patient. Maybe it is as well he was too weak to come!"

Farin nodded. Eric's sister was representing him at this reception, as the steward of Sanjos represented Las Costas. It should have been Lady Alessia, but she had refused to come.

Rosemary sighed as if the thought of Eric were finishing what the music had begun.

"Eric is getting better every day . . ." said Farin consolingly. "He will reward your nursing soon."

"What do you mean?" she asked sharply.

It was Farin's turn to be embarrassed. "Well . . . I don't think he loves Faris anymore . . ."

"Am I so transparent then?"

"No!" protested Farin. "But I know you very well." He looked at her, thinking how strange it was that he should feel more at ease with her than with his sisters. "Besides, it's nothing to be ashamed of. You've seen how Faris has lost her beauty since Jehan died. I doubt that Eric's memories will be able to withstand the living presence of a woman who loves him."

He tried to see Rosemary not as his familiar friend, but as Eric might do. Rosemary was too tall for him, but she would be just the right size to fit into Eric's embrace. She was wearing a jade-colored gown tonight with a pattern of eucalyptus leaves woven into the hem. The vivid shade set off her golden hair. But she looked tired. Maybe as Eric recovered she would get some color into her face again and he would see that she had a beauty of her own.

The music was growing fainter, receding like a departing tide and leaving only the low murmur of conversation to fill the space where it had been. He wondered why they had stopped. Then massed clarions called and sound cascaded into the gap like a returning wave. An astonished babble started as the echoes faded, but stillness spread again from the doorway like ripples from a stone thrown into a pond.

"You were telling me how Faris has lost her beauty?" whispered Rosemary.

Farin shook his head mutely, watching his sister and Caolin enter the hall. He had forgotten how Faris looked dressed in bright colors, and he had never seen her wear anything like this. The brilliant reds and purples of her gown flamed against the underdress, which was of a shade somewhere between black and violet, like the skin of a grape, that echoed the darkness of her hair. Tiny gold buttons marched downward from the throat of the high collar to disappear where the brocade bodice was clasped across her breast, and from wrist to elbow where the undersleeves emerged from the square hanging sleeves. Oversleeves and skirts rippled like the enameled wings of some exotic artificial butterfly.

A soprano recorder began to play all alone. After a few measures, the alto joined it, then the tenor and base, following their leader in a fugue as the members of the court fell into step behind their Queen.

The procession circled the Hall. As it passed, servants lit the rest of the candles. By the time the Queen reached the chair that had been set for her on the dais at the end of the Hall, light blazed from every corner, displaying the sheen of velvets, the glitter of gold or silver thread, the luster of a cabochon jewel glowing on hand or breast.

From his place near the Queen Farin looked around him at the color that flushed men's cheeks, the new light in their eyes. He leaned over to whisper to Rosemary, "Whatever you may think of Caolin this is surely brilliant choreography!"

"Yes, but for what end? Look more carefully at that gown."

The Queen's smile remained etched on her pale face as she

spoke to those around her. She leaned in front of Caolin to greet Lady Jessica and the scarlet of her brocade seemed to bleed into his crimson robe; its metallic traceries could have been drawn from the polished gold of Caolin's hair. Suddenly Farin felt cold.

Plumes waved above the heads of the crowd, as Prince Palomon and his escort approached. The Herald stepped forward.

"My Lady Faris, Mistress of the Jewels and Regent of Westria—I present to you now Palomon, Lord of the Tambara and Elected Prince of the Confederation of Elaya."

Faris rose in a rustle of silks, held out her hand for Palomon to touch in greeting, then sat down again.

"Had you commanded Westria in the south, your beauty alone would have vanquished us." Palomon's teeth flickered white among the black curls of his beard. He nodded to Lord Robert with the faintest hint of mockery. "My Lord Commander, my congratulations on your victory."

"It was a narrow one," said Robert, bowing slightly. "You maneuvered very cleverly."

"Not cleverly enough it seems," Palomon said silkily. His gaze moved from Robert to the Seneschal, then back to the Queen, and he stepped aside to introduce his entourage. Then the Herald brought forward those members of the Council who were to participate in the treaty negotiations. When the introductions were complete some invisible signal set the musicians playing again. There was a general movement toward the food.

One of the Guildmistresses brushed by Farin, talking to her husband. "And did you notice those sleeves?" she said, "Elayan cut! And no weavers of Laurelynn ever patterned that brocade!"

"But dear, perhaps the cloth was booty taken in the war . . ." said the man, as the couple passed out of hearing.

Rosemary frowned. "I hope there's not much talk of that kind."

Without answering Farin steered his companion toward the table and managed to abstract two goblets and a pitcher of wine. Rosemary scooped up some cakes and they withdrew to a window seat.

This time the musicians were playing the pavane at the proper speed. Faris and Caolin led the line of dancers dipping and swaying the length of the Hall. Faris' eyes glittered feverishly. Caolin's strong hand guided her through the variations as the music, precise and brilliant, elaborated on its basic theme.

They danced well together, given the differences in their heights, but Farin remembered how Faris had danced with Jehan, like two halves joining again.

"Farin—who is that man—the one standing by the door?" Rosemary's question brought him to the present again. He looked around and saw Ercul Ashe munching a cake with a complacent smile.

"Yes, that's Ercul Ashe. *He* seems to have recovered from the battle well enough!" said Farin. Certainly, with his greying hair sleeked back and his fur trimmed tunic buttoned demurely to the chin, the Deputy Seneschal bore little resemblance to the tattered creature Farin had rescued from Brian's pavilion.

"He looks too secure," said Rosemary. "Why should he be so easy when everyone else in Westria is either angry or anguished. Go talk to him, Farin—"

Farin's own smile faded as he remembered ravens conversing with the dead in the grey dusk of the battlefield. "Ercul Ashe left the camp as soon as I released him . . . he never saw what his words had done . . ." he said slowly. He gave Rosemary's hand a squeeze and moved toward the door.

The guests were drawing aside to leave the center space clear. Farin edged around them as a troop of performers bounded onto the floor brandishing short wooden swords and hand-bucklers painted red or blue. The bells fastened to their wrists and ankles chimed merrily as they paired off for the stylised sword dance. Ercul Ashe looked up as Farin approached him, his smile becoming a trifle more open as he saw who it was.

"Sir Farin!" the Deputy bowed deeply. "I have not thanked you for my deliverance—indeed I was so distraught it was some hours before I realized who you were! I have not wanted to intrude upon you, and of course I have been much occupied." A discreet nod indicated the dancers and the crowd. The dancers were whirling and weaving, opposed swords tapping a counter-rhythm to the drums.

"Yes, it is a brilliant affair," agreed Farin carefully, wondering how to lead up to his subject. When he had seen Ashe before the man had been reeling with fatigue and fear. What motivated him now that he was secure on his home ground?

A boy came by with a pitcher of wine. Farin held out his goblet and motioned to the lad to refill that of his companion. It was red wine this time, a heady vintage from near Sanjos. Well, perhaps that was fitting, thought Farin, feeling the strong stuff ease the tension in his throat.

"Thank you—" Ashe acknowledged his compliment. "It was not easily accomplished in so short a time." He sipped at his wine.

"I can imagine," replied Farin, "the Seneschal must have driven you hard."

"Driven? My lord has no need to *drive* his staff. They know what he expects of them," Ashe said proudly. Farin was reminded of the tone in which women boasted of their labor pains.

"But there was so much to do . . ." he offered encouragingly.

"My lord anticipates all contingencies," said Ercul Ashe.

Rat-a-tat-tat went the wooden swords. The bells of the dancers jingled like mail.

"I wish he had anticipated Palomon's maneuvering on the battlefield!" Farin fought to keep his tone merely regretful; this was as hard as pitching his voice to deliver a difficult song!

Some unknown emotion curtained Ashe's gaze. Farin felt his heart begin to pound, sensing that his words had slipped past the other man's guard as the dancers' swords slipped by their opponents' parrying. Could he make it easier for the Deputy to blame Caolin?

"I am glad that I got you out of the camp when I did—" Farin said meditatively. "When men are grieving they do not always stop to weigh the evidence. Some spoke against you when they heard who had suggested the battle plan . . ."

Ashe's face did not change, but he became very still. "And what of you, Sir Farin? Do you think I intended treachery?" he said quietly.

Flushing a little at the baldness of the statement, Farin shook his head. "I was there when you spoke to Lord Robert. I believe that you believed the plan would work." he said, a little more strongly than he had intended. The dancers wheeled, and the red-clad warriors began to drive the others the length of the room.

"Someone else could have betrayed the plan. Were you the only one who knew what you intended to say?" Farin went on.

Another man would have laughed or grown angry. Ercul Ashe only pursed his lips and lifted his thin brows.

"If you heard me at the camp you also heard me say that I have worked with my Lord Caolin more than seven years. After serving such a master, do you think a child like you will trick me into betraying him?"

Farin blushed in earnest now, realizing how transparent his attempts to manage the conversation must have been. The red dancers beat their foes around the room with regular smacks of sword against sword or shield. Farin had heard just such a terrible music in battle. But it had been silent, afterward.

"Did you see the battlefield?" he asked sharply, meeting Ashe's eyes for the first time. "The pasture was churned to red mud, and the horses stumbled on severed limbs. I saw a coyote dragging off an arm whose hand still gripped a bow. It was a woman's arm . . ."

"Such things happen in war—" Ashe began weakly, but Farin cut in.

"Do you wonder that I want to know if our movements were betrayed?"

"No . . ." Ashe sighed and took another swallow of wine. "But the book where I found the plan was in the oldest part of the library with the volumes that tell of the devices of the ancients—The book was thick with dust, and I told no one about it on my way south. Even Caolin was too busy to listen to me."

Farin felt his heart sink. They had been so sure Caolin was at fault somehow. But, Farin did not think that Ercul Ashe could feign such sincerity.

"I have wondered too . . . I would not have men think me a traitor . . . but it *must* have been chance . . ." The words came almost too low for Farin to hear.

With shouts of triumph the dancers in the red tunics drove the blue-clad warriors from the room.

"Think about it still, Master Deputy. There may be something you have forgotten. For if someone has hidden behind the shield of your integrity, then traitor is the name you will surely bear!" Farin's words were lost in the burst of clapping with which the audience saluted the end of the dance, but Ercul Ashe turned away abruptly. Farin knew that he had heard, and did not have the heart to call him back.

The dancers had come forward to take their bows, red robes interspersed with blue. Idly, Farin wondered why those colors had been chosen. Blue might indicate Elaya, but then the winners should have worn Westrian green. When everything else about this evening had been calculated so carefully it was hard to imagine the colors were pure chance. The crowd swirled, making a path for Caolin to lead the Queen to the door. His crimson robes glowed in the blaze of the candlelight, almost overwhelming the splendor of her brocade.

Red is the Seneschal's color . . . and the banner of Las Costas is blue! Anger shriveled the pity Farin had begun to feel for Ercul Ashe and he looked quickly around him. But the room was emptying. The Elayans had left in the wake of the Queen, and the Deputy Seneschal was also gone.

"Your servants have gone . . . that is good. I hardly hoped to find you alone . . ." Caolin spoke from the shadows by the door.

In a single fluid movement Prince Palomon came to his feet, already drawing the sword that had been leaning against the wall. The door latched gently as Caolin stepped into the light. Palomon stared at him for a moment, then let his sword slip back into its sheath like a cat withdrawing its claws.

"I did not hear my guards announce you—" the Prince said dryly.

"Your guards do not know that I am here." Caolin drew a second chair up to the low table and sat down. The table bore an inlaid chessboard whose filigreed pieces stirred Caolin's envy even now, when all his will was focused on his purpose here.

Palomon's expression became subtly more ironic. "Shall I display a common curiosity," he asked, "or question my guards? You have succeeded in interesting me, Master Seneschal, or else I would call them now. Men name you sorcerer . . . is this a demonstration of your skill?" The candelabra on either side of the table flickered uneasily and shadows danced and scuttled around the room.

Caolin smiled, refusing to be disturbed by the other man's veiled mockery. When the Prince did question his guards he would find that they thought they had admitted Rodrigo Maclain. He might well begin to wonder, then.

"Do you believe that I am a sorcerer?" he asked blandly.

Palomon's shoulders twitched in a movement too delicate to call a shrug. "Such a title has no meaning for reasonable men—Will you have some wine?" Without waiting for an answer he filled a second goblet and pushed it across the table to Caolin. With one tapered finger he caressed a chess piece of colored ivory. "Will you play with me?"

Caolin sighed and shook his head. "If only we had the

time . . . But though my errand is less pleasant it may be more profitable—It seemed to me that a meeting of minds might be desirable before we meet on the Council floor."

Palomon's finely arched brows lifted again. "You expect me to make promises unadvised?"

"Do you mean without listening to your advisors mouth opinions and then turning the words until they believe that your ideas are their own?"

Palomon's eyes sparkled suddenly, but he did not reply.

"Besides," Caolin went on, "*I* am alone."

"*You* are not the Lord of Westria."

It was Caolin's turn to shrug. "Not in name . . ." He wondered if Palomon, who had inherited the rank that gave him the right to wrest power from among the other princelings of the Royal House, resented the Seneschal's assumption of authority.

The Prince gave him another oblique glance. "You imply that you control the Queen—are you her lover?"

Caolin stared at him, unable to keep the blood from leaving his face and returning so swiftly that the shadows swirled around him like a dark tide. He remembered . . . Faris in Jehan's arms . . . the simulated Faris struggling beneath him on the Red Mountain . . . the many other women who had come from Jehan's bed to his own . . .

Why was he so shocked by Palomon's suggestion? Why had he never consciously considered the possibility on his own? A hidden doorway in his own mind gaped suddenly, like the mouth of a well, and he dared not look in. And yet there could be no better way to keep power than by seducing—by marrying the Queen!

"Do not be offended—" the Prince said delicately. "Since the lady has lost her husband it would be a natural thing—though I understand that your Westrian women often take a man's role and rule alone . . . For instance," he went on, "Who will hold Las Costas now that their belligerent lord is gone?"

"His widow, according to custom." Caolin took a long swallow of wine, realizing that Palomon's comment about the Queen had only been made to lead up to this.

"And do you think that the Lady of Las Costas would suffer your governance if she knew whose messenger had betrayed Lord Brian's position to me?"

"I had thought you understood . . ." Caolin said patiently. "Elaya and Westria hold each other in check. We can only gain from this Council if we are both prepared to make a sacrifice . . ."

Palomon waited silently. His face seemed carved from some dark wood.

"And I have no need to beg your discretion in any case." Caolin continued. "You cannot prove that the messenger was mine. You rule alone, but you were elected. Those who raised you to the throne can cast you down." Caolin sat back, searching the Elayan's face for any response. A gust of wind rattled the window, then passed on.

"You have called us both reasonable men . . ." the Seneschal added. "Surely we are too reasonable to deal in threats or mysteries." He leaned across the table, striving to hold the other man's gaze. "Listen to me, Palomon. We can gain no more from this conflict. Though it will be some time before you can threaten us again, we cannot afford to follow up our victory . . ."

Palomon laughed shortly, turning his goblet back and forth by the stem. "You are being very frank—do you want to be *my* minister?"

Caolin shook his head, weighing his words. "Men like the late Lord Brian must be driven, but I had hoped to speak with you on equal terms."

The Prince raised his head and he stared at Caolin beneath half-closed eye-lids, giving somehow the impression that he was looking down at the Seneschal.

A vein throbbed painfully in Caolin's forehead. Just so had Brian looked at him. *Softly now*—he told himself, though his fingers had closed around his ring of office until its facets bit painfully, *this man traces his ancestry back farther than Jehan could do. He would be a King if Elayan pride would suffer so public a lordship. But he has the reactions of a chessmaster. He will not be obvious . . .*

He met the Elayan's scornful gaze, held it, passionless, until Palomon shrugged and looked away. Caolin picked up an ivory knight from the chessboard.

"Palomon . . ." he said softly, "is there anyone in Elaya who is your equal on this board?"

The Prince's eyes sparkled suddenly and he laughed. Caolin set down the chesspiece and eased back in his chair.

"Very well—" said the Prince as if continuing the previous interchange, "but if Westria and Elaya are equally impotent, why have you come to me?"

"Our nations may be immobilized, but you and I are not. I will not quarrel over a few miles of land . . ." Caolin shifted in his chair and it squeaked thinly, as if Brian were groaning in his grave.

"You would give us Santibar?" whispered Palomon.

"If my position here were strong enough, I could ensure that by the time you are ready for war again, the fortress would be easy prey," said Caolin carefully.

"What do you want?" Palomon leaned forward.

For a moment the question hung between them. A candle spluttered as the flame reached a flaw in the wick, then resumed its steady glow.

"I need the support of the people of Westria . . . For instance, I could become very popular by giving them the head of the man who had Lord Brian shot down . . ." Caolin took another swallow of wine. "But I have no wish to deal with your brother, who from all accounts is a belligerent fool."

A smile flickered on Palomon's full lips.

"If I should . . . marry the Queen . . . recognize me as Lord of Westria. But for now, give me symbols—" said Caolin, "reparations in gold and an apology for invading Westria. Insist that you will negotiate only with me."

"My own people would take my head if I did that!"

"What are words? Do your people need to know exactly what was said? If you hint to your councilors of secret concessions they will support your interpretation of what occurred. And a trade agreement will regain you the gold . . ." Caolin's wine glowed like the stone in his ring in the candlelight. Darkness surrounded them, separating them from the world.

The Prince of Elaya was still frowning into his goblet. "But a public apology!" His nostrils flared with distaste.

"Your Army destroyed the fortress called the Dragon's Claw . . . I could delay its refortification . . ." Caolin breathed carefully, as if any movement would break the delicate chain of persuasion he was forging between himself and the other man.

Palomon drew back suddenly and set down his goblet with a click. "You offer promises, but you ask *me* to pay . . . and then to wait for you to keep your word."

Anger flared in Caolin's belly. Palomon jerked away as if

he had been struck. The Seneschal's ring blazed as his hand clenched on the table's edge.

"I have promised you—and I always keep my promises *precisely*, Palomon!" Caolin hissed.

The Prince of Elaya tried to laugh, but his heavy lids did not quite hide the trouble in his eyes. "I believe you . . ." he said softly. He bent to pick up a chesspiece which Caolin's movement had knocked to the floor.

"And yet—" he added, a gleam of real humor suddenly relaxing his face, "I still would like to play at chess with you!"

Caolin smiled and forebore to tell him that he already had.

IX

The Morning Star

Early morning light slanting across the Lady Mountain left the intricate silhouette of the nearer ridge in shadow while the blue-hazed farther slope soared luminous against the sky. The Master of the Junipers felt his throat tighten and he wondered why he was so moved. It was only rocks and trees, though it might for a moment seem a veil drawn across the face of a world whose substance was living light. Once, he had been able to see that world.

He heard a ripple of laughter behind him. Most of the Queen's household had come with them to see the infant Prince receive his milk-name. The party had crossed the Bay yesterday and passed the night at the foot of the Mountain, for Faris had refused to sleep at Misthall.

The Master sighed. He had not been to the Lady Mountain since Faris was married to the King, and she . . . what place could either of them go that would not blur before their eyes with memories?

He looked back. Rosemary and Farin rode beside the litter which was bearing Eric up the Mountain. Farin had slipped his harp from its case and was improvising while he rode, guiding his horse with his knees. Behind them came Faris, and Branwen with the baby bound into a basketry cradleboard slung from the saddlebow.

The cradleboard was indeed a work of art, with its woven patterns brightened by red and blue feathers from woodpecker crests and jays, with a white deerskin to wrap around the child. A woman with a face like polished manzanita wood had left it at the Palace soon after the baby's birth with the message—
"Now that one of our blood will rule the Powers of Westria, let him be cradled as a child of the people . . ."

Then Berisa had told them of the Karok grandfather whom her younger brother and sister had never known. A descendent of the tribal People who were the original human inhabitants of Westria would rule . . . The Master realized suddenly that such a thing had not been since before the Cataclysm. His pulse quickened and his awareness reached out to the steady spark that was the child, perceiving for a moment the wonderful confusion of shape and color that swirled before the baby's eyes as he was borne up the path.

Quickly he withdrew again. The baby would have enough to assimilate today without the presence of an adult mind. But not for the first time he wondered at the ease with which that contact had been made. If he himself had ever begotten any children he was not aware of it. Would linking have been as easy if the baby had been his? Could any infant be reached so? Or was this relationship special—the one blessing of this dreadful time?

Rosemary's warm laugh distracted him.

"No, Eric, we are *not* going to join the dancing down at the Sacred Grove!"

"But the Lords of Seagate always go there to celebrate Beltane. I'm strong enough . . ." Eric protested.

"And will you still feel so strong after you have played your part in today's ceremony?" she asked tartly.

Farin interrupted her—"Don't be insulted, Eric. What Rosemary really fears is that one of the tree-maidens will carry you away!"

Eric laughed. "I *have* heard stories . . . Beltane is like the Feast of the First People in that way."

The Master smiled too, for he had served a year in the Sacred Grove and he had his own memories of the dancing at Beltane.

Sound shimmered from Farin's harp, silencing them. He began to sing:

"A King went out hunting, out hunting alone—
One day in the springtime, when the grass it was green—
And found there a maiden who sat on a stone
With the flowers all around her so fair to be seen.

'Ah maiden, no one could be fairer,' said he—
One day in the springtime, when the grass it was green—
'Come now to my castle and dwell there with me,
With the flowers all around you so fair to be seen.'

'I am Princess of Flowers, and may be no man's bride—
One day in the springtime, when the grass it is green—
But I'll be your love if you'll stay by my side,
With the flowers all around us so fair to be seen.'

The Kingdom lamented and counted him slain—
One day in the springtime when the grass it was green—
But the lovers alive in the greenwood remain
With the flowers all around them so fair to be seen."

"If Jehan had stayed with me in the north, he might be alive today!"

Startled, the Master saw that Faris had urged her horse forward to pace beside his own. "My dear . . ." he began.

"Can't I be allowed to forget?" she asked bitterly. Pitiless, the morning sunlight betrayed the false color on her lips, glistened on the dusting of powder with which she had tried to hide the shadows beneath her eyes.

"You cannot reject the past without rejecting yourself, but you can live each new day one hour at a time . . ." He offered her words worn smooth in the watches of his nights—the litany with which he tried to exorcise his own memories.

She shook her head. "Not today. Today I must put on the Jewels. How can I do it without him to share the burden?" her voice failed.

And how can I speak the words and conduct the ritual, when I feel nothing waiting to receive my prayer? The Master's fragile content shattered. He struggled to keep from voicing his despair.

"Stop it!" whispered Faris. "Must I bear your pain too?"

For a moment grief reverberated between them. Then the Queen spurred her horse viciously. The contact broke as a covey of quail exploded from the brush beside the path and the black mare leaped forward.

The Master's horse snorted and stumbled as Caolin's mount shouldered by, and the Master flinched, glimpsing contempt unshuttered in the Seneschal's eyes. For a moment the two faces flickered between him and the road—the Queen's brittle mask of beauty, Caolin's face, fuller than it had been, with all the betraying lines smoothed away.

The Master's unease focused to a sudden passionate resentment of the confidence with which the Seneschal had gone after the Queen. He clucked to his horse to catch up to them, then reined in. No—not now, when Caolin's amused smile could distort every word he said. No, he must try to find Faris alone.

"I will come in a moment—only leave me alone!"

Her words still trembling in the brittle air, Faris stumbled to the summit of the Lady Mountain, listening to Rosemary's footsteps fade. Numbly she set down the case in which the Jewels waited for her touch. She caught her breath on a sob, then stilled again as she heard only the wind, tuning itself to the contours of the Mountain with a thin high note that wavered on the edge of sound.

Far below the waters of the Bay glittered blindingly, a restless reflection of the light that had fired the bowl of the sky to a translucent sapphire glaze. Light glanced from the waters, from facets chipped in the rock of the mountainside, from the polished surfaces of madrone leaves.

The others were gathering in the meadow, waiting for Faris to put on the Jewels so that the ceremony could begin.

She stared helplessly around her, remembering how she had stood on top of the Father of Mountains and seen Westria laid like a golden promise at her feet. But this sunlight burned her eyes. Across the water the Red Mountain seemed about to shoulder free of its crumpled foothills. The slopes that lapped the Lady Mountain heaved like the waves of the sea.

For a moment the world whirled around her. Her balance was gone, and she fell, bruising her knees on the stone. *What is happening to me? What have I done?* She felt the easy tears sting her eyes, but there was no one to comfort her.

A vagrant scent of sun-warmed grass caught at her memory. She had done this before—wept into the bosom of the Mountain because she feared the ceremony that would unite her to the King. But now Jehan lay lost in the shadows of the Sacred Grove, and she had come here to give a name to his child.

And I am still afraid of the Jewels . . .

The wind song had deepened to a low hum that seemed to vibrate from the solid rock beneath her. She laid her palms against the weathered stone. There was a power here too, she thought, that supported her without judgement or demand.

"Lady of the Mountain," she whispered, "lend me your strength!"

Peace built around her, as fragile as a bubble of blown glass. Faris held her breath, motionless upon the still point of the turning world.

Why are you afraid?

Faris sought inward for an answer, and shuddered as she remembered the sweet sense of power that had stirred within her when she put on the Jewels before, and the triumphant smile on the face of that other Faris who had looked out from her mirror, mocking her. Somewhere within her, the Lady of Darkness was still there.

Then the trill of birdsong, the hum of the bee's flight, even the murmur of the wind, dulled and disappeared. Peace, palpable and enduring as the mountain itself, barriered her from the world.

For a moment Faris waited, poised on the edge of commitment, then she moved into that clarity where will and need are one. She opened the box that confined the Jewels.

Power throbbed around her, shaking the fragile boundaries of her control. But the stillness of the Mountain remained within. She imagined it rising around her, an inner barrier which would distance even the seductive power of the Jewels. She put them on, then got to her feet, carefully, as if she balanced the whole weight of Westria, and started down the hill.

Men and women turned as Faris came toward them. She assumed her place across the circle from the Master of the Junipers and held out her hands.

To her left, Lord Robert waited, and Eric to her right, responding to her offered hand with a swift movement that set the embroidered arms on their tabards glittering in the brilliant sun. Rosemary and Lady Alessia completed the circle as they took the Master's hands.

Those who had come to witness the ceremony gathered around them. Faris glimpsed the flare of Caolin's crimson robe, and saw, standing at attention near his mother, the amber-eyed boy who was Brian's heir. She felt their excitement as one feels the distant throb of the sea. But she was still barriered against its force.

The Master's invocation drew to a close. ". . . and therefore, Maker of All Things, make us open to Thy will. For Thou art the source of all strength and safety, and our promises are only manifestations of Thy power." His voice wavered on the words. "In the Names of the four elements and of the Covenant of Westria, let us begin."

Hands unlinked. Lady Jessica stepped into the circle past the little table by which the Master stood, followed by Farin with the baby clasped awkwardly in his arms. The child squirmed and looked around him with bright dark eyes.

"My Lords, my Ladies—" the Master bowed to each side of the circle. "You have come here, in the names of the Provinces of Westria, to stand sponsors to this child at his first naming, and to pledge to guard him until he is grown. Will you undertake this trust?"

Agreement echoed around the circle, but Faris held still, held to her circle of peace until her part should come.

"Will you promise to care for this child as if he were your own?"

"I will . . ."

"Will you see that he is taught the history of the Cataclysm and the meaning of the Covenant by which we live?"

Question and answers sectioned the brilliant stillness, the Master's voice fined to a cutting edge by strain, the replies of the sponsors falling one upon the other like notes in a trumpet call.

"And when he feels himself ready to bear the name of a man, will you bring him to be initiated and sworn to the Covenant of Westria?"

In the blaze of noontide they stood shadowless. Light shimmered on Rosemary's golden braids, flickered coppery on Alessia's leashed curls, picked glints of bronze and silver on Eric and Robert's bent heads.

The Master's voice deepened, falling through the sunlight.

"What shall the child be named?"

Faris felt her throat close. Light swallowed her words. What name—what name could transform him from 'the baby' to a person whom she could not ignore? She had thought to call him *Dolor*, for her sorrow . . .

"Who are you?"

The baby turned in Farin's arms, and Faris could not tell if she felt the clear flare of his spirit, or saw light kindle in his eyes.

"Star . . ." her reply sang to meet that brilliance. "He shall be called Star!"

The infant was still watching her, something achingly reminiscent of Jehan in the brilliance of his eyes. But his brows were too straight for that likeness. He was himself . . . Her vision blurred, extrapolating from the baby's rosy features the broad forehead and muscled jaw of a man.

"My star! My son!" her spirit called to him.

The Master of the Junipers turned to the baby and bowed. "I salute you, Morning Star of Westria, for someday you shall bear the Jewels of Power. Therefore we must do more than name you—you must learn to know the Jewels."

The Master's gaze lifted to Faris. She felt his tension eroding the surface of her control and tried to smile, drawing the strength of the Mountain around her once more.

Farin laid the baby in Rosemary's competent embrace. The Master took an earthenware bowl of corn pollen and traced on Star's forehead the circled cross of Westria.

"In the name of Earth I bless you, son of this land. Grow **strong** as its bedrock, fertile as the soil, upright as the growing **things** that seek the sun!"

Faris felt the earth quiver. Through the soles of her feet she **sensed the** layered rock beneath her, the network of roots that **latticed the** earth, the life that sprang in every leaf and blade **of grass.** But her fingers were already unclasping the Earthstone **from about** her hips, and that awareness faded as she laid it **for a moment** on the belly of her child. Star's eyes turned to her, round and astonished, until she took it away.

The Master carried the Earthstone back to the table, and brought a silver chalice of rainwater as Jessica took the baby from Rosemary and carried him to Eric. Faris turned after her, feeling her stomach churn as the Sea Star, without the Earthstone to balance it, began to wake.

I am your Mistress—be still! she thought swiftly, willing her muscles to relax.

"In the name of Water I bless you, son of the sea. Grow mighty as the pounding waves, responsive as the tides, gentle as the falling rain!" The water on the Master's finger made a crescent on Star's brow, partially wiping the pollen away.

Faris' breasts throbbed with milk, her ears roared with the sound of the sea. She remembered how she had been the sea, bearing this child to birth. Tears filled her eyes. But already she was unbelting the Sea Star, and touching him.

Farin bore the baby across the circle to Robert, but Faris fought for breath while wind blew back her hair. Her ears opened to the whisper of wind around the Mountain, the cry of a hawk miles away, to the aromatic scent of the incense with which the Master was blessing the child.

She bit her lip, struggling with the power of the Jewel. Her barriers were thinning, and she sensed the force locked in the crystal at her breast, fought the temptation to let it break free.

"In the name of Air I bless you, son of the skies. Grow free as the wind, harmonious as music, wise enough to name all things—even yourself when the time shall come!"

The Wind Crystal lifted from Faris' breast as if borne by its own silver wings. As she laid it on Star's chest the crystal and the child's eyes blurred in a single point of light. Through the rustle of voices came his cry.

Faris felt his confusion, sensed a tumult of images for which Star had no words, and poured toward him love and reassurance until he stilled. Then Jessica carried him toward Alessia.

As Faris turned to follow, sunlight blazed across her sight, kindling the Jewel of Fire to life upon her brow. She walked toward Alessia through air like a sea of flame, battling the awe of those who watched and the power that pulsed through every nerve until it seemed that she too would burst into flames. Her body was a shell of blown glass, too fragile a vessel to contain such a fire.

"In the name of Fire I bless you, son of Light. Grow terrible as the lightning, companionable as a candle flame, brother to all who are warmed by the fire of life."

Faris' fingers closed on her coronet. She reached to touch it to Star's brow. But suddenly the air between them seemed filled with flames.

"His gown is burning, beat out the fire!" A woman's scream echoed from past to present in her memory. *I must not let him burn!* Again Faris twisted in agony as the fire retraced its pathway up her arm. But still she reached for Star, not knowing if he were hers, or the housekeeper's child she had saved long ago. Then her hand closed on his cool flesh and she let go the Jewel of Fire.

Darkness . . .

Faris' mind still resonated with images of pain and splendor—the Master's anguish, Star's delight, the terrible beauty of the Jewel of Fire. She knew her brother's arms were supporting her, but she could not see. As the pounding of her heart stilled she understood that there was no fire, and that it had been her own son whom she had touched with the Jewel.

My son . . . the ferocity of her passion to save him astonished her. *I love him,* she thought in wonder, *my own sweet Star!*

"Behold, ye people of Westria, the Master of the Jewels

who is to come!" The Master's voice was lost in the cheering that washed over Faris, piercing her naked soul.

The baby began to cry and she heard the Master trying to comfort him. "My son—let me go to him!" she whimpered, struggling in Farin's arms. But no one heard.

"What is wrong with her, what can I do?" Farin's panic lashed her and she screamed.

"I will take her."

Faris felt her brother's uneasy relief. Strong arms lifted her. The voices faded, and presently the torrent of emotions that had battered her began to weaken, as if some other will were blotting them away.

"Be still . . ." Faris realized that she had been hearing that dry voice for some time, with her ears alone. "There is a wall around you. You cannot hear or feel. You are safe with me . . . I will not let the Jewels hurt you again . . ."

Faris shuddered, knowing how nearly the Jewels had mastered her. She felt the earth solid beneath her, and she breathed to the rhythm with which cool impersonal fingers caressed her hair. Gratefully she sank into the silent dark.

After a long time, Faris opened her eyes. She was lying in the shade of a laurel tree. Beside her, Caolin sat with his back against its trunk, one arm resting easily across his bent knee as if he had been there for a long time. As the laurel leaves flickered, sunlight revealed the carven features she had come to know so well, shadow dissolved them into mystery. Which face was his? She sighed as awareness of her own body began to return.

"How do you feel?"

She struggled to sit up. "My head aches . . . but numbly." Just as, she thought, the salves had kept the agony of her burned arm at bay. But this time it was her mind whose protective covering had been stripped away. Dimly she sensed the life of the tree, but nothing from Caolin, beside her. Had he also kept those other minds from touching hers?

"Caolin . . . thank you for protecting me," she said softly. "And thank you for sparing me your emotions now. Your barriers must be better even than the Master's used to be . . ."

His eye-lids quivered as if that had touched him, but he continued to smile at her. "I did what I could to help you," he said neutrally. "Are you ready to go back?"

Faris looked down at the meadow, busy now with people

setting up the feast. A blue curl of smoke threaded the trees.

"So many minds . . ." she shook her head, but her breasts were taut with milk, and her arms hungered suddenly for the weight of her child. "Where is Star?"

"With the Master of the Junipers, I suppose," replied Caolin. "Don't worry, they have probably fed the child. I am surprised that the Master has not grown breasts to suckle him!"

He is my *son!* Faris felt resentment flare, not entirely because she knew the agony that waited for her if the baby had no appetite to relieve the pressure in her breasts. "I have to go. Will you stay with me and help me shield?"

"We will not be separated by any will of mine," he said, watching her, "but there are those who will resent it if we seem too close."

"No!" Faris gripped his sleeve, seeing her promised protection being torn from her. Caolin did not move, but the wind-tossed branches loosed a flood of sunlight that blinded her so that she could not see his face. Her need spoke. "No, I will not let you go!"

"Rosemary, let go of me!" Eric thrust her supporting arm aside. He took several careful steps toward the horselitter that had been braced up on logs to make a bed for him and sat down, and only the pallor around his mouth and a rapid pulse beating in his throat told Farin what it had cost him.

"You are tired—we're all tired. I only wanted to help you . . ." said Rosemary quietly, still standing where he had left her.

"By protecting me like a hen with one chick?" Eric snapped.

The image of Eric flapping downy wings set a bubble of laughter growing in Farin's throat and he turned away to stifle it. But Rosemary and Eric took no notice of him.

"Such help will make me an infant again! Go back to the baby, if that's what you want—I am not your child!"

"No, thank the Lady!" she retorted. "I wish your mother joy of you when you go from here to Bongarde! And I hope you go soon, before I regret that I gave you your life again!" Shaking, she whirled, stood a moment trying to control her features, then stalked away.

Farin took his hands from his ears, held there as if they could dull the impact of the shouted words. Eric was staring after Rosemary, his face almost as flushed as hers had been. Somewhere farther down the slope a flute twittered mockingly.

"Don't tell me I'm ungrateful—" said Eric, glaring at Farin as he had glared at the Elayans on the battlefield. "I'm going mad, always being cosseted and cared for."

"Did you have to be so harsh?" asked Farin peaceably, leaning against the madrone tree. "Rosemary was exhausted already and the ceremony was a strain for her. You may be getting well, but who will take care of her if she falls ill?"

Eric eased down on the bed, wincing just a little, and pulled a pillow beneath his arm. "Take care of Rosemary?" he repeated blankly.

Farin shook his head in disgust. *She loves you, and if your brains weren't made of granite you would have seen it long ago . . .*

A rabble of boys dashed past them, followed by an excited dog. "Badger, you come back here!" a woman called.

Farin, wondering if she was calling a boy or the dog, turned and saw it was Alessia of Las Costas.

"My lady!" he scrambled to his feet and bowed.

She stopped, recognized them, and after a moment's hesitation marched up to Eric.

"Sir Farin, my Lord Eric . . . do your wounds trouble you still?"

Eric grimaced. "I am only a little tired—"

"Don't try to get up, lad. You need not pretend with me— I nursed Brian often enough to tell when a man is in pain." She held herself upright as a maiden, but there was an etching of lines around her weary eyes, and bitterness had worn its grooves at the corners of her mouth. For a moment her glance held Eric's, then he sighed defeat and lay back again.

"They tell me you were wounded at my husband's side." Alessia said.

Eric's eyes did not falter now. "My lady, I brought two griefs from that field—that Lord Brian fell, and that we were friends for so short a time. I think . . . I fought him before because he was what I wanted to be . . ."

"I believe you." Alessia said softly. A muscle twitched in her cheek. "I am glad he had so good a companion." She looked around. "Badger, come here!"

One of the boys emerged from the tumult, and meeting his mother's glance, came slowly toward them. His steps hastened a little when he saw who waited there. He had his mother's auburn hair, but Brian's belligerent eye.

"My son—give Lord Eric your hand."

As Badger began to comply, Eric tugged free Brian's ring, put it into the boy's hand and closed his fingers around it. Badger looked at him in astonishment, but Alessia grew so white that Farin put out an arm to steady her.

"Badger, listen to me—" said Eric gravely. "When your grandmother died, your father went to King Jehan and swore to be loyal to him, and the King gave him this ring. Now the King is dead, like your father, but when that baby you saw named today is grown, he will be *your* King. Now your father knew it would be a long time before Star can give you a ring of your own. So Lord Brian told me to bring his ring to you. Will you swear to serve Star as your father did Jehan?"

"I swear it," said Badger clearly.

Eric swallowed and added, "Your father was a good lord to his people and the best fighter in Westria. Do not forget him. And when you are old enough to swing a sword, come to me if you wish, and I will show you how to use it . . . If your mother agrees," he added uncertainly. Badger was nodding with shining eyes.

"You do us honor—I know no one else so worthy to teach Brian's son!" Alessia's eyes were wet, but her voice was steady now.

"Mama, the ring is too big," said the boy. "You keep it— I shall lose it if I try to put it on."

Alessia bit her lip and held out her hand. "We will get a golden chain, darling, and hang it around your neck until you are grown."

A ball flew past them and Badger's eyes followed it, though he held himself still. "Go now and play—" Alessia told him. "I will stay and talk to Lord Eric for a while."

But for several minutes no one spoke at all. Farin's nostrils flared as the wind brought a scent of roasting meat their way and he wondered if he could leave to get something to eat.

"I hope you did not mind . . ." said Eric finally. "Lord Brian asked me to take the ring . . ."

"Mind?" Alessia's brows bent. "I wondered about it, but I supposed the ring had been on my lord's body when they burned—"she broke off and sat down on the edge of the bed as if her will were no longer quite sufficient to hold her upright. Wind rustled in the madrone leaves overhead, then passed on.

"They told me only that you found them, Sir Farin—" her

gaze returned to Eric. "But no one knew how it happened. Tell me how my lord died."

His eyes on the ground, his scarred hand clenching and unclenching in the blanket, Eric began to speak. Listening, Farin's mind peopled the barren battlefield with warriors. But they seemed distant now, their anguished faces ennobled by the sunset glow. Even the figure of Brian, scything his way through the ranks of his foes, was shadowed with tragic beauty by his approaching doom. *Not an epic but a lament . . .* thought Farin.

In the mists of the morning, Lord Brian stood proudly, but now in the darkness . . . He closed his eyes, searching for the line that teased him and the lift of the haunting melody.

"And then I saw him fall—" Eric finished, resting his forehead on his crossed arms. Mourning doves cooed in the madrone tree, lamenting the slow fall of the sun.

"Why cannot I believe it was only the chance of war?" said Alessia. "I know that even the greatest tree may be brought down. But the Seneschal sought my lord's death before . . ."

"What?" said Eric and Farin together. Eric sat up again.

For a moment Alessia frowned, then met their eyes. The westering sun kindled flames in her russet hair. "My lord swore silence to the King, but they are both dead now . . . I do not think that oath binds me. Last fall Caolin forged a letter to make King Jehan think Brian a traitor, then arrested and would have killed him but for the intervention of the King!"

The wind was blowing harder now, chilling the brightness of the afternoon. Farin ground the heels of his hands into his eyes to halt the tears and the rush of memories he thought he had locked away. *"That* was what he would not tell us! That was why he went out into the rain!"

"Farin, what is wrong?"

But now in the darkness . . . Farin's inner lament was halted by the spoken words. He looked up, saw through a haze of tears Jessica, and Robert looming behind her. Their eyes went anxiously from Farin to Eric and Alessia.

"Did you know that your brother took the fever that killed him going out to save my lord from Caolin's treachery?" asked Alessia in a tight voice.

"Lord Robert, did you ever learn who betrayed the plan that Caolin's Deputy persuaded you to follow? Did you know that Caolin had sworn Brian's death? Brian told me so," said Eric, croaking with the effort to keep his voice low.

Farin's heart began to pound, heavily, like a distant battle-drum.

"Brian and the Seneschal were always quarreling," said Robert, the worry lines deepening around his eyes. "The Lord of All knows what I would give to know what went wrong, but what proof have you that Caolin . . . I cannot believe—"

"What can't you believe, Lord Robert?" asked Caolin.

The hand of a traitor has stricken him down . . . Farin's throat closed. After a moment Eric's dropped jaw snapped shut. Caolin surveyed them all with a sardonic smile on his lips, but there was no smile in his grey eyes. The wind whipped his robes around him like a flame in the sunset light.

For a moment there was no sound but the rustle of the wind in leaves, as if the trees themselves were whispering tales of treachery. All of them stared at Caolin. Farin wondered if he looked as guilty as Eric, as defiant as Lady Alessia, then thought, *but* we *are not the guilty ones!*

Lord Robert was the first of them to stir, assuming the dignity of the Ramparts as if he had drawn their protection over him from three hundred miles away. Lady Jessica clung to his arm.

"I will believe nothing until I have proof before me, my Lord Seneschal," he said mildly. "I suggest you do the same."

Some of the menace went out of the air and Farin dared to breathe. But he felt the tension in Alessia, as if sparks would spit from the waves of her hair.

"I am not so moderate," she hissed. "You may think yourself secure with Brian gone, but his spirit cries out against you."

Caolin shook his head gently. "I pity your grief, my lady, but Prince Palomon's crossbows killed your husband, not I . . ."

"But your servant told them—"

Farin clutched at Eric to silence him, stepped in front of the bed as if his slim body could hide that of his friend.

"Is this by any chance a conspiracy?" There was an edge to Caolin's soft laugh.

Staring resolutely past him, Farin saw his sister approaching with the baby in her arms, followed by the Master of the Junipers and Rosemary. The world seemed to slow. He had an eternity in which to watch Faris' expression change, to hear her ask the inevitable question, to recognize his own dread.

"I think they do not like Jehan's choice of a Seneschal . . ." replied Caolin.

Farin winced as the Queen's terror lashed him, sensed the

desperate appeal with which she turned to Caolin and saw the gleam of triumph in the Seneschal's pale eyes as he smiled at her.

"Yes, I want him gone, and more than that!" cried Alessia. "I want him to pay for my husband's death!"

Faris turned on her—"And who will pay for the death of mine? Brian forced his way into Jehan's sickroom and after their quarrel Jehan fell sick again—Lord Brian deserved to die!"

"Faris!" Farin's protest was echoed by the Master of the Junipers, but Faris did not seem to hear them. Everyone was talking at once.

"But Faris," Eric's exclamation rose above the rest, "did half the army deserve death too? Would Jehan—"

She glared at him. "Do you think your scars give you the right to change Jehan's will?" Star had begun to whimper but Faris only held him more tightly.

"You are all trying to confuse me!" the Queen's gaze moved from Eric to Alessia and the others while she fought for breath. "Are you trying again to seize independence for the Provinces now that Jehan is gone? May the Jewels destroy me if I alter the disposition Jehan made of this land! Caolin is Seneschal, and a united kingdom is my son's heritage. I will defend them both if I have to replace every Lord Commander in Westria!"

The baby had begun to shriek protest at the unleashed emotions crackling around him. The rush of wind through the trees echoed the voices of the crowd that had been attracted by the argument.

"Faris! Be still!" The voice of the Master of the Junipers rasped across the clamor. "Accusations should be aired in Council, not in a public brawl. You cannot attack the Lords of the Provinces this way!"

Faris stared at him, awkwardly patting the baby, whose face was purpling with rage.

"My Lady—consider Star—" the Master said more gently. "Your anger is upsetting him." He held out his arms to take the child.

"No!" Faris stepped backward until she bumped into Caolin, whose crimson robes flared around her in the wind like a nimbus of flame. "Perhaps I cannot deal with the Provinces now, old man, but I can deal with you! They only want my kingdom, but you would steal my son! Jehan's will made no provision for you, and I think you have stayed here too long!"

Farin tried to reconcile his knowledge of his sister with the madwoman he saw. The Master's face was bared like a skull in which only his eyes lived.

"Faris . . ." his whisper was lost in the wind.

"I am your Queen," she shouted, "and I tell you to go!"

The light went out of his eyes. "Very well. I cannot stop your self-destruction. Only remember your own words when you despair and call out for me, for I shall not be here!" He spoke as if the wind had shaped itself to words.

"I will make my own mistakes, then, for I swear I will deny my own name before I see your face again!"

The Master turned away.

"So . . . the great adept of Awahna, the pride of the College of the Wise, is humbled at last!" Triumph blazed through Caolin's control.

The older man paused a moment, looking up at the Seneschal. His shoulders twitched the words away. Farin strained to hear his reply.

"You are alone now, Caolin . . . for your own sake be careful, and remember that Jehan loved you."

Silenced, Caolin looked down and the Master continued to walk away. Rosemary ran after him as his grey-brown robe blurred into the shadows under the trees.

Caolin put his arm around the Queen, stroking her hair. After a few moments she stilled and let him lead her away.

Farin felt his own strength leaving him and he clutched at the madrone tree. The light was fading, but the sky was still scarred with bands of fire.

"Robert, that man is dangerous," said Jessica firmly. "I know that Jehan trusted him, but he is dangerous now."

Lord Robert sighed, looking after the receding figures of Caolin and the Queen. "Perhaps, but without evidence, what can I do?"

"And if you *had* evidence?" asked Alessia.

"What do you mean?" asked Robert. Jessica took his arm, and as Alessia began to talk the three moved away.

Eric's trembling shook the framework of the bed. "Has Faris gone mad? How could she do that? How could she be like that?"

Farin shook his head. "I don't know . . . I don't know her anymore . . ." He sat down on the edge of the bed. "But I'm glad you are going home. Jessica is right—I'm the Queen's brother, which should protect me . . ." he paused, wondering if the woman who had banished the Master of the Junipers was still his sister in any sense that had meaning now. How cold the wind had become.

"Well, you and Robert and Alessia should be safe in your own Provinces . . ." he went on, "but I'm glad that Caolin didn't see Rosemary with us today."

"Rosemary?" Eric's hand tightened on Farin's arm.

"Caolin knows now that *we* are his enemies—" said Farin patiently. "If he could bring Brian down in the midst of his Army, what could he do to Rosemary alone in Laurelynn? We'll keep looking for evidence for Robert, and send word to you in Bongarde if we have any success."

Eric's eyes glittered in the shadows. "I'm going back with you to Laurelynn," he said abruptly, looking across the field. Farin saw Rosemary coming slowly toward them and bit back his reply. Perhaps something good might come out of the disaster of this day.

As he stood up a last ray of sunset slanted beneath a cloud and flared on the Jewels of Westria, still lying on the altar where the ceremony had been.

Caolin looked down at the four Jewels of Westria spread out upon his table, glittering in the candlelight. He had not realized that they would be so beautiful. For two days they had lain hidden in his saddlebags while he fought the desire to go and look at them and the fear that the Queen would open the redwood casket she had brought home from the Lady Mountain and find the pieces of common stone he had put inside.

But now he stood on the Red Mountain, and the Jewels gathered and returned to him all the light in the room. The stillness seemed to increase the weight of the darkness outside.

"*I* have the Jewels . . ." the candle flames bent to his whisper. Light stirred in the depths of the Earthstone like new leaves in a forest stirring in the sun as Caolin turned it back and forth between his long fingers. Deliberately, he laid his palm across the surface of the stone.

He felt a strange heaviness, and a prickling whose source he sought vainly until he realized that it was not a physical sensation at all. Scarcely daring to breathe, he set the Earthstone down.

At the College of the Wise, the other students had set messages for each other in the rocks of the path and discerned strange tales from twisted bits of metal left from the ancient times; but to Caolin they had only been metal scraps and stones. In the ceremonies they had used him to handle objects too charged with power for any of them to touch, as a man without nerves to sense pain might be asked to take a hot kettle from the stove.

Quickly he reached for the Sea Star, and felt a tremor in his own belly. For the second time power tickled the surface of his soul. Carefully he put the Sea Star on the table again and stepped back a little, staring hungrily at the Jewels.

"I can *feel* them!" His voice cracked on the words as his mind leaped inevitably to the question of what would happen if he put them on. The hairs lifted on the back of his neck and his skin chilled. *No—you are not their Master* . . . He remembered the apprehension in Jehan's face whenever he put them on. *They are too dangerous* . . . *keep them safe* . . . *keep them here* . . .

Caolin pulled the curtain aside and looked out. But the wind had drawn a cloak of cloud across the stars. He could hear it sighing across the mountainside as a man sighs for some forgotten loss. Where was the Master of the Junipers now?

He had feared him for so long, and in the end how easily he was rid of him! Caolin let the curtain fall, his eyes drawn back to the Jewels.

"Well, old man, what did you expect me to do? You have left the Jewels, and the Queen, and the kingdom in my hands!" He laughed. "Well, I will guard the Jewels—and the Queen? I think she is ready to come to me . . ."

He remembered how Faris had clung to him and tried to imagine embracing her, but his mind conjured only memories of Jehan kissing her, image flowing into image until he saw only the slow turn of the King's head, and an echo of old passions darkened his eyes.

I wanted Jehan . . . he answered the question Palomon had set him at last, *but he is gone, and the world is an empty house which I must furnish somehow* . . . All that remained of Jehan were his kingdom, his Queen, his power. By taking them, could he touch Jehan somehow?

"But they will try to stop me—that bitch Alessia and Robert and the rest—I must marry Faris so that I cannot be dismissed . . ." *And the Jewels?*

Their beauty teased him, but he shook his head. Yet perhaps

there was a way he could draw on their power now . . . His gaze moved to the door to his temple, that he had not opened for almost six months now.

Dead air flowed from the open door. The stale scent of the incense Caolin had used in his ritual set nightmares stirring in his brain, his barriers powerless against visions that came from within. He waited, trying not to breathe, until the candle he held burned steadily once more.

Then he gathered the Jewels in a cloth and took them inside, setting each on the altar of its own element, not pausing until his foot struck against the boar's head that still leaned against the altar of the Lady of Fire.

No . . . he shook his head, denying his memories, and set down the Jewel of Fire. But the glass eyes of the boar took fire from the candle flame and followed him. *You killed Jehan* . . .

"No!" Caolin shouted then, grasped the dead thing and stumbled through the other room and flung open the door, his muscles straining painfully as he cast the boar's head wheeling into the darkness to disappear somewhere on the slopes below.

Shaking, he collapsed into a chair. The door slammed behind him; his mind reverberated with that accusation, in Brian's voice, and in his own.

After a time Caolin forced himself to get up. The wind of his passage had blown the candles in the temple out, but the scattered glitter of gold and bronze from the Jewels on the altars reflected light from the other room. Carefully he locked the temple door. The wind had increased, rattling the catches of his windows as if it sought a way inside. Shivering, Caolin drew his blankets around him and lay down.

Jehan . . . *oh my dear lord* . . . *how simple things were when I only grieved because I could not find the road to Awahna, and you told me that you loved me* . . . He comforted himself by recreating that first encounter, and in the midst of his memory, slid into sleep.

He was walking in the forest with Jehan, all the past gone like some evil dream in the sweet interplay of speech and silence . . . Their voices soloed to the orchestra of whispering trees and distant waterfalls. Grey cliffs rose above the pillared pines, converging toward a blaze of azure sky that marked some wonder that the trees still hid.

"Are we going to Awahna now, my Lord?" he asked.

Light dawned in the King's face. "Caolin—I have always known what you desired."

But Caolin saw his shadow, suddenly, stretch black upon the path as changing hues of light streamed from behind him. When he turned, there were four brilliant figures beckoning— tree-brown, sea-blue, wind-silver, red as fire—their eyes were gems, their fingers shone with power.

In his ears, a whisper from Jehan—"Awahna holds the Jewels' reality . . ."

But Caolin had no will to move until they faded like a rainbow in the sun. Then he turned.

But then, Jehan was gone.

Caolin woke in the dim emptiness between night and day, his body shuddering with soundless sobs, for Jehan's face was still vivid before him, and now he remembered how much he had lost.

The Master of the Junipers stirred painfully. The fresh damp smell of the air told him that dawn was coming even with his eyes closed, but his muscles were stiff with sleep and the strain of the two days' swift walking it had taken him to leave the lands of men behind.

For the price of a blessing, a trader from Seahold had sailed him all the way to Rivered with his cargo of salted fish. Since then he had been afoot, pushing himself onward. But now he was in the mountains, and though the Lord Commander of the Ramparts was called their guardian, men did not rule here.

A bird called, three notes rising in a question and breaking off, as if she were afraid to wake the sleeping world.

Be still! the Master told himself. *This is why you came away. Be still and forget everything that is not here and now . . .*

He opened his eyes. A pale golden light was diffusing across the grey sky, like hope in a weary heart. He made himself get to his feet, shivering, and turned slowly clockwise, saluting the guardians of the four directions and lifting his arms to the lifegiving light of the sun as he had done every morning since he entered the College of the Wise. Then he began the danced meditation that balanced the body with the forces of the universe.

The Master's foot slipped on a loose stone and he came to a halt, gazing unseeing at the trees. *Has even this failed me now?*

First it had been a shadow between him and the Mistress

of the College. Now he understood why her leadership had faltered. How could she counsel the priests and priestesses of the College to teach and correct the people when she herself saw only emptiness at the heart of things?

It was hard enough to get through life without carrying other people's burdens, and in a world that no longer held holiness or glory it hardly mattered what one did. How many others in the College had followed her through loss of faith or laziness? How many others throughout the land? Was he the only one who had been deluded?

The Master sank to his knees, his hands digging into the earth. After awhile his sight cleared and he saw that his fingers were clenched around something green—a withered acorn out of which a seedling grew. He sat back on his heels, staring at it. *That is no delusion. It cannot know the dangers, yet still it seeks the sun.*

I was seeking Awahna. Like the seedling, despite all evidence, there is something in me that longs for the Light. Carefully he patted dirt around the little tree and moistened it from his waterskin. Then he bent to drink at the little stream near the place where he had lain down. In his pouch were a knife and flint and steel. He knew where things grew in this land that would keep life in him. For a while . . .

The Master straightened, gazing at the misty silhouettes of the hills emerging into the brightening day. Somewhere among them the road to Awahna lay. Logic told him that he would never get there.

But as he gazed upward he smiled, for the mountains were filled with light.

X

Dream—and Nightmare

Faris slipped toward wakefulness as Star stirred in the cradle beside her bed, her emerging awareness replaying the events of her dreams. She watched herself move through a richly colored world of animate forms whose meaning hovered on the edge of understanding.

The baby squeaked, then gathered his strength for a wail. Faris stretched out her hand to the cradle, setting it rocking as she sat up.

"There, my love—be still—I'll feed you soon!"

Her dreams still glowed in her memory. *I ought to tell Farin,* she thought, but he was not speaking to her these days. *I should write them down . . .*

She reached for a fresh diaper and bent to change the baby. When she was finished she opened the window, breathing deeply of the cool dawn air. Already the weather was warming, though it was not yet June. Too soon, the morning freshness would disappear.

But the damp air set her coughing—she had been very ill for the week after Star's naming, but she had hoped to be over that by now.

The baby, realising that his hunger was still unsatisfied, began to cry again. Faris carried him to the rocking chair, pulling down the loose neck of her nightgown to bare her breast. Her nipple hardened in the cool air and she sighed with pleasure as the baby's lips closed on it and her milk began to flow.

She held him close, stroking with wondering fingers the dark silk of his hair. A thrust of her foot set the chair to rocking. Vaguely she remembered that there had been a time when she had not loved him, as she remembered the quarrel after his naming—like a bad dream . . .

Softly she began to sing.

"Oh why are you fretting, my darling, my child?
Are you not yet to this world reconciled?
Lie still now and listen, for music is near
And the harping and piping will banish all fear . . ."

She should send for Farin, she thought. Star burped and let go of her breast and she shifted him to the other side.

"And are you yet waking? Upon Mama's breast
Lay your head, and her heartbeat will lull you to rest.
Your father will bear you to sleep's shining hall,
And there you may hear the best music of all."

Her voice faltered on the last verses but she forced herself to finish.

"My little one, *you* will never feel your father's arms around you unless you meet him in your dreams . . ." she whispered, blinking away tears. But Star had fallen asleep, his pink mouth a little open, tiny fingers clutching a fold of her gown. Gently she detached his hand and laid him back in his cradle, suddenly desperate for something to distract her from her memories. The dream . . . she should record it.

She looked around her for paper, saw only Jehan's Journal, which she had not opened since Star was born. There had been blank pages at the end. Faris had meant to tear out the empty pages, but seeing Jehan's writing again her movements slowed, a sentence caught her eye and she began to read.

. . . a lord must have more than courage. He must govern
with justice, judging himself no less rigorously than
the least of those he rules . . .

The words were written hesitantly, with much crossing out. But Faris recognized them, remembering how Jehan's voice had rung through the Hall when Eric was invested as Lord Commander.

He must act not from prejudice or even preference, but must
give the accused the benefit of the doubt until he traps

himself, and then pronounce what the wrongdoer himself has chosen for his doom . . .

The notes broke off, then, and after a little space she saw another line whose strokes were heavy and even as the calligraphy on a warrant of execution.

But who will judge me?

"Oh, my beloved," Faris said softly, "for what fancied sins did you blame yourself? And if you deserved censure, what of me? Our child will be my judge if I cannot preserve his heritage." She riffled back through the pages of the Journal as if seeking inspiration, but found only a carefully copied poem.

Fair as the lily flower, fairer than the dawn,
Thou, whose grace with beauty fills my days,
Fair as the springtide when winter's cold is gone,
Lady still grant me on thy sweet face to gaze . . .

Abruptly she closed the book, having no need to search her memory for the night when Jehan had sung her that song. After a few moments she turned to the mirror on her wall, examining her reflection. "Jehan is gone, but I am not. Am I still beautiful?"

The face that glimmered in the glass was no longer that of a girl, and yet it was not old despite the silver in her hair. Stripped of softness, the lines of her cheek and jaw seemed ageless. Faris thought—*I am a woman now,* and then, *will I live out my life alone? Do I want to?*

Jehan himself had told her not to mourn him too long, but where could she find a lover who would be worthy of his memory? Whom could she trust not to take advantage of her love?

Eric? No—she must not take him from Rosemary a second time.

Caolin? The thought teased her imagination. She could hardly imagine that cold man stirred by passion, and yet he had been kind to her. How astonished everyone would be . . .

No, she thought, some would be furious. Memories of the Naming Feast began to surface and she saw once more the anger in the eyes of Eric and Farin as they confronted the Seneschal. Why did they hate Caolin? Did they hate her too? Even the Master of the Junipers had deserted her. She had been ill and terrified that afternoon, surely he must have known that she had not meant him to go!

Star snorted softly and turned in his sleep. Faris sighed. "I can live without a lover, but not without love . . ." She touched the cradle gently, and as it began to rock the baby stilled. "My little Star—you are the only one whose love for me is sure!" She frowned. "Somehow Caolin and the others must learn to be friends again as we were when Jehan was alive."

Caolin's eyes moved quickly down the page.

. . . and so it would give me great pleasure to have you as guest for an evening of music on the last night of May . . .

The Queen's handwriting skimmed across the paper, the pen strokes light and apt to swirl unexpectedly.

Caolin folded the invitation carefully and set it on his desk, nodding to the messenger. "I will send her my answer."

"We were discussing the refortification of the Dragon's Claw . . ." Ercul Ashe reminded him. "You must authorize release of the supplies." Papers rustled in his thin hands as he began to list the resources that would be required.

Caolin thought of the elaborate language of the treaty Prince Palomon had signed, and the very simple promise on which he had given the Elayan lord his hand. A memory of candlelight warred with the sunshine spilling across his desk.

"I will authorize supplies, but not for the fortress—it is the road that must be repaired," he told his Deputy.

Ercul Ashe looked up. "So that they can attack us more easily next time?" Some emotion stirred beneath his still features like a hidden fish in a lake, but his voice was, as ever, neutral.

Caolin frowned. "Elaya will not attack. Both countries need the trade. Make up the list for me to sign." He listened absently as his Deputy's pen scratched across the paper, then opened the Queen's letter once more.

An evening of music in the warm night air . . . Would there be colored lanterns as there had been at the Feast of the First People almost a year ago? And would Faris lie down for him as she had for Jehan? He felt his flesh stir, remembering how the King's hands had moved upon her body. Faris was the Queen. Surely she would be something more than the other pieces of female flesh that had come from Jehan's bed to his own. He had touched no one for six months.

This woman had been Jehan's . . . Resolutely Caolin suppressed recollection of the dreams of the King that had haunted him since he had taken the Jewels. Surely they were no more than the results of his own self-doubt, now, when everything he had ever desired was coming to his hand like a hawk to her master's fist—the Jewels, the Queen, the land of Westria.

The door opened suddenly. Someone spoke from the shadows of the hall.

"How domestic! How refreshing to come in from the dusty streets and find you sitting cool and peaceful with your dog at your side!"

Caolin's hand moved automatically to cover the letter as he looked up. His eyes narrowed, but he relaxed as he recognized Ordrey, who booted the door shut and dropped into a chair. Ercul Ashe sniffed at the faintly alcoholic atmosphere that surrounded the other man, and continued to write.

"I did not expect you today," said the Seneschal. "Are you tired of your holiday?"

"No. But I would enjoy it more if people could forget the damned war . . ." Ordrey stepped over to the sideboard and poured wine into a goblet. He drained it in one swallow, filled it again and took it back to his chair.

"What happened?"

Ordrey shrugged, then glanced mockingly at Ercul Ashe. "I wouldn't visit the taverns for a while, dear colleague, if I were you . . . Do you know what stories they are telling about the battle of the Dragon Waste?" He sipped at his wine.

Ashe stopped writing and Caolin stilled, alerted by some tension in the way the Deputy gripped his pen. *Does he suspect how he was used?*

"You're not going to ask me how the gossip goes? You feel that the Lord Seneschal's chief Deputy has no need to fear the murmurings of lesser men?"

Ercul Ashe started to add a word to his list and his quill pen split, splattering ink across the page. He reached for another and began to trim it with precise, vicious strokes.

"Ordrey—" Caolin began a warning.

"People know who suggested that wonderful strategy to Lord Robert." Ordrey said kindly, avoiding Caolin's eyes. "I scarcely dare admit I'm acquainted with you, much less that I.

went with you on that ill-fated journey." The penknife jerked and half of the new quill drifted to the floor. Ercul Ashe sat, staring down at it. Ordrey began to laugh.

"Ordrey, be still!" Caolin's anger throbbed in the air. He held Ordrey's pale eyes until the flicker of amusement in their depths had died, waited until Ercul Ashe's dull gaze sought his as well. Ashe was a fool, but no one could learn anything from him. Ordrey, on the other hand, knew everything. Caolin wondered whether his loyalty would equal Ronald Sandreson's, if it came to questioning. Eric or Alessia would give much to learn what Ordrey knew.

"If you are frightened we must send you to safety . . ." said Caolin softly. "When Ercul manages to finish this list he is making, we will need a courier to take it to the border. You should be safe enough on the South Road!"

Ordrey began a theatrical grimace, then schooled his features, meeting Caolin's eyes. He set the goblet down.

"And what about me?" asked Ercul Ashe.

"You?" the Seneschal raised one pale eyebrow. "But you have nothing to conceal . . ."

"If Ordrey has nothing to conceal, why did Caolin send him away?" Eric pushed himself to his feet and took a step toward Farin and Rosemary. Concern flickered in the girl's eyes, but Eric had been out of bed for nearly three weeks now, since shortly after the Naming Ceremony.

"Perhaps they were both joking," she replied. "The man is Caolin's messenger—is it so strange that he should be sent off again? Surely Ordrey knows that nobody will harm him merely for serving as escort to Ercul Ashe!"

Eric crossed the room to Farin, who sat in his usual place on the window ledge. It was morning and sounds of carts and street merchants crying their wares drifted through the open window.

"No. Not for that—" said Farin slowly. "But there is *something* . . ." He closed his eyes, remembering the bewilderment in Ercul Ashe's face when the man had come to him that morning.

"For three days I have thought about it, Sir Farin, and I am convinced that Ordrey and my Lord Caolin were laughing at me. I lie awake and ask myself why?" Then the picture was replaced, as if he had turned a page in his memory. Farin

remembered Brian's camp, and a man laughing as Ashe struggled in his bonds.

"Ercul Ashe told no one but the Commanders what his idea was, before or after the Council of War," said Farin. "But I heard him say to Ordrey that Robert had accepted his plan. Dust can be sprinkled over a book . . . What if Caolin already knew about that strategy, and *Ordrey* betrayed it to Palomon?"

Farin looked up at his friends. Rosemary was frowning thoughtfully, but Eric's big hands closed and unclosed. *Caolin was wise to send Ordrey away* . . . thought Farin, watching him.

"Eric! You cannot go after him—not yet!" exclaimed Rosemary, who had been watching him too. She grasped his arm and abruptly let go again, coloring. "I'm sorry." She looked away. "I forget I'm not your nurse anymore."

Eric's hands stilled. A muscle twitched in his cheek as he looked down at her. "No. You are right. I cannot do anything until I am a man again . . ."

"Mousetraps and snares . . ." sang a hawker in the street below. "Live traps for every creature—mousetraps and snares . . ."

"*I* can go." Farin said into their silence. "We must find some real evidence, you know. Ercul Ashe will be watching his master now, but I doubt that Caolin will strew his floor with incriminating documents."

"But Ordrey knows you!" objected Rosemary.

"He knows the Queen's brother who plays the harp Swangold. But will he know a wandering bard who sings the common songs of the road? I'll darken my skin and pull a cap over my hair." Farin got down from the window ledge.

"I wanted to go in any case—I've another idea . . ." Two pairs of grey eyes turned to him expectantly. "With or without evidence it will be hard to move Lord Robert against the Seneschal while everyone is still praising him for winning that treaty from Elaya. We must turn the people against Caolin!"

"If you think you can do that, Farin, you grow as proud as he is!"

"What do you mean to do?" Eric sat down on his bed again.

"Well—" Farin flushed. "I have made a song. It's the song about Brian that you asked me for, Eric—" He took a deep breath and his light voice filled the room with a haunting melody.

"The sun rose like flame through the mists of the morning,
Below, men awaited the doom of the day,
And saw, stretched before them their foe's camp
  abandoned—
No life but the blackbirds and sparrows at play.

Oh where are the warriors, and where are the maidens,
And where is the hero who led them to war?
Their blood and their ashes now nourish the wasteland,
And the Lord of Las Costas will lead them no more."

"The rest is about the battle, and there's a verse telling how a hooded man carried the word to Palomon, and asking who sent him there . . ."

Eric whistled. "Even the Queen's brother won't be safe once Caolin hears that!"

"Well, I wasn't going to sing it in Laurelynn . . ." Farin colored again. "But if an anonymous harper starts it in the south, and if people like it . . . the traders will carry it across Westria before two weeks are gone!"

"There's one problem," said Rosemary. "If you are tramping the South Road you'll miss the party Faris has planned for next week. What will you tell her?"

"Will she even notice I am gone?" Farin answered bitterly, remembering how his sister had struggled in his arms and how Caolin had borne her away.

"Farin! You know that's not true. Faris wants to say she is sorry."

Farin shook his head. "No. You read her invitation. She wants everything to be the way it was before. But the King is gone. Brian is gone, and she herself sent the Master of the Junipers away. Do you think I can sit beside her without her picking up everything I feel?" His pulse was racing.

"Don't you think *I* feel—" began Eric, but Rosemary interrupted him.

"He's right. He and Faris are twins. It will be hard enough for you and me to barrier our thoughts from her! But Farin, be careful," she added. "I've heard stories about Ordrey . . ."

Farin avoided her eyes, remembering the whispers he too had heard. His long musician's fingers curled defensively into his palms.

"Yes. Well—you two enjoy the party, but watch out for Caolin!"

* * *

Little lanterns shone among the green plums in the trees by the edge of the lake, sparkling on silver and crystal and glowing on the rich clothing of the Queen's guests. A glitter of light edged the wavelets pulsing outward from the barges moored just offshore as the musicians settled into place.

Faris glanced nervously around the semi-circle of chairs and cushions arranged to face the lake. Across from her Lord Robert and Lady Jessica were talking softly to Elinor of Fairhaven, while Master Ras of Santierra spoke to the concertmaster, who had not yet joined his consort of musicians on the barge.

Caolin had taken a chair to her right and a little behind her. He was dressed simply but richly tonight, in a new linen robe of dull rose worked with silver.

Rosemary and Eric had not yet arrived.

One of the servers knelt before her, offering a tray of goblets that held chilled wine. Faris took one, smiling her thanks, and drank quickly. Branwen had already told her that Farin had left Laurelynn. Closing her eyes, Faris could still see the resentment in the girl's face, as if the Queen had driven him away. Her throat ached—Farin had not even come to her to say good-bye.

Were Eric and Rosemary going to stay away too?

Then Faris heard Jessica call out a greeting and sighed in relief as she saw Rosemary coming through the lamplit trees. Her blue gown billowed as she hurried forward. For once Rosemary had left her hair unbraided and it cascaded down her back like a river of gold. Faris smiled. Surely tonight Eric would look at Rosemary and find her fair.

Eric was coming more slowly behind her, leaning on a staff. His eyes followed Rosemary and he joined her on the other side of the semi-circle from Caolin.

Well—at least everyone was here.

Faris gathered the folds of her sleeveless over-robe and moved to face the company, the corded silver silk dragging behind her. The interlace of peach and plum blossoms that bordered it gleamed in the lamplight, matching the peach-colored gauze of her undergown.

"My Lords and Ladies—" Faris waited as the conversations stilled, stifling a need to cough. "I thank you for your company. I hope that you will find the refreshments and the music we have prepared for you equally enjoyable." She gestured, and the concertmaster raised his wand. The first strains of music drifted across the water as she sat down.

Flutes and horns and viols sang out each in turn, then joined their voices in interlacing strands of melody. The white-robed servers moved gracefully among the guests, offering them patés and pastries, sliced fruit or cheese and a selection of wines. Faris' taut nerves began to ease.

Rosemary watched the musicians, but Eric was watching Rosemary. Yet he sat a little apart, as if he were afraid to touch her. Faris could feel his longing, as she could feel Rosemary's wall of unhappiness. Perhaps that was why the girl did not realize that what she most desired was within her grasp.

Faris smiled to herself, feeling like a village matchmaker. *And what match would I make for myself?* she wondered then. Without turning her head she could see Caolin's profile. His eyes were closed, his features modeled by his abstraction to an unaccustomed purity. *Is that the true Caolin? The soul hidden behind his perpetual mask?*

The music concluded and applause broke the stillness like the wingclaps of startled birds. Another composition followed, then an intermission when the servers offered new delicacies. The guests got up and stretched, and walked back and forth along the edge of the lake.

"Your musicians play well, my Lady—" Master Ras of Santierra bent before Faris, then straightened, his dark face shining. "But I had hoped to see your brother tonight—I have heard much praise of his skill."

"He had a sore throat and dared not come," said Rosemary, glancing sidelong at Caolin.' Faris looked at her sharply—had Branwen been lying? But no—she could *feel* that Farin was far away. She turned to hide her hurt. Let them think she believed them.

"This evening is like something in a dream . . ." said Jessica, smiling kindly at Faris. "The air is so warm, and the lights on the water are so beautiful."

"I had an interesting dream a little while ago," said Faris brightly, seeking to fill the silence. The others turned to listen to her. Desperately she sought to recapture the vividness of the dreams she had recorded in the Journal.

"I was walking in a garden . . ." she began, "and with me went a horse, an eagle and a boar. Soon the horse galloped away, but the eagle rested on my shoulder and I fed it from my hand. Time passed, then the boar attacked the eagle and destroyed it. Then it and I were left alone together, and night fell . . ."

She looked at them helplessly. Perhaps Farin could have found words to recreate the fear and wonder of that dream, but she had not the power. There had been another dream that night, but what use would it be to try to recount it now?

"It has the ring of a prophecy—" said Lady Elinor. "Have you tried to interpret it?"

"Perhaps they could guess its meaning at the College of the Wise," said Lord Robert gravely.

"Perhaps," answered Faris. "I only dream . . . if any could tell me its meaning, I would reward him well." Suddenly embarrassed, she felt Caolin watching her and looked away.

Faris had feared that Caolin might quarrel with Eric or Rosemary, but everyone was keeping to generalities tonight, and if no one was swearing friendship, at least there was no hostility. Caolin had hardly spoken at all.

She fingered the milky opals in her silver necklace, her touch waking their rosy glow. *They are only gems . . .* she thought, *not the Jewel of Fire. Why does the air seem so warm?* She unclasped her over-robe and let it fall across the back of the chair. Her gown was cut low across her breasts, the full sleeves gathered at the wrists in the northern fashion instead of hanging free like those of the others. She envied the coolness of open sleeves—but if she had worn them they would have revealed her scar.

"Dreams can be strange indeed," said Master Ras. "Once I dreamed a mastersong, but when I woke I had no paper to record it, and after, I could never remember how it had gone. What about the rest of you?" He gestured around the circle. "What do you dream, my Lord Seneschal?"

Caolin lifted his head abruptly, something anguished momentarily revealed in his grey eyes. "I dream of the King . . ." he whispered before his gaze was shuttered once more.

Her heart wrenched, remembering her own dreams of Jehan, Faris signaled for the music to begin again. This time it was a group of singers from the Ramparts, miners who wove a close harmony around a melody as rhythmic as if it had been composed to hammer blows. Lord Robert put his arm around his wife and leaned back, smiling. Eric shifted uneasily on his cushions, as if pained by his wounds.

Branwen came through the trees with Star in her arms. Faris

felt her breasts throbbing in response to the sight of the baby and pulled down the neck of her gown to feed him. In a moment his fussing stilled.

"There, my son—" she whispered. "You will not starve. Mama will take care of you . . ." Her glance moved watchfully around the circle, where the music had stamped the faces of Caolin and the others alike with its own identity.

The singing ended. Jessica rose and came to Faris, bending to stroke Star's cheek. Then she smiled and folded her arms across her breasts.

"You remind me that it is time for me to feed my own little one. But I am glad we came. The evening provided a welcome interval of harmony."

"Thank you." Faris smiled back at her, once more astonished by Jessica's perception.

When they had gone the Queen called for the consort to play again. She finished feeding Star and gave him to Branwen to return to his bed. Then she whispered to the servers to leave the wine pitchers and go.

She refilled her goblet and drank again, her awareness expanding as the music went on. She could feel the pleasure of Lady Elinor and Master Ras, and Caolin seemed content. She glanced at the Seneschal's still features. *Do I really want him for a lover? Or do I only fear to remain alone?*

She bit her lip and focused on Rosemary, whose unhappiness was becoming steadily more apparent. The musicians were playing a popular song about unrequited love. When it was done, Faris signalled the musicians to be still.

"Rosemary—" she said swiftly, "we should let the players rest awhile. Do you remember how we used to sing together at the Hold?"

Her friend shook her head. *"You* have a lovely voice, but I have not sung for too long . . ."

"But I am afraid I will cough in the middle of the song," said Faris truthfully. "It must be a duet." She racked her memory for something suitable.

"Please, Rosemary, I would like to hear you sing," said Eric.

"You would?" Rosemary turned uncertainly to the Queen, her cheeks a little pinker than they had been. "What do you want to do?"

A fragment of melody surfaced. "The Parting Hymn that we learned at our Initiation and Nametaking," she said. Once more she saw the meadow at the foot of the Father of Mountains, and the ranks of young men and women flushed with pride in their newly chosen names. The hymn had seemed to express everything they had learned.

Rosemary nodded. "Very well. But your voice is higher, so you must begin."

Faris took a long swallow of wine, letting its sharpness quell her cough, and its warmth dissolve the last of her nervousness. Then she started, relaxing as Rosemary's warm contralto joined her in the second half of the line, then wove over and around her ascending melody.

> *"Lest we forget, our voices join in harmony*
> *Once more before we part, before we part.*
> *What we have shared will never fade in memory,*
> *But live in the eternal present of the heart."*

The tune shifted key in the middle so that the second verse started a note higher than the first.

> *"May your path be fair, yet in the chain of living,*
> *Men are no more than links, no less may be—*
> *Blame not the world, for no way but by giving*
> *Yourself to her rhythms, may you be truly free.*
> *Our tangled lives are no haphazard blending;*
> *Strangers, we neither meet nor part by chance.*
> *Fortunes which seemed to whirl us towards an ending*
> *But add another figure to the dance."*

Faris saw the others watching them and wondered, *In what pattern are our lives entwined now?* It seemed to her that Rosemary's voice faltered then, but she went on, soaring into the final verse of the song.

> *"Singly we sway, unbalanced passions sundering*
> *Our hearts, and yet we hope, when all is done,*
> *To find ourselves, where is no need for wondering,*
> *Poised in that Love wherein all loves are one."*

Rosemary stood up on the last line, fist to her mouth, staring at Faris. "How could you ask me to sing that—how could you, Faris, when you know . . ." she broke off on a sob, then gathered her skirts and ran off through the trees.

Eric struggled to his feet and stood staring after her, his face losing the little color it had held. Appalled, Faris went to him. "Eric!" she whispered urgently. "Do you love her?"

He looked down at her though nothing in his manner showed that he realized who was standing there. "Yes . . ." he said wonderingly. "Yes."

"Then in the Lady's name go after her!" Faris grasped his arm and pushed him in the direction Rosemary had gone. Faris sank into her chair, shaking her head, and reached for her wine. At least Rosemary would get her chance now. When she looked up again Lady Elinor and Ras of Santierra were standing before her, trying to hide their smiles.

"My Lady—now we must go as well. We thank you for your hospitality, and a most . . . entertaining . . . evening." Master Ras bent respectfully over her hand.

There was a silence when they had gone, broken only by a tentative croak from a frog in the reeds further down the shore, and the creaking of the barge.

"My Lady—" the concertmaster called across the water. "Will you be wanting us to play any more?"

"What?" Faris roused herself. "Oh—I am sorry. Of course you may go, and thank you. Your music was beautiful." She thanked them again when the rowboat had ferried singers, players and instruments to shore. Only a few of the little lamps remained alight now, like belated fireflies resting in the plum trees. The concertmaster bowed, then straightened, glancing uncertainly at Caolin, who was staring across the water.

"I would be happy to escort you back to the Palace, my Lady, if you will honor me . . ."

Faris smiled and shook her head. "There's no need. The Lord Seneschal will bear me company."

And then there were only herself and Caolin. The night was striking up its own music—the multi-voiced chorus of frogs, the tambourine of crickets in the grass, the humming of insects and the whirr of descending wings from those that hunted them.

The evening was over. Why then was she still sitting here with a sense of anti-climax souring her pleasure? She smoothed the silky gauze of her gown across her thighs, feeling the flesh beneath—the evening had been too warm for a petticoat. But had that been her only reason for choosing this gown?

She remembered what her mirror had shown her as she dressed for the evening—how the peach-colored gown had lent pink to her cheeks, how its soft folds had revealed the body beneath them . . . *I was going to be so fair he could not resist me,* she thought bitterly, *the one woman who would succeed where everyone else had failed.*

Caolin had not moved. His head was silhouetted against the starlit sky, his hands clenched in the folds of his robe. She considered the man—the pale silky hair cut short at the neck, his smooth skin and the lean height of him, like an image carved of marble and gold. Could these things attract her, who had known Jehan? Faris took a swift swallow of wine.

"I think that the evening went well . . ." she said aloud.

He turned to face her, the flickering shadows mocking her memory of his face. He spoke abruptly. "My Lady—did you know that I came here tonight intending to make love to you?"

For a moment she had no words. Her heart was thudding slowly, heavily. She pushed herself to her feet and took two steps toward him, standing where the remaining lamplight would reveal her body underneath the gown.

"Caolin . . ." she said softly. "My name is Faris."

His grey eyes focused on her, meeting her gaze fully for the first time. "Faris . . ." some of the tension seemed to go out of him with the breath. "Well, I will give you truth, Faris," he said as she tried to read his face. "I have loved no woman. I do not love you now."

Faris nodded. "I have loved only one man. But I think we need each other."

"I need you to maintain my position—" Caolin said bitterly, "to do the things Jehan left in my charge. I must be sure of you—do you understand?"

He was pleading with her. Faris shook her head in bewilderment. Did he want her to refuse him?

"I need your help to do as he bid *me,* and I do not want to be alone."

"But you were Jehan's!" he half turned away.

Faris sighed. "Do you think Jehan would disapprove?"

"No—I don't know!"

Must I do it all? The night had stilled around her, but suddenly Faris felt a surge of desire, and after a moment identified its source, as one might identify a fragment of melody, as Eric and Rosemary. She realized that she had dropped all her own barriers now. From Caolin she sensed faintly confusion and fear. Would he open himself if he made love to her?

"Caolin . . ." Faris reached out and took his hand.

He kissed her then, without gentleness. She had not expected his touch to bring her ecstasy, but she was grateful for his warmth and the security of strong arms around her at last.

After a little he released her. His face was intent, as if she were a problem he had to solve. He stroked her hair, then began to remove the pins, one by one, until the massed coils fell like shadow about her shoulders. Delicately, his finger traced the curve of her cheek, wandered over the smooth skin of her neck and across her breast, slipping beneath the edge of her gown and easing it over the curve of her shoulder.

Faris stilled, all her nerves flaring in response to a sequence which she had learned from Jehan. Abruptly she knew—*We have both loved only one man* . . . But she had no time to wonder, for Caolin was pulling her down on the carpets that had been laid over the grass, fumbling with his tunic and her gown. His body thrust against hers. Gasping, Faris lowered her hand to guide him and reached out with all the power of her mind for his, forcing her way through barriers weakened by his desire.

"Jehan!" She sensed his inner cry, and with the name something gave way in him like skin splitting along the line of an old scar. Caolin's body convulsed away from hers. Into her mind poured images—*a boar's head . . . the boar striking Jehan down . . . a woman who was and was not herself, whose flesh melted in a dark agony of fire* . . . Shrill laughter seared all the hidden places of her soul.

No—the laughter was Caolin's, crouched on his hands and knees above her while she whimpered and tried to curl away from him. His hand vised her shoulder. Faris shuddered with horror and pity, understanding now what he had done and how it had crippled him. The completeness of his former self-control was the measure of his violence now.

"You are the Dark Lady, come to torment me!" he cried. "I know you, Demoness—you were sent to destroy him, to destroy us both, but I know you now!"

Faris twisted and the thin stuff of her gown tore, freeing one arm. She struck out at him. "I am Faris—Faris the Queen."

He let go of her and sat back staring. His silence held her still.

"No—you cannot be the Queen," he said at last, "for you are flawed, and she was beautiful . . ." His voice had gone utterly without tone.

He has seen my scar! Her moment of comprehension was destroyed by her own hidden fears. Shivering, Faris tried to cover herself with the rags of her gown.

Caolin did not speak, and after a time she forced herself to look at him. He was still kneeling beside her, but the glow had gone from his eyes. Now, his gaze was that of a man who sees a serpent in his path.

"Caolin—" she whispered, but his voice absorbed hers as if he had not heard.

"You *must* serve me now." His calm was more terrible than his rage had been.

Faris sat up. "I am still Queen of Westria, however flawed," she said bitterly. "Have you gone mad, Caolin?" But of course he must be mad, after what he had done.

"Mad?" Caolin laughed gently. "You are the one who drove all your friends away—exiled the Master, earned your brother's hatred, drove Eric to another woman's arms. But it does not matter. I can compel you to do my will . . ."

He lifted his hand so that his ring of office caught the light of the last lamp. Faris stared at the ruby light. He moved it left and right, and her head turned. She understood what was happening now. He had done this to her before, and her will fluttered against his compulsion like a trapped butterfly. But his words resonated in her memory. She could not get free.

"You see?" Caolin laughed again. "Shall I make you walk naked through the streets of Laurelynn, displaying your scar? I have bent your will several times already, so that I could make peace with Palomon . . . you have no defense against me now."

His voice lowered, became more intimate. "Shall I order you to hold your son's arm in the fire? You *will* be mad, then . . ."

Faris stilled, her eyes fixed like a trapped rabbit's on Caolin's ring. In some untouched gulf of her mind her thoughts struggled desperately. *It is true . . . I must have consented or he could not hold me . . .*

She felt the invading pressure of Caolin's will forcing entry, as she had broken through his barriers moments before. She tried to scream as flames filled her inner vision, billowed around her. She heard a child shrieking in terror, saw fire lick at silken garments, fasten on the tender flesh beneath, as she had seen it when she was a child and again when Star was Named.

Lady of Fire, help me! She cast herself forward, beating the flames.

The last of the oil lamps went out.

The fire was gone, and the ruby spark that had held her eyes had disappeared. For a moment Faris blinked stupidly at the darkness. Then she scrambled to her feet and ran, blundering blindly among the trees.

Caolin's harsh laughter followed her. Without understanding she heard him say—"Are you afraid of me, Faris? You should be! I am the boar you saw in your dream! I destroyed Jehan!" He gasped for breath, then called again, "You will obey me, Faris, for the sake of your child!"

Sobbing soundlessly, clutching at the rags of her gown, Faris stumbled toward the Palace, pausing only to retch into the bushes beside the garden door. She pushed through it, then barred it behind her, shutting out the rasp of Caolin's laughter at last.

But she was already forcing herself up the stairs, though the breath seared her throat, not stopping until she reached Star's cradle. In the dim glow of the nightlight she could see the perfect curve of his cheek. His peaceful breathing was the only sound in the room.

Slowly the vision of his flesh blackening in the flames faded away. Faris' hands clenched as she fought the urge to clutch him to her breast. But if she touched him he would sense her agony and cry, and Branwen would come in and ask her what was wrong.

"No. No one must know . . ." Shuddering, she stripped the gems from her neck and ears, wrapped her chamberrobe around her, then locked the door to the adjoining room.

"I could accuse Caolin of rape—" The bruises where he had gripped her were beginning to throb. If it only had been rape! She had far rather have had him penetrate her body than this violation of her soul. Her stomach churned as she saw herself as he had pictured her—distorted and vile. *How could Jehan have loved me? How could he have made me Mistress of the Jewels?*

The Jewels!

Faris straightened, fire throbbing along her veins as she remembered their power. *Caolin called me the Dark Lady,* she thought, *now he shall see the Dark Lady indeed!* Unsteadily she went to her dressing room, and opened the redwood Jewel chest. She fumbled at the green silk covering of the Jewel of Fire.

There was only a chunk of serpentine.

Unbelieving, Faris snatched away the cloths that had wrapped the other Jewels, and found only stones. Had the Master of the Junipers taken them to be revenged on her? Or was it Caolin?

The room blurred. Her knees betrayed her, but Faris scarcely realized that she was falling. Her body grew rigid as her anguish exploded in a soundless scream.

In the Inn of the New Moon on the southern road, Farin woke suddenly, eyes straining to pierce the darkness, quivering with his sister's pain.

As the force of the call faded and the pounding of his heart eased, Farin thrust aside the cloak in which he had wrapped himself to sleep. He must return to Laurelynn.

Trying not to wake the other sleepers in the chamber, he picked up his pack and harpcase and started toward the door. He turned back to leave on his bed a few coins from the handful he had earned singing that evening, then opened the door carefully and went down the stairs.

Soon he was on the road to Laurelynn, shivering and searching the east for any sign of dawn.

The Master of the Junipers cried out in his sleep, then sat up, hands to his ears as if he could shut out the dreadful cry which his had echoed.

Faris! I must go to her!

Once more he seemed to see the tormented face with which she had sent him away, and he heard his own voice once more—*"Only remember your own words when you despair and call out for me, for I shall not be here . . ."*

He rested his face in his hands. He was days from Laurelynn. For good or ill, by the time he could reach Faris, whatever danger threatened her would be past. She needed help now. It had been a long time since he had asked anything from the Lord of Light. Did he dare pray for someone else? But he had abandoned care for his own life when he sought this wilderness. What happened to him did not matter now.

The Master composed his limbs for meditation, sent his spirit questing inward. He flinched at the drop into darkness, but he did not resist it now.

The abyss was measureless. After a time his own name was lost to him, and all memory of light as well, but still he held to the image of Faris. And then there came a moment when he was at rest. Warm darkness opened to receive him, and then at last he released consciousness of himself, and of her, and was free.

From the interaction of light and darkness the world is born . . .

The forest was beginning to emerge from shadow as light grew somewhere in the east of the world. The Master of the Junipers started, becoming aware of his own self-awareness, then he smiled.

Oh Mother of Darkness, help Faris now . . .

The darkness that had engulfed her lifted gradually. Faris forced herself to get up, shivering in her sweat-soaked robe. But her spirit hovered somewhere beyond the nausea and the cold and the fear, in a detached clarity in which mind and soul possessed an eternity in which to consider what she must do.

"I cannot let anyone know that the Jewels are gone—if the Master of the Junipers has them they will be safe, but Caolin would use my lack of care as more evidence of my madness . . ."

And he would be right, too, responded her inner commentator.

"And if Caolin has the Jewels . . ." For a moment she could not find words to express the consequences of that. In their brief traumatic touching of minds, she had seen enough to know that Caolin was now a sorcerer.

The Jewels tempted me to become the Lady of Darkness—to what would they tempt Caolin?

Faris shook her head. "I could take to my bed again, but how long could I refuse to see him? As soon as we met he would bind my will and I would be lost."

The Master of the Junipers warned you of this when he begged you to continue your training. You can barely barrier lesser minds, and Caolin may be even stronger than the Master!

"I wish I had died giving birth to Star—no one could have made use of me then!" The dark waters of the lake would give her rest.

And everyone would conclude you had gone mad from grief, and who would protect Star from Caolin?

No—whatever solution she found, it must protect Star and it must protect Westria. If her own survival were necessary to achieve these goals, then it would have to protect her as well.

Faris went back into her bedroom, needing to reassure herself that Star was still safe, then turned to the window. She shivered in the cool air, wondering how much time remained until dawn. She coughed and turned away.

"I have acted foolishly in the past, and who would believe my word against Caolin's? I must find a way to discredit him and prove my sanity!"

Suddenly Faris recalled Caolin's boast that he had destroyed the King. She forced her mind back to the events surrounding Jehan's death. She pushed damp strands of hair back from her face and reached for his Journal, seeking the final pages that she had never dared to read. The King had written a great deal after the boar had struck him down.

Oh my beloved! she thought, reading, *I saw you as a god— would you have been happier if you could have admitted to me that you were only a man?*

She went on, slowing as she reached Jehan's discovery of Caolin's treachery.

"Even then Caolin wanted power!" she exclaimed, her hands clenching on the book. "Sweet Lady! Why did Jehan leave me and the kingdom in that man's hands?"

She came to the last entry, whose writing wavered weakly, distorted by pain as if it had been written in the King's blood. *Because he loved him* . . . came the answer then. Faris re-read the words aloud.

> My watchers sleep. How long have I been wandering? No—it is the fever, now . . . Where are you, Caolin? I touched your soul—But you are still there, and your soul burns like a coal in the ashes.
>
> Fire burns veils from my eyes. I did not mean to give you the leavings of my love. I loved you and Faris differently. What could we three have done together if I had only understood in time?
>
> I will give you my power and my Queen—even set my land in the balance to redeem the harm I have done. You and Faris must save each other, Caolin!

When she had finished, Faris closed the book, for Jehan had written no more. Then she cast herself on her bed and wept at last, for Jehan, for herself, and for Caolin.

"I tried—my dear, I tried! I would have loved him, Jehan . . ." she whispered brokenly. "And now your agony binds me. How can I save Star and the kingdom without destroying Caolin?"

Outside a bird twittered then fell silent again. Soon others would wake to herald the sun, and the moment when her decision must be made.

"If I learned to use the powers the Master always said I had, Caolin could harm neither me nor the child," she said at last. "But even at the College of the Wise we would be vulnerable to him or to others who might wish to use us in a struggle for control. There is only one place where I could study in safety. Awahna . . ." The lamp flared as if the name had given it new life.

"I will go to Awahna and leave Caolin with no competitor. For his own sake he will guard Westria. But he must not be too secure, so I will tell no one where I have gone!"

She choked down laughter, began to search hastily for the things she would need. Rummaging through chests, she thrust her silken gowns aside, for she was not going as a Queen. She took the plain tunic she had worn at the College of the Wise to serve as shirt and petticoat, and an old skirt and worn boots and a brown shawl of Branwen's.

What else? She scooped chains and bangles from the gem chest to trade for food upon the road. In a separate compartment she found the King's ring. Kissing it, she hung it around her neck on the chain with the golden cross that Jehan had given her.

Faint sucking noises came from the cradle, then ceased as Star found his thumb, but that would not satisfy him long. Quickly she folded a rough blanket lengthwise on the bed, began packing it with diapers and baby gowns.

Star whimpered. Faris stopped her work and forced herself to calm as she sat down to nurse him, rocking him gently as her mind cast back and forth over what she had done. Would it be enough to disappear? Should she leave some kind of clue for those with eyes to see?

When the baby was done, Faris changed and dressed him and laid him back in his cradle, where he followed her movements with bright dark eyes. Night was fading now. Birds sang cheerfully in the orchard. She picked up Jehan's Journal and tore free the pages on which she had recorded her dreams. To the last one she added a single line—

"Caolin has shown me the meaning of my dreams."

She placed the papers on the table. Then she tied the blanket roll and slung it behind her, drew the shawl over her head, and looked in her mirror a final time. With her greying hair braided down her back and the coarse shawl shading her face, she looked like a peasant woman old before her time. No one would connect her with the fair young Queen of Westria of whom bards sang.

Then she tucked Star in his blanket, and went out, leaving the door ajar. The eastern sky was brightening to gold. Faris felt her heart lift, fancying she saw the light of Awahna shining before her. Nothing could hinder her now, for at last she was going where she wanted to be. She smiled, remembering how she had dreamed that she set a laurel seedling in her garden, then carried it east to escape a storm and replanted it in the mountains where it grew strong and tall. Though he might never know it, Caolin had shown her the meaning of her second dream as well.

The sun lifted over the rim of the Ramparts a hundred miles away, and Faris and her child passed unnoticed through the gates of Laurelynn.

XI

The Trial

"My Lord I am sorry, but the Queen cannot be found." The Captain of the Guard of Laurelynn bowed and took a step backward.

"You are sorry!" Caolin turned on him, "She must be *somewhere!* Are your men blind? Surely in one day and a half a woman carrying a child could not get far. Send men to search all of the main roads within a day's ride of Laurelynn, and all the by-ways as well!"

"Yes, my Lord." The guardsman's brick-colored uniform jerkin was already darkening with perspiration. "But we have searched already . . ." he began, then faltered as the Seneschal rose from his chair. "Yes, my Lord Seneschal—we will look again!" Sweating, he backed out of the room.

I must find her before she tells anyone . . . Though the afternoon heat throbbed in the room Caolin shivered, remembering how his memories had been drawn from him when Faris touched his body, and his soul.

"My Lord Seneschal, I have couriers waiting if the messages are prepared." Another man stood in the doorway.

Caolin looked inquiringly at Ercul Ashe, whose pen completed a flourish as he nodded, folded the paper and added it to the pile on his desk.

"They are ready," said the Deputy. "One for each of the Free Cities." He stood, absently massaging his writing hand, while the man clattered down the stairs. The offices around them throbbed with orders and speculations, while the city buzzed like an overturned hive whose queen has been removed. A thousand voices repeated a thousand variations on the same refrain—

The Lady Faris is not in Laurelynn . . . The Queen and her child have disappeared . . .

"Should I begin to draft the formal proclamation now, my Lord?" The cool voice of Ercul Ashe breached Caolin's abstraction.

"What? Oh yes—I suppose we must tell them something." The Seneschal ran his fingers distractedly through his hair. Where would Faris seek help?

Caolin straightened. "Find someone who knows the cabin of the Master of the Junipers on the Lady Mountain and send him to look there!"

The Deputy nodded and called to one of the clerks who was waiting in the hall. Caolin felt the office spin around him and realized that he had not eaten since the day before. He poured wine and raised the goblet to his lips, but he could not drink.

If she had left a note accusing me I would be in chains by now . . . Caolin grimaced. *Why didn't Faris accuse me? Does she think that uncertainty will make me betray myself?*

He closed his eyes, but he could not forget Faris' pinched face or the disfiguration of her arm. She was flawed, he reminded himself. She should never have been made Queen.

Did I sense that Jehan had suffered some contamination? He wondered suddenly. *Was that why I destroyed him? It was her fault, then . . .*

"They found nothing when they dragged the lake . . . no trace of the Queen in the City at all . . ." said Ercul Ashe, the faintest question in his tone. Caolin rested his head in his hands, ignoring him. Where was Faris? What more could he do to locate her?

He had sent a message pigeon to one of his agents in the south the previous evening, when someone had at last told him that Faris was gone. He hoped that it would reach Ordrey. Gerol was with him—until they returned he could not even set the great wolf on the Queen's trail!

"It is strange that the Queen should have run off this way . . ." Ercul Ashe spoke again. "But illness can unhinge the mind. Did she seem well, that night?"

Caolin slowly lifted his head, staring at the other man as Gerol would have considered a trapped hare. "The Queen was quite unharmed when she left me. I do not know where she has gone. And I never lie . . ." he replied in a still voice. All the frustrations of the past two days focused on the Deputy's curious face.

"I spent half the morning repeating this to Lord Robert of the Ramparts while he wrung his hands because he did not know what to do." Caolin's voice gained in volume as he leaned across the desk. "And now, little man, will you make yourself my questioner?" he roared, easing around the desk toward Ercul Ashe, who scuttled for the door, his composure shattered at last.

The Seneschal stopped short as the door slammed, leaning on the desk with rigid arms. Pain throbbed at the base of his skull. He started to lick dry lips and discovered that his mouth had been contorted in a snarl. He shook his head, trying to evade the pain. All his energy had focused on finding Faris. But what would happen when she was found?

I destroyed Jehan . . . I swore to serve Faris and the child as I had served the King . . . I never lie . . .

Caolin's head drooped until his fair hair brushed the top of the desk and he groaned, knowing that once he had found them his own oath bound him to kill both Faris and her child. But no one must ever know—his own survival, Westria's security, depended on forever concealing what had become of the lost Queen.

Faris pushed her way through the willow branches to the edge of the road, coughing in the red dust that billowed around her, watching the diminishing figure of the horseman who had raised it.

"They are still looking for us—" she told Star, hitching him up against her shoulder. She shivered inwardly, wondering what instructions Caolin had given his messengers. She had to get off the road, to find someplace where she did not need to fear each passer-by.

"We should look for a place to spend the night . . ." she said stoutly. "I had hoped that we could stay with some farmer, but it is not safe yet, so soon, and so close to the road." She sighed, looking around her.

The haze of dust lent substance to the long rays of rosy light that slanted across the Valley from the western hills. There was a red-gold sparkle from among the reeds to her right where the Darkwater meandered in its shallow bed. If she followed it a little longer she would come to the fork where the Mercy rushed down from the mountains to join it, and the beginning of the Pilgrim's Road. Then she would be safe.

But she was not there yet, and though a ride from a farmer had shortened today's journey, she was still weak from a year's soft living. She had awakened aching in every muscle after a night on the damp ground, and her cough was back again. Tonight she could hope for no more than some thicket that might shelter herself and her child from the dew.

Faris climbed down from the raised roadbed, and began to make her way across the fields. Her skirts swished softly against the golden stalks of wild oats whose grainheads were already ripe enough to catch in the rough cloth as she went by. She breathed in the aromatic scent of sun-cured hay and was reminded of the fields around her home. Slowly, something in Faris' spirit began to ease. The drowsy silence of the land filled her until, like the world around her, she was ready for the evening's rest. She thought that though she had known both ecstacy and great grief within the past year, since she had met Jehan she had not known peace.

The golden land stretched before her, glowing as if it had absorbed the light along with the heat of the sun. It was as she had seen it from the peak of the Father of Mountains a year ago. But then she had been looking down on the earth. Now she was a part of it, and this small part which she could see yet encompassed the whole.

For a moment she forgot to move, suspended in the stillness, awareness turned inward as she sought a knowledge that barely eluded her grasp.

Awahna . . . Awahna was there—if only . . .

And then Star nuzzled against her neck and the moment was gone.

"Oh my baby . . . we shall have to take the long way after all!" she whispered, her eyes blurring with tears.

It was then that she noticed before her the overgrown wheel-ruts of a road. Curious, she followed its windings towards a clump of Valley Oaks. They framed a small building of white-washed adobe, roofed with a motheaten thatching of reeds. But there were new patches of plaster on the walls. Someone still cared for the place, old though it was.

Cautiously, Faris opened the door. She blinked at darkness and a blaze of light which gradually resolved themselves into a shadowed entry and an alcove lit by a window that faced west. Her steps echoed on the worn tiles as she moved forward, trying to make out the hint of color on the farther wall.

Then the angle of the sun changed and the colors flared to life before her—a fresco showing a man, dressed simply in a robe of an adept, holding a staff as if he were a shepherd or a King. The artist had painted shadows behind him the better to display his aura of light. There were wounds in his hands and feet, and his eyes were like those of the Master of the Junipers. But his bearing was Jehan's.

Faris laid Star gently upon the low altar and bowed, for she recognized that she had come to a shrine of the Guardian of Men.

"Fair Lord, I thank you for this hospitality and ask your favor for my child . . ." she murmured, then stood silent until through closed eye-lids she felt the light fade with the setting of the sun and the Presence that had glowed within her awareness recede.

She straightened and carried Star to the other end of the little room, where she spread her blanket and left him while she gathered wood and cooked a simple meal of porridge and dried fruit. In the stillness of the night she dreamed that the Guardian had come down from the wall and was standing beside her, holding out his hand. He led her to an opening in the mountains where grey cliffs rose like pillars to an azure sky.

She had been there in her dreams, walking with Jehan.

But now the Master of the Junipers waited to welcome her. She ran toward him, laughing, *You see, I have found the way at last* . . . and opened her eyes to the golden light of dawn.

Sunlight filled Eric's chamber, but it was no brighter than the light in his eyes when he looked at Rosemary. Farin rested his forehead against the polished curve of his harp, repressing an urge to strike the happiness from those two glowing faces, as if they had no right to joy, with Faris gone.

"It's almost as if she knew something was going to happen to her—" said Rosemary softly, "and wanted to see us settled first . . ." Eric turned to her and lifted her hand to his lips.

"Faris is *not dead!*" said Farin. "Don't talk as if she were!"

Eric's face was troubled as he looked down at him. "Well, of course we all *want* to think she's alive—but the search has gone on for six fruitless days! How can you be so sure?"

Farin rested his chin on the harp and frowned. "There's something—a thread of awareness—between us. I felt her despair the night she disappeared. I would feel the pain of her death. Oh why did I go away?!" His fist struck the window sill beside him and he looked at it in surprise as the numbness gave way to pain.

Eric sighed. They had gone over all this too many times.

"She must have run away . . ." Farin continued after a little while. "She did that after our mother died." He sent a bitter glance at Branwen. "If you had given the alarm immediately—" he began.

"I didn't want to cause talk!" she exclaimed. "The Queen needed no more gossip about her odd ways . . . and when I found that Rosemary was not in *her* rooms I thought they had gone out together and forgotten to leave word!"

She looked reproachfully at Rosemary, who blushed and glanced self-consciously at Eric. Some detached part of Farin's awareness noted that he had been right to think love would make Rosemary beautiful. Even the flush of heat and the pearling of perspiration on her forehead did not diminish her new splendor.

He sighed, running his hand along the smooth curve of the harp. *But to me, Swangold is fairer still,* he thought. He had not believed that he could miss a mere instrument so much. Even if he had to paint over her gold to disguise her, when he took the road once more he would not leave her behind.

Farin stopped the thought, surprised to realize how naturally he assumed that he would be going away again. *Well, until I find Faris, there is no life for me in Laurelynn . . .*

He forced his attention back to the conversation.

"Caolin must know *something*—" exclaimed Branwen. "The concertmaster told me he left them alone together . . ."

"At Faris' request," answered Rosemary. "And the concertmaster would be quick to air any suspicions—he doesn't like the Seneschal."

They all jumped as a soft knocking rattled the door. Eric swung it wide, peering down the shadowed staircase. Farin stiffened as a shape materialized from the shadows—grey robe and greyer hair. He recognized Ercul Ashe.

The man eased into the room and looked behind him. "Is anybody there?" he asked anxiously. "I don't think I was seen."

"Why?" asked Farin, coming up to him and taking his arm. "Are you suspected?" His heart had begun to pound heavily in his breast. The Deputy had never been willing to come to him before.

"No . . . I am sure my lord is too distracted to think of me." Ashe sat down in the chair Eric offered him. "And yet—

I cannot tell *what* to be sure of anymore!"

"Is it the Queen?" asked Rosemary urgently, "Has Caolin—"

"What? No—I'd swear he is as desperate to find her as any of you. After all, his authority depends on his status as her minister."

Farin swallowed. "But you have learned something—" he asked softly, "something that we must know . . ."

"I think—" Ercul Ashe looked up at them with tormented eyes, and his voice became a thread of sound, "I think that my Lord Caolin has become a sorcerer!"

Farin repressed an urge to laugh. After all, *something* had frightened the little man.

"What has he done?" asked Eric, who did not seem to find it funny at all.

"Is it not sorcery to wear another shape than your own?" said Ercul Ashe.

Farin felt the hairs lift on his neck.

"He was angry with me for asking too many questions," the Deputy explained. "I thought he was going to strike me, and then it was not Caolin, but a wolf preparing to spring . . . I thought it was my imagination, then . . ."

"But not now?"

"No. Not since I remembered how people have mocked me, saying they saw me at times and in places I had no memory of. So I questioned them . . ." he forced out the words. "Now, I think that the Lord Caolin sometimes goes about in my shape instead of his own.

"He has *used* me! He has used my face and my reputation to serve his need without my knowledge or my will. I was only a convenience . . ." Lines etched in his face by years of dutiful service were dissolving under this strain.

Farin swallowed and looked away, not wanting to see the older man's shame. He wondered, *How would I feel if my lord had defiled my loyalty so?*

"But Master Ercul—why would he do that?" asked Eric at last.

The Deputy Seneschal sighed. "I can think of one reason. For a time I had meetings with an agent of Prince Palomon's— nothing treasonous—it was only to feed false information to Elaya!" he added, seeing the look on Eric's face.

"When war was declared my lord told me to stop going, and I was glad. But—" he looked around the circle of intent faces, "the keeper of the Inn of the Three Laurels tells me that I continued the meetings until after the peace talks, when Prince Palomon returned to Elaya!"

Eric was pacing back and forth like a caged mountain lion. "I always thought that Palomon's apology came too easily—" he observed harshly. "What do you suppose Caolin promised in return?"

"Unless we find written evidence we will never know," said Rosemary.

"And unless we can prove that Caolin is playing at sorcery, all the witnesses in Laurelynn can only swear that they have seen Ercul Ashe!" Farin objected.

Rosemary leaned against the window ledge, her bright hair backlit by the afternoon light. "I wish the Master of the Junipers were here. He would know what powers the Seneschal has . . ."

"What about the Mistress of the College?" offered Branwen. "When the Council meets in two weeks she will be here. Could she examine Caolin?"

"I hardly dare ask her—" said Rosemary, biting her lip, "and if Caolin has become so powerful, I wonder if she would succeed."

Farin moved away from them, feeling suddenly cold. Had Caolin used sorcery on Faris? He had imagined the Seneschal strangling her secretly and bundling her body into the lake . . . But what if mental violence had caused that anguished cry?

I would have protected her! he thought, and then, *But I was not here . . .*

"I must go—" said Ercul Ashe. "I am expected."

"You have done more than we could have hoped!" exclaimed Rosemary. "Be careful—you must not let Caolin suspect your change in loyalties."

The Deputy Seneschal got stiffly to his feet, drawing dignity around him. "My loyalties have not changed," he said simply. "I serve Westria."

Some impulse of responsibility drew Farin to accompany him down the stairs and watch him disappear into the crowd. As the young man turned to go in a man with the bearing of a soldier limped by, leaning on his companion's arm. They were singing—

> *"Alone with the ravens, a warrior lies wounded—*
> *He is shaking with fever, his blood stains the ground.*

> *He groans with the burden of farewells unspoken,*
> *Knowing not if by friend or by foe he'll be*
> *   found . . ."*

Farin's lament for Brian had come to Laurelynn.

Faris laid the back of her hand against her forehead, then readjusted her broadbrimmed hat against the sun. Did she have a fever? Her skin was hot and dry, but so was the air she breathed. Sun striking the rock cliffs to either side of the road made a furnace of the arroyo the Mercy had cut through the hills.

Her pony stumbled and Faris pulled him up with one hand, clutching automatically with the other at Star, who lay bound against her by her shawl. She had bought the beast, and her hat, at a holding near the town of Gateway with the last of her silver bangles, but though riding had eased her feet the animal walked no faster than she could, and its jolting gait made her ache in every bone.

But she had seen no searchers for several days. Had they forgotten her already? She coughed harshly and dug her heels into the pony's sides.

For four days she had followed the Pilgrim's Road through the billows of the foothills where the crimson of the earth overpowered the dull green of the occasional live-oaks or pines. But the mountains rose ahead of her now, ridge upon shadowed ridge of fir and spruce and pine.

Faris groped for the exaltation that had sustained her at the beginning of her journey, but it had been drained from her by the endless weary days. Now the road was climbing steadily while the gorge became deeper and the cliff fell away abruptly to where the Mercy frothed white over the rocks far below. The height brought a welcome breeze, but Faris' head still ached dully, and she blinked at the glare. She looked down, and dizzied, closed her eyes again.

If I were to fall no one would see. No one would ever know what had become of me . . . Faris shivered then and hoped it was from fear. Star squirmed and protested, and she forced herself to loosen her grip on him.

"I cannot be ill! I must not—not now! What would happen to you?" she cried. "I have been traveling too hard, that is all. I have been on the road for almost two weeks. I should find somewhere to rest. Awahna cannot be so very far away!"

But the thin air of the mountains seared her lungs, and the road wound onward to the end of the world.

"The Lord of All be thanked that the testimony is over—I thought they would be thinking up new excuses for not finding Faris till the end of the age!" Rosemary leaned back against the painted pillar that supported the porch of the Council Hall and sighed.

"I am thanking the Lord for you, Rosemary!" said Eric seriously. "If you had not asked your father to suggest a noon recess, Caolin might be Regent by now. Of course Lady Alessia and I would have voted against him, but I don't know about the others. He made it sound like such a *reasonable* suggestion . . ."

Rosemary laughed. Farin hoisted himself up on the railing and sat kicking his heels against the rungs. The rose-colored bricks of Laurelynn looked faded in the noon glare. It had been three weeks since Faris disappeared.

"This afternoon's debate will decide it for good," he said slowly. Too vividly, he remembered how the Seneschal had looked, with his fair hair cut precisely to skim the little up-standing collar of his loose linen robe. He had not seemed to notice the heat, thought Farin, feeling perspiration make a rivulet down his back.

"I think that Caolin has made a mistake," said Rosemary. "Given time to think about it, people who tolerated him as Seneschal may not want to see him on the Regent's throne."

"I hope so," answered Farin. Men and women were still coming out of the Council Hall, talking excitedly. Farin fanned himself with his loose sleeve, wishing the clouds banked in the west would cut off the sun, or build up to a storm—anything to break the tension that had been building all day.

"But can a Regent function without Caolin? *I* would not want the job!" exclaimed Eric, running his fingers through his tumbled hair.

"We expected Faris to do that job," Farin said bitterly, "and to bear her grief for Jehan as she bore his child." He felt suddenly chilled and alone. *Oh my sister . . . will you ever forgive me for deserting you?*

"There's always Robert . . ." muttered Eric. "He might do it if there were no other acceptable choice, and if someone testified against Caolin. Oh, I know I promised not to call on Ercul Ashe unless I could protect him from his master," he answered Rosemary's worried frown, "but if Caolin remains in power I cannot help his Deputy, and without the little man's evidence how can we break the Seneschal's power?"

"*We* may not have to . . . look!" Farin pointed to a slash of crimson that wove through the multi-colored tapestry of the crowd—Caolin and his staff crossing the courtyard to the Chancery. But people were edging away from them. Farin could feel their suspicion, their curiosity. Someone cried out, "Remember the Dragon Waste!" Then they heard a snatch of song that strengthened until the words of the chorus came clear.

> "Oh where is our Lady, who once walked in beauty?
> And where is the Star who brought hope to our sky?
> Oh ask the red spider who spins in the City—
> With so many secrets, perhaps he knows why . . ."

Farin saw Caolin stop and stare around him until he in turn recognized the group on the porch. Farin clutched at Eric's arm, shaken by the malice in the Seneschal's eyes.

"It's not fair—" he breathed between fear and laughter. "I didn't even write that verse to the song . . ."

The people fell silent, watching Caolin pass, remote and lordly, seeming equally oblivious of their praise or blame.

"What would they do if they thought he might become Regent over them?" asked Eric, frowning.

Farin bit his lip. His stomach was bitter with the knowledge that the journey which had cost him his chance to help Faris had not even bought anonymity. Not that it mattered anymore . . . The place in his soul that had been empty since the death of the King was filling now with hatred for Caolin.

Fragments of new verses began to surface in his mind and the world steadied around him. "I will tell them," he said, smiling thinly. "And I think that Caolin may soon be very sorry he asked for that job."

"No—you must not."

Farin looked around and realized that Branwen had joined them. He wondered how long she had been there.

Her tone sharpened. "You know that the Seneschal never forgets an injury. Let someone else bring him down!"

Farin swallowed. Branwen had grasped his arm and he was uncomfortably aware of her body. He could not help but remember the night before the boar hunt when he had lain with her. But that did not explain the terror in her eyes.

"Somebody must try," he spoke as gently as he could. "Would you rather that Caolin's anger fell on *them?*" He gestured toward Eric and Rosemary.

"Yes!" hissed the girl. Her blush had paled and every blemish showed on her sallow skin.

Farin pulled his arm from her grip, understanding now why he had been avoiding her. Her desire stifled him, heavier than the humid air. She not only wanted his body, she wanted *him*.

"I will be safe enough. I am leaving Laurelynn to search for my sister as soon as this Council is done."

Spots of color flared on Branwen's cheeks. "I thought I had only your harp to compete with. I should have known that my real rival was the Queen."

"You had what you wanted—" Farin replied furiously. "And that was as much as any woman will get from me!"

His hatred for Caolin, his guilt for having failed Faris, his love for the golden harp, merged in a single moment of vision in which his future stretched before him like a fair white road. Thrusting Branwen away, Farin jumped down from the porch and began to push through the crowd.

The people of Westria moved to let him pass, whispering his name. Farin began to smile, memory of his quarrel already fading. For the crowds would still be waiting when he returned with his harp—waiting for him to move them to his will as he played for them.

Caolin considered the councilors of Westria enthroned on the eight sides of the Council floor, and the representatives of their Estates who sat on the rising benches behind them.

How shall I move them? he wondered. *How shall I shape them to my will?* He rose with the others as the great horn was blown and the Council declared to be in session once more.

Now . . . he thought, feeling his mouth dry and the blood tingle in his veins. Was this how Jehan or Brian had felt, facing their foes across a battlefield?

"This morning we discussed mounting a search for the Queen that would cover the entire kingdom," said Caolin. "Since this must affect all of your territories, I would like to request the Council's authorization." He looked at them inquiringly. *And when they find her?* He shied from memory of the orders he had given Ordrey.

"I thought that this morning we were discussing the Regency, my Lord Seneschal," Alessia observed tartly. Her basilisk eyes glittered beneath the dark fires of her hair. "There is still a motion to be voted on."

Caolin suppressed a sigh. He had hoped to distract them from that, since his move to gain power in name as well as in deed had failed. He shrugged deprecatingly. "It was proposed as a matter of convenience. But it was my understanding that the Council felt it too soon to consider such a move."

"Yes, surely it is too soon," said Lord Robert eagerly, looking up from his study of the polished slates on the floor. "It is barely three weeks since the Queen . . . went away."

Caolin sniffed. If Robert was his competitor for the Regency he was certainly not enjoying the prospect. In the silence Caolin caught the sound of singing from outside the Hall. His glance went to the bench behind the Queen's throne from which Sir Farin had glowered at him for the past three days. The young fool! He should have taken steps to silence him . . .

Now Lord Eric was on his feet, looking to Rosemary for reassurance as he cleared his throat. "My Lords and Ladies of Westria—at the final Council of our King, Jehan named the Lady Faris as Regent for their child. But he added that if anything should go amiss, we must decide for the future ourselves."

Jehan! Caolin's glance fled to the shaft of brilliance that fell from the skylight of the Council Hall to the empty hearth on the floor, but he saw only the light of midwinter illuminating the worn beauty of Jehan's face. *Oh my dear Lord . . . why did you leave me alone?*

"This kingdom must have a leader who is chosen by law, not by default. Let us decide now!" Eric cried.

Caolin began to frown, but Frederic Sachs was on his feet almost before Eric had sat down, and the Seneschal relaxed again. A judicious combination of flattery and fear had made the man his servant long ago.

"You were the Queen's champion, my young Lord—do you now fancy the mantle of the King?"

Eric reddened. There was a spurt of malicious laughter from some in the crowd as Sachs went on. "Surely our Lord Seneschal, who has borne the weight of the kingdom since the King died, is best fitted to wield this power. Let him be confirmed in it!"

Sachs looked to Caolin for approval and the Seneschal tried to smile. But he realized that there was no way to avoid debating the Regency now. He winced inwardly as Lady Alessia took the floor.

"My fellow Councillors, I have felt closer to the Queen than any of you can understand, now that I guard my own son's heritage. But for that reason I can afford no sentiment. You see the empty places here which last year held so many good men." She gestured around the Hall at the gaps on the benches.

"Do you of the cities wish to take their places, as you accuse Lord Eric of wanting another's power? I do not believe so—" said Alessia, "I believe we were all equally grieved by the battle in which my lord was slain. Now we are weakened and when Elaya attacks us again we will need a warrior at our head."

Eric stood again. "The Guardian of Men knows that I have no desire for *anything* that was the King's!" he stammered, his eyes on Rosemary. "I would not take the Regency if you offered it to me. But I agree with the Lady of Las Costas. I would willingly follow my Lord Theodor, who is senior among us, or Lord Robert, who was our Commander in the war."

"A Commander who let half his army be slain?" shouted someone.

"Through following a plan suggested by Caolin's Deputy!" snapped Alessia.

Caolin felt movement behind him, but knew he must not turn.

"I didn't know . . . I didn't know . . ."

The Seneschal stiffened, recognizing the voice of Ercul Ashe.

"Be still, man," whispered one of his companions. "No one has accused you."

"No. I am lost . . ."

Caolin's hands clenched. The hysterical fool! Swiftly he cast back, trying to remember whether Ashe knew anything that might be damaging. The Deputy had been a clerk in the Office of the Seneschal when he himself took service there. For years he had been Caolin's most trusted assistant. No one must question him!

"Nay, my Lady—I accepted the plan," said Robert heavily. "The responsibility is mine. Yet Lord Eric spoke well. I will give my allegiance to my Lord of the Corona, if he will take the job."

Forgetting Ercul Ashe, Caolin leaned forward. It was coming now, for surely no one would choose a man who needed a staff to rise from his chair!

Theodor straightened in his seat as if his dead youth were returning to him. After a moment he smiled.

"I am grateful for your confidence, but even if the Council should offer it, I must not take this role. Last year Brian spoke of the dangers of having a lord who knew only some of his lands. I opposed his solution to that problem, but his analysis does apply to me," he sighed. "The Corona is so far from the kingdom's center that I could not serve as Regent without neglecting it. And I have passed the best of my fighting days. You will need a younger man to lead you—a man who continues to struggle even in the face of defeat because that is where his duty lies."

Lord Theodor levered himself to his feet. His eyes lingered for a moment on the empty thrones of the King and Queen of Westria, then he turned. "I propose to you, therefore, that Lord Robert of the Ramparts be made Regent of this kingdom until such time as we find the Queen or her son."

There was a tense silence when he was done. Caolin stared at dust motes whirling in the sunlight, thinking furiously. Who would have believed the old man could refuse? Now Robert would be forced to agree—already he sat with his head bowed beneath the weight of his approaching responsibility.

Who could trust so unwilling a candidate? wondered Caolin. *Is it so wrong for me to want the power? I could use it so well for Westria!*

The other members of the Council and their followers were watching him, now, in a stillness that extended even to the crowd outside. Caolin nodded.

"I believe that it is now my duty to call for a vote." He was a little surprised that his voice should be so even. As he looked from face to face, he wished he could have just a few moments alone with each of them before their choice was made. With his knowledge, and perhaps the help of the dark fire in his ring, surely he could compel support from them! But numbers protected them now.

"Is it the will of this Council that a new Regent for Westria be chosen at this time? And if so, who shall this Regent be?" Caolin took a deep breath and turned to the Lady Alessia, on his left.

"I vote to make Lord Robert Regent now," she said flatly.

Well, the Seneschal had expected that. "Master Sachs?" he asked.

"The Free Cities choose the Lord Caolin."

"My Lord Eric?"

"Robert was my Commander—I'll serve him again," said Eric quickly.

Caolin's eyes slid past the King's empty chair directly across the Council floor from his own, and he bowed to Lord Theodor. "As you made this proposal I assume that you vote for Robert?" he asked ironically, and hated Theodor when the old man nodded and smiled.

"And the College?" Caolin's heart began to pound as he considered the dark, ambiguous face of its Mistress. She, alone of that company, might have been able to compel truth from him. She was looking at him now with a detachment that was almost sorrow.

"The College of the Wise chooses the Lord of the Ramparts."

Because you can rule him as you will never rule me? Caolin bit back the words, turned to Lord Robert last of all.

"And you, my Lord—will you vote for yourself?" he asked gently.

"How can I feel worthy of this task?" Robert exclaimed. "Let me abstain!"

"How embarrassing . . ." said Caolin, striving to hide the hope that struggled for birth. *Perhaps, even now . . .*

He went on, "I must agree with you. And I think that when the Queen is found she will not be happy to learn that her office was usurped so soon. I vote to delay this decision until another time."

"The tally is three 'ayes', two 'nays' and one abstention," said the clerk. Comment rustled through the Hall like wind in the trees.

"Not much of a majority," murmured Caolin.

"Robert, you must change your mind!" cried Eric. "Listen to the people!"

Subconsciously Caolin had been aware of a mutter like that of an approaching storm. But it was voices, not thunder, whose confusion was settling to a rhythm, a chant . . . Lord Robert's name. In a moment everyone in the Hall was echoing it.

After Caolin had made Palomon sign the peace treaty they

had cheered *him*. *Well*, he thought with a remnant of self-mockery, *Palomon's concessions were as hollow as Robert's victory*. He watched the play of expression on his rival's face—alarm giving way to the grim resignation of a man who turns at last to face his foe.

Robert would not refuse election now. Caolin had but a moment to salvage his plans . . .

"Very well," said the Lord of the Ramparts at last. "I will do it, and may the Guardians of Westria help us all."

"The vote is four 'ayes' to two 'nays,'" said the clerk. "Lord Robert is chosen Regent of Westria."

Before anyone else could move Caolin strode toward Lord Robert. He needed only to convince one person now.

"My Lord Regent! So that there may be no doubt of your election, I do now pledge you my loyalty before the Council and people of Westria!" He moved into the shaft of sunlight, willing them all to see his sincerity.

"For fifteen years I served the King, and I know the weariness of the man who sits *there* . . ." he pointed at the empty throne. "It will not be lighter for Lord Robert because he bears only the staff and not the crown. In all the world there is no land like Westria, where there is such good ground for all the arts of peace to grow!" Caolin turned, addressing each sector. He was a little surprised to realize that he was trembling, for what he was saying was true.

"Our neighbors envy our wealth and our golden fields. And yet there are things here that cannot be defended with the point of a sword . . ." He stared at Eric, wondering if he could understand. Carefully he began to delineate the delicate networks that interwove to form the fabric of Westria, and the precise management that was necessary to balance them.

"Some of this you know, my Lord, for you have ruled a portion of the land—" he turned to Robert again, "but you will have much to learn." He bowed his head. "I think that the decision of this Council is therefore a wise one, for it leaves two to bear the burden which might have borne one down. That is why I offer you my service, my Lord!" He met Lord Robert's tear-bright eyes and forebore to add, *as I gave it to the King*.

Then he waited, schooling his face to show no sign of triumph, while Robert rose and held out his hand. "Caolin . . ."

"No!" shrieked Alessia. "You cannot confirm him, Robert—he is Brian's murderer!"

"No!" came an echo, and Caolin saw Farin standing in the doorway with his harp glittering balefully in his arms. "Faris fled from him in fear!"

"No!" Eric found his voice. "He has betrayed us to Palomon!"

Truth! The accusations struck Caolin as Palomon's arrows had struck Brian. *But there was no proof for them!* Shaking with fear and fury, he looked at Robert in appeal.

The new Regent strode past him onto the polished floor, shouting for silence in a voice that would have carried across a battlefield. It shook the Council Hall, and stilled the ominous humming of the crowd that had followed Farin.

"Those are grave accusations! You have chosen me to lead you, and so I tell you—substantiate them now or be still!" Robert stared. "Well?"

"My Lord was proud and sometimes prejudiced," Alessia spoke in a low voice, "but he did not lie. He told me that Caolin had forged a letter to make the King think him a traitor, and when the Seneschal's men would have murdered him, to save him Jehan went out into the rain and so caught the fever of which he died. And later, before the battle, Caolin swore to Brian that he would contrive his death."

"My Lord Regent, will you believe the ravings of a woman mad with grief?" hissed Caolin. Farin stepped farther into the Hall, and Caolin realized who had been leading the mob outside. Robert turned his anxious gaze on him.

"My sister and I are linked in mind, and the night she disappeared her terror awakened me!" Farin said simply.

"Are you sure you were not awakened by jealousy?" Caolin began.

"But the Seneschal was the last one to see the Queen," interrupted Rosemary. "In the morning there was only the note that said, 'Caolin has shown me the meaning of my dreams . . .' Faris was gone!"

The light that shafted through the windows seemed to have turned to fire. Caolin turned to Rosemary. "And where were you when all this was going on?" he asked silkily. "Why don't you tell us what you and the noble Lord Eric were doing in the bushes while the Queen suffered whatever befell her, alone." He ignored Eric's protests.

"You tell a fine tale to excuse your negligence, but several days' of testimony have proven that it was the Queen's desire to stay with me. By the Lady of Fire, my Lords, why should

I harm her? If Faris were here now you would not dare to deal with me so!"

"Lady Rosemary is my promised wife!" Eric exploded. "Anyone who accuses her of . . . of anything, will answer to me!"

"First you must support your own accusation. I believe . . ." said Robert distastefully. "Can you prove what *you* say?"

Eric exchanged glances with Farin. "I have a witness," he replied, "but I will not ask him to speak unless his safety is guaranteed."

Caolin stiffened. A witness? Witness to what?

Lord Robert frowned. "Very well, he has my protection . . . if he is here . . ."

"I am here . . ." The reply was faint, but Caolin heard it. Others heard too. The Seneschal followed their stares to his own sector of the Hall and saw, white as cheese and shaking like an aspen leaf—Ercul Ashe.

"No! You are mine! Who brought you to this treachery!" Caolin dared not move, for how could he even trust the ground to bear him, now?

"You did, my Lord Seneschal," said the Deputy, steadying. It seemed to Caolin that he was seeing him for the first time, a fragile ugly man who stood as if his spine were steel.

There was no sound as Ercul Ashe came down from the Seneschals' benches to face the Regent of Westria.

"Lord Caolin is a sorcerer who binds men's wills and blinds their eyes," said the Deputy. "I know an innkeeper who will swear that on an evening when I was in my chamber, someone who wore my shape came to his tavern to meet with Palomon's spy!"

"You are so terrified of being charged with betrayal of the plan for the battle of the Dragon Waste that you turn on me!" Caolin fought to keep his voice low, though a roar of outrage was building that threatened to drown out anything he might say. "You would have done better to trust to my protection, Ercul Ashe. *You* suggested the meetings, *you* were the only one who visited Hakim MacMorann, and what proof can *you* offer regarding what *you* said to him?"

Caolin turned quickly to Lord Robert. "My Lord Regent—" he said wryly, the tone of one adult to another. "Is this all the proof that can be set against fifteen years of service to Westria?

It is insufficient even to bring a case in a court of law!" He stared at the other man, willing his belief, for the fire that had filled the air ran in his blood now, demanding release.

Robert looked at the tumult around them, biting his lip. His face seemed suddenly as grey as his hair.

"You are right . . . there is no proof that can bring you to trial, Caolin," Robert said painfully. "But with the welfare of the kingdom on my shoulders, how can I let you remain in the office you now hold?" He gestured toward the ranks of hostile faces. *"They* will never trust you now, and if I upheld you they would not trust me!"

"No." Caolin shook his head. "You need me too much . . ."

"Caolin, I *must* dismiss you now . . ." Robert was pleading.

The Seneschal stared around him. "And do *all* of you agree?" The air throbbed with dark fire. As the silence grew he looked at them, marking his enemies.

Ercul Ashe, who had betrayed him. Alessia . . . Eric and Rosemary and her old father . . . the Mistress of the College and Frederic Sachs and the rest. He was shaken for a moment by the hatred in Farin's face, the image merging sickeningly with his memory of Faris struggling in his arms. And then he saw the Dark Lady he had embraced on the Red Mountain, and he knew that he was free to use Her power now.

He pulled the chain of office from his neck and flung it to the floor in a clashing of soft gold. "I would have served you to my life's end, but you yourselves have written the fate that will come to you now." With an effort he fought the desire to tell them he held the Jewels of Westria. He had warned them—when they saw their destruction approaching they would know from whom it came.

"You will go then?" asked Robert wonderingly.

"I will go, with no recompense for my services but the holding the Queen promised to whoever interpreted her dream." Caolin felt his smile slipping, and turned hastily.

"But where—" began Robert. "Stop him!" shouted Eric and Farin as one.

"Oh no!" cried Caolin turning on them, "No one shall ever hold me again!" Somebody shrieked and people scuttled out of his path. Power was throbbing in his veins, flaming along every nerve.

As he emerged from the Council Hall he saw sunset on the

streets of Laurelynn, and knew that like himself, the city already burned.

"I am burning . . ." said Faris clearly. "I am burning like Jehan, and soon I shall be consumed and float away." The air glowed around her like fire but she felt no pain.

And then Star began to cry again.

Faris jerked as if waking from sleep, staring around her. It was sunset. Ruddy light glowed on the slabbed trunks of the pines, and laid a golden sheen across the forested slopes below. She was in the mountains. She was sitting on the ground with her back against a tree. She was thirsty.

The baby still whimpered fretfully, but Faris had heard something else and remembered why she had stopped here. Leaving Star nestled in her shawl she crawled toward the rush of the stream, collapsed beside it and put her face into the water, drinking as if she could never be filled. After a little she managed to sit up again, and though the world still held the afterglow of a summer's day, suddenly she was shaking with cold. She coughed, bracing herself against the pain in her chest.

Then she crawled back to Star, and still shivering, put him to her breast. He seized her nipple, sucking painfully, but after a few moments he let go and butted frantically against her chest. Sweat began to run down her face.

"My little love, what shall I do?" She moved him to the other side, feeling the easy tears start as the milk in this breast failed as well, and she could only rock him when he began to cry once more.

Even in her weakness she knew that he was lighter than he had been when their journey began. His face was pinched, and after a few moments he seemed to lose even the strength to wail. Once more the cough tore her chest. She held her arm across her mouth and when she took it away saw that her sleeve was stained with brown.

The road stretched mockingly onward, golden in the sunset light. *Fool's gold . . .* thought Faris bitterly. She recognized her symptoms now, for she had suffered through two bouts of pneumonia as a child.

"We must find people. This road is rutted—someone must live near. They will take care of you . . ." Faris closed her eyes for a moment, marshalling her strength.

When she opened them again the light had deepened. In the sunset hush of the mountains she heard the barking of a dog. Shivering, she began to bind Star clumsily against her breast.

Her horse had wandered off two nights ago, or perhaps it was more, for the days were confused in her memory. But she would not have had the strength to mount it now. She crouched, shaking, fighting the temptation to sink down into the dreamless dark. *Help me* . . . she prayed to that darkness, and then for a little while was still.

"Hullo—"

Painfully, Faris looked up and saw a tow-headed boy about ten years old, with scratched legs and a faded home-dyed tunic stained with berry juice.

"Are you coming to visit us? We don't get many strangers— just pilgrims sometimes, from the towns. I have never been to a town but my father has. He is Gilbert Stonebreaker, and this is Stanesvale." He picked up his basket.

Faris gripped his arm. "Can you help me up?" she croaked, "I am ill—" The boy twitched like a nervous horse but he did not pull away. Awkwardly he helped her to stand and let her lean on him as they made their way down the hill. Dimly she was aware of a log house, the smell of goats and a sudden flurry of dogs. She staggered as the boy broke away from her and stood swaying, clutching at Star and praying that she would not fall.

"Mother, mother—there's a sick old woman with a baby— come and see!"

Faris felt strong arms go around her and forced herself to look up into a woman's face, with weather-ripened cheeks and merry eyes.

"Milk . . ." she whispered. "I must have milk for the child." The effort to speak rasped her chest and she began to cough. She let them take the baby from her, feeling rather than understanding the kindness in the woman's stream of words.

Then she closed her eyes and let the darkness surge over her at last.

Shadows leaped like demons from Caolin's lamp to the room's dark corners as he pulled out another drawer of files and began to add its contents to the heap on the floor. Somewhere men were shouting. Caolin stiffened, but the sound faded. His muscles eased and he began his work again. They had hunted him through the streets of Laurelynn while he took shape after shape to confuse them, misdirecting them at last to the eastern road.

Soon he would take the opposite direction. They would not think to look for him on the Red Mountain. He had come here one last time for his books, and to destroy anything that might set them on his trail.

That had been his intention. But that was not what he had done.

Caolin looked at the sheaf of papers in his hand—his notes on the officers of Rivered. They were Lord Robert's men, but he doubted that the Lord of the Ramparts possessed such knowledge of their background and performance, their ambitions and their secret sins, as he had collected here.

"All this is my work!" He saw the shelves with their bound reports and stacks of files, the fruits of fifteen years of service to Westria, realizing for the first time what a priceless repository they were. "Do they expect to steal my labor once they have cast me aside?"

But they have done it already . . .

The papers slipped from his grasp and he stood staring down at them, shivering a little, and knew that he had returned to his office because even now, after all his words of defiance in the Council Hall, he could not believe that it was true. This place of all others was his refuge, his battlefield, his own— where in the turmoil of the day or the stillness of the night he had used all his powers as they were meant to be used.

And I will never come here again . . . He ran a finger along the polished wood of his desk; touched the box of quill pens, like arrows in a quiver. He sank into the great chair behind his desk, settling into the comfortable hollows his own body had worn there.

"They hailed me as Seneschal and now they curse me as sorcerer," he said softly at last. "I would have given them everything, but they want nothing from me, therefore they shall have nothing of what I have done for Westria. *They* have named me evil, and evil I shall be . . . I have no choice, now . . ."

He got to his feet, held the lamp high and began to tip out oil over the pile of papers on the floor. He heard a door click, the echo of a footstep in the hall—he must not be found here! He groped for a new shape, visualized the little clerk who kept the door.

"Durren! What are you doing here? I saw a light and wondered—" the papers stirred as the door to the office opened and shut again. Caolin recognized the voice, precise and a little disapproving, of Ercul Ashe. He fought to hold Durren's form as hatred strung his nerves.

"Master, forgive me for not getting consent—I thought there might be some evidence here . . ." Caolin ducked his head submissively and began to sidle toward the door, setting the lamp back on the desk so that the farther end of the room was in shadow.

He reached it, touched the key.

"Very well. Did you find anything? Do you know where he is?" Ercul Ashe's voice sharpened as he peered at the other man.

"Yes . . ."

Caolin turned the key in the lock and slipped it into his belt, then straightened, letting the form of Durren slip away. The Deputy staggered back, staring at the man who had been his master. His mouth formed the word 'traitor' silently.

Caolin shook his head. "You are the traitor, Ercul Ashe— to Westria and to me." Suddenly he was entirely calm. He had accepted his destiny and been rewarded with the life of his enemy.

"I didn't know that Ordrey already knew the plan!" Ashe found his voice. "I was only your puppet—I was innocent!"

Caolin shrugged disdainfully. "Are you still bewailing that battle? It let me make a lasting peace where a greater victory would only have brought more war! I cloaked my deeds to hide them from fools like you, who would not understand how they served Westria!" He began to laugh harshly and laughed again, seeing Ercul Ashe grow pale. Shadows groped from the corners of the room.

"You call me traitor, but your tender pride has deprived Westria of *me!* If it *was* pride—" he peered at the Deputy. "What did they promise you for this deed? Worm! Do you think to take my place?"

Ashe shook his head. Another step backward brought him to the wall, and he stood, twitching, while Caolin mastered himself again.

"Do you know . . ." he said softly, "that once I killed a man whose only crime was loyalty to his master? And you have betrayed *me* . . . You claimed protection, but where are your fine friends now? Fate has given you into my hand. Sooner or later it will give me the others too."

Ercul Ashe licked dry lips, tried to straighten and stop the tremors that shook his body against the wall. "Are you going to murder me? I *was* loyal to you . . ." his voice cracked. "But you were different when the King was alive."

Caolin stopped short, remembering how it had been when he could look on Jehan and see the Lord of Light—before he had embraced the Lady of Darkness and been lost. *Jehan!* Darkness swirled around him and for a moment he poised, reaching out to the emptiness where love had been.

Then Ercul Ashe snuffled convulsively and Caolin's vision focused again.

"But the King is not alive, and no one can save you, or me . . ." He lifted his ring so that the garnet glowed in the lamp's dim light, caught the Deputy's desperate gaze. "You are your own murderer, Ercul Ashe . . . and your heart will stop at the touch of your own hand . . ."

He stared at the other man, using him as a mirror to build this image one last time, and as in a mirror, Ercul Ashe saw himself approaching with death written in his eyes.

Ercul Ashe stretched out his hand and rested one cold finger above his heart.

Staring into the other man's eyes, Caolin saw awareness return an instant before his body registered its agony. He drew back his hand swiftly, fearing to share the other's pain. But there was nothing, only the waiting until the untidy twitchings of the body at his feet were still.

"My Lady of Darkness, accept this sacrifice," he said dully. "Ercul Ashe, farewell."

He bent then and dragged the body to the heaped papers, splashed more oil across them and touched the pile with flame. It seemed to him that it was a fitting pyre. Fire pulsed back at him; light and shadow leaped and merged around him as if the room and all its furnishings were no more substantial than his lost dreams.

He groped for his bag and fumbled for the key. The flames were licking at the base of the bookshelves now. Then he unlocked the door and slipped like a shadow along the passageway, through the twisting streets, away from Laurelynn. Behind him the night sky filled with angry flames, distracting those who had been seeking him.

When he reached the Red Mountain and the Jewels they would know where he had gone. But it would be too late, then.

XII

The Way to Awahna

Suddenly, the morning air was filled with butterflies. The Master of the Junipers missed a step and grasped at a branch of manzanita. Golden wings brushed his cheek and for a moment his spirit fluttered joyfully. Then a little breeze stirred his hair and swirled the butterflies into the pure azure of the sky. Reluctantly the Master's tethered soul returned to him, but he was still smiling as he looked down and saw the tattered carcass the butterflies had been feeding on.

There is nothing to be afraid of here . . . His breathing steadied as he realized that the body had been that of a deer. *Surely there are worse fates than to nourish butterflies!* Today was Midsummer. In the coming months the butterflies would mate and lay their eggs and die, and in the spring the cycle would begin anew.

Did I really fear to find Faris' body? He wondered as he continued down the mountainside. And yet what made him think he would find the Pilgrim's Road, much less the Queen?

On the second night of his journey he had dreamed of meeting Faris at the gates of Awahna, and waking, had been certain that was where she would try to go. But what if he had been wrong? He stumbled onward until he rounded a shoulder of the mountain and saw below him the winding ribbon of the Pilgrim's Road gleaming in the morning sun.

He stopped short, his heart thudding heavily in his chest. "Now, let me find a holding, and let them give me word of the Queen. And then I will be done with doubting Your purpose, Lord!"

"Why?" Caolin brought his hand down upon the stone parapet that edged the platform at the top of the Red Mountain.

He felt the shock of the blow, but no pain. His pain was all internal, now.

"Why was I raised so high if I was not meant to reign?" He had evaded his pursuers, but he could not escape the questions that tormented him. He leaned out over the sheer cliff face. Wind plucked at his robe, rocking him. Just a little farther and he would not be able to balance again . . .

Why not let go and bring an end to pain?

Below him Laurelynn shimmered mockingly in the heat of noon. Caolin sobbed, unable to look at it, unable to look away. His vision darkened—he saw the rose-brick towers of the city melt and run like blood into the river; the ploughed fields sprouted bones like stalks of corn.

Caolin collapsed back onto the platform, his fingers digging into the cracks between the stones. *They will not let me serve Westria and I dare not die,* he told himself. *I must do something so terrible that the things other men care for can never tempt me again!*

His laughter was muffled by the stones. Some still voice within him whispered that this was madness. But that was just as well, he thought, for he would have to be mad to put on the Jewels and wield them to the destruction of Westria! After a time he managed to sit up, aching in every bone. He shut his eyes against the burning noonday glare. *The Light rejects me! I must find shelter from the sun!*

Crouching like some creature of darkness caught out by day, Caolin stumbled back to the beacon-keeper's lodge. Margit tried to help him, but he thrust her aside, made fast the door behind him and drew the curtains.

Then he threw himself onto his bed to wait until the terror of the light should pass away.

Faris turned her head to watch the play of light and shadow that formed and then erased Caolin's face. She was lying in the shade of the laurel tree on the Lady Mountain . . . no, she was in a house, and the dappled light was cast by the sun that moved slowly across the rustling leaves outside. But where was Caolin?

She drew breath to call him, winced and remembered where she was and why. It was quiet now, but there had been some sound to awaken her—the heavy front door opening and closing again. From beyond the curtain she heard a murmur of voices.

"The blessing of Midsummer be with you. I am Megan of Stanesvale, the holder here." There was a pause. Outside, the wind whispered to the pines.

"The child in your arms—was he brought here by a stranger, by his mother? Is she still here?"

Faris' breath caught painfully and she fought to suppress the spasm of coughing that would prevent her from hearing that voice again.

"His mother?" said Megan. "I thought she must be, for all her silver hair. She came here yesterday, fainting with fever. The baby was starving too, but goat's milk seems to agree with him."

"Yes . . ." the other voice trembled. "Thank you. I have been seeking them."

Rough as granite and sweet as honey—Faris would have known that voice at the thin edge of the world. She let out her breath and the coughing took her, so that she scarcely knew when the curtain was pulled aside and the Master of the Junipers came in.

For a moment the shock of his recognition breached her weakened barriers—she saw through his eyes her sweat-matted hair and haggard face on the pillow, the thin hands that clutched the sheet. *Like Jehan!* he was thinking. *No, it shall not happen again!* The Master reached to test her forehead, held the fragile bones of her wrist to find her pulse. He felt fever, and a flutter like the heart of a frightened bird.

Faris forced herself to open her eyes, unable to bear his pain. "You're real!" her voice strengthened. "I thought I had dreamed you again . . ."

The Master looked down at her, his face working as he tried to return her smile. How thin and brown he had become! She saw now that his robe was tattered and frayed, his face scratched above the ragged growth of beard.

"I was going to Awahna . . ."

"Yes. I know." His lips twitched. "So was I." He began to examine her more thoroughly, his gaze growing abstracted as the physician replaced the friend. Faris tried to speak, found her mouth too dry, and had to wait while the Master gave her water from the earthenware mug beside the bed, then held her until she had finished coughing again.

"I must tell you why . . ." she said at last. "I had to go where Caolin could never follow me!" Swiftly, she told him what had passed between her and the Seneschal, pointed to her bundle, where Jehan's Journal still lay.

"I had sent you away, and there was no one I could trust in Laurelynn. What else could I do? I must learn enough to protect my child and save Caolin too!"

"Save Caolin?" the Master exclaimed. "How can you think of it? I felt your agony a hundred miles away!"

"And the pain of what Jehan and I did to *him?*" breathed Faris.

He slowly shook his head. "No . . . I saw Caolin daily and never guessed at the canker that was eating his soul . . ."

Faris lay back, breathing carefully. The bed seemed to be tilting beneath her. She struggled against the dark tide of fear. The Master held her hands until she could feel strength flowing from him to her.

"Before you can save Caolin you must save yourself." His voice had deepened, steadied—it was the priest's voice now. "You are the perfect child of the Maker of all Things. Fill your mind with the pattern of what you were meant to be!"

The picture he held in his mind began to take shape in hers; she saw herself as she had been last summer in Laurelynn, though even then, she could not remember having been so beautiful.

"The body reflects the mind. You must rule your own mind, and you shall be free."

"To wield the Jewels of Westria, the wearer must first rule his own soul," read Caolin. "He must know the qualities in himself that correspond to the attributes of each element. The Jewels will link him to all that the elements rule, but he shall rule the elements by self-mastery . . ."

Caolin set the book down on the table. In his mind something settled almost audibly into place. He looked around him, for the first time since early that morning seeing and understanding what he saw. It was nearly sunset, and the light that filtered through the curtains was red as fire.

Sometime during that afternoon he had left his bed and begun to read, seeking in that mechanical activity a distraction from the chaotic thoughts that would have drawn him into a madness from which he could not have returned.

He caressed the worn leather cover of the book. There lay

his answer—the power of the mind! It was his fortune, his defense, the one thing that had always been his own.

If he had put on the Jewels the night before, they would only have amplified his own hatred and fear. But tonight surely his mind's cold passion could master them. Despite the folklore that told how the Jewels would overwhelm anyone who had not been initiated to their mastery, he had found no evidence that their use required anything more than training and confidence.

Caolin began to walk around the room, easing muscles tensed by the hours he had spent huddled in the chair. Now he was remembering the contents of the books at which he had stared.

"This world in which we live is neither as solid nor as immutable as it appears," the *Book of Julian* had said. "It is a patterning of powers, and the Mind is the greatest Power of all. The master of the Jewels does not *use* them, he *becomes* them, and they become him—healing or destroying according to the health or dis-ease of the one who wields them. Let the Jewel-lord therefore search his soul well before he wears them, as he would search for any flaw in a sword that he has taken into his hand, for if there is a weakness, it will surely betray him . . ."

Had Jehan ever read that? Was that why he had feared to use the Jewels? And Faris, so weak that Caolin could rule her with a glance—how could she hope to use their power? *But I am strong!* he thought. *I have no hidden flaws!*

He pulled back the curtains from the window and opened it, breathing deeply of the cooling air. His eyes moved to the closed door of his temple, where the Jewels waited for his touch to awaken them.

"But I must go carefully . . ." He had raised his hand as if he were taking oath. Now he lifted the other and looked at them, shuddering. They were grazed and bloody, their whiteness streaked with grime. His robe was torn, dust-smeared. Quickly he stripped and poured water to wash himself.

The cool droplets glittered like the red stone in his ring. In the west, the sun was sinking toward a sea that glowed like a lake of fire. Soon, pastures in holdings all over Westria would blossom with the bonfires of Midsummer Night. But the power of the sun was broken. Men's pitiful imitations would not save them now! When Faris emerged from whatever hole she had run to, there would be nothing for her to rule.

Caolin dipped his sponge into the basin and passed it over his body again and again, letting the water dissolve all the evil memories of the past twenty-four hours as it washed away their stains, until only his purpose remained.

Washed, shaved and at peace with the world, the Master of the Junipers finished his portion of the Midsummer feast. The western sky still glowed with the memory of a brilliant sunset, but upon the long table, candles burned cheerfully.

"Papa—can't we light the bonfire now?" asked the oldest boy. The other two chorused agreement, glancing hopefully from their mother, sitting at the end of the table nearest the hearth, to their father, who brooded opposite her. The candle-light glowed on the pewter goblets, the rich grain of wooden bowls.

"Not yet—it is not quite dark, and Mica has not finished his pie," answered Megan. She turned to the Master. "The lady looks much better now."

The Master nodded. "Yes. The dandelion root tea you made for her has helped, and if your sons can find me chapparal, tomorrow I will brew an infusion that may clear her lungs. I think the crisis of her illness will come soon."

Star stirred in his cradle and Megan went to him, lifting him expertly to her shoulder while she reached for a leather bottle of the sort they used to feed motherless lambs. She sat down again in her carved chair, humming softly, and held the bottle for him to suck.

The Master considered the baby nestled in the mountain woman's arms and thought how easily he had adapted to this substitute for his mother's care. With his dark head laid against Megan's breast, he might have been her own.

"Even after the crisis—" the Master said thoughtfully, "it may be long before the . . . lady . . . is well enough to go on."

"I'm sorry to hear it," said Gilbert, the gruffness of his tone making his words ambiguous.

"So am I!" retorted his wife. "It does me good to hold a babe in my arms once more." Some old pain showed for a moment in Megan's face, and Gilbert's grim look softened.

"They tell me that you were wounded at the battle of the Dragon Waste," the Master of the Junipers said quietly. The woman might be holder here, but if only for her sake, he must win over her husband as well. Gilbert grunted.

"If you like, I will examine you—that child's father was a notable warrior," he gestured toward Star, "and I often tended him." The Master realized suddenly that though he might always carry the pain of losing Jehan, what he had read in the King's Journal that afternoon had lifted some of the guilt he had been carrying as well.

For a long moment the other man's eyes held his, then Gilbert tried to smile. "I had accustomed myself to going halt-legged till I die . . . I can wait until the lady recovers," he said.

Megan's smile showed her relief. "Last night in her fever the lady spoke of an enemy," she said. "Was that delirium? She would not tell me her name. Who is she, and what does she fear?"

The Master shook his head. "It will be safer for her, for you all, if you do not know. The child's father is dead, and there are those who will destroy both him and his mother if they are found." Faris had forgiven Caolin, but she knew his secrets now. The Master could not believe that Caolin would forgive the Queen.

"Did he die in the battle with Elaya?" Gilbert's eyes glittered.

The Master considered him. "He died in the service of Westria."

"Mama, it *is* dark now, and I am done with my pie!" said the youngest boy. His brothers pushed back their benches as their father nodded, and clattered after him to the door.

Gilbert rose, reaching for the staff that leaned against his chair. Through the window one star glittered like a jewel in the pale evening sky.

"I will watch by the lady and the child." said Megan to the Master. "Go with them and bless the lighting of our Midsummer fire."

Caolin lifted the taper to light the candles on the Altar of Earth, then moved to the altars in the other three corners of the room until his temple was filled by a steady, shadowless glow. His gaze rested on the Jewels, in that moment drawn as much by their beauty as by their promised power.

He had bathed and dressed in a clean gown of undyed cotton and eaten the bread and fruit that Margit had set out for him. Now, standing in the midst of his temple, he willed himself to calm. His masters at the College of the Wise had taught him better than they knew, he thought, and he had not wasted the years since then. As his breathing deepened he let awareness of all outside this room slip away.

"Through the power of my Will, I encompass all things. There is nothing in the universe that does not exist within Me . . ."

Caolin stood upright and balanced, each muscle at ease as he began to map the domains of the Elements within his own soul.

Who am I? What am I? At the college such questioning had been part of the discipline of the students preparing to journey on the other planes. But such travelling had been forbidden him, until now, when he had the Jewels to dissolve the cataracts upon the vision of his soul.

He had no mirror here, but he pictured to himself what a glass would have shown—a tall man, smooth-limbed and clean-shaven, with pale fine hair and eyes like the winter sea. That was the body Jehan had loved . . . But he was not concerned with his body now.

He considered the four altars and the Jewels they bore, stopped, facing north and the first of the elements. *Now, I am concerned with the shape and coloration of my mind and soul.*

He took a deep breath and stepped forward.

"I claim the Power of Earth, immovable, unbending. Like the earth I have endured the assaults of my enemies. I stand like a mountain peak in a storm; I am as hard as stone, and their swords shall shatter against my unyielding will . . ."

He paused, remembering the gentler qualities ascribed to this element—nurturance, permeability—but those were for women. Nothing in him responded to them. He set his hands against the naked stone of the Red Mountain that formed the floor of his temple, as if he could absorb its strength through the skin of his palms.

After a few moments he moved to the Altar of Water where the crystal flagon and the Sea Star alike refracted the candle-light.

"I claim the Power of Water: the force of the flood; the inexorability of the tide; the patience of the falling rain, for like the rain, my will can wear rock away . . .

"I claim the Powers of Air!" Caolin bowed before the third altar now. "For the power of the wind is the power of the will, and air bears the words by which I shape reality."

He circled back to the altar on which the Jewel of Fire cast back the candles' flame. "I claim the Powers of Fire: fire to consume my enemies; fire falling from heaven like a striking sword!" He willed away the memory of times when he had invoked the Lady of Fire to bless his love, for he could only call on the Dark Lady now. For a moment Her face glimmered within the Jewel, mocking him with Faris' eyes.

He had invoked power—the active, masculine strength of each element that corresponded to his own identity. The Masters of the College had preached the need for a balancing of male and female to control such forces as these. But surely they were mistaken. Power could only be mastered by power . . .

Quickly, Caolin bowed to each of the Jewels in turn. *When I have put them on I will call the winds, and strike clouds together to spark the lightnings. They who have seared me with their hate and cast me into the dark shall have their fill of fire and darkness!*

Light blazed suddenly in the darkness in which Faris had been drifting. Cool hands lifted her, drawing the sweat-soaked sheet away and sliding a fresh one beneath her. She bit her lip as the movement restored awareness of which joints and muscles, which bared nerves, were most vulnerable to pain.

Then they replaced the coverlet and tucked it snugly around her. Faris lay very still, waiting for her blood to stop pounding, waiting for the world to go away.

The candle moved so that it no longer hurt her eyes. "Can you open your mouth, Mistress? I want you to drink this now." Faris felt the hard rim of the cup against her lip. The drink was tart, with an aftertaste of peppermint. She drank again and Megan smiled.

"Thank you," whispered Faris. "Is my child well?" Her breast ached for the warm weight of him though she knew that she had not even strength enough to hold him now.

"Yes, he does very well. Tomorrow I will bring him to you." Megan waited until Faris had emptied the cup. "I will be going now—it is nearly midnight—" she said to the Master, "but you must call me if there is need."

He nodded. "Come to relieve me when it is dawn."

Faris felt a breath of air caress her cheek as Megan pushed the curtain aside and passed through. "I have been such a trouble to her, and to you too, from the beginning," she sighed. "If I had let you teach me to control myself and the Jewels, I would have been able to deal with Caolin . . ." Some memory stirred in her mind as she spoke—something else the Master ought to know . . .

"No—" he was saying, "we laid too much upon you too soon. But no failure is forever. Now you have to repair your body so that we can begin again. I know that you want to sleep to evade the pain," he went on. "But right now you need to be *here,* in your body, using all your abilities to heal yourself!"

"My abilities?" she echoed mockingly.

"Yes—" the Master said gently. "You have great awareness—turn it inward to comprehend your own ills. You respond to beauty—hold to the image of your own. You have a gift for right action in a crisis that a warrior would envy—use it to marshal your own forces against your foe!"

"What do I look like, to you?" Faris asked, as if he were a mirror in which she might see her soul.

The Master closed his eyes, deliberately misunderstanding her. "I see your body patterned in light, but where the colors should be clear and glowing and the energies should flow smoothly I see them muddied, trickling sluggishly as a river flows when men forget the Covenant and choke it with debris."

She sighed as he focused on her again. "What must I do?"

"First, you must become aware of the earth supporting you. Feel the pulse of her energies as if you were lying directly on the soil. Then, visualize a shaft of golden light flooding down from that place where all is brightness, pouring through you, filling you with power . . ."

As she tried to comply, Faris perceived a tingling along her veins, a varying pressure as if a wind were blowing across her chest and outward along her limbs. She realized that the Master of the Junipers was passing his hands back and forth a few inches above her body with a stroking motion, as if he were brushing grains of sand away. Imperceptibly her pain began to ease.

Faris' eyes closed. Her awareness focused on the movement through her body of those currents of power. *There is a battle going on within you,* came the Master's thought. *You must visualize the forces that will come to your defense.*

"You are the center of the circled cross, in which the elements are joined!" he said aloud. "Use their power!"

Faris felt a throbbing in her chest and found it easy to imagine the struggle there. She breathed painfully, concentrating on drawing the golden light to help her, and awareness of the world around her passed away.

She knew that she had done this before—this grasping and focusing of power—she felt the Jewel of Fire burning her brow, felt the surge of balanced energies as she and Jehan strove to drive back the unlawful flames . . .

Once more she was standing in the Sacred Wood, on the Lady Mountain, in her chamber in Laurelynn, bearing the four Jewels. *The Jewels!* She struggled to tell the Master, but she could not break free.

Caolin has the Jewels!

Standing on the platform at the pinnacle of the Red Mountain, Caolin unwrapped the four Jewels of Westria, named them and put them on:

Earthstone . . .

Sea Star . . .

Wind Crystal . . .

Jewel of Fire . . .

His skin prickled as power began to swell through his nerves. He breathed deeply, deliberately, images flaring behind his closed eyes. Then he trembled, for he felt something beyond the reach of his senses, like a sound too high for a man to hear, an itch too deeply set to scratch, darkness in which one might strain forever to see. Was his isolation too great for even the Jewels to break through?

Be still, he told himself, *be open . . . wait . . .* He stood, yearning for the touch of power as once he had waited for Jehan's mind to touch his.

And like an answer it came.

Caolin's shout ripped the air, reverberated across the transient woods and fields and through the imperishable framework of which the land called Westria was only the appearance that mortal men could see.

I am Master of the Jewels! I, Caolin!

In the Sacred Wood, the Lord of the Trees was aware of him. From the depths of the western ocean Sea Mother flowed upward to float on the surface, waiting. Perched on an outcrop of the Ramparts, Windlord half-spread his great wings to catch the first stirrings of the storm. And in the forested slopes below him, the Great Bear stirred from the shadows in which he had lain, grunting a question that rumbled like thunder across the night.

On the many levels of the Place men called Awahna, the

Powers that ruled the elements focused suddenly upon the Red Mountain.

And Faris, wandering between the worlds, heard Caolin's words, and crying out, broke abruptly from her dreams . . .

Startled into wakefulness by the shout, the Master of the Junipers grasped Faris' shoulders, calling her name. Her pulse was bounding like a frightened doe. Was this only a nightmare or had the crisis of her fever come?

"Be still—it is over now . . ." He squeezed the extra water from a cloth, laid it across her brow.

"No . . ." she got out at last. "Caolin . . . took the Jewels, and he has put them on!"

The Master sat back, letting go of her. Caolin and the Jewels?

"They . . . were the only thing left to him . . . of Jehan's," said Faris. "I am afraid of what he may do."

The Master stared at her. Her harsh breathing was the only sound in the room. He wanted to tell her that there was no danger—Caolin, who had failed to reach Awahna, could never hold the Jewels. But what if it had not been lack of ability, but some other, deadlier flaw that had kept him from his goal? The Master shook his head, fighting a horror, trained into him at the College, of the idea that one who was unsworn and uninitiated should touch the Jewels.

"I thought . . . he would be satisfied to rule Westria," Faris said a little more easily. "It is my fault. He is on the Red Mountain now . . . I must try to reach him." She closed her eyes.

"No! Remember what I told you! Your body could not survive if you left it now!" He stared at her, shocked anew at her fragility as she lay swathed in the folds of Megan's gown. "No," he repeated. "I will go to him. Will you promise to stay and watch by me?"

Faris nodded. "Until you return."

The Master leaned back in his chair and shut his eyes, shuddering as his spirit struggled to leave a body that was unprepared to let it go. There was a moment of anguish, as if he were trying to squeeze through a closing door, and then he was free.

He oriented himself, found the line of light that led toward Laurelynn. But he scarcely needed a guide—the astral plane pulsed with currents of energy that flowed toward a single point where a glowing crimson figure gestured his commands. The Master neared him and sent out a mental call.

For a moment the rush of energy faltered. Caolin stared at the Master, and the older man shivered, sensing the mixed passions in Caolin's soul. Did he realize what the forces he played with could do?

"Stop—you will destroy Laurelynn!"

"I know . . ." Caolin laughed. *"Did your mistress at the College send you to plead with me? It will do no good! The Queen is gone and Robert has cast me aside! Go seek the lost Queen and tell her that no one will rule in Laurelynn now. Find Faris, and if she will listen to you tell her how she has betrayed Jehan!"*

The Master tried to approach him but the force of the Jewels blasted him away. He recoiled along the path by which he had come and jerked back to awareness of his own body, clutching at the arms of his chair.

And in that unguarded moment Faris touched his mind and read all that had passed between him and Caolin.

"He was right—it is my fault! Others cannot fight my battles anymore."

Still dizzy, the Master shook his head. "You will give up your life for nothing. You cannot stand against one who wields the Jewels!"

"And if he is allowed to go on?"

"I think that the forces he plays with will overpower him at last. He will be destroyed . . ."

"He, and what else? What will happen to Laurelynn and the heart of Westria?" she asked. The Master swallowed dumbly, visualizing a shattered city beneath a sundered sky.

"You see—" she said quietly. "I must go to him. What does my life matter if Caolin destroys all that I was trying to preserve? He holds the Jewels, but they are not his. I *feel* them, even now. Perhaps they will still respond to me."

Faris ignored the Master's protest as she continued, "Everything is quite clear now. I thought to learn the ways of Power, but I was not made to endure a lifetime of the subtle struggles that surround the Crown. Only when the great danger comes do I know what to do. But I will live if I can, I promise you, for Star's sake . . ."

The Master's awareness reached out to her and he knew that this was not delirium. She was arguing like a warrior volunteering to stand rearguard against an overwhelming foe.

"I am going—" Faris repeated, "but I will fare more swiftly if you guide me, and more easily return . . . Will you help me?"

With sick recognition the Master remembered how Jehan had asked his guidance on the final road. But he could not deny the Queen's reasoning. He reached out to take her hand. "Yes . . ."

Yes—wind creature—come to me now . . . Caolin reached for the cloud, calling it like some shy bird he wished to coax to his hand. Already he had forgotten the Master of the Junipers, for the balancing of the elements required all his attention. Delicately he nudged the western winds behind the cloudbank and commanded them to push it toward Laurelynn.

Every sense was bombarding him with messages—the pressure of grains of soil against the probing rootlets of a tree; the slow heave and suck of waves on the shore; wind singing through an owl's wing-feathers as it stooped on some hapless scurrying thing; a young man's arousal as he drew his girl away from the light of the Midsummer fire and into the shadows where their bodies joined—as the Jewels linked him to the life of Westria.

But he refused to acknowledge these things. As the power of the Jewels increased, so did Caolin's concentration. He had nearly forgotten his physical body now, for he had shifted unawares from the material stones of the peak to the focus of power which represented the Red Mountain on the astral plane.

Faris hovered above the sprawling rooftops of Stanesvale, exulting in the freedom of her energy body and the blessed absence of pain. She perceived herself drawn upon the darkness in lines of light, and only the luminous silver cord that emerged from beneath her ribcage connected her to the wasted physical body below.

The Master of the Junipers waited for her nearby. She could feel the life-pulses of tree and beast in the mountains, the dreaming souls of the people in the house. Love for them all welled in her heart, poured out to them and to her child, asleep in his cradle below.

But the power of the Jewels was drawing her. *I am ready, my brother,* she told the Master. *Let us go.* She took his hand, and they passed along the lines of light, toward the storm that swirled between the Red Mountain and Laurelynn.

"*Caolin!*"

For a moment his attention faltered. The lightning bolt meant for the gates of Laurelynn hissed across the river's surface like a thwarted snake and ignited a dead tree at the water's edge. Warning blazes flickered in the fields already, circling the town. Faris felt the people's terror, their bewilderment as they gazed at this sudden storm.

"Caolin! Please stop—for the sake of Westria—for the love you bore Jehan!"

When Caolin perceived her Faris knew it, for as it had been by the Lake of Laurelynn, his mind was open to her and she recoiled from what she saw. Why had she ever thought that he would hear? What had made her think he might obey? She shivered, and he knew her fear, and laughed.

"There is no name that you can call upon to stop me now! Were you hidden with that snivelling priest? I wonder that you dare to seek me here, since you fled from me before. Indeed, I welcome you—now you will see what your own act has done . . ."

She knew that it was true, that she had failed—failed him, failed Jehan, failed Westria. She stood alone and wretched in the dark.

"Stop thinking of yourself—" the Master's thought pierced her despair—*"you do not matter now."*

For a moment Caolin seemed shaken. Then he turned away. *"It is too late—the choices are all made. You cannot tempt me to repentance anymore. I am damned, and you can neither save nor stop me, for I am the Jewel-Lord now!"*

His attention left her, but she felt him gather up the winds, and fling bright lightnings at the city's spires. She felt the varied forces of the Jewels pulse through her, the familiar pressure of their power, as she had felt them in the Grove, and on the Lady Mountain, not so long ago.

Caolin reached out to move a cloud, and Faris swept it back at him, instinctively, as she would have brushed a hornet from her child.

She jerked at the backlash of power. Looking down, she saw white radiance flare at her breast, and at her waist, her loins, a blue and amber glow. Something burned like flame above her brow. Wondering, Faris knew she bore the Jewels. Though Caolin might hold the stones themselves, *she* had been sealed to them, and on this plane, she, also, held their power.

"Caolin!" her call rang through all realities. *"I can command you now—I, Faris, am the Mistress of the Jewels!"* She

struck aside the stormclouds, sent them thundering like maddened horses off across the hills.

Caolin stilled, and turned, considered her. *"I would have spared you, Faris, even now. But now I see I must destroy you too . . . Did you think this power was all my own?"* His gaze went inward. He was trembling.

Behind him, something blotted out the stars.

Vision reversed, made darkness visible—a woman's face, a cloud of mantling hair, eyes like dead coals, and skin a dully radiant veil across dark fires within. The Master whimpered. Caolin bowed. But Faris knew the face once seen in Caolin's memory, seen in her mirror once, in Laurelynn, when in despair she had put on the Jewels.

"I am the Queen of Darkness, and My power that of Eternal Night. This is My hour. Your dream of light is ended—you denied Me when I lay within, but will no more, who know Me for your twin . . ."

The Lady's laughter broke across the night, sucked backward in a glistening slick tide till reason slid foundationless; identity drowned, mad and drunken, in that shoreless sea. And Faris, drifting in that dark embrace, knew how Caolin was tempted, and understood . . .

"Faris, come away! Your body is weakening . . ." Faris clung desperately to the Master's appeal, to the syllables of her own name.

"Faris! You must break free!" The Master's horror of the Lady's darkness reinforced her own, and a sudden clear anger flared in her.

"I must stop Her or She will destroy Westria—She is the dark face of my soul!"

"To do that you would have to absorb Her into yourself again, and you have not the strength or the time . . . Faris, come back while you still can!"

Lines of light shivered across the face of the land as Caolin shook the foundations of Laurelynn. The air quivered with the renewed tumult of the storm.

But the eyes of the Lady of Darkness swallowed light. *"Come to Me, and find oblivion far deeper than the lake of Laurelynn . . ."*

"Lady of Flowers! Lady of Fire! Lady of Light!"

Faris reached inward for their images, for the Names of all the goddesses who had possessed her when she was made Queen. Brilliance blinded her, rainbows flared behind her eyes, refracting myriad visions, scents, and songs . . .

"*Sister, we are here, we are you, we are One . . . Light and Darkness are the two wings of the world . . .*"

And Faris knew Herself, and knew the thing that in her had been missing, and embraced the Darkness, and was made whole and free.

She was darkness . . . She was starlight . . .

She was the storm's fury, and the stillness at its heart . . .

She spread her wings above the city then, and Caolin's fury, striking her in vain, was now deflected to its source again . . .

Now the storm boiled about the peak. Faris felt Caolin's anguish and rage. Her thought sought him—

"*Calm the elements, Caolin!*"

"*I cannot . . .*"

"*Then call them in a gentler form.*"

"*I do not know how . . .*"

"*Then strip off the Jewels!*"

There was no response from Caolin. The Red Mountain erupted in fire. Its slopes shook. Their quivering transmitted tremors across the land. Escaping his will, the Jewels rioted. The forces that formed the frame of the world vibrated, faltered, rhythm gone.

"*I . . . will . . . not.*"

Faris felt his answer, his anger, his anguish that she could not ease.

She rose like a bastion over Laurelynn. She spread her protection across the battered land. The essence of the Jewels, that was her own, she set against their lawless counterparts—absorbing, enduring, transmuting, extending power in a thin veil that, pricked by Caolin's pain, failed finally—the Jewels struck again.

Then, suddenly, there was an ease from strain. The load that she had carried now was shared. Light stood against her darkness like a counterweight, and darkness balanced the beauty of her light. Action and reaction, partnered now, reimposed a rhythm on the world. For she was not alone . . .

"*Oh, my beloved . . .*"

"*Oh, my severed soul . . .*"

She knew him then—the sum of all her shattered memories—eyes alight with laughter, a caress, the scent of roses, the sweet mingling of half-awakened bodies, tender, tempered strength, transmuted pain . . . *Jehan* . . .

Touching him, she knew all that his written words had tried

to say, and he knew what Caolin was, what he would be.

"*Beloved, we must help him . . .*"

"*Yes, I know.*"

For a last time their joined thought sounded, "*Caolin—we forgive you, save yourself now!*"

"*You cannot forgive me—I destroyed you both! How can I forgive you?*" Caolin's answer was plucked on the highest note of pain.

"*Take off the Jewels, and live, until one comes to give and take forgiveness in our names!*"

They felt his struggle as they felt the forces that tore at him, searing his body as they seared his soul.

"*Help me . . .*" on the edge of perception came the plea.

Faris and Jehan moved toward Caolin. Force and fullness, strength and subtlety, mated with the Jewels' warring powers and for a moment stilled them. Jehan and Faris blessed him with their love.

And in that instant of freedom, Caolin took off the Jewels.

Freed from that faint restraint at last, the Jewels joined with the powers they ruled, were whirled away—wild, unwilled were outward borne; dispersed in a last pure pulse of power . . .

The Jewels were gone. The Master of the Junipers, unshielding his awareness, could sense nothing but the varied manifestations of the elements they had ruled. The reverberations of the battle were already fading, and around him peace was settling on both the physical and spiritual dimensions of the land.

Dimly he could sense Caolin, like the dull glow of a coal burned nearly to ash. He was alive, but the backlash of the powers that had escaped his mastery must surely have devastated the mind that had wielded them. It would be long, before Caolin could be a threat again.

Before him, shaped against a sky that flowered with stars, the Master saw the King and Queen. They were shining, and he thought that all the times that he had seen them paired—in the Beltane ritual, at their meeting in the Great Dance in the Sacred Wood, enthroned in the Council Hall of Westria or bearing the Jewels as they faced the forest fire—all had been only foreshadowings of this mated sovereignty.

Then they moved a little apart. "*My beloved, I must go back now.*"

The Master's joy ebbed as he looked at her. "*You cannot*

come with me . . ." he told her. *"The silver cord is broken—you have been away too long."*

The night shivered with her bewildered pain as Faris looked about her and understood that at some time during the struggle with Caolin, the ribbon of light that had bound her spirit to her body had disappeared.

"There is nothing left within that world for me—" the Master faltered. *"My Lord, my Lady, let me come with you!"*

"My dearest friend!" Jehan looked at him, returning in that glance all the love the Master had ever given him. His features were still those of the man the Master had known, perhaps more so—closer to being a perfect expression of the spirit that the Master had glimpsed in his face as he lay dying six months before.

"You are the only one of us left to guard the child, the only one who can preserve the memory of what we have done . . ." came the thought of the King.

"My Star! My child! Who will hold him now? I bore him, but you lifted him into life—oh Master, you must love him for me now!" Tomorrow, some child would find the ground strewn with crystals and never know they were the tears of the Queen of Westria.

"Keep him hidden and safe until he has grown strong enough to claim his inheritance. Let him grow free from those who would seek to use him, or spoil him as I was spoiled with too much false affection," added Jehan. *"Keep him secret, lest knowledge of him tempt Caolin once again."*

The Master hesitated, wracked by his own agony.

A light was growing in the eastern sky. The Master turned, and saw it was not dawn—the hills themselves were luminous. He saw a shining road that led between two piers of stone, and recognized the Gateway to Awahna . . . But he saw that the trees and waterfalls of the Valley where once he had walked had been only a veil to shelter mortals from the bright substance of Reality.

"We will return for you when your task is done. It will not seem long."

"It will seem long to me . . ." the Master assented at last. *"I will guard the child. But when he has achieved his kingship, I will follow you."*

And there came a sound . . .

His spirit stilled to hear the harmonies, that chord by chord built, yet were not resolved, as if the Lord of Air harped on the wind. Moving to that music, Faris and Jehan were leaving him. Their figures lit the dark, and shadowed glory on the living light. Across the harping, one clear trumpet call rang like a summons.

Voices answered it, and then the singers came, dancing like sunsparks on a rippling stream. It seemed to him that some had faces that he once had known. The Master wept because he could not speak to them, because he could not sing their song.

"Glory to the Lord and Lady, to the children of the sun— Glory to all living souls that manifest the Holy One . . ."

The music deepened. Earth became a drum, cadencing a new processional, shaken by feet too great for mortal earth to bear. The Master saw, and hid his eyes, but in his heart the gods were recognized . . .

"Glory to the Powers of Heaven, who rule the spheres in majesty—Glory to the Lords of Life who sit in splendor on the Tree . . ."

And yet he did not know when they were gone, for the Light was every color . . . it was none . . . the music was all melodies . . . yet still . . . and, gods and souls forgotten, his own will was lost and found within a greater one.

"Glory, glory, gloria . . ."

One came.

One moment was Eternity.

Darkness and Light, and all that was were One.

Epilogue

"Praise be to the Guardian of Men—you are with us again!"

The Master of the Junipers opened his eyes on a strange room that was luminous with the soft light of an opalescent dawn. The air held a moist freshness as if it had recently rained.

There was a movement nearby and Megan bent over him. He closed his eyes again, reaching for the phrase of melody that had shaken his soul, his mind grasping vainly at the words of the song. The light of this world was so much less than the illumination from which he had come.

"Are you ill?" came the woman's voice. "I went in to see if the lady had been disturbed by the storm and found you both like ice. It took an hour's chafing to get warmth into your limbs, and as for the poor lady—"

The Master forced himself to focus on her, realizing that his cheeks were wet with tears. He must tell her that he knew that Faris had already completed her journey to Awahna . . .

"No—" Megan sounded alarmed. "Don't try to speak. You are still looking at me from a hundred miles away." She poured tea from a stoppered stone jug into a cup and held it to his lips. It was hot, and gradually he felt awareness of his body return.

"I am sorry . . ." he whispered, then stopped, for how could he make this woman understand what had happened here?

"You do not have to explain," Megan said calmly. "I have no training in these things, but I am a child of these mountains, and I have seen too many folk pass to and from Awahna not to recognize the marks of the other world . . ."

She looked down at her work-roughened hands. The Master watched her, recognizing now a strength in her that was one manifestation of that power which he had so recently experienced in its pure form.

"What will you do with the child?" Megan asked suddenly, still staring at her clasped fingers. "My womb will bear no more, and that little one is already dear to me. If you have no other place for him, will you let me raise him as my own?"

He stared at her. The King and Queen had left him to guard their heir, but would it be safe to take him back to Laurelynn? Caolin still lived, and though his strength was in ashes now, he might one day recover his powers and with them the ambition that had nearly destroyed him, and Westria. When he returned to Laurelynn he must go to the Red Mountain to look for Caolin. He would need care, and now, defeated and vulnerable, he might even be healed, and Faris' sacrifice would not be in vain.

Yes, Caolin could be dealt with, but there were others, with greater right in the world's eyes, or greater desire for power, who might prevent the Master from keeping the trust Faris and Jehan had laid upon him.

He reached out to Megan with all the strength left to him, reading in her a strength and steadiness that came from the hills in which she had been bred.

"I think I could find no better fosterage—" he said at last. "Take care of him, for the sake of—" he had almost said, *for the sake of Westria* . . .

"For the lady?" asked Megan. "I will take care of him for his own sake, Master!"

He lay back then, fighting his exhaustion, wondering if despite all their precautions, she had guessed Faris' identity.

After a little the woman spoke again. "We have prepared the lady for burial. We honored her as well as we knew how— in a while, when you are able to rise, perhaps you will come and look at her?" she asked diffidently.

But it was bright morning before the Master went into the room where the body of the Queen of Westria lay, though drawn curtains left it dim. They had set candles of scented beeswax around her, and the bed was covered with asters, late poppies and varicolored lilies so that it looked like a meadow filled with summer flowers.

The Master gazed down at the body, seeing all the marks of her suffering cleansed away. Megan had dressed her in the robe she had brought from the College of the Wise, and combed out her hair to cover the pillow in mingled waves of shadow and silver. And yet this was only an imperfect image of the completed beauty he had seen in Faris' face the night before.

So the *Death* he had read for her in the cards so long ago had meant the death of the body after all, but it had also been in truth a card of transfiguration. Now the promise he had seen then was fulfilled, and she was the *High Priestess*, the Bride of the Prince who is no longer of this world, initiate of all the mysteries.

Let the elements take this body I have loved . . . he thought as his hands moved in blessing and farewell, *as they have taken the Jewels of Power she bore, and as her spirit has passed to the keeping of the Maker of All* . . .

From the next room he heard Star's small contented cradle-song, and Megan's lullaby. A light wind passed through the opened window and parted the curtains, and the Master was for a moment blinded by a haze of light. When he turned, the wind was swirling loose petals from the scattered flowers to hide the body, like the wings of butterflies.

Index to Characters

Sir CHARLES of Woodhall, a holder of the Corona.

Lord DIEGUES DOS ALTOS, a holder of the Ramparts.

Sir DIETRICK of Wolfhill, a holder of the Ramparts.

DURREN, doorkeeper at the Chancery in Laurelynn.

Lady ELINOR of Fairhaven, cousin of Lord Theodor, member of the Commission to Santibar.

Mistress ELISA, priestess at the Hold in the Corona.

Lady ELNORA of Oakhill, a holder of the Ramparts, guide at Battle of Dragon Waste.

ERIC of the Horn, Lord Commander of Seagate.

Mistress ESTHER, chief priestess of Elder in the Ramparts.

Sir FARIN HARPER (of Hawkrest Hold), brother to Faris.

FARIS of Hawkrest Hold, Queen of Westria ("the Lily of the North")

FIONA FIREHAIR, a legendary beauty of Westria.

FREDERIC SACHS, Speaker of the Free Cities in the Council of Westria.

GERARD of Hawkrest Hold, father of Faris, Farin and Berisa.

GEROL, a wolf, the companion of Caolin.

GILBERT of Stanesvale, husband of Megan.

The Mistress of the GOLDEN LEAVES, an adept at the College of the Wise.

GORGO SNAGGLETOOTH, a trader between Westria and the Brown Lands.

Lady GWENNA, wife of the Lord Mayor of Laurelynn.

HAKIM MacMORANN, a trader and spy for Elaya.

HAKON, Lord Commander of Seagate, father of Eric.

HILARY GOLDENTHROAT, a legendary poet of Westria.

Lady HOLLY of Woodhall, daughter to Sir Charles, later wife of Andreas.

HUW, Rosemary's owl.

JEHAN Starbairn, King of Westria.

Lady JESSICA of Laurelynn, wife to Robert of the Ramparts.

JAIME of Palodoro, a holder of the Royal Domain, packmaster.

Master JOAQUIN, Lord Mayor of Laurelynn.

JONAS FERRERO, a smith in Tamiston, in the Ramparts.

JONAS WHITEBEARD, a trader and spy for Westria.

JULIAN Starbairn, "the Great," third century King of Westria, founder of royal line.

The Master of the JUNIPERS, chaplain to King Jehan, adept of the College.

Lady KIMI of Longbay, a holder of Seagate, member of the Commission to Santibar.

Sir LEWIS of Marsh Hold, Herald of Westria.

LINNET, milk name for the oldest daughter of Sandremun and Berisa of the Corona.

MADRONA, former name for the Mistress of the College of the Wise.

Sir MANUEL of Orvale, Controller of Highways.

MARA, Queen of Normontaine.

MARGIT, a deaf-mute, servant to Caolin.

Lady MARIANA of Claralac, a former mistress of King Jehan.

Mistress MARTINA, a holder in the Royal Domain.

Mistress MEGAN of Stanesvale, a holder of the Ramparts, Star's foster-mother.

MICA, milk name for the youngest son of Megan of Stanesvale.

Sir MIGUEL de Santera, Commander of the Fortress of Balleor near Santibar.

MIK WHITESTREAK, bodyservant to the King in Laurelynn.

ORDREY, confidential agent for Caolin.

PALOMON STRONGBOW, Lord of the Tambara and Prince of Elaya.

PATRICK, Steward of Misthall.

PHILIP of Rivered, oldest son of Robert of the Ramparts, briefly Jehan's squire.

RAFAEL, squire to Jehan, killed by raiders in the Corona.

Mistress RAMONA, a priestess in Elder.

Sir RANDAL of Registhorpe, a holder of Seagate.

Master RAS of Santierra, Master Bard, member of the Commission to Santibar.

ROBERT of Holyhill, Lord Commander of the Ramparts.

Lord RONALD SANDRESON of Greenfell, cousin to Lord Theodor of the Corona.

Lady ROSEMARY of Heldenhold, daughter of Lord Theodor.

Lord RODRIGO MACLAIN, an emissary from Elaya.

Sir RUDIARD of Applegard, Ambassador from Normontaine.

Lord SANDREMUN of Heldenhold, son of Lord Theodor.

Sir SERGE of Greenforest, a knight of Seagate.

STEFAN of the Long Ridge, son of a holder of the Corona.

SOMBRA, Faris' black mare.

STORMWING, Jehan's white stallion.

TANIA RAVENHAIR, daughter of the Miwok chieftain Longfoot, in the Ramparts.

THEODOR of Heldenhold, Lord Commander of the Corona.

THUNDERFOOT, Eric of Seagate's black stallion.

The Master of the TIDEPOOL, an adept at the College of the Wise.

WALDAN of Terra Linda ("Mole"), a former soldier of Westria.

Sir WALTER of Wilhamsted, a holder in the Royal Domain.

WAREN, a clerk in the Chancery in Laurelynn.

THE DRAGON REBORN

Sequel to The Great Hunt

Book Three of *The Wheel of Time*

by
Robert Jordan

Praise for *Eye of the World*

"A powerful vision of good and evil...fascinating people moving through a rich and interesting world." —Orson Scott Card

"Richly detailed...fully realized, complex adventure." —*Library Journal*

"A combination of Robin Hood and Stephen King that is hard to resist...Jordan makes the reader care about these characters as though they were old friends." —*Milwaukee Sentinel*

Praise for *The Great Hunt*

"Jordan can spin as rich a world and as event-filled a tale as [Tolkien]...will not be easy to put down." —*ALA Booklist*

"Worth re-reading a time or two." —*Locus*

"This is good stuff...Splendidly characterized and cleverly plotted...The Great Hunt is a good book which will always be a good book. I shall certainly [line up] for the third volume." —*Interzone*

The Dragon Reborn
coming in hardcover in August, 1991